Prelude to Glory

VOLUME 7

The Impending Storm

Prelude to Glory

VOLUME 7

The Impending Storm

A NOVEL BY

RON CARTER

BOOKCRAFT

SALT LAKE CITY

PRELUDE TO GLORY

Volume 1: Our Sacred Honor
Volume 2: The Times That Try Men's Souls
Volume 3: To Decide Our Destiny
Volume 4: The Hand of Providence
Volume 5: A Cold, Bleak Hill
Volume 6: The World Turned Upside Down
Volume 7: The Impending Storm

© 2003 Ron Carter

BOOKCRAFT is a registered trademark of Deseret Book Company.

Visit us at deseretbook.com

Library of Congress Cataloging-in-Publication Data

Carter, Ron, 1932–
    The impending storm / Ron Carter.
      p.   cm.
    ISBN 1-57008-993-0 (hardbound : alk. paper)
    1. United States—History—Revolution, 1775–1783—Fiction.   2. Washington, George, 1732–1799—Fiction.   I. Title.   II. Series: Carter, Ron, 1932– . Prelude to glory ; v. 7.

    PS3553.A7833146   2003
    813'.54—dc21   2003006959

Printed in the United States of America   18961-7108
R. R. Donnelley and Sons, Crawfordsville, IN

10   9   8   7   6   5   4   3   2   1

This series is dedicated to the common people
of long ago who paid the price

This volume is dedicated to the people employed
by the publisher, who have been so helpful, patient and
dedicated to bringing this series to the highest
standard possible. Among them are Cory Maxwell,
Jana Erickson, Emily Watts, Brad Pelo,
Garry Garff, and Richard Peterson, to name
a few but by no means all. Without them this
effort would have been impossible.

None had anticipated the catastrophic plunge of America into the economic and political chaos that followed the new nation's world-shaking military victory over the British. The national government disintegrating, state governments defiant, worthless currency, border tariff wars, bankruptcies rampant, bitter disputes over river rights, and sectionalism were ripping the union apart. There was talk of dividing America and reunion with Great Britain. Courthouses in Northampton, Worcester, Concord, Taunton, and Great Barrington had been stormed by farmers to stop foreclosures. The self-destruction of America had begun. November 5, 1787, with heavy heart, Washington took up his quill and wrote to his brilliant fellow Virginian and congressman, James Madison:

> *My Dear Mr. Madison:*
>
> *At this critical moment let . . . us look to our national char-acter, and to things beyond the present period. . . . Wisdom and good examples are necessary at this time to rescue the political machine from the impending storm . . .*

PREFACE

Following the *Prelude to Glory* series will be substantially easier if the reader understands the author's approach.

The Revolutionary War was not fought in one location. It was fought on many fronts, with critical events occurring simultaneously in each of them. It quickly became obvious that moving back and forth from one event which was occurring at the same moment as another, would be too confusing. Thus, the decision was made to follow each major event through to its conclusion, as seen through the eyes of selected characters, and then go back and pick up the thread of other great events that were happening at the same time in other places, as seen through the eyes of characters caught up in those events.

Volume 1, *Our Sacred Honor*, follows the fictional family of John Phelps Dunson from the beginning of hostilities in April 1775, through to the sea battle off the coast of England in which the American ship *Bon Homme Richard* defeats the British ship *Serapis*, with Matthew Dunson navigating for John Paul Jones. In volume 2, *The Times That Try Men's Souls*, Billy Weems, Matthew's dearest friend, survives the terrible defeats suffered by the Americans around New York and the disastrous American retreat to the wintry banks of the Delaware River. Volume 3, *To Decide Our Destiny*, leads us across the frozen Delaware River on Christmas night, 1776, with Billy Weems and his friend Eli Stroud, to take the town of Trenton, then Princeton. Volume 4, *The Hand of Providence*, addresses the tremendous, inspiring events of the campaign for possession of the Lake Champlain–Hudson River corridor, wherein British General John Burgoyne, with an army of eight thousand, is defeated by the Americans in one of the most profoundly moving stories in the history of America, at a place on the Hudson River called Saratoga. Volume 5, *A Cold, Bleak Hill*, leads us through two heartbreaking defeats in the summer of 1777, one at Brandywine Creek, the other at

Germantown, and then into the legendary story of the terrible winter at Valley Forge, Pennsylvania.

Volume 6, *The World Turned Upside Down*, brings us through the realization by the British King and Parliament that they have underestimated the strength of the Americans in the northern colonies. Upon the resignation of the commander in America, General William Howe, they order General Sir Henry Clinton to take command and move the war effort to the South. The French and Spanish join forces with the United States, and the entire course of the war changes.

Away from the battles, we find General Benedict Arnold and his wife, Peggy, entering into their treason with British Major John André, resulting in the arrest and death of John André, while Benedict Arnold escapes to become a British officer.

In that volume, the British conquer Savannah, Georgia, then Charleston, South Carolina, and General Cornwallis, given command of the British forces in the South by General Clinton, begins his march north. Crucial battles are fought at Camden, then King's Mountain, and at Guilford Courthouse, with General Nathanael Greene commanding the American forces in a delay-hit-run-delay tactic that slowly exhausts the British forces. General Cornwallis moves his beleaguered army to Yorktown, Virginia, protected by the guns of the British navy while he refits his men. But when the French navy engages them and drives the British ships away, General Cornwallis is landlocked, and General Washington makes his historic march from New York to Yorktown. With French soldiers assisting, the Americans place the British under siege, and ultimately General Cornwallis must surrender his entire command.

The war is over. It remains only to quell a few British who will not accept defeat, before moving on to the signing of the peace treaty.

In this volume, we discover that the defeat of the British at Yorktown results in a horrendous split in the British government, with King George III determined to hold the American colonies, while his cabinet is split on the question, and Parliament is against him. The result is the most dramatic house-cleaning in the history of English politics, when the entire cabinet is dismissed and a new one appointed. Instantly the cabinet and parliament vote to abandon America, and peace negotiations commence, with a resulting treaty in 1783. America has become a free and independent nation.

It is then the new nation is shocked by the harsh reality of their victory. The United States are bankrupt, with a congress that is powerless to raise revenue or compel unity among the states. Immediately the several states begin bickering over border tariffs, river rights, and money. Most states print their own currency, as does Congress, and within months the paper money is valueless. Veterans are discharged from the Continental Army without the pay they had been so ardently promised and must return home penniless. Without money they cannot pay the debts they had accumulated over the years they were serving their country, and bank foreclosures and bankruptcies reach horrifying levels. Robert Morris and Haym Salomon, the two financial geniuses to whom George Washington turns for help, quickly understand that without taxing powers being vested in Congress, the United States is doomed.

Slowly but steadily the United States is descending into a chaos that will destroy everything the Americans fought for. The best and brightest among them realize something must be done, but as yet, no one has dreamed what it will be. Then, in August of 1786, an event occurs that puts the issue squarely before the entire country. A discharged army captain named Daniel Shays leads 1,200 veterans against the courthouse in Northampton to stop the court from entering more bankruptcies and putting the debtors in prison. Concurrently, others storm the courthouses in Worcester, Concord, Taunton, and Great Barrington. Men are shot dead and wounded.

A fundamental change has to occur, or all is lost. James Madison of Virginia begins writing letters. There will be a gathering of representatives from all states at Philadelphia on the second Monday of May 1787. This assembly will address the ills that must now be resolved.

The Constitutional Convention has convened.

Chronology of Important Events Related to This Volume

1781

January 17. American General Dan Morgan engages British Colonel Banastre Tarleton at Cowpens, South Carolina, and, through a brilliant military stratagem, soundly defeats the infamous Tarleton, destroying nearly his entire regiment.

March 1. The Articles of Confederation are ratified.

March 15. Americans under command of General Nathanael Greene engage British soldiers at Guilford Courthouse, where the Americans are defeated; however, the British losses are high, and the British are seriously crippled in their southern campaign.

September 5–8. French ships sent by King Louis XVI under command of Admiral de Grasse to aid the Americans, engage and defeat the British fleet in Chesapeake Bay. With the loss of the British navy for support, General Cornwallis, with his entire army at Yorktown, is landlocked and subject to attack by the Americans under General Washington and French General Rochambeau.

September 28–October 19. General Sir Charles Cornwallis is placed under siege by American and French forces, who pound him with cannon for weeks. October 19, 1781, Cornwallis surrenders his entire army to save his soldiers. The surrender essentially concludes the fighting in the Revolutionary War.

1782

February 23. Sir Henry Clinton, commander in chief of British forces in America, is replaced by General Sir Guy Carleton.

March 27. The most horrendous wrenching in the history of the British government occurs when the entire cabinet of King George III is thrown out of office, to be replaced by a new cabinet that favors abandoning any further hostilities with the United States.

April 12. Peace conferences commence between Great Britain, France, and America, in Paris, France.

April 12. The British soundly defeat the French navy in the Battle of the Saints, West Indies.

November 30. Provisional and preliminary peace treat is signed in Paris, between Great Britain and the United States.

1783

January 20. Britain, France, Spain, and the Netherlands sign a general armistice and hostilities cease between them.

September 3. The Paris Peace Treaty is signed by Great Britain and the United States in Paris. The Peace Treaty of Versailles is signed by Great Britain, France, and Spain in Versailles.

November 2. General George Washington delivers his farewell address to the army.

November 3. Congress commences the disbanding of the Continental Army.

November 25. General Washington bids farewell to his officers at Fraunces Tavern in New York City.

December 23. General Washington resigns his commission, bids farewell to Congress, and returns to private civilian life.

1784

January 14. Congress ratifies the treaty of peace between the United States and Great Britain. The American Revolution is formally concluded.

1785

May 18. The Mount Vernon Convention convenes at Washington's residence.

1786

August–September. Daniel Shays leads 1,200 men to stop all legal proceedings concerning bankruptcies and debtors at the Northampton Courthouse in Vermont. Concurrently other men storm the courthouses in Concord, Taunton, Worcester, and Great Barrington for the same purpose.

September 11. The Annapolis Convention is convened.

September 14. The Annapolis Convention adjourns with notice given to all states of a proposed convention to be held on the second Monday of May 1787, at Independence Hall, Philadelphia.

PART ONE

London, England

November 25, 1781

CHAPTER I

*T*homas Reeves Hocking turned up the collar of his heavy black cape, pulled his tricorn low on his head, and hunched his thin shoulders against the bite of the raw, late November wind at his back. Feet spread for balance, he turned on the deck of the small packet boat *Alice* to glance back down the broad Thames River, rough and gray in the swirling late morning fog, as though by the peering he could see across the English Channel to the French port of Calais from whence he had come. The small vessel had left France earlier that morning with four passengers, two canvas sacks of mail, and the three-man crew—all silent, white-faced, as she plowed north across the Channel, pitching and bucking in the great whitecaps that put her decks awash, with the bitter easterlies whistling in her sails and rigging. Hocking had no recall of the hours he had spent in the tiny, damp hold, hearing only the constant roar of wind and feeling the shudder of the tough little craft as she took the relentless pounding of the sea. Sitting on a plank bench, staring at the half-inch of water that constantly lapped at his shoes on the floorboards, he reached too many times to feel the sealed message in the breast pocket of his coat. His only clear recollection of the torment of the crossing was his constant awareness of the terrifying message he carried. It numbed his brain and froze his heart within his breast.

Yorktown—Cornwallis and his eight thousand—gone, dead, captured—Graves and our fleet—defeated in open battle on the Chesapeake Bay by de Grasse and his French

3

fleet—we lost on the sea and we lost on the land—the Americans—that ridiculous gathering of rabble beat us—how? how? how?

The unthinkable reality filled his head, ringing like an unending chant. The sick gnawing inside had finally driven him up onto the pitching deck to grasp the handrail and stand shivering with the fog collecting freezing on his dark, shaggy eyebrows and thin, sharp face. He watched unseeing as the small vessel worked its way through the jumble of boats and ships of every flag and description, which endlessly plied the waters of the great waterway that gave the world access to London, the capital city of the greatest military power on earth. The Thames River traffic went about its business, seemingly oblivious to the fact it was Sunday, when all right-thinking Church of England adherents were in their churches, or their homes, peering judgmentally down their noses at those who dared defy the edicts of the Great Jehovah concerning the Sabbath.

Hocking glanced at the flags on the masts of the monstrous gather of ships that undulated on the river swells—India, Spain, France, Holland, Germany, the West Indies, Greece, Africa, Portugal, Scandinavia—and an odd thought passed unbidden through his mind:

How many gods, how many religions, are represented here on this river? Or is it just one? One who is seen differently by each of the many who is seeking? Which Sabbath, which holy day, is the right one? Catholic? Protestant? Oriental? Hebrew? Indian? Asian? African? And what would happen to the business of world trade if every port in every country were shut down on the Sabbath, or the holy day, of every religion? Impossible. The business of the world must go on. The message I carry must be delivered today. It will likely wreck the British government. Maybe—probably—change the course of the history of the world. Sabbath or no, it will not wait. It must reach Germain today, before the thunderbolt strikes through Walpole and the newsmongers. And after Germain? Only the Almighty knows.

He wiped at the beads of moisture clinging to his heavy brows and his face, aware that it was a mix of freezing fog and nervous perspiration.

Hocking scarcely noticed the little boat passing beneath London Bridge, then Southwark Bridge, and begin to turn left as it passed beneath Blackfriars Bridge, on past Whitehall to Westminster Bridge where the helmsman brought her hard to starboard and worked through the press of watercraft to tie up rocking at the Westminster docks, near the houses of Parliament and the abbey. The crew spilled the sails, set the gangplank rattling onto the dock, and then set about lashing the heavy, wet canvas to the arms. The captain, short, stout, round face weathered like leather, pointed his four passengers to the gangplank, then seized the two mail pouches to follow them.

Hocking descended the gangplank, and the moment his soaked shoes were on the ancient, black timbers of the dock, he turned trotting into the bustle of people of every description, working his way through the throng to the wet cobblestone street, searching for a hack for hire. He waved frantically, and a driver with a scarf tied over his hat and beneath his chin came back on the reins of his old horse, and the rig rocked to a halt. Hocking called up to him, "Lord Germain's residence at Pall Mall, and be quick about it," jerked the door open, and vaulted inside. The hackman's eyes widened slightly and he muttered to himself, "Lord Germain, is it now? Aren't we the high an' mighty!"

He clucked, slapped the reins on the rump of the wet hide, and the indifferent horse set out at a trot, iron shoes ringing on the wet cobblestones while the metal rims of the wheels set up a steady yammering and the aged hack swayed on its leathers. The driver worked north past St. James Park, then easterly toward the Pall Mall district, to pull up short in front of a low stone building that showed weather stains from two centuries of winters and summers. Hocking had the carriage door open and was on the ground before the hack driver wound the reins around the whipstock. He shoved coins into the hand of the startled man and bolted for the entrance where a pair of guards stood at attention in sodden uniforms. The soldiers recognized the shape and quick, quirky movements of the wiry little man, and one reached for the iron handle to swing the heavy, black oak door open. Head drawn in, shoulders still hunched against the bite of the cold wind, Hocking strode into the ante-room, removed his tricorn to throw the moisture onto the floor, and went to the desk of the aging receptionist.

"Thomas Reeves Hocking to see Lord Germain. Urgent."

The elderly man nodded. "On what business, sir?"

Hocking could not mask his impatience. "His Majesty's business."

"Is Lord Germain expecting—"

Hocking cut him off, eyes flashing as he leaned slightly forward. "No, he is not, but he knows who I am. Tell him Hocking . . . Hocking the courier . . . has just come from Calais. I carry a message from our agent in the court of King Louis of France. Tell him!"

The old, gray eyes opened wide. "King Louis? France?"

"Tell him. Hocking. King Louis."

Wordlessly the aged man rose from the chair, and in the labored way of the elderly walked down a corridor, swaying slightly on legs that would no longer bend easily, heels tapping a slow cadence on the worn marble floor. Hocking heard a door open, then close. Twenty seconds passed, and the door opened, then closed again. Fifteen seconds later the old man appeared and motioned.

"Lord Germain will see you. Follow me."

Hocking waved him off. "No need. I know my way."

Five seconds later Hocking rapped on a door, it yawed open, and he was facing Lord George Germain, Secretary of State for the American Colonies, under authority of Lord North, First Lord of the Treasury in the cabinet of King George III. It took Hocking a moment to understand why Germain and not his ever-present secretary had answered the door. It was the Sabbath; the secretary was not on duty.

Germain stood tall, strong, clear-eyed, capable, despite his sixty-six years. A complex man, his life had been a strange mix of heroism as a selfless officer seriously wounded at the Battle of Fontenoy early in his career, but who for reasons never established, failed to instantly follow orders at the later critical Battle of Minden in 1759, during the Seven Years' War with France. His thirty-minute delay allowed the beaten French to regroup, and though the British carried the battle, they failed in a rare opportunity to utterly destroy a large segment of the French army. Blame for the failure to seize the moment was laid at Germain's feet, it being generally held that had he followed orders instantly, the French would not only have lost the battle, but would have suffered a catastrophic defeat. To clear his name, Germain demanded his own

court-martial, which resulted in his being stripped of all military standing and ordered never to serve His Majesty in any military capacity for
the remainder of his life.

Possessed of an odd mix of disarming congeniality and melancholy
bordering on depression, he was loved and admired by some, loathed and
despised by others. But whatever the mix, it was never questioned that he
was an excellent administrator with keen perceptions, a soldier with a
superior sense of military matters, and gifted with an innate sense of the
politics required to make things happen. Thus it was that in 1775, when
Lord North began his search for a fresh candidate to fill the position of
Secretary of State for the American Colonies, he found no one in the
British Empire better prepared than George Germain, his court-martial
and punishment notwithstanding.

For a moment Germain's cool, penetrating stare fixed the diminutive
courier where he stood. Then his expression softened.

"Come in."

Hocking stepped into the cavernous office. The gray stone walls
bore paintings, maps, a flag from Germain's first military campaign, and
tapestries. A fire crackled in the massive, blackened fireplace, over which
a large painting of King George III hung, an unmistakable evidence that
above all, Germain understood politics.

Germain gestured to a chair facing his huge walnut desk, and took
his place in his own leather upholstered chair. "You carry a message?"

Hocking drew the parchment from within the folds of his damp
cape and coat and reached to offer it to Germain.

"From Paris."

Germain read the strain in Hocking's voice and the flat look in his
eyes perfectly. He broke the scarlet wax seal and unfolded the document.
For more than one minute he sat stock-still, reading and rereading the
terse message while Hocking breathed light, watching every movement,
reading every expression that flitted across the stony face. Then Germain
dropped the document on his desk and leaned back in his chair. For long
moments he sat motionless, staring at the document as though it were

something alive, while he brought his disoriented thoughts to some sense of order. He raised his face to Hocking and gestured to the paper.

"You know the contents?"

"I have not read the document. I know the message."

"Cornwallis went down?"

"At Yorktown. Captured. His entire command, dead or prisoners."

"Our fleet? Our ships that were ordered to the Chesapeake to get him off the land if necessary?"

"Defeated. Driven off by the French."

"De Grasse?"

"De Grasse and de Barras. They defeated Graves and Hood."

"General Clinton in New York—didn't he send reinforcements?—attempt some relief, some rescue?"

"Graves sailed his fleet to New York for repairs. Clinton tried to refit the ships and send Graves back to rescue Cornwallis, but Graves arrived at Yorktown about a week too late. All three armies and both navies were gone—ours, the Americans, the French. The town was all but deserted."

Germain drew a great breath and let it out slowly, controlled. "Do the French know all this? King Louis? Vergennes, his minister?"

"They've known since before November twentieth. It was November twentieth when Vergennes told Benjamin Franklin."

"Franklin's still in King Louis's court representing the colonies?"

"He is."

"How long have you known about Yorktown?"

"I heard the rumor three days ago. I waited for proof. I got it early this morning."

"What proof?"

"The official dispatch from Clinton to yourself should arrive sometime overnight, or early morning."

"Arrive here? At this office?"

"Yes."

Germain leaned forward, face intense. "Are you certain?"

"Certain."

Germain straightened in his chair, and Hocking saw the heavy decisions begin to form in his eyes as he spoke.

"Return to France immediately and keep this office advised of further developments. Should you need anything, ask at the outer desk. In the meantime keep all matters we have discussed confidential."

Hocking rose abruptly. "Yes, sir."

Germain followed Hocking to the door and held it open, gazing at the floor with his mind racing as the sounds of Hocking's quick footsteps on the flagstones faded and the huge door into the street opened and closed. He strode quickly down the hallway to the aging receptionist who stood to meet him.

"I will need a hack immediately."

"Yes, sir."

Five minutes later Germain braced himself against the wind, closed the door behind him, and trotted to the waiting hack to cup his hand and shout orders up to the driver.

"The residence of Viscount Stormont, Portland Place. Waste no time!"

Clattering on the cobblestones, the hack careened northerly across Oxford Street, onto Portland Place, and the driver came back hard on the reins to bring the blowing horse to a standstill before an ancient stone building with great chimneys on both ends. Germain was on the ground, hurrying before the carriage stopped rocking. He banged on the heavy door with a clenched fist and spoke to the plump servant the moment it opened.

"I must have audience with Lord Stormont this moment."

The startled man bobbed his head once, turned, left the door open, and ran up the hallway. One minute later Lord Stormont came striding down the hall working at buttons on his vest, eyes wide and inquiring. Neither man wasted time on protocol.

"What's happened?"

"No time. Dress for this weather and come with me. I'll tell you on the way."

"Where are we going?"

"To get Thurlow for his advice, and then probably on to see North!"

Stormont stopped in his tracks, mouth gaping open. He recovered and clacked it shut. "Thurlow? North? Something's happened in America!"

"Get dressed."

In minutes Stormont returned, fastening the latch on his cape, and both men hurried out the door into the wind to clamber into the carriage and slam the door. The driver swung it around to return to Oxford Street, then easterly to Bloomsbury. While the passengers clung to the windowsills to hold their seats, Germain related the catastrophic story to a stunned, incredulous Stormont.

The two men stood in the wind and waited for Lord Chancellor Thurlow to answer the pounding on his door. Two minutes later the three men were in his sumptuous library, face-to-face. Stormont remained silent with Thurlow, waiting for Germain's lead, faces a blank.

Neither Thurlow nor Germain had forgotten that in their beginnings, they had been formidable political enemies. But in the deadly game of high level politics where deals and careers were decided in clandestine meetings held in small rooms at night, each had grudgingly learned to respect the rare political skills of the other. While there was never warmth between them, each knew the counsel of the other would be candid and sound. And this time, Germain needed to hear the counsel of Thurlow. He came directly to it.

"Cornwallis surrendered his entire command at Yorktown."

Instantly Thurlow's face became the practiced, neutral mask of a master politician.

"I see. When?"

"October nineteenth."

"On what authority do you have this?"

"Hocking. Our agent in Paris."

"Certain?"

"Certain."

Thurlow paused, searching his memory. "Our fleet. What happened to our fleet?"

"French warships under de Grasse drove them out of the Chesapeake."

"That left Cornwallis landlocked?"

"Yes."

"Who defeated Cornwallis on land? Certainly not the Americans."

"The Americans with seven thousand French infantry under General Rochambeau."

"Rochambeau! Perhaps the best general in France." Thurlow raised a hand to command silence. "Just a moment. Weren't Washington and Rochambeau at New York, holding Clinton?"

"No. Rochambeau was at Rhode Island. When de Grasse moved his fleet up from the West Indies to the Chesapeake to engage our fleet under Admiral Graves, Washington made a forced march south to trap Cornwallis if de Grasse succeeded. Rochambeau brought his French with Washington. De Grasse succeeded, and Cornwallis fell."

"Clinton did not rescue Cornwallis?"

"He tried. Too late."

"How many did we lose?"

"In the beginning Cornwallis had about eight thousand in his command. We lost them all. Killed or captured."

Uncharacteristically, Thurlow rounded his mouth and blew air. "We lost Burgoyne and his eight thousand at Saratoga in '77, and now Cornwallis and his eight thousand at Yorktown in '81."

He paced away toward the huge fireplace, hands clasped behind his back. For ten seconds the only sound was the wind sucking at the chimney. Then he turned.

"We can survive the loss of Cornwallis and his army, but I doubt we can survive what this will do to Parliament and His Majesty. Parliament is already divided. Shaky. Rockingham and Shelburne and Hillsborough are moving away from the King over the time and the money we've invested in this American adventure. Six years! Two armies! Millions of pounds! This couldn't have happened at a worse time."

Germain nodded and Thurlow stood stock-still, eyes burning like embers, as he continued. "North has to know immediately, and whether he has the stomach for it or not, he will have to take it to His Majesty. It would damage North if this news reached the King and Parliament through Horace Walpole and his newspaper. It may damage him no matter what he does. He has to know now."

Thurlow's stare held Germain for several seconds of dead silence while each man considered the enormity of the calamity. Then Germain slowly turned to Stormont, waiting.

Stormont returned his blank stare and nodded. "I agree. Which of us goes to Buckingham?"

Germain drew air and slowly released it. "My responsibility."

He sat in abject silence for the southerly drive down Drury Lane, then west on Strand, inventing and rejecting sentences he could use to break the earthshaking truth to North. The driver sawed on the reins and the horse came to a nervous stop on Downing Street before the residence of Lord North, First Lord of the Treasury, perhaps the most powerful office in His Majesty's cabinet. As in a daze, Germain braced himself against the wet wind and knocked on the great door. Three minutes later he was standing in the library of Lord North.

Seldom in the history of the political hierarchy of the British Empire had two more disparate men faced each other. Germain tall, square-shouldered, erect, athletic, handsome, engaging. North shorter, rotund, face round and jowled, protruding eyes, clumsy of movement, wide-mouthed, thick-lipped, and his speech flawed with a lisp. Germain skilled at war, North skilled at peace, and very near beyond redemption in his bungling of the American theater of England's quest for world dominance. King George had brought North into his cabinet in the hope that though North was personally incapable of directing a war, he had the political skills to find and utilize officers who could, Germain among them.

The draw of the wind at the fireplace was the only sound as North waited. Then Germain's words echoed in the huge, stone-walled library.

"I have received a message from our agent in Paris."

North's breathing slowed, eyes widening as he waited for the thunderclap he sensed was coming.

"General Cornwallis has surrendered his entire command at Yorktown."

For five full seconds North stood like a granite statue. Then he shook his head slightly and whispered, "That is impossible."

"The French fleet defeated our naval forces under Admiral Graves. The Chesapeake is held by the Americans."

The air and half the life went out of North. He staggered backwards two steps into the leading edge of his desk and caught his balance. His right hand flew to his breast and his breathing constricted. His face became white, then began to grow red. Germain took a step forward, prepared to grasp him, fearing the man had suffered a stroke.

"Shall I summon your physician?"

North's eyes opened wide, protruding in disbelief, and then he flung his arms outward and turned and began to pace in great, long strides, nearly shouting, "By the Father, it is all over! It is all over! It is all over!"

Germain stood balanced, ready to seize the man should he topple over.

North turned suddenly, face red, eyes flat with shock. "King George! Does His Majesty know?"

"I do not believe so."

North's mind was racing. "Parliament meets Tuesday. The Privy Council will be gathering at the Cockpit tomorrow! Oh! Oh! The Empire! We are destroyed! Destroyed!"

He began to pace again, as though his great strides could outdistance the nightmare.

Germain waited until he slowed. "Should you take this up with His Majesty before it reaches him from the streets?"

North gasped. "Has it reached the streets?"

"Not yet."

"Then I must gain audience with His Majesty at once." He paused, and for the first time forced his shattered thoughts into some semblance of coherence. "Have you received any official dispatch from Cornwallis? Or Clinton?"

"I am expecting Clinton's official dispatch yet today."

"I cannot go to His Majesty without an official document. The instant it arrives you must deliver it here, to me, no matter the time."

"I shall. What do you wish me to do in the meantime?"

"Make as little of this as possible. Should the newsmongers come clamoring, dismiss it as an unsubstantiated rumor. I shall take the official notice from Clinton to His Majesty immediately I have it in my hands."

Germain nodded. "What is your present vision about continuing the war in America?"

North's voice rose in defensive intensity, and he jabbed a fat finger into the air. "I warned them! I warned Parliament last winter. Repeatedly! Repeatedly, mind you! As First Lord of the Treasury, I cannot . . . *cannot* . . . finance the war in America for another year. Nothing could be more clear than the fact we must find a way to resolve that conflict immediately . . . *now* . . . or abandon it!"

Germain's breathing slowed as the echo of the words in the great library died. For a time that seemed an eternity, he faced North in silence, whose jowls were clamped shut and trembling. The only sound was the crackle of the fire, and the lonely moan of the wind while both men allowed the words to take tentative root in their brains. Each knew that what was happening could wrench the British Empire into pieces.

Germain licked dry lips, and the sound of his voice startled both of them. "I shall go back and wait for the dispatch from Clinton." North remained silent, motionless, while Germain turned and walked from the great room. The boom of the huge door closing behind him sounded like the clap of a death-knell.

The wind died in the evening, and by ten o'clock the fog had lifted. At midnight the heavens were a black velvet dome with points of light that reached into eternity when the knock came at Germain's door. He received the folded parchment, addressed to himself, bearing the seal of General Sir Henry Clinton, nodded to the messenger, and closed the door. For half an hour he sat alone and unmoving before the fireplace, while his understanding of what was happening to the British Empire broadened with each rereading of the heavy parchment. At one o'clock he climbed into his waiting hack and slammed the door. At half past one, in the still, dark cold of approaching winter, he walked steadily from the carriage to the front door of North's office building, identified himself, and was granted entrance. A light was burning in the library when Lord North answered his knock.

Without a word Germain passed the document to North, who raised his large, protruding eyes and waited in silence while Germain spoke.

"It is confirmed. Admiral Graves was defeated at the Chesapeake. General Cornwallis surrendered his entire command."

North bobbed his head once. The shock that had been in his eyes eleven hours earlier was still evident, but under control.

Germain continued. "Do you wish anything further from myself?"

"Not at this moment. I have arranged audience with His Majesty at eight o'clock in the morning. He will know of this before the meeting of the Privy Council."

Germain pondered for a moment, then hesitantly pushed the matter beyond his proper bounds. "Do you have a plan?"

Instantly North understood Germain was probing for an answer to the question on which the Empire would stand or fall. Germain, during his service as the Secretary of State for America, had made it abundantly clear he would never agree to abandon the war to retain the North American colonies. Never. North, however, had refrained from declaring himself until developments in the wild, unpredictable war made it clear whether the treasury of the nearly bankrupt Empire could afford the unending drain of millions of pounds sterling. Now he was alone, facing Germain, and Germain had chosen this moment to put the issue out in the open, squarely between them.

Was this the time to begin what could result in the polarization of the political structure of England and end up ripping the Empire into pieces? North made his decision. His sentence was measured.

"I do not believe we can afford to continue the war in America." His eyes dropped for a moment while he decided there was nothing else to say. He raised his face to look steadily into Germain's eyes in silence, waiting. For the first time, the conflict between the two men, which had been lurking in the shadows, was open, declared, irreversible. Neither could calculate where it would lead, nor did they try.

Germain broke it off. He nodded. "I shall be available should there be need," he said, then left the room.

In deep reflection, North closed the door behind him, then turned back into the room to spend the night pacing, trying to understand the implications of what had happened. But he could not force his brain to find the end of it. The rooster was cracking out his announcement of a new day approaching when North went to wash himself and don his best finery for his meeting with King George III.

With London awash in chill morning sunlight, North sat slumped in his hack as it made its way from Pall Mall to Buckingham Palace. He stared straight ahead as the uniformed guards swung open the huge, wrought-iron gates to admit his rig, and he remembered nothing of walking the few steps from the swaying hack to the front door, then down the hall, where waiting, immaculately dressed and mannered servants introduced him into the royal library. The opulence of the appointments in the high-ceilinged, vaulted room went unnoticed by North as he made his way to the great, ornately carved desk to await the arrival of his sovereign.

King George III was not the son of King George II, but the grandson. The firstborn of King George II was Frederick Louis, the Prince of Wales. The hapless child was small, ugly, frail, awkward, egocentric, and openly hated by both his father and mother, who publicly stated they would prefer the child dead. He lashed back at his father by joining the opposition party and engaging in a life of debauchery rarely known, even among that high strata of British society that abounded in degeneracy of every kind known to the human race. In time he married, and on June 4, 1738, his wife, the Princess of Wales, gave birth to a sickly child who was given the name of George at his baptism, one month after his birth. Young George had both the virtues and vices of an ordinary citizen, but never did he have the character, or the vision, to reign as king from the most powerful throne in Europe. While the boy was yet an adolescent, his grandfather, the King, became incurably insane, and on October 25,

1760, died suddenly. His father, Frederick, the Prince of Wales and the next in line to inherit the throne, had died nine years earlier, in 1751. Thus the mantle of the throne fell on the firstborn of the next generation, young George III, at the age of twenty-two. He was handsome, engaging, often witty, and totally captivated with being the King. He could not then know that his lack of capacity, combined with the crushing weight of ruling England, would drive him to neurosis, and that, coupled with the genetic disease porphyria, would eventually drive him mad, to die a lunatic.

He was forty-three years of age that bright, cold November morning when he walked from his private chambers to his library to keep his early morning appointment with Lord North. He was troubled, aware something calamitous had occurred, sufficient to drive his First Lord of the Treasury to request an unprecedented eight o'clock Monday morning, private meeting to be held in the King's quarters. Precisely what had happened was not yet known to him. He was wearing his familiar powdered wig and finery nearly beyond description as he opened his private entrance into the library and walked to his desk.

North stood instantly and waited while the King walked to his chair, sat down, adjusted his purple, gold-trimmed silk robe, and raised his eyes.

"I presume there is some reason you have requested this . . . ah . . . unusual meeting."

North bowed slightly and remained standing. One did not take a seat until invited by the King. He spoke with his slight lisp evident. "Your Majesty, there is. It is with deepest regret that I deliver this dispatch to you from General Sir Henry Clinton."

Instantly King George started in his chair. "From America?"

"Yes." North held the folded parchment out, waiting for the king to receive it. The monarch spoke without reaching.

"What has happened?"

"It is in the dispatch, Sire, from the hand of General Clinton."

"I am asking you. What has happened?"

North was trapped, left without choice. His protruding eyes rolled as he spoke. "Sire, General Lord Charles Cornwallis and his entire command have fallen. October nineteenth, at Yorktown, in the colony of Virginia. Our naval fleet was defeated by the French on Chesapeake Bay, and have sailed to New York. They are apparently returning to England."

The King came off his chair like a coiled spring. "Cornwallis? His entire command? How many? Ten thousand?"

"Eight thousand, Sire. All killed or captured. General Cornwallis is himself a prisoner."

"That can not be! Simply impossible." He snatched the dispatch from North's fingers. "This dispatch is a fraud!"

"Sire, I assure you, the dispatch is authentic. I have conferred with Lords Stormont and Thurlow and Germain before bringing the news to this chamber. They agreed. You must know of this before the Privy Council meets this morning. They will learn of this before the day is out, and such news will be common gossip by sunset. Parliament meets tomorrow. Only the Almighty knows what they will do with this."

The monarch's clenched fist slammed onto the table, eyes flashing as he exclaimed, "You know what they will do with this! Rockingham and Shelburne and Hillsborough will demand that we abandon the American colonies! Six years! Millions of pounds sterling! Tens of thousands of lives! All for naught!" He began to pace, gesturing, exclaiming, his shouted words echoing off the hard stone walls.

"I want it known that I *will not* abandon the Americas." He spun and thrust a finger at North. "I am aware of your statements that the treasury cannot maintain this war another year. I must know—what is your position on continuing the war for America?"

North drew a breath to gain time. "To withdraw would be a disaster most difficult to justify."

The King shook his head. "That is not an answer. What is your position?"

North settled and spoke bluntly. "Your Majesty, as matters now stand, I do not see how we can continue with it."

"You oppose me on this?"

"I oppose no one. I think only of the Empire."

"Germain? Where does he stand?"

"Sire, I believe that is a question for Germain to answer."

"Then I shall ask him." The King stopped his pacing and brought himself to the fringes of control. He locked North with a stare that was alive with electricity. "Regardless of your private misgivings, I am charging you with the responsibility to make it known to the Privy Council today, and Parliament tomorrow, that I will never consider abandoning our campaign for America. Am I absolutely clear?"

North hesitated for an awkward moment, then said, "I understand, Sire."

Only then did the angry monarch open the written document and stand with feet spread to read it in total silence. He read it again, then folded it and flung it onto his desk.

"You are excused."

"Yes, Your Majesty."

Bowing, North backed himself to the door and shambled out of the room in his awkward, ungainly fashion. During the entire encounter, the King had not asked him to be seated.

The Privy Council, composed of men whose credentials and experience in affairs of the kingdom and the world qualified them to advise Parliament and Crown, had been an institution in British government for nearly five hundred years. Their charge was to address and debate matters of crucial importance to the Empire, and impart their wisdom. Little did they know that the morning of Monday, November 26, 1781, was to burst upon them like the sword of the Almighty striking from the heavens.

The Privy Council was called to order with Germain sitting in stoic silence, watching every expression, waiting for the lightning bolt to strike. North made the announcement of General Cornwallis's fall, and for the first time in Germain's memory, the more than two hundred men of prominence first gasped, then sat motionless in dead silence for a full five seconds before talk erupted. Decorum vanished and bedlam reigned.

Men gestured, spoke without being recognized, pointed, exclaimed. For minutes the deeply ingrained British discipline vanished. Slowly the tumult subsided and the meeting came back to order. Germain watched and listened to the comments, all gravitating toward the same conclusion.

"There is no hope! All is lost."

"We must abandon the Americas!"

"We can not maintain our armies in India, Minorca, the West Indies, and support our war with Holland if we continue to send millions to America. And what of the Channel? With the French ships prowling constantly, defending our own shores is our paramount duty."

"Let the colonies go! We must protect our investment and our trade in the West Indies at all cost."

Watching every move like a hawk, Germain caught a glimpse of Anthony Storer passing a written note to Carlisle, and made it his business to quietly obtain and read the note at the recess: "What we are to do after Lord Cornwallis's catastrophe, only the Almighty knows."

By early afternoon the news was in the street, and Lord Gower heatedly spoke of the shock now evident on the faces of the commoners. He saw the dismay, distrust, disbelief in their faces as they shouted, "The wisest and most intelligent are all asking each other what is next to be done, and the wisest and most intelligent can give no answer!"

The debate raged on with Germain listening, watching the direction the country was moving. The wealthy in the Empire—those who contributed most to the treasury and who expected a return on their investment—slowly distanced themselves from the position taken by King George and his ministry. They could see their millions disappearing into a black hole called America, without hope of ever recovering their investment, or a return thereon, while other, more lucrative holdings of the British Empire were going begging.

The gap between King and Privy Council widened and solidified, becoming irrevocable. It was the unanimous opinion of the members of the Council: England should abandon all thought of bringing the American colonies to heel, and the reasons were simple and compelling. Britain was a victim of its own ambition. It had opened too many farflung frontiers, engaged too many countries in war over too long a time. The Empire's interests in India, Gibraltar, Minorca, the Mediterranean, the Orient, West Indies, Spain, Holland, France, and the Americas each demanded a greater share of the dwindling wealth and available manpower. The futile struggle to retain the American colonies had to end! Hard decisions had to be made before complete bankruptcy brought the whole trembling structure down. Were the Americas of top priority in a ranking of England's possessions? No, said the Privy Council, the West Indies with the rich rum and sugar and slave trade are of more value. Let the colonies go. Save the West Indies.

The King, and Germain, dug in their heels for the battle. On His Majesty's request, Germain drafted and circulated a well-reasoned, sensible memorandum, declaring that with the superiority the British presently held at sea, Nova Scotia, Penobscot, New York, Charleston, Savannah, and East Florida could all be held and maintained by the British forces then in place, and with very little additional investment, an attack could be made on the rebel coasts, with assistance coming down from Canada to defeat the Americans.

The memorandum fell on deaf ears. Germain understood that the realities of the crisis were not fatal. What was fatal was the people's loss of the will to fight on. They had had enough. Six years, millions of pounds, and thousands of lives, with no end in sight, was too much.

Abandon America. Save the West Indies, and the other British colonies.

December 8, 1781, the Cabinet voted to send only new, raw recruits to America to bolster the flagging military; investing seasoned troops was a waste. December 14, in the House of Commons, Germain thundered that the ministry was unanimous against abandoning America. Instantly North shattered the illusion of a united ministry by resigning his seat as First Lord of the Treasury, but he did not abandon his place in either the Privy Council or the King's cabinet. He simply moved back and took up a lesser seat. The same day, the rupture in the ministry became irreparable when the subject of the plans for America was brought on in the House of Commons for debate and a vote. The opponents of

Germain and the King disemboweled the entire matter with a planned and perfectly executed silence. The matter was closed without a word. The gulf between King and Parliament widened.

With heavy heart, Germain accepted the inevitable. If the ministry were to survive, it would require finding sacrificial scapegoats. In dark corners and small rooms, the names of Germain, the chief protagonist for holding the American colonies, and the Earl of Sandwich, head of naval operations who supported Germain, were the two selected for blame. Germain heard the deadly whisperings. Before Christmas, he secretly beseeched the King to release him; he had been prudent with his fortune, and with the peerage he would receive upon his voluntary retirement, he could live comfortably, with honor.

It was not to be.

King George was outraged. He did not quarrel with Germain's voluntary retirement, but he was nearly neurotic in his insistence that whoever replaced Germain would have to be committed to continuing the war to hold America, as Germain had been. The King might make do without Germain, but he could not maintain his stance on the Americas unless Germain's replacement was as committed as Germain himself had been in support of the American offensive. King George summoned Lord North.

"You may replace Lord Germain, but you will do so with a man equally strong in support of saving the Americas!"

The widening rift between the Crown and Prime Minister instantly became public. The head-on collision brought the wheels of British government to a grinding halt. With no way to force movement in the government, North could do nothing but let Germain remain in his position.

December 23, the House of Commons voted to replace the unfortunate General Sir Henry Clinton from his position as commander of military forces in America, but as for a replacement? Parliament favored General Sir Guy Carleton, who had so long struggled to maintain a strong British presence in Canada, and who had lately voiced deep reservations about continuing the battle to conquer America. But so long as

Germain remained Secretary for the American Colonies, Parliament could appoint no one. On that same day, December 23, 1781, North was again summoned to a private conference with the King.

The meeting was icy. Protocol and formalities were neglected as the King spoke.

"I have had a lengthy conference with General Benedict Arnold."

North gaped. Benedict Arnold? A private conference with the King? North settled as the King continued.

"General Arnold has proposed a plan that will bring the colonies to their knees. He informs me they are destitute. Bankrupt. Their troops are beginning to mutiny. Already Washington has been forced to put down one mutiny and execute the mutineers. Arnold correctly calculates that if we will maintain our present course in America, they will capitulate because they have no money to continue. The army will simply quit and go home. We can win in America if we will simply maintain a presence there. I want that message delivered to the Privy Council and the House."

The message fell on deaf ears. Benedict Arnold? Can a traitor be trusted?

In despondency that approached depression, King George found himself with no other choice. To save any hope of retaining some modicum of respect from the Empire for the throne, he would have to compromise. Once again he summoned North.

"You will meet immediately with the Secretaries for both the Northern and Southern Departments, Stormont and Hillsborough. Peace negotiations with the American colonies will fall on their shoulders should that necessity arise, and I must know their disposition toward granting America the full independence the rebels now demand."

North called both men to his private library and startled them with his calculated indecision. He presented himself in the posture of being morose about the direction the war had taken and horrified at the depletion of the country's treasury. He opined that what little control England still held over the Americans was worthless, and he openly declared that the King was in total disagreement with him. He concluded by retreating into a wait-and-see attitude in the forlorn hope that somehow something unexpected might rescue the Empire. Stormont and Hillsborough departed the meeting stunned and befuddled, but they did not change their determination to bring an end to the war for America.

December passed into January, 1782, with Lord Germain bewildered at the deadlock in London. Lodged in nearby Drayton, on January 10, he wrote that he was in a state of waiting, " . . . as if all were peace and quiet. Lord North perhaps is doing the same; but if he intends to make any change among us, it is almost time to let us into the secret." On January 15 he could no longer endure the state of limbo that had seized the land. He returned to London and requested, and was granted, audience with the King on January 17. He put the critical question to the King directly.

"Sire, am I to still regard myself as Secretary of State for America?"

Caught in the crossfire of the white-hot battle, the King narrowed his eyes and retreated.

"That decision has not yet been made."

Germain revolted. Trembling to control himself, he spared nothing. "Your Majesty, I will never retract my refusal to grant America independence! I will leave office now on my terms, rather than be forced to it later on their terms. I must have an answer!"

Stunned at the audacious outburst, the King fumbled for a moment. "I shall confer with North. You have my word he will summon you immediately to resolve the matter."

The summons arrived at Germain's quarters the next morning, January 18, 1782. Germain made no attempt to disguise his resolve, nor his impatience. He was waiting for North at the appointed time and place on Downing Street. But when North came, he did not come to the room where Germain was seated, waiting. Rather, without a word, he walked on down the hall to take up his place in a cabinet meeting on Admiralty matters! His assistant timidly approached Germain.

"Lord North has repaired to a cabinet meeting on issues of the Admiralty."

Germain was confounded! A cabinet meeting? Admiralty matters?

He understood he had been invited to a private, pivotal meeting with North. Jaw clenched, Germain was ushered into the cabinet meeting, where he sat silently, struggling to control his rage. The meeting ended, North stood, bowed to his peers, and walked out with no visual sign that he even knew Germain had been present.

In a monstrous passion, Germain stormed back to his quarters and wrote a scathing letter of resignation to the King. Robinson, an intermediary, begged him to withhold it until Monday morning, January 21. During the four-day wait, it was discovered that the King had written North regarding Germain, as promised, but the letter was delivered to North with several warrants. Buried in paperwork and pressures, North had tossed the entire packet to a clerk, and had never seen the letter. When the King heard of North's neglect, he sent him a severe rebuke, and North repentantly arranged to meet with Germain the following day, January 22. Germain came, and his words cut like a cavalry saber.

"Do I remain Secretary of State for America?"

North spoke with resolve, bulging eyes narrowed. "At the moment, yes. However, it is impossible to continue the war. America is lost to us. It is vain to hope that we can prevent granting them independence."

For long seconds the two men stared at each other before Germain drew the line. "Then you must begin looking for another Secretary of State for the American Colonies."

North slowly answered. "I shall, but it will not be an easy task. Jenkinson has already advised me that he will not accept the office. You must continue until the matter is resolved."

In the deadly game that was now out of control, North realized his duty to inform the King of Germain's position. The King went into a rage, shouting, "If Germain is to be removed for opposing independence, then I must be removed as well!"

Shaken to his very foundations, North found himself stumbling, groping, unable to remedy the fact that the Privy Council and Parliament were both on the cutting edge of revolt against their King. He must divine a way to reconcile the King's refusal to abandon America with the rock-solid decision of the House of Commons to the contrary. Using every resource and all his energy, he could conceive of nothing that would succeed.

On January 30, North received a sealed correspondence from Germain. "I demand the response I was promised regarding the position of Secretary of America. The mails are being prepared for America as well as the West Indies, and proper instructions are an absolute necessity for the commanders in chief, as well as an answer to the request of General Sir Guy Clinton to resign. Lacking such, this department can not function."

Germain received no answer. The following day, on his exit from the Cockpit, North simply stated that the request was reasonable, but he could do nothing, since Jenkinson had again refused to accept the position. From that moment, Germain considered himself relieved as the Secretary of State for the Americas. On February 9, 1782, he bade an emotional farewell to his staff and office and closed the door behind him as he left the building for the last time.

The issue of what to do with the Americas ground on in the House of Commons. The first week of February, 1782, the King held a paper-thin margin of twenty-two votes in his support among the House members, but the opposition was rapidly pushing their attack on him and his stubborn refusal to abandon America. The conflict was quickly moving from an historic battle to an onslaught. North was nearly physically ill from fear. On February 27, lightning struck. The opposition to the Crown in the House of Commons again forced a vote on the question of abandoning the war against America. This time the majority was against the King by nineteen votes.

In a hopeless effort to retain something from the earth-shattering defeat, North proposed that the entire policy regarding the Americas should be reconsidered, with those opposing the Crown invited to participate. It was not to be. On March 4, 1782, the House of Commons passed a resolution that " . . . all who should advise or try to prosecute offensive war in America for the purpose of reducing the colonies to obedience by force are to be deemed enemies of this country."

It was over.

The opposition turned to Rockingham and Shelburne, who had been the core of the opposition to King George and his ministry. North requested of the King that he be released from office; the King refused. Rockingham and Shelburne moved ahead like a juggernaut. They scheduled a vote for March 20 to determine what was to become of the present ministry. Desperate to save face, North implored the King to permit his resignation, to spare him being forever remembered as dismissed by a vote of the House of Commons. The King refused; however, on March 20, the day of the vote, he relented. When Lord Surrey arose in the House to propose the removal of all the ministers, North rose with him, and after heated debate, North prevailed. He resigned. As he walked past those gathered at the door, he said simply, "Goodnight, gentlemen. You see what it is to be in the secret." Without another word, he departed that august body and walked out into the night.

On March 27, with the Marques of Rockingham now named First Lord of the Treasury, and the Earl of Shelburne his Secretary of State over Home and Colonial Affairs, England witnessed a wholesale slaughter of the ministry never before seen in the history of the Empire. Of the entire cabinet that had served with Lord North, only one survived in office—Thurlow.

The Rockingham ministry appointed Richard Oswald, an elderly, one-eyed Scot, with Henry Strachey, the Undersecretary of State, to represent England at a peace treaty conference to be held in Paris. The purpose was to meet with representatives of the United States of America, to grant the rebels full independence on such terms as were mutually agreeable. The American delegates were Benjamin Franklin, John Jay, John Adams, and Henry Laurens. Secretary for the British delegation was Alleyne Fitzherbert, with Benjamin Franklin's grandson, William, serving as secretary for the Americans.

The war for the Americas was over. The will of the British Empire to longer endure the stubborn refusal of her colonies to submit to their authority had been undone by the fall of Yorktown and the surrender of General Cornwallis and his entire army. The house of cards had tumbled. Embarrassed and humiliated before the world, they had done the only thing left to them. The purging of their own government of all who had participated in the profound debacle had been spectacular, brutal, and unprecedented. Men who on one day had held the keys of power to the mightiest empire in the world, were on the next day stripped of any vestige of their glory, to become things of ridicule and scorn. They were gone. All of them.

England had thrown the dice, and lost. Her rebellious children, now orphans, had won.

Notes

Lord North, First Lord of the Treasury during times relevant herein, and one of the most powerful men in the King's cabinet, is accurately described as to both his very unimpressive personal appearance, and his political attitudes and capabilities, which were sufficient to manage the ministry in a time of peace, but clearly rendered him incapable in a time of war (Mackesy, *The War for America, 1775–1783*, pp. 20–21). Lord George Germain is accurately described, including his startling history, his impressive physical appearance, his commanding presence, and his superior capacity to serve as Secretary of State for the American Colonies in the cabinet (Mackesy, *The War for America, 1775–1783*, pp. 46–57). For an excellent chart of the royal cabinet as it existed at times relevant in this chapter, see Mackesy, *The War for America, 1775–1783*, on the unnumbered pages following the Preface, pp. xxvi.

King George III is as described. Physically appealing as an adult, he had a sense of wit and charm, but never the capacity to rule a kingdom such as England. His ancestors had clear episodes of mental illness, which George III inherited, and manifested from time to time in fits and sustained periods of incompetence and insanity (Leckie, *George Washington's War*, pp. 26–40).

The events, dates, persons involved, and the time line that describe the news of the loss of the British army under command of General Cornwallis at Yorktown, when the terrible message reached London, who received it, and the tumultuous and disastrous aftermath that ensued, resulting in the total destruction of the King's cabinet, and the replacement of it with men who supported the proposition of granting independence to the rebellious American states in an effort to save the British interests in the West Indies, are as herein set forth. The key participants, and the role they played in the entire episode, are as described, including North, Germain, Stormont, Thurlow, Shelburne,

Rockingham, King George III, and others. Most of the meaningful statements credited to these major players in this chapter are verbatim, or very near verbatim, quotations from the historical records. In this chapter, this writer has described the momentous fall of the North ministry as a "wholesale slaughter," while Piers Mackesy described it as a "massacre"; a very powerful description from the modest and revered Mackesy (Mackesy, *The War for America, 1775–1783*, pp. 433–76; Leckie, *George Washington's War*, pp. 659–60).

Benedict Arnold, the hero-turned-traitor, did have audience with King George III, as herein set forth, as well as with other leaders in the Privy Council and Parliament, in which he proposed that the collapse of the American army was imminent due to a total lack of money. There actually had been two mutinies which required Washington and General Anthony Wayne to execute at least six American soldiers, all of which was true. Further, if England could have maintained even a token offensive, they would have won the war by default of the Americans. His efforts were too late, however, and his plan was never given serious consideration by any other than the King, and Arnold never rose to a position of much influence (Mackesy, *The War for America, 1775–1783*, p. 468; Martin, *Benedict Arnold, Revolutionary Hero*, p. 430; Randall, *George Washington, A Life*, pp. 390–91; Higginbotham, *The War of American Independence*, pp. 403–5).

With the fall of the ministry of Lord North, and the rise of Lord Rockingham, the British commissioned Richard Oswald and Henry Strachey to travel to Paris to negotiate the independence of the United States, with Alleyne Fitzherbert as their secretary. The United States authorized Benjamin Franklin, John Jay, John Adams, and Henry Laurens, with William Franklin as their secretary, to represent America (McCullough, *John Adams*, pp. 273–85).

Readers may be interested to know the rest of the story of Benedict Arnold. He spent time in London where he was included in the circle of high political figures, including personal audience with the King, however with little substantial influence. He decided to relocate his family to Nova Scotia, Canada, where a large community of British sympathizers, called Tories, had gathered after fleeing from America. He attempted several mercantile ventures in Nova Scotia, with little success, and returned to London, where he continued his efforts in the mercantile and privateering business, without success. With asthma, gout, and disabling pain in his twice-wounded left leg destroying his health, he slipped into a week of severe illness and died on June 14, 1801, in London, his life and fortune gone, his widow, Peggy, and their children in destitute condition in a foreign country. A folklore rumor suggests that in his last moments, he beseeched God to forgive him for his treason against America and requested that he be buried in his American general's uniform. The story is unfounded, and the best historians take the position that it is not true, as does this writer (Martin, *Benedict Arnold, Revolutionary Hero*, p. 431).

Horace Walpole was considered one of the leading sages of the London news industry and commented continuously on the British-American conflict (Leckie, *George Washington's War*, pp. 194–96, 367, 380, 460).

CHAPTER II

*T*he late November cold wind quieted in the night, enough that a light frost settled over the small American and French military camp at the fishing village of Gloucester on the north bank of the York River in the southern reaches of Virginia. What was left of the tiny tobacco trading village of Yorktown lay directly south, across the broad expanse of the river, which flowed east into Chesapeake Bay and on into the dark waters of the Atlantic beyond.

In the blue-black of five o'clock A.M., a young drummer stood shivering beside the flagpole to bang out reveille, then trotted back to his tent to drop his drum, then hunker down next to the small fire in the nearby ring of smoke-blackened rocks, palms thrust outward to catch the warmth. He watched as the camp stirred, gathering the will to rise one more time and face the grinding monotony of building the morning cooking fires, frying stale cornmeal mush, boiling fourth-day coffee beans, inspection, drill, and moving freight. Six years of soldiering had taught the American army the hard truth that most of military life was relentless, mindless obedience to a daily routine that became sheer torture.

He grinned at the soldiers as they curled in their blankets, cursed the cold, and loudly but sincerely offered to shoot him—or better yet, hang him—if he beat on that cursed drum one more time. Just one more time, and his mother would receive a letter: "It is with great glee that we inform you of the death of your favorite son, who was shot dead while sounding reveille."

One hundred yards due west of the flagpole, Caleb Dunson stirred beneath the pine boughs of his lean-to, swallowed sour, and waited while the recollection of where he was solidified in his brain. For a brief time he lay wrapped in his ragged, threadbare blanket, allowing himself the luxury of savoring the little warmth, and of letting his thoughts come as they would. In the darkness, random images formed in his sleep-fogged mind, and he did not forbid them.

Mother at home in Boston—the night he ran away from home to join the Continental Army at the age of sixteen—the lust for revenge on the red-coated soldiers who had shot and killed his father at the battle in Lexington—the battle at Brandywine, where he had shot and bayoneted men so close he could smell the fear on them—the beating he had taken from the bully Murphy—Dorman teaching him to use his fists—the sickening satisfaction of beating Murphy to the ground—the flawless beauty in the face of Nancy, the British spy who used him—the fight in the woods when Murphy and another man ambushed him—the realization he had killed both of them—his court-martial and acquittal—leaving his New York company to join the American army in the South—his capture and escape—Primus the fugitive black slave who had saved his life during the escape—joining Francis Marion and his small band of patriots—the battles at King's Mountain and Cowpens—joining the Americans and French at Yorktown—the great Chesapeake sea battle between the French and British—the siege of Yorktown—Washington sending a small force across the York River to Gloucester at night to stop "Bloody Tarleton"—the musket flashes in the fight before dawn—Tarleton's retreat—digging in to hold Gloucester—the surrender of British General Lord Charles Cornwallis at Yorktown—

It all came in a jumble of fleeting images.

He half-opened his eyes to peer out at the shapes taking form in the approach of sunrise—the skyline, the trees, the lean-tos at the place where the Americans were camped, and the scarcely discernible canvas tents of the French set in orderly rows, one hundred fifty yards to the east.

Good soldiers, the French. Turned Yorktown in our favor—good men—good officers—Rochambeau one of the best.

He straightened in his blanket and lay on his back to stretch leg muscles stiff from being curled for warmth half the night. His thoughts rolled on.

The British surrender of October nineteenth—watching the redcoats march into that field to lay down their arms—their brass band banging out "The World Turned Upside Down"—the hatred in their eyes at the sight of the French—the quiet afterwards—the strangeness of having no one to fight and wondering what they should do next.

He came wide awake and sobered as the image of his older brother came clear and sharp in his mind. *Matthew, tall, dark, serious, a born leader, expert navigator, and six years away from hearth and home fighting for independence—married to Kathleen—one square, blocky child—a toddler son who was clearly the grandson of John Phelps Dunson—Matthew, who led the French to victory in the crucial sea battle of the Chesapeake and then came to find him on the Gloucester side of the river after the British surrender.*

Twenty-four? Can Matthew be twenty-four? And can I be twenty? I haven't thought on it since I left home.

He reached to the bottom of the blanket and felt for his shoes and socks, buried next to his Deckhard rifle in the pine boughs he had spread on the ground for a bed beneath the slanted roof of the lean-to. The socks were stiff and had holes in the toes and heels, and the battered shoes were cold as he put them on and tugged at the laces beneath the blanket while his thoughts ran on.

Billy Weems—like a lifelong brother—coming with Matthew to find him after the surrender—Billy the faithful, the steady, the sensible—round, homely face, sandy hair, unbelievably strong, with thick shoulders and barrel chest and tree-stump legs, now a lieutenant with a sergeant named Turlock, who had been nearly killed by a cannon blast at the storming of British Redoubt Number Ten on the York River just five days before the surrender—with them a man dressed like an Iroquois Indian with a tomahawk thrust through his weapons belt and a long Pennsylvania rifle—speaking little, missing nothing, eyes penetrating, handshake firm—Billy calling him Eli—Eli Stroud, who had lately lost his wife—the odd feeling that Billy and Matthew had known Eli for a long time.

To the east, the sky was rapidly coming to a deep red, making a silhouette of the bare branches of the thick forest of trees. The first arc of the sun transformed the hoarfrost crystals into tiny prisms of red and gold and blue, and for a few minutes the gray, wintry world sparkled. Then the frost was melted, turning the bare ground of the camp slick and clammy. The morning wind arose, sweeping down the river to the Chesapeake, dissipating the wispy ground-mist.

Caleb took a deep breath, threw back his blanket, and came to his feet with the fluid, rolling move of a natural athlete. He rose to full height, just under six feet, and shrugged into his coat. The grunted, terse grumblings of those around him were beginning as he shook out his blanket, folded it, and laid it at the foot of his pine-bough bed, then carefully laid out his rifle, powder horn, and bullet pouch ready for inspection. The Deckhard rifle had been given to him by the small band of fierce freedom fighters in South Carolina commanded by Francis Marion—the Swamp Fox—before the battle at King's Mountain. Caleb preferred it to the standard musket, with its shorter range and lack of accuracy. Loading the Deckhard, which required pouring powder from the powder horn down the barrel, seating the ball on a greased linen patch, punching it into the muzzle with a starter, then driving it home with a hickory ramrod, was slower than loading a musket, but the deadly accuracy up to four hundred yards more than compensated for the time lost.

He found a place at the small, running brook that served his New York company, then knelt and caught his breath as he splashed freezing water onto his face, head, and neck. He dipped water into his mouth and spat it onto the forest floor as he rose to stand, water dripping from his dark brown, six-week growth of beard onto his coat and shirt. He backed away from the stream to give way for the next man while he wiped at his face with his coat sleeve. He untied the leather thong at the back of his head, smoothed his long brown hair as best he could, caught it together and retied it. For a moment he stood still, peering, searching upstream fifty yards to the place where the Black company shared the stream.

Primus, average height, average build, large eyes showing white in his round, black face, was there with the others in his company, taking his rotation at the creek. He and Caleb exchanged glances, but nothing more, before each went to his own pack to get his wooden plate and spoon and cup, and walk to the fire. The two men stood hunched in their separate breakfast lines, shivering while vapors rose from their breath, then holding out their bowls and cups to receive a large spoon load of steaming mush, two strips of fried sowbelly, and a smoking cup of bitter, colored water generously called coffee.

With half a dozen other men, Caleb sat in silence on a log near the cooking fire and dipped his spoon into the mush, blew on it for a moment, then gingerly touched it with his tongue. It was still too hot when he took the first mouthful, and he sucked air. He looked to the east where the sun was making filigree of the bare tree branches, and studied the rows of stacked crates, eight feet wide, six feet high, and a quarter mile long, and then looked at the cleared, flat place where the cannon were held. Beyond were the wagons and skids and sleds used to haul the freight down to the docks, and beyond them were holdings of the hundreds of horses and oxen that pulled them.

How many rows of captured stores remained? One hundred fifty? How many more tons? Six hundred? How many heavy guns? One hundred? And across the river at Yorktown, what? Sixty more cannon? Another five hundred tons of stores? How many horses? Three hundred? Oxen? One hundred?

He shook his head at the remembrance of the bewildering time following the surrender of the British on October nineteenth. French Admiral de Grasse was under orders to return with his fleet to the West Indies to wreak havoc among the British ships and territories there. His leaving forced a pivotal decision. When he sailed out into the Atlantic, would the land forces remaining at Yorktown and Gloucester wait for the British navy to return with warships to rescue Cornwallis? If the Americans remained, British General Clinton could and would bring down his fleet and his army and guns from New York, and with his superiority in numbers and cannon win in a pitched battle. So, should the Americans and French remain at Yorktown, or leave? And if they were to leave, what would they do with the mountain of desperately needed supplies and cannon they had brought, combined with those captured from the British? Should they burn it all and spike the cannon, to be certain the equipment and stores did not fall into British hands? If not, then what was to be done with it?

The answers, and the orders, quickly came down from General Washington:

Move the supplies by ships, out the mouth of the York River into the Chesapeake, then due north to the tiny hamlet called Head of Elk in Maryland, the northernmost settlement on the great Bay. There they would be safe from any British fleet that might return to Yorktown to attempt to rescue Cornwallis and avenge their humiliating defeat. Removed to Head of Elk, the supplies and guns would be easier to protect and more accessible to the American and French troops in the north. To make the haul, the Americans and French would scavenge what few American and French ships they could find.

General Rochambeau graciously volunteered to remain and take command of the operation, while General Washington would take the bulk of the American forces, with a few French, north to lock and hold British General Clinton on Manhattan Island and the Hudson River. Billy and Eli were among those ordered to move north with General Washington; Caleb and Primus were to remain with General Rochambeau to move the freight up the Chesapeake; Matthew was ordered to sail with de Grasse to assist in navigating the tricky channels and reefs in the countless islands of the West Indies, and to act as a courier for General Washington with a small, swift schooner.

For Caleb and those who were to remain, the unanswered question was what would happen if British admirals Rodney, Graves, or Hood brought gunboats into the Chesapeake while the cargo ships were in full sail? The unarmed American and French transports, and their crews, would be doomed. The nervous Americans anchored two small schooners at the mouth of the Chesapeake, each with one cannon bolted down on the deck, and stationed a man with a telescope in the crow's nest around the clock. The captains were ordered to fire three, timed cannon shots if a ship were to heave into sight with the dreaded Union Jack snapping in the wind.

With the orders given, General Washington and his army marched out, traveling north, and General Rochambeau took command of the sweaty, tough, monotonous labor of moving more than a thousand tons of military stores, and hundreds of cannon, to the Gloucester and Yorktown docks to be loaded into the holds, and stacked on the decks of the handful of tiny frigates and schooners they had commandeered. Thence up the Bay to unload, and return for the next load.

Thirty-two days had passed since the men first hitched reluctant horses and indifferent, splayfooted oxen to the wagons and skids and sleds, and began moving the freight down to the docks. The small ships, crammed with munitions and supplies, with cannon lashed down on their decks, rode deep and slow in the water, moving out into the Chesapeake and north for the two-day journey to Head of Elk, and they rode high and light and churned a ninety-foot wake on the return trip to Gloucester and Yorktown. Their crews stood silent at the rails, listening for the distant boom of three timed cannon blasts, and watching for sails of warships showing the red, white, and blue bars of the British flag flying from the mainmast.

The distant cannon shots did not come. None of the vaunted British warships appeared to avenge their humiliating losses at Yorktown.

Caleb squinted one eye to swallow the last of his breakfast coffee, stood, wiped at his dripping nose, drew a deep breath, and walked to the stream to wash his utensils. He set them in their place on his blanket for inspection and joined others as they entered the rope enclosures where the horses were held. With their shaggy winter hair growing daily, the horses tossed their heads and snorted, then settled and waited while the men buckled on the halters and led them to the wagons. They backed them up beside the wagon tongues, wheelhorses first, and began the process of mounting the horse collars, then the harnesses, connecting the tugs and traces, and finally snapping them to the singletrees, then to the doubletrees. The drivers climbed into the seats and sorted and threaded the six, long leather strands between their fingers while the crews clambered into the wagon beds and sat down. The drivers clucked and slapped the reins on the rumps of the wheelhorses, and the wagons creaked into motion toward the great rows of crates.

From his place in the jolting wagon, Caleb saw the officers walking rapidly towards a crude, one-room log building used for worship, realized it was Sunday, the Sabbath, and remembered the order issued by General Washington more than three years before, May 2, 1778. On the Sabbath, all officers were to attend religious services at the place most convenient to them, as an example to their troops.

Quietly Caleb shook his bowed head and a cynical smile crossed his face. *The Sabbath? Worship who? God? What God? The God that let the British kill Father? The God that was somewhere else for the past five years while tens of thousands of men spilled their blood—crippled, maimed, dead? The God who talks about love and heaven while he lets men filled with hate destroy each other in the purgatory of war? Worship such a being?*

He shook his head once more. *Let the officers do the worshipping. Moving a thousand tons of freight and cannon will go right on, and it won't be the officers that do it. For most of us, the Sabbath will be just like yesterday, and tomorrow, and God isn't going to do a thing to change it. If he's so almighty why doesn't he stop the pain? Why? Why?*

The drivers came back on the reins and talked the horses to a stop. The crews dropped to the frozen ground with their breath rising in the cold, morning air. They lowered the tailgates of the wagons and positioned the thick, fourteen-foot hickory planks, slanting from the wagon beds to the ground. Hard, callused hands seized the handles of the freight hooks while others reached for forty-foot sections of one-inch hawsers to loop around the three-hundred-pound crates. The men paused for a moment, took a deep breath, and commenced the brutal labor of using the hooks and hawsers to drag the crates up the planks and stack them in the wagon beds for the haul to the docks. Stopping for the midday meal was a tiny island of comfort in their world of sweat and strain, and the obligatory, one-hour daily drill at three o'clock was a blessed relief.

Sunday passed into Monday, and November blended into December without fanfare or notice. Lacy ice formed on the banks of the Chesapeake. The men carried hatchets to the creek to cut through the ice for camp water. They built small, crude huts for warmth, and the first blizzard of winter came howling in from the Bay before Christmas. By mid-January, temperatures hovered at zero. The Chesapeake was a glare of ice, and the small ships had to break a channel north and keep it open. The great stockpile of crates and supplies and cannon steadily dwindled at Gloucester and Yorktown, while they grew at an equal pace at Head of Elk.

It was the first week of April, with an almost indiscernible feel of spring in the air, when Caleb and his company loaded the last of the oxen onto the three ships remaining at Yorktown. They weighed anchor and sailed out into a blustery wind that sang in the rigging and whipped the bay into endless choppy whitecaps. Midmorning two days later they led the oxen single file down a broad, makeshift gangplank to the tiny dock at Head of Elk, and then unloaded their gear. In the afternoon they cut pine saplings and boughs and fashioned their lean-tos. The sun was touching the western rim when they lined up for evening mess at their new camp. With steaming bowls of mutton stew in hand they sat down on logs to eat.

The great task was finished. Little was said, but from time to time as twilight approached, every man among them glanced at the huge mountain of stores, and cannon, and livestock they had moved over the course of a brutal New England winter. They wiped at their beards with hands that were cracked, and they looked at each other with eyes that shone in silent pride at what they had done.

In approaching twilight, Caleb walked past the orderly rows of French tents, to the place in the woods where the small gathering of black soldiers made their camp. Some stared in stony silence while others, who knew him, nodded an acknowledgment. One pointed to the north, where Primus was kneeling, spreading his blanket on a bedding of pine boughs. He turned as Caleb approached, and the two sat down cross-legged beside each other on the blanket. No words of greeting were necessary between them.

Caleb gestured toward the supply depot. "We're finished. Decided where you'll go when the war's over?"

For a time Primus stared at his hands, clasped in his lap. "North. No cotton fiel's or indigo or slave masters."

"Know anybody up there?"

Primus shook his head and remained silent.

"Thought about trying to find your wife and child? Back down south somewhere?" Caleb saw the pain come into the white eyes and the black face.

"They gone. Like cattle. Won't never find 'em. Gots to start over. New."

"Might be hard. Not many black people up north. Not like where you were raised." Caleb saw the longing, the yearning, and it tore his heart when Primus shrugged his answer.

"Don't matter much. Black is black, north or south."

Caleb drew his knees up and circled them with his arms. "Maybe I can help. In Boston. If you decide to go there."

"Maybe New York. Philadelphia. Maybe Boston. Anyplace where bein' there won't cause no trouble. Jes' a place to earn my way with no hurt."

"You let me know. Hear?"

Primus turned to look at him. "I hear."

Caleb came to his feet and walked away without looking back.

The men sought their blankets early and stared thoughtfully into the dark as the drummer rattled the ten o'clock tattoo. One by one the lanterns in the lean-tos and huts and tents winked out, and the quarter-moon rose over a dark, silent camp.

Notes

Following the victory at Yorktown, French Admiral de Grasse remained in the Chesapeake for a short time to protect the bay from British warships while the task of moving the supplies from Yorktown to Head of Elk was begun, then sailed out in compliance with his orders to attack British ships and holdings in the West Indies (Caribbean). French General Rochambeau remained to finish the work in the Yorktown vicinity. General Washington marched north with most of the Continental Army and some French infantry to check British General Clinton at New York (Freeman, *Washington*, pp. 494–95).

CHAPTER III

*D*aylight on the Chesapeake came in a gray overcast that turned the sun into a dull red ball rising in the east. Sometime in the night the salt breeze from the Atlantic had died, and morning came with an eerie, dead calm, and a damp chill in the air. All nature seemed to be holding its breath. No birds of spring moved in the silent trees. No squirrels darted and scolded. The oxen stood transfixed, facing east, while the horses pranced and whickered, nervous, ears pricked and moving, sensing what was coming. Soldiers and sailors at the Head of Elk encampment walked silent through the breakfast mess lines with narrowed eyes, peering south and east, searching the skyline for the first glimpse of the low, level, ominous purple cloud that would be moving steadily toward landfall.

Caleb held his wooden bowl and cup to receive his morning ration of thick, boiled oats and coffee, and sat on a log with three others from his company to blow on the smoking mush for a moment. He glanced about at the eyes and faces of the men and the way they moved their hands, trying to gauge how close the entire camp was to the breaking point. The five months of a harsh Chesapeake winter had taken its toll. The bland sameness of the daily food rations made mess call a matter of choking food down to maintain strength. Mail had arrived once, in January, and men with wives and children in distant homes did not know if their families were alive or dead or starving or freezing in the cold and snows of a New England winter. Only small, disconnected bits of news of the fortunes of the war had trickled into camp. No one knew whether the Americans and British had fought it out in the north or whether the French and the British navies had collided in the West Indies to settle the stand-or-fall question of which country would control the American coast, and consequently, dictate the terms of what was left of the war.

The mind-numbing monotony of inspection, mess, drill, and standing day and night picket duty guarding the mountain of supplies salvaged from Yorktown and Gloucester had turned the men surly, edgy, intolerant. Arguments erupted over nothing, then became heated, then exploded into bitter fights. Eight days before, four men in the same company had each claimed a small piece of seared pork at the evening mess. Tempers flared. One reached for his bayonet, and within seconds, two of them were groaning on the ground, doubled over, holding their midsections, close to dead. Scattered talk of mutiny had been heard in the quiet of the darkness after the tattoo drum sounded. The two questions that gnawed at the men incessantly were *what* and *when?* What would trigger open rebellion, and when would it happen?

The sound of raised voices brought the head of every man in the company swiveling around to peer toward the docks, wide-eyed, suddenly alert, fearful the revolt had begun. They came to their feet to stare down the slight incline to the water where a knot of men were gesturing, pointing south, past the place where their own small fleet lay at anchor, unmoving in the flat, glassy waters of the Bay. All eyes raised to study the Chesapeake horizon to the south for a full minute before they saw the tiny speck. Another minute passed before it became a schooner moving slowly toward them, sails limp in the calm preceding the approaching storm. She was driven by six long oars, three on each side, stroking in rhythm.

Mess Sergeant Darren Orme, aging, gray hair and beard, stoop shouldered, nose badly broken years earlier when a mare had kicked him, pointed with his large, wooden mush ladle, still coated with the morning's cooked oats.

"Which flag?" he rasped in his high, backwoods voice. He turned to

Caleb. "Dunson, these eyes aren't what they once was. Is she ours? French? British?"

For long seconds Caleb studied the incoming fleck. "Can't tell."

"How many? We got the whole British fleet comin' in here?" Mortal concern was plain in his eyes.

Caleb shook his head. "Looks like only one."

"One?" His grizzled old face wrinkled. "Most likely a scout snoopin' to find out if we're still here."

Caleb rounded his lips to blow air for a moment. "Maybe."

Orme turned back to the cook fire. "Well, this gawkin' and guessin' isn't goin' to change nothin'. We got chores. You men get at it."

The morning mess crew went grudgingly back to the kettles of steaming water to wash their utensils, while the other men went to the stream to rinse their own before turning to the relentless morning grind. Caleb tossed the water from his bowl and cup and spoon before he laid them on his blanket, then walked to the woodyard. He picked up a heavy splitting ax and waded through a blanket of ankle-deep wood chips to the nearest chopping block, picked a rung of pine from the stack, set it upright on the battered block, set his teeth, and swung the ax hard. In this army, only two things were certain: there would never be enough food, or enough firewood.

An unusual hush held the camp as the men worked, constantly turning their heads to study the small craft creeping slowly up the bay, cutting a "V" in the glassy waters made black by the thickening overcast. Behind the craft, a thin purple line was creeping upward on the eastern horizon. Ten minutes passed before an officer with a telescope shouted, "American flag. She's ours!"

Every man in the company stopped to stare, with one question riding each of them. If the ship is American, why is she alone? A heavy foreboding crept into them as they stood still, watching the small incoming schooner.

Suddenly Caleb's eyes narrowed and his arm shot up to point. "She's too low in the water! Been damaged. Bowsprit's half gone. Two arms on the for'ard mast are crooked. She's been shot up."

Anxious eyes probed the lines of the creeping schooner and began picking out the tiny black dots in the slack sails, where cannonballs had punched through. At five hundred yards they could see the splinters of the shattered stump of the bowsprit. Behind it, two cannon muzzles thrust through gun ports that had been cut on the main deck. Behind the makeshift gun ports, the railing was blown away in several places. The lower and middle arms on the forward mast were shot into two pieces. The hull showed four crude, jerry-rigged repairs where six, thirty-pound British cannonballs had smashed through above the waterline.

"She gonna make it?" It was Primus's voice, coming from behind Caleb, to his right.

Caleb rubbed the back of his hand across his mouth, judging. "She'll make it."

The men watched with growing interest, reading in the damaged ship the unmistakable signs of a heavy sea battle. In their minds they were hearing the roar of the cannon and seeing the blood-slick carnage as grapeshot and cannonballs smashed into ships and ripped into the bodies of men. Slowly the wounded little ship came on, the three long oars on each side working in a slow cadence, their dipping breaking the smooth surface of the becalmed bay. At one hundred yards the officer with the telescope sang out, "*Henrietta!* Her name's *Henrietta!*" Men all up and down the line looked at each other with the question in their eyes, but no one recognized the name.

With the ship still fifty yards from the dock, Caleb narrowed his eyes and leaned forward. Incredulous, he blurted, "That captain! It's Matthew!"

Primus stared hard at the tall man standing erect at the bow, hatless, both hands on the rail, dark hair tied back, dark beard, his disheveled uniform spotted with dried black blood, calling orders to his skeleton crew as they lined the ship with the main dock. Primus squinted at the recognition of Matthew from their brief meeting at the battle of Yorktown.

They heard the shouted command, "Ship oars," and the long oars came dripping out of the water and raised to the vertical position to let the ship slow and glide thumping against the thick black timbers of the dock. Two-inch hawsers were thrown snaking from the ship, and eager hands looped them over the weathered pilings. Caleb and Primus had moved toward the dock and were jostling their way through the gather of men, as the crew of the *Henrietta* set the gangplank. They saw Matthew turn to his crew, his voice rising as he called orders.

"Dead and wounded first."

From behind him came four men, dirty, barefooted, shirts and trousers speckled where blood had splattered and dried. Two of them each carried a blood-soaked canvas bag sewed shut with the stitching of a sailmaker. Matthew led them down the gangplank onto the dock. Weariness and anguish showed in his eyes as he faced the silent men gathered before him. His voice came loud and demanding.

"Where's a doctor? Your hospital? Get your doctor."

An officer quickly pushed to the front. "Just here," he said, pointing. "Follow me!"

Instantly a path opened through the crowd, and Matthew stepped to one side. He gestured to the four behind him to follow the officer, while he walked back to the gangplank, waiting for three more men who came in single file. The first carried a man in his arms like a sleeping baby, and Matthew's jaw clamped shut at the sight. The left arm of the unconscious man was missing below the elbow. The left foot was also gone, above the ankle. The stink of gangrene reached out from the dirty bandages. Behind him came a man leading a sailor whose face and head were swathed in strips of dried-blood-soaked sheeting. The injured sailor walked with halting steps, feeling his way, blind and deaf. The last man was half carrying a sailor who had both arms splinted and wrapped tightly to his ribs. Behind them came three other men, unwounded but dirty and exhausted.

Matthew got them all ahead of him on the dock and followed them past the soldiers who stood quietly, watching, eyes dropping to the ground at the sight of the man who would go through the balance of his life in a world of silent blackness, and judging whether the gangrene that reached them like the stench of death would kill the unconscious man.

None saw, nor did they think of the glories of war as the wounded and dying passed by.

Without a word Caleb and Primus fell in behind Matthew to follow him the two hundred yards to the crudely built, makeshift log hospital. Sergeant Orme followed, with half a dozen men of the breakfast mess crew. A nurse held the door open as Matthew and his crew passed through into the twilight of the interior, while Caleb and Primus stopped at the door. Two doctors met Matthew at the first row of bunks, frames built of pine limbs with bottoms of woven ropes. Half the beds held sick and disabled men who propped themselves up on one elbow to watch the procession pass by. The strong odor of dysentery, carbolics, and stringents hung in the air like a pall, and Matthew and his men breathed light.

The doctors took one look at the dead and wounded and drew a deep breath. The tall one, round shouldered and bespectacled, turned on his heel, and led the small column back to the corner of the large room where log partitions walled off a surgical suite. The shorter one, balding, husky, followed, face a study in controlled pain and anger. Inside the partition, the tall one removed his spectacles, rubbed bloodshot eyes, and turned to Matthew.

"I'm Doctor Muhlman. I'm in charge here."

Matthew nodded. "Captain Matthew Dunson. Can you take on our dead and wounded?"

Muhlman sighed. "The dead should go on down to the church for burial. We'll take the wounded here." He gestured with his head toward the unconscious man with the missing arm and foot. "Gangrene. We'll start surgery in the next ten minutes. We'll be lucky if . . ." His voice trailed off, and he did not finish the sentence.

Matthew interrupted. "Do you need me here? I've got to see the commanding officer as soon as I can."

Muhlman's eyebrows rose. "You have more wounded?"

"No. But there's a storm about three hours behind us. Someone's got to get your ships and this camp ready."

"That bad?"

"Yesterday it was close to a typhoon."

"You go. We'll take care of this."

"Do you want my able men to help?"

"No. We have enough."

"I'll be back as soon as I can."

"Go."

"Where's the church? For the two dead."

"Leave them here. We'll handle it."

"Thank you, sir."

Muhlman gave hand signs, and the shorter doctor nodded. Two nurses turned on their heels and went to the medicine cabinet in the corner to begin selecting bottles and instruments to lay out on a clean cloth. Matthew turned to his ten able-bodied men and gestured, and they followed him back through the rows of sick, glad to be free of the stench and the morbid feel of the dimly lit room. Matthew strode to the cluster of bearded men gathered near the door and spoke to the nearest one.

"Could you tell me where to find your—"

He stopped in mid-sentence, wide-eyed. "Caleb!"

Caleb shifted his weight from one foot to the other. A casual grin tugging at the corners of his mouth, nearly hidden by his beard. "Matthew. Nice to have you come visit."

Matthew reached to seize his shoulders. "Are you all right?"

Caleb shrugged. "Good. Suffering a little from boredom, maybe, with everybody else around here. Until you came paddling that schooner." He sobered. "I saw your dead and wounded. There was a battle?"

"A big one. We'll talk later. I have to get to the commanding officer."

He shifted his feet to move before he looked past Caleb at the round, black face of Primus.

"Primus! I'm surprised to find you here."

Primus nodded. "Nice to see you again, Cap'n Matthew."

Matthew turned back to Caleb. "Where's the commanding officer?"

Caleb pointed. "Over there, maybe three hundred yards. Name's Colonel Humphrey Edvalsen."

"Where's General Rochambeau?"

"Left on orders weeks ago. Want me to take you to Edvalsen?"

"Yes. Now."

Caleb turned to Sergeant Orme. "All right with you?"

Orme bobbed his head. "Get back as soon as you can."

Matthew broke in. "Sergeant, do you have any food you can spare? My men haven't eaten since yesterday morning."

Orme shrugged. "Mush. Coffee. Maybe some black bread."

Matthew turned. "You men go with the sergeant. I'll find you later."

Caleb and Matthew, with Primus following, worked their way through the press of men, moving as fast as they could.

"You have something for Edvalsen?" Caleb asked. "Orders?"

"Not orders. Information. From Admiral de Grasse."

"De Grasse? What happened down there?"

Matthew shook his head. "A battle. De Grasse was beaten."

Caleb gaped. "He *what?*"

"Some bad mistakes. The French lost."

"Are the British coming here?"

"Maybe. I doubt it. Where's Colonel Edvalsen's tent?"

"No tent." Caleb pointed to a small, crude log building of green lumber, jointed with mud and dried sea grass. "There." One minute later the three of them stopped before the door and faced the picket. He eyed Matthew, then spoke in a soft Southern dialect.

"You have business with the Colonel?"

"Captain Matthew Dunson, lately with Admiral de Grasse down in the West Indies. I have critical information for the commander of this camp. I presume that is Colonel Edvalsen."

The picket looked at Caleb, then Primus, and it was impossible to miss the look of condescension that crossed his face as his eyes passed over the black man. Primus lowered his gaze to the ground, as he had done all his life when in the presence of a white man who looked at him as though he were less than a human being.

The picket broke it off. "Both these men with you?"

"This is my brother, Private Caleb Dunson. He was at Gloucester, and he's been here since with the New York Company. Primus is one of us. Time is against us. I need to see Colonel Edvalsen."

"One moment." The picket knocked then entered the dimly lit room, and thirty seconds later returned.

"The Colonel will see you and your brother."

Caleb tensed and shifted one foot, balanced, ready, and spoke quietly. "Primus is a soldier in the Continental Army. He goes where we go."

For a moment hot anger flared in the picket's eyes, then passed. "I didn't mean anything. It was an oversight."

He stepped aside, and Matthew pushed past him, Primus next, and Caleb behind, as they entered the room and blinked while their eyes adjusted to the dim light. They stopped four feet from a rough-hewn desk, and came to attention. Edvalsen rose from his chair to face Matthew. He was average height, average build, with a trimmed beard, wearing a uniform that needed laundering. He was smoking a pipe that added to the blue haze already in the room. Even in the dim light, they could see a scar that ran horizontally on his right cheek, the evidence of a British musketball that had creased his face but could have killed him.

Matthew saluted. "Captain Matthew Dunson, United States Navy. I arrived less than an hour ago bearing sealed information from Admiral de Grasse, intended for your eyes, as well as others."

Edvalsen returned the salute. "Colonel Humphrey Edvalsen, commander of this encampment." His flat New England accent left no doubt he was not from the South. He gestured. "Have a seat, gentlemen."

The three of them drew up chairs fashioned from green pine wood.

Edvalsen spoke. "You have a writing?"

Matthew handed him a packet of tightly tied oilskin, and for three minutes the only sound in the dim room was the rustling of parchment as Edvalsen read and turned pages. He raised surprised eyes to Matthew.

"The French were beaten down in the West Indies?"

"Yes."

"You were there?"

"I was navigator on De Grasse's ship. Yes."

Edvalsen leaned forward on his elbows. "What happened?"

"De Grasse was under orders to invade Jamaica and drive out the British. He had thirty-three ships of the line and enough troops to do it, but Admiral Rodney's fleet joined Admiral Hood and brought the British fleet to thirty-six warships."

Edvalsen set the parchment aside, listening intently.

"April 9 the British set out to catch the French. Admiral Hood and his squadron got separated from Rodney. For two days the French had their chance to entirely destroy Hood's squadron, but de Grasse decided against it and held his course for Jamaica. Hood rejoined Rodney, and the two fleets entered into all-out battle near the Isle of the Saints. Thirty-three French against thirty-six British. The British captured five French ships, including de Grasse's flagship. Right now, de Grasse is a prisoner in the hold of Rodney's ship."

Slowly Edvalsen leaned back and tapped the document, incredulous. "De Grasse a prisoner, after what he did to the British here? Impossible!"

Matthew said nothing, and Edvalsen continued.

"The message says de Grasse ordered you to carry this message to Washington. Why weren't you taken prisoner with de Grasse?"

"When de Grasse realized he'd lost everything, he ordered me to get through the British gunboats to warn General Washington that the British navy controls the West Indies. If they decide to come north, there is nothing to stop them. They could blockade every harbor."

"How did you get through the British?"

"Took the fastest schooner we had and made a run."

"That's the vessel you tied up at the dock?"

"Yes."

"Pretty badly mauled."

"We went through a massive sea battle to get out."

"You know General Washington is not here. He's up north, on the Hudson."

Matthew started in surprise. "I was told he would be in Philadelphia. You're certain he's up on the Hudson?"

"Certain. Why did you stop here?"

"We had no choice. We lost two arms on the for'ard mast, and were hulled six times. Two crew members dead, three crippled. The schooner would never have made a New England harbor."

"You stopped here for repairs?"

"Not just repairs. It is essential you know the British might come up the Chesapeake to recapture the supplies you have here. And, we need to leave the *Henrietta* here and take one of your ships. It's imperative General Washington know as quickly as possible what happened to de Grasse. I think the British have decided to hold Jamaica and the West Indies at all costs, and they'll probably hold their fleet down in the West Indies. But if I'm wrong—if they do come north—they could hit you here and go on up to cripple the entire Continental Army. Maybe destroy it. General Washington has to know."

For five long seconds Edvalsen stared at Matthew, thoughts running. "Will you need replacements for your dead and wounded?"

"Depends on which ship you can spare. From what I saw in your harbor, I'll need at least five men." He gestured toward Caleb and Primus. "I'd like these two and three others. I suggest we use volunteers because it's possible we could run into British gunboats before we get back down the bay to the Atlantic. If we do, I'll have to try a run through them. I'll need a full crew."

Edvalsen's eyebrows arched. "You know these men?"

"My brother and a friend."

Edvalsen paused to gather his thoughts. "I'll get your volunteers."

Matthew raised a hand. "One more thing. We came in ahead of a storm that will hit here in about three hours. Coming up from the West Indies. We were not far from the western edge of it. It was close to a typhoon. I suggest, sir, that you get your ships ready for it."

Edvalsen stood, then leaned forward, palms flat on the desk. "I'm a soldier, not a sailor. Can you handle it?"

Rising himself, Matthew said, "Yes, sir, with your permission."

"You've got it."

"First, can you authorize me to leave the *Henrietta* in exchange for one of your schooners or frigates that's seaworthy?"

"Take your pick."

"Unless there's something else, I'd better get down to the docks."

"Wait." Hurriedly Edvalsen scrawled words on a paper, folded it, and handed it to Matthew. "That's authorization to take one of our ships, and to take command of the men at the docks to get braced for this storm. If anyone asks, show them that."

"Thank you, sir." Matthew folded the paper as he strode from the room out into the gray overcast and started toward the docks, Caleb and Primus following. The slightest stir of a freshening Atlantic salt breeze brushed their faces, and the flag at the top of the forty-foot pole stirred. Matthew stared toward the east. The purple cloud that had been low on the distant horizon since daybreak was now a towering black curtain less than five miles away, blotting out the sun, turning day into dusk, moving steadily toward them across the northern reaches of the Chesapeake. Even at that distance he could see the winds and torrential rains churning the bay to a froth and hear the ominous roar.

"She's coming," Matthew said. "We've got to get the ships tied tight to the docks. Those winds will beach them if we don't, and if they're tied too loose they'll batter themselves to pieces against the pilings. Let's move!"

The three broke into a sprint for the docks, and thirty yards before they reached the water, Matthew was shouting orders above the mounting howl of the wind and rain, and men were jumping.

Notes

As described in chapter 1 of this volume, in the closing months of 1781 and the first months of 1782, the British concluded that their greatest interest in the Americas was their valuable possessions and trade in the West Indies, with Jamaica their greatest prize. Accordingly they ordered thirty-six of their warships under Admirals Rodney and Hood to protect Jamaica from capture by the French. The French ordered Admiral de Grasse, who in early April 1782, had thirty-three warships together with a large number of troops in the waters of the West Indies, to invade and seize Jamaica. On April 9, 1782, the two opposing navies collided and for days engaged in a running battle, de Grasse attempting to reach and seize Jamaica, and Hood and Rodney attempting to stop him. De Grasse suffered embarrassing losses when two of his ships, the *Jason* and the *Zele*, collided in the night, disabling the *Jason*. Later, during the night, the *Zele* again collided with another ship and lost her foremast, totally disabling her. Additionally, the *Caton* was damaged by cannon fire in a skirmish and had to withdraw, as did two other ships that could not keep up with the fleet. With his command thus reduced, de Grasse chose to engage the British, who now had substantially superior numbers of able warships. A fierce battle ensued in which de Grasse's flagship was captured with four other French vessels. De Grasse was imprisoned by Rodney, and the British won a major victory. Had they chosen, the British could then have sailed north, blockaded most American ports, and badly crippled the American army. However, consistent with the decision of King George and Parliament, the British chose to remain in the West Indies to protect their possessions there, including Jamaica (Mackesy, *The War for America, 1775–1783*, pp. 456–59). For a listing of the ship count, see page 457 of Mackesy.

Head of Elk, Maryland
April 1782

CHAPTER IV

*B*y midmorning, there was no sun. By noon there was no daylight. The world was in deep twilight, blurred by rain so heavy men
struggled to breathe. It came horizontal, driven by screaming easterly
winds that bent trees to the west and tore some from the earth. Great
limbs, ripped and shattered, were scattered, rolling. Lesser branches and
the leaves of spring were stripped away to come whistling, gathering in
heaps where wagons, or buildings, or the long rows of crated supplies
stopped them. Half the tents sheltering the French soldiers snapped their
tie ropes or jerked the pegs from the ground to go tumbling, snagging,
flapping furiously in the tumult. Most of the simple lean-tos of the
Americans were swept away. Horses and oxen in the great pens turned
their rumps to the wind and stifling rain and stood dumbly, heads down,
enduring the storm. Men sought places where a wagon, or a building, or
a cannon, or a crate, offered protection, and they sat on the ground,
leaned forward, backs to the rain, hands clasped over their heads to wait
out the spring storm.

In midafternoon the howl of the wind climaxed and then began to
diminish, and the torrential rain slowed. It was past five o'clock when
men could rise and stand in the wind and stare into the steady down-
pour, awed, cowed by the terrible power of the storm. For a time they
walked slowly through the destruction, humbled in their souls by a sense
of their own smallness.

Their hair and beards and clothing dripping, Matthew and Caleb and their small crew worked their way from the crated supplies through the mud and wreckage to the docks, standing quiet as they peered at the ships. The *Henrietta* rode deep in the water, slowly settling. Two of the other ships had splintered railings where the heaving water had thrown them against the dock and the pilings. One ship looked like a crippled bird, with the main and forward masts snapped and dangling. Matthew set his teeth at the sight of the battered ships, and he and his crew quietly walked to examine the eight frigates and schooners that appeared to have ridden out the storm undamaged. A little after six o'clock, with the heavy overcast thinning and the rain and wind tailing off, Matthew turned to Caleb.

"I'm going to see Edvalsen. Can you take these men to evening mess with your company?"

Caleb left with the crew while Matthew turned to pick his way through the badly mauled camp to Edvalsen's quarters. The picket at the door, soaked and dripping, disappeared inside for a moment, then gave Matthew entrance. Edvalsen stood behind his desk in the yellow light cast by a single lantern on his table. His uniform was soaked, and the smell of wet wool hung sharp in the air. Matthew came to attention, Edvalsen gestured to a chair, and the two sat down facing each other.

Edvalsen cleared his throat to speak. "I never saw a camp in such a mess. What's your report on the ships?"

"Three with damage. Two with railings gone, one with two masts gone."

Edvalsen heaved a sign of resignation. "Can the masts be repaired?"

"Not repaired. Replaced, but it takes time. A mast reaches completely through all decks of a ship, to a notch in the keel. The decks will have to be removed where the mast passes through, and the damaged mast lifted out. A new one will need to be lowered into place and set with huge bolts and braces. It will take good carpenters and sailors who know how. Do you have them?"

Edvalsen tossed one hand up and let it drop. "We'll manage. The other two, with the railings damaged?"

"Two carpenters can fix those in one day."

"Is there a ship fit to carry you north?"

"The *Carrie*. She's light and sound, I judge around eighty tons. Should make good time. I'll have to cut two gun ports in her bow and get the cannon from the *Henrietta*. That can be finished by midnight. Any objection to my taking her?"

"None. Can the *Henrietta* be salvaged?"

"Yes. In the battle down in the West Indies she was hulled by cannonballs six times, and she lost two arms. But the masts were untouched, and she's sound. If your men will get her pumps working tonight they can raise her high enough to make repairs within two days."

"When do you plan to leave?"

"Daybreak."

Edvalsen's eyes opened in surprise. "What about the storm? Isn't the wind wrong?"

"Storm should be about blown out. We can tack our way into the wind. It's British ships that concern me. If they have the Chesapeake bottled up, they could be trouble for all of us. If we run into them I'll turn and come back to warn you. If I haven't returned within two days, it means the Bay is open. Understood?"

"Understood. Do you need provisions?"

"Some. I have your written order."

"Show it to the commissary officer. He'll get you what you need."

The two men stood and Matthew leaned to shake Edvalsen's hand. "Thank you, sir."

"Good luck."

In a steady wind and cold rain, four carpenters walked up the gangplank onto the dark deck of the *Carrie*. They set lanterns hissing in the rain and in the yellow light began with crosscut saws. By nine o'clock they had finished cutting the gun ports in the railing on both sides of the bowsprit, and by ten o'clock the two, twenty-four-pound cannon were on her deck. By midnight the recoil ropes holding them in position were bolted to both sides of the gun ports and strung around the butts of the guns; the ramrods, budge barrels, and cannonballs were all in place. By five o'clock, with the rain easing and the wind dying, there were enough provisions in the hold of the little ship to sustain twelve men for twenty days. At six o'clock, with the unrisen sun turning the eastern clouds a dull purple, Matthew held a lantern high at the bow and gave the order.

"Cast off!"

Bearded men on the dock worked the heavy, dripping hawsers from the brackets and threw them over the undulating rail of the ship, where strong hands caught and coiled them. The little schooner slowly separated from its mooring, and Matthew gave the next order.

"Unfurl the top sail on the mainmast!"

Barefooted sailors sixty feet above the deck hooked their feet over the ropes in the rigging to jerk the knots of the ropes lashing the sails to the yardarms, and the soggy canvas dropped into place. Beneath them, strong hands seized the ropes dangling from the sails and lashed them to the lower yard. The sound of the sails popping full rose above the whisper of rain on the bay, and instantly the *Carrie* took on a life of her own. Shafts of golden light from the rising sun came gleaming through gaps in the ragged clouds as Matthew gave the orders, and the little vessel began the slow process of tacking south, back and forth, port then starboard, on a wind coming in from the southeast. By seven o'clock the wind had shifted and was coming in directly from the east. Matthew then unfurled all the canvas and set the sails to catch the steady breeze, and the little schooner leaped south, trailing a wake more than one hundred yards long. Matthew took his position in the bow, feet spread and set, searching the dark water for logs and trees torn from the mainland and driven into the bay, large enough to crack the keel of a ship at full speed. Without looking back he gave hand signals to the helmsman, who spun the five-foot wheel port or starboard, as Matthew pointed.

At nine o'clock, with every man in the crew watching and waiting, Matthew sent the first man into the crow's nest, seventy feet up the mainmast, telescope in hand, under orders to watch for anything flying the British Union Jack. Ten minutes later the shout came from above, "No sails in sight." At noon his relief man took the telescope and settled into the tiny, round, waist-deep bucket. At three o'clock the third relief man took up the position to repeat the call, "No sails in sight."

Every man on the tiny ship let out held breath. They took their evening meal in the confinement of the little mess hall, and while three took up their positions for first watch, the others went below decks to their gently swinging hammocks to rest before their four-hour duty. In full darkness Matthew gave orders to furl all sails except the top mainsail; running afoul at full speed of a massive tree floating in the black of night could crack the keel, and a cracked keel could not be repaired in the water.

A little after nine o'clock a rising wind from the northeast swept the dark heavens clear. Unending points of light sprinkled the black velvet, and then the Big Dipper hove into view above the northeastern horizon, pointing to the North Star. Matthew took his bearings, called to the helmsman, and the little ship sped steadily south, directly down the center of Chesapeake Bay.

When the two o'clock watch changed, Matthew went to his small, confined quarters, stretched out on a bunk that was two inches shorter than he, slipped off his shoes, and slept the deep, dreamless sleep of exhaustion. The clanging of the bell calling for the six o'clock watch change brought him back on deck, to stand at the bow. He called the order, "Unfurl all canvas!"

Three minutes later the sails popped full and the *Carrie* was flying. The morning mess was finished when Caleb and Primus came to stand beside Matthew. Caleb was scratching his beard, hair awry, clothing still damp.

"You expecting British ships at the mouth of the Bay?"

Matthew's forehead furrowed. "Maybe."

"How far ahead?"

"We're right where the bay narrows." He pointed west. "Over there is the York River. Yorktown. Gloucester." His hand shifted to point south. "Down there is Lynnhaven Bay. Before we reach Lynnhaven,"—he shifted his point to the east—"we come to Cape Charles, over there, and south of Cape Charles is Cape Henry. Between them is the entrance into the bay. If the British mean to seal up the Chesapeake, that's where they'll be."

"How soon?"

"We'll be there in less than half an hour."

"If they're waiting?"

"We go back to warn Edvalsen."

Caleb could not suppress a grin as he pointed to the two cannon in the bow of the tiny ship. "Sure you don't want to fight it out?"

Matthew shook his head, grinning back at Caleb. "I'm sure those two guns would terrify any British naval officer."

A hint of a smile crossed Primus's face. "If we have to shoot those guns at those big British warships, I hope we movin' awful fast."

Matthew chuckled. "So do I." He sobered and turned to call out, "Take your posts. We're coming to the mouth of the bay." He cupped his hands to shout up to the man in the crow's nest. "Watch sharp to the east. That's where they're most likely to be."

"Aye, sir."

The men stood rooted, staring south and east until their eyes watered, searching, waiting for the dreaded shout from the crow's nest, "Sails ho!"

Matthew watched as the lighthouse at Cape Charles came into view, and they were past it half a mile before he turned to the helmsman. "Hard to port. Take a due east heading."

"Aye, sir." The man spun the wheel and watched the compass before him until the needle pointed directly to his left. The ship leaned to starboard as she heeled to port, coming around directly into the wind. The men in the rigging began the tricky, arduous work of handling the sails to tack into the wind, while those on the deck and the lookout in the crow's nest strained their eyes for the first sign of sails with the colors of the British Union Jack fluttering from the top of the mainmast. Matthew watched to the south, then the north, dividing the distance between Cape Charles and Cape Henry as the little craft entered the Atlantic. She held her course out into open water for two miles, running free and clear. All eyes turned up to the man in the crow's nest, and then the shout came down.

"No sails in sight."

A spontaneous cheer arose from the *Carrie*, and Matthew called his next order.

"Take a course due north."

"Aye, sir."

Again the little craft leaned to starboard as she heeled to port, coming around to a due north heading. The crew set the sails to catch the east wind, and the little vessel leaped forward. Caleb looked at Matthew, standing in the bow with the salt wind in his face and hair, feet spread, a rapture on his face that Caleb had never seen, and it came to him. Men who venture the sea on sailing ships know. A trim schooner flying with her canvas tight, and a deck rolling with the seaswells in open water, is a wondrous, free, living thing. Matthew was where he belonged, master of his world.

The spring sun was halfway to its zenith in a blue sky when the call came from the crow's nest. There was a strange sound in the voice.

"Cap'n, there's somethin' comin' over in the nor'east skyline. Looks like a ship, but she's too low, and there's no masts. None."

Instantly Matthew was at the starboard rail, his telescope extended, slowly sweeping the skyline to the east. Minutes passed before the tiny speck appeared to those at deck level, and Matthew hunched forward, studying the black silhouette.

"What is it?" Caleb asked.

Matthew shook his head and said nothing as he concentrated. A time passed before he spoke.

"I think it's a cargo ship. My guess is she was caught in the storm and demasted altogether. Looks like she has no canvas at all. She's too low in the water. She has a longboat in the water towing her on a line. I think she's trying to make landfall before she sinks."

"Any flag?"

"None. No mast." He turned to the helmsman. "Take a heading east by nor'east and hold her steady."

"Aye, sir."

No one questioned going to help the crippled ship. The unwritten law of the sea.

The speeding *Carrie* had closed to less than two miles from the creeping hulk when the shout came from the crow's nest, "Cap'n, I think she's dumping her cargo!"

Matthew raised his telescope and for several seconds held it steady, studying the black shape. Suddenly he sucked air and lowered the telescope. His face was distorted, eyes blazing, jaw clenched.

Caleb turned, startled. "What's wrong?"

Matthew's voice came hot. "She's a tight packer!"

"Tight packer?" Caleb asked, puzzled.

"A slaver! Blacks packed in the hold so tight some can't lay down to sleep. They're throwing blacks overboard."

Caleb jerked in disbelief, then glanced at Primus. Primus moaned and hid his face in both hands, then turned and walked away, out of sight. Caleb reached to jerk the telescope from Matthew's hands, and for ten seconds he studied the incoming ship. White-faced, shaking, he lowered the telescope, saying nothing because he could not speak. The rest of the crew, barefooted, bearded, were transfixed at the rail, staring in shocked disbelief. Every man among them had heard such tales from old sailors, but none were prepared to see it. Matthew went to his quarters to reappear instantly with his large brass horn to communicate over long distances.

The bow of the *Carrie* cut a twelve-foot curl as she skimmed onward through the dark Atlantic waters, steadily closing the gap with the crippled ship. At one mile the crew could hear the screams and cries of the blacks being thrown into the sea. At half a mile the sound of a voice through a captain's horn reached them, heavy with a Dutch accent.

"Hallooo. Who are you? Repeat, who are you?"

Matthew raised his horn. "The *Carrie* out of Head of Elk, Maryland. American. Who are you?"

"The *Helga* out of Rotterdam. Dutch. For what purpose do you approach?"

"Assist. You appear to be demasted and sinking."

"We will make landfall. We have sickness on board. Come no closer."

All eyes turned to Matthew, waiting. He raised his horn. "We're coming alongside."

"Repeat. Sickness on board. Come no closer."

Matthew turned to the helmsman. "Steady as she goes." He turned back and once again raised his horn. "What sickness?"

"Plague."

"We can help. We're coming alongside."

"Do not come alongside."

Matthew turned to Caleb, puzzlement plain on his face. "Something's wrong. Load those cannon with grapeshot and bring them to bear on the man with the horn."

For a moment Caleb hesitated in surprise before he answered, "Aye, sir." He turned and gave hand signals and led four men to the guns.

At four hundred yards Matthew turned back to the oncoming ship. "Repeat. We're coming alongside."

The answer was instant, loud, profane. "This is an act of piracy!"

Matthew called, "It is an act of mercy."

At two hundred yards, the men on the *Carrie* could see the black men and women in the ocean, some floating face down, others still swimming, fighting to keep their heads above water, mortal terror in their wide, white eyes. Matthew called orders.

"Spill the mainsails!"

Within seconds the ropes securing the great main sails were jerked free and the canvas relaxed, flapping in the wind until the sails were drawn up and lashed to the arms. The *Carrie* slowed, scarcely moving forward in the water. Matthew gave his next order.

"Hard to starboard. Take her in among those in the water and pick up those still alive."

"Aye, sir."

The *Carrie* swung hard to starboard, passed the longboat towing the mortally wounded *Helga*, and crept slowly into the midst of the bodies in the sea. The crew began throwing ropes and pulling the living on board, dripping, emaciated, terrified, huddled together. The crew launched their single longboat to reach those too far for the ropes. Primus was beside Caleb, listening to the dialect of those who stood shivering, murmuring among themselves, turning flat eyes to the crew, and at Primus. In twenty minutes the deck and hold of the little schooner were jammed with the living, and Caleb took count. He turned to Matthew and spoke quietly, and Matthew could not miss the controlled fires burning behind his eyes.

"Eighty-nine living. Sixty-six dead in the water."

For a moment Matthew made his calculations. "One hundred fifty-five. He has more in his hold."

An angry voice came bellowing from the larger ship. "That is our cargo. I charge you with piracy."

For the first time Matthew peered at the man. Stocky, thick-shouldered, thick necked, with a broad nose, heavy beard, face burned brown by sea and sun. Matthew correctly judged him to be the first mate, not the captain. Matthew did not use his horn.

"We're coming on board." He spoke to Caleb without turning. "Get those two guns backed out of their ports and swing them around to bear directly on that officer and his crew. Do it now."

Caleb turned and gave orders.

The thick-shouldered officer shouted, "I order you to withdraw. If you attempt to board we will resist with arms."

Matthew waited ten seconds while the two guns came into position. "Do as you wish. Our cannon are loaded with grape."

The Dutch officer visibly recoiled back one step. "You would not fire on a Dutch ship carrying a legal cargo."

A light came into Matthew's eyes. "Would you care to find out?"

Tension held for five seconds while the first mate decided he did not wish to find out if the Americans would fire the big guns. Silently he backed away from the rail and gave a hand signal to his crew to stand down. Matthew turned to his waiting men.

"Grappling hooks."

Six of the three-pronged hooks arched over the gap separating the ships to clatter onto the deck of the *Helga*. In that instant the men threw their weight into the ropes to drag the hooks back to the rail where the prongs grabbed and held. Within minutes the ships were lashed together at the rail, and Matthew led ten of his men over the hooks onto the deck of the larger cargo ship, careful to stay out of line with the cannon behind them, where Primus and two men were hunched over the big guns, linstocks smoking and ready. Matthew walked directly to the man with the horn who stood sullen, trembling with anger, and faced him. Caleb took a position at Matthew's right, slowly flexing both hands at his sides. The thick-shouldered first mate licked dry lips and turned his head far enough to be certain his crew was behind him, ready. There were thirty-one of them.

Matthew wasted no time. "I am Captain Matthew Dunson, United States Navy, commander of the *Carrie*. Your name and rank, sir?"

By the rules of the sea the Dutch officer was required to answer. He rasped it out, "Jakob Stenman. First mate of the *Helga*."

"Your captain?"

"Dead. In the storm. When the mainmast came down it cracked the hull and killed the captain. He was buried at sea."

"Your ship's surgeon?"

"Dead. Swept overboard when he tried to reach the captain."

"Your cargo is slaves?"

"That is not your business to know."

"It *is* my business. You threw one hundred fifty-five human beings overboard. Sixty-six are dead. If they were part of your cargo, the eighty-nine who are alive belong to whoever picked them out of the water, and at this moment they're on my schooner. If they were not part of your cargo, you and your crew are guilty of sixty-six murders. So which is it? Cargo or murder?"

For five seconds the space between Matthew and Stenman was charged with something alive. Behind Stenman, his thirty-one men turned their heads far enough to stare down the muzzles of the two, twenty-four pound cannon less than fifty feet away, each loaded with twenty-four pounds of lead balls one inch in diameter. At that range they would blast a twenty-foot section out of both railings and mutilate half the Dutch crew in an instant. Hovering over one gun with dead eyes was a black man holding a smoking linstock six inches from the touchhole, and over the other gun stood a lean, sun burned, bearded man licking his lips, clutching a linstock eight inches from the touchhole.

The Dutch crew murmured, then settled, waiting for orders. The first mate stood silent, seething with rage.

"Which is it," Matthew demanded again, "cargo or murder? I won't wait."

"Cargo."

"I claim the eighty-nine on my schooner. I'm going below to see if there are more."

"You have no right to go below," the first mate bellowed.

Matthew pointed west, toward the coastline, and the cutting edge in his voice was unmistakable.

"Landfall is more than three miles. This ship will never make it. I'm going to give an offer one time, and you're going to accept it or reject it, I don't care which. I'll tow you back to Cape Charles where you can salvage your ship. But before I do, I'm going below and taking one man with me. Make up your mind."

The Dutchman's face became livid as he trembled with anger. He fumbled for words, then blurted, "You can not . . ."

Matthew turned on his heel and spoke to his men. "Return to the *Carrie* and make ready to get under way." He called to Primus, "Stand by the guns. If anyone in this crew moves, fire." Matthew and those with him had taken two steps when the first mate stopped them.

"Go below. Then you must tow us to port."

"Keep your crew right where it is while we're below decks. If one man moves, the cannon will fire." He turned to Caleb. "Let's go."

Matthew walked past the silent Dutch crew to the door that opened into the narrow staircase leading below decks. The instant he swung the door open he was plunged into a stench like nothing he had ever experienced before. It hit him like a wall, driving him back a step to turn his face away and clap his hand over his mouth and nose. He breathed fresh air deep for a moment, then turned to once again try the stairs. Caleb followed him down into the blackness.

The only light was that which followed them through the door. Their eyes adjusted as they descended into the abyss. They were four stair-steps from the bottom when their feet struck water, and they realized the hold of the *Helga* was shipping more than three feet of the Atlantic Ocean. They lowered themselves into the stinking, slimy mess, and pushed away from the staircase, straining to see in the darkness. They felt something bump against their legs and slowly understood they were bodies, floating face down, and then in the dimness they realized there were others, some standing alone, some clinging to each other, and then in the dim light they could see their eyes, white in their black faces, past fear, past terror, waiting only to die.

Matthew paused and realized that weeks of human feces and urine were mixed with the sea water, and he could smell the terrible corruption of dysentery that had eaten the linings from the bowels of the blacks to ooze uncontrolled into the mix in which Matthew and Caleb were standing. The stench in the air was something palpable, forcing them to squint their eyes as tears ran down their cheeks into their beards. Fighting to hold down their gorge, they sloshed through the fetid murk eight feet before Matthew turned back. Caleb turned to follow, then stopped to bend forward, peering at something in the slimy mass. It took him a few seconds to make it out, and he gasped, and then he retched sour where he stood. He was staring at a mother, naked and dead, still clutching her dead infant to her breast.

White hot anger rose raging in Caleb's breast and burst from his throat in the sound of a wild animal. A low moaning came from unseen voices all around them, and Matthew turned to signal Caleb to follow him. They climbed back up the stairs with the stinking muck clinging to their clothing from the waist down and emerged into the sunlight. Matthew walked away from the door and left it open, with Caleb following. He strode directly to Stenman and his voice purred.

"There is no plague down there. It's dysentery. You starved them to death. Get them on deck. All of them. Dead or alive. Now!"

Stenman's jaw thrust out in defiance. "I refuse."

Matthew turned to call to Primus. "Fire!"

Instantly Stenman's hand shot up. "Do not fire! We will bring them up." He turned to his crew. "Bring the cargo on deck. All of them."

Open resistance erupted among the Dutch crew. "We will not go down! There is death in the hold." They backed away and began to spread out. Caleb took one look and stepped to the two nearest him. Caleb's feet were spread and his arms were at his sides, loose and easy.

"Get down those steps. Now." His eyes were points of light.

The man nearest him shook his head and made a lunge. He had moved less than a foot when Caleb's right fist caught him flush on the point of his chin, and he was falling unconscious when Caleb's left hand broke his nose. The man next to him reached for his belt knife but before he could bring it up, Caleb hit him above his left ear. The man's head snapped to the right and he went to his knees, but not before the knife raked Caleb's left rib cage. Caleb hit him once more in his right temple and the man toppled and his knife clattered to the deck. Red blood came flowing to soak Caleb's shirt as he plucked up the knife and turned to face the next man. Caleb was holding the knife low, cutting edge up, balanced on the balls of his feet, and Matthew saw in his face that he would kill the man in an instant if he made the wrong move. The man saw the look in Caleb's face and made his choice. He settled, and the crew of the *Helga* stopped, confused, unsure.

Matthew gave orders to Stenman. "You remain here with me. Put your bos'n in charge of your crew. Tell your men that when they have brought up all who are down there, dead or alive, they will get a pump and a hosepipe and wash them all clean. Then they'll prepare the dead for burial at sea, and prepare food from their own stores to feed the living. They will give the blacks their blankets to keep them warm tonight. Tell them you will remain with me on the *Carrie*, and if they do not obey those orders we will hang you from the mainmast yardarm. Tell them."

Stenman choked down his outrage, then repeated the orders in Dutch. The crew stared at Matthew, incredulous, then slowly moved toward the door into the hold. As they began the descent, Matthew turned to Caleb. "Get the medicine chest from my quarters on the *Carrie* and meet me on her deck."

Caleb turned and was gone as Matthew spoke to Stenman.

"Take me to your captain's quarters and show me his war chest."

Stenman's eyes bulged. "You are going to rob us?"

"Move!"

Three minutes later Matthew had an iron-strapped, one-hundred-eighty-pound war chest on the floor of the captain's quarters and was counting Spanish dollars and British pounds sterling. He made a mental tally of the money all cargo ships carried to pay the crew, make repairs, and buy food in the long and dangerous crossing of the Atlantic. He closed the lid, snapped the huge iron lock shut, and turned back to Stenman.

"Back on deck."

Outside he spoke to two of his own men. "There's a chest in there on the floor. Bring it."

The two men entered the small quarters to reappear carrying the heavy ironwood chest between them, and Matthew pointed them over the railings onto the *Carrie* before he spoke to Stenman.

"You follow them. I'm right behind you."

Half an hour later, with Caleb sweating, gritting his teeth, Matthew tied off the last of twelve stitches he had used to close the cut on Caleb's ribs, clipped the gut thread with surgical scissors, washed Caleb's side with alcohol, covered the wound with clean linen, and wrapped him from armpits to waist with bandage. He helped him into his last clean shirt, buttoned the two buttons, and looked his younger brother in the eye.

"That feel all right? Too tight?"

Caleb shook his head. "Fine."

"Where did you learn to handle your fists like that?"

Caleb shrugged. "I learned."

Matthew paused, collecting his thoughts and selecting his words. "I think you would have used that knife to kill that last man if he'd moved wrong." He stopped for a moment, searching for a gentle way to say what he must, and there was none. "That's how a killer thinks. I didn't expect that from you."

Caleb did not look at Matthew. He lifted his left arm, testing it against the dull pain in his ribs. "The man stopped. The crew settled. It worked."

Matthew stared long and hard, then let it go. In the few days he had spent with Caleb, first at Gloucester, then sailing down the Chesapeake and finding the crippled *Helga*, Matthew had sensed something he had never before felt in Caleb. The boy he had known was almost gone. In his place was a man that was in many ways a stranger. Part of it, maybe most of it, could be explained by the inevitable change that occurs in every man who must face the sick horrors of cannon and musket tearing soldiers to pieces in battle, and the awfulness of killing or being killed. But there was something else in Caleb, something deep down and hard, indistinct in the shadows of his inner being that left Matthew probing, unable to define it, unable to let it go. It gnawed at him.

He pushed it aside. He would wait. While he was putting things back into the medical chest, he spoke once again.

"I don't know what we'll do with these blacks once we reach Cape Charles." He paused to look about the decks of the small schooner where the blacks were standing or sitting in groups, wrapped in blankets to hide their nakedness, and for warmth. They had been fed their first hot meal of decent food in two months.

Matthew went on. "The ones we took out of the water are legally ours. The ones we got out of the hold are still owned by Stenman. What do we do? I can't stay with them at Cape Charles, and I can't take them all north. There are one hundred seventy-two of them here and on the *Helga*. Far too many for the *Carrie* and there's no time to get a bigger ship. They're all sick with dysentery. Some will die. I can't stop to take care of them because my orders are to find General Washington."

Caleb raised both arms, worked his left arm, testing the restraint of his wrapped chest. "Looks like we have a problem."

Matthew said, "Let's talk to Primus."

Caleb turned, found Primus, and waved him over. For a moment the three sat in silence before Matthew spoke.

"Can you understand these people? Talk to them?"

Primus nodded. "Some."

"Where are they from?"

"Africa. Maybe the coast. On the west. Strange dialect but I get some of it. Most of it."

Matthew paused while he collected his thoughts. "We can't take these people with us. The ship's too small and there's no time. If we leave them at Cape Charles, back at the entrance into the Chesapeake, what will happen to them?"

Primus's eyes opened wide. "Bad. All bad. Can't talk American. Got no clothes. No place to go. Nothing to eat. Sick. Dying. They be taken for slaves by the firs' white man finds 'em." Primus bowed his head with a sadness in his face, knowing the hopeless truth. In this country, his people were considered less than human.

Matthew cleared his throat, then continued. "Let me make a suggestion. What would happen if you and Caleb stayed with them? Moved them north, overland? Up the Chesapeake, through Virginia, on to Massachusetts, or maybe Vermont. Somewhere north where we can get help for them?"

Caleb stiffened, stunned. "You mean walk? No food, no clothing? Walk that distance with those sick people? Through slave country?"

"No. Ride." He pointed to his cabin. "I have the war chest from the *Helga* in there. Over six thousand Spanish dollars, and nearly sixteen hundred pounds British sterling. More than enough to buy wagons and horses to carry these people. Food, clothing, blankets, medicine."

"You mean to take the Dutchman's money? Robbery?"

"I don't know if it's robbery. I'm ready to call it a settlement for towing their ship and crew to a safe port. But no matter what we call it, I'll use some of that money if it will save some of these people. There'll be enough left to get the Dutch crew home."

A reckless grin crossed Caleb's face. "Sounds fair to me."

Matthew moved on. "It's risky. I can spare you two, and two more men to help with the livestock and wagons. You'll have to teach a few of the Africans how to drive horse teams. There's a dozen things could go wrong. I won't order you to do it. You'll have to volunteer. You two, and two more."

Caleb stood, favoring his left side. "Give me a minute." He walked away, among the crew, to return in three minutes.

"We got the volunteers."

Matthew nodded. "One more thing. These Africans are our property. I'll have to make a bill of sale to you giving you legal title, in case someone stops you and demands proof that they aren't runaways. I'll have that ready when we put you ashore. As captain of the *Carrie* I also have authority to pick my officers. I'll give you my written commission as first mate. If anyone challenges you, it might help if you're an officer in the United States Navy."

For a moment Caleb stood still, shaking his head in wonderment. "Me? A slave owner and a naval officer?" He raised a hand and continued. "What about Primus?"

Matthew looked at the African long and hard. "He's a free man. I will not put his name on a bill of sale that makes him property."

For a brief moment a light came into Primus's eyes as he understood what Matthew had said, and then it faded, as it always did.

Notes

British Admiral Rodney was ordered by the Crown and Parliament to protect British interests in the West Indies (Bahamas) and Jamaica particularly. French Admiral de Grasse, after his victory over the British in the Battle of Chespeake Bay, was under orders to attack British interests in the West Indies and capture Jamaica if possible. British Admiral Hood joined Rodney, which raised the British ship count to thirty-six, three more than the French had. Then through a series of unusual mishaps the French lost the use of five of their ships, and the British engaged them. The result was the capture of Admiral de Grasse's ship and five others, and a resounding British victory in the West Indies, wherein Admiral de Grasse himself was taken prisoner. The engagement commenced April 9, 1782, as herein indicated. The battle was referred to as the Battle of the Saints, because it was fought near the island of St. Lucia. The *Carrie* and the *Helga* are fictional vessels, as are their crews.

General Washington was deeply concerned that when they could, the British would return to blockade all American ports on the eastern seaboard. For this reason he was anxious to remove all supplies and munitions from Yorktown and Gloucester to a place where the British would be less able to recapture them. Head of Elk, Maryland, was selected. However, the British had determined to abandon the Americas to protect their interests in the West Indies, and did not reenter the Chesapeake. For a complete analysis see Mackesy, *The War for America, 1775–1783,* pp. 444–58. See also the map on page 340, which includes the Chesapeake Bay, Head of Elk, Cape Charles, and Cape Henry; Freeman, *Washington,* pp. 493–95.

For a discussion of sailing ships, their construction, the art of tacking, the language commonly used, and other detail as set forth in this chapter, see generally Cutler, *Queens of the Western Ocean;* Jobe, *The Great Age of Sail,* p. 151 and other supporting pages.

Slavery was a legal business at the time set forth in this chapter, and ships from most foreign ports, including the Dutch, regularly entered American waters and ports with slaves bound for American markets. The throwing of slaves overboard for reasons of sickness or ship damage or lack of food, occurred regularly. The inhumane, deplorable conditions in the hold of such ships, where the slaves were held, were as described. In the years between 1760 and 1800 such ships were often called "tight packers" because the slaves were packed so tightly in the hold.

For information regarding the locations in Africa from which slaves were obtained, and the number of slaves from each, between the years of 1662–1867, as well as a listing of the nine countries most prominently involved in the slave trade, see Klein, *The Atlantic Slave Trade,* Appendix A.I, pp. 208–11.

CHAPTER V

★ ★ ★

*T*hey came sweating on cantering horses, the three of them, in single file on the road winding its way through the thick forest of the Hudson River Valley toward the American Continental Army camp at Newburgh, sixty miles north of the city of New York, on the west bank of the great water highway. An American captain leading with a white flag on a pole thrust into a stirrup socket, a British major in full dress uniform, riding ramrod straight, proud, chin high, and an American sergeant following, his long Pennsylvania rifle unslung and resting across his thighs, thumb on the hammer, finger on the trigger. They rode wordlessly, eyes constantly moving, watching in the heat of the late spring day, on jaded mounts that showed a crust of dried, white lather where the bridle straps chaffed their jaws and the saddle girths worked their bellies.

They rounded a curve where the packed dirt road moved away from the great river, then straightened, and they saw the first rows of white tents two hundred yards ahead where the trees thinned on the south edge of the army camp. Two pickets, a private and a corporal, stepped into the road, muskets at the ready, bayonets fixed. The private stood silent while the corporal challenged the riders.

"Who comes there?"

The American captain pulled his horse to a stop, and the others reined in. "Captain Nicholas Carruthers. Pennsylvania Second. Bringing a British messenger to General Washington."

The corporal's eyes widened. "A prisoner?"

"Not a prisoner. Messenger. Under this white flag. He has a sealed letter."

"For Gen'l Washington? A letter? From who?"

Carruthers masked his irritation. "General Sir Guy Carleton. Commander of British forces in the United States."

The picket started. "Carleton? I thought Clinton was down there. Can I see it? I'm supposed to see it."

Carruthers shook his head. "No. For the eyes of General Washington only." He took a deep breath. "We've come sixty-two miles since four o'clock this morning. These horses are used up. So are we. The general needs this message. Do we pass, or not?"

"I'm supposed to look at that message. I can't just—"

Carruthers leaned forward, his eyes hard, voice menacing, "What's your name, Corporal?"

The picket reached nervous to wipe at his mouth. "You can pass, sir. You can pass right on." The two on the ground stepped aside. Carruthers tapped spur and raised his reluctant horse to a ground-eating trot, followed by his tiny column of two. While they were yet fifty yards from the first tents, the rasping sound of saws grinding rungs of wood from dead pine trunks and the ring of axes at the woodlot, splitting the rungs into kindling reached them, then slowed, then stopped. The crew of sweating men, stripped to the waist, paused to peer at the odd sight of a white flag over what was clearly an American captain, a British major in full military uniform, and a grizzled sergeant, riding spent horses past them into the heart of their camp.

Sixty yards to the east, Sergeant Alvin Turlock of the Massachusetts Fourth Regiment turned from the detail of men that was setting up the huge iron tripods and kettles for evening mess and squinted to study the strange sight of two Americans bringing a British officer to the small log home that served as headquarters for General George Washington. They passed the forty-foot flagpole with the American flag hanging limp in the afternoon heat and drew rein before the hitching posts, where four bay horses were already standing hip-shot. Two enlisted soldiers were tending the mounts while two more stood picket duty at the building entrance.

The three weary riders dismounted to stand stiff-legged, straightening their backs in the fashion of men who have been too long in the saddle, handed the reins of their horses to a waiting private, and walked to the door where two armed pickets stopped them. From a distance, Turlock turned his head slightly to the right, straining to hear what he could with his good left ear. He heard the voices, but could not make out the words. He watched the door open, and the three disappeared into the dim light inside.

"Somethin' peculiar goin' on," he muttered to himself. He turned back to his evening mess crew. "Well, whatever it is, evening mess won't wait. Awright, you lovelies, get yer backs into it. Fires to build, venison to cut, potatoes to cut. Leave the winter sprouts on 'em and put 'em right on into the mix."

Favoring his right leg, the wiry little sergeant limped to the nearest tripod to hoist a heavy, round, smoke-blackened, three-legged kettle onto the iron hook that dangled on a chain from the apex of the tripod.

He turned to two privates and pointed to four battered wooden buckets with rope handles. "Fetch the water." He gestured to two enlisted men near the stacked kindling. "Get the fire goin'. This meat won't cook itself."

Steam was rising from the kettles when the lanky sergeant who had ridden as armed escort for Carruthers and the British major came striding toward Turlock, rifle held loosely in his right hand.

"You Sergeant Turlock?"

The man was tall, angular, with a huge square jaw and sunken eyes. His jaw had been broken as a boy, and he talked from one side of his mouth. His voice was high, and he spoke softly.

Turlock answered. "Yes. You?"

"Sergeant Ephraim Quillen. Pennsylvania Second. I come in with Cap'n Carruthers and that British major."

"I saw."

"They said I might get supper with your company."

Turlock shrugged. "Got a bowl? Cup?"

"Over on my horse."

"Get in line when we call. Venison stew and black bread and the bitterest coffee in the army."

Quillen grinned. "It'll have to go some to beat what I been drinkin' down the river."

"Down the river?"

"Near Fort Lee on the New Jersey side. Watchin' to keep the British set in New York."

"Fort Lee? That's right across the river from New York. The British thinkin' about comin' across the river? Or maybe up this way?"

"Naw. Other way around. You haven't heard?"

"Heard what?"

"The British Parliament cleaned out that whole bunch that was bent on beating us. All of 'em. Gone. Done it last month, almost overnight."

Turlock stood in silent disbelief. Quillen went on.

"Then they put in a new bunch that's given up on beating us. We aren't worth the trouble, they said, and decided the only thing on this side of the Atlantic worth keeping is Jamaica and a few islands down in the West Indies. Rum. Sugar. So they said, forget the United States. Send our navy and soldiers down there to keep the profits coming from the sugarcane. That's what they done."

"You know this for true?"

Quillen nodded. "That's what I'm told."

Other soldiers had begun to drift in, listening. For a moment Turlock stood still, his mind racing.

"What's that British major doing up here under a white flag to see Gen'l Washington?"

Quillen shook his head. "Don't know. Nobody told me. I was sent along with my rifle should someone take exception to our comin'. But I got a notion about it."

"What notion?"

"It won't be no surprise to me if he's here to invite Gen'l Washington to some sort of a peace talk."

Turlock's head jerked forward. "You mean we're gettin' close to the end of this war?"

"My best guess."

Turlock rounded his mouth and blew air. "I was startin' to think I'd never see the day."

The call came from behind him, loud. "Mess is ready!"

Fifteen minutes later sergeants Turlock and Quillen were seated on a log blowing on smoking chunks of venison and potato, singeing their lips as they tried the first load from their wooden spoons. For a brief moment Quillen glanced at the right side of Turlock's head, then back at his steaming bowl. Without turning, Turlock spoke.

"Quite a sight, isn't it?"

Color rose in Quillen's face. "Didn't mean to—"

"It's all right. Take a look. I got to look at it ever' day."

For five seconds Quillen studied the right side of Turlock's head. The skin was pitted and parchment-stiff, with a spiderweb of small cracks that showed pinpoints of dried black blood. His beard was spotty on that side, and his right ear was partly missing where dead gristle had been cut away. Random strands and small clumps of hair had tried to grow.

"None of my business, but it looks like you was standin' awful close to somethin' when it blew up."

"October nineteenth of last year. British Redoubt Number Ten at Yorktown. We stormed it before dawn. Cannon about four feet away went off. Seems like I didn't need somethin' like that to make me uglier'n I already was, but that's what happened. Couldn't hear on the right side for near three months, and I still got to turn my head some to hear things straight. Memory partly gone, but she's comin' back. Hair and skin on that side'll never be the same."

Quillen stared in awe. "You was with the ones who took those two redoubts?"

"We took ten, the French took nine."

"I was on the west side of the Yorktown fight. We heard about what you done at those redoubts over on the east. Couldn't hardly believe it."

"Well, that's what happened."

Suddenly Turlock raised his head and lowered his spoon, watching something behind Quillen. Quillen turned to see a lieutenant trotting toward them and glanced at Turlock for an explanation.

"One of Gen'l Washington's aides. Wonder what he wants."

The young lieutenant stopped at the first cluster of men taking their evening mess. They stood and came to loose attention as he spoke, and Turlock turned his head to hear.

"The general wants to see a Lieutenant Billy Weems and a Scout Eli Stroud. Anybody know the whereabouts of either of them?"

Turlock stood and called, "You looking for Weems?"

The man came trotting. "The general wants him. Know his whereabouts?"

"Yes, sir." Turlock pointed. "He's at the officer's mess, right over there. Reddish hair, built strong."

"Stroud?"

Turlock shrugged. "He's wherever you find him. Weems might know."

The young, smooth-faced officer turned on his heel and was gone at a run. Turlock sat back down and stirred his stew for several seconds.

"Wonder what that's about?"

Quillen interrupted. "You know this Weems?"

A faint, wistful smile passed over Turlock's face. "I do."

Thirty minutes later, with the sun casting long shadows eastward, Billy Weems and Eli Stroud faced the pickets at the door of Washington's headquarters and Billy spoke.

"Lieutenant Billy Weems and Scout Eli Stroud. We were told to report to General Washington."

Without a word the picket swung the door open and stepped aside. Billy led as the two entered the small, austere room with walls of unpeeled logs and mud chinking. Directly facing the door was a plain table made of pine planks. Behind it sat General George Washington. Billy stopped three feet short of his desk, Eli on his left, and saluted.

"Lieutenant Billy Weems of the Massachusetts Fourth, sir. You remember Scout Eli Stroud. We were ordered to report to you."

General Washington rose, graying hair pulled back and tied behind his head. He wore his full dress uniform, wrinkled, showing sweat stains. His pale blue-gray eyes were steady, and in them was the light of recognition. At the moment he could not remember how many times he had called this pair into his office for scouting assignments he would trust to no others. Eli, dressed in beaded buckskins and moccasins, tall, dark hair, dark-skinned from more than twenty years of summer sun and winter snows, regular features, prominent nose, a white man orphaned as an infant and raised by the Iroquois to age nineteen to be an Iroquois warrior; gifted in his knowledge of the woods, educated by the Jesuits to speak all six Iroquois dialects, together with French and English, fiercely independent, a three-inch scar from a long ago battle prominent on his left jawline, a born leader. Billy, from Boston, clad in homespun trousers and an officer's tunic, shorter, barrel-chested, powerful beyond most men, round homely features, steady, called from the ranks of the enlisted to become a lieutenant based on merit alone. Washington could not remember Eli Stroud ever saluting anyone, or Billy Weems failing to do so.

Washington gestured. "Be seated."

Both men drew up straight-backed pine chairs and sat facing Washington, who took his place in a high-backed, scarred, leather upholstered chair. They could hear the birds and insects of spring through the open window as the two waited for their commander in chief to speak.

Washington pointed to two documents on the table in front of him. They saw the concern in his eyes as he picked up one document and spoke.

"I received this less than one hour ago from a British major who carried it here from New York under a white flag."

Washington paused, judging how much of the contents he should reveal, then went on. "I've been concerned—deeply concerned—that our Congress and officers would begin to think the war had ended when General Cornwallis surrendered at Yorktown. I feared we would become less diligent in our opposition to the British and give them time to rally and rebuild."

He paused for a moment, then went on. "You're aware that we've positioned the Continental Army to encircle the British in New York and control the Hudson. That's why I'm here, in Newburgh. Our whole intent is to prevent them from moving in any direction without our knowing it. We simply can't afford a surprise attack in the southern regions, or for that matter, to the west."

Billy nodded.

"Now this letter arrives from New York. Carried by British Major Theodore Durfee. It is signed by General Sir Guy Carleton."

Billy started. "General Carleton from Quebec? In New York? I thought General Henry Clinton was in command there."

"No longer. General Carleton has replaced him." Washington leaned forward on his forearms to spread the document flat. "Let me read to you." He located the proper place and traced with his finger as he read.

" . . . I am joined with Admiral Digby in the commission of peace, and we are most anxious to reduce the needless severities of war."

Eli blew air. "A peace commission? They're asking for peace talks?"

Washington nodded and remained silent for several seconds, then continued.

"I'm suspicious. I don't know if this is an effort to get us to stand-down during negotiations while they get ready to attack, or whether it's genuine. If it's genuine, they'll have to come to terms with Congress, not with me, but it is my duty to determine if this is what it claims to be."

Again he paused. Eli settled back into his chair, mind leaping ahead, sensing what was coming. Billy remained motionless. Washington plucked up a second document and leaned forward, picking his words.

"Four days ago this letter was delivered to me." He raised it. "From French Admiral de Grasse. He wrote it during a major sea battle in the West Indies. De Grasse was certain the British would win. This letter was sent to warn us that if they did, they could send part of their navy north to blockade all of our major ports. Cripple us. He wanted to warn us."

Eli pointed. "How was the letter delivered?"

"De Grasse gave it to a young captain in our navy. An excellent navigator I had assigned to assist de Grasse in the West Indies."

Washington saw Billy straighten in his chair as he continued. "He was given command of a fast schooner and sailed her out of the battle, badly damaged. He stopped at Head of Elk to warn our forces there, then traded ships and came on north to Philadelphia, and overland to find me here."

Billy raised a hand. "The name, sir? Of the navigator?"

"Matthew Dunson."

Washington saw the surprise and recognition in Billy's face, and asked, "You know him?"

"All my life, sir. Is he safe?"

Washington nodded. "Safe, and in Philadelphia with what few ships we have, awaiting further orders. Fine officer."

Billy closed his eyes for a moment, then relaxed.

Washington tapped the two documents on the table with a long index finger. "These two documents raise a serious question. Can the British be asking for a peace parley as a delay tactic while they move their navy from the West Indies up here to blockade our ports? Or could they intend moving part of their army, or all of it, out of New York in preparation of an attack?" He leaned forward. "I must know, and there is only one way to be certain. Go see."

Billy glanced at Eli, who sat motionless.

"I've called you here for that purpose. You two are going down to New York to observe conditions directly, then report back to me on two questions: First, do the British have their West Indies fleet at anchor in New York harbor? Second, is there any indication they are preparing their army for a major campaign?"

Billy spoke. "How soon do you need a report?"

"Three days."

Eli nodded. Billy answered. "Yes, sir."

"I want you to leave tonight."

Again, Eli nodded and Billy answered. "Yes, sir."

"What will you need? Horses? A boat? Provisions?"

Eli glanced at Billy and something unspoken passed between them, then Billy answered. "A canoe. Two telescopes."

Washington's eyebrows arched for a moment. "You can travel well enough downstream in a canoe, but what about upstream? Won't you need horses?"

Eli answered. "The Hudson runs both ways, depending on the Atlantic tides. They'll be coming in two days from now. For a while the river will run backwards, halfway to Albany. A canoe can take us both ways. If anything goes wrong, we can get horses from the British."

Washington said, "Of course. I had forgotten about the tides. Will you need rations? Ammunition?"

Billy answered, "I think we'll be all right, sir."

"I'll have two telescopes for you in fifteen minutes. Is there anything you need to ask me before you go?"

"No, sir."

"Report directly to me when you return, day or night."

"We will, sir."

"You are dismissed."

Billy and Eli stood, and Billy saluted. "Thank you, sir."

Washington watched them turn and walk from the room, out into the early shades of evening, then reached again for the message from General Carleton.

Outside, Billy and Eli angled west toward the dwindling cook fires of the Massachusetts Fourth Regiment, where Sergeant Alvin Turlock saw them coming and stood waiting.

"You seen Gen'l Washington yet?" He turned his good ear to listen.

"Just came from there."

"Where you off to this time?"

"Down river. We'll need a little dried meat and some cheese and bread."

"How about a few potatoes? Shriveled and got sprouts from winter storage, but by now I doubt you'd know how to eat a good one."

"We'll take 'em."

"When you leavin'?"

"As soon as we get our weapons and blankets and two telescopes from the general."

"I'll have a sack ready when you come back."

The steady drone of crickets and the croaking of bullfrogs in the marshes and bogs reached through the deep dusk as Turlock handed a burlap sack to Billy and he swung it over his shoulder. The bandy-legged little sergeant stared up into his face, dim in the shadows, ignoring the fact he was speaking to an officer. "Got the telescopes?"

"Right here."

"You two be careful, hear?" He watched them disappear into the shadows before he turned back to the low evening campfire.

They walked silently down the incline to the river where Eli picked a light, birch-bark Iroquois war canoe from the sixteen that were tied to the pier. They laid their weapons and the telescopes and sack in the bottom before Eli stepped into the bow and settled to his knees. Billy grasped the gunwales in the rear and launched the craft, splashing, then jumped inside, dripping, to take up his paddle. Ten minutes later they were near the center of the mighty Hudson River, stroking to a slow rhythm, enough to move them slightly faster than the current to maintain control.

Unnumbered stars speckled the black domed heavens as they passed the lights of West Point on the heights of the west bank. A three-quarter moon rose on the eastern rim to cast a broad, quivering trail of silver light that followed the canoe, bobbing tiny and frail on the surface of the mighty river. Both men looked upward for a time, then at the black, fearsome water on which their fragile craft danced, then at the sweep of endless forests that covered the broad valley on either side of the river, and a consciousness of their own smallness swept over them.

Fort Clinton was a faint outline on the west bank; to the east, not far from the river, they saw the faint glow of the hamlet of Verplanck. They passed Stony Point on their right, the only sound the quiet dipping of their paddles as Eli silently worked the bow and Billy the stern of the craft. It was well past midnight when the single light at Tarrytown to their left gleamed tiny in the night, and they drew close to the black shoreline, watching and listening as they glided silently on. The moon was settling toward the southern horizon when they turned into the mouth of a small, unnamed creek, beached their canoe, and concealed it in thick foliage. Without a word they took meat and cheese from the sack, buckled on their weapons belts with the sheathed knives and Eli's tomahawk, picked up their rifle and musket, and set a course due east through the forest. Eli led, with Billy following, marveling as always at how Eli moved in the blackness and thick foliage without sound, as though guided by something only Eli understood.

Eight miles later, the breaking of dawn found them on their bellies, lying invisible in the thick green ferns on a bluff overlooking the British encampment at White Plains, three hundred yards below. They listened to the familiar rattle of the morning drum pounding out reveille and watched as the troopers threw back the tent flaps to walk out into the glory of a calm spring morning in the great Hudson River Valley. Wildflowers were everywhere, thronging the open meadows and lining the banks of the streams and brooks that flowed westward into the river. The pines were so green they seemed deep blue against the brightness of the oak, beech, ash, and chestnut trees that carpeted the rolling hills as far as the eye could see.

For a time the two remained motionless, studying the lay of the British camp, remembering. They were seeing White Plains as it was on October 28, 1776, when the British caught the ragged, beaten remains of the Continental Army on the flats and cut them to pieces—drove them into a panic-driven retreat back to the south. They were remembering the nightmare of the fight at Long Island two months earlier on August 27, which had broken and scattered the untrained Continental Army, and the catastrophe at Fort Washington on Manhattan Island that followed on November 15, which all but annihilated the smashed remains of the American army.

Billy stirred and pointed, and Eli nodded. Both reached for their telescopes and extended them to begin a slow study of the entire installation. Sixty tents, eight regulars per tent: four hundred eighty regulars. Twenty officers' tents, five officers per tent: one hundred officers. The horse herd was held in a pen formed by ropes strung in the trees. One hundred thirty-four horses, more than half of them draft animals for pulling wagons or cannon. The twenty cannon were formed near the horse pen in two opposing lines, muzzle to muzzle. The wagons were lined in twelve rows of five each behind the cannon: sixty wagons. The gunpowder was in barrels stacked one hundred fifty yards from anything else, covered with tarps, with two pickets always on duty. There was no way to count the barrels, but each man made his own estimate of the amount, according to the size of the mound. The crates of food supplies were divided into three areas: two for the enlisted, one for the officers. The drill and parade ground was worn to the deep brown soil; there was no grass.

Slowly the scouts shifted to relieve set muscles, then settled again to watch the movement of the regulars and the officers. The British finished and cleaned up the morning mess, then stood for inspection. Twenty men marched in formation to feed and water the horses. Four of the men tied sixteen horses on short ropes to a line strung between two trees while two more men strapped on the thick leather aprons of a blacksmith. They began the methodical labor of drawing the feet of the horses up between their knees, then jerking the nails from the worn shoes to toss them clanking into a pile. Then they set out sixty-four new, caulked shoes and jammed them into the white-hot coals of the forge, waited until they were glowing, then began the careful work of pounding them into the shape of the hoof of each horse.

To the north a wood detail stripped off their tunics and commenced the never-ending drudgery of sawing and splitting more firewood. One company of regulars assembled on the parade ground in ten ranks of ten, and Billy and Eli could hear the barked commands of their sergeant as he put them through their daily drill. They had started the cook fires for the one o'clock mess when Billy collapsed his telescope and slowly withdrew from the crest of the rise and Eli followed. Without a word they rose to a crouch and retreated silently through the thick spring foliage until they could no longer hear the pounding of the blacksmiths' hammers or the shouted commands of the drill sergeant, and they hunkered down behind the decayed trunk of a great pine, fallen in a long ago time.

Billy spoke in hushed tones. "See anything that says they're getting ready to move?"

Eli shook his head and said nothing.

"Only five hundred regulars. Not enough. The main camp's got to be down on either Manhattan Island or Long Island."

"Or Staten." Eli squinted up at the sun. "Not quite noon. We need some rest if we're going to take a look at Long Island tonight."

With Eli leading, they retraced their steps in silence, stopping to listen, moving, stopping. They covered the eight miles back to the river and their canoe with the sun just past the zenith, and sat down. Eli spoke quietly.

"The only tracks besides ours were two Indians that passed going south sometime yesterday morning. Mohawk. Could have been scouts, but I doubt it because they didn't return. No British patrols. Nothing. They're not getting ready to move."

Billy nodded, and Eli continued. "We tip up the canoe and you sleep under it. I'll take first watch."

At four o'clock in the afternoon Eli nudged Billy and traded places in the cool of the shade of the canoe. At eight o'clock Billy roused Eli, and they sat listening to the rasping of crickets all about them and the clamor of frogs reaching from bogs along the river. With night birds performing their incredible nightly pirouettes overhead, they ate cooked mutton, cheese, and chewed down a raw, shriveled potato. They drank long from their wooden canteens, then sat lost in their own thoughts until the last hint of the sun was gone, and the forest was covered by a shroud of deep purple and black.

"It's time," Eli said, and they both rose. They buckled on their weapons belts, Billy tied the burlap sack beside his belt knife, they picked up rifle and musket, and hoisted the canoe overhead. Twenty minutes later they were in the canoe, Eli on his knees in the bow, Billy serving as tiller. Together, they threw their shoulders into it, driving the light craft out into the current of the great river.

The three-quarter waxing moon rose as they passed Dobb's Ferry to their left, on the west bank of the river, and caught the salty tang of the sea strong in the air. The heavens were an unending spread of celestial wonder as they passed the lights of Philipsburg. They came within fifty yards of the east riverbank as they approached the north head of the East River, and they silently held to the center of the narrows as they passed Kingsbridge and followed the curve of the river to their right, due south. Half an hour later they passed Harlem to their right and remained in the river center as they worked on south, past the entrance into Long Island Sound, down to Kip's Bay, where they swung due east to beach the canoe on the south bank of the inlet. They hid it in the forest, took their weapons, and beneath a moon that cast the world in silvery twilight, set a course due south, walking overland toward Brooklyn and Gravesend.

It was midnight when they slowed, listening to the sounds of the night as they crept forward up an incline approaching Brooklyn. They were remembering the steamy, sultry day of August 26, 1776, when they had last been on the banks of the East River, part of a terrified, shattered remnant of a lost army with their backs to the river and ten thousand British regulars one mile in front of them. In the dusk General Washington had turned to Colonel John Glover, commander of the Marblehead Brigade of fishermen, and asked if he and his regiment could move what was left of the Continental Army across the river to Manhattan Island during the night. The little fisherman nodded, gathered every vessel on the river that would float, and the miracle was done.

The two silently positioned themselves on the rise called Brooklyn Heights, and for more than ten minutes used their telescopes to search for campfires. There were none. Across the East River they could see lights in New York, one mile distant, and north of the city were scattered flecks of light reaching north for more than two miles.

They moved on south, following little known trails through the woods, past Flatbush, on to Gravesend, and once again stopped to search for campfires. They counted ten. Silently Eli gave hand signs, Billy nodded, and they separated, each circling opposite sides of the camp. Just over one hour later Billy stopped, bowed his head, closed his eyes, and concentrated. From the east it came—the haunting, distant call of an owl. Fifteen minutes later the two were on their haunches, speaking in whispers.

"Anything?"

Eli shook his head. "No pickets. No patrols. Nothing moving. You?"

"The same. This camp is not expecting to move any time soon."

"Are they on Staten Island?"

They covered the three miles due west at a trot, to stop on the west bank of Long Island, one mile from the near shore of Staten Island. For more than twenty minutes they glassed the far shore, looking for anything that would betray a British camp. There were three small lights, nothing more. They glassed once more, looking for the masts or the running lights of ships, and there were none.

There was frustration in Eli's whisper. "Nothing. No camp, no ships, nothing. That leaves Manhattan Island. We have time to get back up to the canoe before dawn if we go now. Kip's Bay is about five miles above New York City, on this side of the river. We might be able to cross the river to Manhattan Island in daylight, if the British don't have pickets or patrols up there. I haven't seen any yet, not at White Plains, not Brooklyn, not Gravesend, not Staten Island."

He moved, irritated, unable to reach a conclusion. "No lights? No patrols? No pickets? No ships? Are they that sure of themselves?"

Billy shook his head, puzzled, in doubt. "We'll see."

Dawn found them sitting next to their hidden canoe, in the thick cover of the New England forest on the south bank of Kip's Bay, working on cooked mutton, cheese, and raw potato. Billy smacked the corncob stopper back into his canteen. "My turn for first watch. You sleep. This could be a long day."

Beneath a bright noon sun they set the canoe in the water and minutes later beached it at the mouth of the bay. For ten minutes they studied the traffic on the East River—a few deep-water, three-masted ships, a multitude of barges riding low in the smooth water, loaded heavy with lumber, coal, and grain, two garbage scows, and many rowboats moving people north and south up and down the river, a few east and west, across it. They counted seven Indian canoes with the high, sweeping curves front and back, constructed of birch bark stretched over a hickory frame, sinew lashing it together, and sealed with pine tar.

Eli rounded his mouth to blow air. "You'll have to take off your officer's tunic to make the crossing."

"I know."

"If we're caught you'll be out of uniform. Hung for a spy."

Billy shrugged out of his tunic and laid it in the bottom of the canoe. "If I'm caught. Let's go."

There was little notice paid them as they worked their way across the river. They were just another canoe carrying an Indian and a white man wearing a sweated cotton shirt among the many craft on the watery highway that bounded the east side of Manhattan Island. The nose of the canoe struck the sand of the riverbank, and they both stepped splashing into the chill water to drag it ashore past the tree line, out of sight in the woods where they hid it in the ferns and undergrowth. They took their rifle and musket, and the now nearly empty burlap sack, and walked directly west until they came to Post Road, the dirt road that divided Manhattan Island on a north-south line. Carts and wagons loaded with spring vegetables, eggs, chickens, rabbits, milk, grain, and fresh meat rumbled south toward the city, while a few empty ones traveled north. A few mounted horsemen rode among men on foot, each preoccupied with their business of the day, paying little attention to others. There was not one red coat in sight. Without hesitating, Billy and Eli blended into the mix with a swinging stride, unnoticed, just another Indian and white man going south on business of their own.

They were three miles north of the city when the first British patrol came marching, a perspiring captain leading ten men in two columns. The traffic opened for them as they marched squarely up the center of the dirt road in dusty boots and sweated tunics. Billy and Eli stepped off the road and watched them pass, then kept moving, unnoticed in the crowd. They were forty yards past the patrol before Eli turned his head far enough to look. The soldiers were still in rank and file, marching north in cadence.

Less than five minutes later Billy and Eli slowed at the first faint sounds of drill sergeants shouting orders ahead. Two hundred yards later they were passing between row upon row of tents pitched in massive fields on both sides of the road. The British Union Jack stirred in the wind on sixty-foot flagpoles. Officers moved briskly between tents and buildings, while regulars saluted and went on with the work of a great military installation. Billy watched to the left while Eli studied the right—counting, absorbing everything they could see. Twelve regiments on the half-mile square parade ground at one time, drilling. The wagon depot, with more than six hundred wagons parked in orderly lines, hub to hub, wagon tongues all turned to the left. More than thirteen hundred penned horses. Four acres of the area stacked twelve feet deep with hay and dried grass for horse and oxen feed. Away from the road, three hundred sixty cannon aligned in twelve rows, and beyond the heavy guns, spaced one hundred yards apart, were six fenced, sunken powder magazines with more than sixty pickets on duty, muskets unslung, bayonets mounted. At the south end of the sprawling encampment were six hundred tons of crated foodstuff in two locations, one on each side of the road.

A sweating driver slowed his wagon, then reared back on the right reins of his four-horse team, and the heaping load of bagged oats rattled off the roadway to be added to the eighty tons of bagged oats already stacked near one of the huge horse pens. A second wagon with twelve quarters of fresh-killed beef covered with old, blood-spotted canvas followed, angling toward a long, low mess hall where men in butcher aprons waited. Billy and Eli watched and counted as the wagons began leaving the road, right or left side according to their load, to deliver their produce and wares to the British, and get their pay. They looked into the bearded faces of American farmers, and the farmers kept their eyes on the rumps of their horses. They had long since learned that contracting their wares for British gold was much more profitable than selling to the Americans for paper money that was rapidly becoming worthless. They refused to look anyone in the face while they drove and unloaded their wagons and stood in line for their pay before returning home with a purse heavy in their pockets while they argued with their violated consciences.

Men riding horses reined off the road and cantered to buildings marked QUARTERMASTER, to make contracts for their summer crops of grain, corn, fruit, and meat. Men in worn shoes and threadbare trousers walked from the road into the great camp to stand nervous, eyes downcast as they asked for work doing anything they could—anything the British deemed beneath themselves—anything that would bring pay in British gold. Digging latrines, clearing rotten straw and horse droppings from the barns, slaughtering mutton, chickens—anything.

Billy and Eli watched them leave the Post Road, and walked on south with the traffic thinning as they moved. They were three miles from the southern tip of the island when they sighted the first of the great estates east of the dusty road. Three-storied brick mansions with huge pillars forming the front portico. Stables in long, low buildings with stalls for sixteen horses. Sculpted gardens and landscapes. Wrought-iron fences and gates nine feet in height. And each of them now flying a British flag and housing British officers. The spoils of war.

West of the road, toward the Hudson, they passed a second British camp, strung out for more than a mile. Again they walked on, silently counting the men, supplies, cannon, horses, watching for any sign that the British might be preparing for a massive movement. The wagons stood in rows, empty.

The farmers with their loads for sale sawed on the reins and their horses turned right, and the wagons disappeared among the tents and buildings. Most of the laborers on foot followed, peering about for the quartermaster to beg for work. A few stayed on the road moving south toward the docks, hoping for another day's work among the ships tied up at the great New York waterfront. Eli and Billy walked among them, silent, suddenly conscious that they were the only ones carrying a rifle and a musket, with a powder horn and bullet pouch slung over their shoulders, and wearing belts with sheathed knives and a tomahawk.

Both knew it was only a matter of time.

They were passing the lower end of the huge encampment when they saw two British officers, one husky with a red beard and a Scottish accent, the other lean and vociferous, on the west side of the road. They were in hot argument, pointing first south to the forest of masts of the great ships in the harbor, and then west toward the lesser ships and rowboats and canoes tied to the wharves and piers along the Hudson. Billy and Eli did not slow, nor look, as they passed the two perspiring redcoats, but three seconds later the raised voices of the two officers suddenly fell silent and both Billy and Eli tensed. They dared not stop nor turn, but they could feel the bony finger of the lean one pointing between their shoulder blades. They walked casually on, but were searching the west side of the road, toward the river, for the place they would break if the officers challenged them.

There was no challenge, and they walked on toward the harbor, listening to the sounds of the few men left on the road and of the men working the watercraft to their right, and the great harbor half a mile ahead. They nodded to a British patrol led by a sergeant with dusty boots and sweat rings beneath his swinging arms, and listened as they passed until the sounds of the measured cadence faded and died. They reached the south end of the island and came onto the great spread of docks and wharves from the west, past what was left of Canvas Town. There were still some blackened hulks of buildings remaining from the great fire that had swept the New York waterfront on September 21, 1776. The holocaust destroyed almost the entire waterfront and one fourth of the city, to leave it open to vagrants and criminals and people of the night who moved in to take up residence in the still smoldering remains. The new occupants had used scorched and partially burned canvas to make hovels where they huddled during the day, to come out at night, and for a long time the respectable citizenry dared not venture into the squalor and robberies and murders of Canvas Town.

Men of all nationalities, in all manner of dress, moved about on the waterfront, loading and unloading ships tied to the piers. Quickly Billy and Eli walked among them, listening to the confusion of languages, watching eyes that conveyed fear or defiance or indifference in faces that were black, yellow, brown, and white. Men with beards or smooth faced, some stripped to the waist, others clad in white loose robes with their heads bound in turbans. Billy gave a head gesture, and Eli followed him away from the water, toward a row of buildings, some rebuilt since the fire, others old, weathered, unpainted with faded, peeling signs that read INDIA LTD. or ORIENT TRADING or AMSTERDAM INTL. or a dozen other names from seafaring nations the world over. Quickly they began the count of the ships, those moored to the wharves first, then the men-of-war riding at anchor in the harbor, mixed with the British military transports.

For twenty minutes they counted, with only those nearby glancing at them from time to time, suspicious of two men who were clearly not of the sea, one carrying a rifle and one a musket, loitering about without any discernible purpose.

They had just finished their count when from their right came the hollow sound of shod horse hooves on the heavy timbers of the docks. Instantly their heads swiveled, and two seconds later they caught a flash of red one hundred fifty yards down the pier. For ten seconds they stood still, and their breathing slowed.

Two tall bay saddle mounts came prancing on the dock, necks arched, fighting the bit in the unfamiliar smells and sounds of the waterfront, ridden by two British officers, one husky, red beard, the other lean and hawkish. Their saddles each had two holsters with the brass-bound handles of pistols thrusting upward. The two officers were spurring their horses through the throng, scowling as they peered into the crowd, looking for two men—one an Indian with a Pennsylvania rifle, the other a white man with reddish hair and a musket.

Without a word, Billy reached to open the door behind him, into the office of CHERBOURG TRADING, and backed in, Eli following. Behind a gated counter where the shipping company did their business, three startled men raised their heads from the books on their desks to look. The nearest one, frail, with black sleeve garters on a white shirt, pushed his spectacles back up his nose and spoke with a decidedly French accent.

"You have business?"

Neither Billy nor Eli stopped. Billy quickly unlatched the gate, and they both barged past the startled men to the rear door of the square, plain office, threw it open, and were in an alley filled with broken and discarded crates and refuse, with the three Frenchmen standing wide-eyed, bewildered in the doorway behind them.

Without a word Billy and Eli sprinted west, toward the Hudson River, glancing to their left down each narrow passageway to the waterfront for the oncoming British officers, but did not see them. They cleared the waterfront and turned north, running hard, dodging through surprised men moving in both directions on the dirt road leading back the way they had come. They had covered four hundred yards when Eli veered to the left, toward the river, and tossed his rifle into the nearest canoe. In a single stroke of his tomahawk he cut the mooring rope as Billy tossed his musket clattering into the bottom of the light craft and seized the gunwales. Thirty seconds later they were digging their paddles deep, stroking toward the center of the mighty Hudson, running with the northbound, incoming Atlantic tide.

They were six hundred yards from shore when they heard shouting and commotion from the shore behind them. They glanced back to see the two bay horses and the officers in a cluster of men staring after them. The officers were shouting, shaking their fists. While Billy and Eli watched they dug their spurs into their mounts and jumped them to a full gallop north, up the river, scattering men in all directions.

Billy pointed and shouted, "They're going for the cannon redoubts up by the supply depot!"

They were one mile from the Manhattan Island shore and two hundred yards south of the four heavy cannon guarding the big depot when they saw the great cloud of white smoke erupt from the first big gun, and flinched at the whine as the thirty-six pound ball passed ten feet over their heads to raise a thirty-foot geyser, forty yards beyond them, followed by the boom of the distant blast. They saw the white smoke leap from the next two guns, and the whine of the cannonballs was not more than five feet over their heads. The two shots raised geysers less than twenty yards to their left, and instinctively both men angled the canoe away from the shore as the last cannon belched smoke and the cannon-ball came singing twenty feet short, close enough to wet them with spray.

Billy was counting the seconds. A good cannon crew could ram the wormer down the hot cannon barrel, then the wet swab to kill all remaining sparks, ladle in the powder, seat the dried grass or straw to hold the powder, drop the cannonball into place and drive the ram home to lock the entire load in place, tap powder from a powder horn into the touch-hole, and touch the smoking linstock to the hole, all in about one minute. The crew on the first gun on the Manhattan shore still had fifteen seconds to finish reloading when a ball ripped into the water thirty feet ahead of the canoe to throw spray in the faces of Billy and Eli, followed by a distant boom from the New Jersey side of the river. Instantly both men looked up at the three-hundred-foot-high granite cliffs of the great New Jersey Palisades, stunned when they saw the smoke rising from one gun on the rim, with four others being brought to bear on them.

Both men knew. It was only a matter of time.

Eli turned. "Ready?"

"Ready!"

The next cannonball from the New Jersey heights cleared their heads by only three feet and the spray wet them, head to toe. The gun on the Manhattan side fired, and the cannonball tore into the water two feet short of the center of the frail craft and tipped it violently. When the two men felt the side of the canoe rise, each grasped his weapon with one hand and gunwale opposite with the other and threw their weight with the force of the water. The canoe reared up on its left side in the water, held for a moment, then went on over, upside down in the white foam from the blast, with a large, visible split in the birch bark from the near miss. Both men clung to the gunwales with all their strength as they hit the cold water, then kicked their way under the fractured, upside-down canoe, and hung to the underside with one hand, their weapon in the other. They made no movement in the scarce light coming through the crack, but let the craft drift with the incoming Atlantic tide, moving north, up the river.

The gun crews on both sides of the river watched the canoe overturn in the great geyser of water, the two men thrown into the water, and then the canoe settle upside down. With their telescopes, the gun crews saw the fracture in the hull. They held their telescopes on the capsized craft as it drifted north with the tide, turning slowly in the water, crippled, showing no signs of life. The bodies of the two men never appeared.

The red-bearded officer nodded his head in triumph. "Dead. Both of them. Sucked down by the river current." He looked at the gun crews, proud, superior. "Quite good. Quite good."

He drew rein on his horse and loped away with his leaner companion following, to report to their commanding officer: Two suspected Yankee spies discovered, and destroyed.

Beneath the canoe, Eli counted breaths. Fifty. One hundred. Two hundred.

There were no more cannonballs, no more distant blasts.

He continued the count to five hundred before he spoke quietly to Billy, "They think we're dead. We stay here until we're past the guns of Fort Washington, then we go ashore on the New Jersey side. Our army holds Fort Lee up on the bluffs. We can go north from there."

Notes

The great fire that burned the waterfront and about one quarter of New York City occurred on September 21, 1776. "Canvas Town" resulted, as described herein (Johnston, *The Campaign of 1776, Part 2*, pp. 118–19; see also Leckie, *George Washington's War*, pp. 281–82).

Following the Yorktown victory, General Washington was fearful the Continental Army and Congress would assume America had won the war and become careless. He admonished them to remain alert and watchful. May 9, 1782, he received a letter from British General Sir Guy Carleton, wherein General Carlton wrote that he was " . . . joined with Admiral Digby in the commission of peace" and most anxious to reduce the needless severities of war, as quoted in this chapter. Washington remained skeptical of the British intent, but soon realized they were not preparing for a summer campaign away from New York, their home base (Freeman, *Washington*, pp. 495–98).

The battles remembered by Billy and Eli of August 27, October 28, and

November 15, 1776, at Long Island, White Plains, and Fort Washington, are chronicled in Leckie, *George Washington's War*, pp. 262–96.

For excellent maps of the areas described in this chapter, see Mackesy, *The War for America, 1775–1783*, pp. 84 and 92.

For a general description of the peculiar way the incoming Atlantic tides affect the Hudson River, forcing it to "run backwards," see Ketchem, *Saratoga*, p. 7.

CHAPTER VI

*I*n deep, warm dusk, Billy and Eli walked through the campfires of the Continental Army near the tiny village of Newburgh on the west side of the Hudson River. They came steadily—hungry, tired men in tired clothes. They stopped at the front door of the log building with the American flag mounted on the forty-foot flagpole. The windows were dark, and there was but one picket standing his watch, young, smooth-faced, intense. He stiffened at their approach.

"Who comes there?"

"Lieutenant Billy Weems and Scout Eli Stroud. We're under orders to report to the general upon return from a scout."

The picket bobbed his head. "The gen'l told me. Wait here." He did a smart right face, marched four steps, then broke into a run toward General Washington's quarters. Less than five minutes later General Washington came striding, the young picket with musket at the ready, trotting to keep pace with him. Billy and Eli followed the general into the office and waited while he lighted a lamp and set it on the desk. Billy saluted, and they both sat at the general's gesture. The yellow lantern glow cast their shadows on the rough-hewn walls.

"I see you've returned. Any injuries?" There was a weariness in the face and eyes of the tall man, but beyond the weariness was the indomitable iron will that drove him relentlessly.

"None, sir," Billy said. He leaned forward to lay the two telescopes on the desk.

"Report."

Eli interrupted. "Do you have a map? It might make things easier."

Two minutes later a large map of the Hudson River Valley, from Fishkill on the north to Staten Island on the south, was unrolled before them with the corners weighted. All three men studied it for a few seconds before Billy pointed.

"Starting here"—he moved his finger as he spoke—"down to about here, is a depot two miles long."

General Washington studied it for a moment. "On Manhattan Island?"

"Yes. Just above New York City."

"Any detail on what's there?"

"Yes." Again his finger moved as he spoke. "About one thousand tents, both sides of the road, eight regulars each, about eight thousand troops. Here, a parade ground, maybe half a mile square. Here, six hundred wagons, empty, lined, and stored." He paused, then tapped the map and continued. "About thirteen hundred horses with four or five acres of feed stacked here. Here, about three hundred sixty cannon, in rows with their muzzles plugged. Over here, six separate powder magazines, sunken, with around sixty pickets on duty. Here, I judge about six hundred tons of crated food."

"Anything at White Plains? Long Island?"

Eli shook his head and leaned over the map to point. "White Plains, sixty tents—about four hundred eighty regulars. Twenty officers' tents—maybe one hundred officers. One hundred thirty-four horses, half saddle mounts, half draft horses. Twenty cannon near the horse pens, lined, muzzles plugged. Sixty wagons, empty, stored. Gunpowder stored aboveground, maybe forty barrels, fifty pounds per barrel. About one ton altogether. Some crated food, but not much."

He straightened for a moment, then continued. "On Long Island, here, there were only ten campfires burning. Almost nothing there. Same with Staten Island, over here. Three campfires. Nothing else."

For several seconds Washington studied the map, making mental calculations. "General Carleton has about eleven, maybe twelve thousand men down there, altogether. Mostly on Manhattan Island. Any indication he's preparing a major move?"

Billy shook his head. "There are eleven British warships anchored in the harbor and none of them look like they've been in battle. Their West Indies fleet is somewhere else. There are near one hundred transports, all with sails furled, riding at anchor. All the ships are high in the water, empty. None of them loaded. Skeleton crews. There are no smaller boats taking stores or munitions to them. The work on the docks is all for business ships. Commercial. From all over the world. No sign of one British ship preparing to load and leave."

Washington straightened to peer into their faces. "You were down on the docks?"

Eli nodded but said nothing.

"When?"

"Yesterday."

"Daylight?"

"Yes."

"Dressed as you are now? With your weapons?"

"Yes."

"You weren't caught?"

A slow grin slid over Eli's face. "It got a little close there for a few minutes, but they didn't catch us."

"How close? Was there shooting?"

"We got away in a canoe. Rode the incoming Atlantic tide up the Hudson. A British cannonball turned the canoe half over and we helped it the rest of the way. Stayed under it while it drifted north, up to Fort Lee. They thought the cannonball got us."

Washington listened intently, then shook his head once. "Anything else?"

Billy answered. "Yes. We walked down Post Road, the length of Manhattan Island. Farmers with all kinds of farm produce were selling to the British. No sign of concern about the British leaving. Normal business day."

Washington released the weights on the corners of the map and it rolled up loosely as he spoke. "I think you've answered my questions. It appears that the British fleet has either remained in the West Indies, or has returned to England, or partly both. If they intended coming north to blockade our rivers, they would have done so by now, and it has not happened."

He paused for a moment while he put his thoughts in order. "There is nothing suggesting General Carleton intends making a major effort to leave New York for any reason. If we're right on both questions, then we have much more freedom to finish our plans for the coming summer campaign."

He heaved a great sigh and for a moment fingered the papers on his desk. Then he came back to the two men before him and spoke directly to Billy. "There's reason to think the war will draw to an end soon. We are beginning with a plan to muster out the officers in the Continental Army. I've assigned that to General Lincoln. I do not know where your name appears on his lists, but you will be advised."

Billy's mouth fell open for one split second before he spoke. "Discharged? Going home?"

"Yes, in the next few months."

"What about the enlisted? Eli?"

"Soon after."

Washington picked up the loosely scrolled map and began tightening it. "Is there anything else?"

"No, sir."

"Thank you for your report. Dismissed."

"Thank you, sir." Billy saluted, Eli did not, and they turned on their heels to walk out into the warm night and the sounds of crickets and frogs and the faint whisper of wings overhead. Evening campfires burned as they walked on.

There was excitement in Billy's voice. "Going home in the next few months. I can hardly think what it will be like to walk up the street in Boston and see my home. Mother. Trudy. I can hardly think of it."

A quiet wistfulness fell over Eli, and Billy caught himself short, remembering that Mary, the light of Eli's life, was gone.

Eli said softly, "I'll get to see Laura. Wonder how big she is now. She was so small when I left. Little ones grow fast. Too fast. I wonder if she'll remember me."

Billy mused, "She'll be a beauty. She won't be long remembering."

Ahead, the raspy voice of Turlock reached them. "I was startin' to fret. You took long enough gettin' back. You all right?"

Billy leaned his musket against a log. "Fine. Anything left from evening mess?"

"You're supposed to eat with the officers, or have you fergot? Well, no matter. Kept some pork an' potatoes over there by the fire. Git your bowls."

They sat on a log with the dancing firelight making shadows and lines on their faces, Billy and Eli eating in ravenous silence, while Turlock talked.

"Heard about the officers? Gen'l Washington says the war might be nearly over. They'll be startin' to send the officers home, and then the enlisted. Can't hardly get hold of the idee I'll be out of this army some day. Don't know what I'll do with myself after six years of this."

Billy stopped chewing for a moment. "You'll figure out something."

"Likely. Maybe move on west. Hear they're goin' to open new land out there. Get my hundred acres of prime forest land like they promised. Raise some vegetables and rabbits on a few acres, and leave the rest to the deer and raccoon." He looked at Eli. "You goin' back up north to your family?"

Eli shrugged. "Likely. Better get my discharge first, though. Ought to be some money come with it, and that hundred acres."

"What'll you do with a hundred acres of forest?"

Eli stopped for a moment. "Maybe give it to my sister and her husband. If it's close enough to where they live. We'll see."

Turlock turned to Billy. "What you figgerin' to do with your hundred acres?"

Billy laughed. "Me? In Boston? Sell it. Give it away. I don't know."

Turlock turned back to stare in the fire. "Only thing is, they haven't told us yet where this land is. I sure hope this isn't like some of them other promises Congress made. We was supposed to have pay this past two years, but we haven't seen hardly any of it. I got over a hunnerd dollars comin'. I sure hope I get it."

Billy nodded. "They'll have to do something, or there'll be trouble."

Eli glanced at him. "It has me worried. Congress can't get money. No power. All they can do is ask the states, and if the states refuse, Congress can't force them. It worries me."

Turlock rubbed his gnarled, callused hands together and stared into the fire wistfully, but said nothing.

They finished their food, washed their bowls, and walked back to the fire.

Billy clapped Turlock on the shoulder. "Thanks for the hot food. First we had since yesterday."

"Sometime you got to tell me about what you saw down there."

"Tomorrow."

"Git to bed."

Eli followed Billy to his quarters and stopped at the glowing coals of the spent fire in front of the tent. "You still have those letters you been writing to the Dunson girl?"

In an instant the face of Brigitte flashed in Billy's mind—the hazel eyes, the nose, the mouth, and a remembrance of the way it felt to hold her, the day he left and she threw her arms about him and held him close as the friend she had known from earliest memory. Friend, not sweetheart. Billy gestured. "Inside with my things."

Eli paused for a moment. "When you get home, give them to her."

There was surprise in Billy's voice. "What brought that on?"

Eli took a few moments to pick his words. "Nothing else in life more important than what can be between a man and a woman."

For a time Billy looked into Eli's face and saw the pain of what he had lost when Mary died in his arms. He saw it, and his heart ached.

"I'll think on it."

Eli shook his head. "Do it."

"She won't have me. Not me. Look at me. She's a lovely lady. She gave her heart to that British captain—Buchanan. He's dead, and she grieves. I'll always be a friend, but that's all."

"Give her the letters. If you don't you'll always wonder what might have come of it. Do it."

"I'll think on it."

Notes

All pertinent notes appear following chapter 5.

CHAPTER VII

★ ★ ★

*W*ith the setting sun casting long shadows eastward, Sergeant Alvin Turlock, Massachusetts Second, pointed, and six privates dumped huge armloads of cut firewood next to the tall tripods from which huge, dented, thirty-gallon, fire-blackened kettles hung on chains. Wisps of steam were beginning to rise from the mix of diced pork from three shoats, chopped fresh cabbages, cut turnips, chunks of potatoes, and creek water. Turlock watched as the four men assigned to cook the evening mess dipped worn wooden spoons to test the mix, and began the process of adding salt—stirring, tasting, adding, tasting, adding. Sad experience had taught them one cannot unsalt the stew. Too much salt, and the mess crew would answer to angry, hungry men. The cooks tested one more time, smacked their lips through heavy beards, nodded to each other, and put the salt bucket down.

Turlock watched as the two men in charge of the two clay bake ovens opened the heavy, black iron doors creaking, and hunched their heads down to squint inside at the forty-eight loaves of bread just beginning to turn golden on top. They used pads of burlap to clang the doors shut and drop the iron crossbars into their slots, then walked to the stacks of cut firewood. Baking bread added two more basic rules to preparing mess: don't burn the bread, and, sift the flour before you mix the dough. Every man in the Massachusetts Second had ravenously eaten bread riddled with weevil in the harsh winters of '77, '78 and '79, but now, with the shooting ended and soldiering having become a matter of mindless monotony, all tolerance for weevil had vanished. Sift the flour and get rid of the weevil, or take your punishment.

Turlock heaved a sigh and sat down on a rung of firewood near the tripods, his thoughts running.

Things is getting edgy—near a whole year with nothin' but that drum gettin' us up in the mornin', mess, drill, cut firewood, mess, drill, shoot fer practice, clean yer weapon, cut more firewood, sit around in the evenin', and wait fer that cussed drum to put us to bed. Most folk see somethin' glorious in this soldierin', but they're the ones that don't know most of it is just the boredom of doin' the same thing over until you're like a plow horse—don't have no thought but the harness—doin' today what you done yesterday and what you'll do tomorrow.

He paused for a moment, then let his thoughts continue.

Gen'l Washington said they're goin' to muster us out, but they sure haven't done it with the Massachusetts Second. I expect they'll get around to us, but in the meantime these men are gettin' surly. Lookin' to either get into a battle to end this war, or just get up and go home.

He shifted his weight to relieve the ache in his lame right leg.

I reckon soldierin's been like this forever. Even back there when them Greeks and Romans fought it out. I guess it was the Greeks and Romans. Greeks and somebody. I seen them pictures in a book—wearin' them skirts and fightin' with them stubby little swords.

A thought brought a wry grin to his bearded face.

I bet them soldiers got froze good wearin' them skirts in the winter. But maybe they don't have winter over there, wherever it is. But I bet them soldiers got edgy just like us, sittin' around waitin' for somethin' to happen. Skirts or not, winter or not, I bet they got edgy. I reckon soldierin's been like this forever. I wonder if Adam had an army. Adam and Eve. If he did, I bet they got edgy, too.

Turlock reached for a stick and stirred at the fire. Sparks showered, then settled, and he stood, calling to the cooks and bakers.

"This mess ready?"

"Fifteen minutes. Maybe twenty."

The tip of the stick had caught fire, and Turlock stubbed it out in the dirt before he tossed it back onto the kindling pile. He was walking toward the bake ovens when he saw movement on the trail to his left, and paused to look. He brightened at the sight of Billy Weems walking toward him.

"Lieutenant, you comin' for evening mess?"

Billy shook his head. "Been over at the colonel's tent with the other officers. Just got orders. We're moving camp downriver to Verplanck." He sat down on a log worn smooth from where the men sat to eat. Turlock's eyebrows arched as he sat down beside him.

"Somethin' happenin' at Verplanck?"

Billy shook his head. "No. General Washington got a second letter from the British General Carleton and Robert Digby a while back. They want a peace treaty."

Turlock turned his good ear to Billy. "What's Washington done about it?"

"Sent the letter on to Congress. Says peace treaties are for Congress, not him."

Turlock snorted. "Congress? That bunch'll talk it to death. We'll be here another ten years."

Billy shrugged. "Washington says the military is going to stay under the control of Congress." He stopped for a moment, then changed direction. "General Rochambeau is bringing his troops up here somewhere, and we're moving down to Verplanck."

Turlock's voice was filled with disgust. "What's down there?"

"Same as here—a place to wait while a peace treaty is worked out, or we go back to war. Washington's worried that the letters from Carleton and Digby are a trick, but he's not sure. If they really want peace he doesn't want to attack, and if it's a trick he doesn't want to get caught unprepared. So he's going to move closer to New York and be ready, whichever way it goes. That's why we're going down twelve miles closer to New York."

"Verplanck is across the river."

"We'll cross it."

"Soon?"

"That's why I came to find you. We start getting ready tomorrow. Tell your men."

Both men flinched at the bellow from the cooks, "Mess is on!"

They stood, and Turlock gestured. "Better git yer bowl. Pork stew and bread."

"Can't. Got to find Captain Rhodes about tomorrow. Crossing the Hudson will take some planning."

"Stroud know about this?"

"Washington sent him down to Verplanck two days ago to be sure there's no British down there to surprise us. Got back last night. No British anywhere near."

Turlock bobbed his head. "Sure you won't stay for mess?"

Billy shook his head. "Take care of your men. I'll eat at the officer's mess."

The morning star was fading in the east when the camp drummer kicked back his blankets, swallowed against the acrid taste in his mouth, and reached for his drum. For reasons no one could ever determine, the sound of a drum carried further and louder in the hour just before dawn than at any other time in the run of a day. Birds two miles away quieted for a moment, and squirrels darting about gathering the ripe nuts and seeds for winter paused, great bushy tails cocked and curled over their backs, beady eyes searching. Mother raccoons gathered their little broods and cuffed them into a silent line. Deer and elk twitched their long ears and stood silent, nervous at a sound not of the forest.

The eastern sky was pink and rose when the Continental Army soldiers at Newburgh sat down on logs and stumps to attack wooden bowls of steaming oatmeal mush and molasses. Morning mess finished, the sun was a great brass ball sitting on the tree line across the Hudson River when the men took a deep breath, hitched at their belts, and began. Officers bawled orders, and sinewy men with hard hands moved. Within minutes the great camp was a confusion of sound and motion.

"New York First, git them crates over here and start packin' the blankets—Cut out them trees—got to have someplace to put the salt pork barrels—Move them sacks of potatoes an' cabbages an' turnips over there and be careful about it—bruises go rotten—Get the salt beef into them barrels and move 'em over there by the salt pork—You men git forty of them wagons and start loadin' the flour barrels—then the salt pork and beef.

"All you men in New Jersey Third, get the horses, four to the wagon, and start hitchin' 'em up—Move the loaded wagons down to the river and unload 'em—We're startin' a depot down there—Boats an' barges'll be along directly.

"Massachusetts Second, load the boats an' barges when they git here an' take everything down the river to the Verplanck landing.

"You men in the Pennsylvania Third, start movin' the gunpowder barrels out of them magazines and be careful. No candles, no lanterns, nothin' that might set 'em off. Git twenty wagons and hitch up the teams and start movin' the powder down to the river depot, two hunnerd yards from anything else.

"New Hampshire Fourth, start movin' them cannon down to the river, and keep a pole through them spokes—don't let none of 'em get away. What we don't need is a runaway cannon bustin' someone's legs or back. Git at it!"

They stopped at noon to eat salt beef and fried bread dough, then dropped into the grass to lay like dead men for twenty minutes before the officers shouted them onto their feet once more. At sundown, exhausted men in sweat-damp clothes ate their evening mess in ravenous silence, then went to their blankets with the western sky still showing daylight.

Days blended into a blur of loading crates and barrels into wagons that moved in a continuous line down the incline to the river and returned with sweating horses lunging into their horse collars, shod hooves tearing into the dark earth for the climb back. Slowly the massive Newburgh camp dwindled, while the new camp twelve miles down and across the river at Verplanck grew to take form and shape.

A hundred men dug new powder magazines and covered them with logs and two feet of earth. Each regiment laid out their section of the campground and dug their latrines. Crude log huts with mud and moss chinking went up in a day for the officers' headquarters. Rows of tents appeared, and firepits were dug and lined with rocks. Almost unnoticed, summer became fall, and the great forests of the Hudson River Valley were transformed as by magic from a carpet of green as far as human eye could see, into a wild, crazy quilt of endless colors that stopped hardened men while they stared at the indescribable beauty and felt their own smallness in the face of the handiwork of nature.

October brought the first heavy frosts, and the first freeze in November found the great campground at Newburgh a vacant clearing with only the dead, brown, frozen leaves of summer blowing in the early winds of winter among the abandoned leavings of an army. The men in the last few wagons turned to look and felt the strange, haunting sadness that broods over a place that was once alive with the sounds of life and living, now littered with only discarded fragments of the lives of those now gone, and silence.

They turned their faces to the river, pulled their ragged coat collars up higher, and started the wagons down the incline toward the spider-web ice on the riverbanks. They came back on the reins, and the horses set their front feet digging, stiff-legged, and dropped their hindquarters as they held the wagons back while they worked down the grade to the waiting barges.

In early December, a gentle snow began to fall in the stillness of a late afternoon, huge, wet, heavy flakes that weighed down the branches of the pines and caught in the hair and shaggy brows and beards of the men. It held through the night, and in first light of day the world had been transformed to a white so pristine bright that the men squinted as they set about clearing away eight inches of snow from the firepits and dragging the heavy iron cook kettles to the tripods for morning mess. Midmorning, the deep gray storm clouds thinned and the snow slackened, then stopped. By noon there were patches of blue overhead, and the quiet, steady dripping of melting snow was a soft undertone through the camp. By evening mess, the grounds were crisscrossed with slushy trails tromped from and to places where the business of the army had to be done.

Turlock was stacking fresh-cut, dry firewood near the evening cook fires when he was surprised by the familiar voice from behind.

"Sergeant, got a minute?"

Turlock pivoted. "Lieutenant! Didn't hear you comin'. Sure I got a minute."

The little sergeant followed Billy away from the fire, into undisturbed snow near a stand of pines, and Billy spoke quietly, eyes narrowed, intense.

"Heard anyone talking hard against Congress? Maybe stirring up trouble?"

Turlock's eyes widened. "No. Not about Congress. A lot of talk about not gettin' paid for a year or two."

"More than usual?"

Turlock scratched at his beard. "Hadn't thought on it. Yes, more than usual. We was told we'd be mustered out months ago, but we're still here, and we aren't gettin' paid. The men are startin' to disbelieve they ever will."

"Any officers saying such things? Anyone trying to organize a committee or some sort of group to make a protest?"

"Haven't heard of it. Why? You heard otherwise?"

"Not me. But others. Will you watch and listen?"

"I'll do it."

Billy started to turn, then stopped. "General Rochambeau and his army stopped at Newburgh yesterday. On their way south to get on the French boats to return to France." He paused for a moment, eyes downcast. "They're good soldiers. Turned the war in our favor. General Washington went up to bid them farewell. He admires Rochambeau and Chastellux. I'm glad he went up to pay them honor."

A far look came into Turlock's eyes. "I doubt I'll ever forget those Frenchmen diggin' those zigzag trenches to put Yorktown under our cannon—or that morning we stormed those British guns at redoubts nine and ten. Those Frenchmen dressed way too pretty, but when it came right down to it, they were real soldiers. Real soldiers. Charged right into the muzzles of those cannon and muskets at number nine. Real soldiers."

Billy nodded. "I remember." He turned. "Keep your ears open. Let me know if you hear anything."

An unexpected thaw set in at midnight, and by afternoon the following day the camp was a swamp of mud and dirty puddles. What little snow remained lay in small patches on the north side of tents and the log cabins and trees. Turlock slogged his company through the chores of the day, quietly listening to their talk and banter, hearing their usual grumbling and murmuring—cursing bad food, bad officers, bad duty, bad pay—all the things he heard every day. The following evening he gathered with his men for mess.

"Awright, you lovelies. Git yer bowls and brace yerselves for this feast."

"Beef brisket an' cabbage? A feast?"

"That just looks like brisket. It's really prime beefsteak. Done just right. And look at this here bread. Golden brown and fluffy, just like yer mother made."

"That's fried dough!"

"Trouble with you men is you don't have no imagination. You're just naturally missin' half of life. Eat and be glad you got it."

Turlock was working with his bowl of steaming food when the quiet words from four nearby enlisted men reached him.

" . . . and he said they're going to write it down and take it to Congress."

"Who's going to write it down?"

"Likely McDougall himself."

"You mean General McDougall? Alexander McDougall?"

"The same. Heard he got arrested by Gen'l Heath a while back because he made a deal with a company named Comfort Sands for supplies, and then mishandled it real bad and the supplies never got delivered. So Heath arrested him and it went to a court-martial."

"McDougall got court-martialed? What happened?"

"Nothin' much. Never does with them generals. Just told him to be a good boy and not do it again."

"What's this about McDougall goin' to write down somethin' and take to Congress? Write down what?"

"Complaints of a lot of officers, and maybe make some demands."

"Demands about what?"

"The officers haven't been paid, and they're fearful now that Congress can't get the money to pay 'em, and they're goin' to demand it or else."

The four men stopped eating. "Or else what?"

The speaker shrugged. "Maybe a revolt. Mutiny. Rebellion. That's what I heard."

The men looked at each other in near disbelief. "Gen'l McDougall doin' somethin' like that? You musta heard wrong. Yeah, you musta heard it wrong."

Turlock slowly walked over to the group, still working at his bowl of corned beef and cabbage. "Where'd you hear all this?"

"All what?"

"McDougall, writing down something."

"Just talk."

"Who?"

The man pointed over his shoulder with a thumb. "New York First. Just talk."

"Any officers sayin' this?"

"Yeah. A captain. Maybe a major."

"Well, you let the New York regiment talk all they want. Just don't get it started here. Talk like that can make trouble."

The quarter-moon was hanging low in the east when Turlock found Billy walking from the log cabin headquarters of Colonel William Schott toward his own tent. Vapors rose from their faces in the darkness as Turlock spoke.

"Just heard talk at evening mess. Rumors from New York First are that Gen'l McDougall and some other officers might be stirrin' up trouble."

"What kind of trouble?"

"Gatherin' up complaints. Gettin' ready to write out some demands and take 'em to Philadelphia to Congress."

Billy spoke slowly. "Rebellion? Revolt?"

"Maybe."

"You heard about McDougall? And Heath?"

"Yeah, I heard. Heath arrested McDougall and got him court-martialed."

Billy drew and released a weary breath. "Bad blood there. I'll let Colonel Schott know what you heard."

Turlock paused for a moment. "Any such things from other regiments?"

"A few. General Washington's concerned."

Turlock shivered. "I'll keep an ear open."

Billy turned to go, and Turlock stopped him. "You worried pretty bad about this business of officers complaining? The McDougall thing?"

A cloud crossed Billy's face. "These troops spent the past seven years winning a fight we should have lost. The country owes them. If Congress can't keep the promises it made to pay them, what becomes of it all? Do we lose everything we gained?"

Turlock saw and felt the fear and the pain in Billy's heart. "Maybe we outsmarted ourselves."

There was a pause before Billy answered. "How?"

"Thought winning the war was the answer to everything. Didn't understand that getting our freedom—independence—might bring worse troubles than we had before. We knew who our enemy was before—they was wearin' them red coats. Who's our enemy now? Who do we shoot at? Our officers? Congress? Ourselves?"

For five full seconds the two men stared at each other in the dark while the terrifying thought settled in. Then Billy turned and quietly walked back in the direction from which he had come, toward the log cabin headquarters of Colonel William Schott.

Notes

August 4, 1782, Washington received a second letter from British General Carleton and Robert Digby, again suggesting peace negotiations. Washington forwarded the letter to Congress, stating that only Congress could conclude peace. Congress then ordered General Nathanael Greene to remain in the South with his command. Suspicious the British letters were a ploy to gain them time and advantage, Washington moved most of his Newburgh army camp twelve miles south, down and across the Hudson, to a small village named Verplanck, to be nearer the British stationed at New York. In December, French General Rochambeau did visit Newburgh on his way to the ships that would carry his army back to France, where he and Chevalier Chastellux were greeted most warmly and with great honors by General Washington. Rumors began to circulate about mounting dissatisfaction, and then anger, among the officers of the American army because they were not being paid, nor was there any prospect that they would be. General Alexander McDougall did enter into a supply contract with a company named Comfort Sands & Co. and quickly came to sharp disagreement over the terms, resulting in a violent argument, following which General William Heath arrested General McDougall for misconduct and brought it to a court-martial in which McDougall received a mild reprimand. Then General McDougall began agitating among the officers to create a writing to be submitted to Congress, making demands for the pay and land they had been promised (Freeman, *Washington*, pp. 498–99).

Philadelphia
Early January 1783

CHAPTER VIII

*C*ongressman Joseph Jones, wiry, round-shouldered, cavernous eyes and jutting chin, threw the thick, stiff parchment document down on the small corner table, clenched his teeth, and jerked out of his chair. He strode to the door of his tiny rented room on the second floor of the boardinghouse two blocks from the Pennsylvania State House, then back to the fireplace, then back to the door, driven by the rising realization that Congress was caught between two gigantic forces that were headed for a cataclysmic collision for which there was no solution and no escape. He pivoted and strode again back to the fireplace, then to the door, then to the small window that overlooked the narrow, winding Philadelphia cobblestone street below that afforded a view of the back wall of Independence Hall. He snatched the curtain back and stared at the brick building two blocks away, obscured by the gray light and blowing snow.

Three terms in that building, and now it all comes down to this.

He turned to look at the document as though it were something alive and deadly.

They're right! Those officers are right! McDougall is right! We made them the promises when we needed them, and they stayed and fought, and now they want their pay. They're right!

He walked back to his chair and plucked up the document to glance once more at the twelve pages, with more than fifty signatures of

Continental Army officers, ranging from generals down to majors. He skimmed some of the requests, then the demands, then their brief statement of the devastating consequences if Congress should fail to keep its promises. He shuddered and threw the document back, skittering across the table to hit the wall.

We made the promises, and we knew we did not have the power to keep them if the states failed to make their contributions. Well, they failed! We don't have the power to force them to do anything, and we don't have the money to pay as we promised. Nor the land! One hundred acres each.

He paused and by force of will brought his anger and fear under control. Slowly he settled in the worn, upholstered chair before the table, and forced some semblance of reason to his thoughts. For a time he stared at the yellow glow of the lamp, then turned to listen to the quiet moan of the wind drawing in the chimney, and watch the flames dance in the fireplace. He glanced at the clock on the desk and shook his head.

Forty minutes and we start the morning session. How many others got a copy of this? What are they thinking? How do I tell my people in Virginia that we can't pay their soldiers? We have to muster them out with Continental dollars that are not worth the paper we printed them on. We can't give them the land we promised because we don't have it—never did. We don't have anything, and we can't get it.

His head dropped forward, chin on his chest.

How do I tell those Virginia regiments that I deceived them? I and the rest of us in Congress. How do we do that?

The sound of rapid footsteps on the stairs and then in the hallway brought his head up, and he rose at the loud knock on his door. He swung the door open to face Charles Thomson, Secretary of the United States in Congress Assembled, who was knocking snow from his tricorn and cape.

"Come in, come in," Jones said, and stepped aside. "Have some hot chocolate against the cold."

Thomson shook his head. "No time." He reached inside his coat and drew out a document sealed with royal blue wax bearing the impression of General George Washington.

"This was delivered in chambers ten minutes ago. Addressed to you from General Washington. I brought it over."

Jones seized the document and with trembling fingers broke the seal. He turned it toward the fireplace for light and silently read.

> My Dear Friend, Congressman, and fellow Virginian:
>
> I write hastily since my duties here spare little time for other than the most pressing business. As you know, under the direction of Congress General Greene has remained in the Southern Department; I took the liberty of moving the Newburgh camp to Verplanck to be closer to New York, affording closer surveillance of the movements of General Carleton and his command. You will recall I received a second message from Gen. Carleton expressing great desire to enter into negotiations, which I forwarded to Congress for their deliberations. I trust the matter is proceeding rapidly.
>
> However, the real purpose of this brief letter is to advise that I am aware there is an increasing spirit of rebellion among the officers of the Continental Army. I have just learned that a lengthy document was forwarded to Congress that includes several pages of extreme complaints and demands, which document bears the signatures of some of our most able and worthy officers, including General Alexander McDougall.
>
> The temper of the Army is much soured, and has become more irritable than at any period since the commencement of the war. What Congress can or will do in the matter does not belong to me to determine; but policy, in my opinion, should dictate soothing measures.
>
> I entrust this opinion to you in the sure knowledge that as a friend to myself, and to Virginia, you will give it every consideration as Congress faces the very difficult task of addressing the document you should have by now received from General McDougall and his associates.

Should you conceive of any way in which I can help, you
have but to give me due notice.

Your ob'dt servant,

G. Washington.

Jones's head snapped up. "Did anyone else receive such a letter from
the general?"

Thomson shook his head emphatically. "No, sir, not that I know of.
Only yourself. I'm aware of your friendship with General Washington."

Jones pointed to the thick document on his desk. "You know that
very early this morning most of us in Congress received a copy of a
document from General McDougall?"

"I'm aware of it, sir. I've read it."

"Have you heard anything over at the hall about McDougall's
demands? How others in Congress view this thing?"

"Only that they're absolutely desperate about what to do."

"You understand what is happening?"

"Yes, sir, I think so."

Jones's voice rose as he spoke and paced. "We promised those men
their pay, and they've waited two years or more to get it. The war is essentially over, and we're about to muster them out, and we can't pay them!
Congress has no power to tax, to raise money, and no power to force the
separate states to contribute either money or land. Congress is a toothless
wolf!"

Jones paused in his pacing and threw his hands in the air, his voice
high, loud. "No one—not the states, not Congress—hesitated when we
needed those men so desperately. We made the promises, and they
believed them and stayed to win the peace."

He swung around to face Thomson squarely. "Now they've won the
peace, and suddenly everyone—*everyone*—seems to have forgotten how
everything depended on those men and how freely we made the promises
we had to make to hold them. Every state has printed its own money! So
has Congress. And what do we have? Fourteen separate issues of paper
money, most of it worthless. Almost no hard money in the entire country
to back it up. Bankruptcy rampant. Business closures in record numbers.

Employment plummeting. States turning on their neighbors with border tariffs on all goods crossing state lines. Border disputes rampant. And no chance—no chance—to keep our promises to those men."

He drew and exhaled a great breath. "Now we have the Continental Army threatening revolt! The very men who saved the Confederation."

He glanced at the clock and forced himself to cool.

"You'll forgive me for raising my voice to you about all this. It certainly was none of your doing."

He walked hastily to the small closet in the corner nearest the window and drew his heavy cape from its peg. "We have to go. It won't do to be late for the morning session. Not this morning."

He threw the cape about his shoulders, closed the clasp at his throat, fastened the first two large buttons, then jammed his tricorn on his head.

"Somehow we're going to have to go through a charade that gives the appearance of an earnest effort to meet the demands of Mr. McDougall and his associates, and hope the passing of time will dull their anger."

He gestured toward the door. "After you, Mr. Thomson." As they passed out into the hallway Jones muttered, "I'd rather be in the hottest corner of purgatory with my back broken than go face what is surely coming this morning across the way in those hallowed halls of Congress."

Notes

In 1783, Joseph Jones was a congressman from Virginia who enjoyed a personal and friendly relationship with George Washington. General McDougall and many others did draft a lengthy document, voicing their anger and listing out their complaints and demands and forwarded it to Congress. General Washington wrote a letter to Congressman Jones warning that the Continental Army was in its sourest mood since the beginning of the war. A large part of Washington's letter is quoted verbatim in this chapter. Congress was without power to raise money by taxes or in any other manner, or to acquire land from the states. The United States was entering into a period of bankruptcy for many citizens, many states, and the United States itself. Most states, as well as the

United States Confederation government, were printing their own paper money. Most of the paper money became worthless. The country was facing an unprecedented economic crisis (Freeman, *Washington,* pp. 498–500; Bernstein, *Are We to Be a Nation?,* pp. 8, 9; Morris, *The Forging of the Union,* pp. 36–46).

CHAPTER IX

★ ★ ★

*S*ergeant Turlock reached to clamp his tricorn on his head against the blustery, raw March wind that swept north up the Hudson River Valley beneath low, rolling, slate-colored clouds, moaning in the bare trees, prying at every tent flap, every door, every window in the Confederation Army camp at Verplanck. He carried his musket in his right hand as he walked toward the officers' quarters, hunched forward, favoring his right leg, nose dripping, coattails flapping. He passed the great, crudely built, log assembly hall and turned west, headed to the row of small huts hastily constructed during the winter for the officers. He had gone ten yards when the first mix of freezing rain and hail came whistling horizontal to sting the left side of his face and beard and soak his coat. Twenty yards later he passed the first officer walking east, head down, cloak billowing out behind, and he passed six more officers in the next eighty yards. He was twenty feet from the familiar tiny cabin near the end of the row when the door opened and Billy Weems walked out into the sleet, head ducked, holding his tricorn in place with one hand, his coat closed with the other. Billy was five feet from Turlock before he raised his head, squinting against the sleet, and saw him approaching.

He spoke loudly, above the wind. "You coming to see me?"

Turlock shouted back, "I was. Where you going?"

"Assembly hall up at Newburgh."

Turlock nodded his head vigorously. "You heard about that Stewart thing?"

"Yes. A few of the officers are gathering up there."

"I heard. That's why I come to see you. What's going on?"

"I don't know. Something about Congress—telling Congress their grievances."

"I heard they figger to write it all out."

Billy nodded vigorously. "Want to come along?"

"I'm not an officer."

"I'll get you in." They leaned into the wind, gritting their teeth against the gale that drove the sleet through their coats as they made their way down the incline to the Hudson River where a barge waited for the next load of officers going upstream. There was no talk as they sat hunched on the benches for the rough, rocking, hour-long trip twelve miles upstream, then made the slippery climb to the nearly deserted Newburgh camp. Billy and Turlock joined a cluster of officers at the door and shuffled forward as the group filtered into the chill twilight of the huge assembly hall. Inside, some of the officers of the Verplanck camp milled about while a few others found seats on the rough pine, backless benches. Wind moaned at the large fireplace on the west wall and leaked, whistling, through the gaps where windows did not fit their frames. The bearded men wiped at their noses, and turned their coat collars up, saying little as they waited. The big rear door creaked open one more time, and the last cluster of officers entered with a blast of freezing wind that fluttered the fire and moved the single American flag on the pole behind the rough-hewn lectern at the head of the hall. Seated near the flag were Major John Armstrong and Timothy Pickering, once adjutant general to General Washington.

After a time, the door to a small room in the left corner, behind the flag, squeaked as it swung open, and Colonel Walter Stewart, recently appointed Inspector General of the Northern Army, and a former personal aide to General Horatio Gates, entered. Every man present knew all too well the history of Gates, the pseudo-hero of the battle of Saratoga and the great coward of the later battle of Camden, South

Carolina, in which he deserted his command under fire and was found two days later, two hundred ten miles distant from the disastrous defeat his men suffered when he abandoned them. Average size, round faced, receding chin, Stewart approached the lectern in a fresh uniform, erect, self-assured, and every officer came to attention. Stewart surveyed them for a moment.

"Be seated."

Benches creaked as the officers sat down.

Stewart's voice came loud to be heard above the sounds of the wind and the pelting sleet hammering at the few windows on the east wall.

"First, I wish to thank you for your presence here today. This assembly is not an officially convened meeting with a military purpose. Rather, it is a voluntary assembly for purposes which have been too long neglected by our military commander and by the Confederation Congress."

The room fell into dead silence. No one moved or spoke. Stewart raised his voice, and he swept his hand toward the assembly in a grand gesture.

"As you know, I stand before you following my return from my recent visit to Congress in Philadelphia. You will recall that in January, two months ago, a writing was delivered to Congress stating in strong terms the dissatisfactions and grievances of this corps of officers. The purpose of my visit was to determine what action Congress had taken in response. While there I had the privilege of entering into deep and meaningful discussions with various leaders of that august group, and I became aware of the crisis that is rapidly approaching."

He paused, and every officer present except Armstrong and Pickering fell into a puzzled silence, glancing at each other with the unspoken question in their eyes: *What crisis?* Turlock turned to Billy, questioning, and Billy silently shook his head.

"I refer to the crisis that now threatens each man in this room! You have answered the call of General Washington and the Congress to serve your country. You left hearth and home and all that mankind holds dear and sacred, to accept starvation, freezing, sickness, and the cannon and musketry of the greatest military force on earth! Through the dark hours of death and defeat, you stood steadfast in your quest for liberty. Liberty! Patriots all! Each and every of you, patriots as never before seen."

Still, no one on the benches moved or spoke.

"Yours is the sure knowledge that you have wrought a victory without comparison in the written history of civilized nations."

Stewart paused for a time, and a low wave of murmuring went through the officers and stopped.

"It is now my duty to tell you the manner in which you are to be repaid by our commander and our Congress. While in Philadelphia, I learned that it is their intent to disband this army in the next short period of time, without the reward which you have so nobly earned and to which you are so richly entitled."

Open talk broke out, and Stewart raised a hand to silence it.

"The reward promised by General George Washington . . ."

Talk erupted.

"The reward promised by Congress itself! . . ."

The officers turned to exclaim among themselves.

"You will not be given the back pay promised you. You will not be given the pensions promised you. You will not receive the land promised you. You will return to your wives and families, to your farms and businesses, to your homes, penniless! Unable to provide the simplest of life's necessities. Paupers! Disgraced! Dismissed like flotsam!"

Turlock started to rise, and Billy pushed him back onto the bench.

Stewart plowed on.

"Fellow officers, you are the ones who placed this nation in the chain of independency, and what have our leaders done? Shown their ingratitude by betrayal! Deceit! Delay! Unkept promises! And now, dismissal with nothing! *Nothing!*"

Billy sat motionless, hand on Turlock's trembling shoulder, listening, sensing the temper of the officers around him as they raised their voices in anger. None had been told the purpose of the meeting. None had come expecting to hear the terrifying claim by the Inspector General of the Northern Army that they were to be dismissed without the pay or the land or the pensions they had repeatedly been promised and which would be so desperately needed when they returned to their homes and families. Had Stewart's statement come from a lesser officer as a matter of casual mess hall banter, they would have laughed and forgotten it. But they were not listening to a lesser officer flippantly tossing out a dining hall absurdity intended to provoke a passing moment of levity. They were in the great assembly hall, listening to stunning, shocking, unbelievable charges being made by the inspector general against their commander in chief and the Continental Congress!

Again Stewart raised a hand for silence, and his voice rang off the walls.

"I am calling for a formal convening of all general and field officers tomorrow, March eleventh, at ten o'clock A.M. The purpose of the meeting is to receive their unanimous approval of a document which is to be hand-carried to Congress. A document which reminds our Congress, and our commander in chief, of all their promises, and requires of them that they deliver to each of us what we so justly deserve!"

He paused to draw a deep breath and order his thoughts.

"There will also be a second document. This document shall advise Congress and our commander that should they continue in their course of delay and denial, the army shall withdraw to a new location outside the United States, and there the army shall establish a new state of its own, beyond the reach and authority of either Congress or our commander. Then wait and see how quickly they come to us on their knees, pleading!"

A breathless hush settled, and then the hall erupted in a deafening din. Officers came to their feet in disbelief, fumbling to understand that the inspector general of their army should utter such blasphemy.

Abandon the United States?

Leave our homeland defenseless?

A new state? Under military authority?

Billy sat transfixed, brain numbed. Turlock was white-faced, frozen, unable to speak or move.

Stewart shouted them into silence, hand raised, finger pointed to the ceiling.

"A new state, but only if we must. There is another way, and I give it to you as an alternative. Rather than form a new state in the wilderness, let them make the peace with England, and then we shall refuse to lay down our arms when ordered by Congress. Maintain our arms. Continue as an army. An army with the power and authority to require Congress and our commander to accept our just demands and requests."

The tumult continued while the officers tried to force their shocked minds to tell them whether the proposals of their inspector general were a plan to achieve justice, or treason. Stewart dropped his hand to the lectern and waited. The uproar continued and Stewart let it run—one minute, two, three. The officers turned to each other, shouting above the drumming of the wind and the sleet to repeat what they had heard, and to listen to themselves to see if it had the flavor of patriotism or the stench of rank blasphemy. Billy remained silent, his hand still on Turlock's shoulder, while the wiry little soldier shook with rage.

The shouting lessened, and Stewart finally called, "Gentlemen! Gentlemen! Gentlemen!" All eyes turned to him, and they quieted.

"I have prepared and printed written notices of tomorrow's meeting for all officers in this camp. I have also prepared a written statement of the plan which I have briefly explained to you, by which we will demand and receive that which we were promised. That document shall be delivered to Congress. Printed copies of both the notice and the plan will be given to you as you leave this hall, and others will be delivered to the remainder of our officer corps throughout the day. You will be expected to attend the meeting tomorrow morning."

He paused for one brief moment, then concluded. "You are dismissed." Stewart turned from the lectern and strode to the small room from whence he had come, followed by Armstrong and Pickering, who closed the door behind them.

For thirty seconds the officers stood in loud discussion while their shattered thoughts came together and they realized they were dismissed. Some began filing out of the large doors at the rear of the hall, where two captains handed each of them the notice of the meeting called for the following morning, together with the printed statement of the case Stewart had prepared against Congress and General Washington. They jerked their tricorns low and walked out into the wind and sleet, trying to read as they walked.

Billy and Turlock accepted their copies of the documents and walked to the north side of the building to huddle close to the wall where the south wind and sleet passed over them. Silently they read the two documents, then read the statement a second time to be certain they had understood the plain meaning of the proposal. Billy looked at Turlock and without a word turned on his heel and trotted down the sloping bank of the river to the waiting barge, Turlock following. Forty minutes later he leaped from the barge to the dock, running west toward the headquarters building of General Washington. He halted before the confused picket while Turlock came running behind him.

"I'm Lieutenant Billy Weems, Massachusetts Second. I have to see the general. Now!"

The picket's brow was furrowed, eyes narrowed in question. "The general is not to be disturbed. What's going on? Officers walking around in this weather, reading something."

Billy thrust the two documents forward. "These. Mutiny."

The picket's head jerked forward, eyes bugging. "What? Mutiny?"

"Mutiny. Do I see the general?"

Two minutes later Billy was in the square, plain room that served as Washington's headquarters, standing at attention before Washington's desk. Turlock was to his left, slightly behind him. The general was leaning back in his chair, blue-gray eyes inquiring.

"You wished to see me, Lieutenant?"

"Yes, sir. I believe it is urgent you read these." He laid the two papers on the general's desk and stepped back.

Washington leaned forward to pick up the damp notice. Quickly he scanned it, then read it in detail. A quizzical expression flitted across his face.

"Where did you get this?"

"An hour ago, in a meeting at the Newburgh assembly hall."

"This is not signed. Who arranged the meeting?"

"Colonel Walter Stewart, sir."

"The inspector general? For what purpose?"

"It's in the second document, sir."

Washington squared the second document on his desk and for two minutes the only sound in the room was the wind at the fireplace and windows, and the pelting of the sleet. Washington did not move until he had finished the reading twice. He raised his eyes to Billy, and there was controlled thunder and lightning leaping from them.

"This is also unsigned. Who wrote it?"

"I don't know, sir."

"I doubt Colonel Stewart wrote it. Was anyone with him?"

"Major John Armstrong, Junior, sir, and Timothy Pickering."

"General Gates?"

"I did not see him, sir."

For a moment Washington leaned forward on his forearms, face down in deep thought. Then he raised his eyes. "How many officers were at the gathering this morning?"

"I would judge between forty and fifty, sir."

"What was their reaction?"

"From what I saw and heard, they were . . . shocked . . . in the beginning, but it seemed the longer they listened to Stewart the more the shock wore off. I think they began to consider some of the things written there. I think most of them will attend the meeting called for tomorrow morning, and a lot of other officers with them."

Washington locked eyes with Billy. "Is there serious discontent among the officers?"

Billy did not flinch. "Yes, sir. There is."

"Where do you stand in this?"

Billy's answer was instant. "I didn't join this army for pay or pension or land. I believe what Colonel Stewart is doing is treason, sir. I refuse to be part of it."

"Is there anything else you should tell me?"

"Not that I can think of, sir."

Washington looked at Turlock. "Sergeant, do you wish to add anything?"

"No, sir. Yes, sir. Billy—Lieutenant Weems—told it right. I didn't join this army for pay, either, sir."

"Thank you, Sergeant. You men are dismissed."

Billy interrupted. "Sir, is there anything we can do?"

"Yes. Go back to your regiment and conduct yourselves in a normal fashion. Should you see or hear anything else I need to know, bring it to me."

"Yes, sir." The two turned on their heels and walked back through the heavy, plank door, out into the weather.

Inside his small, austere office, the iron will of George Washington clamped down on the seething rage within. Slowly he forced his mind to settle and waited for that certain inner sense to tell him he was in control of himself and seeing the affair for what it was. He began putting his thoughts in order, examining them from every angle to be certain of the logic and reasoning.

Stewart—once an aide to Horatio Gates—still is—Gates was behind Stewart going to Congress—they've talked since—they're responsible for this mutiny—Stewart's persuaded Armstrong and Pickering to join his plan—Armstrong is the best writer among them—he has to be the one who wrote these documents.

He leaned forward, elbows on his desk, closed his eyes, and buried his face in his hands while his thoughts continued.

This is what Hamilton and Morris and Wilson saw coming when they approached me with their plan to use the anger of the military to force the states to give the Confederation broader powers—sufficient to stop this uprising—but their plan was wrong—the states wouldn't stand for giving the powers those men wanted to Congress— and it is likely they will now be ambitious about reminding me of their plan—must be careful in handling Hamilton and Morris and Wilson.

He reached for a conclusion.

Both mutiny and treason—if Gates and his confederates succeed, they'll tear the United States apart—must be stopped—but how—how?

Washington dropped his hands from his face and for a long time sat with narrowed eyes staring unseeing at his desk. Then he picked up his quill and with studied strokes wrote:

10th March 1783
Colonel Hamilton:
I am aware of the meeting proposed for all officers by an anonymous writer for ten o'clock A.M. tomorrow, March 11, 1783, at the Newburgh assembly hall. This is to advise I will personally take the matter in hand.
Cordially your ob'dt
G. Washington.

He stood and strode to the door and swung it open, and his startled secretary came to attention.

"Would you please have this delivered to Colonel Alexander Hamilton at once? He is now a representative in Congress, at Philadelphia."

"Yes, sir."

"Until further orders, I am to be disturbed by no one except Lieutenant Billy Weems."

"Yes, sir."

At noon General Washington summoned his secretary and handed him a carefully drafted document.

"See to it this is copied in numbers sufficient to post it immediately at all places the officers will see it. Instruct all general officers they are required to read it aloud in the officers' barracks as soon as possible, and this evening at officers' mess."

"Yes, sir."

By two o'clock the wind and sleet had stopped, and the thick overhead clouds had thinned to show patches of blue. By three o'clock the camp was flooded with sunlight, with wisps of steam rising from the puddles of melting sleet. At four o'clock, Billy Weems was startled by a knock at his door. He opened it and faced Eli Stroud, dressed in his leathers with his rifle at his side and some folded documents in his left hand.

Billy stepped back. "Come in."

The door closed and Eli raised the documents. "You seen these?"

"Yes."

"Do you officers know any more than what's here?"

"Should be three papers. One is a notice of the meeting tomorrow. The second one calls for treason. The third one is from General Washington. You got all three?"

"I do. I never saw anything like it. Can you tell me anything more about what's going on?"

"The papers speak for themselves. But I have my own idea about it."

"What is it?"

"Gates wants to replace Washington."

"Looks that way. And after that I think he wants to set up a government controlled by the military, and he wants to be the commander in chief."

Billy nodded silent agreement and Eli went on.

"How are the officers seeing all this?"

"Some one way, some the other. Most want what they were promised. I don't know what they'll do when they have to make a choice."

"You read what General Washington says?" He held up Washington's writing.

"All of it. Called that business of creating a new state an act of disorderly and irregular conduct on the part of whoever proposed it and condemned the proposal for the meeting tomorrow morning. Ordered that it not be held. He set up a meeting for all officers next Saturday, the fifteenth. Ten o'clock in the morning. In the Newburgh assembly hall. He's going to be there."

Eli interrupted. "So is Gates."

"I saw that. The general asked Gates to conduct the meeting. That surprised me."

Eli shook his head. "No, I think Washington has become the fox. By handing the meeting to Gates, Gates is going to think Washington has sympathy with his side, and Gates will have his entire crowd there. If that happens, I expect Washington will put a stop to this Gates thing for all time. I believe that's how Washington figures it."

Billy fell into a few moments of thoughtful silence. "Makes sense. The question is, what's going to happen if Washington comes down hard on the Gates people? Will the officers take it? Will they revolt? Walk out? I know for certain they want what was promised them. That's what the McDougall affair that started this whole thing was all about."

Eli took a deep breath. "I never expected this, but it looks like Saturday is going to turn this country one way or the other. The army runs it, or we keep our liberty." He slowly shook his head, and spoke thoughtfully. "The British couldn't stop us. Now it looks like our own army intends to pick up where the British failed. Think on it. General Washington has to try to put down his own army, to save this country. In my worst thoughts I did not see this one coming."

Billy spoke quietly. "Neither did I. We better be there."

The following morning, within five minutes of the roll of the reveille drum, the three documents, two from Armstrong, one from General Washington, had seized the minds and the tongues of every man in camp. Every tent, every hut, every place two or more men met, the talk rolled on, sometimes heated, sometimes quiet. In blustery March weather, soldiers completed their regular daily functions woodenly, without thought, while the chatter spilled out. After evening mess, men gathered around campfires to continue the debates. Quiet voices could be heard long after the ten o'clock drum tapped out tattoo.

Time lost meaning as the days dragged on. By Friday it seemed no one could remember a time when Gates's mind-wrenching proposal of drawing the army off into the wilderness to form a new state had not been the core of existence in the military. Worse, if the proposal would force Congress and General Washington to deliver their pay, land, and pensions as promised, what was wrong with it? General Washington's condemnation of it was only to be expected, since it was now clear that neither Congress, Washington, nor the separate states could keep their promises, nor did they intend to try.

The rattle of the Friday night tattoo drum had echoed and died in the far reaches of the black forest when Eli rose from his blankets to stand in the night breeze, peering up at the three-quarter moon in thoughtful reflection.

Most of these men want their pay. That's fair. Most of them do not want to mutiny to get it. None of them want treason. That is as it should be.

He watched clouds forming, riding the breeze to drift past the face of the moon. In the moment of passing they were transformed from deep purple to silver, and then they were gone.

What will they do tomorrow if this all comes to a choice? Will they mutiny to get their pay? If they mutiny, what will Washington do?

Clouds darkened the moon and held, and for a few moments Eli became an Iroquois Indian, reading the moon and the clouds, judging the transient March weather.

Maybe rain tomorrow. Maybe not. At least clouds. Cold. And wind.

He brought his thoughts back to the dark thoughts of what morning would bring.

Eight years—thousands dead—men and women—blood—too much blood— pain—suffering—all for an idea—liberty—we won—defeated the British—and now, it looks like our own army has become our enemy.

For a long time he peered up at the moon, watching the gathering clouds cover it, cutting off all light.

Why is it that somehow the best things in life are the hardest to hold onto—my mother and father, gone when I was two years old—Mary gone—at war most of my life—the French or the British or the Mohawk—and now, liberty—it seems like we paid a big enough price in the past eight years to win it—now it looks like we have to fight our own army to keep it—why is it so hard to keep the good things?

From far away came the baying of a wolf, then another, and another, as they took their turn in the relay that would bring down a deer or an elk. Nearer, an owl inquired with its soft "whoooo." Eli lowered his eyes to peer into the blackness of the Hudson River forest, reading the sounds of night as though it were full daylight. Then he raised them again, watching the gathering clouds blot out the stars and the eternity beyond. His thoughts ran on.

All His handiwork—He put the price on the good things—the only question is, are we willing to pay it?

He lowered his eyes and dropped back to his blankets. *Tomorrow morning—we find out more about the price of liberty—and if we're willing to pay it.*

Dawn broke with a chill March wind moving, billowing gray clouds up the valley. Morning mess was little more than a forum for final arguments on what was to come. Eight o'clock found officers gathering in groups and clusters, talking among themselves, gesturing with raised voices from time to time. By half past eight they were loading into barges at the dock and pushing off into the broad, slate-gray expanse of choppy water. At twenty minutes before ten o'clock Billy and Eli stood at the door of the large, low, Newburgh assembly hall where two captains inspected them for weapons before one gestured toward Eli and spoke.

"Are you an officer?"

"Scout."

"For whom?"

"General Washington."

Billy interrupted. "I'm Lieutenant Billy Weems. Massachusetts Second. This is Scout Eli Stroud. He's the one General Washington sent to scout Verplanck before we moved from here down there. He's with me."

The captain studied Billy for a moment deciding whether he could allow a scout into a meeting limited to officers only. He made up his mind.

"Lieutenant, you're responsible for him. If anything goes wrong, you're the one who will answer. You can enter."

They entered and moved to one side to study how the benches were placed, then the pulpit, then the chairs behind. Eli glanced at Billy, who nodded, and they separated. Eli walked casually along the left wall to the front of the great room while Billy walked along the right to the first row of benches. They both leaned their backs against the wall to remain standing, casually watching. From their position they could look into the faces of all the officers seated on the low pine benches. Each was less than twenty-five feet from the lectern and twenty feet from the four chairs behind it. Behind the chairs, in one corner, was the small room reserved for the participants; in the opposite corner was a door leading outside. Billy and Eli had access to everyone who was to conduct or speak, and to the escape door.

They remained standing, leaning against the wall, waiting and watching as the hall filled. At ten o'clock the door into the small room opened, and there was a great rustling sound as every officer in the room rose to his feet and came to attention. General Horatio Gates entered, followed by Major Armstrong, then Timothy Pickering. There was an instant, involuntarily intake of breath in the room as General George Washington, towering over them all, also entered. Every eye was on him as he followed the others to the chairs, and they remained standing while Horatio Gates took two steps to the lectern. Tending towards heaviness, round features, jowls beginning to sag, Gates smiled grandly before he spoke.

"You may be seated."

No one moved until General Washington was seated. Then Armstrong and Pickering took their chairs next to his, and the officers sat down on their low, backless benches, silent, waiting.

Gates continued. "This meeting is convened upon orders of our commander in chief, General George Washington." He paused and turned toward Washington in the classic tradition of a showman. Washington did not move.

Gates turned back. "General Washington has requested that I make a statement. As you know, the United States has a peace commission in France, engaged in arranging a treaty of peace with the British. When the treaty has been signed, Congress shall begin the process of dismissing this army."

There was a pause, then Gates went on. "You are aware that serious . . . questions . . . have arisen regarding the terms under which both the officers and enlisted will be discharged. Various promises have been made to the entire army in the past, which lately have become . . . troublesome, since it is now thought by many that those promises cannot be kept."

For the first time, murmuring broke out from the floor, then quieted.

"True to his duties as commander in chief, General Washington has convened this meeting for the purpose of clarifying both his position, and that of Congress, regarding their responses to the recent . . . inquiries . . . they received, and have considered."

He drew a handkerchief from his sleeve and mopped at his brow. "It is therefore my distinct honor to present to you General George Washington."

Gates stepped aside and waited while Washington rose from his chair and walked to the lectern, towering over Gates, his prominent nose and jaw in sharp contrast to the round, fleshy features of the smaller man. Gates nodded, turned, and sat down.

To Billy and Eli, and those who knew him, the expression on Washington's face, and the small, unnoticed movements of his fingers and his feet, evidenced the fact he was agitated, struggling within. He removed a paper from his tunic, smoothed it on the lectern, studied it for a moment, then raised his head. His voice reached every corner of the hall.

"My fellow officers. I have prepared a written presentation. With your permission, I will read that which I wish to say."

Billy and Eli were not watching Washington. They were searching the faces of the officers, watching, waiting for the first one who showed signs of rebellion, mutiny.

Washington began.

"I have carefully read the unsigned document distributed by an anonymous author on March tenth, instant. I have examined it many times, and have formed my conclusions with much thought and deliberation.

"It is clear to me that the author of that address was motivated by impulses bordering on mutiny. Perhaps treason!"

Shocked silence filled the room. Not one man moved.

"The themes of that writing appeal to base and fleeting feelings and occasions, and were guided by the most insidious of purposes."

Armstrong's mouth was hanging open, his face deathly white.

"It is beyond my imagination that someone in this army has prompted his fellow officers to not only leave—abandon—their wives and children, but to desert their country in the most extreme hour of her distress!"

Gasps were heard throughout the hall.

"I cannot contemplate anything so shocking as suggesting that this body turn their swords against Congress, plotting the ruin and sowing seeds of discord between the military and the civil authorities that guide this country. In the name of heaven, what can this writer have in view? He is neither a friend of the army nor of the country! Rather, he is an insidious foe of both!"

Murmuring broke out. Washington did not hesitate but raised his voice.

"The anonymous writer of this perfidy has calculated to impress the minds of the readers with an idea of premeditated injustice in the sovereign power of the United States, and rouse all those resentments which must inevitably flow from such a belief."

Open talk broke out. Billy and Eli tensed, peering into the faces of the officers, waiting for the first one who raised a fist or spoke in anger.

Washington lifted his face from his written speech and stood erect, waiting, watching, giving the officers time to vent themselves. They quieted, and he again began to read. A softness came into his voice.

"Let me entreat you, gentlemen, on your part, not to take any measures which, viewed in the calm light of reason, will lessen the dignity and sully the glory you have hitherto maintained. Let me request you to rely on the plighted faith of your country, and place a full confidence in the purity of the intentions of Congress."

Murmuring arose, then slowed, then stopped, and Washington continued. He read slowly, giving each word its due.

"You will, by the dignity of your conduct, afford occasion for posterity to say, when speaking of the glorious example you have exhibited to mankind, 'Had this day been wanting, the world had never seen the last stage of perfection to which human nature is capable of attaining.'"

Washington stopped. Gates, Armstrong, and Pickering dared not move. Billy and Eli were scanning the officers facing the lectern. Their faces were a mix of inscrutable emotions.

For more than ten full seconds the silence held before Washington reached inside his tunic to draw out a second paper. He smoothed it on the lectern and once more raised his head.

"I wish to share with you a letter lately received by myself from my friend Joseph Jones. He is a congressman from the State of Virginia and a patriot in the finest sense of the word."

He tipped his head forward to read and began.

"I take quill . . ."

He stopped, dropped his face lower, squinted, and started again. "I take quill in hand . . . to . . . share with you . . ."

He stopped again, to pick up the paper and raise it closer to his face, and start once again.

" . . . share with you . . . the sad state of affairs that . . ."

Every eye in the room was on Washington. There was not a sound, nor a movement. No man among them had ever seen or heard of the general unable to read a letter. Three seconds became five, then ten, and still Washington held the paper near his face, straining to make out the small, closely written words.

Then he laid the paper down and raised his right hand to a pocket in his vest, where he fumbled for a few moments before drawing out a small pair of spectacles that had been delivered to him in the month of February by Doctor Rittenhouse. No one knew he had them; none had ever seen him put them on. Slowly he unfolded the temples of the fragile, wire-framed spectacles, and set them on his nose. He adjusted the temples behind his ears, and looked out over the faces of the stunned officers before him. Their eyes were wide in shock. George Washington? Spectacles? A mortal? No man among them had ever thought of him as a mortal. Not their General. Other men grew old. Not George Washington. Immortal. Indestructible.

An electric charge filled the hall as the officers stared in silence, minds reeling as they gaped in disbelief at their commander wearing spectacles.

For a moment Washington peered at them, suddenly understanding the blank expressions. He raised a hand to wipe at his mouth, then spoke simply and softly from his heart.

"Gentlemen, you must forgive me. I have grown gray in your service, and now it appears I am growing blind."

For three full seconds there was no sound, no movement, and then open talk filled the room. Eyes moistened, and battle-hardened soldiers unashamedly wiped away tears. Both Billy and Eli were staring at their commander as though seeing him for the first time. Every man in the hall knew in that instant that none of them would ever forget the emotion that swept through them, rallied them, brought them together once again as a band of proud patriots. Washington folded his papers, inserted them back inside his tunic, and steadily walked down the center aisle of the room and out the door where his aides were waiting.

Nearly disoriented, Gates rose and walked to the lectern. Always the politician, he sensed the temper of the gathering and knew he dared not say one word that would disparage General Washington, or his address. Carefully he called the assembly to order.

"My fellow officers, our commander in chief has spoken. I trust his words have brought a unity among us."

A major in the first row rose and strode to the lectern beside Gates.

"I am certain General Gates agrees that we should come together in a unanimous vote of confidence in General Washington."

The hall rang with shouts of "Hear, hear, hear!"

"I propose that a committee be formed here and now, under the chairmanship of General Henry Knox, and that Major Samuel Snow be directed to draft a vote of confidence in the justice of our Congress and to request that General Washington pursue our interests with them. Further, that we repudiate the sedition found in that document submitted by the anonymous writer and commit ourselves to supporting an orderly presentation of our affairs to our civil leaders."

Once again the hall echoed with "Hear, hear, hear."

Timothy Pickering rose and came to the lectern. "I object to the—"

He got no further. The hall fell into bedlam. Officers with raised fists shouted him down. Pickering's face distorted in fear as he backed away from the lectern and dropped into his chair.

General Henry Knox, the short, rotund, librarian-turned-cannoneer, who had been unswervingly dedicated to Washington from the day the shooting began eight years earlier, and who had seen the army through every major battle they fought, strode quickly to the lectern. "I accept the nomination to chair the committee, and I herewith appoint Major Samuel Snow to draft the vote of confidence in General Washington and Congress, as heretofore moved."

"Hear, hear!"

Major Samuel Snow sprang to his feet. "I accept the appointment!"

Knox bellowed, "This meeting is adjourned."

The back doors were thrown open, and the officers began spilling out into the wind, exclaiming, gesturing, as they began to understand they had been part of something that would be told and retold as long as there was a United States.

Inside, Billy and Eli waited until the hall was empty before they walked to the back doors, out into the weather, and turned to close them. They were approaching the barge when Billy broke the silence between them.

"I never saw anything like that."

Eli shook his head. "One man. Stepped into the breach. Likely saved the country."

There was little talk as the barge bucked the wind and white water on its return to Verplanck. The wind died at sundown. In full darkness Major Samuel Snow sat down at a small desk in the corner of his quarters, adjusted the flame in his lamp, and reached for his quill and bottle of ink. Later he paused to listen to the regimental drum sound tattoo and continued his writing. At eleven o'clock he laid down his quill, rubbed weary eyes with the heels of his hands, stretched his legs, and rose from his chair. He sat back down long enough to read the four-page document he had drafted under the title of "A VOTE OF

CONFIDENCE IN OUR CONGRESS AND OUR COMMANDER IN CHIEF." He would read it again in the morning, make whatever additions or corrections were needed, and submit it to a committee he would have selected by ten o'clock.

He reached to unbuckle his shoes, paused, straightened, and reached for his daily journal. Once again he took up his quill and carefully wrote on the next clean page of the book.

" . . . There was something so natural, so unaffected in the general's appeal as he sought our understanding of his need for the spectacles as to render his spontaneous words superior to the most studied oratory. It forced its way to the heart, and you might see sensibility moisten every eye."

He sprinkled salts on the wet ink, waited for a moment, swept the salts away, and read the words once again. For a moment the feeling that had driven him to his feet in the assembly hall with his fellow officers surged once again in his breast, and he reached to wipe at his eyes. He nodded his satisfaction, closed his journal, and turned down the wick on his lamp.

Notes

Colonel Walter Stewart, Inspector General of the Northern Army and a former aide to General Horatio Gates, visited Congress in Philadelphia and returned to the army camp at Verplanck, New York, to report his findings to his circle of close friends, including Major John Armstrong Jr., Timothy Pickering, who was once General Washington's adjutant general, and likely to General Gates. His report was that Congress, and General Washington, were both incapable of delivering what they had promised to the officers upon their discharge. A notice was quickly sent out to the officers inviting them to a meeting at the Newburgh camp, Monday, March 10, 1783, together with an "address" which it is thought was written by Major John Armstrong Jr., in which statements were made that were tantamount to treason. Alexander Hamilton, Governeur Morris, and Wilson became aware of it and attempted to persuade Washington to use this unrest to persuade the states to grant Congress the power to put down the discontent. Washington refused their plan. A second meeting was advertised by these men for the following day, Tuesday,

March 11, 1783, inviting all officers. General Washington quickly learned of the meeting and read the "address," which included among other things a proposal that lacking obedience from Congress and General Washington to their demands, the American army should abandon the United States, draw off to a distant place, and set up their own state, or, alternatively, refuse to lay down their arms; in essence, take control of the government. A furious Washington quickly ordered the meeting canceled and arranged his own meeting for Saturday, March 15, 1783, in the Newburgh assembly hall, and ordered General Gates to conduct the meeting. In said meeting, General Washington stunned the entire assembly by angrily condemning the efforts of the Gates-Armstrong-Pickering faction to essentially dismantle the United States, and strongly implored the officers to wait but a short time longer to give Congress time to meet their obligations, which he was certain they would do.

In closing his remarks, General Washington attempted to read a letter received from his personal and trusted friend, Congressman Joseph Jones. Because the writing was small, General Washington could not read it. From a vest pocket, he drew a pair of glasses given to him by a Doctor Rittenhouse two months earlier, and put them on his nose. Not one man in the room had ever seen him use glasses, nor had any of them ever considered that General Washington could ever be subject to such infirmities as failing eyesight. It stunned the entire crowd into silence. Washington, sensing the tremendous power and drama in the moment, quietly made the brief statement that turned the officer corps in his favor. Essentially, he stated that he had grown old in their service, and now it appeared he was growing blind. Many of the officers wept. Washington walked out, and it was then they spontaneously appointed General Henry Knox to head up a committee, and Major Samuel Snow to draft a resolution casting a unanimous vote of confidence in Washington and Congress. It is thought by many of the most respected historians that this event was pivotal in establishing the principle that the United States would remain subject to civil, not military, authority; and it essentially saved the nation. The entry made that evening in the journal of Major Samuel Snow is quoted verbatim herein.

The speech given by Washington as recited in this chapter is abstracted from the best records available on the question, as are the remarks attributed to Stewart, Armstrong, and General Gates. As far as is possible in this abbreviated summary, many parts are verbatim quotes (Bernstein, *Are We to Be a Nation?*, pp. 30–33; Freeman, *Washington*, pp. 368, 498–501; Morris, *The Forging of the Union*, pp. 47–49; Higginbotham, *The War of American Independence*, pp. 409–12).

Verplanck Army Camp
June 1783

CHAPTER X

*T*he reveille drum had not yet sounded when the knock came at Billy Weems's door. For a moment he sat fully dressed at the tiny table in the corner of his officer's quarters, speculating who could need him in the dead-quiet predawn purple of an early summer morning. He glanced at the paper on which he had begun writing just moments earlier under the light of a lamp, read the salutation, "My Dear Brigitte," turned it face down, and stepped across the small room to open the door. Captain Armand Rhodes of the Massachusetts Second Regiment faced him in the doorway, face yellow in the lamplight. Billy came to attention as Rhodes spoke.

"I saw a light." He took a printed NOTICE from several he carried beneath his arm, and offered it to Billy. "Read this, and follow the instructions."

"What's it about?"

"Orders for mustering out the army. Today."

Billy's heart leaped. "The orders finally came?"

Rhodes nodded. "Be sure your men are notified where to be and when."

"I will. Anything else?"

"Not right now. I have to get these notices out to the other companies. Any questions, find me."

"Thank you, sir." Rhodes turned away and Billy left the door open.

The first of the morning birds had begun their declaration to the world that another dawn was breaking and they were staking out their territorial claims against all comers.

There was a tremble in Billy's fingers as he sat back down at the table, laid the document flat, and began to read.

" . . . March twelfth instant Captain Joshua Barney arrived in Philadelphia aboard his schooner *Washington* bearing the official text of the Pact signed by British and American diplomats in Paris on November 30, 1782. Pertinent parts are as follows:

"Final terms are to be inserted in, and to constitute the treaty of peace, proposed to be concluded between the Crown of Great Britain and the said United States; but which treaty is not to be concluded until terms of a peace shall be agreed upon between Great Britain and France, and his Britannick Majesty shall be ready to conclude such treaty accordingly. PROVIDED HOWEVER, that the independence of the United States is herewith acknowledged and is the initial article of said treaty; all hostilities are to cease forthwith; prisoners are to be exchanged.

"FURTHER, it is acknowledged that on January twentieth, 1783, the other sovereign nations party to this agreement, namely France and Spain, did enter into the said Pact as signatories, which now binds all parties.

"FURTHER, on April fifteenth instant, the United States Congress ratified and approved the said treaty, and on the nineteenth of April instant, all hostilities between the parties formally ceased."

Billy paused to raise his head, putting his thoughts in order. *The British and Americans agreed to stop the shooting last November, and France and Spain agreed to it in January. Our Congress ratified it and all hostilities stopped on April nineteenth.*

Something caught in his memory and he paused for a moment to search for it. April nineteenth. *April 19, 1775! The day John Dunson and Tom Sievers and Matthew and I went to Concord! The day the shooting began! The day I was shot and bayoneted, and John was shot and died. The war started on April nineteenth, and now it's ended on April nineteenth! Nearly unbelievable.*

He brought his thoughts back to the paper in his hand.

"Each officer in the Massachusetts Second Regiment will have his command present in the assembly hall following the midday mess, at two o'clock P.M. where they will be instructed in the details of mustering out. Other regiments will be mustered out in an orderly succession on a schedule that will be printed and circulated timely."

For the first time the words took on meaning. His heart leaped, caught in a rush of thoughts and emotions. *It's over! The bloodshed is over! We won! Home—mother—Brigitte—Trudy—Matthew—home—home—freedom. We won!* He sat still, letting it run. Slowly the flood of thoughts settled and he was aware of but one all-encompassing, humbling impression. *The Almighty was there through it all—eight long years of suffering and bloodshed—He was there.*

In that private place where he lived alone with himself and his conscience, Billy knew. History would give the impossible victory to the Americans, but it belonged to the Almighty. Billy swallowed at the lump in his throat, and gave it time to settle before he finished reading the document.

"Officers of the Massachusetts regiments are to instruct their commands—be present at the Assembly Hall—two o'clock P.M. for mustering out."

Quickly he set aside the beginnings of his letter to Brigitte, turned down the lamp wick, shrugged into his officer's tunic, and walked out the door into the dawn. For a moment he stopped in the warm, clean, still air. The heavens were a dome of endless gray-blue overhead, and the forest a carpet of rich green, flooded with the reds and golds and blues of unnumbered summer flowers. The music of the birds filled the air as they flitted on business known only to themselves, feathered like royalty with every color in the rainbow. For a moment Billy paused, humbled by the renewal of life that was all about him, awed by the handiwork of his Creator.

He was thirty yards from the morning breakfast fires of the enlisted men of his company when the familiar, high, twangy voice reached him.

"All right, you lovelies. You're still in the army, and morning mess won't cook itself. Git to it."

Billy grinned in his beard as he watched Sergeant Alvin Turlock straighten and turn toward him. Turlock's eyes narrowed as he studied Billy.

"You look like the hawk that caught the frog. Somethin' goin' on?"

"Just got orders from Captain Rhodes. The mustering out of some of the army starts today. Two o'clock. Assembly hall. Have this company there."

Turlock's head jerked forward. "The orders finally come? For certain?"

"For certain."

"This army is being mustered out today?"

"Part of it. At two o'clock."

Turlock raised both hands above his head. "Hallelujah! I was beginnin' to think the Almighty had forgot us. Praise be!"

"Be sure every man gets the order right. Two o'clock today, at the assembly hall."

"They'll get it right. We'll have 'em packed and ready to go long before that."

Billy spoke as he turned. "I'm going to find Eli."

He trotted the worn dirt path to the huts that sheltered the twenty scouts of the Massachusetts Second Regiment, to find Eli standing near the morning cooking fire, his rifle leaning against a tree, intent on reading a copy of the NOTICE. Eli raised his head to locate Billy as he came on and gestured to the document in Billy's hand.

"I see you got the notice."

"Yes. Today's the day."

"Heard about how they intend paying the soldiers? Some have two years' pay coming."

"I don't know about the enlisted. General Washington persuaded Congress to pay the officers their back pay and pensions over the next five years."

"So I heard. I hope they can do it. But what about the enlisted? These men haven't got enough money to get them home."

Billy shook his head. "I don't know what to expect. We'll find out this afternoon. Two o'clock at the assembly hall."

Eli folded the NOTICE and slipped it inside his shirt. "I'll be there."

The news raced through the camp like a lightning strike. Every tent, every hut, every place men gathered, loud, raucous talk filled the air. For the first time in memory, not one man complained about the cooking as they gathered and wolfed down their fried mush and hardtack. Drill was forgotten. Men washed their utensils and set them out to dry, then went to their tents or lean-tos to sort out their personal possessions from those owned by the United States Army. They laid out their blankets and began placing their belongings on them in preparation for rolling them up for the journey home.

They finished their midday mess and for the last time washed the huge kettles and tipped them upside down to drain and dry. Sweating in the heat of the sun directly overhead, they pulled down the tall, smoke-blackened tripods and stacked them near the woodpile. They did not add wood to the cook fires, which soon burned to glowing coals, then smoldering, gray ashes. They noticed the strange quiet of the absence of axes splitting firewood.

At half past one o'clock Turlock shouted his men together. "Fall in for a count. Wouldn't do to leave a man or two behind."

Five minutes later he shouted his next order. "For'ard . . . *harch!*"

There was an unexpected pride in them as they stepped out for the last time as a company of soldiers in the Continental Army. Their backs were a little straighter, their step a little more firm, and there was a certain swing to their arms and a trace of a swagger as they followed Sergeant Turlock to the assembly hall, where other companies were gathering, some already inside. He gave them the last order they would receive from him.

"Company . . . *halt!* Fall out and take a place inside the hall."

He led them to the door and held it for them as they entered. They waited for a moment while their eyes adjusted to the gloom in the great room, which was lighted only by half a dozen small windows on each side. They stacked their muskets against the wall with the others already there, then took seats on the low, rough, backless benches. An American flag hung unmoving on a pole beside the lectern. Behind and to the left was a small room for those who were to conduct the meeting. The room was filled with a low undertone of talk. Just before two o'clock, the doors opened again and early summer sunlight flooded in while the last two companies entered to find seats.

At two o'clock the door to the small room squeaked as it swung open, and Captain Armand Rhodes walked directly to the pulpit, followed by Major Ulysses Dastrup and Colonel Josiah Spencer. Every man rose to his feet and came to attention. Average size, round-faced, receding chin, Rhodes carried a small wooden box that he placed on the floor beside the lectern, then straightened, and faced his command.

"Be seated, gentlemen."

Benches creaked as the company sat down.

"I have been ordered by Colonel Spencer to conduct this matter. It will be necessary to call roll. The sergeants will answer for each company."

He called the companies in order, and each sergeant answered, "All present or accounted for, sir."

He set aside the Regimental Roster Book. "All companies are reported present." He paused for a moment, then took a deep breath.

"As you know, today we gather for the last time as soldiers in this regiment, and in this army."

Murmurs arose, and he waited until they quieted.

"On behalf of myself and Major Dastrup and Colonel Spencer, I want each of you to know, it has been an honor to serve with you. You have given your best in a victorious cause. It is doubtful any of us sees clearly and fully what you have done for your country, and for the world."

The enlisted men moved and settled, sweating in the hot, dead air, waiting for the core of the business at hand, and Rhodes moved into it.

"I am ordered to inform you that for good reason, you are being placed on furlough today."

Spontaneous exclamations broke out.

Furlough?

Not discharge?

We were told we are going to be discharged. Paid. Going home with our money and our land!

Rhodes raised a hand and waited for the tumult to recede.

"Let me explain. At this time there are still some parts of the peace treaty that must be agreed upon before it is complete and final. If you are discharged now, the Continental Army will cease to exist, and there will be no one to resist a British attack, should the peace agreement fail. Congress has learned that the peace treaty is now being framed by our representatives in Paris, and for that reason has concluded they can send you home at this time, but with furloughs, not discharges. When the peace treaty is signed, the furloughs will be considered discharges.

"Have I made this clear?"

Men came to their feet calling out.

"Can Congress pay us when the peace treaty is signed?"

"Furloughs for how long? Tell us how long before we get our pay."

"I got a wife and five children been waiting two years for my pay. What do I tell them?"

"How are we going to be paid? Continental paper money? Worthless! We want hard specie—gold or silver!

"Gen'l Washington promised. Congress promised. Where are they now?"

Rhodes stood behind the lectern, hands gripping each side, white-knuckled, mouth clenched shut, eyes downcast as he waited until he could be heard above the fading uproar. His voice came hot, loud, commanding.

"You will be seated and remember that you are soldiers!"

Slowly the men sat back down and the room quieted. Rhodes went on.

"Thank you. With your furlough papers, you will be given a voucher for three months' back pay. You can redeem the voucher any time after six months, in your home state."

For a moment there was a breathless hush; then the room exploded in another uproar.

"Three months? I haven't had pay for two years!"

"How do I pay my way home?"

"What of my debts on my farm?"

"A wife and five children! How do I provide? Charity?"

The tumult rose to an angry crescendo, and Rhodes let it run on for a time before Colonel Spencer squirmed in his seat and Rhodes raised both hands to shout the hall into silence.

"You men know there is nothing I can do about this. The United States government is without money! None! General Washington has forced Congress to issue their written promise to see you get something! He can do no more."

For a moment Rhodes wavered, then drew a deep breath and spoke from his heart.

"You were promised. I know that. You stood and shed your blood when it had to be done. I was there with you. I swear before the Almighty that if I could, you would each go home now with every cent you are owed, and the pensions you were promised, and title to the land you were promised, and a full discharge. But there is nothing I can do. I can only ask that once more, for the last time, you forbear."

Once again he gave the men time to vent their frustrations.

"May I now finish the terms of the furloughs?"

There was a murmur, then silence.

"You may keep your arms. Your muskets. Keep your cartridges and cartridge boxes. Keep your canteens and blankets. What little hard money we have in camp will be divided equally among you, and you can claim your share from the quartermaster. It isn't much, but it is all that can be done. Before you leave this camp, go to the commissary. The food we have left will be divided as equally as possible among you to help you on your way home."

The silence held as Rhodes finished.

"As for the furlough papers and the pay vouchers, there is one for every man here, in this box, bundled for the sergeants to come and get. They will be responsible for distributing them according to the name on each furlough. You are invited to remain in this hall to distribute the furloughs, or to move outside if you wish. Are there any questions?"

Men looked about, but none raised a question.

"Again, it has been my great personal honor to serve with you. I trust you will remain the good soldiers you have been by waiting for your pay. The sergeants are free to come and get the bundle of furloughs for each company and distribute them. That is all. May the Almighty bless each of you."

He stopped, swallowed hard, and waited while every man stood and came to attention. Then he turned from the lectern and followed Major Dastrup and Colonel Spencer back into the small room and closed the door.

The troops turned to each other, and their deep disappointment and mounting fears spilled out to fill the hall with loud, hard talk and angry gestures. Turlock made his way through the din to the wooden box beside the lectern, searched out the tied bundle of folded papers with his name on it, and pushed his way back to his men. He motioned, and they followed him outside into the heat of the afternoon, where he called names aloud while men reached for their furlough papers and pay vouchers. Those who could read paused to study their own paper first, then read aloud for those who could not read for themselves.

They gathered back at their section of the sprawling camp and began arranging their belongings on their blankets. None expected the odd spirit that swept through them as they tied the loop cord to the ends of their blankets to sling them across their backs.

Going home! The horror of war left behind. Wives. Children. Laughter. Farms. Work. The family cow. The plow horse. A bed with sheets. Rustlings in the kitchen before dawn with the aroma of frying bacon and griddle cakes reaching every corner of the small log home. Hot Sunday dinner at their own table with a clean, white tablecloth. Neighbors. Their own tiny hamlet. The feel of good earth at spring planting. Growing their own crops. The eternal joy of harvesting the fruits of their labors. The smell of grain in the bind for winter and potatoes in the root cellar.

Then the battle-hardened, bearded men looked at each other, and for the first time understood there would be pain in their parting. Four, five, six, eight years together, sharing starvation, freezing, sickness, wounds, tears of sorrow, tears of joy, defeats, and finally the victory that rocked the world. They had never reckoned that their lives had become so intertwined. They were brothers, bound together as surely as they were bound to those who awaited them at home.

They spoke little as they said their good-byes and embraced for the last time. They turned quickly to wipe at moist eyes, then straightened, squared their shoulders, and walked steadily toward the quartermaster building to collect their token pay, then on to the commissary for their tiny ration of the bundled food. Turlock waited and watched them leave until the last man in his company disappeared in the forest. For a time he stood rooted, peering about as though he did not know what to do next. Then he drew a great breath, squared his pinched shoulders, and said aloud, "Well, that's the end of it."

With his blanket roll slung on his back and his musket in hand, he made his way through the nearly empty camp to the officers' quarters, to the small hut, where the door was standing open. He saw Billy inside and rapped on the door frame.

"Sergeant! Come on in. I was coming to find you. Is the company gone?"

"I'm the last. Figgered to see you before I go."

Silence hung for a moment before Billy spoke. "Where will you go?"

Turlock shrugged. "Pennsylvania. Vermont. Don't matter much. Anyplace I can build a little cabin and do a little work. Maybe Philadelphia. New York. Where there's ships. I spent better'n a year learnin' to be a sailmaker. Pretty good one. I'll be all right. How about you?"

"Back to Boston. Maybe I can get my old employment back. Keeping accounts."

For a moment neither man spoke, and then the wiry little sergeant thrust out his hand. "Billy, you take care of yourself. I don't expect I'll ever forget the things we been through together. Maybe some day I'll be in Boston, and I'll find you. See how you are. Be good to yourself."

Billy took the smallish, gnarled hand in his own, and looked into the face, scarred on the right side, beard and hair splotchy. "I will. I promise. You've got to promise that if ever you need anything, you'll come find me. Do I have your promise?"

"You do."

Neither expected the surge that filled their breasts. Billy swallowed hard. "God bless you, Sergeant."

"And you, Billy."

Turlock turned and walked back into the sunlight, and Billy came to the door to watch him disappear on the dirt path into the woods, walking west toward the Hudson River. For a long time he stood there while scenes of battles, and freezing camps, and starvation he had shared with Turlock came and went before his eyes. He turned back to his bunk and finished rolling his belongings into his blanket, tied it, slung it over his back, and walked out and closed the door for the last time.

It was near four o'clock before he found Eli at his hut, one of the last scouts to leave camp. Eli was slinging his tied blanket over his shoulder when Billy approached and spoke.

"Leaving?"

"North. I have a daughter up there that I haven't seen for too long. She's likely walking by now. Talking. You? What's your plan?"

"Home. Boston. Maybe take up my old employment. Account keeping."

Eli nodded. "You still have those letters? For the Dunson girl?"

"In my blanket."

"Going to deliver them?"

"I don't know yet."

"Your choice. But if you don't, you'll always wonder."

Billy waited for a moment, deciding whether he should raise a question that had been in his mind for more than five years. He cleared his throat.

"Do you remember when you came to this regiment, back on Manhattan Island?"

"I do."

"You said you came to find out two things. One was about Jesus. The other was about George Washington. Did you find out?"

For an instant, surprise showed in Eli's face, and then he stopped to stare off into the forest for a time before he answered.

"Partly. I found out General Washington is a rare man. Rare. I don't expect ever to meet another like him. And I found out a little about Jesus."

He paused, then asked Billy the question. "How many men have we seen killed?"

Billy shook his head. "I never thought on it. Hundreds. Maybe thousands."

Again Eli paused, ordering his thoughts. "All the killing weighs heavy. It's a hard thing. A bad thing. All the peace, all the good I've known in life, has come to me from those who have charity. I think that's what Jesus taught. I've learned that."

Billy fell into a moment's silence, then nodded, and the moment passed. The two men locked eyes, and in that instant they silently said the things that needed to be said between them.

Billy spoke. "You'll get down to Boston sometime. Find me."

"I will. You know the way north up to my sister's home, and you're good in the forest. Will you come?"

"I learned the forest from you. I'll come every chance I get."

"Give those letters to that girl."

Billy smiled. "I'll think on it."

Eli picked up his rifle, straightened, nodded to Billy, turned, and walked steadily away, up the north path into the woods, and was gone.

For a moment Billy stood where he was, then shouldered his musket and turned to follow the dusty path east into the forest.

Notes

The chronological sequence set forth in this chapter is accurate. November 30, 1782, a preliminary pact was signed between England and the United States agreeing to a cessation of hostilities; final terms of the peace were to be added thereto. March 12, 1783, news of it was delivered to Congress in Philadelphia by Captain Joshua Barney in his schooner, *Washington.* January 20, 1783, France and Spain agreed to the pact. March 26, 1783, news of the joining by France and Spain reached the United States. April 15, 1783, Congress ratified the pact. April 19, 1783, exactly eight years from the day the first shots were fired at Lexington and Concord, the pact was formalized.

Disbanding the army was done under the supervision of General Washington. Congress had no money and could not pay the soldiers as promised. Under the influence of General Washington, the officers were promised a five-year pension, and the enlisted men were given a pledge from Congress that they would receive three months of pay from their home state, said payment to be made six months in the future. They were not discharged, but given furlough papers that would become final when the Paris Peace Treaty was finally finished in detail. Then their furlough papers would be deemed a discharge. The failure of Congress and General Washington to meet their previous promises was the beginning of a national crisis (Freeman, *Washington,* pp. 501–2; Higginbotham, *The War of American Independence,* pp. 406–12).

The mustering out process as herein described is accurate, as is the description of the feelings of the men as they parted for the last time (Martin, *Private Yankee Doodle,* pp. 279–81).

Philadelphia

June 1783

CHAPTER XI

*T*hey came in the sweltering June heat, a column of angry, mutinous, American militia soldiers from the Pennsylvania Third Regiment, sweating from their two-day march east, through the eighty miles of rolling Pennsylvania hills that separated their military camp in Lancaster from Philadelphia. They wore their uniforms, or as much of one as they owned, and they carried their muskets and bayonets, and on their belts they wore their cartridge boxes. As they came into the cobblestone streets of Philadelphia, citizens cautiously peeked out of homes and shops to watch them pass, silent, fearful of why armed soldiers were in their streets once again.

The soldiers marched to the barracks of the Pennsylvania militia, and Major Artemus Bates, leading the militiamen, barged through the doors of the headquarters building, into the office of the commander. The startled colonel recoiled, then sprang to his feet blustering, shouting, "What's the meaning of this! I'll have the lot of you arrested!"

Bates waved the threat aside. "Where are the militia officers' quarters?"

The colonel's face reddened with outrage. "Who are you? What do you want?"

The major's voice purred. "The militia officers' quarters. Where are they? Or do we go find them ourselves?"

The colonel straightened to full height, shoulders square, chin thrust out. "Not a word until I know who you are and why you appear here like a mob!"

"I'm Major Artemus Bates. With me are officers and enlisted militia from Lancaster. We're here to get the pay and pensions and land we were promised. We're going to pay a visit to Congress. You have men here who will join us. Where are the militia officers' quarters?"

The colonel's mouth dropped open for a split second. "You expect some of my militia to join in this mutiny?"

"I expect to talk to them. For the last time, where are their quarters?"

Thirty minutes later the Lancaster militia, with their ranks swelled by two hundred Pennsylvania militia officers and enlisted, filled the narrow, winding street in front of the State House, where the Pennsylvania Executive Council as well as the Continental Congress were in full session. Five minutes later they had it surrounded, bayonets mounted, muskets at the ready. Startled citizenry lined the walks and doorways, pointing, exclaiming, unable to understand the unheard-of spectacle of armed American militia soldiers surrounding their own State House, where the national and state officials were in session!

Inside the building, windows open to catch what little breeze might pass, Elias Boudinot, sitting president of the sweltering Continental Congress, leaned forward, head cocked to hear the words of soft-spoken, diminutive James Madison above the rising tumult reaching through the windows. Suddenly Madison stopped and turned his head to peer out the window. Instantly Boudinot turned to look, as did nearly every member of the Congress. They gaped at the sight of hundreds of their own soldiers in a double line that circled the building, muskets at the ready. For a moment no one moved, then everyone moved and spoke. Boudinot gaveled the floor back to order and turned to the sergeant at arms.

"Go find out what the disturbance is in the streets and report back at once!" He turned back to the floor. "Gentlemen, we will be in a five-minute recess, during which time no one will leave this room."

Seven minutes later the doors burst open and the sergeant at arms marched back into the square, austere, high-ceilinged room, white-faced, two paces ahead of Major Bates. Three armed soldiers followed, and the group stopped ten feet inside the chamber. Every congressman gasped, and then wild, angry talk filled the chamber. The major strode forward five paces to face Boudinot, standing behind the raised desk at the front of the room, trembling with outrage, waiting for the tumult to recede.

"What is the meaning of this?" Boudinot bellowed, face red, neck veins swelled.

"We are officers and enlisted of the Pennsylvania Militia. We've come to make our just demands on this Congress and on the Executive Council of Pennsylvania for the pay we were promised for our service in the army."

Boudinot's fist slammed down on the desk. "That matter has been concluded!"

The major's voice rang off the walls. "Not so! The settlement offered us falls far short of the promise made! We will have our just due. We are here to demand that we be allowed to appoint our own officers to appear before you and present our demands formally."

Boudinot jerked straight. "And if we refuse?"

"Then we will storm this building and hold you hostage along with the Executive Council of Pennsylvania until you do."

"Treason!" shouted Boudinot.

"Justice!" shouted Bates.

Movement at the windows caught the eye of Madison, then others, and they turned to look. The muzzles of twenty muskets were thrust through, some aimed at Boudinot, some at Madison, half a dozen at Alexander Hamilton, slender, silent, watching the intruders like a hawk. The sound of musket hammers coming to full cock echoed in the room. Hamilton had faced violent men so many times his instincts were honed to a fine edge when it came to judging which ones would talk and which ones would shoot. Now he was silently studying Bates, his eyes, his words, his demeanor. Would Bates shoot?

Hamilton made his decision and stood.

"Major," he called, "I am Alexander Hamilton. I served with General Washington through—"

Bates cut him off. "I know who you are. There are muskets pointed at you." The room fell into a silence so thick it hung like a weight on every man present.

Hamilton nodded. "I see them. Shoot if you must, but know that you will hang if you do."

"There will be no shooting until you force it," Bates growled.

The sure knowledge flashed in Hamilton's mind—*he won't shoot*—and instantly he plunged on. "Are you willing to listen to reason? A solution that will satisfy both sides?"

"I've stated our conditions. We will be allowed to appoint our own officers to set our case before both the United States Congress and the Executive Council of the State of Pennsylvania."

Hamilton gestured with a sweep of his hand. "Surely you know that such a proposal will not be legally binding until it is drafted into a formal motion, brought to the floor, debated, and receives a majority vote! That is elementary. Short of that, you will have absolutely nothing! To the contrary, you will be guilty of mutiny, treason, insurrection, and civil disobedience! For three of those offenses, you can be hung! You and every man with you!"

Ridges appeared on Bates's jawline as the words sunk in.

Hamilton gave him no time to reflect. "Think of it! How many men are with you? Three hundred? Four hundred? Four hundred hangings will likely take half the rope in Philadelphia!"

Bates was sweating profusely, and both Madison and Hamilton caught the fleeting hesitation in his eyes as he spoke. "All we want is our just due."

Hamilton walked boldly from his desk to the center aisle to face Bates at ten paces. The muskets were still at the windows, and half of them followed Hamilton.

Hamilton's voice rang with authority. "And you shall have it!" He turned to Boudinot. "Mr. President, I move that the calendar be cleared immediately, and that the demands of these men be reduced to a proper motion to be debated and acted upon according to lawful procedure."

It took Boudinot two seconds to catch up with Hamilton's audacity. "Do I hear a second?"

Twenty voices boomed, "Seconded. A vote!"

"Are any opposed?"

Again the voices sounded. "None! Unanimous in the affirmative."

Hamilton turned back to Bates, finger raised and pointing like a sword. "There, sir, is the answer! A legally enforceable resolution that is fair to both sides. You submit to us your list of officers, and we will act immediately. Do you accept those terms?"

It had happened too quickly. The confrontation, Hamilton's irreproachable logic, and then throwing down the challenge to Bates to submit to lawful process. For five full seconds the only sound was the buzzing of summer insects through the open windows. Then Bates drew a deep breath and asked, "What about the Executive Council? We are making the same demand on the State of Pennsylvania."

Silent men began breathing again while Hamilton gave Bates no time to reorganize his thoughts. Hamilton pointed out the door.

"You will settle that with them, sir, not us. They are just up the hall, second door on the right."

For a moment Bates stood silent, unable to find a way out of the box he found himself in. Without a word he pivoted and started for the door, when Hamilton's ringing voice stopped him.

"You can do as you see fit with the Executive Council of this state, but in the meantime, order your men to stand down. The local citizenry will not tolerate their state house and the Congress of the United States being held hostage. Worse, it is only a matter of time before more Continental troops arrive to restore order."

Hamilton's feet were planted, his head erect, eyes blazing. "In short, sir, move your command to some other place. At once."

Anger flared in Bates's face at the direct order, and he trembled with rage, on the brink of ordering his men to smash out the windows and take the room by storm, shooting if they must. After a few moments he brought his anger under tenuous control, stiffened, then shifted his weight from one foot to the other. "*We* will decide when we withdraw!" he thundered. "Until we do, we are going to take possession of the city powder magazine until you meet our demands."

Hamilton threw one hand in the air. "Take the magazine at your own risk. We must have your list of the officers who will present your claims."

"You'll have it by morning."

"Deliver it here to President Boudinot."

Bates turned on his heel and marched back out the door, his three soldiers following. Behind him, the muskets disappeared from the windows, and the hall fell into silence as the congressmen concentrated on the sounds of marching feet moving down the hall to the room where the Pennsylvania State Executive Council was meeting. They heard the big door open, then slam shut, before the United States Congress lapsed into bedlam.

Boudinot pounded his gavel until order was restored, then turned to the secretary.

"Mr. Secretary, write a brief summary of what has just happened here, directed to General George Washington. Be certain to mention we were threatened with cocked muskets by upwards of four hundred of our own troops!" He paused to collect his thoughts, then pointed his gavel at the secretary. "And include the following: 'They have secured the public magazine, and I am of the opinion that the worst is not yet come. Congress respectfully directs that Continental troops equal to the task instantly be ordered to this city to restore order, using whatever means necessary, unless the Pennsylvania Executive Council succeeds in putting down this rebellion with Pennsylvania militia.'"

From the floor came resounding approval, and Boudinot let it die before he continued.

"Did you get it all? Every word of it?"

"Yes, sir."

"The moment the ink is dry, get the best horse and the best horseman in this town and have him prepared to carry that document to General George Washington. If the Executive Council fails to get their Pennsylvania militia to protect this Congress, that messenger leaves immediately."

"Yes, sir."

Boudinot turned back to the congressmen. "Take your seats. I hereby propose that we adopt a unanimous resolution that unless the Pennsylvania Executive Council takes effective measures for supporting the public authority to protect the United States Congress, we remove this body to the city of Princeton, in the State of New Jersey, to conduct its business in Nassau Hall. Do I hear a second?"

"Seconded."

"Do I hear a request for a vote?"

"I put the question."

"All in favor?"

The walls shook with the shouted "AYE!"

Boudinot stood. "It now remains only to find out if the Executive Council can persuade their own militia to get that mob out of here."

Within the hour the congressmen watched from their windows as the armed soldiers fell into rank and file and marched east, toward the city powder magazine. Ten minutes later a sealed, written message arrived, signed by John Dickinson, President of the Pennsylvania Executive Council.

" . . . and I am mortified to report that I can not count on the Pennsylvania militia to protect the delegates of the United States Congress . . ."

Hamilton leaped to his feet, fist raised, voice hot with anger. "Disgusting! To the last degree, weak and disgusting!"

Fifteen minutes later a small, wiry boy of seventeen, dressed in the buckskins and moccasins of a backwoodsman, handed his rifle and powder horn and shot pouch to a sergeant holding the cheekstrap on the bridle of a deep-chested, leggy gray mare.

"Be obliged if you'd hold those things for me, Sergeant. I'll be back for 'em."

The boy thrust a packet of documents wrapped in oilcloth inside his shirt, rubbed the jaw of the mare, then her ears, and spoke to her low and gentle.

"Good girl. Good girl. We're goin' for a ride, you and me."

He stripped off the saddle and blanket and grinned as he leaped effortlessly astride the mare, bareback, then gathered the reins and looked down at the sergeant. "Three days. I'll be back."

The bearded old sergeant was still holding the cheekstrap. "Danny, you got near a hunnerd miles to go, and it 'pears most of it'll be in the dark. Pace the horse so she don't give out. Follow the river east 'til you cross Neshaminy Creek, then go on up and cross the Delaware above Trenton. Angle northeast and you'll come to the Raritan, and then on over to the Hudson, and up to Verplanck. Them rivers 're goin' to be runnin' high and fast with the spring snowmelt, so you be careful. Hear me?"

"Yes, sir, I hear you. I been most of them places when there was fightin' goin' on. I figger I'll make Verplanck tomorrow afternoon late. Give the mare one day to rest, and be back the next day. Much obliged fer you takin' care of my things, and yer advice."

The boy reined the mare around, thumped his heels into her ribs, and raised her to a trot, her iron shoes clattering on the cobblestone streets of Philadelphia, throwing sparks. He passed through the outskirts to where the roads were dirt wagon trails winding through the thick summer forests, following the great Delaware River east. Without a saddle, he rode light and easy, man and horse working as one. He raised her to an easy, ground-eating lope and felt her pulling at the bit, wanting to run. He held her back, talking to her, patting her neck. "Got to save some, girl—a long way to go."

He jumped the mare into the swollen Neshaminy Creek with the sun still in the western sky, and slid off to one side, holding onto her mane as she swam. With the sun below the western horizon, he walked the mare into the broad expanse of the Delaware River, and once again slipped from her back to hang onto her mane while she held her head high, feet and legs reaching, stroking for the far shore, five hundred yards distant. She clambered out of the fast-running water in deep twilight, sides heaving. He gave her twenty minutes to settle and pull green grass, then once again was on her back, moving northeast. It was past two o'clock in the morning when he put her into the Raritan River under a half-moon. She came out of the water dripping, and he held her to a walk for twenty minutes, then a trot, then her easy, effortless lope, pacing her, saving her for what was ahead. The sun was high when he saw Manhattan Island two miles across the Hudson. The mare splashed through water up to her belly at Popolopen Creek with the sun past its zenith, then across Murderer's Creek and Qassaic Creek. The sun was low, directly at his back as Danny reined the weary horse up before the headquarters building at Verplanck military camp. He paused only long enough to rub the hot neck. "Good girl."

He waited while the picket stepped inside the building, and three minutes later was standing across the desk from General Washington, the sealed oil packet in his hand.

"Sir, I'm Daniel Yarbrough, scout with the Continental Army at Philadelphia, under orders to deliver this to you." He laid the packet on the desk.

Washington glanced at the packet, then back at the boy, puzzled by his buckskin shirt and breeches and moccasins.

"A scout? When did you leave Philadelphia?"

"Yesterday about this time."

Washington's eyes narrowed. "You rode all night? What's this about?"

"Well, sir, it's all in them letters. But if you're askin' me to report, I can tell you there was a whole company of militia from Lancaster come marchin' in yesterday, and they talked about two hunnerd militia into joinin' 'em, an' they surrounded the state house. Held Congress and the Executive Council prisoner for a while. Then they went down and took over the city powder magazine, an' that's when someone from Congress got holt of me and sent me here with them letters. It's all there, sir."

Washington came to his feet, leaned forward on stiff arms, palms flat on his desk. "Am I to understand that some United States soldiers held Congress hostage?"

"Yes, sir, that's what you're to understand. Uh . . . beggin' the General's pardon, sir."

"When did you last eat or sleep?"

"Yesterday before I left. But it's the horse needs tendin', sir, not me.

Come over a hunnerd miles. Four rivers. Needs about a gallon of oats and some hay."

Washington sat down abruptly, deftly wrote four lines on a piece of paper, dropped his quill, and handed the folded paper to Danny.

"Take that to my secretary. He will direct you where to get food and rest for yourself and your mount."

"Yes, sir."

"You are dismissed."

Danny walked out the door as Washington broke the seal and drew out the first of the papers. His face hardened as he read. When he finished, he slammed his open palm down on his desk and rasped out, "Infamous! Outrageous!" He did not leave his desk until the Hudson Valley was locked in deep dusk, and he was back at his desk before the morning drum banged out reveille. By seven o'clock a messenger was running through camp with a written order to be delivered to General Robert Howe. By eight o'clock, Howe was standing before Washington's desk, bewildered, waiting for some explanation of the emergency that required his appearance before morning mess. Washington wasted no time.

"There was a general mutiny by some Pennsylvania militia at Lancaster. Yesterday they marched on Philadelphia and joined with a large segment of militia to surround the state house where they hold Congress and the Pennsylvania Executive Council hostage until their demands are met. They are after full pay and other compensation, which neither Congress nor Pennsylvania can provide. The Executive Council could not force them to disperse."

Howe gaped.

"At the earliest moment possible, you will lead fifteen hundred troops, fully armed, to Philadelphia, where you will take all steps you deem necessary to put down this mutiny, including the force of arms or hanging those responsible."

Howe stood white-faced, speechless, and Washington concluded.

"The mutineers have seized the Philadelphia powder magazine.

Congress has resolved to abandon Philadelphia and resume session in Princeton."

Howe stammered, "Unbelievable, sir."

"If we do not act swiftly and decisively, it could bring down the United States. Send me daily dispatches until this matter is resolved. Do you understand?"

"Yes, sir."

The following morning Washington parted the curtain of the front window of his headquarters to watch General Robert Howe lead his column out, with their supply wagons and four cannon bringing up the rear in the heat and dust. For three days the dispatches arrived with no news other than the miles covered, and the standard sick call for each day. On the fourth day, Washington sat down at his desk and concentrated on the three pages written by General Howe.

In a shameful withdrawal, amid humiliating catcalls and obscenities shouted by the throng of mutineers, Congress had wound through the streets of Philadelphia in an unprecedented exodus to the city of Princeton, where they resumed their business in Nassau Hall.

With little reason to remain in Philadelphia, the mutineers had withdrawn, to return to their barracks in Philadelphia and to their camp in Lancaster. The all-important list of officers they wanted to present their claims before Congress was never delivered.

On July fourth, 1783, the seventh anniversary of the signing of the Declaration of Independence, a second written message arrived on Washington's desk.

It was over.

A mix of relief and apprehension flooded through Washington. An episode fraught with catastrophic potential had been averted, true enough, but that was vastly overshadowed by a deeper question. Was this the end of a thing that could shatter the United States, or the beginning?

Perplexed, Washington shook his head. How does one lead good, brave men through the gall of battle for eight years, only to find it necessary to confront them with the force of arms to save what they had so valiantly fought to obtain? How?

He sat down at his desk and opened a drawer to withdraw a document he and his staff had labored over. It was the last and most important of a brief series of writings that most had begun to call his
"Circulars to the States." This last document had been printed and circulated to the army and the thirteen states just days earlier, and had
instantly been referred to as "Washington's Legacy."

Slowly, thoughtfully, silently, he read it.

" . . . There are four things which I humbly conceive are essential to
the well being, I may even venture to say, to the existence of the United
States as an independent power:

1st. An indissoluble Union of the States under one Federal Head.

2nd. A sacred regard to public justice.

3rdly. The adoption of a proper peace establishment, and

4thly. The prevalence of that pacific and friendly disposition among
the people of the United States which will induce them to forget their
local prejudices and policies, to make those mutual concessions which
are requisite to the general prosperity, and in some instances, to sacrifice
their individual advantages to the interest of the community."

There was a deep sadness in his eyes as he dropped his head forward
to stare blankly at the desktop.

What more could I have said—or done—to make this country see what is so plain
if only they will clear their vision of all divisiveness? Our own military, holding Congress
hostage! Pennsylvania unable to control its own militia. Making impossible demands. No
end to it. When will they see?

He replaced the document in his drawer and by the power of his will
forced himself to survey the never-ending stack of papers that enslaved
him, ruled his world. Battles could be measured by the time between the
first shot and the last one, but not so the paperwork needed to run an
army. No one could remember when the paperwork started, and everyone understood it would never cease. Each day brought its own unrelenting load, and the worst nightmare known to a commander was the
chaos that buried him like an avalanche if he failed to handle it.

Weariness lined his face as he sighed and reached for the first document. He was composing an answer to a dispute over a supply contract when an unexpected knock brought his head up.

"Enter."

His personal secretary, Major Thaddeus Shaffer, tall, soft-spoken, stoop-shouldered, stepped into the room.

"You wished something?" Washington asked.

"Sir, I'm sorry to interrupt. This message just arrived from Robert Morris. It is marked 'Urgent.'"

Washington tensed and laid down his quill as Shaffer laid the document on his desk.

"Is there anything else?" Washington asked.

"No, sir."

"You are dismissed, but be available on a moment's notice."

"Yes, sir."

Washington seized the document, broke the seal, and read it twice to be certain of its content. Then he called, "Mr. Secretary!"

The door opened instantly and Shaffer entered to stand at attention.

"Mr. Morris will arrive here within the hour. With him is a man by the name of Haym Salomon. See to it refreshment is available, and once he is here, I am not to be interrupted except for dire emergency."

"Yes, sir."

Robert Morris was the wealthiest man in the United States and considered by most to be the most powerful, gifted merchant on the continent—a financial genius. Ambitious, confident to a fault, bold in taking risk, nerves of steel, no respecter of persons, Morris had connections with every leading merchant in America and abroad. Kings and monarchs knew Robert Morris. Banks around the world were eager for his business. When the United States found itself bankrupt and plunging into the black abyss of unending debt in 1781, Washington had turned to him for salvation, and Morris had responded. Congress abandoned its three-man financial committee, created the office of Superintendent of Finance to replace it, and appointed Morris to be the first Superintendent, with a clear ultimatum: unscramble the mess.

In record time he established the drastically underfunded Bank of

North America, commenced the issue of Continental paper dollars with too little gold to support them, demanded the states pay their own soldiers, hammered on French and Dutch banks until he obtained large loans to maintain solvency in the newly formed bank, threw out the system of army regimental commissaries with all the corruption it had spawned, instituted the contract system for supplying the army, and with a series of bookkeeping entries that baffled even the most experienced merchants, raised enough money to pay for the battle of Yorktown and essentially end the war.

It took him just weeks to identify the root of the problem. The United States Congress did not have the power to raise revenue! It could levy no taxes! The national government could only request funding from the States, beg them if necessary, and if the States could not or would not deliver, the national treasury emptied in a matter of days, sometimes hours. In 1782, furious creditors from major cities all over America proposed a mass meeting in either New York or Albany to create a uniform plan that would force Congress to pay their long overdue contract claims.

Morris was incensed. How, he reasoned, can the government continue to make promises to pay the army, and contractors, without the commensurate power to obtain the money? He attacked Congress with the simple truth of it, arguing loudly that since Congress was charged with the responsibility of maintaining an army, it had the inherent power to levy taxes to do it. A desperate Congress agreed. A law imposing an impost tax of five percent on goods imported into the country was passed, and while the ink was still wet on the parchment it was hastened to the thirteen states for their approval, since the Articles of Confederation required that all such laws passed by Congress must receive unanimous state approval. Twelve states approved instantly, Rhode Island alone rejecting it. The single rejection doomed the tax measure, and with it, any hope of rescuing the United States from the havoc of financial ruin.

Morris was furious at the idiocy he was seeing in the politicians. They had mandated him to rescue the United States from bankruptcy, then denied him the single tool needed to do it. Livid, he resigned.

The politicians? They threw up their hands in supplication, begging him to remain in office until a successor could be appointed, knowing it was impossible to replace Robert Morris. Reluctantly he stayed, declaring the entire time that it was futile.

In the midst of the desperate chaos, George Washington received reports of a second man whose financial wizardry and impeccable credentials were legendary in the world of international business. Haym Salomon. Born of Jewish parents in Lissa, Poland, in 1740, Salomon had early demonstrated an affinity for business and accumulating wealth. When mobs rose against the Jews in Poland and burned the town of Lissa in 1767, he emigrated to America, only to discover that traces of the same mindless prejudice existed in his new country. He joined the Sons of Liberty, a shadowy New York group dedicated to opposing the British, and was twice arrested and imprisoned by the British for aiding the American cause. By disguise and clever artifice he escaped and fled, leaving behind his wife and six children and six thousand pounds British sterling. The moment he could he rescued his wife and children and continued in his lucrative business as a merchant, serving the American cause. Small, slender, quiet, master of seven languages, including English and his native Yiddish, he slowly built a reputation that spread throughout the states and all major foreign ports and banks. Steadily his accounts swelled with wealth. News of his abilities and commitment to America reached George Washington, who immediately importuned Robert Morris: get Haym Salomon.

Reluctantly, the independent, opinionated Morris invited Salomon to a private meeting. Commitments were made. Salomon threw his genius and entire fortune into the effort to fund the great revolution, and time and again provided the gold that Robert Morris needed when the crises came. It was the robust Robert Morris who became known as the Financier of the Revolution, but it was the quiet, steady, gentle Haym Salomon who propped him up when he faltered.

Seated behind his desk, hunched forward, deep in frustration over the myriad written angry demands and complaints from creditors and unpaid American officers, Washington started at the knock on his door.

"Enter."

Thaddeus Shaffer opened the door, hawkish face a mask of intensity. "Sir, Misters Morris and Salomon have arrived."

Washington laid down his quill and straightened in his chair. "Show them in."

Washington rose as Morris entered, husky, round-faced, charismatic. He was followed by Salomon, small, slender, hunched, unobtrusive, sallow-faced, breath rattling from illness. The near total difference between the two men was striking. Washington had never seen Salomon until that moment, and he covertly studied the man, gathering his first impression.

Typical of his tendency to dominate, Morris marched to the desk, thrust out his hand, and spoke first.

"General, it is good of you to receive us on such short notice."

Washington reached to shake his hand, then that of Salomon, and spoke to Morris. "Not at all. It is good to see you again, Mr. Morris." He turned to Salomon. "It is my great pleasure to finally meet you, Mr. Salomon. Won't you be seated?"

The simple pine chairs creaked as they took their seats.

Washington abided the usual formalities. "Would you care for some refreshment? My secretary has arranged for it."

Morris shook his head. "Thank you, we shall not be here that long."

Washington dropped his eyes for a moment, then went on. "I received your message, marked urgent. Is there something pressing?"

Instantly Morris focused, became animated. "There is. It has to do with that business in Philadelphia. Holding Congress hostage."

"Disgraceful. I understood it is concluded."

Morris shook his head vigorously. "It isn't concluded. Oh, it's true enough that the mutinous soldiers have gone away and that Congress is safe in Princeton. But that in no way is a conclusion to it."

Washington spread his palms on his desk. "What are you telling me?"

Morris leaned forward, eyes flashing, words tumbling. "Let's put the Lancaster-Philadelphia disaster in context. To do that I have to go back."

He cleared his throat and for a moment ordered his thoughts.

"You recall I used loans from France and Holland to support the Bank of North America."

"I recall."

"$1,272,842 went to the Confederation government in loans to keep the army supplied during the war. To support that, I issued notes. In the banking world they were called Morris Notes, or Morris Warrants. They were issued over my signature and backed by my reputation, and they directed the Treasurer of the United States to pay them when due, in gold. Those notes were circulated in the business world, and eventually fell due. I went to Congress and warned them they had to be paid. I pled with Congress to impose poll taxes, land taxes, liquor taxes—any number of ways to raise the money to pay the notes."

Washington's face was a blank mask as he listened, tracking.

"Congress failed. They finally sent out a plea to the separate states to raise eight million dollars to pay the notes. They got four hundred thousand, some $7,600,000 short. The entire financing structure collapsed."

Morris straightened in his chair and continued, voice rising with emotion.

"I scarcely need to remind you of the deplorable condition of this army during the war years."

Washington nodded.

"No food. No gunpowder. No salt. No blankets. Men freezing to death. Starving. Do you remember your estimates of how much flour and how much meat this army required each year?"

"I do."

"One hundred thousand barrels of flour. Twenty million pounds of meat. In one winter, 1,500 horses died simply because the army could not find fodder! And the men ate half the dead horses!"

Morris fell silent, and Washington slowly leaned back, while visions of scarecrow men, standing barefoot in the snow, eating tree bark, passed before his eyes—the wagon that passed through camp at Valley Forge each morning, collecting the frozen bodies of those who died overnight of exposure, starvation, sickness—three thousand of them in five months—a sergeant appearing before him in rags, pleading for flour the army did not have to feed his men who had not eaten for eight days in the dead of winter.

Washington's words were scarcely audible. "I was there. I know."

Anger nearly choked Morris. "Those men—the ones who survived—suffered beyond anything I have ever seen. And they did it because they would not quit! What they were fighting for meant more than their suffering!"

Morris was nearly trembling. "Most fought for more than two years with little or no pay. Twenty cents a year! That's what the lucky ones got. The rest got a promise."

He stopped to regain control. "So when Congress appointed me Superintendent of Finance and directed me to set things right, I provided temporary relief to avoid a catastrophe, and I told Congress there was but one permanent solution: levy taxes. They tried, and failed."

Morris drew a great, weary breath, and for a moment a dead silence held the room. Then he leaned forward, and his words hung in the air like a cloud.

"The problem has nothing to do with money. It has to do with a government that is structured for catastrophic failure. There isn't the slightest chance the thirteen states are going to agree unanimously on anything to do with money, and lacking that unanimous agreement, the government is not, and never will be, capable of paying its debts because of its own Articles of Confederation! It is doomed. Absolutely doomed."

There it was! As clearly as mortal man could say it.

Morris picked it up once again.

"The Confederation government has been reduced to the status of a beggar. It must beg the states for money, and the states do not have it. The only other source of money is through the voluntary gifts—charity, if you will—of individuals. I have given my entire fortune in the cause." He turned to Salomon. "This man has bankrupted himself of his fortune and ruined his health in paying government debts. I know you have freely given most of your private fortune, and refused to take one dollar in pay for your services in leading this army for the past eight years."

He threw one hand in the air. "Heroic! But not enough, and never will be."

He stopped, and Washington waited for his conclusion.

"May I reach the bottom of this. It is simple: Americans abhor the thought of a strong central government—a king, a monarch, an all-powerful parliament. They fear and detest the idea of any one person or any institution being vested with power to control them. Each state has learned to handle its own government, and none of them, no, not one, can conceive of giving up local control in favor of a strong central government."

He stopped for a moment. "It is my opinion that the problem that resulted in that Lancaster debacle is the fact that Americans are shackled by their own minds. They cannot rise above localism! The revolution forced the individual states to unite against a common enemy, but their minds have not yet conceived that such a union can survive only if given the powers to do it. As deplorable as it may seem to them, that includes taxation."

Morris sank back in his chair, and it seemed the air went out of him. His head tipped forward, and for a time he stared at his hands, working one with the other.

Washington studied him for several moments, then looked at Salomon. The little man met his gaze, eyes clear, face firm, and Washington knew he was looking into the soul of one of the great patriots of the entire revolution.

"Mr. Salomon," Washington quietly said, "I would value your views."

"I have not discussed this with Mr. Morris, but sir, he has stated it well. No government institution can long survive if it can not maintain itself, and that requires revenue. Until our people accept that and make provision, the financial crisis that is now shaking this government to its roots will continue."

"Thank you, sir." Washington turned back to Morris. "Is that the urgent business that brought you here?"

Morris nodded. "That, and one more thing. I am of the firm conviction that no state can, or will, make the necessary contribution to meet the immediate need. If that is true, sir, it is my opinion that the Lancaster rebellion is but the beginning. Temporary measures may stall it for a while, but in the end there can be only catastrophe."

"I see. Is it in your mind to continue to function in the office of the Superintendent?"

"Yes, I will remain. I will do everything I can to delay the inevitable, but again I say, until the root problem is solved, there is nothing I or anyone else can do to avoid the final result."

For a time Washington stared at his desktop while his mind set things in order. "You realize this matter is beyond my commission. I command the army. Congress commands me. Only Congress can address such problems."

"I know that, sir. I have driven Congress to a near frenzy with my demands and arguments. And to what end? They now dread my very appearance in their chamber. I came here for another reason altogether."

Morris leaned forward, and there was an uncommon intensity in his face. "General, sir, make Congress wake up! They might listen to you. This country—the world—is on the brink of the greatest advance in thinking in recorded history, on the question of governments. Make them listen!"

For a moment the three men sat motionless, Washington startled by what sounded like a direct order from Robert Morris, Salomon dumbfounded, Morris shocked at his own audacity. Morris continued.

"But whatever you do, do not let the failure of Congress tarnish you. You've given too much. Don't let their foolishness diminish you."

Time meant nothing as Washington sat silent, considering Morris's frank, unvarnished request that he somehow persuade Congress to rise above itself, coupled with what was nothing less than a deep need in Morris to protect him. It came to Washington that Morris and Salomon had appeared before him in one, last great effort to save their country from ruin. The truths they had laid bare rose in his breast, terrible, appalling, as the three of them sat in silence, and then the feeling faded and was gone. Washington cleared his throat.

"I suggest we do not speak of this meeting outside this room. I will make an entry in my personal journal, in which each of you will receive the credit you have so richly earned. Was there anything else?"

Morris shook his head. "Nothing from me, sir." He turned. "Mr. Salomon?"

The little man reflected for a moment. "May I say, the suffering my people—the Jews—have endured has taught us many lessons. One is that from great pain comes great understanding. I do not know if I will live to see it, but I believe this country will rise above its own weaknesses. We will survive. We will flourish."

The declaration caught both Morris and Washington by surprise. For a moment neither man dared speak. Then Washington nodded.

"Is there anything else?"

"No, sir."

"Gentlemen, your concern is justified and your presentation deeply moving. I'm grateful to you for bringing them. If there is nothing else, you are dismissed."

Three minutes later Washington stood at the window of his crude office, curtain drawn back, watching the backs of the burly Morris and the slight Salomon as they walked to their waiting carriage. He watched them open the door, step up into the van, close the door, and wave to the driver. The dust from their departure had long settled before he turned from his window, sat down at his desk, reached for his quill, and drew out his personal journal.

" . . . this day I have had the high privilege of conferring with two of the finest patriots in the American cause . . ."

Notes

A substantial number of mutinous American militia from Lancaster did in fact march eighty miles east of Philadelphia, where they were joined by many from the Pennsylvania militia. They gathered at the Pennsylvania State House, where they surrounded the building and held Congress and the Pennsylvania Executive Council hostage pending agreement that their demands for a hearing of their grievances. Alexander Hamilton and James Madison were among the delegates in Congress. Elias Boudinot was the President of Congress, and John Dickinson was President of the Executive Council. The mob made their demands, Congress deferred, and John Dickinson stated that the Pennsylvania militia would not protect any of them, quoted nearly verbatim herein. Alexander Hamilton thereupon declared the "to the last degree weak and disgusting!" as quoted herein. However, the confrontation between Hamilton and the leader of the mob, named Major Bates, as herein described, is hypothetical, intended to inform the reader of the matter as it truly developed.

Immediately prior to the Lancaster uprising, Washington had completed the draft of his final message in his "Circulars to the States," which was promptly denominated "Washington's Legacy" and is partly quoted verbatim herein.

The issue involved in the uprising was as described, the promises made to the soldiers by Congress and Pennsylvania regarding their pay and benefits from their war service. Some had not been paid for two years. Others had been given printed money called "Continental dollars," issued by Congress, however, it took over 500 such Continental dollars to be worth one cent, which meant some soldiers received twenty cents per year for pay. Besides Continental dollars, each state had been issuing its own currency, and most of it was not backed by hard coin or gold. The result was a terrible chaos in the financial affairs of the country, both state and national. To solve the problem George Washington succeeded in getting Robert Morris to become the first Superintendent of Finance for the national government, an office created by Congress in their desperation to solve what they saw coming as described.

At Washington's insistence, Robert Morris contacted Haym Salomon, a Jewish financial genius, who gave his all to help the country in the financial calamity that threatened its very existence. It was through the efforts of these two men, Morris and Salomon, that enough money was provided to see the country through to the victory at Yorktown. It is not known that Robert Morris and Haym Salomon ever both met with Washington as herein described, but it is known that Morris delivered to Washington the critical message that he was certain the various states would not make the money contributions requested of them to avoid catastrophe. Much later, in November 1797, Washington found Robert Morris in debtors prison, the result of giving his wealth to support his country. Haym Salomon, his health broken from his unending efforts to save the American cause, died of illness on January 4, 1785, at age 45, leaving his wife and children penniless. A monument to honor the contributions of the three men, Washington, Morris, and Salomon, in their selfless giving to save America, has been erected in Chicago.

Bernstein, *Are We to Be a Nation?*, p. 39; Morris, *The Forging of the Union,* pp. 40–42, 50–54; Higginbotham, *The War of American Independence,* pp. 299–305; Freeman, *Washington,* pp. 502–10, 733; Davis, *Sectionalism in American Politics,* pp. 40–58; Milgrim, *Haym Salomon, Liberty's Son,* pp. 6–8, 84, 113–16, and see the Chicago monument with the figures of Haym Salomon, George Washington, and Robert Morris, p. 117.

CHAPTER XII

★ ★ ★

*T*he thought rose in the mind of Kathleen Thorpe Dunson to set her glowing, and it repeated like a chant—*he's coming home, he's coming home, he's coming home!* Wild anticipation swept through her, and she plunged into a torrent of mental inventions of how Matthew would arrive, and when and what he would be wearing, and what he would say, and what she would be wearing, and what she would say, and she clenched her hands beneath her chin, picturing the moment when he would sweep her into his arms and kiss her, and they could give expression to all the longing that had been building in their hearts since their separation, and it would come rushing over them like a great, irresistible tidal wave. He would arrive in the late afternoon and burst through the door, dashing and handsome in his naval uniform, and she would be devastating in her finest gown, and he would be tender but manly, and she would be demure but yielding, and she would have the table spread with the finest, shining white linen with needlepoint all around, and folded napkins, and the most expensive silver place settings. There would be goblets of the best English crystal and dozens of scented candles on great candlesticks, and she would have ham and breast of turkey waiting in the oven, and steamed oysters, candied yams, buttered potatoes, relishes and condiments in silver serving trays, and tarts and cakes, and he would be entranced by the richness in the air, and his eyes would glow with love as he understood that this was her humble offering at his homecoming. And she would take him by the hand to lead him into the small room where their little son, John, would be sleeping in his crib, and a look of wonder would steal into Matthew's eyes as he reached to gently touch the dark thatch of hair, and he would turn to look at her and there would be worship in his face as he gathered her into his arms and . . .

"Half past four o'clock and all's well in good weather."

He's coming home at half past four, and the turkey and ham are ready and I must change—half past four—and the tarts and cakes are cooling and—half past four . . .

A tiny, faint voice came from deep within—*four o'clock in the morning—the bellman not Matthew—the bellman—*

Kathleen stirred and slowly opened her eyes, struggling to come from the immaculately prepared table in the dining room to the world of reality in the blackness of her bedroom.

Four o'clock—Matthew coming—

A warm morning breeze moved in from the Atlantic across the Boston Peninsula to stir the curtains at the window and bring the familiar scent of salt sea air and the sounds of ships' bells from the harbor. Kathleen swallowed dry and waited for the invented images to fade and those of the coming day to clarify.

The bellman—not Matthew—Monday—wash day in Boston—he war changed many things—but not wash day in Boston—going to be hot today—must get up soon to start the fires for the wash water . . .

Her eyes closed, and she drifted into that warm, comfortable place midway between sleep and consciousness, where reality is dulled and secret dreams arise. She did not stir again until the bellman's call of half past five came from the cobblestone street in front of the great Thorpe home that had become hers following the banishment of her traitor father and the death of her mother in England. She threw back the sheet that covered her, swung her feet out onto the huge oval braided rag rug and into the woolen slippers at her bedside. She was tying the belt on her robe over her nightgown when she entered the parlor and walked to the fireplace where she used the brass fireplace shovel to open the bank of coals. She added tiny pine shavings to the glowing embers, blew gently with the leather bellows, then added more small sticks and shavings until the flames came licking. Back in her bedroom she dressed in a sturdy, gray, ankle-length cotton skirt and blouse, buckled on her high-topped leather work shoes, tied a white bandanna about her head to hold back her long, dark hair, and slipped into a heavy, full-length work apron.

With the sun half risen, she poured the last bucket of well water into the huge black kettle, added two large chunks of wood to the fire beneath it, glanced at the heavy wooden washtub and the two rinse tubs on the long, sturdy wash bench, and walked back into the house. She stole silently into the room where John lay sleeping, then went through the house, gathering clothing and table linens into a large woven-reed basket. She walked silently down the hall to carry it out to the washbench near the tripod where wisps of steam were beginning to rise from the kettle. For a moment she paused to peer at the sky, judging the weather. The morning breeze had died, and Boston was locked in hot, humid, dead air. In every direction, thin, straight columns of gray smoke drifted upwards from fires heating wash water all over the peninsula. It was going to be another hot wash day in Boston town.

At half past seven she used a long-handled dipper to move water from the steaming kettle to the big wooden washtub. She cut shavings of brown laundry soap from the bar into the water, stirred until it frothed, then loaded the first heap of clothing into the mix and punched it down with a peeled hickory stick to let it steam and soak. Ten minutes later she had the rinse tubs filled with hot water, then took twelve trips to the well to haul water in the heavy, waterlogged bucket to refill the kettle.

While the wash soaked and the water heated, she fed a fretful John his breakfast of mush and applesauce, changed his diaper, dressed him, and pressed her cheek against his forehead, feeling his temperature. *Too warm—it's those two big molars coming in.* For a time she sat in the parlor rocker with him in her lap, gently rubbing his swollen gums with her little finger.

"Does that feel good?" she crooned to him, and he whimpered when she stopped. "I know—I know," she said and once again rubbed the tender gums, humming while she rocked him. She rose and walked to his room, held him on her hip while she stripped his bed with one hand, then went to her room to strip her own bed, and then moved out to the laundry tubs, John on one hip, the basket on the other, where she set the bedding on the washbench. She tied a fifteen-foot cord from the back of John's shoulder straps to one of the posts supporting the clotheslines, set him in the grass, returned to the first load of soaked laundry, jammed the corrugated washboard into the water, drew a deep breath, rolled up her sleeves, and began.

Gather a garment in both hands, up and down the board twenty times, wring it out, into the warm rinse water, take the next garment, up and down twenty times, wring it out, into the warm rinse water—fifteen minutes later she straightened, hands on her hips to relieve her back for a moment, then dipped out the dirty, cool wash water and refilled the tub with hot. Cut soap, stir, jam in the bedding, punch it down with the stick, and move to the rinse tub. Up and down with the first garment, wring it out as hard as she can twist, into the second rinse tub, pick up the next garment. Twenty minutes later she dropped the last garment into the last rinse tub, dipped the dirty rinse water from the first rinse tub, refilled it, moved to the second rinse tub and began the sloshing and wringing out of the finished load. Into the basket, over to the clothes-line, fill her apron pockets with wooden clothes-pegs, two in her mouth, and hang the finished load. Empty the second rinse tub, refill it, then back to the scrubboard and start over.

By ten o'clock small curls of her dark hair clung to perspiration on her forehead. She added kindling to the fire, picked up the wailing John, and went from the heat of the sun into the cool of the house. Seated in her rocking chair, she gathered her son to her, comforting him and rub-bing his gums while she rocked gently, humming to him in her own little heaven. His fussing gradually ceased and his eyes closed, and she watched as his head tipped slightly forward, and he slept. She rose smoothly to her feet, walked down the hall, and laid him on his stomach in his bed. He stirred, and she placed the flat of her hand on his back and hummed for several seconds while he settled and began to breathe deeply.

Five minutes later she was back at the big washtub, perspiration running as she worked the heavy, water-soaked sheets up and down, one section at a time. At half past noon she wrung out the last rinsed sheet, dropped it into the basket, raised her apron to wipe the perspiration from her face, and walked back into the house. She ate bread and cheese and cold mutton while she fed John, changed him, rocked him while she rubbed his gums, and at fifteen minutes past one o'clock walked squinting back into the bright sunlight and the heat and humidity waiting in the backyard. She tied the cord to the back of John's shoulder straps and set him in the thick grass where he sat down and began pulling it and stuffing it in his mouth.

"No, no," she scolded, and cleaned out his mouth with her finger, then stood him on his feet. He followed her as she felt the clothes on the line—still damp—then carried the last basket load to the single line that was open and began shaking out the sheets to hang them.

Need wind to dry these—hope wind comes—

With her back to the kitchen door, she had set the third clothes-peg when John stopped moving and fixed his eyes on something behind her. She glanced at him, puzzled for a moment, then turned as she heard her name.

"Kathleen."

Matthew stood not ten feet behind her in his white shirtsleeves, tall, feet spread slightly, long dark hair tied back with a leather thong, face glowing. For an instant Kathleen stood rooted, unable to believe he was there, and then without a word she fled to him to throw herself into his arms and clasp him to her with all her strength. For long moments they stood thus, saying nothing, while the yearning that had been denied so long rose within to drive out every thought but one.

They were together, and they were home.

She drew back her head and kissed him, and kissed him again. Only then did words come.

"You're home. You're home."

He was beaming. "I'm home."

"Are you all right? Not hurt? Crippled?"

He shook his head. "Fine."

"Oh, Matthew!" she exclaimed, "I was going to have the dining room all so beautiful, and food, and dressed in my best—"

He reached to press two fingers against her lips to quiet her. "I don't care about that." He drew her to him.

She shook her head. "I'm all wet! Perspiring! A real mess."

He placed one hand against her damp cheek. "Does it matter?"

"No."

They stood in their embrace until John made sounds and Matthew turned his head. "Is this John?" he asked, incredulous. "I wouldn't have known! Look how he's grown." He broke from Kathleen and lifted the boy into his arms, studying the square, handsome little face, watching the dark eyes that peered at him as a stranger.

"He's cutting his back teeth," Kathleen said. "Fussy."

"He looks like Father."

"More every day."

"Is he sound? Healthy?"

Kathleen laughed. "Yes."

The baby pushed himself back from Matthew and leaned toward Kathleen, and she reached for him.

"He doesn't remember you. It's been two years. Give him time."

Suddenly Matthew looked at the clotheslines and the washtubs as though seeing them for the first time.

"You're washing!"

"Monday in Boston."

"Let's finish."

Together they hung the last of the finished sheets, and while Kathleen went into the house to nurse and tend John and put him down for his afternoon nap before she changed into dry clothing, Matthew emptied, rinsed, and stored the washtubs and kettle and the tripod. Then he quietly entered the house to gather his bags and officer's tunic from the parlor where he had dropped them, and walked softly past John's door to the bedroom as Kathleen was walking out. She stopped, took his tunic from his arm, and whispered, "Let me help you."

She was hanging his tunic in the closet when she noticed small stitches on the sleeve, and she walked back into the bedroom to hold it up in the light. It was faded, threadbare, patched in five places, and there was a small tear near the right cuff. She turned to Matthew.

"I don't know if this is worth mending."

For an instant he hesitated. "I'll have to get another one."

He saw the flash of concern in her face before she turned to the closet to hang it with his other clothing. As they continued to unpack his bags, she said nothing, but he saw the anxiety rising in her eyes as she handled his shirts and trousers. They were clean, but they were thin, mended. His shoes and boots were worn, in need of soles. She watched him unfold a small tissue packet, and draw out his royal blue watch fob with the gold needlepoint lettering, "M D," the one she had worked so long and hard to make for him when they were but youngsters. Tenderly he placed it in a drawer and was turning when he noticed her expression, soft, with eyes brimming.

"It saw me through," he said quietly.

She pointed, and on her table was the small, beautifully painted snow owl he had carved for their gift exchange those many years ago.

"I know," she answered.

He took an oilcloth packet in one hand, her arm in the other, and led her quietly down the hall, past the door of the sleeping child, into the dining room.

"Cider in the root cellar?"

"Yes. Would you prefer coffee?"

"Too hot for coffee," he answered. He laid the packet on the table, picked a pitcher from the kitchen cupboard, and walked out the back door to return with it half full of cool cider. Kathleen brought glasses, and they sat at the table. Matthew poured the apple juice, tasted it, and set his glass down, savoring the richness.

"I've waited a long time for that," he said.

Kathleen nodded, and for the next half hour they were lost in small talk and laughter about everyone and everything that had been building inside each of them since their last parting. Then Matthew sobered, and Kathleen fell silent, sensing a need in him.

Finally he spoke. "The root cellar is more than half empty."

A shadow crossed her face. "I know."

"Is there a reason?"

She worked her glass between her hands, staring at it for a moment. "Money."

He drew and released a breath. "For how long have you lacked?"

"Months. Maybe a year."

"I feared that would happen. How have you lived? Paid your way?"

She shrugged. "Washing. Ironing. Sewing. Needlepoint. Caring for children of others."

"For whom?"

"The military. The wealthy. Anyone."

"I didn't mean to let that happen. I had nothing to send."

"Nothing to do with you. Half—maybe most—of the women in Boston have been forced to it. There is no money anywhere. No gold or silver. Nothing but worthless paper money. Do you know the cost of a pair of boots for you?"

"No."

"Six hundred dollars. A common frying pan, one hundred twenty-five dollars. A kitchen fork, thirty-seven dollars. There's no way to deal with it. I don't get paid for my work in money. I get potatoes, or meat, or this cider. No one has money."

For a long time Matthew stared at his glass before he raised it once more, drank, then set it down.

"Coming from the wharves this morning, I saw the offices of three shipping firms closed down. Out of business. Two were big ones—been there since I can remember. Bankrupt. Walking down Fruit Street there were half a dozen—maybe ten or twelve—shops closed. Doors and windows boarded. Most had court papers nailed to the doors. Bankruptcy."

Kathleen nodded but said nothing.

Slowly Matthew unfolded the oilskin packet and laid two documents before Kathleen.

"One of those is my pay for the past eighteen months. It's a pledge by Congress that the State of Massachusetts will pay me in money if I'll wait long enough. The other is my military discharge. What I'm telling you is I'm coming home with nothing but a promise that I will get my pay sometime in the future, and that I am now a discharged naval officer with no pension. I'm empty-handed, without employment, and from the look of things in Boston town, there is not a soul that can employ a navigator. If three shipping firms have closed down from bankruptcy, there are going to be qualified navigators and ship's officers begging for work. Willing to accept anything they can get, at any rate of pay that's offered."

He stopped and stared vacantly at his glass before he continued.

"Maybe I can trade work of some kind for food, but what I don't know is how we're going to pay the property taxes on this home. That takes hard money." Slowly he shook his head. "I don't know where to go to get hard money."

She covered his hand with hers. "We'll find a way."

He stared into her eyes. "Where? How?"

"I don't know. And it isn't important that we stay in this house. We can sell it and that will give us some money. We can buy another smaller home. We have each other. And the baby. That's all we need. We'll be all right."

For a moment they looked at each other, him struggling to understand her blind faith, her feeling his fear at what he saw coming.

They both started at the rap on the front door. He looked at her, inquiring, she shook her head in surprise, and Matthew started for the door when it opened. Before him stood his mother, and behind her, the twins, Adam and Priscilla, and Brigitte. For an instant they all stood in silence, and then Margaret rushed to seize him, and everyone spoke at once. Margaret clutched him to her, and she kissed him on the cheek, then she hugged him again with all her strength. She broke from him and held his arms while she inspected him, head to toe.

"You're all right? Not harmed?"

"I'm fine."

Margaret turned to Kathleen. "We had to come. Just had to. I waited for a while to give you two a little time together, but we couldn't wait any longer."

Matthew interrupted. "We'd have come down later on. How did you know I was here?"

"Adam saw from the engraver's. He's apprenticed. Engraves silver. He couldn't leave work to catch you."

Matthew turned to Adam and Prissy in disbelief. The twins had been eight years of age when he left eight years earlier. He had seen them twice since, the last time just two years before, but nothing had prepared him for what he now saw. Prissy had turned into a beautiful young woman, while Adam was nearing full height, close to six feet. His hands, feet, and Adam's apple were all far too large, his arms and legs and face too long; but it was clear that when they all caught up with his growth, he was going to be a strongly built, handsome man. Prissy had been a knobby-kneed child, but now? Before him stood a demure young woman, pretty but reserved, even somewhat bashful. She was obviously different than the more outgoing Brigitte—quieter, more thoughtful, but striking in her own right.

Matthew exclaimed, "Is this Adam? And Prissy? What happened to my little brother and sister?" Matthew shook his head. "Adam, you've become the man of the house!"

Adam blushed and stared at the floor for a moment, then extended his hand and said in a voice deeper than Matthew would have imagined, "It's good to have you home."

Prissy stared steadily at him, eyes glowing, and he reached to grasp her shoulders.

"Look at you, Prissy! You've grown up. A beauty."

Prissy dropped her eyes for an instant as only a woman can, and Matthew drew her to him in an embrace, and she held him for a moment while Margaret stood to one side, beaming with the joy and pride that only a mother can know.

Matthew turned to Brigitte, and instantly knew. She had survived the loss of her first love, endured six years of war, and faced the daily grind of worry and unending work to put food on the table. She had passed from a youth to a mature, beautiful, grown woman. He reached for her and she stepped close to embrace her brother and kiss him on the cheek.

"Welcome home, Matthew. It's so good to see you again."

"And you," he said.

Kathleen broke in. "Matthew, if you'll fetch more cider, I'll get the glasses."

Ten minutes later they were seated about the dining room table, working on two pitchers of apple cider in the midst of chatter. While the talk tumbled out, Matthew noticed little things. Margaret's dress was faded, her hands red and rough. Adam's jacket was patched at the elbows. The hem of Prissy's dress had been undone to lengthen it. Brigitte's dress showed wear in the sleeves and yoke, and her hands were those of a laborer. He saw it and his heart ached, but he said nothing of the years they had silently suffered the burdens of war.

He turned to Margaret. "Have you heard from Caleb?"

"Not recently."

Matthew nodded. "Might be a while. I left him at Head of Elk with about ten wagons loaded with slaves. He's bringing them north."

Margaret set her glass down with a thump. "He's *what?*"

The room quieted. "We came across a slave ship at sea. It was sinking. We brought the slaves ashore, and Caleb started north with them. Nothing else we could do."

Margaret's eyes narrowed. "How did Caleb come to be with you on a ship at sea? Are you telling me everything?"

Matthew shook his head, grinning. "No. I'm not. That would take all night. We'll talk it all out later."

Chuckles surrounded the table for a moment before Matthew continued. "What of Billy?"

Margaret shook her head. "Expected home any time. Trudy and Dorothy are watching every day."

She looked at Kathleen. "Is the baby all right? Still teething?"

"Asleep. Fine. A little fever. I'll wake him."

Margaret raised a hand. "Let him sleep."

Adam spoke hesitantly to Matthew. "We heard about Yorktown. Were you there?"

Talk quieted. In that instant Matthew was hearing the blasting of the big guns and seeing men maimed and killed by exploding cannonballs. He answered. "Yes."

"The sea battle?"

"Yes."

"Was it bad?"

Matthew understood the boy was asking him to describe the roar of the cannon and the shredding of the sails and shattering of the yardarms and masts of the ships; of the men who were killed and the ships that were sunk—the great drama of an historic sea battle. For a few moments Matthew studied his glass, then made his answer.

"We won."

Adam somehow sensed that Matthew was going to say very little about the momentous battle that ended the Revolutionary War. He did not understand why, only that he had seen a reluctance in the eyes of his brother. He reached for his glass and said nothing.

Kathleen spoke. "Margaret, can you stay for supper? Please? I have ham and cheese in the root cellar and—"

Margaret raised a hand. "No, this is a time for just the three of you. We only came for a minute, but we'll help clear your wash from the lines before we go."

"I can do it. Matthew and I."

"Oh, come on, it will only take a minute if we all—"

Matthew cut in. "We'll do it, Mother. You've no doubt got wash on your own lines."

Margaret frumped, "Well, we offered." She spoke to the other children. "Come on. We've got work to finish and supper to put on the table."

They all followed her to the door where she stopped and turned. Her eyes were filled with deep gratitude as she reached once more to embrace her firstborn. "Son, it's so good to have you home. Come down later if you can." She looked at Kathleen. "Bring the baby."

"I will."

They all walked to the large gate in the high white fence that enclosed the Thorpe home, and Matthew and Kathleen stood side by side in the late afternoon sun, each with an arm about the other as they watched and waved until the family disappeared in the afternoon traffic of the narrow, crooked, cobblestone Boston street.

They walked arm in arm back into the house, where Kathleen stopped to listen. "John's awake," she said and started towards the arch-way into the bedroom wing. Matthew caught her by the arm, and she saw the cloud in his face.

"How long have Mother and the others been like that?"

"Like what?"

"Old clothing. Patched. Hands of laborers?"

"I never thought about it. Four years. Five."

She saw the muscles set in Matthew's jaw for a moment before he said, "Let me see your hands."

She did not move. "They're fine."

He reached to raise her wrist and for the first time looked closely at her right hand. It was rough and red from five years of hot water and soap and splitting kindling with an ax and planting and nurturing a garden and doing wash and ironing and sewing and needlepoint for anyone who could trade food for her work.

For a time Matthew stood with her hand in his, tenderly touching it, smoothing it, and then he released it and turned to walk away. Kathleen saw and felt the pain in him, and she yearned to take it away, but she did not know how.

Notes

The Dunson family is fictional, however, the homecoming of Matthew as described herein is typical of what the discharged soldiers experienced. Paper currency was near worthless, and coin or gold was almost non-existent. The cost of boots, a frying pan, and a fork as quoted herein are accurate. The exchange of work for food and other necessaries for living was common

(Milgrim, *Haym Salomon, Liberty's Son,* p. 84), and see all citations regarding the horrendous financial condition of the country as cited in the endnotes of the previous chapter.

It will be remembered that Kathleen Thorpe Dunson's father, Doctor Henry Thorpe of Boston, was secretly a traitor to the American cause. While this series uses the name Henry Thorpe, the true name of the traitor was Doctor Benjamin Church, a wealthy and powerful figure in the politics of Boston. Caught in his treason, he was tried in a Massachusetts court, convicted, and his sentence was banishment from America for life. He disappeared, never to be seen again by his family. See volume 1 of this series, *Our Sacred Honor,* chapters 7 and 9, and the endnotes for chapter 19.

The bellman, sometimes called the "rattle-watch," walked the streets of New England towns through the night, accompanied by a boy apprentice, calling out the time at intervals, as well as the weather (Earle, *Home Life in Colonial Days,* pp. 362–63).

In the revolutionary time period, Monday had been established as "wash day" in Boston (Earle, *Home Life in Colonial Days,* p. 254; Ulrich, *Good Wives,* p. 28).

Boston

Late June 1783

CHAPTER XIII

*B*illy was yet six miles from the Boston Peninsula when he caught the strong, familiar scent of salt sea air riding the five o'clock morning Atlantic breeze, and unexpected memories came in a rush in the predawn darkness.

The small white house that was the only home he had ever known—Mother and Trudy—the narrow, winding, cobblestone streets—the sounds of ships' crews in the harbor—his work desk at the Potter & Wallace Counting House on King Street—the tidy white church—Reverend Silas Olmsted—Matthew—Brigitte.

He touched his coat pocket where he kept the oilskin packet of faded, battered letters he had written to Brigitte over the past years, and once again his need to open his heart to her collided with his fear. A beautiful, accomplished woman, and a homely, common man? He shook his head, pushed away the pain, and continued his stride on the crooked dirt road leading east through the thick Massachusetts forest toward The Neck, the only ground passage connecting the peninsula to the mainland.

Dead ahead, the black velvet of the heavens slowly yielded to a deep purple, and the earth separated from the sky. Something in the forest to Billy's left bolted, thrashing through the thick foliage away from the road, and Billy looked, hitched his bedroll a little higher on his back, and walked on.

The high, light rift of clouds above Boston were caught up in reds and yellows from a sun not yet risen when Billy strode past the first of the great two-wheeled carts loaded with sacked flour for the Boston markets, and within minutes there were other men driving teams of oxen and horses that leaned into their yokes or collars to move the carts loaded with winter hay, or wheat, or cider, or beef, or milk and cheese, or smoked hams and bacon, steadily on toward the buyers in town. The first arc of the sun was shining in Billy's eyes and casting long shadows westward when he passed through The Neck.

Half an hour later he was in the dirt streets on the western fringe of the town, and then he was into the cobblestones among the familiar sounds of iron-rimmed cart wheels clattering toward the shops and onto the docks, and the morning people calling to each other as they hurried to and from homes and shops. It struck him as odd that there seemed to be fewer of them than he remembered.

He was more than a block away when he saw the white picket fence of home, and he broke into a trot. He hurried through the gate and up to the front door to knock twice, then open it and walk in. As always, the austere little house was spotless. For an instant he stood still, caught in the incomparable feel of being in the place of his beginnings. Then he called, "Mother!"

There was only silence, and he walked quickly through the tiny dining room, into the kitchen, and out the back door into the small backyard. The garden was in and growing, and there were fresh, white wood chips around the chopping block, and half a cord of fresh-cut firewood stacked against the back wall of the house. He got a small piece of cheese from the root cellar, then walked back into the kitchen to take a piece of bread from the bread box, drop his bedroll on the floor, and sit down at the dining table. He finished eating, drank water dipped from the kitchen water bucket, and sat in the quiet for a time, speculating where Dorothy and Trudy would be at the hour of eight o'clock on a summer's morn.

He shrugged, picked up his bedroll, walked down the narrow hall to his bedroom, and opened the window curtains to let the morning sunlight flood in. As he untied and opened his bedroll, he glanced at all the little things that were the mosaic of his childhood and youth. He put his razor and razor strop on the closet shelf, and his soiled clothes and the old blanket in the wicker basket on the closet floor, and sat on the bed for a moment, leaned forward, elbows on knees, remembering the days he had lain in that bed more dead than alive with a musketball hole through his left side and a bayonet wound beside it. Matthew refused to leave him for a week, sitting at the bedside during the day, sleeping on the floor at night, until he knew Billy would survive.

He stood, took the oilskin packet from his coat, and carefully placed it in the bottom drawer of his dresser before he hung his threadbare coat in the closet, rolled up his sleeves, and walked into the backyard to pick up the ax.

He had cut half a cord of kindling before the kitchen door opened, and his mother and sister walked out. For a moment the three stood transfixed, and then Dorothy was holding him to her with her eyes closed, and Billy had his arms about his mother while Trudy stood nearby, not knowing what she should do.

Dorothy's heart was overflowing at the sight and touch of her son—home—home after six long years of not knowing if he was dead or alive, or crippled, or whether she would ever see him again. She clung to him while her soul filled with the supreme joy of knowing that he was there, and he was whole. She pushed him back, and put her hand to her mouth. For a moment, she couldn't speak at all, her voice choked by the ache in her throat. She gazed at her son through the tears that welled up in her eyes and began spilling down her cheeks.

"Billy. Oh, Billy. You're home!"

"I'm here."

Dorothy wiped at her cheeks, and then she laughed at the heady relief of having her firstborn safely back. "Would you look at me. Crying." She turned to her daughter. "Trudy's been waiting, too."

For a moment Billy stared at his sister in shock. The little girl of eight years before was gone. Trudy was a grown woman. He reached for her, and she stepped inside his arms to hold him, and he felt her tremble as she spoke.

"Billy. We've prayed so hard. I can't tell you . . ."

"I know. I know. I've prayed too."

For a time they stood there, basking in the glow, and then Billy said, "I need to wash. Splitting that wood raised a sweat."

He drew water from the well to rinse the sweat from his face, then followed them into the kitchen for a towel before he turned to Dorothy.

"You were gone early this morning."

"Had to deliver some ironing to Silas. Millie's ailing. Can't get out of bed. I fixed some soup for her."

Billy straightened. "What happened to Millie?"

"Stroke of some kind. Affected her eyes. Some days she can hardly see. Silas spends most of his time taking care of her."

Concern showed in Billy's face. "Sorry to hear that. Is Silas all right? Can he still take care of his church duties?"

"Aging. He takes care of the Sunday services, but he doesn't get around as much as before. I help with the shopping." She turned to Trudy. "Fetch four eggs and that piece of ham from the root cellar, and some cheese and milk."

Billy interrupted. "I'll help."

Talk about small things mellowed as they moved about the tiny kitchen. Billy started a fire in the stove and fed kindling while Dorothy and Trudy set a skillet to warm, then cracked the eggs, and diced ham and cheese for an omelet. Billy helped set the table, and Dorothy brought the steaming platter to the table while Trudy poured milk. They brought a loaf of bread on a cutting board, then butter and strawberry preserves. Dorothy pointed and Billy took his place at the head of the table—a place that had been his since the day a man in seaman's garb appeared at their front door, working his hat in his hands, refusing to raise his eyes as he told them that Bartholomew Weems, first mate in a fishing fleet, Dorothy's husband and Billy's father, had been lost at sea. Too early Billy had become the man of the house. Dorothy took her place to his right, Trudy to his left. They clasped their hands beneath their chins and bowed their heads, and Billy softly returned thanks to the Almighty for the simple bounties of their table.

Billy could not remember a meal that had tasted so good, or one that had reached so near to the very core of his soul. He spread home-churned butter on Dorothy's bread and added her strawberry preserves and ate it in a grateful silence that bordered on reverence.

As he ate, his mother gazed at him, seeing in his plain, homely face and sandy hair the echo of her long-lost husband. The wonder of it all nearly overcame her. Her son was home from war. Eight long years of living every day in mortal fear of receiving a letter from a Massachusetts regiment officer were ended. Billy was there at the table, sound, caught up in the love that she had put into everything in her little home.

Trudy was dipping steaming water from the stove into the wooden dish tub when she asked, "Billy, were you in the fighting? Yorktown?"

He didn't immediately answer, and Dorothy saw him considering the question. A veil seemed to drop over his eyes.

"Yes. I was there."

Trudy stopped. "Was it bad? Like we heard?"

Dorothy saw the remembrance of the cannon and the muskets and the bayonets and the screams of maimed and dying men flash in Billy's eyes, and she spoke before Billy could.

"There'll be time for such things later."

Billy looked at her for a moment, then quietly said to Trudy, "I don't know what you heard. We did what had to be done."

With the gift of her mother's intuition, Trudy sensed she had ventured into the forbidden. She stopped with the dripping dipper held poised, and said, "Billy, I didn't mean . . . I'm sorry. So sorry."

He smiled. "It's all right. There'll be time later. We'll talk."

Dorothy suddenly focused. "You must have clothes that need washing and mending!"

"There are a few things in my room, but they'll wait." He gestured to the stacked dishes. "You wash, I'll dry."

The warm talk about anything and everything flowed, with laughter and pauses, while Billy silently studied the unbelievable transformation that two years had worked in his sister. She had a round, unremarkable face, and tended to be stocky, much like their mother. She spoke from time to time, but there was much that she held inside. And like her mother, there was a gentleness and a rightness that shined through to touch all around her.

Billy watched as Dorothy placed the dishes back in the kitchen cupboard, and said, "You must have things to do this afternoon."

She gestured. "Ironing. For Josiah Wiltham. Promised I'd deliver it this afternoon."

"I'll get the irons."

Billy added wood to the stove and set the four flatirons on the plates to heat while Dorothy carried an armload of stiff, washed shirts and linens to the kitchen table. While Billy set up the ironing board, Trudy began dipping her hand into a bowl of water and flicking droplets onto the clothing, then rolling the sprinkled garments tightly to mellow. Dorothy waited for ten minutes, shook out the first shirt, reached for the first iron, moistened her fingertips and tapped the face of the iron to check the heat, and the three of them settled into the routine they had followed since Billy could remember. Billy tended the fire in the stove and rotated the irons, taking the cooled iron from his mother and handing her one that was hot in its place. Trudy kept the pile sprinkled and carefully folded and stacked the finished items as Dorothy handed them to her.

Billy had not expected the feeling of deep satisfaction that quietly emerged as they worked together in the heat of the kitchen, saying little, exchanging glances, watching the clean, finished stack of laundry grow. It was as though chatter would have been a sacrilege. Halfway through the work, Dorothy gestured to Trudy, who picked up the flatiron and shook out a sprinkled shirt while Dorothy dampened the next one. Billy's eyes widened in surprise as he realized that Trudy was no longer a child. Dorothy had patiently trained her, taught her to do a woman's work, and he marveled at the skill he saw in her.

At midafternoon Trudy finished the last tablecloth, folded it, set it on the pile, and turned to Dorothy. "I think we're finished."

Billy nodded. "I'll get the basket."

Ten minutes later the ironed wash was neatly stacked in the Wiltham family's woven reed basket, with a clean cloth tucked around the top. Billy picked up the basket while Dorothy and Trudy worked with their hair for a moment before they put on their sunbonnets, and the three of them walked four blocks, through the heat and humidity of a summer's day in Boston, to deliver their work to the home of Josiah Wiltham. Billy was startled but said nothing as Dorothy received her pay—a side of smoked bacon for the root cellar. They were walking homeward on the shady side of the street when Billy spoke.

"You were paid with bacon?"

Dorothy nodded. "They have so little money."

A twinge of concern rose inside Billy. "Is it usually that way? Trade work for food?"

"For most of us. The only money is paper, and it's nearly worthless."

"The businesses in town?"

"The same. No money."

Billy opened his mouth to speak once more, then thought of Trudy, and fell silent as they wound through the narrow streets to their home. As they passed through the front gate Billy noticed for the first time that the sea air had pitted and peeled the white paint on the fence. They were in the house before he asked casually, "Any paint for the fence?"

Dorothy shook her head.

"Any money to buy some?"

Again she shook her head.

Billy read the flash of deep concern, bordering on panic, in his mother's face as she looked at him, and his breathing slowed as the truth struck home. He had assumed the shortage of hard money was limited to the states and the Continental Congress. Only now did he realize it had reached much further. He felt a grab in the pit of his stomach but said nothing as they entered the house. In the coolness of the parlor he turned to his mother.

"I haven't bathed for days. Would it be all right?"

"Of course."

Half an hour later the big wooden bathtub was in the center of the kitchen floor behind sheets that were hung from wires to shield it from the rest of the house, and Billy was pouring heated water from the stove into the tub. For a long time he sat with his knees under his chin, slowly working with the brown bar of strong homemade soap while he forced fearful thoughts to clarify in his mind.

How many people were without hard money?

How many businesses?

How far did the lack of gold and coin reach?

The sun had set and the supper dishes were finished when he quietly spoke to Dorothy.

"Could you come to my room for a minute?"

They left Trudy reading by lamplight in the parlor and made their way to his small room where they sat on his bed. For a time Billy stared at the floor, silent, before he spoke.

"I didn't want Trudy to be here for this." He raised his eyes to Dorothy's. "Do you have any money?"

"No. None."

"For how long have you lived like this? Trading work to stay alive?"

"Oh, I don't know. Fifteen months."

"Is there any money in Boston at all?"

Dorothy shook her head. "Paper money. Worthless. I don't think anyone has real money. Gold or coin."

There was a long pause before Billy asked the next question, and Dorothy sensed the intensity in him.

"How about Potter & Wallace? My old employer. How is the counting house getting along?"

Dorothy dropped her eyes and began working her hands together, slowly. "You knew Cyrus Wallace passed on before you left. Hubert Potter kept the business going until three years ago. Then he began losing big accounts."

Billy's breathing slowed. "Why? How?"

"His big accounts closed their doors. He lost six or eight two years ago. Another five last year. He had to let his employees go because he couldn't pay them, and finally he closed the counting house. Potter & Wallace is gone."

Slowly Billy straightened. "Where is Hubert Potter?"

"Passed on. He had a stroke eight months ago. Died the last week in January. I think the loss of his business killed him."

Dorothy had not raised her eyes from her hands. Billy went on.

"Any other businesses closed?"

Dorothy nodded. "Seems like half the town's closed. Six or seven of the big shipping lines have closed their offices down at the docks. The little businesses that depended on them are gone. Men everywhere are looking for work. They'll do anything they can find to stay alive. Farms all around are being taken by the banks."

They sat for a long time, Dorothy staring at her hands, Billy looking at the floor, before he spoke again.

"Do you know if there are bankruptcies?"

"Too many. Far too many."

"I should have known."

"How could you? You've been gone."

He spoke softly. "On the way home, I tried to buy food. Nobody would take the paper money the army gave me. I had to trade my musket to eat. And my bayonet. On the way into town this morning there were fewer farm carts coming in."

Dorothy took a deep breath and turned her face to him. "You're home. Nothing else much matters. I don't know what we're going to do about all this, but I know we'll live through it somehow. We'll be all right."

He looked into her eyes and realized as never before that she had endured the terrible struggle of a widow trying to provide for herself and her two children, from the black day the man appeared at their door with the message that broke her heart: her husband was dead.

Tenderly Billy took her rough hand in his and for a time he held it and touched it gently. "We'll be all right." He heaved a great sight. "Is Matthew home?"

"Yes. Four days ago."

"Is he all right?"

"Fine."

Billy nodded. "I'll go see him tomorrow. We'd better go back to the parlor. Trudy will wonder."

Later, in the blackness of his room, Billy threw back the sheet and swung his feet to the rag rug. He had to strike the steel to the flint three times to draw a spark large enough to ignite the shredded linen, and another few seconds to transfer the flame to the lamp wick with a sliver of burning pine. The small yellow light dispelled all the demons of darkness that had tormented his sleep and awakened him, and he glanced at the small clock on the shelf beside the bed. It was fifteen minutes before one o'clock. For a moment he studied the clock. It was a John Phelps Dunson clock, beautifully carved, and accurate within thirty seconds each month. A gift from Matthew and his father, a master clockmaker and gunsmith, fifteen years before.

He turned from the clock and sat in his nightshirt, leaned forward, elbows on his knees, and the remembrances came flowing.

He was back at his desk in the Potter & Wallace Counting House, keeping records for owners of many kinds and sizes of businesses that were vibrant and thriving until hard money failed. Lacking gold or coin to support their credit, some withered, and he experienced again the pain of watching them die. The stoop-shouldered Hubert Potter was there, sharp face scowling as he shook his finger in the faces of his six employees and pounded it into them—there are many reasons a business will fail, but none so certain as to find itself lacking in gold or hard coin to back its credit. The lifeblood of commerce is gold. Hard coin. That's what feeds and clothes a family, or a city, or a country. Never forget that, he had repeated. Never!

Hubert Potter was a dour, hard-headed, practical New Englander, but for all that he had a sense of fair play, and a heart. When Billy left Boston to join the battle for liberty, Potter had promised him his old job upon his return. And now, Potter was gone. Somehow it had never occurred to Billy that Hubert Potter would ever die. Billy shook his head. Maybe the only thing that could have taken him was the loss of his beloved counting house.

Now, Potter's words rang in Billy's head.

The lifeblood of commerce is gold. Hard coin. That is what feeds and clothes nations. Never forget.

The thought brought questions that struck fear into Billy's heart.

How far has the lack of hard money spread? How many businesses and farms are gone and how many more are threatened? How many states are in trouble? Is the Continental Congress in trouble? How bad? How do I feed and take care of my family? Pay taxes? If Potter & Wallace is gone, where do I find work?

He recoiled at the next thought.

How many failed businesses and farms will it take to destroy the United States?

He sat for a long time staring vacantly at the wall in the yellow light of the single lamp before he turned down the lamp wick.

I'll see Matthew tomorrow. Maybe he'll know more.

Notes

For the ironing of clothes in colonial times see Ulrich, *Good Wives,* p. 28.

For the process of taking a bath in a wooden tub in the kitchen, see Pool, *What Jane Austen Ate and Charles Dickens Knew,* p. 201.

For the habits of women wearing bonnets in colonial America, see Earle, *Home Life in Colonial Days,* p. 285.

The reader will recall that Billy Weems was employed by the Boston firm of Potter & Wallace to keep business accounts, as what we would now call an accountant. See volume 2 of this series, *The Times That Try Men's Souls,* p. 48. Both Billy and the Potter & Wallace firm are fictional.

CHAPTER XIV

*B*illy never knew how the Dunson family learned of his homecoming, or that the Weems family was coming to see Matthew. He only knew that at nine o'clock the following morning, Margaret and her children were at the great Thorpe home standing with Matthew and Kathleen and two-year-old John at the gate, waiting for the Weems family to arrive. The morning street traffic paused to stare down their Boston noses at the unseemly sight of women hugging women, and a man hugging a man openly for all of Boston to see, amidst tears and exclamations of joy. Inside Billy, something that had been dormant too long came alive as he clutched Matthew to him, and the two embraced without a word. Billy faced Brigitte, confused, not knowing what he should do, when she stepped to him and threw her arms about him as a beloved friend. For a moment he stood stunned, and then he wrapped her in his arms and held her while his heart pounded.

Margaret clasped him to her as one of her own. "Oh, Billy. You don't know how good it is. We've worried."

Billy stopped short, staring at Adam and Prissy. "What happened?" he stammered. "You were . . . you've grown up!"

Everyone laughed.

"Come inside," Kathleen exclaimed, "while breakfast is still hot."

Billy looked at Matthew. "Breakfast?"

Matthew shrugged. "Blame the women, not me."

The house was filled with the aroma of baked ham, steaming griddle cakes, maple syrup, coffee, and milk. The huge table was set with white linen and china and crystal and silver. Billy stopped short, wide-eyed and staring, struggling to absorb it all. He looked at Kathleen.

"What's all this . . ."

She cut him off. "You're home," she exclaimed, and gave him no chance to respond as she pointed and continued, "Matthew, you there at the head of the table. Billy, the other end of the table. Dorothy—you put your family there, and Margaret, yours goes there."

They each stood by their chairs until the room quieted and Matthew spoke.

"Let us kneel."

Each knelt beside their chair, clasped their hands, and bowed their heads.

"Almighty Creator of us all, for delivering Billy back into our midst, we thank Thee. For the bounties of this table, we thank Thee . . ."

Matthew finished the prayer, everyone repeated his "amen," and the women wiped at misty eyes as they all arose to take their places at the table. For more than half an hour the cares of the world were forgotten as talk flowed and laughter abounded around the table. Platters of smoking ham and steaming griddle cakes made the rounds, were refilled, and made the second round.

Billy asked Matthew, "Are we missing Caleb?"

"You'll never guess. We put him ashore at Head of Elk with about ten wagon loads of African slaves and told him to move them north to a place they would be safe."

Billy's head thrust forward. "You *what?* Where did you . . . how did you come by ten wagon loads of African slaves?"

"Rescued them from a sinking ship." Matthew laughed out loud. "We claimed them as abandoned cargo, and I signed them over to Caleb as his property so he could show ownership if anyone challenged him. And I also made him first mate on an American ship of war. So we've got an American officer who owns ten wagon loads of slaves moving them north somewhere. Caleb has turned out to be a man of stature and property."

Billy chuckled. "Whoever would have thought?"

Coffee was poured, and they all sat for a time, sipping, talking, while they let their breakfasts settle and gathered themselves for the business of cleaning up and returning to the daunting burdens of the world in which they now lived.

Prissy and Trudy swept John into their arms and spirited him away into the parlor to dote on him, while Adam stood, unsure whether on this day he was a child, or a young man. Margaret spared him the pain of making the decision by pointing at the table, then the kitchen, and he began to carefully stack the china and carry it to the kitchen cupboard. Matthew set out the tub for washing dishes and went for water from the well while Billy put the kettles on the stove and poked kindling into the firebox.

Forty minutes later the women hung damp dish towels on the kitchen line and removed their aprons.

"Well," Margaret said, "that's finished. I'll get the men."

She walked to the backdoor and called, "You two have talked enough. We have water that needs to be dumped."

Matthew and Billy carried the wash and rinse tubs to the far back fence to dump the water into the grass while the women fled the heat of the kitchen to sit at the table in the parlor. When the men returned, Matthew faced Kathleen.

"Billy and I need some time. Could we be gone for an hour or two?"

Kathleen looked at the other two women, and Margaret shrugged. "Just as well declare this a holiday." They all laughed.

"An hour or two," Kathleen said, and the two men walked out the front door into the late morning heat. They walked steadily east, toward town, aware that there was less morning street traffic than usual for Boston. They had gone the first block before Billy spoke.

"Spent much time in town in the last four days?"

Matthew nodded. "Yes."

"Is it bad?"

"Bad."

Billy glanced at him. "Mother said Potter & Wallace closed. Them and a lot of others."

"Too many. Bankrupt. Seized by the banks."

A little time passed before Billy asked, "Anyone have any money?"

"No. Probably a million dollars in paper money in Boston, and it's worth nothing."

"State money, or Continental?"

Matthew shook his head. "Both. Some will take Massachusetts paper money at a ninety percent discount. No one will take Continental paper money at any discount."

Billy took a deep breath. "How were you paid when you were discharged? Massachusetts money or Continental?"

"Neither. A written promise from Congress to pay me in the future. You?"

Billy answered, "The same. I had to trade my musket and bayonet to get food to come home."

Matthew shook his head and said nothing.

They entered the south end of King Street and walked steadily on until they came to the closed office of Potter & Wallace, where Billy slowed and stopped. He was not prepared for the desolate feeling that rose in his breast when he saw the chain on the front door handles and the paper nailed to the door declaring the business closed under bank seizure. He cupped his hands about his eyes and leaned close to the glass in the door to peer inside. The interior was stripped of everything— tables, desks, lamps, wall murals, filing cabinets—everything. A knot rose in his stomach at the remembrance of the vibrant office he had known, and he turned away, unwilling to stare longer at the dark void inside.

They turned onto Fruit Street and walked to the wharves and docks that lined the south, east, and north sides of the Peninsula. The familiar smells of the sea and decaying fish washed up from beneath the heavy timbers, along with the aromas of spices from the Orient and rum from the West Indies drifting from the ships undulating at anchor in the harbor and tied to the docks. Dockhands of every hue and dress and language sweated as they moved the goods of the world to and from ships. But there were great vacant gaps along the docks where ships should have been tied, and the bustle of dock laborers was thinned. Those nearest Matthew and Billy paused to study them as they passed, and in their eyes was the fear that somehow these two intruders would rob them of the few days' work they had begged for and the few pennies it would put in their pockets.

Billy looked at Matthew, who shook his head and remained silent as they moved on. They passed Griffin's Wharf, with three hundred yards of open, vacant space where ships should have been moored, and Billy looked to his left at the shipping firm offices facing the sea. The doors of India Trading Limited, Worthington Corporation, and Tappan Partnership were all chained shut, and there were papers tacked to them. They walked on to Long's Wharf, then the North Battery, both directly in line with the shipping channel leading to and from the Atlantic. Four more office doors were chained shut with court papers nailed to them, two of them formerly the largest shipping firms in Boston.

They rounded the east end of the Peninsula and came to Copp's Hill where they counted two more offices that were closed, windows vacant, bank papers tacked to the doors. They turned west to walk past the Mill Pond, where Matthew gestured and they sat down on a worn bench.

"You've seen it," Matthew said quietly. "Nine shipping firms gone. Boston's in trouble. Serious."

"You tried to find a position?"

"Since the day I got home." Matthew shook his head. "Nothing. Not in the business of ships. I've tried to find other work. Anything. I'm still looking."

"Heard anything from Caleb?"

Matthew shook his head. "Not a word. Don't know where he is."

"Are the farmers around here in trouble?"

"Bad. Bankruptcies. Bank seizures."

"How about other cities? States? New York? Pennsylvania? Connecticut?"

"The newspapers say they're about the same as here. States are beginning to set up border tariffs on incoming goods to raise money. There've been bad disputes between them. The same with the major rivers. Quarrels over which states have the fishing and shipping rights."

For a time Billy sat in silent reflection while the seagulls squawked and argued over the remains of fish and refuse left on shore by the tides. Finally he turned to look at Matthew.

"Are the states going to pull apart? Are we going to lose everything we thought we had won in the past eight years?"

Matthew slowly shook his head. "I don't know. That's the direction it's all moving right now. Congress doesn't have the power to change it. The states know nothing except independence. It's possible they could go to war with each other. I can't see the end of it. I only know I have mouths to feed, and I can't find a way to do it."

"You have any money?"

"Almost none."

"Root cellar?"

"Mostly empty."

"Same with us. Am I going to have to leave Boston to find work somewhere? Move inland? You have any plans for work?"

A rare, cynical smile passed over Matthew's face. "No. I've talked with three shipping companies about a position as navigator, or captain, or first mate, or even bos'n. Nothing. I talked with a bank. They've foreclosed on so many shipping companies they'll give you one of them if you'll just assume the debts against it. Nobody's interested, because the debts are double what the line is worth, and there's no hard money to pay them. Just worthless paper currency that nobody will take. No way to pay the crews. Buy goods for resale. Food. Sailcloth. Rope. Repairs. Insurance. Books of account." He shook his head. "The shipping business is dying, and Boston with it."

"Same with counting houses. Potter & Wallace is gone, and one of the other two big ones in Boston is closed. I suppose I can learn something else, but what? The lack of hard money is bringing down the whole country."

Matthew glanced out at the Boston Back Bay. "The only thing I have is the promise of Congress to pay me some day. A lot of discharged officers are discounting those papers by ninety percent to get money to live on."

"I have the same paper. I might have to take the discount and sell it."

For a time they sat in hopeless contemplation, minds working, twisting, turning, trying to find a crack in what seemed to be a solid wall. Suddenly Billy straightened, and Matthew turned to look at him, waiting.

Billy's face was drawn down in question. "Just a minute. Did you say some banks would give a shipping firm to anyone who would assume the debts against it?"

Matthew nodded but said nothing.

"What would happen if two discharged officers put up two written congressional promises for future payment in gold or hard coin to buy a shipping company?"

Matthew's eyes widened and Billy went on.

"While I was with Potter & Wallace I had connection with most banks in Boston, one time or another. Some of them will remember me. I can tell you right now, any right-thinking banker would a lot rather have a written Congressional promise to pay in gold sometime in the future, than a note they know is absolutely worthless because it can be paid with paper currency that is worth less than the cost of the paper. What do you think?"

Matthew sat bolt upright, his mind leaping ahead. "It hadn't occurred to me."

"You run the ships. I'll run the office."

Matthew swallowed while his thoughts raced. "How do we buy merchandise? Who do we sell to with no hard money available?"

"I don't know. But if things are as bad as they look, a lot of merchants are going to be willing to make any agreements they can to stay alive. They'll have to share the risk, and some will do it."

"But who buys?"

"Maybe someone in the South. Virginia. The Carolinas. They don't have manufacturing down there like we do up here. Plows. Nails. Stoves. Anything manufactured."

Matthew thoughtfully rubbed his palms together while he slowed his mind. "I don't know. Nine shipping firms have already closed down because they couldn't find a way to survive. If they couldn't survive, why could we?"

"You may be right. So let's look at the alternative. We stay out of the shipping business and go looking for work where there is none. How far would we have to go from Boston to find something that will feed our families? Philadelphia? New York? Richmond? Charleston? Savannah? Maybe we could get land up in Vermont and farm it. Move our families up there. Any ideas?"

Matthew shook his head. "Let's take a little time and think on it."

"I agree."

They both rose and walked west, with the great green grassy slopes of the Boston Commons one block to their right. They were halfway home before Matthew broke the thoughtful silence.

"There's one more thing. Congress sent Benjamin Franklin and some others to France to work out the terms of the peace treaty with the British. They've been at it for two years now, and the news is the terms are concluded. They're just waiting to get it in writing and signed by all three countries—America, England, and France. I know John Adams was there, and that he arranged a loan from Holland that saved us after Yorktown. Maybe Franklin and Adams and Jay have arranged for other loans. Maybe from Spain, or more from Holland. If they did, and the loans are big enough, maybe there will be enough gold or coin to save the country. At least for now."

A time passed before Billy answered. "Maybe. But in the meantime, I'm going to talk to banks about using congressional promises as collateral for buying a shipping business."

Matthew nodded. "I'll talk with some companies about the same thing."

"Talk with Kathleen. And your mother. I'll talk with my family."

They walked on in silence, down the twisting street, not noticing the heat of midday or the people or the carts passing by. In their minds they were pushing and pulling and twisting the doubtful question of whether a bank, and a shipping business owner, would ever consider accepting a written promise from the Continental Congress to pay in gold at some future time.

Maybe. Maybe.

And behind that question was another.

Had Benjamin Franklin, John Adams, John Jay, and Henry Laurens gone one step beyond the peace treaty with France and England and persuaded someone—anyone—to loan the newborn United States millions of Spanish dollars or Dutch guilders or French livres to save the infant nation from collapse?

Maybe. Maybe.

They walked on through the narrow streets of Boston toward home, hating the indecision, hating the "maybes" that were leading them from the secure life they had known, steadily downward into a black, bottomless abyss.

Notes

For an excellent map of the Boston Commons and The Neck and Boston Peninsula, showing the various wharves in colonial times as named in this chapter, see Freeman, *Washington,* p. 229.

By order of Congress, Benjamin Franklin, John Jay, John Adams, and Henry Laurens negotiated the peace treaty with England, called the Paris Peace Treaty because negotiations were conducted in Paris over a two-year period. Franklin's grandson, William Temple Franklin, had been selected by Benjamin Franklin to act as scribe and secretary (McCullough, *John Adams,* pp. 278–80).

The selling or bartering by discharged soldiers of their muskets and equipment, as well as their written promises from Congress or their home state to pay them, was a common practice to get enough money for the long walk home (Martin, *Private Yankee Doodle,* pp. 279–89).

Passy, France

Early August 1783

CHAPTER XV

*T*he weight of his seventy-seven years, and the gout that plagued his legs, and the sultry heat of a late July midmorning in Passy, France, all came together to make rising from a chair, or sitting down on one, a matter of teeth-clenching torture for Benjamin Franklin. Wearing his robe and slippers, he used his cane to hobble to the table in the home he had acquired in the village bordering Paris, and laboriously settled onto his breakfast chair. His once muscular frame and square face now tended toward paunch and flesh. His eyes were a study in the lifelong discipline of shielding secrets and schemes known only to himself, and his jowls were beginning to sag. For a fleeting moment he regretted his recklessness the previous night at the sumptuous banquet and ball hosted by the Dutch Embassy in Paris.

It wasn't attending that he regretted. It was his abandon, his lack of self-discipline. He was the darling of the continent of Europe! Inventor, author, scientist, printer, businessman, politician, sage, philosopher, genius, he was the most intriguing, charming, famous person in their world, age notwithstanding! In the grand palaces and halls of kings and princes and ambassadors and foreign ministers, where every man and woman had spent a fortune on silks and satins and tailors and powdered wigs and hairdressers to be certain they were the most desirable, elegant creatures in sight, Franklin's plain, brown, colonial suit, and his refusal to wear a powdered wig drew subtle, venomous comment from the men, while it drew the most famous of the richly gowned women to him like flies to honey. If anyone wished to know where Minister Plenipotentiary Benjamin Franklin of the United States was in the unending Parisian social whirl, they simply asked which embassy was hosting the nightly banquet and ball, went there, and sought out the largest cluster of richly appointed women. Franklin would be in the center, standing out like an aging turkey among young peacocks, smiling, kissing hands, shamelessly flattering every woman within earshot, whispering confidences into waiting ears, entering into the quadrilles and waltzes with the most dazzling dancing partners, toasting with the costliest champagne in France, holding forth until past two o'clock in the morning, and groaning with remorse as his crippled legs and hips took the bumpy cobblestone ride back to his residence in Passy.

For a moment Franklin looked out the window beside the table, taken by the myriad of roses and lilies set in banks and rows in the small garden. He tucked the large white napkin beneath his ample chin, poured steaming hot chocolate into a china cup, and closed one eye to gingerly sip at it. He smacked singed lips and reached for a thick slice of toasted brown bread and a knife to spread butter and strawberry jam. Hot, sweet chocolate sided by rich French bread and butter, topped with too much strawberry jam was his panacea for his wastrel ways. He was using a small spoon to dig the last morsels of a poached egg from the shell when a knock came at his door.

"Yes," he called, "I'm here. Come in." He turned, smiling, calling to his grandson in the parlor. "William? That you?"

"Yes, sir. Just came to report that—"

"Come in here," Franklin called. "Have a chair. Some toast and jam. The French have a way with strawberry jam."

The young man appeared in the doorway. "Just came to remind you that the others will be here at eleven o'clock. Is there anything you wish me to do that is not done?"

Franklin pursed his mouth in thought. "You have six copies of the final draft of the treaty?"

"Yes."

"My notes?"

"Yes."

Franklin shrugged. "That should be all."

"Good. I'll come for you when they're in the library."

Franklin gestured. "Won't you have some of this bread and jam?"

"I've had breakfast, thank you."

Thirty minutes later William again rapped at the door, then assisted Franklin with his cane down the hall and into the library. Franklin nodded to the others as he made his way to his large, overstuffed chair near the stone fireplace, leaned his cane against the padded arm, and slowly lowered himself into the cushions.

"Ah, there," he sighed as he looked about, smiling. "Gentlemen, it's good of you to come. Hopefully we can conclude this business of the treaty. William, do these gentlemen have copies of the final draft? Do you have one?"

"Yes."

"May I have my notes?"

William handed him two sheets of paper, and Franklin spent several seconds working with his spectacles as he read them. He raised his head and looked at the four silent, waiting men.

To his left, John Jay. Tall, slender, hawk-nosed, hawk-faced, born to wealth in New York, Jay moved with a slight, unconscious air of haughtiness. A keen mind and a native tendency to speak his thoughts freely brought him to Congress, where he had distinguished himself. His peers selected their rising star to represent the United States in Spain in the hope his talents could sway the courteous but intractable King Charles III to loan gold or Spanish dollars to the desperate American cause. Jay not only failed, he was embittered at the condescending Spanish aloofness that proved to be an impenetrable wall. He was all too happy at the end of his second year to receive orders to abandon the failed Spanish effort and join Benjamin Franklin and John Adams in Paris in their monumental efforts to strike a peace treaty with the defeated British. He arrived with renewed enthusiasm and became one of the few living men who got on acceptably well with John Adams, who was ten years his senior.

John Adams of Massachusetts. Shorter than average, stocky, regular features, receding hairline, he was also obstinate, defiant, and opinionated. When John Adams reached a conclusion on anything, it became instantly and irrevocably the only conclusion for all right-thinking, reasonable men. To be sure, his dedication to the American cause, vision, and industry was constant and recognized by his peers to be rare indeed. But from all outward appearances, it never occurred to Mr. Adams that he could commit error in his thought processes, and his self-confidence was exceeded only by his colossal ability to ignore the credentials and station of those whom he chose to shred to make himself understood; and that included King Louis XVI himself, to whom Adams sent notes and letters that at once demeaned the King and elevated Mr. Adams. Mr. Adams's methods of conducting politics and negotiations had much more in common with the hammer of a blacksmith, than those of a skilled statesman. It was Mr. Adams who ripped into the peace negotiations so vociferously that the Comte de Vergennes of France, the prime minister appointed by King Louis XVI to handle all matters of state, furiously delivered three monstrous letters.

The first was to Mr. Adams himself: "His Majesty does not stand in need of your solicitations to direct his attention to the interests of the United States."

The second was to Mr. Benjamin Franklin, together with a collection of the notes and letters Mr. Adams had written to enlighten both the King and Vergennes. With the Adams notes and letters, over his own signature, Vergennes had bluntly informed Franklin, "His Majesty expects that you will lay the whole before Congress."

The third was to La Luzerne, the French representative in Philadelphia where Congress was in session: "You are directed to do all possible to have Mr. Adams recalled."

Thoughtfully Franklin wrote his own missive to Congress, candidly and brutally calling out the fact Adams had badly mauled just about everybody involved in the peace effort, thoroughly wrecked a substantial part of what had been accomplished, and appeared to be blindly dedicated to finishing his destruction. Franklin concluded his letter:

"Mr. Vergennes, who appears much offended, told me yesterday that he would enter into no further discussions with Mr. Adams, nor answer any more of his letters . . ."

It was at that time that Mr. Adams was spared what had the makings of either his political demise in France, or a devastating international incident, by voluntarily announcing to Franklin that he was departing Paris at once, in favor of going to Holland to see ". . . whether something might be done to render us less dependent on France."

No one was more relieved than Vergennes to see Mr. Adams depart France, and Vergennes instantly and happily provided the passports and documents to accommodate his leaving. Eventually Mr. Adams succeeded in persuading a reluctant Holland to recognize the United States as a free and independent nation, securing for the newborn member of the international community, a loan from three Dutch banks of two million dollars at five percent per annum interest. Then he returned to his duties in Paris, to learn of the letter written by Franklin to the United States Congress. Furious, he fumed, recovered, and passed it off by declaring to himself that the sole motive Franklin would ever have in writing such a horrific accusation was Franklin's base jealousy of Adams.

Henry Laurens. Tall, well-built, handsome, brilliant, once vice president of the state of South Carolina, Henry Laurens had been ordered by Congress to Amsterdam in late 1780 with a secret draft of a proposed treaty between the United States and the Netherlands. Disaster struck when Laurens's ship was captured by a British man-of-war and alert British seamen saw Laurens throw the document into the sea. They fished it from the water and presented it, along with Laurens, before a British court. The charge was high treason. The secret treaty, innocuous at best, was enough for the British court to convict Laurens and sentence him to be held prisoner in the Tower of London indefinitely, with orders that "no person whatever speaks to him."

There Laurens remained, languishing, health in serious decline, until the Americans shocked the world at Yorktown by capturing General Charles Cornwallis and his entire army in October 1781. An exchange of prisoners was arranged—Cornwallis for Laurens—and thereupon

Congress ordered Laurens to proceed to Paris to assist Franklin and the group then concluding the terms of the peace treaty with England. Plagued by ill health, and struggling to recover from two years of solitary confinement in a cold stone tower, Laurens was at times subdued, quiet, reflective, but in all, valuable in his efforts to secure the terms of peace.

Of the group of Americans, it was John Jay who most often provided the oil to calm the troubled waters that sometimes roiled between Benjamin Franklin and John Adams, and it was Franklin's profound insights into the nature of human beings and his extraordinary grasp of the ways of the world that undergirded much of the thought that structured the treaty.

With young William Temple Franklin, grandson of Benjamin Franklin, serving as secretary and scribe, this collection of strongly opinionated, talented men had met for nearly two years with the two men appointed by King George III, Richard Oswald, assisted by Henry Strachey. Oswald, an elderly Scot who, though blind in one eye, had amassed a fortune in government contracts, tended to favor the independence of the Americans. A disturbed Lord Shelburne, First Lord of the Treasury in the cabinet of King George III of England, sensed Oswald's weakness, and immediately sent Henry Strachey to assist Oswald, with orders to "stiffen Oswald's resolve."

For well over a year these opposing teams had met in formal negotiations, either at Jay's lodgings at the Hotel d'Orleans on the Rue des Petits-Augustins on the Left Bank, or at Adams's Hotel du Roi, or at the Hotel de Valentinois at Passy when Franklin's gout would not tolerate the carriage ride into Paris, or at the quarters of Oswald at the Grand Hotel Muscovite on the Rue des Petits-Augustins.

With Adams relentlessly pounding, Jay lending nominal support and reconciliation between the others, Laurens raising a more moderate voice, and Franklin providing insights, it soon became obvious, although never articulated, that the two Britons, trained in politics as they were, fell short of being a match for the four self-educated Americans. With stubborn resolve the Yankees won major concessions as the two opposing groups slowly forged the concluding terms of the treaty. Franklin let it rest for a few weeks while the British team returned to London to report to their own King and Parliament, then, as senior member of the American delegation, called his associates to meet with him in the library of his residence. Franklin knew only too well how second thoughts and crafty maneuvers in such matters could lay waste the finalized work of years. Under any circumstance, Franklin was not going to allow Adams, or Jay, to hold the two nations hostage at the last moment by stubbornly refusing to sign the treaty until one of their discarded pet proposals was added to the finished document. It did not take long for Franklin's nimble mind to devise a scheme to accomplish this, and at the same time avoid giving offense to either Adams or Jay: He called them together in his quarters for a meeting to solidify their understanding.

Franklin glanced at his colleagues and smiled amicably. "Gentlemen, it now appears the formalities of signing the treaty will occur sometime in September. Ahh, it occurred to me that our worthy opponents might attempt to recover some of what they've given us by laying down an eleventh-hour ultimatum. Either we concede on some of the major points, or they refuse to sign."

Adams was vociferous. Jay was loquacious. Laurens was thoughtful. Franklin was noncommittal.

"It seemed to me that we would be wise to anticipate such a man-euver. So I requested your presence here for a brief review of the terms as they now stand. If we are clear in our minds on all points, and if we are united, we will be much better prepared for any such nonsense should it occur. Rest assured, if Mr. Oswald or Mr. Strachey finds a difference among us, they will waste no time driving a wedge. Don't you agree?"

There was no question. All agreed.

"Very good. Now, let's run a brief review to be certain there will be no divisions among us. You each have a copy of the major elements of the treaty, and I invite you to follow me. Should there be any questions, now is the time to resolve them.

"Let us begin. The British have conceded that the United States is an independent nation, to be recognized and dealt with as an equal in the community of nations."

Franklin looked at each man in turn, and each nodded assent.

"Moving on. The United States has the primary right of navigation on the Mississippi River." He paused for a moment. "Time and the needs of commerce will prove this to be an invaluable asset to the growth of America. Agreed?"

There was silent agreement.

"Next. Americans will have free rights to take fish of all descriptions on the Grand Banks off Newfoundland."

Franklin looked at Adams, who had made it abundantly clear that the New England fishermen would have those rights, or there would be no treaty. Adams glowed with his victory, and Franklin said, "The New Englanders shall be forever grateful, good sir." He turned back to his notes.

"Most critical. The British shall cede all territory between the Appalachian Mountains on the east, and the Mississippi on the west, to the United States, free and clear of any and all claims of any description."

The men looked at each other, still staggered by the fact that this provision instantly doubled the size of the United States. All heads nodded in agreement.

Franklin again studied his notes for a few seconds. "Extremely critical. All private debts contracted by Americans with British merchants prior to the outbreak of hostilities between the two countries, shall remain valid and enforceable."

Again Franklin paused and looked at John Jay. "Are you at peace with this, sir?"

For a moment Jay hesitated. It was he and Franklin who had argued that all such debts had been more than counterbalanced by the American properties seized or destroyed by the British in the course of the war. It was Adams and Laurens who had taken the view that debts incurred in good faith should be paid, regardless of the ravages of American property by the British during the terrible war years.

"Yes," Jay finally answered, and Franklin went on.

"And finally, gentlemen, we have the very unpleasant issue of whether or not the United States shall pay compensation to the Loyalists whose property was seized or destroyed when they refused to stand with us and fled to safety elsewhere." He shook his head. "I can think of a great number of alternative solutions to the Loyalist problem, most of which include giving them something far removed from compensation."

John Jay cracked a wry smile, and John Adams spoke hotly. "Would some of those solutions include a rope?"

Franklin grinned. "I drafted at least six such solutions, but didn't have the heart to deliver them to our worthy opponents. Besides, it was obvious we had to make some concessions to Mr. Strachey. He had to return to London with at least one bone to throw to King and Parliament. After all, we doubled our size, got the Mississippi, and can fish the Grand Banks forever. Giving the Loyalists some token compensation for loss of their property will be a pittance compared to the profits we will reap from those gains."

He pursed his mouth for a moment before continuing. "So. Are we agreed that the United States will not pay; however, we will request the separate states to provide some form of compensation for property confiscated by the states?"

He waited until all heads had nodded agreement.

Everyone in the room recognized the signs when Franklin cleared his throat, leaned back in his chair, and adjusted his spectacles; something profound, or enigmatic, or both, was coming. The room fell silent as Franklin leaned forward and spoke with measured tones.

"Gentlemen, do any of you have unspoken reservations on any part of this treaty?"

There was movement and a thoughtful silence in the room for a time while each man considered the question.

Franklin continued, and there was iron in his voice. His eyes were flat, expressionless. "Now is the time to commit yourselves. It would be a disaster to reach the day of the formal signing and discover there are terms yet to be decided. Or that there are yet differences among us concerning those terms already agreed."

Adams recognized they had just heard the real reason Franklin had called the meeting. He started to speak, but remained silent as he realized the trap had already been sprung. He could not object without contradicting the commitments he had made but moments earlier, a thing his vanity and pride would not allow.

Franklin started with John Jay, and met the eyes of every man in turn, asking the silent question, and receiving the silent answer.

They were agreed.

Franklin drew and released a great breath, and his expression changed in an instant. Once again he was the sagacious, sometimes amiable, sometimes offensive, sometimes jocular, always unpredictable, Franklin.

"My thanks to you all. My sense of it is that history will pay homage to each of you for your contribution. I know of no treaty that embraces such profound possibilities as the one you have helped create."

He drew his watch from his pocket and studied it for a moment, then turned to his grandson.

"William, it's five minutes before noon. Would you be so kind as to go to the kitchen and ask my housekeeper if lunch is ready? Mrs. Fontaine promised she would have something suitable for this occasion by twelve o'clock sharp." He smiled as the young man left the library. "Gentlemen, this sort of thing gives me a ravenous appetite. Will you join me in the dining room?"

Notes

The persons described in this chapter, their appearance, personal characteristics, background, experience, and participation in the process of negotiating the peace treaty between the United States, France, and Britain, are all accurately set forth. The places the negotiations took place are correctly named. The hot confrontation between John Adams and the French Comte de Vergennes is accurate. The letters sent by Vergennes, Franklin, and Adams are as described, and parts are quoted verbatim herein. John Adams did leave Paris for

Holland, where he secured a two million dollar (five million Dutch guilders) loan for the United States. He returned to Paris thereafter, discovered the letters sent by Vergennes and Franklin to the American Congress, was infuriated, but finally passed it off as being the product of Franklin's base jealousy of Adams. The British delegation, Richard Oswald and Henry Strachey, are accurately described. Strachey was sent by Lord Shelburne, First Lord of the Treasury, to bolster Oswald, a one-eyed, wealthy Scot, who was felt to be too lenient with the Americans. The basic terms of the treaty are as discussed herein. The interplay between Franklin, Adams, Jay, and Laurens is correctly described. Henry Laurens, once vice president of South Carolina, was captured by the British en route to Europe to join in the negotiations, tried for high treason, convicted, and sentenced to be imprisoned in the Tower of London, with orders that he was to speak with no one whosoever. He was later exchanged for the British prisoner, General Charles Cornwallis, and despite poor health was sent on to Paris for the last portion of the peace treaty negotiations (Bernstein, *Are We to Be a Nation?*, pp. 33–34; McCullough, *John Adams*, pp. 239–80; Leckie, *George Washington's War*, p. 228; Mackesy, *The War for America, 1775–1783*, see the chart of the British Cabinet found following page xxvi in the forepart, showing Lord Shelburne as First Lord of the Treasury).

CHAPTER XVI

*F*ollowing the tumultuous upheavals in England leading up to the year 1629, the despotic King Charles I granted a royal charter to an insistent group of Puritans determined to seek a new life in the wilds of a vast, unexplored, primeval land far to the west, across the barrier of the wild Atlantic Ocean. The charter included those lands on the new continent from three miles south of the Charles River to a point three miles north of the Merrimac River, and extending from the Atlantic Ocean westward to the Pacific Ocean.

Therein Charles made two seemingly insignificant mistakes that eventually changed the history of the world.

First, the language of the charter omitted the usual ironclad rule that the seat of government for the newly formed colony would remain in England. The result was simple. The seat of government was with the new colony, in the new land. In short, the Pilgrims and Puritans were given a free hand to govern themselves, independent of British control. Thus, by simple oversight, King Charles I had planted the tiny seed that blossomed into the American Revolution, for once those Pilgrims and Puritans tasted the sweetness of self-rule, they would never again willingly submit to a foreign authority, including their own Mother Country.

Second, at that time, the world thought the Pacific Ocean was but a short distance from the Atlantic Ocean; most assuredly not three thousand miles away. King Charles had no way to know that in granting claim to all the land west of the tiny colony he had given away hundreds of millions of acres of some of the richest land on the face of the earth.

The small band of Puritans crossed the stormy Atlantic, titled themselves "The Massachusetts Bay Company," and chose John Winthrop, a just and goodly man of wealth and education, to be their first governor, with Thomas Dudley the deputy governor. Within days of his arrival in the colony, Governor Winthrop toured the grant of land, and found himself on a peninsula called Shawmut by the Indians. With access to the Atlantic Ocean on three sides, Winthrop saw at once that the peninsula offered unparalleled access for sea-going commerce and trade. When he discovered a spring of clear, sweet, running water on the peninsula, the matter was settled. It was here that he would build his own estate and the town that would become the center of the new colony.

The name of the town would be Boston.

Through the shifting winds of politics, the Salem witch trials, conflicts with angry Indians, the radical views of the zealots Roger Williams, Anne Hutchinson, and Henry Vane, harsh winters, hot summers, a failed attempt to impose taxes, and an abandoned effort by King Charles I to revoke their charter, the fledgling town prospered and grew. By the turn of the seventeenth century it was a major seaport in the new world. By 1750, it was among the leading cities in the thirteen colonies. On the eighteenth day of April, 1775, it witnessed the march of eight hundred British regulars from the Boston Commons across the Back Bay to Lexington and Concord, and their return the night of the nineteenth day of April, an army shattered and defeated by rebellious American countryfolk. By 1782, the city had survived the ravages of the war and seen the British abandon America. By September of 1783, it was a frightened, dying town, with bankruptcies rampant, and too many desperate unemployed walking the streets, willing to take any work that would pay even pennies a day.

In the afterglow of a sun already set, Billy Weems stood waiting at the backdoor of the large stone home of Erastus Pembroke, near the Boston Commons, wiping at the sweat on his face with a damp shirtsleeve. His ax was leaned against the door frame, and to his left, stacked against the back wall beneath a sheltering overhang, were six cords of split kindling, half soft pine, half hard oak, stockpiled against the cold of oncoming fall and winter. Beside the kindling was a huge covered box, half filled with the burned ashes Billy had carefully swept from the two great fireplaces in the mansion. Sometime in November, when the box was full, Billy would spend two days mixing the ash with lye and hot water to make soap for the winter.

Erastus Pembroke, bent with age, white-haired, had inherited the home, and a fortune, from the Pembroke estate, and rumor held that despite the war and the destitution that now gripped the United States, he still had most of the original coin from the wealth of his forebears. Because he was never seen frequenting a bank, it was whispered that the family treasure was buried, either on the grounds surrounding the home or in a secret vault behind the tons of stones and cement that formed the two massive fireplaces. Erastus, a childless widower for thirty-three years, conducted his business of investments from his library, used servants to shop for all household needs, avoided direct contact with the world whenever he could, and paid for everything in coin, some of them Spanish dollars bearing dates in the late seventeenth century.

Rapid footsteps sounded inside the mansion, and Billy waited while the heavy-hinged door swung open. A portly man with a face devoid of emotion held out his thick hand.

"One half-dollar."

One half-dollar for cleaning two large fireplaces and splitting six cords of wood, three of them oak hardwood, was less than half a fair price. Billy reached for the coin, and the house servant avoided his eyes as he dropped it into Billy's open palm.

Billy spoke as he pushed the money into his pocket. "Thank you. Will you have need for more wood?"

"You will receive word."

"The soap? In November?"

"One dollar."

"Thank you."

The door closed firmly as Billy shouldered his ax and walked the narrow path that led from the servants' entrance to the street. He turned to his right and strode steadily west into the onset of dusk, head down, preoccupied, struggling with the fear that now gripped half the town: how would he put food on the family table during the winter? Pay the taxes?

He walked, oblivious to the nearly indiscernible change that spoke of the storms of fall and the snows of winter that were coming. He did not notice the first tints of yellow and red that had touched some of the leaves on the trees lining the Boston streets. Squirrels already showing the beginnings of their winter hair darted, curled tails cocked over their backs, as they scolded the few passersby, but Billy did not hear them. He came to the white picket fence that still needed paint he could not buy, pushed through the gate, and walked into the small home.

"Is that you, Billy?" Dorothy called from the kitchen.

"Yes. Has Matthew been here?" he answered, as he passed through the archway into the kitchen. He opened the cupboard above the window and drew out a jar from the top shelf, dropped the half-dollar into it, then replaced it.

Dorothy watched and turned her head at the pittance Billy had earned for a full day's hard work.

"Yes," she answered, "he'll be back in half an hour. Get washed. Trudy and I have already had supper."

Minutes later he sat down at the dining room table to boiled cabbage and the remains of a mutton roast from the previous Sunday. He said a hasty grace, and in pensive silence mechanically ate his supper. Dorothy saw his need to be alone and quietly busied herself and Trudy in the kitchen. Billy finished, stacked his dishes, and brought them to the kitchen cupboard. He was reaching for the dish washing tub when Matthew's knock came at the door. Thirty seconds later the two were seated at the dining table, with Dorothy and Trudy standing in the kitchen, arms folded, heads bowed, listening intently. Matthew wasted no time or words.

"The British and Americans signed the peace treaty September ninth."

Billy came to instant focus. "How do you know?"

"A schooner just arrived from Calais."

"Just the British and Americans? What happened to the French?"

"The Americans signed without them. Franklin and Adams and Jay thought we needed to assert ourselves independent of France. It offended the French."

Billy started. "After what France did for us? Without them we'd have lost the war!"

Matthew threw one hand in the air. "It's done. Franklin went so far as to ask France to loan us more money. Six million livres. They didn't answer. There is no more money coming from Europe to help us, at least not right now. And even if France does relent and loan us the six million livres, it's not enough to make a difference."

Billy shook his head in shocked amazement but remained silent.

Matthew took a heavy breath and leaned forward, eyes narrowed. "That's not the worst of it. July second—nearly a month before the treaty was signed—the British issued an Order of Council that prohibits absolutely all American ships from trade with the West Indies."

Matthew stopped and watched Billy's eyes widen, and then Billy straightened and leaned back in his chair.

"The West Indies? How much of American shipping trade has been to the West Indies? Half?"

"More than half. Salt, fish, timber, rice, indigo, meat, cloth, whale oil, nails, shipbuilding—there's hardly an end to it. Now it's all illegal. Finished as of July second."

Billy's mind was leaping ahead. "How will the West Indies get—" He stopped, then exclaimed, "Smuggling! They've thrown the whole thing open to smugglers! The fools! The entire British navy isn't big enough to stop the smuggling that's going to start!"

"It's coming."

"Why? What's the gain for the British?"

Matthew shook his head. "Only the British know. I think this is partly their way of hurting us because we won the war, and partly a way to get the profits of dealing with the West Indies."

Billy shook his head. "What profits? Do they think they can ship goods from England as cheaply as we can from here? Or even from Nova Scotia? Wait until the traders in the West Indies find out the cost of freight from England or Canada. They won't survive. Can't the British see that?"

"I don't know. I think they'll make short-term gains that will hurt us, but in the long-term . . . disaster."

For a time the two sat in stony silence, stretching their minds beyond what had been for all their lives, to the horrendous shock of what had come to pass.

Matthew wiped at his mouth. "One more thing. Until now all ships built in American shipyards were considered British. They could use all ports that admitted British ships, both here and in Europe." He shook his head. "No more. Now we're an independent nation, and all our commercial ships have to make new agreements with all ports."

Billy was incredulous. "That'll take years."

"And millions of dollars."

For a moment Billy's shoulders sagged, then squared once again, and he quietly asked the foundation question. "Is there any reason to think we can feed our families by going into the carrying trade?"

In the kitchen, Dorothy and Trudy raised their heads, focused, waiting.

"Eight years ago, the answer would have been no. But now, with things the way they are, the real question isn't about the carrying trade. The real question is, what else is there? Businesses, farms, banks, shops— closing everywhere, bankruptcies, good men begging for work."

He stopped, and the house was filled with dead silence for a time, and then Matthew continued, his voice filled with the desperate, angry sound of a man left with no way to survive.

"Do you know of anything that will be better than a shipping firm? Farming? Manufacturing? Mercantile? They're in worse condition than shipping. What do you know better than keeping business accounts? What do I know better than the sea?"

Billy began to slowly rub his palms together, probing for a ray of light in the blackness, and there was none.

Matthew went on. "There are a few things in favor of shipping."

Billy stopped rubbing his palms and looked at Matthew, waiting. In the kitchen, Dorothy and Trudy were barely breathing.

"There are a half dozen shipping firms that can be bought for just about nothing. Take over the debts."

Billy said nothing.

"There are good crews on the docks that will go to work for nothing but a promise to pay them if you make a profit. They'd rather take the risk of having something later than knowing there will be nothing at all."

Billy asked, "Customers? You said the British and most European ports are closed. Who will buy?"

"Don't go to Europe. Trade up and down our own coast. New England manufacture for Southern rice and tobacco."

"Tobacco's been down."

"It's coming back."

"How do you buy New England manufacture?"

"I don't know yet. But I do know there are manufacturers that will be bankrupt in six months if they don't do something, and I think they'd be just like the sailors on the docks. They'd rather take a risk on getting something than live with the fact they'll get nothing if they don't take a chance."

Billy straightened, mind working. "You're talking about something like a partnership. Get a ship owner and a crew and a seller and a buyer all together and make a deal. We all take a chance we can make a contract work. If it does, we all get paid. If it doesn't, we're no worse off than we are now."

"I can't think of anything better. Can you?"

Billy shook his head. "No. Talked to any shipping firms?"

"You remember Covington and Sons?"

"Yes. I did their books of account for one year."

"They're in trouble. Talking about closing their office. Either the bank takes it back, or they enter bankruptcy."

"I heard."

"They have six ships. Carried a lot of indigo and rice to Holland and France until the market died. I talked to Thomas Covington again yesterday. Offered to take his business if he'll accept the written promise Congress gave to pay my two years' salary in the future. He's thinking about it. I know he'll ask for a written guarantee that if Congress doesn't pay, I will. I told him I wanted to think on it, but I would not guarantee pay in less than eight years."

Billy's eyes were narrow slits as he listened, working with the pieces of the puzzle, making judgments as Matthew went on.

"His ships are sound—I've gone through them."

"Six ships? That will cost. What price is he asking for his business?"

"Take over the bank loan. He can't pay it. That's around sixteen thousand pounds, British sterling. His problem is that the notes he signed are falling due and he can't pay. The question isn't how much his ships are worth, the question is how can he avoid losing everything when he fails to pay his notes? Without money to make deals, the whole country's been working on credit. If Covington can't pay, his credit reputation will be ruined, and if that happens, he'll likely never get back into business at all."

"If he can't pay the notes, how can we? We don't have the money either."

"We don't pay the notes. We give him the promise of Congress to pay me, and he gives that to the bank and his creditors. It all depends on whether they will accept it."

"If all that happens, who buys the goods?"

"Someone in the South. They have almost no manufacturing down there."

"Can they pay in hard money?"

"Likely not, but they can pay in tobacco and rice."

"Where do we sell tobacco and rice?"

"Sell to British firms. There's a big tobacco market in Europe, and the West Indies are already starting to feel the need for rice. They've got slaves down there that are starving, right now. American ships can't sell in the West Indies, but British ships can, and they'll learn soon enough that they can buy rice here and sell it in the West Indies a lot cheaper than shipping it across the Atlantic."

Billy smiled, then chuckled out loud, then sobered. "While I was with Potter & Wallace, if a client had walked in with a business plan like this one, I'd have sent him somewhere else to keep their books of account. Have you counted the times the word *if* has come up in all this?"

"Every part of it is an *if*. But the biggest *if* is, what do we do if we don't make this work?"

There was a pause before Billy answered. "I don't know."

"What about Covington? If he comes back with a counteroffer, what're your thoughts?"

"Depends. If it's much worse than what you've offered, maybe we should look somewhere else."

"I'll do that. Why don't you ask around at other business account offices? Try to find manufacturers who might be interested."

"Agreed."

Matthew stood. "You have enough money to stay alive a few weeks?"

"Close. Earned half a dollar today."

"How?"

"Split six cords of wood. Cleaned two fireplaces."

"Six cords? For half a dollar? For who? Who would do that to you?"

"Erastus Pembroke."

"Yes, Pembroke would do that. I didn't know you knew him."

"I don't. Someone told him they knew a man who could split six cords of wood in one day for half a dollar, and clean two fireplaces besides."

Matthew started for the front door, Billy beside him.

"I get the feeling that winning the war was the easier part of this business of becoming independent. We had General Washington. He did his part. The question is, who's going to step up to lead us now?"

Billy opened the front door. "I imagine Washington will be around, but I doubt he's ready to take on the sort of trouble we're in right now."

Matthew sighed. "So far, nobody seems to know what to do. I know Hamilton and Robert Morris have about given up on it."

"Washington's been visiting a lot of people and places he's had to neglect the past eight years. When he finishes maybe he'll find a way through all this."

For a moment Matthew pondered. "Maybe. I wonder where he is right now. If he does take the time, do you think he can find a way?"

"I think he's south, near New York. Wants to see the officers he served with one last time. Maybe address Congress. He's a soldier, not a banker. Or merchant. I don't know if he can find a way out of the trouble. I don't know if any one man can do it. I don't even know if it can be done."

Matthew stopped outside the door. "One thing. We can't wait to find out. You ask around the counting houses about merchants. I'll cover the docks about shipping firms. Something will happen. It has to."

Notes

The practice of doing business on credit, that is, promissory notes that were passed from one merchant to another, as described in this chapter, was common in 1783. Lacking hard money, such promissory notes were essentially used as currency (Bernstein, *Are We to Be a Nation?*, pp. 8, 9).

The disastrous collapse of the American economic system that began in the late 1770 time frame had reached catastrophic proportions by 1783. There was almost no gold or hard coin to support all the paper currency, which became essentially worthless. On July 2, 1783, England did issue an Order in Council that barred American ships from doing business in the West Indies, an act that seriously crippled American shipping. September 9, 1783, the peace treaty was signed in Paris by England and America, without notice to the French that such was happening. Adams and Franklin both felt America needed to assert herself as independent from France, which was taken as a serious insult by the French. The result was that American ships lost their right to enter foreign ports as British ships, but were required to establish their own credit and rights with foreign ports. It was another serious setback. Merchants in nearly every industry were catastrophically damaged by the loss of trade.

For a succinct, accurate description of the calamity, including charts and tables setting forth the reduction of shipping in certain crucial industries, see Morris, *The Forging of the Union*, pp. 130–61.

CHAPTER XVII

★ ★ ★

*T*he twenty American army officers came in ones and twos, on foot and in carriages, in the cold morning sunlight of late November, down the crooked cobblestone streets of New York City to lower Wall Street, then on to Fraunces Tavern at the corner of Broad and Pearl streets. They came strangely quiet, unexpectedly subdued, pondering the startling request of their commander in chief to gather for a meeting. It was not an order. It was an invitation to those officers still remaining in or close by New York City. The last of the defeated British army had sailed out of New York harbor but hours earlier, and the American officers had rather expected celebration and dancing in the streets, but instead, General Washington had requested their appearance at the tavern to share with him a last meal together. They could not remember him ever issuing a request. For eight years he had issued orders. They came questioning, unsure.

Their boots thumped hollow on the stairs leading up to the long, dark paneled room on the second floor of the tavern where a large table was spread for a banquet. They gathered into small groups, some sitting, some standing, prepared for the usual barracks banter and jocularity of comrades in arms. None anticipated the odd quiet that settled over the room to make boisterousness seem inappropriate. They spoke little as they peered about with the growing awareness that the event was reaching far beyond expectation.

General von Steuben, ever efficient, drew his watch from his vest pocket to check the time. He was twisting the stem to wind it when the door opened, and General Washington entered the room. Instantly every man in the room was on his feet, standing at attention. It was then that the realization struck home. This was their last gathering as the hard core of officers who had stood with the tall man in the doorway, through the dark years to the bright morning of victory. This day would close a chapter in history that had changed the world forever, and before them stood the man with whom they had carried the whole of it on their shoulders for eight years. This was the benediction of the Revolutionary War.

None had ever seen the expression they now saw on Washington's face. The blue-gray eyes swept the room with a sense of tenderness, and there was a discernible gentleness in the set of his jaw and chin. He nodded to those nearest as he made his way to his seat at the head of the table, and they waited until he had taken his chair before they all sat down as one. The room fell silent as grace was said and then the chefs came with their prepared platters of steaming beef and ham, potatoes, yams, nuts, berries, cheeses of all kinds, and breads. They set them on the table and stood back while the officers quietly passed them and began filling their plates while memories of scenes they thought they had forgotten came rushing to push all thoughts of food from their minds.

They saw Washington in the agony of defeat on Long Island, then White Plains, and Manhattan Island, and they saw his shattered, panic-driven army running southwest across New Jersey to cross the Delaware River to McKonkie's Ferry on the Pennsylvania side in the desperate hope the river would somehow stop the red-coated British regulars and the blue- and green-coated Germans with them. They saw him as a shadow on the wall of his tent at night on the frozen banks of the river as he paced inside, shoulders shaking as he wept in the knowledge that he had failed his men, and his country. They remembered his impossible order that on Christmas Day, 1776, he was taking what was left of his freezing, starving, barefooted command back across the Delaware in large Durham freight boats, at night, in the midst of a howling blizzard— men, horses, and cannon—and they were going to take Trenton from the fourteen hundred German Hessians sent by British General Howe to hold the Continental soldiers on the riverbank until the entire army was dead. They remembered the midnight crossing—the nine-mile march by barefooted men who left blood from their feet in the snow and ice—the attack at eight o'clock in the blizzard on December twenty-sixth—the ninety-minute battle—the American cannon clearing King, Queen, and Quaker streets—the loss by the Germans of four hundred soldiers and the surrender of the one thousand remaining in their command.

And they remembered most of all the impossible announcement by Washington that the Americans had suffered only two wounded enlisted men and two wounded officers in the frenzied, house-by-house, street-by-street, face-to-face fight in the tiny village; not one American had lost his life. None would ever forget the certainty that swelled in their breasts that the Almighty had crossed the river with them, and been in the streets with them, that stormy December morning when they had risen from the ruins of catastrophy to defeat a command from the most powerful army in the world.

They saw General Washington sitting his gray horse like a statue on the wooden bridge that spanned Assunpink Creek at the south end of tiny Trenton village, as Colonel Edward Hand of the Pennsylvania militia led his six hundred men in a classic retreat down the streets of the town at dusk, stubbornly holding at each house, each barn, each shop, slowing the infuriated General Cornwallis and his eight thousand troops to a standstill. They saw the cannon flashes in the deep purple of oncoming night as the American cannoneers blasted the first ranks of the British to stop them in their tracks and prevent the redcoats from pinning the American army against the Delaware River and annihilating it altogether as night fell.

They remembered the midnight march around General Cornwallis's camp, then north to attack Princeton. Burned into their memories forever was the sight of Washington, one of the best horsemen in the state of Virginia, turning in his saddle to listen to the rattle of musketfire a mile behind, and the ride he made at stampede gait on his tall gray mare, to rally the green, retreating Pennsylvania militia. Riding in front of the terrified Pennsylvanians, he talked them across an open meadow six hundred yards wide, into the face of a British command under British Colonel Mawhood, row upon row, waiting for the Americans. Mawhood held until the Americans were so close he could see the buttons on their shirts before he raised his hand to give his command to fire, but he was two seconds too late. Washington shouted his order first, and the American volley ripped into the stunned redcoats, scattered them running in a frantic, disorganized retreat. Princeton was taken.

They again heard the muskets and cannon at Brandywine Creek, and then at Germantown, where thick morning fog had confused the battle lines beyond any hope of coordination.

They remembered, and they sat in the warmth of the fireplace, and the security of the tavern, and they looked at the choice food piled smoking on the platters, and on their china plates, and they quietly stopped working with their forks as remembrances of December 19, 1777, came bright and vivid. General Washington was there on his tall bay gelding, caped shoulders and tricorn hat white from the falling snow, face set like granite as he watched his battered army file past to the place called Valley Forge, twenty-six miles northerly from Philadelphia, where General Howe was headquartered with his British army.

The large, sunken eyes of sick men starving to death one day at a time—serving picket duty in January wearing a summer coat at midnight at nine degrees below zero, barefooted, standing on a felt hat to keep their feet from freezing to the ground—cutting off their own dead, black, swollen toes with belt knives to stop the spread of gangrene—eating tree bark—and then eating nothing for eight days—the wagon rumbling through camp every morning, gathering the stiff bodies of the dead, three thousand of them in five months—hacking mass graves with axes in the frozen ground—the dead carcasses of hundreds of starved horses and oxen in camp . . .

Yorktown—the unceasing roar of the heavy guns for fifty-seven days that began when the French navy drove the British battleships from the Chesapeake to leave British General Cornwallis and his army landlocked in the tiny village while the French and American cannon laid siege to them day and night, ceasing only when the British could take no more.

The somber officers were jolted from their memories when General Washington stood. They looked at him and were aware that he had shared their time of quiet reflection. He poured a crystal goblet half full, raised it, and waited while each officer did the same. They all stood, and when the general drank, they drank with him, a silent toast to what they had shared. They were still standing when the general spoke.

"I cannot come to each of you," he began, and his voice cracked and broke, and he stopped. Tears came to his eyes, and he did not bow his head, nor wipe them away. He tried to speak, and again he could not. Every man in the room felt tears come welling, and they did nothing. Battle-hardened veterans, who had endured every form of the torments of war and been in the midst of men dying from cannon and musket-shot, stood with tears running, heads high, unashamed.

Washington shook himself visibly, and they saw the iron will rise in him for the last time in their presence. He cleared his throat and swallowed and continued. "I cannot come to each of you, but shall feel obliged if each of you will come and take me by the hand."

Chairs rattled as they commenced. The officer nearest the general was General Henry Knox, the short, stout librarian who had stepped forward in 1775 to become the commander of the Continental artillery. It was Knox who had brought the cannon from Fort Ticonderoga in the dead of winter, to Boston, to put the British under siege. It was he who had set the guns at the north end of Trenton to blast the streets clear of Hessians. His guns had been in every major engagement, finally joining in the destruction of the British at Yorktown. Through all the starving and sickness and cold, Knox had never failed his general.

Now the blocky man stepped forward and looked up into the face of his commander, and thrust forth his hand. Washington reached to shake it, and in that moment Washington knew the shake of a hand would never tell what he felt in his heart for these men. Impulsively, Washington wrapped his arms about the stout man and drew him close and kissed him on the cheek, and General Henry Knox embraced his general with all his strength, weeping openly.

Behind General Knox stood General Freiderich von Steuben, the German officer who had learned soldiering from the greatest of them all, Frederick the Great of Prussia. It was von Steuben who had performed the miracle in the purgatory of Valley Forge in ten weeks by transforming the chaos that was the Continental Army, into a precision team that caught the British that spring and beat them at the battle of Monmouth Courthouse.

Washington turned to von Steuben, and the two men embraced, neither caring that the tears were flowing.

Each officer in turn came to the general to embrace him. None had ever known their general to embrace another man, nor had any ever seen him weep. Each knew he was part of something that had never occurred before, and would never occur again, something that reached past protocol or pretense, into the purest fountains of honest emotion. They were seeing a part of their general that for eight years he had been forced to seal off from the world, to save his country. They saw it and realized they would never again be allowed to peer into the heart of such a man.

When the last officer stepped back from Washington, the tall man walked to the door, stopped, and turned. His jaw was quivering, and he could not speak, nor did he try. He raised his arm and as his eyes passed around the room, pausing for a moment on each of them, he gave them a final salute, turned, and walked out of the room.

Notes

For a concise summary of General Washington's final farewell to his officers at Fraunces Tavern, see Freeman, *Washington*, p. 507.

For an excellent, famous painting of the scene, see Fleming, *Liberty!* pp. 340–41.

CHAPTER XVIII

★ ★ ★

𝓐 thick, wet, silent snow was falling to muffle and distort the early evening sounds of Boston harbor. Caleb Dunson slipped the tie-rope of his bedroll over his shoulder, picked up his Deckhard rifle wrapped and tied in a blanket, and took his place in the small cluster of passengers working their way across the wet deck of the French frigate *Jeanette*, to the gangplank slanting down to the dock. The first mate checked Caleb's name off the passenger list, nodded, and Caleb walked down the slick, snow-covered planks, using the cleats to set his feet against slipping.

An odd feeling of something missing, something wrong, hung in the air. Walking away from the frigate on the heavy, ancient timbers of Clarke's Wharf, Caleb slowed to peer both directions, noticing for the first time through the curtain of huge snowflakes the number of ships tied to the wharves, and the number of masts of ships anchored in the harbor, undulating on the gentle sea swells. He spent a moment studying the dock laborers loading and unloading the ships, wet snow on their shoulders and in their hair and beards and eyebrows. There were too few ships, and too few men. He looked at the dark doorways and the alleys where men stood in the shadows in wet, tattered coats, desperation plain in their faces and sunken eyes. He could not recall a time when the Boston harbor was not alive with the swaying masts of ships and the echo of the shouted orders of the bos'ns and the freight masters and the profane clamor of the dockhands and the bellowing of captains of pilot boats and ships on their huge, brass horns. The heartbeat of Boston was the harbor, and it was half-deserted, dying.

With the wet snow sticking, he strode steadily west along the waterfront, watching the fronts of the old buildings with peeling paint, counting the windows that were dark and the doors that were chained shut with court papers tacked to them. Black silhouettes stood to watch him pass. He came to Long's Wharf, then on to Griffin's Wharf, with a growing knot in the pit of his stomach. One in three of the shipping firms were out of business, either by choice or by court-enforced bankruptcy. Either way, the truth was that the town in which he had been born and raised was in deep, maybe fatal, trouble. In his life such a possibility had never occurred to him, and as he turned north toward home, a feeling of dread rose in his chest.

He passed from the sounds of ships and men into the quiet stillness of heavy snow in the narrow cobblestone streets with his thoughts turning to home. Mother. The other children. How long had it been? Four? Nearly five years? One letter. In five years, one letter to his mother. For a moment he felt guilt, and he bowed his head, wishing he had written to his mother more often. What distance would there be between them? What would she say? What would he say? What would—

In the eerie silence of falling snow he felt more than heard a faint sound from behind, and he moved with a survival instinct honed to the finest edge by years of mortal combat. He spun to his left, feet spread slightly, the wrapped rifle grasped before him with both hands, balanced, ready to move any direction, seeing all before him in an instant. Through the snow a bulky shadow eight feet away was hurtling toward him with a second shadow ten feet to his right, moving slower. Caleb swung the rifle butt and he felt the solid hit and the first man went down and Caleb twisted to his right to bring the rifle barrel around hard and in the instant before the impact of the hit on the second man he saw the knife coming up and the rifle barrel hit first and the knife stroke missed and the man staggered back and Caleb was on top of him, plunging the rifle butt once, twice, and the man lay still. Caleb pivoted back to the man behind him, who was on his hands and knees, trying to get his feet under him but could not, and Caleb put his foot against the man's shoulder and pushed him over sideways in the snow, and the man threw an arm upward to protect his head, his voice sounding high, fearful, thick with a Scottish accent.

"Don't hit me no more! Don't hit me!"

"Who are you?"

"Don't matter."

Caleb raised the rifle butt over the man's head. "Who are you?"

"McKinrow."

"Who's he?" Caleb pointed to the still form, black in the white snow.

"My brother."

"He had a knife."

"I didn't know that. He's not right in the head."

"He meant to kill me."

"He don't understand things."

"Who sent you?"

"No one."

"Then why?"

"Get money for food. Nothin' to eat in four days. I got a wife and three children."

"Get up."

"You won't hit me again?"

"Get up. Get your brother on his feet."

The man rolled onto his hands and knees, then got one foot set in a kneeling position, and rose, unsteady at first. He stumbled to his brother and rubbed snow on his face until he moved and groaned.

"Lon, git up. Git up."

He caught his brother under his arms and heaved him to a sitting position, then onto his feet, still groaning, moving his head, trying to understand where he was and what had happened. McKinrow looped his brother's arm over his shoulder to hold him upright, then turned to Caleb.

"We goin' to the jail?"

"Don't move."

It took Caleb two minutes shuffling his feet in the snow to find the homemade knife. The wooden handle was cracked, and the blade rusted and dull. He picked it up and the man spoke again.

"Mister, I need to know. Are we goin' to jail? I got to git word to my wife and children somehow."

Caleb shoved the knife in his coat pocket. "Where are they?"

"Over on the Mystic River. Across the Back Bay."

"Why did you try to rob me?"

"Lost our farm. Bank took it. Been tryin' to get work anywhere—farmin', fishin', on the docks—anywhere. Seems like the banks and the courts has closed down half the state. Nobody got no work for us."

"What's wrong with your brother?"

"Got a piece of a British cannonball in his head. Yorktown."

Caleb's eyes widened. "He was at Yorktown?"

"Both of us. He got hurt at Redoubt Number Nine."

"You were there? At number nine? When we took it?"

"Yes. Both of us."

"Who commanded the charge?"

"That Frenchman. Lafayette. We was assigned to him that night. Fought alongside the French. They dressed too pretty, but they fought good." McKinrow paused for a moment before he continued. "Was you there?"

"Across the river. At Gloucester."

There was surprise in McKinrow's voice. "You with the ones that drove out Tarleton?"

"Yes."

"Oh, I wish I could've seen that. I wish I could've."

For a few seconds they stood facing each other in the silence of the falling snow, confused, groping for what either of them should say next. Caleb broke the awkward silence.

"You discharged?"

"Both of us."

"You get your pay?"

McKinrow shook his head. "A promise on a piece of paper. Wasn't worth nothin'. Traded it in for food for the family. Lasted three days. Haven't had much to eat since."

"You have a house? A place to live?"

"A shed. Part of a barn. Over near Winter Hill. Farmer says we can stay there if I keep the barn cleaned out and feed and water his animals."

"Five of you?"

"Five."

"You robbed anyone before?"

"No. Never tried. Don't know how to rob." Caleb sensed shame and a pleading in the man's voice as he continued. "If it wasn't for the children . . . I had to do something."

The brother groaned, and McKinrow shook him lightly. "You all right?"

The man's speech was halting, slurred. "Them cannon . . ."

McKinrow held his face close to his brother's. "No cannon. We're in Boston. Boston."

"Boston? . . . I thought we was . . ."

"It's all right."

McKinrow turned back to Caleb. "He'll be all right. Sometimes he hears and sees things, since Yorktown."

Caleb shook the snow from his coat and worked a leather pouch from his trouser pocket. He picked at the knotted leather thongs until the pouch was open, then drew out four gold coins. He looked at them for a moment, then thrust them at McKinrow.

"Take these. Get some food. Take care of your wife and children. Get him to a doctor if he needs one."

McKinrow gaped. "You aren't takin' us to the law? Jail?"

"Go home."

McKinrow took the money in his hand, and his eyes widened. "Mister, there's more'n twenty pounds sterling here. That's more money'n I seen in three years."

Caleb jerked the drawstrings on the purse, knotted them, and thrust it back into his pocket. "Go home."

McKinrow stammered, "After what we done? How do I pay. . . . what . . . who are you, mister? The Almighty answered our prayers, and I got to know your name."

The thought flashed in Caleb's mind—*The Almighty? He had nothing to do with it. I did.*

He hitched his blanket roll on his back, turned on his heel, and walked away in the hush of the falling snow with his wrapped rifle in his hand and an old, useless knife in his pocket. He dug the knife from his pocket and threw it in a snowbank and did not look back. In his mind he was seeing and hearing the night attack on the British Redoubt Number Nine as he saw it from Gloucester, across the York River, the night of October 17, 1781. The heavy guns blasting, the cannon flashes lighting the black night sky, and the distant shouts and cries as two armies clashed across the river. He saw it in his mind, and then he saw a Scot holding up his brother in the snow in Boston because his brother had come away from the battle with a piece of a British cannonball in his head, and he heard the desperation and the shame in the voice of McKinrow because his country could not pay him, and he lost his farm, and then his pride, and had tried to rob to feed his children. Walking in the beauty of a gentle snowfall that turned the trees and fences and buildings of Boston into a white wonderland, Caleb saw it all, and he walked on toward his home where his mother would be waiting, and his brother and sisters, in a home with a fire in the fireplace, and food.

He had not expected the stir that rose in his heart at the sight of lights in the windows, nor the rise of excitement as he pushed through the front gate and walked to the door. He reached for the latch, then paused, and knocked. He heard the familiar rapid footsteps inside, and then the door was open, and the warmth and smells of wood burning and a supper finished an hour earlier reached to enfold him, and his mother stood before him. She threw her hand up to cover her mouth, and for an instant could neither move nor speak, and then she seized him and clasped him to her with all her strength. Caleb held his rifle with his left hand and wrapped his right arm around her to hold her close and they stood thus for a time before she began to murmur, "Caleb . . . Caleb . . . Caleb." Then she drew back from him and wiped at her tears.

"You're all wet! Come in! Come in!" She stepped back and while Caleb shook the snow from his hair and his coat and bedroll, Margaret turned to call, "Brigitte! Bring the children! Caleb's home!"

Caleb had time to close the door, drop his bedroll, lean his rifle against the wall, and shrug out of his coat before they came through the archway into the parlor, slowing at the sight of him. Brigitte stopped for a moment, struggling to connect the man before her with her younger brother whom she remembered when he was sixteen. Then she walked to him and threw her arms around him and buried her face in his shoulder, and he held her close.

"Caleb. Oh, Caleb! We didn't know if you were dead or alive."

He smiled. "I'm alive."

Margaret was standing to one side, beaming, hardly able to contain herself when the twins came walking across the parlor, wonder in their eyes. They had been nine years old when Caleb had disappeared, a sixteen-year-old boy who was shattered and embittered at the killing of his father by the British in the battle of Lexington and Concord on April 19, 1775. Before them now was a man, strong, striking, confident, with eyes that masked remembrances of terrible hardships and battles and life and death.

Prissy walked to him with a sense of hesitancy. "It's good to have you home." She didn't know whether she should embrace him or shake his hand, and he grinned and reached for her to pull her inside his arms and hold her tight. She threw her arms about his neck and held him as he spoke.

"Prissy. Grown up. Beautiful. I can hardly believe it."

She stepped back, head ducked while she fought to control a tight smile of purest pleasure at his words.

Adam stepped up. He swallowed and his Adam's apple seemed to distort his entire neck. "Caleb, I'm glad to see you." He knew it sounded wrong, and for a moment he fumbled and then blurted, "It's good to have you home." He thrust out his hand.

Caleb looked at him and understood Adam did not think it seemly for men to embrace each other, and he reached to shake the hand firmly.

"I hardly knew it was you. You've grown up. Done right well. I'm glad to be home."

He released Adam's hand, and Adam stood there with his too-long arms hanging at his sides, not knowing what to do next, and Caleb read him perfectly and he stepped close and threw his arms about him, and for a moment Adam stood startled, motionless, before he raised his arms and put them around his brother.

Margaret stepped in. "Bring your things. Your room's ready. Get into some dry clothes." She turned to the girls. "Get out the supper ham and potatoes and set a place at the table."

Minutes later, warm ham and potatoes and peas, with thick-sliced bread and home-churned butter and Brigitte's berry jam were waiting on the table, beside a pitcher of buttermilk. They bowed their heads while Margaret said grace, and then time was forgotten as Caleb reached for the ham platter. He began to eat slowly, savoring every morsel with a reverence known only to those who have seen and endured near total starvation, while the women watched with deep pleasure. Talk began and then came like a flood, with everyone asking questions of Caleb while he tried to chew and swallow and answer. Margaret joined in, but in the exhilaration of having Caleb home, no one noticed that she was intently watching every expression that passed over Caleb's face and in his eyes, listening to his every word and how he said it, silently probing for an answer to the question that had been in her heart since that night long before when he had tried to leave without her knowing. With a mother's instincts she had surprised him in the darkness of the parlor as he opened the door to go, and they had shared their embrace and said their farewell. She had given him her blessing, and he had walked out into the starry night, a boy filled with confusion and anger, blaming the Almighty for the death of his father and the leaving of his brother, Matthew. A boy distancing himself from God, moving steadily toward a world filled with bitter, black hatred for many things his father, and his family, held sacred. From that day, there had been an urgent need in her to know that he had found his way back. She listened with her mother's heart, waiting.

The talk went on until she said, "Here we are, Caleb finally home and we won't let him eat. Brigitte, pour him some more buttermilk, and let's be a little more considerate."

Adam interrupted. "Can I ask a question?"

Caleb nodded.

"That long thing in the blanket. Is that a musket?"

"Rifle."

"Where did you get it?" Adam's eyes were wide, expectant.

"South Carolina."

"You were down there?"

"With Francis Marion."

Adam started. "The Swamp Fox? You were with him?"

"Yes."

"In any big battles?"

Only Margaret caught the subtle change in Caleb's face.

"There was some trouble."

"Any battles?"

"There's time for that later."

Adam fell silent, wondering why neither Matthew nor Caleb would talk about the great, thrilling battles.

Prissy pointed. "Brigitte made the berry jam."

Brigitte grinned. "Prissy baked the bread."

Caleb smiled at both of them. "Three women in the family. Best cooks in Boston."

The women all laughed, and Adam reached for a slice of bread. Margaret raised a hand to correct him, then let it drop, and Adam reached for the butter plate and jam bowl while Margaret ignored him. Caleb was home, safe and whole. The house rule against eating after supper would wait until tomorrow.

With supper finished and the dishes washed, dried, and in the cupboard, Caleb went to his room, turned the wheel on the lamp, and unwrapped the Deckhard rifle. He wiped it with a dry cloth, then set it in the far corner of the closet. He gathered the wet blanket with his damp coat and clothes and carried them out to the parlor where he and Margaret hung them on the backs of chairs and set them on the hearth to dry. Caleb added more wood to the fire and they all drew up a chair to sit near the warmth.

Margaret spoke. "Matthew said you went north from the Chesapeake with some slaves. That was more than a year ago."

"Eighteen months. They were just arrived from Africa. We took one hundred fifty-five of them off a sinking slave ship. Sixty-nine were dead. Drowned when the Dutch threw them overboard."

The women gasped, and then the room fell silent. Margaret saw the cloud cross Caleb's face, and the flash of anger before he continued. "We bought ten wagons and horse teams with the money we got from the slave ship and took them north."

"You? Alone?"

"No. Primus was there. He's a slave from South Carolina. Ran away to join us and fight the British. He came with me. I would never have made it without him."

"Where did you take them?"

Caleb sat motionless for a time, while the knots in the pine firewood popped and sparks danced.

"Nova Scotia."

Margaret started. "Where?"

"Nova Scotia."

"Up in Canada?"

"Yes. We tried to find a place down here somewhere, but . . ." He shook his head slowly. "No one would let us stop. Even in Vermont. No one. After what I saw on that slave ship—Matthew and I—I wasn't going to let someone make them slaves."

"Are there Africans up there? In Nova Scotia?"

"Yes. Two or three thousand of them."

"You let them go? Could they speak English?"

"Not at first. I used more of the money from the Dutch ship to buy some land up there, enough that they could stay together and farm.

Primus stayed with them. He's worked farms before, and after we got some homes and buildings built, there was enough money left to buy some cattle and pigs. I stayed until they learned enough English to get by. They worked hard. They'll be all right. Primus is there with them."

Adam leaned forward, eyes wide, voice strained. "The Dutch were throwing them overboard? Into the ocean?"

A few seconds passed while Caleb picked his words. "There was sickness on board."

"Didn't they have a doctor? I thought all ships had doctors."

"They did, but he died. So did the captain."

"Overboard? Just threw them into the ocean?"

Caleb nodded but remained silent. A look of stunned revulsion passed over Adam's face, and he shuddered.

Margaret said, "How did you get home from Nova Scotia?"

"Took passage on a French frigate. Arrived late this afternoon."

"You must be tired."

Caleb smiled. "The warmth is making me drowsy."

"Would you like some cider? We pressed some good cider this fall."

"That would be good."

Adam put on his coat to go into the backyard and bring a pitcher of chill cider from the root cellar. Talk mellowed and time was forgotten until Margaret pointed at the large clock on the mantel and exclaimed, "Why, it's past ten o'clock! Where has the evening gone? We've kept Caleb up far too long for his first day home." She turned to the children. "Get ready for bed, and we'll have prayer in my room."

Ten minutes later they gathered around Margaret's bed, all in their long nightshirts except Caleb. He still wore his regular clothes. Margaret did not question it as they knelt, and then she turned to Caleb. Her smile, and her words, were casual.

"It would be good if you offered the prayer."

Caleb smiled and nodded toward Adam. "He's been the man of the house for quite a while. Maybe he should do it."

A stab of cold fear pierced Margaret's breast, and Brigitte looked first at Margaret, then at Caleb, and dropped her eyes to stare at her hands clasped before her. Margaret nodded to Adam.

"Your turn."

Adam bowed his head. "Almighty Father, we thank thee for delivering Caleb back to us . . ."

The house was quiet when the mantel clock struck eleven, with Caleb seated in a large upholstered chair before the hearth, head leaned back, staring into the blue and yellow in the glowing embers of the dying fire. He was stocking-footed, still in his street clothes. He heard the whisper of woolen slippers in the hallway of the bedroom wing of the house and watched his mother enter through the archway, white in her nightshirt, hair in a single braid down her back. Without a word she sat in the chair to his right and for a time stared into the fire.

She broke the silence.

"A lot to think about?"

He slowly nodded his head but said nothing.

"Matthew needs to talk with you. Something about the slaves and money."

"I know. I'll talk with him tomorrow."

"You haven't seen his son. John Matthew."

Caleb's face softened. "No."

"I can see your father in that little boy."

For a moment Caleb's breathing slowed, but again he said nothing. In that instant Margaret knew she could not press him. Not tonight. She moved on.

"You saw battle?"

A look came into his eyes—a mix of defiance, and hatred, and pain, and Margaret thought she saw hopelessness.

"Yes. I saw battle."

"Killing?"

He nodded but held his silence.

"It's over. You're home. Can you leave it behind?"

"Some of it. Maybe. I hope so." He fell silent for a moment, then went on. "Is Billy home? Is he all right?"

"He's home. He's fine."

Margaret took a deep breath. "Be patient with us. For nearly six years we haven't known if you were dead or alive. We need to know about those years."

Caleb turned to look into her face. "I'll try. You be patient, too."

"We'll try."

She stood and for a moment she looked down at him, and then she turned and walked from the room. It was past midnight when Caleb opened the door to peer outside. The snow had stopped, and the half-moon was a blur behind thinning clouds. He returned to the parlor to quietly bank the coals in the fireplace and silently went to his room.

It was three o'clock in the morning when Margaret's eyes opened and she lay still, searching in the black of her room for what had awakened her. From down the hall came the soft sounds of mumbled words, and she rose to put on her slippers and walk down the polished hardwood floor to Caleb's room. He was talking in his sleep. She listened intently for a time, but could make out only one phrase that was repeated many times. " . . . watch the left flank . . . watch . . . left flank."

She stood in the dark hallway for a time, waiting for him to shout and come out of his bed fighting a battle that existed only in his mind, but the mumbling faded and died, and she went back to her bed.

At half-past seven, the morning prayer and breakfast were finished, Caleb had cleared a path through the snow to the front gate and out into the street, and Prissy was drying the last of the morning dishes. Caleb came from his room in his heavy coat and paused at the kitchen archway.

"Will Matthew be home?"

Margaret shrugged. "I think so. You going there?"

"Yes. Business. Nova Scotia."

"Dinner's at one o'clock."

"I'll be back."

The wintry sun was half-risen on a white Boston that was surprisingly warm, with the sound of water dripping and running from melting snow and icicles. Caleb walked the path to the gate, out into the street, filled his lungs with clean cold air that carried the salt tang that reached as far back as his memory could go, turned to his right, and walked briskly up the street with the snow crunching. He turned in through the gate of the Thorpe home, to the front door, and knocked. Seconds later the door opened and Matthew stood before him. For a moment neither moved and then Matthew reached to embrace his brother and draw him inside.

"Are you all right? Eighteen months. I was getting worried."

Caleb grinned. "Fine."

Matthew turned. "Kathleen, come see who's here."

She appeared in the kitchen archway in her heavy nightshirt, tall, dark hair a tumble on her back, and in her arms she held John. She stood still for a moment, threw her free hand to her mouth, and exclaimed, "Caleb! Caleb! You're home. We've been so worried." She nearly ran across the parlor to throw her arm about him and he held her, and she backed away to look at John, her eyes glowing with pride and love.

"Caleb, meet your nephew. John Matthew."

Caleb stared at the sleepy-eyed two-year-old in his nightshirt, hair awry, one arm about his mother's neck, and the boy stared back at Caleb with the frank look of a child suspicious of a total stranger. Then the boy leaned his head over against his mother's cheek, and reached to hold her while he glanced alternately at Caleb, Matthew, and Kathleen, unsure whether he accepted the man standing before him.

Matthew smiled and Kathleen laughed. "He doesn't know you. Give him a little time. He'll be in your lap going through all your pockets."

Caleb reached to touch the boy's arm, and John shied away. Caleb shook his head. "He looks like Father."

"More every day."

Matthew said, "Take off your coat. Have you had breakfast?"

Caleb rounded his cheeks and blew air. "Yes. I think those women at home intend feeding me to death."

Kathleen laughed. "I have to go take care of John. Maybe you two could use the library."

The two pushed through the French doors into the chill, dark-paneled library, and Matthew went to the stone fireplace where he used flint and steel to strike sparks into shredded linen, then blew lightly and added slivers, then sticks, until the fire was crackling. The two brothers sat in upholstered chairs near the hearth, hands extended, palms turned outward toward the fire while the room warmed.

Matthew asked, "When did you get in?"

"Last night."

"You're all right?"

"Good."

"You had trouble with the Africans? It's been eighteen months."

"No trouble." He paused for a moment. "Took them to Nova Scotia."

Matthew straightened, incredulous. "Where?"

"Nova Scotia. Couldn't find a place for them down here."

"Who took them in?"

"No one. We kept four of the wagons and teams and sold the other six and used most of the rest of the money from the Dutch ship to buy some land. We built some barns and homes. They're farming. I stayed long enough to be sure they could speak a little English and could survive a Canadian winter and turned them over to Primus. He'll take care of them."

"He's up there with them?"

"Yes. I think he intends finding a ship that will take them all back to Africa. If he does, he'll sell the farm to pay their passage."

Matthew slowly shook his head. "Seven years ago we declared that the Creator made all men equal, and we fought a war because of it. How is it we have to send Africans to Canada to keep them from being slaves?"

Caleb stared steadily into the fire, and his words came quiet and deadly serious. "Seems like someone made a mistake. Either the Declaration of Independence, or the United States, or the Creator. Someone."

Matthew turned his head to his brother, eyes narrowed, glittering, and Caleb could not miss the sharpness in his voice. "Be careful. Rising above slavery doesn't come easy. The Creator called out Moses, and it took him forty years."

Caleb shrugged it off, and Matthew took a new direction.

"Do you have any of the Dutch money left?"

"A little. About one hundred forty dollars in gold coin."

Matthew leaned back, speaking more to himself than Caleb. "What's the right thing to do with it?"

Caleb's answer came instantly. "I got a look at the docks and some of the town yesterday coming home. Shipping firms closed. Court notices on the doors. The harbor and wharves half-deserted. Shops closed. Good men in the streets begging for work. That's what I saw. Am I right?"

Matthew nodded.

"Is gold coin hard to come by?"

"Nearly impossible."

"I saw Mother's hands. And Brigitte's. They've been working too hard. Are they bringing in any money?"

"They trade work for food. I've been splitting their firewood and handling the Monday wash water."

"Are you bringing any money into this house?"

"Not much. No."

"Billy?"

"Same. Splits six cords of wood once a week for half a dollar. Trades work for food. Continental paper dollars are worthless. No one has money. It's the same everywhere."

Caleb paused for a moment before he went on. "The banks? Can they be trusted?"

"No. Too many are closing."

Caleb took a deep breath. "Well, as far as I'm concerned, the one hundred forty dollars goes into Mother's money jar in the cupboard."

"It's not our money."

"Where's the Dutchmen we took it from?"

"Gone. I've got the name of the shipping firm and the name of the ship. I could send it to them."

"Not if I have a say in it. Do you remember what we saw that day? Dead bodies in the sea. Dead men and women and babies in the hold of that ship. Sick. Starved. No light. No air. Up to their waist in seawater

and their own filth! Those slavers getting rich and fat. You think I'm giving that money to them for what they did? No, it stays with Mother."

"You'll have to tell her where you got it."

There was an edge to Caleb's voice. "I will. It's my pay for the past
eighteen months of my life."

For a moment Matthew studied his brother's face, then settled back
in his chair and once again changed direction.

"Do you have any thoughts about getting work?"

"Is the newspaper shop still open? My old employer?"

"No. Closed nearly a year ago."

"If you and Billy can't get steady work, I don't have an idea what I'll
do. Maybe have to leave Boston."

"And go where?"

Caleb tossed a hand up. "I don't know. Philadelphia. New York.
Charleston."

"Philadelphia's worse than here. New York the same. I don't know
about Charleston or other cities in the South."

"Maybe go inland. There has to be farmers or someone that needs
to hire."

"I doubt it. There are a lot of men from the Appalachians and up
north that have come here looking." Matthew leaned forward, elbows on
knees. "Caleb, this whole country is in trouble. We won the war. Now it
looks like we're going to lose the peace."

Caleb shifted his feet. "What are you going to do?"

"Billy and I have been talking. Maybe there's a way to get a shipping
firm. He runs the office, I run the ships. If we can get the ships, then
maybe there's a way to get a cargo to go down south, and one to bring
back up here."

Caleb shook his head. "Buy the cargo? With what?"

"Not buy. Find someone willing to pay us to carry it. There are merchants here and north of here that have manufactured goods they'll sell at
cost, just to get their money out of them. Same with some merchants
down south. If they'll both cooperate, we can take the manufactured

goods south, and bring rice or tobacco back. They get their money out of their goods, and we get our pay for the shipping."

Caleb stared at the floor for a moment before he spoke. "How far have you gone with this plan?"

Matthew shifted in his chair, and Caleb saw the anxiety rise in him. "We've talked with the old Covington and Sons Shipping Company. Six ships. Good condition. I went over each of them. Been trading in Europe and India. Sometimes in China. They're going to be taken by the bank or by bankruptcy if Covington doesn't find a way to pay the loan. Covington wants to sell. They'll turn all their assets over to anyone who'll pick up the bank loan."

"How big is the loan?"

"Just under sixteen thousand pounds British sterling. Far below the value of six seaworthy ships."

A reckless grin crossed Caleb's face. "You got sixteen thousand pounds British sterling in Mother's money jar?"

Matthew ignored it. "We talked to the bank—Billy and I. The bank has taken over so many businesses that couldn't pay their loans that they're willing to do almost anything to get rid of some of them at any price. The bank doesn't want Covington. We made them an offer."

"What offer?"

"Billy and I both have the written promise of Congress to pay our last two years' officer pay. We offered them those notes at full value, and agreed to pay the balance of the loan within eight years."

"What did the bank say?"

"They want time to present it to their full board."

"If you can't pay off the balance in eight years?"

"We think we could sell four of the ships if we had to and get enough to nearly pay off the bank. We told them that. They're considering it."

"Trade with Europe is risky. The Atlantic's a big ocean. Too many ships never return."

"We won't trade with Europe very much. We'll do our shipping up and down our own coast."

"Someone on the French ship that brought me here said the British have stopped all trade between the West Indies and the United States. Is that true?"

"Yes."

"Won't that cripple your ideas on shipping?"

"We won't trade with the West Indies. We'll trade with legitimate merchants on the mainland."

"And if the legitimate merchants smuggle your merchandise into the West Indies for big profits?"

"If we know about it, we'll stop dealing with them."

"Sounds to me like a lot of smugglers and pirates are going to get fat running merchant ships past the British gunboats at night while legitimate shippers go bankrupt."

"Probably."

"Dangerous. You going to mount cannon on your ships?"

"Not if we can avoid it."

For a few minutes Caleb stared into the fire, carefully going over the pieces of the plan, and then he turned back to Matthew.

"I don't think I ever heard such a loose plan. Any chance it will work?"

Matthew leaned forward, elbows on his thighs, rubbing his hands together slowly, staring at them.

"I doubt I ever heard of such a plan either." He stopped working his hands and turned to Caleb. "The only thing that justifies it is the hard fact that neither Billy nor I can think of a better one. If you can, I'd like to know about it."

For a time Caleb did not answer, and then he spoke quietly. "A long time ago I worked for a newspaper that's out of business now. And I've spent six years learning to kill or be killed, and taking Africans to a safe place. I can't think of anyone who would hire me for what I've learned to do. So I doubt I can add much to what you and Billy have put together."

Matthew's eyes fell for a moment. "If the bank decides to take the risk, it's possible there would be a place in it for you."

"You're the sailor. Not me."

"You can learn."

"That depends. In the meantime, maybe I'll have to leave home. I can't stay there and be another mouth to feed."

"One hundred forty dollars in gold coin will feed the family for a long time."

"A lot longer if I'm not there."

"That's between you and Mother."

Caleb stood and stretched. "Well, it looks like I came home to a lot of surprises. Some bad, some good. Adam and Prissy've grown up. Your son's a handsome little fellow. You and Kathleen seem happy. We're all trying to figure out how to keep from starving to death. The whole country's in trouble. Seems like if the war was all we thought it was, we ought not to be facing such a total disaster."

Matthew shook his head. "I know, I know. But we've got to remember, we still have the important things."

"Like what?"

"Our health. Family. Freedom. We'll find a way out of this. It'll all work out somehow."

Caleb started for the French doors at the same instant they opened, and Kathleen entered with two glasses of buttermilk on a tray.

"You two have been talking so long I thought you might need something cool."

Caleb glanced at Matthew and held up a hand. "Thanks, but I had so much breakfast I'm still full."

Matthew said, "Maybe some other time."

Kathleen caught the interplay between the men and a shadow of question crossed her face. "Is there something I should know?"

Caleb shook his head. "No. I promise the next time I come I'll be ready for buttermilk."

Kathleen shrugged, turned, and walked out the door, and Caleb followed. She went back to the kitchen as the two men walked to the front door where Caleb donned his coat and buttoned it.

He opened the door to brilliant sunlight sparkling off endless snow crystals, and the sound of water running everywhere. He paused at the door long enough to turn to Matthew.

"Let me know how things work out with the bank and Covington."

"I will."

Notes

The desperate economic condition of the United States and the city of Boston has been explained and documented in preceding chapters. The characters and events in this chapter are fictional.

Winter Hill is a small village on the west bank of the Mystic River, not far from Charlestown, across the Back Bay from Boston. See Freeman, *Washington,* map facing page 229.

CHAPTER XIX

★ ★ ★

*T*hick fog rolled in like a curtain at midnight, followed by a twenty-degree drop in temperature at four A.M. By eight o'clock every rope, sail, mast, arm, and spar on the few ships in Boston harbor was sheeted with ice, and the skeleton branches of every tree in the streets and yards of Boston were sparkling as they drooped low with a thick coating of ice.

Caleb pulled up the collar of his coat, thrust his hands in his pockets, and hunched his shoulders against the raw morning as he walked along the waterfront toward Griffin's Wharf. Cold was one thing, and wet was another, and Bostonians could stand either. But when the two occurred together, the chill went clear to the bone, and even the hardiest of those in town bundled heavy and walked rapidly.

He shivered as he picked his path on the treacherous ice that covered the docks, vapor rising in a cloud from his breathing as he worked his way through the few men working on the wharves. He kept his eyes left, looking for a tiny shop with a hastily made wooden sign that said something about printing. He did not expect it to be set back from the street, nor did he expect it to be on the door of what had once been a storage shed attached to one side of a fish packing house. He turned toward the unpainted door, then stopped long enough to glance forty yards up the waterfront to where a knot of bearded men in ragged coats had gathered near a ship tied to the dock, shouting at something that was happening inside their circle. He watched for a moment, then turned to the small wooden sign above the door with the words PRINTING—NEWSPAPER that had been scrawled in block letters with a large lead pencil. He pushed through the door and stopped for a moment to let his eyes adjust to the dark of the cold, dingy room that was rank with the smell of printer's ink.

A rustle came from one corner, and he peered as a sparse man stepped toward him.

"What can I do for you?"

"I heard you were trying to start a print shop, or a newspaper. Thought I'd see if you could use a hired man. I've had experience."

The tall, angular man shook his head. "Tried. It failed. Not enough business. I'm just getting the press and print ready to load. I'm leaving."

"Need any help loading?"

"Sure, but I can't pay. I'll manage."

"Could I leave my name? In case you change your mind?"

"Save the trouble. I'll be out of here by tomorrow evening."

Caleb nodded. "Thanks, anyway. Good luck."

He walked back out into the freezing morning and closed the door and picked his way through the ice on the aged, black timbers to the front of the fish house where he slowed to study the uproar of the crowd of men to his left. Caleb turned toward them, and had gone half the distance when he understood. A fight on the docks never failed to draw a crowd, and two men in the center of the circle were settling a difference with their fists and knees. Caleb walked to the outer edge of the circle for a moment to look and listen, and was turning to leave when someone screamed, "A knife! He's got a knife!" and the crowd shrank back, scattering. Caleb turned back, hands still in his pockets, and saw a large man, well over six feet tall and above two hundred fifty pounds, with a fish knife clutched in one hand, standing over a smaller man, reaching for his hair. The big man's mouth showed traces of blood, and the smaller man, writhing on the ground, was bleeding from a badly broken nose, a deep cut above one eye, and a smashed mouth. The bigger man caught the blood-matted hair in one hand and started a stroke with the fish knife when Caleb shouted, "Hey!"

The big man's head jerked around to glare at Caleb, and the circle quieted as he bellowed, "You want to get cut too?"

In that instant Caleb was seeing the last bully he had met—Conlin Murphy, who had beaten him unconscious six years earlier simply because Murphy was a vicious brute and Caleb was a gangling sixteen-year-old innocent. And he was remembering Charles Dorman, the man who saw the beating and spent a year teaching Caleb how to use his fists. In his mind flashed the day in June 1778, when Murphy again called him out in front of the whole regiment at Valley Forge, and he had battered Murphy to the ground, bloody, unconscious, and filled Murphy with a smoldering hatred and a vow to kill Caleb—and the day in the woods near camp when Murphy and two other men ambushed him. The desperate, two-minute battle left Murphy and one of those with him dead, and the third one running back to the commanding officer to tell a tale of murder. The court-martial had cleared Caleb of any wrong-doing, but left him with a history that included killing two American soldiers in a fight.

It all came flooding to him as he stood peering at a big man who had beaten a small man and was ready to kill him with a fish knife.

Caleb moved forward. "You've beat your man. He's down. That's enough."

The man snarled, "Get away." Again the knife started its downward stroke and Caleb broke for the big man.

"Leave him alone! You'll kill him." He stopped five paces short of the two of them, peering first down at the smaller man, then up into the wild eyes of a brute lost in blood lust. Caleb moved his feet, balanced himself, and nearly shouted, "You use that knife on him, it will be murder! You'll hang."

The big man lunged, and Caleb saw the knife coming up and shifted to his right and the knife missed and Caleb set his feet and swung hard with his left hand and felt the solid jolt clear to his hips and saw the man's head snap back and blood spurt from his broken nose and he swung with his left hand again and hit the man hard over his heart and the man doubled forward and Caleb swung his right hand from his heels and hit the man's temple just above his left ear and the big man went down sideways, sprawling on the icy black timbers and the knife went skittering fifteen feet into the crowd. Men moved away from it. Caleb straightened, feet spread, both hands ready, and waited, but the big man did not move. Caleb brought his breathing under control and straightened his coat and looked at the crowd, eyes blazing.

"Anyone else want to get into this?"

No one moved in the silence.

"Any of you know either of these men, get them out of here."

A few men nodded and moved closer to the two battered men on the ground, but their eyes never left Caleb. He stood for a few seconds longer, then turned and started back down the waterfront. Those in front of him moved to open a path, and Caleb did not look in either direction as he walked away. He was fifty yards from the quieted crowd when he raised both hands to flex his cold fingers and look at his white knuckles. None was broken. He thrust his hands in his coat pockets and walked on, head bowed, struggling to regain his mental balance after the sudden, unexpected rush of brutality. He heard a high voice calling from behind, and turned. A small, hunch-shouldered, weasel-faced man with a scraggly beard, wearing a threadbare coat with a ragged scarf over the top of his head and tied beneath his thin jowls came trotting, watching his feet on the ice.

"Hold up. Hold up."

Caleb waited. The man slowed and stopped six feet in front of him, breathing heavy, vapors rising in a cloud. He was grinning, eyes glowing from beneath heavy brows coated with ice. He pointed over his shoulder.

"You done it now."

"Done what?"

"Beat Judd! That big man back there. Waterfront bully. You beat him in front of everybody, and when you done it you took away the only thing he had and he won't let it go. No sir, he won't. He'll come lookin' for you. Yes sir, you done it now. Done it proper."

"Judd who? Who is he?"

"Just Judd. Mean—worst on the waterfront. Crippled half a dozen men in fights. One died. Sheriff can't do nothin' about it because nobody dares talk against him."

Caleb looked at the man. "Why are you telling me?"

The little man shrugged. "Figgered you should know so's you'll watch. It'll be all over the waterfront by noon. He can't stand for that. You better watch, 'cause he'll come lookin' sure."

Again Caleb was seeing Conlin Murphy—remembering the oath he swore to get his revenge for the beating Caleb gave him with the whole regiment watching—the ambush in the woods—two men dead. Would Judd become another Conlin Murphy? Would he? Caleb took a deep breath.

"Who are you? What's your name?"

There was a sense of indifference in the man as he answered. "Loman. I'm nothin'. Live wherever I can. Mainly around the waterfront."

Caleb shook his head. "I can't do anything about Judd. He'll have to do whatever he's going to do." He turned to leave when the small, pinch-shouldered little man grasped his sleeve.

"There's a way to stop it."

"How?"

"Challenge him to a fair fight. In front of the crowd. He'll look like the coward he is if he says no, and if you beat him again, he's finished. Either way, you'd be doin' everybody on the docks a big favor."

For several seconds Caleb stood staring back up the wharf, caught in the agony of deciding whether he wanted to risk a reputation as a waterfront brawler, or walk the streets of Boston forever fearful of an ambush by a brute of a man with a fish-gutting knife in his hand. His mind settled.

"I'm leaving."

The little man shook his head. "Too bad. There's three or four cowards just like Judd that are always around him, feedin' off him. They'll come lookin' for you. You won't see them, but they'll see you, and tell

Judd. Watch! Too bad. Too bad. There was money to be had from all this."

Caleb shook his head as he walked away. The little man stood watching until Caleb turned into a narrow, crooked street that angled toward the Boston Commons and was lost from sight.

Caleb walked to Fruit Street, then turned east to stop at the Red Rooster Tavern. He entered, waited until his eyes adjusted to the gloom, and walked to the desk, facing a plump young woman with a scarf holding back her brown hair and wearing a soiled apron over her gray cotton dress.

"Is Mr. Whalen in?"

She shook her head. "He doesn't own the tavern any more."

"Who does?"

"Charles Penobscot. He's not here right now."

"You in charge?"

"I'm his daughter."

Caleb glanced around. It was near noon, and the tavern should have been half filled with men ordering their midday meal and drinking hot buttered rum against the cold and fog. Instead, there were only three silent men seated at different tables, each grasping a rum mug.

"I knew Mr. Whalen. I grew up in Boston. I came to see if he could use a hired man. I can do most anything. Do you know if your father would have need? I'll work for about anything he'll pay."

The girl shook her head. "It's just him and me. Unless we get more business we're going to have to close or sell. Sorry."

Caleb nodded. "Thanks anyway."

He turned his collar high and hunched his shoulders as he walked back into the street and picked his way over the slippery cobblestones, working north and east. By one o'clock he had sought work from the owner of a bakery and a clock maker; neither could pay for a hired man. A little after one o'clock a freezing wind blew in from the Atlantic to set the bare trees in motion, rattling with the ice, and clear out the fog and set the ships in the harbor rocking against their anchor chains. By four o'clock Caleb had worked his way through the entire peninsula. Five other shop owners, including a silversmith and a gunsmith, had no need for hired help at any price. With the wind at his back, he faced into the twilight of a sun already disappeared, walking toward home when the thought came to him.

Money? What did that wharf-rat say? Too bad, because there was money in that trouble this morning? Money? How?

He puzzled on it for a time, head down, working his way through the narrow, crooked streets, and was crossing an intersection when he caught a flicker of movement to his left and he looked. There was nothing in the oncoming gloom of deep dusk. He turned left onto the street where the Dunson home stood, and walked on, watching, while lights came on in windows and curtains were drawn closed for the night. He was two short blocks from home when he again saw movement in the shadows to his left, and he broke into a trot. At the next corner he darted to his left, vaulted a white picket fence into an enclosed yard, and dropped to his haunches, watching everything coming from his right. Ten seconds passed before the black shape of a thin man came dodging from one tree to the next, running toward the corner, where he turned right. Caleb waited until the man had turned before he leaped the fence and sprinted.

The man heard him coming from behind, spun, slipped on the slick cobblestones, went down scrambling, and had regained his feet when Caleb grabbed his coat collar from behind. The man threw up both hands exclaiming, "I have no money. No money."

His beard was a series of food stains, and he was wearing a filthy, patched coat, scarf wrapped about his head, old trousers, and shoes far too big for his feet. He smelled of sweat and smoke and rum and was trembling.

Caleb seized the front of his coat and lifted him clear off his feet and backed him against a sycamore tree.

"You've been following me for half a mile. Why?"

"No, no, no!"

"You've got five seconds before we go to the sheriff."

"No, please, no. Not the sheriff."

Caleb let the man's feet settle to the ground. "Why were you following me?"

"I meant no harm."

"Last chance. Why?"

"I had to. Or get a beating."

Caleb recoiled. "Judd?"

The little man was nearly whimpering. "Don't tell him. Don't tell him."

"Where is he? Right now, where is he?"

"Back at the dock."

"You go tell him. You found me, and I want to see him again tomorrow morning at ten o'clock. Same place. Alone. Tell him, or I'll come find you."

"I will, I will."

"Get your arms up."

The man's arms went straight up and Caleb went through his pockets. There was no knife or pistol.

"Get moving."

"Yes, sir!"

The small man pivoted and darted away and Caleb watched him disappear into the darkness. He stood where he was, watching, listening in the freezing wind until the evening star appeared in the east, and then he walked two blocks past home, turned to his right, and circled back through the streets. He stopped again at the front gate, watching and listening, and then walked quickly to the front door. Inside, he unbuttoned his coat and hung it on a peg, while Margaret came from the kitchen.

"You're late. I was getting worried. Hungry?"

Caleb walked to the fireplace to turn his palms to the warmth. "I could eat."

"Pork stew all right?"

"Good."

Margaret returned to the kitchen and Caleb heard the shuffle of dishes before she returned with a large bowl of steaming stew to set it on the table.

"Any luck today?"

He shook his head. "Seven stops. No one is hiring."

She studied him for a moment. "You'll find work. Seen Matthew today?" She walked back into the kitchen to return with a glass of buttermilk and a platter with sliced bread and a saucer with butter.

"No."

She set them on the table, and Caleb took his place. She sat down facing him.

"He said there's a strong chance he and Billy will get the Covington shipping firm."

Caleb reached for the bread without saying grace, and Margaret did not correct him, nor did she reveal the pain that rose in her heart.

Caleb spread the butter. "Something happened today?"

"The bank sent out someone to look at the ships and go over the books. They're interested."

Caleb spooned stew into his mouth and took a bite of the buttered bread. "Matthew say anything about cargo? What's he going to carry in the ships?"

"I think he said rice from the South. Maybe tobacco from Virginia."

"What will he carry from here down south?"

Margaret shrugged. "Didn't say. You'll have to talk with him."

"Where's Brigitte? The children?"

"Up at Matthew's. Should be home soon. School tomorrow. What's your plan for tomorrow?"

Caleb heaved a huge sigh. "Just like yesterday and today. Look for work."

There was a rustle at the front door and Margaret called, "Brigitte? That you?"

"We're home."

"Things all right at Matthew's?"

Brigitte walked into the dining room with Adam and Prissy following, all working with the buttons on their coats. Their faces were red from the cold. "Fine. He thinks the shipping business thing will happen soon."

"He mention what cargo he would carry down south?" Margaret asked.

"Something manufactured. Nails, or stoves, or plows."

"The baby all right?"

"He's a terror. Into everything."

Margaret laughed as the three of them walked back into the parlor to hang their coats and scarves.

Caleb stood. "Got enough wood for morning?"

"Yes. Adam brought some in."

"Been a long day. I think I'll go to bed."

The room fell silent as Caleb walked through the archway, down to his room, without joining the family for evening prayers. Adam looked at Margaret, and she walked back into the kitchen to the dirty dishes without a word.

Inside his room, Caleb lighted the lamp and removed his shoes. For a time he sat on the bed, staring at the yellow light, working with his thoughts.

Judd. On the dock, alone. Ten o'clock. What will I do?

He removed his shirt and trousers and socks, and settled between the sheets in his long underwear, then twisted the lamp wheel. His thoughts ran on in the blackness, taking on size and fears larger than life. Five years ago he had humiliated Murphy with the entire regiment watching, and thought their trouble was finished. He could not know then how wrong he was; he would have to kill him to end it. Today he had beaten a second bully to the ground, and before the day was finished had flushed a man out of the shadows to learn Judd was looking for him. He lay on his back staring into the blackness, then put his arm over his eyes, fist clenched.

What was I to do? Stand there and do nothing while Judd killed that man? Was that what I should have done? Watch one man murder another? Tomorrow at ten o'clock I meet Judd once more. No matter what he or I say, will it come down to one of us killing the other to end it, like Murphy? Will it?

He drifted into a tormented sleep, tossing and twisting, and in the night Margaret heard him mumbling.

Daybreak found him outside the kitchen door in his coat, swinging the ax to split rungs of pine for the fireplace. He ate hot oatmeal porridge and drank hot chocolate with the family, buttoned his coat back on, and walked out into the street. At nine o'clock he was leaving the office of Jeremy Chandler's book bindery because they had no need of a hired man, and ten o'clock saw him walking past the old, abandoned fish house near Griffin's Wharf, working through the dockhands as they loaded and unloaded the few ships tied to the dock. He was close to the place of the previous morning's fight when he saw Judd's head above the others. He walked on, and men slowed and then stopped, and began to follow him. Thirty feet from Judd, Caleb peered at the face of the huge man. His nose was swollen and twisted and dark, and both eyes were blackened. Caleb walked steadily on, glancing right and left at the ragged dockhands, gathering like jackals to a killing. Far to Caleb's right was Loman, watching intently. Next to Judd was the little man who had followed Caleb.

Men stepped back, and Caleb walked to within six feet of Judd before he stopped. His voice came loud.

"I'm the one who beat you yesterday."

A wicked smile formed on Judd's face, and a tiny trickle of blood started from his battered nose. He reached to wipe at it.

"I know who you are."

"You want to settle this?"

"I'll settle it."

"I won't fight you. No good can come from it. It's over. You win."

Judd snorted, "It's not over until I say."

"Then say. I won't fight. I'll leave. You win. The waterfront is yours."

Judd took a step forward, towering over Caleb by seven inches and seventy pounds. His voice was choked with rage. "You see what you did?" He pointed at his face. "Hit me when I wasn't expecting. You'll look worse when I finish. Maybe dead. Then it will be finished."

Caleb shook his head. "Then do it now with these men watching. I won't fight back. I'll keep my hands in my pockets, and then I'll get the sheriff. You'll go to jail for assault. You want to go to jail?"

Judd shook his head, grinning wickedly. "Nobody here will see anything but a fair fight."

Caleb glanced at the men. Their eyes were shifty, their faces a blank, and suddenly Caleb realized that Judd had warned everybody but his own men to stay away from Griffin's Wharf until he said otherwise.

Rage rose to choke Caleb, and he stood silent until he could control it. "I came here to end this thing without trouble. I'm through. I'm walking away. Leave it alone, and the docks will be yours."

He turned to walk away and heard a heavy grunt as Judd lunged, and he pivoted to his right and ducked as he heard the high, shrill shout, "Stop it! Stop it!" and felt Judd's huge fist land heavy on his shoulder and fall away as Judd's lunge carried him past Caleb. He straightened and faced Judd as he recovered from his missed charge, then backed away, hands still in his pockets as Judd came on once again, massive arms extended to grapple and rend. Suddenly Loman was between them with one hand on Judd's chest shouting up at him, "Stop it! Stop it! You'll go to jail!"

Judd looked down at him and he saw the pinpoint eyes beneath the shaggy brows and understood he dared not smash the little man, and he slowed. Loman kept his hand against Judd's chest, arm stiff, still shouting up into the face of the brute.

"You can beat him if you do it legal!"

Judd peered down at him in wonderment, unable to grasp how he could legally beat a man to death.

Loman did not stop. "In a fair fight. Hands wrapped. Professional. Rules. Someone to keep the rules. Spectators. A purse for the winner. Winner take all. Legal!"

Caleb gaped as it struck him. Money! Loman had said there was money to be had from this. Loman was in it for the money!

Loman kept shouting, shaking a finger in the face of the astonished Judd. "Only one thing. No matter how it turns out, it's over. You will never fight this man again, and he will never fight you again. Do you understand?"

Judd batted his eyes, unable to put it all together in his head. "You mean we fight for money?"

Loman's frustration showed. "Judd, listen! Listen! Yes. For money.

Like a professional. With spectators. Rules. You can beat this man half to death, and no one can ever accuse you for it. Do you understand?"

Judd shook his head, unable to grasp it. "Legal? For money?"

"Yes."

"Where?"

"That's to be decided." He turned to Caleb. "This is the only chance you have to end this thing. If you don't, there'll be another man follow you home and Judd'll find you. When he does, there'll be a killing, one way or the other. Make your choice."

Trapped! Anger and outrage leaped inside Caleb. Fight for money? Like a professional? Dorman flashed in his mind—scarred around the eyes and mouth, no bridge to his nose, brows heavy with scar tissue. He saw it and felt the revulsion, and then from deep inside came the certain sureness.

If he could not find a way to stop it now, it would end as it had with Murphy. The evil of the thing would not be satisfied until one of them, himself or Judd, was dead, unless he could find a way to stop it now.

His thoughts ran on. Would Loman's maniacal scheme stop it?—save a killing?

Caleb turned to Loman. "End it forever?"

"If Judd agrees." He turned to Judd. "One fight with rules. That ends it forever. Do you agree?"

For three seconds no one spoke while Judd pondered. "I'll do it."

Loman turned back to Caleb, grinning in anticipation, eyes glittering. "There you have it. Agreed?"

"Yes. But not in Boston. Across the Back Bay, in Charlestown."

Notes

The characters and events in this chapter are fictional. For the history of the conflict between Caleb Dunson and Conlin Murphy, and the role played by Charles Dorman, see volume 5 of this series, *A Cold, Bleak Hill*, particularly chapters 1 and 31, and parts of volume 6, *The World Turned Upside Down.*

CHAPTER XX

★ ★ ★

*N*ever had there been such a flood of ecstatic buzzing in the small, Chesapeake Bay town of Annapolis!

The citizenry had walked a bit livelier and held their heads a bit higher when Congress adjourned at Princeton, New Jersey, on November 4, 1783, to reconvene at Annapolis on November 26. Hosting the United States in congress assembled created a momentary national stir and provided a slight nudge upward in the Annapolis hotel and tavern businesses and gave the local fledgling newspaper a few headlines and a modicum of bragging rights. But soon enough the citizenry learned that the luster of politics is a thin, transient veneer that can quickly fade into the humdrum everyday business of life. The newfound celebrity of the small town soon dulled and began slipping away.

That was November.

No one in the country was prepared for the bombshell that burst over Annapolis in December.

On Saturday, December 20, startled citizens had slowed in the streets at the sight of a cluster of army officers with gold braid on their tricorns and large epaulets on their shoulders, riding high-blooded horses through the streets toward the state house. In the midst of the group, a full head taller than those around him, was General George Washington, astride his tall, dapple-gray mare, ramrod straight, blue-gray eyes watching everything. The officers tied their horses to the hitching posts in front of a large, white building, and walked beneath the columned portico, through double doors into the entryway, then down the hardwood hallway with their boot heels tapping, to the large hall where Congress was seated.

Upon their entry, the hall quieted. When he could collect his wits, Thomas Mifflin, president of the body, inquired the purpose of the unexpected but most welcome visit. General Washington stood at attention facing him.

"I wish to tender my letter of resignation from the office which this august body conferred on me in the year 1775."

Audible gasps echoed, followed by stunned silence, then a spontaneous outburst of exclamations from every congressman in the room. Washington remained at attention, chin high, eyes locked onto President Thomas Mifflin—the same Thomas Mifflin who had been suspected of collusion with generals Thomas Conway and Horatio Gates in the infamous Conway Cabal five years earlier, in which it was suspected Conway and Gates were covertly attempting to undermine General Washington and replace him as commander in chief of the Continental Army. If rancor against these men still had a place in Washington's heart, it was not evident as he stood on the floor of the United States Congress. He appeared before Mifflin as a servant of his country, subject to the will of the people, through their congress, and its president.

His letter of resignation was read and returned to him. A motion was made, loudly seconded, and unanimously voted in the affirmative: that on Monday, December 22, Congress should entertain the general and his aides with a day touring the city of Annapolis, followed by a sumptuous supper in his honor. Further, that at twelve o'clock noon on Tuesday, December 23, 1783, Congress should receive the general to formally accept his letter of resignation and conduct such other business as he desired to bring before it.

Within minutes of the vote on the motion, the news was outside the state house, and it leaped through Annapolis and the surrounding countryside before the wintry December sun had set. Every shop, every tavern, every ship in the harbor was alive with outbursts and exclamations, and by evening the pending resignation of General George Washington was the single topic that buzzed in every home.

Resign? It had never occurred to either Congress or the nation that he would resign, or even that he *could* resign, for he had risen above mortality! He had become the Revolution! How does a Revolution resign? Through eight years of cannon and musket, freezing, sickness, starving, struggling with an untrained, ragtag army, his inspired vision of a free country and his unwavering iron will had been their anchor, their cornerstone, their rock, leading them steadily on through the storm to the impossible victory over the mightiest military power on earth. In the memory of living men, none could recall a mortal more deserving to be their king for as long as he lived. It was his right!

Resign? The thought struck fear into their hearts. To whom would they turn? Whom could they trust? What was to become of their foundling nation?

On Sunday the general attended church services in a simple, small chapel that was jammed to the walls with citizens seeking to catch a glimpse of him, with a crowd waiting outside to watch him pass to his carriage. On Monday the streets were lined with people of every age, every description, watching, saluting, waving, as the general was escorted through the town. Aides and soldiers had to force a path through the crowd that surrounded the dining hall where the great supper was served, then again through the throng that gathered along the route to the ballroom where the finest Annapolis had to offer in music and entertainment and dancing was provided.

Tuesday morning the general spent in quiet reflection in his quarters, writing notes regarding some details he felt necessary to personally attend, and then composing a few remarks he wished to make to Congress at the time he would formally present his letter of resignation. At fifteen minutes before noon he left his quarters in company with his aides and his escort, and walked through the throng to the state house. At noon he entered the building and proceeded to the doors behind which Congress waited. The hallway was jammed with hushed men and women in their best attire. The sergeant at arms requested that he wait, then disappeared inside the assembly hall. Moments later he reappeared, escorting Charles Thomson, a beloved colleague of the general who had served as Secretary of Congress when Washington had served as a member. The two men clasped hands warmly, then Thomson, now a senior and revered member of Congress, opened the door and escorted Washington into the chamber. President Mifflin designated a chair, and Washington sat down. Citizens of high standing and their ladies were shown in and given preferred seats. Then the doors to the chamber and the gallery were opened to the public. In seconds there was no place to sit, or stand; the room was jammed to the walls, with people crowded into the corridors and halls, fervently hoping for a glimpse of Washington and to catch a few words.

The secretary stood and gaveled the tumult to silence, then turned to President Mifflin, who rose and addressed Washington.

"Sir, the United States in Congress assembled are prepared to receive your communications."

The air was electric. Everyone knew they were witnessing an event that would stand alone in the annals of history for all time. No one dared breathe aloud. Every eye was on the general to catch his every expression, every ear strained to catch his every word.

The general stood, and he bowed! He bowed! He to whom every person in the building would have gladly gone to their knees, bowed to them. Then he drew a piece of parchment from his pocket, carefully unfolded it, and held it with hands that were visibly shaking. He paused for a moment, and then he spoke.

"Mr. President. The great events on which my resignation depended having at length taken place; I have now the honor of offering my sincere Congratulations to Congress and of presenting myself before them to surrender into their hands the trust committed to me, and to claim the indulgence of retiring from the service of my country."

He stopped and he choked, and struggled to regain his composure. He waited until he could control the shaking of his hands. Tears were running down the cheeks of every human being present, and none thought of it, or cared. The great man continued, his voice regaining its strength as he spoke.

"Happy in the confirmation of our Independence and Sovereignty, and pleased with the opportunity afforded the United States of becoming a respectable Nation, I resign with satisfaction the Appointment I accepted with diffidence. A diffidence in my abilities to accomplish so arduous a task, which however was superseded by a confidence in the rectitude of our Cause, the support of the supreme Power of the Union, and the patronage of Heaven.

"The successful termination of the War has verified the most sanguine expectations, and my gratitude for the interposition of Providence, and the assistance I have received from my Countrymen, increases with every review of the momentous Contest.

"While I repeat my obligations to the Army in general, I should do injustice to my own feelings not to acknowledge in this place the peculiar Services and distinguished merits of the Gentlemen who have been attached to my person during the War. It was impossible the choice of confidential Officers to compose my family should have been more fortunate. Permit me, Sir, to recommend in particular those, who have continued in Service to the present moment, as worthy of the favorable notice and patronage of Congress.

"I consider it an indispensable duty to close this solemn act of my Official life, by commending the Interests of our dearest Country to protection of Almighty God, and those who have the superintendence of them, to his holy keeping.

"Having now finished the work assigned me, I retire from the great theatre of action; and bidding an Affectionate farewell to this August body under whose orders I have so long acted, I here offer my commission and take my leave of all the employments of public life."

At that moment a sensation of awe settled over the entire assembly. In their hearts they knew. Never again would they be in the presence of a man who had the world at his feet for the asking, but who was above the human need to seize it. In the darkest hours of the eight years now ended, when the urgent needs of the battlefield demanded that

Washington assume control of the Continental Army without interference of an awkward, cumbersome Congress, this man had never wavered. The free and independent nation he envisioned had to be—*had to be*—governed by the voice of the people through their elected representatives. No one, including Congress itself, could remember the countless times Washington had deferred his own views, his own needs, his own fears, demanding that ultimate control of himself, and his army, rested with the people, not with him. How many governments in Europe had been surrendered into the hands of the military, only to discover too late that such power in the hands of warriors invariably led to the same result—disaster? It was the hallmark of the history of the world. The people knew, and they peered at Washington through their tears, and they were humbled.

Washington drew his commission from his tunic pocket, folded the copy of his very brief address, stepped forward, handed the two papers to Mifflin, nodded, stepped back, and remained on his feet facing Mifflin, waiting.

Mifflin stood, and from his desk raised a sheet of paper on which was written a brief acceptance speech. When he could control his feelings, Mifflin read in a voice cracking with emotion.

"Called upon by your country to defend its invaded rights, you accepted the sacred charge before it had formed alliances and while it was without funds or a government to support you. You have conducted the great military contest with wisdom and fortitude, invariably regarding the rights of the civil power, through all the disasters and changes. You have, by the love and confidence of your fellow citizens, enabled them to display their martial genius and transmit their fame to posterity. You have persevered until these United States have been enabled, under a just Providence, to close the war in freedom, safety, and independence . . . but the glory of your virtues will not terminate with your military command. It will continue to animate remote ages. . . . And for you, we address to Him our earnest prayers that a life so beloved may be fostered with all His care; that your days may be happy, as they have been illustrious, and that He will finally give you that reward which this world will not give."

For a brief moment the hall was gripped in silence. Then Mifflin laid his paper down, and an audible sigh filled the room. Eyes brimming, Charles Thomson approached Washington to hand him a copy of Mifflin's acceptance speech and shake his hand warmly. Washington nodded to his old friend, then turned to Mifflin and bowed once more, then turned first to his right, and then his left, bowing finally to the delegates in Congress. He turned, and with his aides, walked from the chamber.

Immediately Mifflin adjourned the business of the day and dismissed the spectators. When the only persons remaining were the delegates themselves, Washington reentered the hall and personally visited the desk of each man to shake his hand and express gratitude for his services. Few could hold back the tears. No man present anticipated ever again feeling such a surge in his heart as they watched this tall, erect man walk from their chamber and close the door.

Washington made his way through the quiet, waiting throng to his carriage with one vision in his mind: his Martha, and his home, Mt. Vernon. It welled up in his chest and filled every fiber of his being with anticipation and longing. The feel of her arms about him. Her gentle touch, and the love in her eyes. The excited chatter of her grandchildren through her son, Jack Custis, who had become as his own. And the sight of the house, square, solid, amid the outbuildings and orchards and rolling hills. Home. Hearth. Family. The world offered nothing of higher value.

The carriage tilted as the big man stepped in and took his place. An aide firmly closed the door and nodded up to the driver. The whip popped above the matched horses, and the coach moved through the cobblestone streets.

Citizen George Washington, Esquire, was going home.

Notes

The visit to Annapolis where Congress was sitting, and the resignation of his commission by George Washington as commander in chief of the American

Continental Army, at noon on December 23, 1783, as herein described is historically accurate, including Washington's yearning to be home with his wife and family (Freeman, *Washington*, pp. 508–10).

The brief address given by Washington to Congress when he resigned his commission is quoted verbatim, since this author felt it to be one of the great documents to come from that time period. The spelling and punctuation are preserved as they appeared in the original document composed by George Washington (Fitzpatrick, *The Writings of George Washington*, pp. 284–85).

The acceptance speech given by Thomas Mifflin, then president of Congress, is quoted verbatim herein, in nearly full context (Bowers, *The Young Jefferson*, p. 320).

CHAPTER XXI

*D*orothy Weems rinsed the last bowl from the midday dishes, handed it to Trudy to dry, and was wiping her hands on her apron as she walked to the archway to thoughtfully watch Billy. He was seated at the dining table with business papers in two stacks, head bowed, studying a four-page summary of the last fifteen months of business done by Covington and Sons shipping firm. He shifted, raised his head to stare at the front door expectantly, then resumed his intense concentration, shaking his head from time to time at the unmistakable profile of the failing shipping business that was emerging from the paperwork. Dorothy could not miss the set of his jaw and the grim lines about his eyes and mouth.

"Not encouraging?" she asked.

"Bad."

"Are you still expecting Matthew?"

"He's late."

"What is it he's bringing?"

Billy sighed and leaned back, then raised his arms and stretched set muscles. "The bank and Covington agreed to most of our offer. You knew that?"

"Yes. Last week." She walked to stand near his chair, waiting.

"Their acceptance of our offer depended on two things: We must deal in gold or silver, and not in printed money. And we have to find merchants here, and in the South, that are willing to use our ships to carry their goods so we have a profitable cargo both directions. Without cargo, a shipping firm is worthless."

"Is that what Matthew's been working on?"

"Yes. There's a manufacturer here in Boston that's willing to ship nails and salt fish down to a buyer in Virginia, and we have a Virginia tobacco merchant willing to ship tobacco here, if we'll guarantee a sale. It all has to be in hard money, not paper. Matthew's been trying to find a buyer. That's where we—"

Dorothy jumped and Billy flinched at the sharp, distinctive knock on the front door, and Billy was on his feet and moving before Dorothy could turn. He threw the door open and instantly stepped back.

"Come in."

Matthew stepped inside with a sheaf of papers beneath his arm, and Billy closed the door against the December cold. For one split second neither man spoke, and then Billy said, "Well?"

Matthew lifted his tricorn from his head. His mouth was a straight line, his forehead drawn down.

"There's an interested tobacco buyer in New York. Maybe."

Billy's face fell. "Maybe?"

"Maybe. Dutch. He's contracting for three hundred tons of tobacco to be delivered between now and May. Right now he's waiting for a guarantee from a bank in Amsterdam."

"Guarantee of what?"

"That they'll loan him the money to buy. The Dutch have access to all British ports, and this merchant has big customers in London and Liverpool. Paris, too. The problem with the Amsterdam bank isn't the European market. It's here in the United States. Just about everybody over there knows this country is bankrupt, and they're reluctant to give a guarantee that depends in part on American ships and merchants."

Dorothy interrupted. "Take off your coat. You two can sit at the table. I'll be in the kitchen."

Matthew worked with the buttons on his heavy coat, then hung it and his tricorn and scarf on the line of pegs beside the front door. The two men took places at the table, and Matthew laid his sheaf of business papers alongside those already there. Billy leaned forward, forearms on the table.

"Anyone know when the Amsterdam bank will decide?"

"The Dutch merchant thinks they made their decision about four weeks ago. The problem is the Atlantic Ocean. They're just waiting for the ship to get here with the mail."

Billy made instant calculations. "Four weeks? The ship could get here next week."

"Yes. It could. If it does, and if the Dutch bank will guarantee, we'll most likely get the contract to carry three hundred tons of the tobacco from Virginia to New York."

"Nails and salt fish going down, tobacco coming back?"

"That's how it looks right now, but this whole thing is unstable. If we don't get the answer from the Dutch in the next few days, I don't know how long the other merchants will wait. Our bank won't wait forever, either."

"Has our bank said anything? Are they backing out?"

"Not yet. But they're nervous."

"And we can't do anything but wait."

Matthew nodded his head. "That's about it."

Billy closed his eyes and leaned back in his chair, and Matthew ran his hand through his thick, dark hair. Nerves and tension and weariness made lines in the faces of both men as they passed a moment of silence, each making calculations, going over the entire shaky plan one more time, judging the weaknesses and strengths, probing for any way to shore it up, knowing there was nothing more they could do.

Finally, Matthew rounded his mouth and blew air, then pointed at the papers stacked on the table.

"How do you see Covington Shipping?"

Billy shook his head. "They're finished. No bank will touch them."

"That's how I see it." Matthew tapped the papers he had brought. "These papers are from the Dutch tobacco buyer. Named Doernen. Been in business for eleven years. Fairly good reputation. I'll leave this with you."

Billy nodded. "I'll look them over. Will you be home later?"

"Yes."

"All right if I come down when I've finished reading them?"

Matthew stood and walked to the door to put on his coat and scarf. "I'll be waiting."

For more than an hour Billy carefully went through the paperwork on Doernen Company, of Amsterdam. Then he dug the heels of his hands into his eyes, stood, stretched, and went to the kitchen to drink water dipped from the water bucket, then walked to his room to change from his worn woolen slippers to his shoes.

He was seated on his bed closing the buckle on his shoe when a powerful, unexpected thought came into his mind. He snapped the buckle closed, then slowly rose from the bed and crossed the room to the chest of drawers in which his clean clothing was kept. He opened the bottom drawer and drew out the oilskin packet he had placed there the day he arrived home. Carefully wrapped inside were the letters he had written over the past five years, in which he had opened his heart to Brigitte. He untied the leather cord, unfolded the oilskin, and returned to sit on his bed. For a long time he tenderly touched the worn, ragged pages, reading the faded words from a few of them, remembering the times that thoughts of her, and writing the letters he was never going to deliver, had sustained him through one more night, one more battle. Thoughtfully he rewrapped the packet and carried it with him through the house to where his overcoat and scarf hung on the pegs by the front door. He thrust the packet into one of the coat pockets, put the coat on, gathered the papers from the dining table, and walked to the kitchen, where Dorothy was adding split pieces of wood to the stove fire.

"I'll be back soon. Maybe an hour."

"Matthew?"

"Yes."

The brief walk in the cold of a December late afternoon went unnoticed. Kathleen met him at the door, and minutes later he was seated in the library of the great Thorpe home, Matthew beside him, both facing the large, ornately carved desk.

Matthew waited in silent expectation.

Billy tapped the papers. "The Dutch company—Doernen—is probably reliable. I think they understand the tobacco business, and the shipping business. They deal hard but fair. If their Amsterdam bank backs them, I think they're what we're looking for."

Matthew leaned back in his upholstered chair. "Can I tell that to our bank?"

"Yes. And anyone else in this arrangement that wants to know."

Matthew shook his head. "Did you ever think you'd find yourself getting involved in these kinds of business dealings?"

Billy spoke earnestly. "Never. I still can't believe what we're doing."

"Sleep much at night?"

"Not much."

"Have you told your family all about it?"

"Yes."

"I've told Kathleen and Mother. Tried to warn them. They haven't said no."

"I'm not sure they really understand the risk."

"Probably not."

There was a pause, and then Billy dropped his face downward for a time, silently staring at the design in the India carpet under his feet. He raised his head and turned to Matthew, and Matthew stopped all motion. He had never seen the expression that was now on Billy's face.

Billy cleared his throat and spoke softly. "There's something I need to say."

Matthew's breathing slowed.

Billy went to his overcoat and drew out the packet of letters. For a moment he held them, then walked back to lay them on the near edge of the great desk. He pointed at them.

"Those are letters I've written to Brigitte. The first one was five years ago. It was then that I first understood that I had a special . . . strong . . . feeling for her."

He turned and looked his lifelong, closest friend in the eye. Neither knew how long they stared, Billy watching for a sign from Matthew, Matthew stunned beyond words. Billy went on.

"I kept them. Undelivered. I didn't want . . . I wouldn't put them in her hands or say anything to her about them because I couldn't hurt her. I know her feelings for the British captain, Richard Buchanan, and I know he is gone, and her heart with him. I know I will never be the sort of man she wants, or deserves, and I would never do anything that would put a barrier between her and me. I will not risk losing her as a friend."

He stopped, and for a few moments remained silent before he went on.

"It's possible our two families are going into business together, and the business could fail. I thought you should know about these letters before things go any further." Billy stopped, set his jaw, and waited.

For a time the only sound in the library was the crackling of the fire in the fireplace. Matthew stared, his mind numbed beyond thought. His voice cracked when he tried to speak, and he started again.

"Five years?"

Billy nodded.

"And not a word about it to anyone?"

"Eli Stroud knows. And Alvin Turlock. No one else."

Matthew came directly to it, as only lifelong, trusted friends can. "Do you love her?"

Billy thought for a moment. "I don't know. I've never had anything to do with women. I think so. Yes. I think I do."

"You kept all this inside? Why couldn't you tell me?"

"To spare you. Your family. Nothing can come of it."

"Why?"

"Look at her. A lady. Beautiful. She's worthy of a gentleman with breeding. Now look at me. Billy Weems. Just Billy Weems. I'll never reach her. Not where she is. I wouldn't embarrass her with ever letting her know all this."

Matthew spoke with an intensity Billy had never heard in him before. "You decided all this without telling her?"

Billy slowly straightened. "I didn't want to—"

Matthew cut him off, his voice rising. "Do you think she hasn't learned something about what's valuable in this life? Learned something from these past eight years?"

Billy leaned back, startled. "What do you mean?"

"The value of what a man *is*, not how he looks."

Billy leaned forward. "Matthew, look at me. No woman like Brigitte is going to take interest in a man who looks like this. I know that. I've accepted it."

Matthew paused to choose his words. "I look at you, and I see one of the best men alive."

There they were! Words that had lain unspoken inside Matthew all his life. Words he thought Billy understood without hearing them. Words he thought he would never speak. Out in the open between the two of them.

Billy did not speak nor move, because he could not. Matthew went on.

"What do you think Brigitte sees when she looks at you?"

Billy recoiled. For a full ten seconds neither man spoke, and then Billy broke the intense silence.

"I don't know."

"Are you willing to risk finding out?"

Billy weighed his words carefully. "I won't risk hurting her. I won't."

A strange look that was a mix of pain and resolve crossed Matthew's face before he continued.

"Maybe what you mean is that you won't risk hurting yourself, should she reject you. The price of every right thing in this life is risk. Wife. Children. Country. There is risk in all of them. And pain. The rewards are there only for those who are willing to pay the price."

"You think I should tell her?"

"Are you ready to spend the rest of your life wondering?"

Billy drew and slowly released a great breath. "I can't do anything that might hurt her. I *can't*."

"It might hurt her. Or it might bring her the greatest fulfillment she will ever know. The only question is, which? There's the risk. Are you willing to take it? Or are you going to settle for fifty years of not knowing? Of living with an ache that can only get worse?"

The beginnings of fear came into Billy's face as Matthew went on.

"You said Eli Stroud knows. What did he have to say about it?"

"Deliver the letters."

"Didn't Eli lose his wife?"

"Mary died when Laura was born."

"He took the risk, and he knows the pain, and still he told you to deliver the letters."

Billy's eyes widened, but he said nothing, and Matthew went on.

"Do you want me to read the letters?"

"No! . . . Yes." Billy held his head in his hands. "If you want to."

"I doubt it. They're between you and Brigitte."

"But, you think I should tell her?"

"Yes. But that's for you to decide."

For a time Billy sat in silence, working with the new thoughts. Then he stood, picked up the packet, and walked to his coat.

"When you hear from that Amsterdam bank, let me know."

He slipped the packet into the coat pocket and then put the coat on. He said nothing more of the letters; for the moment the matter was closed between them.

Matthew spoke as they walked to the front door. "I will. Tomorrow's the Sabbath. See you at church?"

"We'll be there. Do you know how Silas is getting on? His health? And Mattie's?"

"Mattie's failing. Silas is starting to show aging."

"See you in the morning."

Billy tightened his scarf, raised his coat collar against the crisp night air, and slowly walked home, working with his thoughts. He spoke very little at the supper table and said nothing as he helped gather the dishes to the wooden washtub in the kitchen, with Dorothy watching his every expression, aware he was struggling with something inside. He knelt with Dorothy and Trudy for evening prayer, then went to his room to sit on his bed fully dressed until past eleven o'clock. He was in his bed by midnight, staring upward in the blackness, and he did not drift off into a troubled sleep until after one o'clock.

The Sabbath broke with a frigid sun in a clear, cloudless, windless sky, to transform the frost on the trees into countless tiny prisms of yellow, green, and blue diamonds. Neighbors raised top hats and uttered their typical Boston "Good morning to you" as they walked to church, with vapor trailing behind their heads. The bell in the tower was ringing as they entered the small white building, and their faces had white spots from the cold as the families took their places in their reserved pews. The Reverend Silas Olmsted labored to the pulpit on stiff legs to conduct services and deliver his sermon. It was clear the fire still burned within his heart, despite the diminished strength in his voice. At the conclusion of the meeting, he took his usual place beside the door to bid his congregation his customary good-bye, and they slowed to shake his hand warmly and share their love for this little man who had spent his life as their spiritual counselor.

Outside, the Weemses waited for the Dunsons, as they had ever since they could remember, and for a few moments the two families stood on the cobblestone walk in the usual banter and chatter before they began the short walk home. As the talk died and they said their good-byes, Billy spoke quietly to Brigitte.

"Could I walk with you part way?"

Matthew caught the words, and with no visible sign, listened to hear Brigitte's reply.

For an instant her eyes narrowed in question before she answered. "Of course." She turned to Margaret. "You go on. I'll be home shortly."

Margaret looked at her, then Billy, but did not question it. "We'll start dinner. Don't be long."

Dorothy stood silent, wonder in her eyes.

Billy took Brigitte's arm and steered her away from the few people left in front of the church, to the street on the west. They walked for a time, side by side, each with their hands thrust into their coat pockets, saying nothing. They had reached the corner before a premonition rose within Brigitte's heart, and she slowed.

"You wanted to talk?"

Billy nodded. "Yes."

He stopped, and Brigitte saw him struggle to take charge of himself. After a moment, he said, "Over five years ago I became aware of some feelings inside of me. For you."

He heard her gasp, glanced at her, but went on.

"It was during battle. I lived through it, and when I could, I wrote you a letter."

"I didn't receive it."

"I didn't send it."

"You didn't send it?"

"No. I wrote another. And I kept writing. I wrote about the things happening around me, and the pain of war—killing—and my thoughts about it all."

Again he paused, and she waited.

"And I wrote about my feelings for you. It's all in the letters. . . . Twenty-two of them. . . . I still have them."

He began to walk, with her beside him, and Brigitte turned her head to look at him, then straightened to stare straight ahead, shocked beyond words. Quietly Billy went on.

"I did not intend you should ever see the letters. I did not think I would ever be telling you this. But with our families ready to go into a business that will be difficult at best, and a failure at worst, it seemed to me you should know."

She forced the words. "You wrote of your feelings for me?"

"Yes."

She wanted desperately to ask him of those feelings, but could not.

He went on. "I think I have unsettled you with all this. Badly. I doubt it would be good to talk much further right now. I think it will be better if you take the letters and read them. Start with the oldest first. Take whatever time you need. I only ask that when you've finished, and taken time to understand your own thoughts, you share them with me."

He stopped on the cobblestones, and she stopped, and he looked her full in the face.

"Will you do that?"

"Read the letters?"

"And talk with me after?"

She nodded. "Yes. I will."

"Thank you." He drew the packet from his pocket and offered it to her, and she accepted it and stared at it for several seconds before she put it in her coat pocket. He pointed up the street, and walked her to the gate into her yard, and held it for her as she walked steadily to the front door. She entered the house without looking back, and Billy closed the gate, and turned toward his own home.

Inside, Brigitte walked into the kitchen, where Margaret and Prissy were bustling with the stove and pots of steaming food, and stopped.

"Mother, I'll be in my room for a while."

Margaret had never heard her voice so subdued. "Child, what is it? What did Billy want? Is something wrong?"

Brigitte shook her head. "Nothing's wrong. We'll talk later."

Margaret listened to Brigitte's footsteps fade in the hallway, then heard her bedroom door close. For several moments she stood still, caught between needing to know what had happened to unsettle Brigitte so badly, and Brigitte's right to the privacy of her own affairs.

Inside her room, Brigitte turned up the lamp and drew the packet from her coat pocket, then sat on the bed, still wearing her coat and Sunday bonnet. Her fingers were trembling as she unwrapped the letters, and her heart was pounding when she opened the first one. The paper was yellowed, and the lines fading. She turned it to the light to read.

> My Dear Brigitte:
>
> The fortunes of the battlefield have made me accept the fact that many of us will not be coming home. In the quiet of the night I have thought on this and realized the need to use what time I have, be it much or little, to spend on things that matter. It was to me a surprise to realize that thoughts of you came often, and then they became dear to me. I did not know how strong a place you hold in my heart. . . .

She finished the letter and sat staring at it for a long time. Never in her life had she supposed she would ever read such a thing from Billy.

She set the first letter aside and unfolded the next one, curled, water-stained, fading.

> My Dear Brigitte:
>   Since last I wrote, I have come to understand I cannot send these letters to you, since your heart belongs to another, and in any event, can never belong to me. Still, there is that inside of me that demands I write to you, and I shall continue to do so. I know the words are only for me, but still, the writing of them brings a sense of peace. . . .

She blinked in disbelief. Billy? Billy Weems? He had such feelings? He could write such words? She folded the letter and reached for the third.

> My Dear Brigitte:
>   It seems that the best connection I have to carry me from the insanity of war to my loved ones at home, is the letters I write to you . . .

She continued reading the letters as they came from the packet. Her breath came short as she began with the ninth. In a cramped and labored hand, Billy had written:

> My Dear Brigitte:
>   I find myself in the north woods, not far from the Mohawk River, with my good friend Eli Stroud. We are under orders to find and make a report on certain Indians. We were ambushed by at least nine of them, and in the combat I sustained a rather severe tomahawk wound on the back of my left shoulder. Eli tended the wound, and it appears it will be all right, except that my left arm is tightly bound to my body. I spent two nights

with a heavy fever that brought many dreams, and my
only clear recollection is that you were there . . .

She brought the letter to her breast and her head rolled back. She closed her eyes and murmured, "Oh. Oh."

Margaret's determined steps sounded in the hall, and Brigitte waited for the firm rap on the door.

"Brigitte! Are you all right?"

Brigitte did not move. There was a vacant sound in her voice as she said, "Come in."

Margaret opened the door and set one foot inside the room, then stopped short at the sight of Brigitte sitting, white-faced, on her bed with the letters on both sides, still in her coat and bonnet. Margaret's hand flew to her throat.

"Child! What . . . have you seen a ghost?"

Brigitte could only raise the letter in her hand to her mother and stare into her eyes.

Margaret seized it and blurted, "What is it? Who wrote it?"

Brigitte gestured to those still in the oilskin packet and those she had already read, and shook her head without saying a word. Margaret turned the letter in her hand to the light and looked first at the signature. Her face drew down in profound wonderment.

"Billy? He wrote this?"

Brigitte nodded but said nothing.

Margaret did not move as she read the faded lines. Then she looked at Brigitte in stunned disbelief, and carefully read it again while her mind refused to accept it.

"When did you get these?"

"Coming home from church. That's what Billy wanted to see me about."

"How many?"

"I don't know. Many."

"What do the others say?"

Brigitte pointed. "I've read these. They're like the one you have. I haven't read the rest of them yet."

It took Margaret time to force her thoughts into some sense of order. "How long have you known?"

"Not until today. Now."

"Never a word before?"

"Never."

"May I read some of the others?"

Brigitte gestured and Margaret sat on the bed. For ten minutes there was no sound in the bedroom while Margaret silently read.

Footsteps in the hall brought both their heads up, and Prissy stepped through the open door. "I think the potatoes are done."

"Set them off the stove. Take care of the kitchen. We'll be out in a while."

Prissy asked, "What are all the papers?"

Margaret raised a hand. "Later. Take care of the potatoes. Close the door, please."

Prissy shrugged and closed the door as she left.

Margaret turned to Brigitte. "You had no idea?"

Brigitte looked her in the eye. "None."

Margaret licked dry lips and slowly began to shake her head. "Billy. In a thousand years. . . . That poor boy! Held this inside for over five years. Oh, how I wish he had said something."

She turned to Brigitte and reached for her hand. "I can't imagine the shock to you. Billy. Billy Weems. Have you ever had these kinds of feelings for him?"

"No, Mama. Never. Not once. He's always been Billy. Like Matthew."

"Could you ever feel this way about him?"

"I can't feel anything right now."

"I was wrong to ask. Wait. Give this some time. Do you want me to bring supper in to you?"

Brigitte paused before answering. "No. I don't think so. I'll come out."

"I'll tell Adam and Prissy something so they won't bother you. We'll have supper on in about an hour."

"I want to read a few more letters and then put them away."

"Get your coat and bonnet off. Do you want me to stay here with you?"

"No. I'll be all right. I'll come for supper."

"Call if you need me."

Margaret stood and walked to the door with the question burning in her mind as to why she had not seen this coming—how had she failed to see what was now plain before her eyes? She stopped to look at Brigitte one more time, then closed the door, and walked down the hall to the archway, slowly realizing there were two men named Billy Weems—the boy up the street whom she and her family had known all his life and helped raise as if he were their own, and the stranger who had declared his love for her daughter Brigitte. She did not know if she could ever make the two into one.

She walked into the kitchen and thrust a fork into the potatoes, then turned to Prissy.

"They're done. Get some flour. When the ham's done we'll use some of the potato water and ham drippings for gravy. Supper will be in an hour. Brigitte has a bad pain in her chest. We might have to send Adam to get Doctor Soderquist."

Two blocks to the northwest, Billy sat on his bed, alone in his room, door closed. For a time he stared blankly at the wall, then rose to pace, then walked to the parlor where Dorothy was knitting while she rocked quietly before the fireplace, and Trudy was seated at the table, poring over the Bible.

"Mother, could I talk with you? In my bedroom?"

Dorothy stilled her hands and looked at Billy for a moment. She laid her knitting aside and followed him quietly down the hall into his room, and he closed the door. He sat on the bed and gestured, and she sat beside him.

"There are some things you need to know. It's about me, and some feelings I have for . . . Brigitte."

A mother's intuition rose in her chest, and Dorothy's breathing slowed with the impossible premonition. "Does it have to do with you walking with her after church?"

"Yes. It does. That and more. Much more. I'll tell you."

Notes

The Dunson and Weems families and their affairs are of course fictional as previously indicated.

CHAPTER XXII

★ ★ ★

*O*n the waterfront, the draw of a grudge fight was nearly irresistible.

Among the rich and powerful, gentlemen settled their differences with dueling pistols, or swords, in an agreed-to, secluded place away from the eyes of all but the two contestants, the ones chosen to act as their seconds, a disinterested party selected to conduct the matter, and a doctor to declare one party or the other dead should that become necessary. The entire proceeding was conducted according to a plethora of rules that had to be scrupulously observed to preserve the notion that the killing was a civilized way of settling affairs of honor, and not bald-faced murder.

Not so on the docks. Differences between two bearded dockhands, each of whom was absolutely destitute of wealth or power, and each of whom smelled of drink and sweat and wore shabby clothing, were settled with fists or clubs or freight-hooks, surrounded by a raucous crowd of their peers, gathered for the evil pleasure of seeing the blood of men locked in mortal combat.

Society deemed the former procedure honorable, and the second one despicable, notwithstanding the hard fact that the purpose of both rituals was identical, and generally, at least, so were the results.

Cobweb ice was forming near the shore when Caleb lowered himself into his borrowed rowboat at the foot of Copp's Hill on the eastern tip of the Boston peninsula. In the gloom of early evening he dipped his right oar deep and pulled hard to turn the boat and take a bearing on the lights of the western shores of the Charlestown peninsula, five hundred yards across the channel that separated the two. For the first ten yards he could hear the rasping sound of ice disintegrating against the bow of the small craft, and he felt the slight resistance as his oars punched through. Vapors trailed behind his head as he steadily stroked for the far shore, feet braced to take the leverage as he put his back into it.

The boat ground onto the rocks and sand of the shore, and he shipped the oars and jumped onto the frozen bank to drag it out of the water, then walked up a beaten path onto the docks and slowed to study who was there, and what they were doing. A few laborers were still working to unload two ships by firelight, and paid him no attention. Beyond them, forty yards off the far end of the black timbers of the wharf, stood the burned-out wreckage of the old Hollenbeck Warehouse. It was within the half-burned roof and walls of the abandoned warehouse that Loman had arranged to have Caleb and Judd meet after dark to settle their differences according to the customs of the waterfront, which meant a brawl until one of them was unconscious, or unable to get back onto his feet, or dead.

Caleb hunched his shoulders inside his heavy coat and with measured steps walked steadily toward the crowd that was gathered in clusters around the fires. None recognized him as he passed, and he was close to the warehouse door, which hung at an awkward angle on one hinge, when Loman, in his threadbare coat, stepped outside, agitated, impatient, and thrust a finger in Caleb's face.

"You're late! We've been waiting! There's over three hundred men in here that've paid ten cents each to see this, and they're getting surly." The little man's eyes were accusatory beneath the shaggy brows, and the odor of rum was overpowering on his breath.

Caleb followed him inside the old structure where more fires burned for light and warmth. Men were jammed to the charred walls, talking, gesturing in the dancing shadows, and the odor of rum and smoke and sweat rode heavy in the air. The crowd quieted and a path opened as

Loman led Caleb to an open space in the center of the building, where the old, partially burned wooden floor had been ripped up and thrown out behind the building, leaving a patch of bare earth. Standing to one side of the dirt floor was Judd, wearing an old coat, hands jammed in the pockets, towering head and shoulders above those around him. A wicked leer fixed his face the moment he saw Caleb.

Loman wasted no time. He stepped to the center of the open place and shouted down the crowd.

"We're ready. The rules are that no one can help either man, no matter what. The contest lasts until one of them is down and can't get up. Neither man can use anything but his own hands and feet. No biting, no eye-gouging." He stopped to point to his left at a thick-shouldered man with a dirty beard and heavily scarred brows. "Tagger will see to it no one interferes or breaks the rules."

He turned to Caleb.

"You ready? You want your coat off?"

Caleb unbuttoned his coat and tossed it aside.

Loman turned to Judd.

"Coat off?"

Judd handed his coat to the man next to him, and Loman continued.

"Either of you want your hands wrapped?"

Neither did.

Loman motioned. "Both of you, get out here in the center of the floor."

The two walked out to face each other, Judd a full six inches taller than Caleb, and seventy pounds heavier. A murmur ran through the crowd.

Loman held up an old cloth bag, tied with a scrap of hemp cord. "The purse is fifteen dollars and ten cents, winner takes all. No matter how this turns out, that's the end of it. Do you both agree?"

Both men nodded.

"All right. Start."

Loman backed out of the opening, Caleb raised his hands, and Judd started toward him, hunched forward, arms spread, moving ponderously as noise from the crowd began to build. Caleb began a shuffling circle to his left, eyes locked onto Judd's chest, catching the vision of the whole man as he came on. Judd lunged, reaching, Caleb slid beneath his left arm, and dug his right fist into Judd's belly as he came past. Judd grunted, recovered, turned, and came at Caleb again. The noise from the crowd mounted as Caleb backed away and continued circling, just out of reach, waiting, watching the frustration and anger mounting in Judd's eyes. Clearly, Judd intended gathering Caleb inside his massive arms to break bones and rend flesh, and it was just beginning to break clear in Judd's mind that he could not catch Caleb. He slowed for a moment, then came on with the tumult rising inside the burned-out building.

Ten seconds passed with Caleb gliding just out of reach, and Judd lunging again, arms thrown wide. Caleb crouched under Judd's right arm and caught the bigger man on the point of his chin with his right fist as he passed him, and Judd's head snapped back as Caleb stopped behind him, waiting for Judd to turn, and for a moment Judd stood still, blood starting to trickle from his mouth, confused, unable to find Caleb. When he turned, Caleb hit him over his right ear, and the big man groaned and went to one knee and then got up, head ringing. The din was deafening. Men were shouting for Caleb to finish him, finish him, beat him down.

Caleb moved back, dropped his hands for a moment while the big man took his bearings, then once again crouched and came lunging, this time swinging his fists like clubs, clumsy, awkward, in the desperate hope one would connect. Caleb moved away, shifted to his left, once again circling, waiting, as Judd came on, swinging blind, desperate, raw fear beginning to show in his eyes and face. Patiently Caleb moved back, waiting for exactly the right moment, sensing it coming, and then it came.

Judd swung his right hand in a wide, wild arc at Caleb's head, and Caleb watched it come, judging the timing, and at the last grain of time raised his left shoulder to take most of the blow, and twisted his head away. The massive fist landed high on Caleb's shoulder and slid off and upward, grazing Caleb's left temple, and Caleb threw his head to the right as though struck hard and dropped his hands and went to his knees and toppled over and lay still in the dirt. There was silence for an instant and then bedlam, and Judd came at Caleb, kicking, and Tagger grabbed him and jerked him away. Loman strode to Caleb, crumpled in the dirt, and waited for movement or any sign he might get up, but there was none. Satisfied, Loman held up the purse and tossed it to Judd, and it was over. It had taken less than two minutes.

Lying face down in the dirt, Caleb did not move. He listened while the uproar began to quiet, and he heard the calls from a few that the fight was a fraud to get money and they wanted their ten cents back, and he heard Loman shout back at them that if they thought it was a fraud they were welcome to challenge either Judd or Caleb to a fight for another purse in one week, to satisfy themselves it had not been a fixed fight. None challenged. Slowly the crowd began to break up into small groups and work their way out the door, most complaining they had come to see a real fight, one that lasted half the night and ended with both men beaten bloody. A few passed close to stare down at Caleb, but none stopped. Minutes passed before the ruins of the old warehouse quieted, and Caleb raised his head to peer about in the dim light of the dwindling fires. The last of the crowd was pushing out the doors. The place was nearly vacant.

Loman was standing at his feet. "Why'd you quit?" he sneered, and threw Caleb's coat in the dirt near his hand.

Caleb got to his feet and picked up his coat. He slapped the dirt from it and was putting it on when Loman repeated himself.

"Why'd you quit?"

Caleb buttoned his coat, turned up the collar, and started toward the door, Loman following with hurried steps, talking loudly.

"You gave the fight to him. I saw it. Why?"

Caleb did not look back, and Loman trotted up beside him.

"Don't you know you can get rich with your fists? I can arrange it."

Caleb walked out the door, into the darkness lighted only by the flickering light of scattered fires, and turned right toward the docks and his rowboat.

"Don't be a fool!" Loman exclaimed, and seized Caleb's coat sleeve to slow him. "There's money to be made!"

Caleb stopped in the deep shadows and lifted Loman's hand from his coat sleeve.

"Judd won the purse. By tomorrow morning he'll be the king of the waterfront, and no one will remember who I am. The next man who wants to be king will have to beat Judd, not me. I don't fight for money. It's over."

Loman stepped back, eyes large in the shadowy light. "You don't want money?"

Caleb's voice purred. "Don't talk to me again about money."

"You think you can walk away? Those men will remember. You haven't seen the last of this."

"You got your fifteen dollars. This better be the end of it. If it's not, you're the first man I come looking for."

Loman gaped and backed up a step.

Caleb turned on his heel and walked away, across the docks, to his rowboat.

Notes

The events depicted in this chapter are fictional.

Boston

Late January 1784

CHAPTER XXIII

At twenty minutes before eleven o'clock, Thomas Chase Covington worked the large brass key to the front door of his shipping firm's office with fingers white and stiff in the freeze that had crusted Boston harbor with ice for five days. Wisps of vapor rose from his face as he listened to the familiar clicking of the lock bolt withdrawing, and he pushed inside the cold, bare, waterfront office, located less than fifty yards from Griffin's Wharf. The insides of the frost-coated windows were covered with a dirty film that had collected since the office closed in November, casting the room in a dull, freezing gloom.

Covington struck flint to steel and nurtured the spark in the tiny iron box of charred linen until smoke, then tiny curls of flame, caught and held. Minutes later he backed away from a newly set fire in the blackened stone fireplace, carrying a pine splinter burning on one end, and went to his desk to light the lamp. The desk, his ancient, worn chair, and four others, were all that remained of the furniture that once served a bustling office with six hired men to keep the accounts of thirteen commercial shipping companies, carrying goods to ports all over the world, and six clerks to assist them.

He set his hat on the desk, dragged his chair to the fireplace, and sat with hands extended toward the flames, reaching for the warmth that as yet hadn't spread beyond him into the shadows of the cold, vacant office.

His faded gray eyes stared into the flames, and his rounded

shoulders sagged in utter defeat. Average height and build, he had been a handsome man in times long gone. Forty-two years—his life's work of building a reputable shipping company—three sons raised in the shipping business—all of it gone. The sons scattered in search of work, the furniture sold, the books of accounts boxed and ready for delivery to two young, desperate men who hoped against harsh reality to succeed where the Covingtons had failed. At age sixty-four, with half the discharged Continental Army frantically searching for any work they could find to feed themselves and their families, there was no one—no one at all—who would consider the once proud and prosperous Thomas Chase Covington for a position commensurate with his proven skills, or any position at all. No one.

He ran a hand through his thinning hair and unbuttoned his great coat to pull at his scarf.

Sitting in the silent office with vapor still rising from every breath, the room stripped bare to the walls, he suddenly felt old. A failure. Useless. A castoff. A burden. Today he would sign over what was left of his life to Matthew Dunson and Billy Weems, and then go home to a chill, silent house filled with faint memories of the sounds of three sons now gone, and a wife who had died three years before. He could see no light left in life, nor could he find a reason to live. He held his hands toward the fire, and did and said nothing as he waited.

The opening of the door jarred him from his reveries, and he rose to face Matthew and Billy.

Matthew spoke as he unbuttoned the top of his heavy coat. "Good morning, sir."

Covington's expression did not change as he answered and gestured. "Good morning. Take a seat there at the desk." He dragged his chair back and sat down facing them. He saw no reason to prolong the pain.

"You brought the papers?"

"Right here, sir," Matthew said, and laid a folder on the desk between them.

Without a word the old man opened the folder and for ten minutes studied the documents in silence. The bill of sale for six ships and the office, the assignment of all accounts receivable—all uncollectible and without value—the assumption by Dunson and Weems of the bank notes, the total and final release by Covington of all claims whatsoever against the firm, the unconditional agreement of the bank to release Covington and accept Dunson and Weems in his place—it was all there.

He set the papers down and raised weary eyes as he leaned forward and interlaced his fingers. "There's one thing that developed just over two weeks ago. I contracted to carry a shipment of coal from the North Branch of the Potomac down to the Anacostia River. Two hundred tons. I got a crew off the docks and sent them up there, aboard the *Jessica*. They loaded the coal and got back down as far as twelve miles below where the Shenandoah joins the Potomac, where the *Jessica* was stopped by authorities from both Maryland and Virginia. They've been battling for years over who owns the river, but never like this. Both claim the right to levy a tax on the coal for the privilege of moving it on the river, and neither one is going to release her until their tax is paid."

He shook his head, and forty-two years of dealing with import and export tax and tariff wars came boiling up. "One tax, maybe. But two? Two taxes on the same cargo because Maryland and Virginia both claim the river? Those fools are going to force a war between themselves."

He leaned back and remained silent for a moment while he cooled. "So far as these papers are concerned, I can sign the *Jessica* over to you, but I can't do a thing about giving possession until the tax problem is handled. I have no idea how to go about that."

Billy leaned forward. "How much is the tax?"

"Total between the two states, about one hundred ninety pounds sterling."

"If it's not paid?"

Covington thumped a stiff finger on his desk. "They'll sell the cargo to pay it, and if they don't get enough that way, they'll sell the ship."

Matthew asked, "There's no way to compromise? Negotiate?"

Covington snorted. "Compromise? The two states are bringing cannon to face each other across the river."

Matthew straightened, alarmed. "Have you run into this before?"

Covington's teeth were on edge. "It's happening all over, from Canada to Georgia—wherever a major river divides two states. The states are all bankrupt, or close to it. They've got to have revenue. Taxing river traffic is one way to do it, and neighboring states are fighting over who owns the rights."

He stopped and for a time sat still, looking at the documents. "I didn't expect this to happen. If it makes a difference, I'll understand. You don't have to sign these papers."

Matthew turned to Billy. "What's your feeling?"

"It changes things."

"Enough to stop the transaction?"

"Maybe. If we can't pay the tax and lose the ship, we've reduced the total tonnage we can haul. And we have one less large asset if we have to sell out to pay the notes. It's bound to make a difference, now or later."

Matthew thought for a moment. "Would our bank pay the double tax to keep this deal alive?"

"Maybe. If it means the difference in making this thing work, or losing it altogether, they might do it."

Matthew heaved a sigh. "This whole transaction is a maybe. Do we go ahead?"

For ten seconds Billy held his silence. "I think so."

Covington drew a quill and inkwell from his desk drawer. "I'm sorry about the *Jessica.* I didn't mean to add that to your troubles. Shall I go ahead and sign?"

Billy glanced at Matthew, and they both nodded.

For ten minutes the three of them signed papers in duplicate, one set for each side. Finished, Covington shoved his hands into his coat pockets and settled back in his chair, eyes vacant, face blank as he struggled to know what he should do next. Forty-two years of his life, and all the responsibility of an international business, gone with the stroke of a quill. No place to go, nothing to do, no one at home, no one who cared if he lived or died. If he rose from the chair and walked out the door, where would he go? He cleared his throat to stop the trembling of his chin and drew his hand from his coat pocket to toss two big brass keys, clattering, onto the desk. Matthew and Billy each took one, studied it for a moment, then thrust it into a pocket.

"About forgot to deliver the keys. They both fit both doors. They're the only ones I know of." He turned to point to several boxes stacked in a corner. "All the books are there. They'll show you all the supply houses we've used for our food and ship needs—sails, chains, tools, paint, lamp oil—all of it. There's also a roster of all the officers and crewmen we've used over the past few years, but I don't know where any of them are now. All scattered and gone, so far as I know. I don't know of anything else I have here that will help you get started."

Matthew gathered the papers, divided them, pushed one set to Covington, and closed the others inside the folder. "Where do you want the desk and chairs delivered?"

Covington shrugged. "Keep them. I've no use for them."

The finality of his words brought him to the bottom of despair. He licked at his lips, then wiped his mouth, lost, groping. His face was suddenly that of an old, discarded man with nothing left in life but to die. He slowly rose from his chair on legs that trembled, and walked to the door with Matthew and Billy watching. Matthew turned to Billy and for a moment a silent communication passed between them, and then Billy nodded once.

Matthew called out, "Mr. Covington." The words echoed against the bare walls.

Covington took his hand from the door latch and turned, puzzled, waiting.

Matthew gave him no time. "We're going to need help. No one knows this business better than you. Would you consider being around to give us advice? We'll carry the load, but we need someone with experience to keep us from making mistakes. Serious mistakes. Interested?"

For a moment the old man straightened in disbelief. "Advice?"

"We'll move this old desk into a corner and you can watch and listen. You see us making a bad mistake, tell us. You won't have to handle the day-to-day business. We'll do that. We can't pay unless this thing works. But if it does, you'll get your fair share along with the rest of us."

"Starting when?"

"Monday."

"What fee?"

"We don't know. You tell us what's fair."

"I don't know."

"When you do, tell us. In the meantime, Monday morning?"

The old man's chin trembled, and then he answered, "I'll be here." For a moment he looked at the two young men, and then he opened the door and walked out onto the waterfront and was gone.

Matthew and Billy sat back down at the desk, and Matthew opened the folder to glance through the papers once more before he turned to Billy.

"What about the *Jessica?*"

"We'd better go see the bank. We can't afford to lose the ship."

Matthew considered for a moment. "This thing about the rivers worries me. I knew the states had their differences, but I didn't know they had begun seizing ships. We need to know what's happening."

Billy said, "Same with taxes and tariffs. We're going to be taking Boston goods to Virginia, and Virginia goods to New York. We need to know the tax laws."

Matthew nodded. "The buyers and sellers are responsible for that, not us, but it's our ships that are going to be seized and sold if they make a mistake."

"We've already got one ship in trouble. Two or three would likely ruin us."

Matthew changed direction. "We've got to get a crew and get loaded for the delivery in Virginia. I've made an offer to Theodore Pettigrew to get the crew and serve as their captain. I worked with him during the war, down in the West Indies. Good man. Can you handle the *Jessica* trouble with the bank, and check into the tax and tariff troubles?"

"Yes." He pointed at the folder on the desktop. "I'll take the papers to the bank when I go."

"Anything else?"

Billy turned to look at the boxes in the corner. "I better spend some time with those records while you're getting the crew."

"Any objection if Caleb's among them?"

"None."

Matthew pointed. "The sign above the door says Covington."

"I'll get it changed."

Matthew stood. "See you tonight."

Billy watched him walk out the door, then turned and for several seconds stood still while he studied the interior of the office, trying to comprehend that he was part-owner of a shipping firm, and that this cold, bare, waterfront room was the heart of it. For the first time he began to understand that going from an employee to an owner was a complicated thing. Ownership had been transferred by the simple stroke of a quill, but making it all a reality was going to take time and effort.

Outside on the slick timbers of the wharf, Matthew trotted west, then north, into the narrow, winding streets of Boston, to a small home fronting on the Boston Commons. He rapped at the weathered door and waited until a small woman with soft brown eyes and an infant wrapped in a blanket in her arms opened far enough to see him.

"Matthew! Come in."

She swung the door open and Matthew stepped inside and removed his hat as she closed the door.

"Dora, is Theodore home?"

"No. He's over at Winnisimmet. He heard there might be work over there."

"When do you expect him home?"

"No way to know. Why? What's happened?"

"We signed the papers for the Covington shipping business less than half an hour ago. We need your husband."

Her eyes widened. "The arrangement you and he talked about?"

"Yes."

"Steady work?" She held her breath.

"Steady. He won't see pay for more than a month, and even then it all depends on whether this thing works. It could fail."

Relief flooded through Dora, and she began to breathe again as Matthew continued.

"Do you know where he might be in Winnisimmet?"

"He took the ferry early to see a man named Toolson. He repairs boats. I don't know where he lives."

"I know Zachary Toolson. When Theodore gets home, would you tell him I'm looking for him? I'll be home later. Tell him to come no matter the hour."

"Yes. Oh, yes!"

Matthew started to turn to leave, but could not resist. "Could I see the baby?"

Proudly Dora Pettigrew carefully folded back the blanket to reveal a tiny, pink, newborn infant with a shock of straight dark hair, sound asleep. The little soul stirred, and her mouth sucked for a moment, and then she relaxed. Matthew raised a hand, then restrained his impulse to touch the little face, and he looked Dora in the eyes.

"It's a miracle every time," he said.

Dora beamed and closed the blanket. "I'll tell Theodore you want to see him."

"Take care of the little one."

"I will."

Back in the streets, Matthew slowed to make a plan, then turned west once again and moved rapidly through the streets, toward the home where he'd grown up. Fifteen minutes later he knocked on the door and pushed inside. Margaret called from the kitchen, "Who's there?"

"Me. Is Caleb home?"

Margaret walked through the archway into the parlor, wiping wet hands on her apron. "Out looking for work. What's happened?"

"We just took over the Covington shipping firm. We have work if Caleb wants it."

Margaret raised both hands defensively. "Wait, wait, wait just a minute. What do you mean, 'took over Covington'?"

"Signed the papers. The banks agreed. We need to get moving."

Margaret's eyes widened. "Does Caleb know about this?"

"I talked with him."

"He hasn't said a thing here."

There was a sense of irritation in Matthew's voice. "He doesn't say much anywhere. Know where he is?"

"In Boston somewhere, looking for work. Maybe on the waterfront. He's old enough I don't check on him."

"When do you expect him home?"

"Usually around supper."

Matthew looked at the clock—ten minutes before three in the afternoon—and walked back to the door. "Tell him I need to see him, no matter the time. I'll be either at the Covington office, or home."

Margaret strode to the door as Matthew walked out. "I'll tell him. Are Kathleen and the baby all right?"

Matthew called over his shoulder, "Fine. John's working on more teeth."

"Say hello for me."

At fifteen minutes past three o'clock, Matthew unlocked the door of the Covington office, stepped in far enough to see Billy was not there, then backed into the street and locked the door. He broke into a trot and worked his way through the scattering of men working on the waterfront, past Long's Wharf, then Clarke's Wharf, the North Battery, and continued northwest, following the curve of the peninsula to the pier where the ferry docked on its return trip from the small village of Winnisimmet, located beyond the Charlestown peninsula, on the mainland. The winter sun was low, and he could feel the temperature dropping with each passing minute. He paced and pounded his hands together for warmth while he waited for the ferry to plow through the broken ice that filled the harbor and thump into the pier. The gate lifted, the gangplank lowered, and Matthew stood tall, peering, waiting for the familiar lean figure of Theodore Pettigrew among those walking down the gangplank.

He was not there. Twilight was gathering when the last person stepped from the gangplank and disappeared into the crowd leaving the wharf, and Matthew followed, angling southeast. The evening star was prominent in the east when he once again passed the dark windows of the Covington office, and he thrust his hands in his pockets as he hurried on through the frozen streets to his home. He opened the front door and began undoing the buttons on his coat, waiting for Kathleen's usual call, but it did not come. Instead, she entered the parlor without speaking.

"Everything all right?" he asked.

"Yes. Theodore Pettigrew is waiting in the library."

Matthew quickly hung his coat and hat, and strode into the library, rubbing his hands together as the slender man stood.

"Theodore," Matthew exclaimed. "Thank you for coming. Been waiting long?"

"A few minutes."

"Can I get you something? Hot chocolate?"

"No, thank you."

Matthew pointed and the two sat down before the fire in the fireplace.

Matthew continued. "Dora told you?"

"Yes."

"Are you still interested?"

"Yes."

Matthew leaned forward. "What about the crew you spoke of? Thirteen men? Are you still in touch with them?"

"Most of them."

"How long will it take you to gather them?"

Pettigrew considered for several seconds before he spoke. "At least ten of them by tomorrow, early afternoon."

"Do they know what we're offering? They don't get paid if this project doesn't work."

"They do."

"They accept those terms?"

"It's better than what they've got."

"You'll serve as captain?"

Pettigrew nodded. "I will."

"Does Dora agree?"

"Yes."

"Can you and the crew start soon?"

"I can start as soon as everyone has agreed."

Matthew pondered for a moment. "Can you have them at the Covington office by tomorrow at two o'clock?"

"I think so. Yes."

"I'll have Billy there. Is there anything else?"

"If there is, we'll handle it tomorrow."

Matthew stood. "See you then. Thanks for coming."

The two men walked from the library to the front door, and Matthew waited while Pettigrew wrapped his scarf and buttoned his coat. He swung the door open and the yellow lamplight cast a huge, misshapen triangle out into the frost crystals. Pettigrew paused for a moment. "See you tomorrow."

"We'll be waiting."

Matthew watched him disappear into the darkness and listened while the front gate clicked shut before he stepped back into the house to close the door. Kathleen was waiting in the parlor.

"Did you sign the papers?"

"Yes."

"Is Theodore willing to help?"

"Yes."

"Have you eaten today?"

"No. Too much going on."

"I'll have your supper as soon as you wash."

Matthew was using half a slice of homemade bread to wipe his plate clean when the knock came at the door. He was off his chair instantly, hurrying to the door to throw it open. Billy was waiting. Kathleen stood in the kitchen archway, missing nothing.

"Come in," Matthew exclaimed.

Billy stepped inside and stopped. Matthew gestured.

"Come sit at the table."

"This won't take a minute."

"You talked to the bank?"

Billy's face was set. "Yes. They have to present the question of paying the double tariff on the *Jessica* to their board. That could take some time."

There was alarm in Matthew's voice. "How much time? We've got to move on this thing."

"Two weeks. Maybe more. But that's not the worst of it."

Matthew set his jaw. "Go on."

"They don't think the board will approve."

"And if they don't?"

Billy's voice became brittle. "It might be enough for them to back out."

"They can't!" Matthew exclaimed. "They've already signed the papers."

"When they signed, they didn't know that one of the ships was on the Potomac under a tax seizure. They say that's a material breach. If they'd known, they probably wouldn't have signed."

For several seconds Matthew sat still, frustration plain on his face. He continued. "I've arranged for us to meet with Theodore Pettigrew and his crew tomorrow at the office at two o'clock. What do we tell them?"

Billy shook his head and remained silent.

Matthew took a deep breath and let it out slowly. "All right. We sleep on it, and take it a day at a time. I'll see you in the morning at the office at eight o'clock. Any better idea?"

"No. See you in the morning."

Matthew held the door while Billy walked back out and disappeared into the darkness, then closed it and walked back into the parlor to pace before the fireplace for a time. For ten seconds Kathleen stood still in the kitchen archway, watching him, and then she spoke.

"There's trouble with the bank." It was a statement, not a question. "They might back out."

"Can they do that after they signed the papers?"

"They didn't know at the time they signed that both Maryland and Virginia had seized one of the ships on the Potomac River. Both states are holding it for taxes. Billy and I learned about it this morning."

"That ship on the river? The Potomac?"

"Yes."

"Won't the bank pay the tax and get it back?"

"They might not. The whole board has to approve, and that will take two weeks. Maybe more. We don't have that much time. And if the board refuses, we're back where we started."

"What are you going to do?"

Matthew tossed both hands in the air. "I don't know. Wait 'til tomorrow and see what we can come up with. I meet with Captain Pettigrew and his crew tomorrow afternoon."

Kathleen walked to the table and began gathering Matthew's supper dishes. She finished washing and drying them with Matthew still pacing in the parlor. For a time she sat quietly at the table, feeling his anguish, not knowing what to do. Finally she went to the bedroom and quietly checked on John, then returned to the parlor.

"John's asleep. I think I'll go to bed. He'll be up early."

Matthew stopped pacing and turned to her. "I'm sorry this has to happen. I just don't know what to do."

"It's all right. Do what you must."

"I'll come for prayer."

He followed her to their bed where they knelt, and Kathleen quietly offered their evening prayer. Matthew added his amen, then stood. "Go to bed. I'll come when I can."

"I know."

Kathleen was about to slip into bed when a knock sounded at the front door. She retied the sash to her housecoat and stepped into the darkened hallway, watching as Matthew opened the door. Caleb stood framed in the yellow light, hands thrust into his coat pockets, vapors rising from his breath, and small white spots from the cold showing in his face.

Matthew stepped back. "Come in."

Caleb entered and stood waiting.

Matthew said, "Mother told you?"

"The business with Covington? Yes."

Kathleen came forward. "You two want to use the library?"

Caleb shook his head.

"Would you like something hot? Chocolate?"

"Just had supper at home."

Kathleen nodded, and disappeared down the hallway to the bedroom as Matthew went on.

"We signed the papers today. Earlier you and I talked about getting a crew. Are you interested?"

"When?"

"Now. The next two or three days. You know we can't pay unless this works."

"I know that. Yes. I'm interested."

"You know about Theodore Pettigrew? He'll be the captain."

"You told me before."

"He'll meet with us tomorrow at the Covington office at two o'clock. Can you be there?"

"Yes."

"There's been some trouble with the bank."

Caleb's eyes narrowed. "What trouble?"

A hard look came onto Caleb's face as he listened to Matthew's explanation of two bordering states in a tariff war over who owned the rights to the river that bordered each of them, and both states holding a ship hostage until a double tax was paid. In his mind he was hearing echoes of the taxes that British King George had demanded of his colonies ten years earlier. Those taxes had started a war.

Caleb's voice came firm, hard. "The bank won't pay the tax to save this deal?"

"We won't know for at least two weeks."

Suddenly Caleb raised a hand. "Wait a minute. You're getting a crew together tomorrow, and don't even know if your arrangement is final?"

Matthew shook his head. "We move now, or lose it."

Caleb shifted his feet. "It might be better losing it now than later, after you've taken on a crew and a cargo."

"We'll see. Will you be there tomorrow?"

Caleb drew a deep breath and let it out slowly, thoughtfully. "I'll be there. I want to hear how you sell this whole thing to Pettigrew and his crew." He turned and opened the door. "See you tomorrow."

Matthew watched until he was gone, closed the door, and thoughtfully walked back to stand at the fireplace, staring into the dying flames for a time, and then he began to pace. At half past eleven o'clock, Kathleen walked into the parlor wearing her housecoat and woolen slippers. Her long, dark hair was in a single braid down her back, and her arms were folded as women do. She came to Matthew, still pacing before the ebbing fire.

"Come to bed. You need rest."

He stopped and faced her. "I wouldn't sleep. Only keep you awake."

She reached to take hold of his arm.

"Matthew, this will all work out. I know it will."

He looked at her, tall, beautiful, with the firelight playing softly in her dark eyes and hair. The Covington shipping business and the banks and the *Jessica* faded until she was the only thing in his life. He reached to place his fingers against her cheek, and spoke to her softly.

"I'll be all right. You go on to bed. I won't be long."

She gazed up at him, and then she said, "Hold me for a minute."

For a time they stood before the fireplace, locked in an embrace, he drawing on her strength, she giving as only a wife can give. Finally he released her, and she stepped back, smiled, then turned and walked into the dark hallway.

Dawn broke frigid in a clear, cloudless, sky. No breath of air stirred, and by seven o'clock the entire Boston peninsula was a forest of smoke columns rising from a thousand chimneys to climb straight into the blue heavens. At fifteen minutes before eight o'clock, Billy Weems turned the brass key in the door of the Dunson and Weems office, entered, and walked to the coals banked in the fireplace. He set a water bucket on the desk. Another bucket was filled with clean, folded rags. Five minutes later Matthew walked in to help him build a fire in the fireplace. By half past eight they were seated at the old desk, still wearing their heavy coats, shoulders hunched, hands deep in their pockets as they waited for the warmth to penetrate the old, square, bare room.

Billy came directly to the pivotal question. "Any thoughts about how to handle the bank and the *Jessica* problem?"

Matthew drew a deep breath. "I've thought about it. I have one question. When you were there yesterday, did the bank keep the signed papers?"

"Yes."

"Then the deal stands, at least for the next two or three weeks while their board decides yes or no."

Billy reflected. "Probably so."

"Legally, I think we've got the right to go ahead."

There was doubt in Billy's voice. "Risky. If anyone in this goes to the bank for verification, it could be bad trouble."

"It could, but in a contest, I think we'd win. We told them about the *Jessica*, and they didn't ask us to put a hold on anything. They didn't say the deal was off. They kept the papers. I think they've given consent to all this, even after they knew about the *Jessica*."

Billy brought his hands from his coat pockets and laid them on the tabletop. "I've dealt with too many banks and too many people with money when I was with Potter & Wallace. When you get to the bottom of the business world, the power is with the money. What's legal is too often what the money says is legal."

Matthew settled. "Do we stop now?"

Billy leaned back in his chair. "It's an out-and-out gamble, and it's mostly out of our control. That's a perfect setup for disaster. If we go ahead now, only one thing falls in our favor. With as many people as we have in this thing, the bank might have second thoughts about stopping it, once it's in motion. I think we gamble. Get the cargo loaded and on the way. Get the suppliers into it. The crew. The merchants. Get this thing in motion. That's business, and banks understand that. It's probably the best chance we have."

"We go ahead?"

"Let's go."

"I agree." Matthew gestured to the two piles of business records on the desk. "Got those sorted?"

"All of them."

"What's your plan for the day?"

"Contact all the suppliers—most are here in Boston—and firm up our credit arrangements. Get to the harbormaster and transfer Covington's port authorization to us. Maybe stop at the bank just to let them know we're watching."

Matthew pointed to the kettles and rags. "I'll get the place cleaned up and try to find some more chairs and desks. Might have to use shipping crates for a while. Pettigrew and most of his crew will be here at two o'clock. Caleb's coming. Can you be here?"

"I'll make time for it."

Matthew drew out his pocket watch and for a moment glanced at the royal blue, velvet watch fob with his initials and a small heart stitched in gold needlepoint, which Kathleen had made for him when they were both awkward adolescents.

"Five minutes past nine. Those offices opened five minutes ago. Let's get at it."

Billy walked out the door and Matthew laid his coat across the desk. By ten o'clock he had swept the office and had two kettles of water boiling over the fire. By eleven o'clock all the windows were washed clean and winter sunlight was streaming through to cast bright trapezoids of light on the floor. By twelve o'clock, twelve heavy, battered wooden shipping crates, four large ones, eight small ones, had been gathered from the discard of the waterfront and positioned near the fireplace for warmth. At ten minutes before one o'clock, Matthew finished sweeping the floor refuse into the fireplace and leaned the broom against the wall. At five minutes until two o'clock, Pettigrew entered to stand near the fire. By five minutes past two o'clock, Billy, Caleb, and eleven men of the crew were standing inside the room, with the eleven sailors talking quietly among themselves, waiting. One of them studied Caleb for a moment, then nudged the man next to him, spoke something quietly, and then glanced at Caleb once more.

Matthew faced the men and the room became silent. "Mr. Pettigrew, do you have any more men coming?"

"No. There are two more that can't be here. I'll talk with them later."

Matthew looked over the crew. "All right. Can I have your attention."

For fifteen minutes he spoke while the men listened in absorbed silence. He left nothing out—the loose financial arrangements, the merchants, the banks, the *Jessica*, the fact that no one would get paid unless the venture succeeded, the fact that the crew would have to load and unload three hundred tons of nails in kegs and salt fish in barrels, then load and unload three hundred tons of tobacco. Loading, unloading, and covering the miles up and down the coast would take thirteen men more than six weeks.

He turned to Billy. "The business arrangements are yours."

Billy took a breath and began. The harbormaster had transferred Covington port privileges to them, the suppliers had agreed to provide the food, sails, rope, lamp oil, fresh water, blankets, and all other essentials on credit, and the merchants involved had arranged handling all the money to buy and sell the cargo. The profits would be delivered in New York at the close of the transaction, and brought back to Boston to be divided. Everyone would get their fair share then, and not sooner.

Billy stopped and looked back to Matthew, and Matthew picked it up.

"That's where we are. I tell you once more, this whole arrangement can go wrong in half a dozen places. You better take some time to think it over before you make your answer."

Pettigrew looked at his men, and a few of them gestured to the door. Two glanced at Caleb, and Pettigrew caught the flat expression in their eyes. He turned back to Matthew.

"We'd better go out on the dock for a few minutes."

Matthew nodded agreement and gestured, and the men filed out into the light foot traffic of the waterfront while Matthew, Billy, and Caleb waited inside. For twenty minutes the crew stood on the black timbers, fifty feet from the door, vapors rising from their heads as they talked in turn, gesturing, stamping their feet for warmth, glancing from time to time back at the office. Finally, Pettigrew nodded, turned on his heel, and strode back to open the office door.

"Matthew, could I see you alone?"

Matthew glanced at Billy, caught the question in his eyes, and followed Pettigrew out the door, where Pettigrew stopped and spoke quietly.

"There's a problem. It's your brother. Two men saw him in a fight right here on the waterfront not long ago. Heard of a second one over at Charlestown."

Matthew recoiled in shock, and Pettigrew stopped for an instant before he went on in a steady voice. He did not flinch. "I won't tolerate a troublemaker in any crew I command."

Matthew raised a hand to stop Pettigrew. "Caleb a waterfront brawler? I don't believe it."

"Two good men say they saw the first one. Half a dozen heard about the second one."

For a moment Matthew stood transfixed. "Give me a minute." He turned on his heel and walked back into the office, closed the door, and walked straight to Caleb, standing near the fireplace. Billy was seated at the old desk.

Matthew's voice was controlled. "Two men in Pettigrew's crew said you've been in two fights lately on the waterfront. Is it true?"

For an instant an expression of puzzlement crossed Caleb's face, and then he replied, "Yes."

Billy rose to his feet, gaping.

Matthew went on. "Pettigrew won't tolerate a troublemaker in his crew. He's right. Neither will I. What happened? Were you drunk? I've never known you to drink."

"No. Not drunk."

"What, then?"

"I was down here looking for work. A bully was going to kill a man with a fish knife. I stopped him."

"That's all?"

"No. He sent a man out to get me. I agreed to fight him a second time, at Hollenbeck's burned-out warehouse at Charlestown, to put an end to it. That's all."

"The same man? Twice? What's his name?"

"Judd. That's all I know."

"Come with me. We've got to settle this."

Matthew turned on his heel and strode back out the door with Caleb and Billy both following. He gestured to Pettigrew as he passed him, and the four of them marched to the crew. The men were standing with their hands thrust into their coat pockets in the cold. Matthew turned to Pettigrew.

"Captain, which two men saw the fight?"

Pettigrew motioned with his head, and two men stepped forward.

"You saw Caleb in a waterfront fight?"

"Yes, sir."

"The other man's name?"

"Judd."

"Is it true this man, Judd, was going to kill a man with a fish knife?"

"Judd had a knife."

"Caleb stopped him?"

"Yes, sir."

"Was it a fair fight?"

"Yes, sir."

Matthew paused to order his thoughts, then plowed on. "There was a second fight?"

"We heard about it. Didn't see it."

"Hollenbeck's old warehouse?"

"Yes, sir."

"Judd?"

"Yes, sir."

"Any other fights?"

"Not that we know of."

Matthew turned to Pettigrew. "I doubt this had much to do with a typical waterfront brawl. Do you agree?"

"I don't know enough about it yet, but it sounds like you're right. Still, I don't want a troublemaker on my ship. You know the rule."

"I do. I'll be responsible for Caleb. If he can't abide your orders, fire him. Is that fair?"

"Fair enough."

A voice came from the midst of the crew. "Captain, sir."

Pettigrew turned, seeking the man who had spoken. "Speak up, man."

A husky man with a heavy beard stepped forward. He had an old, ragged scarf wrapped over the top of his head and tied beneath his chin. His coat was threadbare, his shoes worn through. He spoke with a thick Scottish burr.

"It took a while to sort it out, sir, but I met this man once."

Caleb turned toward the man, eyes narrowed as he studied him. The man went on.

"I didn't see either fight, but I can tell you, sir, this man is no waterfront brawler. I'll vouch for him. Any time."

Pettigrew stared at the man for a moment. "Where did you meet him, McKinrow?"

"Don't matter, sir. All I got to say is he isn't no troublemaker."

Caleb's eyes widened in stunned surprise. The voice! McKinrow! The Scot who had tried to rob him in the dark, in the street near home! The man with the addled brother, Lon, who had a piece of a British cannonball in his head from storming Redoubt Number Nine at Yorktown. One of Pettigrew's men?

The others in the crew turned to stare at McKinrow for a moment, then back at Caleb, then at Pettigrew. Pettigrew turned to Matthew.

"You'll be responsible for him?"

"Yes."

"When do you want us here to start loading?"

Matthew pondered for a moment. "Come inside. We'll lay it out."

They closed the door to the office and drew the old shipping crates near the desk and sat silently, listening intently. For forty minutes Matthew, Billy, and Pettigrew traced the Atlantic shipping lanes between Boston, the tiny village of Jamestown on the James River of Virginia, and New York. Slowly they went through the give and take of hammering out the best plan they could, and then Matthew stood.

"Let's put it all together. I go up the Potomac to try to get the *Jessica* released. Billy, you order and lay in all the supplies these men will need for the haul down to Jamestown, then up to New York, and back to Boston. Captain Pettigrew, you and your men will load the *Rebecca* with the nails from Bartlett Manufacturing and the salt fish from Bjornsen Fisheries. You unload at Jamestown, reload with tobacco from Scott, Ltd., and unload it at Doernen's dock in New York. Doernen will pay you, and you bring the money back here to be divided among us on the schedule as agreed."

He stopped and quickly ran his finger one more time over the routes the *Rebecca* had to follow.

"If anything goes wrong, get word back to this office as quickly as you can."

He took a great breath. "Have we missed anything?"

He glanced around the room at the sober, silent faces.

"All right. We start in the morning. Eight o'clock."

Everyone rose and quiet talk broke out among them as the crew filed out the door into the chill of the afternoon sun, and scattered. Matthew closed the door and turned to Caleb, frustration clear in his voice.

"I had no idea about this thing with Judd."

Caleb shrugged. "It happened. I didn't plan it."

"Who is he?"

"Never seen him before, and haven't since that night at Hollenbeck's."

Matthew bored into him. "Is he a bully? It sounded like it."

"You could call him that. Yes."

"Big?"

"Good sized."

"Bigger than you?"

"Maybe six inches and seventy pounds."

Billy straightened at the desk, and for a moment Matthew stared. "You beat him?"

There was an edge in Caleb's voice. "Yes. I did."

"Where did you learn to use your fists?"

"From a man named Charles Dorman. One of the best in England. I was in his New York regiment. He spent a year teaching me."

"Why would he do that?"

"Because he saw a bully just like Judd beat me half to death when I was sixteen, and he could not abide a bully. No one's beaten me since."

Matthew stood transfixed, slowly realizing there was much about Caleb he did not know, nor understand. "Is there anything else I should know?"

For several seconds Caleb reached back into his memory. "Yes. In June of '78 that bully I told you about—name was Murphy, Conlin Murphy—called me out in front of the whole regiment at Valley Forge. I beat him. Later he tried to kill me out in the woods with a rock. Him and two other men. There was a fight. I had no choice. I got the rock and killed Murphy and one of the others. I didn't mean to kill them. The third man ran and told the commanding officer I had murdered two men. There was a court-martial. All charges were dismissed."

Slowly Billy rose and walked to stand quietly near the two brothers.

Matthew went on. "Anything else?"

"No. That's all I can think of."

There was compassion in Matthew's voice. "I didn't know. I didn't mean to—"

Caleb cut him off. "Don't concern yourself."

Matthew waited for a moment. "What was that Scot— McKinrow—talking about?"

"Nothing. He tried to rob me just after I got to Boston. I stopped him. He has a wife and three children that were starving and a brother who has a piece of a British cannonball in his head from Yorktown. The brother can't think straight. I gave the man a few dollars. It was nothing. I'd forgotten it."

Silence held for a moment while both Matthew and Billy accepted Caleb's words, and then Matthew spoke once again.

"Do I have it all? Is there more?"

"No. Nothing more."

"Can you avoid trouble with Pettigrew's crew?"

"I won't start any trouble. I can't be responsible for what they do."

Billy glanced at Matthew. "That's fair."

Matthew concluded. "Be here at eight in the morning."

Caleb bobbed his head once, turned, and walked out the door into the late afternoon chill.

For more than a minute both Billy and Matthew stood still, looking at the door where Caleb had disappeared. Then Billy walked back to the desk and sat down, and Matthew looked at him.

"I never thought I'd hear such things about Caleb."

"Neither did I." Billy pursed his mouth for a moment before he went on. "Some people seem to attract trouble. I hope Caleb's not one of them."

There was a sound of quiet awe in Matthew's voice. "Beat some bully named Conlin Murphy. Killed him and another man. Now he beat another bully named Judd. I don't like it."

Billy's voice was nearly a murmur. "Then he gave money to a man who tried to rob him. Interesting."

For a time each of them was lost in his own thoughts, and then Matthew said, "Ben Franklin invented that iron pole that draws lightning—his lightning rod. Is Caleb a lightning rod for trouble? Is he?"

Notes

The critical conflicts between states, each claiming rights to regulate traffic on a river that serves as a common boundary for both is factual, as detailed in Bernstein, *Are We to Be a Nation?*, pp. 88–98.

The state of Virginia levied a tariff or tax on all tobacco exported from within her state boundaries, as set forth herein (Nevins, *The American States, 1775–1789*, p. 559).

CHAPTER XXIV

★ ★ ★

*M*arch brought an unseasonably warm Chinook wind
sweeping from the south, up the Hudson River basin, into the great
St. Lawrence River drainage system. It held for three days and three
nights, turning the forests of northern New Hampshire and Vermont
into quagmires, and the deep snows of winter into rivulets that filled the
streams, and then the rivers, in their journey to the sea. The scattered
hamlets and the tiny farms carved from the woods became bogged in
deep mud, and the dim, crooked wagon trails connecting them became
ruts that reached to the axles of a loaded wagon.

Those who bore the daily work of feeding livestock, milking the
family cow, birthing the new heifer, splitting more kindling, and clearing
the snowpack from sagging roofs, cursed the mud that turned the world
into an endless torment, but deep inside there was a rise of spirit. It
would likely freeze again, and snow again, before winter surrendered to
spring, but the grip of winter had been broken. Spring was coming to
claim the world once again with new life. They cursed the mud, but there
was a lift in their souls.

Just less than one mile east of the farm Ben and Lydia Fielding had
cleared in the northern reaches of the Vermont forests, Eli Stroud tied
the family horse to a tree, grasped his Pennsylvania rifle in his right hand,
and dropped to his haunches for half a minute to listen and watch the
rhythms of the forest. Squirrels darted and scolded, jays and bluebirds

challenged and argued, and sounds of dripping and running water were everywhere. A huge porcupine waddled toward a rotted tree stump to rip into it for worms and grubs, then stopped to raise its nose, testing the strange taint in the air. The scent of man brought him around to stare toward Eli with eyes too weak to find him. Of all the creatures in the forest, only three had no fear of humans: the bear, the wolverine, and the porcupine. The bear because of its incomparable strength, the wolverine because it did not know the meaning of fear, and the porcupine because of a cantankerous disposition that turned its shield of barbed quills into weapons that inflicted unforgettable pain. All knowledgeable creatures, including man and the bear, gave ground to the porcupine. Eli silently watched the animal turn his back and waddle on, contemptuous of the human he could smell, but not see.

Eli raised to full height, and without thought, all his learning of the forest came alive. He saw all that moved ahead of him and heard all sounds, and it all took its place instantly. Silently he moved ahead, instinctively picking his way so that his moccasins made no sound, watching through the bare branches of the trees for movement. He had covered thirty yards when he again went to his haunches behind a waist-high outcrop of rough Vermont granite, and carefully laid his rifle over the top. He dropped to one knee and raised his head far enough to peer south sixty yards, where a stream flowed, and a stand of pines partially hid a place where a large dome of natural salt broke the surface of the forest floor. He cocked the rifle and waited, motionless, silent, with the Chinook wind in his face and the late morning sun warm on his shoulders.

Timid snowshoe rabbits, fat with their heavy white winter coats, came to drink at the stream and work on the salt for a moment, then disappear. A raccoon passed, pausing long enough to grasp salt crumbs, poke them into her mouth, drink, wash her face, and move on. Twenty minutes passed before Eli came to a focus. Long ears had moved in the trees, and ten seconds later a young spike buck moved cautiously to the salt, ears flicking, twisting, listening to sounds that only his enormous ears could hear. He was standing broadside when Eli slowly brought his finger to the trigger of the rifle and laid his cheek against the stock, then brought the blade on the front of the barrel into the notch at the rear, judged the shot at sixty yards, allowed nothing for the breeze that was blowing directly into the muzzle of the rifle, buried the gun sights in the deer's neck just below and behind the ear, and squeezed off the shot.

The crack silenced all other sounds and echoed off through the bare tree branches, and the young buck dropped where he stood with his neck broken by the .50-caliber ball. Eli rose and walked forward, tapping fresh powder from his powder horn into the muzzle of the rifle as he moved. He worked the hickory ramrod to seat the powder, then the greased linen patch, then the round lead ball, and drove them home. He tapped more powder into the pan and snapped the frizzen closed, ready for the next shot, should a panther or a bear or a wolverine challenge him for the meat before he could get it onto the horse, and home.

He stood over the fallen deer and touched the open eye with the tip of the rifle barrel. The eye did not blink, and he stood the rifle against a tree. He walked the few paces to the stream, cupped his hands full of water, and returned to release it on the head of the dead deer. In Iroquois, he thanked the animal for its sacrifice—that he, and his sister, Lydia, and her husband, Ben Fielding, and the children, might have fresh meat to keep them strong, and he commended the soul of the deer into the hands of Taronhiawagon, the Iroquois God. All this he did with little thought, from seventeen years of training as an Iroquois warrior. It did not occur to him that the brief Iroquois ceremony might offend Christianity.

Ten minutes later he had cut the scent sacks from the inside of the hind legs of the deer, and was leading the patient old bay mare west on the wet, spongy forest floor, rifle in hand, with the carcass tied across the packsaddle. He came into a clearing, walked past the small cabin he and Ben had built for Eli twenty-five yards east of the Fieldings' house, and stopped at the low barn. Ben came picking his way through the mud from the house to help hang the carcass from a barn rafter and put the mare in her pen while Eli got a tub and a bucket of fresh well water. Eli had his belt knife in his hand, ready to open the deer, when he heard the door of the main house open, and his sister, Lydia, called.

"The children want to know if they can watch. They need to get out of the house."

Eli stepped into the sunlight and for a moment looked at his sister, tall, striking, her honey-brown hair pulled behind her head. The children were clustered around her, already in their coats, eyes pleading. Hannah, in her tenth year, with her mother's eyes and her father's generous mouth, holding the hand of Samuel, her seven-year-old brother who had Ben's spread of shoulders and unruly shock of hair. Beside Samuel stood his brother Nathan, four years old, with his dark hair and dark eyes. And next to him was Laura, Eli's daughter, almost four years old, who every day reminded him more and more of her mother, Mary, who had given her life in the birth of her daughter on July 12, 1780.

Eli considered for a moment. Should Nathan and Laura watch the cutting and detail of dressing a deer? Four years of age? Old enough to know this part of life? He made up his mind.

"All of them?" he asked.

"Yes."

"Do they promise to stay out of the way?"

The children's voices were a resounding chorus, "We promise!"

"You won't cry when I have to cut the deer?"

"No."

"All right. Stay out of the mud. Lydia, send the sack for the offal, and some rags."

Beaming, the children covered the twenty yards at a trot, trying to step where the patchy snow still held. Eli's heart swelled as he watched them come.

Without a word he began: Carefully punch through the hide where the brisket ends, slip his hand inside the cavity with the knife blade pointing outward to avoid slitting an intestine, cut upward to the vent, make a circular cut around the bung, put the large wooden tub beneath the carcass, and drop the entrails into it. Remove the head, make the cut that divides the brisket, down the throat, then use the ax to split the brisket bone and open the lower end of the hanging carcass. Cut the diaphragm on both sides, loosen the lungs and heart, and drop them in the tub on top of the entrails. Set aside the heart, kidneys, liver, and sweetbreads, then use the ax to open the skull to remove the brains and put them with the other offal. Drag the tub with the entrails to the pig-pen beside the barn and dump it into the pig trough for the sow and her eight weaner pigs. Fetch a bucket of water from the well, wash the offal, put it in the sack Lydia had sent with Hannah, tie it shut, and set it on clean straw. Back to the well for two more buckets of water to wash the inside of the carcass twice with the rags, then pry it wide open and jam three, thick, peeled pine branches inside, crosswise, to hold it open and let the body heat out, so the flesh would not go bone-sour. Finally, another bucket of water to wash his hands and knife, and the ax, and wipe them dry with the rags.

Eli straightened and looked at the children. The expressions on their faces were a rare mix of fascination, wonder, revulsion, and acceptance. None had uttered a sound in the half hour they had watched.

Hannah ventured a question. "When do you take off the skin?"

"In a few days. Let the meat age a little, and cool out. We'll salt down the hide for a few weeks until the hair starts to slip, and then we'll make some moccasins. Would you like to have some moccasins like the Iroquois?"

Hannah's eyes grew large. "Honest?"

"If Ben and Lydia agree."

Samuel stammered, "Like the Indians?"

"Just like the Indians."

Samuel spun on his heel and sprinted for the house shouting, "Mama, Mama!"

Eli grinned, shoved his knife back into its sheath, picked up his rifle, and swept Laura up with his free arm and followed Hannah and Nathan back to the house. They stomped the mud off their feet before entering, and Lydia met them, laughing.

"What's this about Indians? Samuel says he's going to be an Indian."

Grinning, Eli laid his rifle on the table and set Laura on the plank floor. "Well, now, that could be. There's enough hide on that deer to make about two pair of small moccasins. If you and Ben agree, maybe Hannah and I and Samuel can do something about that."

"We'll see." Lydia pointed. "Ben's working on the smokehouse. He said the snow put a leak in the roof. When will the deer hams be ready to go in?"

"A few days. Depends on the weather. I'll go split some hickory for the smokehouse fire."

The sun was deep into the western trees when Ben and Eli went to the barn. They finished milking the Jersey cow and feeding the livestock in full darkness and washed before they came to the supper table. They bowed their heads while Ben said grace, and the instant the "amen" was said, Samuel turned to his father with desperate pleading in his wide eyes.

"Eli says he can make some moccasins. Just like the Indians. Can I have moccasins? Please?"

Ben glanced at Eli. "From the deer hide?"

Eli nodded.

Ben fell into thought for a moment, and Hannah said quietly, "Me, too?"

Ben glanced at Lydia and a silent communication passed between them. A judicious look came onto Ben's face as he spoke.

"Pass the potatoes."

Instantly Hannah handed him the wooden bowl of steaming potatoes.

Ben cleared his throat. "There are certain things that have to be understood about children wearing moccasins."

Hannah's shoulders slumped. *Here it comes.*

"First off, they can't be running around the woods away from the clearing because if they do, the Indians might snatch them because they think they're Indian children, with those moccasins."

Hannah closed her eyes in resignation. *That's nonsense.*

Samuel blurted, "They might steal us? Like they did Uncle Eli?"

Ben looked at him like Solomon. "They might."

Samuel's eyes were sparkling. "Honest? Go live with the Indians?" Visions of the deep forest and bears and battles danced in his head.

Ben reached for the mutton platter. "Second, children who wear moccasins have to do their chores without one single complaint, because that's how Indian children do."

Lydia was battling an outburst of laughter. Eli had his face down to hide a grin while he worked on his food. Laura and Nathan were sitting like small statues, wide-eyed, trying to understand what was going on.

Ben chewed on his mutton for a few seconds before he continued. "Third, they can't argue and quarrel with each other, because when Indian children do that, the chief puts them in a canoe and sends them down the river and no one ever sees them again."

Samuel's eyes were popping. "What river?"

Eli raised his head to look at Ben, waiting to hear what river he was talking about, since there was no large river nearby.

Ben's brow furrowed for a moment before he answered. "The Whatsit River."

The corner of Hannah's mouth curled in contempt. "Where's the Whatsit River?"

Eli was still watching Ben. Lydia held mutton on her fork, waiting.

Ben pursed his mouth for a minute. "Well, only the Indians know that. That's why no one ever sees the children again."

Hannah put her fork down in disgust. "You're making this up."

Ben looked wounded, and his voice raised considerably. "I am not! I read it in the Bible!"

Hannah stared at him accusingly. "Where in the Bible?"

"Revelation. Right there at the first, where it talks about all the four-headed monsters. That's where the Whatsit River is. Right where those monsters are. Those are the monsters that get the children and we never see them again."

Lydia could no longer contain herself, and she burst into laughter. Samuel flinched, and Hannah shook her head. Eli laid his fork down and chuckled out loud.

Hannah could take no more. "Can we have the moccasins?"

Ben looked puzzled. "What moccasins?"

"The ones Eli is going to make for us."

Ben's expression instantly changed to one of understanding. "Oh. *Those* moccasins. Yes. You can."

With the supper dishes done and the children in their long night-shirts, the family knelt around the table for evening prayer. The children hugged the grown-ups, and climbed the stairs up to the loft where they went to their beds. Outside, the Chinook wind still held, and the children drifted to sleep with the sounds of melting snow dripping from the eaves of the roof.

Soon Eli stood and picked up his rifle. "I think I'll go to bed."

Lydia followed him to the door and watched him cover the short distance to his own small cabin. She watched until the light glowed, dull behind the curtain drawn over the window near the door, then turned away. More than an hour passed while Lydia fussed and puttered in the kitchen, having her quiet time to let the cares and troubles of the day fade while she gathered inner strength for tomorrow. It was half past nine o'clock when she sat down at the dining table with the large family Bible. For twenty minutes she pored over the letters of Paul, raising her head often as she pondered the meanings that came to her. She closed the Bible and spoke to Ben, seated before the fireplace, deep in his own thoughts.

"Time for bed. I'll bank the fire."

"I'll do it." He rose and reached for the small iron shovel in the fireplace rack.

For a moment Lydia watched him, then went to the window by the front door to draw the shade aside for a last look into the yard, as she always did. The dull light still glowed in Eli's window. She turned to Ben.

"Eli's lamp's still burning."

Ben glanced at the clock on the fireplace mantel. Five minutes before ten o'clock.

"He's usually in bed by now. Any reason you know why he'd still be up?"

Lydia shook her head, and there was alarm in her voice. "None."

"I'll go see."

Lydia was moving toward her coat as she answered. "Let me go."

Ben considered. "I'll stay with the children."

Lydia put on her coat and heavy shoes, draped a shawl over her head, took a lighted lantern, and picked her way to the cabin to knock on the door. A few moments later it opened far enough for the light to frame her, then swung wide open. A look of puzzlement crossed Eli's face as he invited her in, closed the door, and hung his rifle back on the pegs above the door frame.

There was concern in his voice as he spoke. "Everything all right?"

"Yes, with us. Your light was still on."

"I was reading." He gestured to the small, crude table fashioned from white pine.

She looked. The Bible lay open in the pale light of a lamp.

"Oh. I'll go if you're all right." She had her hand on the bolt to the cabin door when Eli spoke.

"Have you got a few minutes?"

She nodded. "Of course."

He pointed to the table. "I've been reading from the New Testament about Jesus. His resurrection. He says everyone is going to resurrect." He laid his hand flat on the table and turned earnest eyes to Lydia.

"Will Mary come out of that grave? Will she look like she did before? Will I see her again?"

Lydia's breath came short. "Where are you reading?"

"John. New Testament. Fourth chapter."

"Jesus said we'll all resurrect, and we will. You'll see Mary again, just like she was."

"How do you know?"

Lydia did not hesitate. "In my heart. Past anything else I know in this life. You'll be with her again, and Laura. The three of you."

Eli looked deeper into Lydia than anything she had ever experienced, and then he slowly nodded. "I can wait."

She stood. "Is there anything else?"

He smiled. "No."

"Sure?"

"Sure."

"Go to bed soon?"

"Soon."

She turned on her heel, and he stood in the door to watch until she reached her own house, and Ben met her at her own door. They waved across the black, muddy yard, and closed the doors.

The warm wind held through the night. Mud and puddles slowed morning chores. With the livestock fed and the bucket of thick, frothy Jersey milk divided, half on the breakfast table in a pitcher, half cooling in the root cellar for butter and cheese, Lydia called them to the table for fried eggs and thick slices of bacon, and bread and butter and milk. Samuel waited until Lydia said grace before he turned to Eli.

"Is the deerskin ready yet? For moccasins?"

Eli shook his head. "Won't be ready for maybe six or eight weeks. We just have to be patient."

Samuel's face clouded. "Will I still be little?"

"Yes. It just seems long, but it really isn't."

Eli's word was enough, and Samuel said, "Oh," and stuffed his mouth with bread.

The breakfast dishes were finished, and Lydia and Hannah had the children up in the loft making the beds when Eli and Ben walked out the front door into bright sunlight and the warm wind. Birds everywhere were declaring territorial rights, and red and gray squirrels, fat with their thick winter hair darted and scolded. The two men picked their way through the mud to swing open the big door into the low barn and walk inside. Eli leaned his rifle against the inside wall, and each took a three-tined, wooden pitchfork and separated—Eli to clean out the horse stall, Ben the milking stanchion. They finished, spread clean straw, Eli picked up his rifle, and they were walking back out the door when Eli slowed and stopped, and turned his head to listen in the wind. Ben looked at him with the silent question, and Eli hesitated, then raised an arm to point due south.

Two hundred yards distant, across the clearing, came a rider mounted on a brown gelding, with a long rifle balanced on the pommel of his saddle. He wore buckskins and moccasins and a full beard, and it was clear he had seen Ben and Eli. The lone rider was followed by a sleigh, drawn by a laboring bay mare. Seated in the sleigh was a man wearing a tall beaver hat and a beaver-skin coat. He was handling the reins with both hands, awkward, rough. There was lather gathered about the mouth of the horse where the bit had worked, and the horse had its neck arched, throwing its head, fighting the pressure.

Ben's head dropped forward in astonishment. "What in the name of heaven . . ."

Eli shifted his rifle enough to slip his finger inside the trigger guard and lock his thumb around the hammer, and the two men waited. When the rider was twenty yards away, Eli drew his hand from the trigger guard and hammer, and raised it to the square to show he held no weapon, and the man on the horse did the same. The strange procession came on, to stop ten feet from Ben and Eli, and it was Ben who spoke while Eli peered past the men, probing the forest behind them for any movement he did not understand.

"You have come some distance," Ben said. "Do you need water and feed for your animals? Food for yourselves?"

The rider answered. "We would appreciate it. We are looking for a man."

"Could I know his name?"

"Eli Stroud."

Ben started, then quickly settled. "You have business with him?"

"We do."

"Your names?"

"I'm Carlyle Stringham." The man turned and gestured toward the mud-splattered sleigh. The runners, built for snow, were battered and bruised from too many rocks and stones in the melting snow. "This is Randall Weatherby."

Ben considered. "I'm Ben Fielding. This farm is mine. This man is Eli Stroud. You're welcome to step down and come into the house. There is water and hay in the barn for your animals."

Twenty minutes later the men made their way from the barn to the house, where Lydia met them at the door with the children standing behind her, shy, wide-eyed in wonder at a fair-sized, bearded man carrying a rifle like Eli's, followed by a sparse, smaller man, sweating, wearing a hat that resembled a stovepipe and a coat that made him look like a grizzly bear fresh out of winter hibernation. He apparently did not have the presence of mind to take it off in the warmth of the Chinook and the sun. The men cleaned the mud from their feet, then walked into the log home.

Ben gestured. "This is my wife, Lydia, and these are our children. Lydia, this is Mr. Stringham and Mr. Weatherby. They have business with Eli."

Lydia bowed. "May I get some cider?"

"That would be good," Ben said, and Lydia spoke to Hannah, who hurried out the door for the root cellar.

"May I take your hat and coat?" Ben asked, and hung them on the pegs beside the door. Eli leaned his rifle, with that of Stringham's, against the wall by the front door, and waited. Hannah burst through the door with a large pewter pitcher clutched between her hands and set it on the cupboard while Lydia brought cups to the table, followed by the pitcher of sweet cider. She gave Hannah a silent signal, and they moved the children away from the table as the men sat down. Weatherby held a thick leather folder in his hand, and did not place it on the table as he picked up his cider. He drank, then turned to Lydia.

"Ma'am, that was good. Very good."

Lydia smiled and nodded but said nothing.

Weatherby turned back to Eli. "I have to explain. I've come from New York where we wear those hats and coats." He gestured toward them, hanging beside the door. "I thought I would be traveling through deep snow up in these north woods, so I came in that sleigh. I didn't expect this warm wind and sun. And I don't know much about handling a horse."

He paused, drank once more, and continued. "I got halfway here, and got lost, so I hired Mr. Stringham as a guide. He's the one that got us through."

Eli's estimate of Mr. Weatherby took a long step upward at the honesty.

Weatherby went on. "You're wondering what brought me here." He laid the leather folder on the table and opened the cover. "I'm a barrister. An attorney. From New York City. Lawrence Weatherby is my father. He's had his law office on Wall Street in New York for over fifty years. Years ago, my father was attorney for Rufus Broadhead. Mr. Broadhead was the father of Mary Broadhead. Mary Broadhead married into the Flint family, and her husband lost his life in what was called an accident."

He stopped to look at the first document in the folder. "This is a copy of the marriage certificate between her and Mr. Flint."

Ben looked at Eli, who was staring at Mr. Weatherby.

Weatherby continued in his matter-of-fact monotone. "Both the Broadhead family and the Flint family lost their entire fortunes. Mary Flint was forced into service as a nurse in a British hospital in New York. The doctor in charge was a Colonel Otis Purcell of the British army. Otis Purcell took a very proper, very paternal view of Mary, and while he was dying from a stroke, wrote a brief statement, which meets the requirements of a will. He left his worldly possessions to Mary Flint." He picked up the second document. "This is a copy of that will." He picked up the third document. "At the time of Purcell's death, a British general named Jeremy Hollins was the party who discovered the body of Doctor Purcell, with the will still in his hand, and General Hollins generously drafted an affidavit stating what he had found, and where he found it, and alleging he believed it to be the last will and testament of Otis Purcell. He gave that document to Mary Flint."

Weatherby drew a deep breath and droned on. "Based on the will and the affidavit, Mary tried to get some of the money that belonged to Otis Purcell. It was being held in the London–New York Bank, Ltd., in New York City. The British government intervened, and their courts in England issued a hold order on those funds, partly because a distant cousin of Otis Purcell, a man named Alfonso Eddington, filed a claim in a court in London, for all property of the deceased Otis Purcell. Mary came to my father with the issue. He advised her to get him copies of the will and the affidavit of General Hollins. He also advised her that in his opinion, it would be extremely difficult for her to perfect her claim in an American court, since the money had been the property of a British officer, and the conflicting claim was being made by a British subject. That all occurred about six years ago, when the war was in progress and the Americans were far from winning. Mary Flint delivered the two documents my father asked for, and then she disappeared."

Weatherby stopped and reached for the cider pitcher. "May I?"

Ben nodded, Weatherby poured, drank, set the cup on the table, wiped at his mouth, then went on.

"Father filed a case for Mary Flint in a New York state court. That court issued an order against the bank, instructing them to hold the contested money right there in New York until the conflicting claims of Eddington and Mary Flint could be resolved." Weatherby laughed, a sudden, sharp burst. "That New York bank didn't know what to do. One order from the British court, and another from the American court, in direct conflict. So they just sealed the account and waited."

For the first time Weatherby paused long enough to look into the faces of everyone at the table, including Stringham's, who was mesmerized.

"Am I going too fast?"

Eli shook his head. "Go on."

Weatherby shrugged. "In 1781 the war ended. In 1782, Eddington died, and the British signed a peace treaty with us. Last year about this time, Father petitioned the American court in New York for an order declaring the money in the account to be that of Mary Flint, based on the written documents of Purcell and Hollins."

He tossed his hands up to let them drop thumping on the table. "Eddington was dead. There were no British courts left in New York. There was no one to contest it! The New York court signed the order.

The money became the property of Mary Flint. The question was, where was Mary Flint? Father asked me to find her."

He began referring to notes and documents in the folder. "The path led to Morristown, where she worked as a nurse under the direction of a Doctor Albigence Waldo. I found an entry in the records of the American camp there that Major Waldo had performed a marriage ceremony on July 6, 1778, joining Mary Flint to Eli Stroud. It took some time, and if I say so myself, some expert detective work to find out where I could locate Eli Stroud. That investigation led me here."

He stopped and stared at Eli.

"Are you the husband of Mary Flint?"

"I am."

"May I talk with her?"

"She died four years ago."

Weatherby recoiled as though he had been struck. "Oh! Oh! I didn't know. I am sorry, sir. So very sorry."

Eli nodded. "I understand. No need."

Weatherby pursed his mouth in thought. "If she has passed on, you may need a second affidavit from someone who witnessed the marriage. Is there such a person that you can find now, four years later?"

"Yes. Billy Weems. A lieutenant in the Continental Army. He gave her in marriage at the ceremony. He lives in Boston."

"Excellent. Are you certain he'll cooperate? Sign an affidavit?"

"He will."

"Then, as her lawfully wedded husband, you inherited all her property at the time of her passing. The money in the New York bank is yours, sir, if you can give evidence from some third party of her passing."

Eli glanced at Ben, then back at Weatherby, but said nothing.

Weatherby continued. "Where did she pass on?"

"Here. In this house."

"Where is she interred? Buried?"

"Outside. In the family burial ground."

"Is there a record of her passing on? Anyone outside the family who might know?"

"Yes. She died giving birth to our daughter, Laura. Laura is over there."

Weatherby turned to look at Laura, standing next to Lydia, and Eli saw the pain in Weatherby's face as he murmured, "Beautiful child." He turned back to Eli.

"Who outside the family might have been here?"

"Parthena Poors. A neighbor. Parthena midwifed at the birth."

Weatherby leaned forward, focused, intense. "Do you know if she kept a record of the passing of Mary and the birth of Laura?"

"Yes. She did."

Relief flooded through Weatherby. "Could you get a handwritten statement to that effect?"

"I think so. Yes."

"Good! Excellent! Get it in writing. Then, sir, you will have to bring the document to New York City, along with the affidavit of Mr. Weems concerning your marriage. The Weatherby law office is on Wall Street. Find us. I will represent you in court, to have the money turned over to you. It's rightfully yours."

Lydia had her hand over her mouth, eyes wide in shock. Ben eased back in his chair, face a blank.

Eli stared at his cider cup for a few seconds, then raised his eyes to Weatherby.

"How much money?"

Weatherby picked the next document from the folder. "Here's the accounting. Otis Purcell left thirty-two thousand, three hundred, twelve pounds British sterling to Mary Flint."

Lydia gasped, Ben stiffened, mouth open, Stringham jerked erect, and Eli laid his hand flat on the table. Weatherby's face sobered.

"However, there have been expenses, costs, and fees. We received no money from Mary when she retained my father, because she had none, so the law firm has advanced all that was needed. Father had to appear in the British court one time—London—and I have had over five years of periodic work on this case. There have been court appearances—oh, it's all here. Let me give you the amount that remains after all costs and fees."

He turned to the fifth page of the accounting, ran his finger to the last line, and read.

"You, sir, have twenty-eight thousand, nine hundred, eighty-eight pounds British sterling in the London–New York Bank, which becomes yours upon delivering proof of your marriage to Mary Flint, and her passing. And I recommend heartily that you waste no time claiming it, because there is no telling how long the London–New York Bank will remain solvent, since it is essentially a London-based institution."

Eli asked, "Are they still in business?"

"Oh, yes. I don't want to alarm you. Your money is there, and it is safe for a time. But with the direction this country is moving, I'd suggest you not delay. I'm leaving a copy of the accounting with you. Should you disagree with any of it, make notes. We'll discuss it when you come to my office in New York."

Weatherby stopped, straightened his documents, and drew out a thick packet closed with string. "There is a duplicate of each of the documents in this file." I leave it with you." He closed his folder and sat back. "Well, I believe that concludes the business that brought me here, sir."

Eli looked at the heavy packet, then picked up the copy of the accounting document and glanced at it. "One thing. Why did your father and you do all this? Put up all that money without knowing you'd ever get it back?"

Weatherby reached to scratch his head. "Father never said. I think it was because he was too old to join in the war, and this was one opportunity to sting the British. It wasn't much of a sting, but I think it made Father feel good. It did me."

Eli looked at Ben, then back at Weatherby. "I'll be at your office soon. I'll get Billy to sign a paper that he was witness to the marriage, and get a writing from Parthena Poors that she was here when Laura was born and Mary died. She's the midwife for anyone within about seventy miles of here."

"Good."

"How do I repay you, Mr. Weatherby?"

"When you get the money from the bank. My billing is in your hand."

"I owe you more than that."

"No, you don't. I got everything you owed me when the New York American court issued that order impounding the money, and I served it on the British barrister who represented that man Eddington. The expression on that barrister's face—" Weatherby stopped to smile, then chuckle. "No, sir, I got most of my pay that day. You don't owe me."

Weatherby sighed and stood. "Well, there's no reason to take more of your day. I can cover quite a distance before dark if Mr. Stringham will be good enough to guide me back. I feel sorry for that horse out there, the one that pulls the sleigh. New York barristers don't get much training in driving sleighs in the Vermont forest, especially when the snow's nearly all melted. Hard on the horse. I feel bad about that."

The others stood, and Lydia spoke. "You'll stay for the midday meal, won't you?"

Weatherby turned to her and bowed. "Ma'am, after tasting that cider, you can believe I would if I could. But I need to be on my way. I thank you for your courtesy."

Lydia was not to be denied. "Can I send some food with you? We have some smoked venison ham in the root cellar. And some cheese. Cider. I have bread."

Stringham cleared his throat and wiped at his mouth, and Weatherby looked at him, and turned back to Lydia.

"I think that would be nice. Yes. That would be good."

Thirty minutes later they all gathered near the barn, where the mare stood nervously between the shafts of the sleigh, and Stringham held the bridle of his saddled gelding. Weatherby attempted to struggle into his coat, then gave up the effort, and tossed it into the sleigh seat, with his hat, next to a large sack of food Lydia had prepared.

"That coat belongs in New York, not here," he said as he climbed into the sleigh and took up the reins.

He paused for a moment. "I'll expect you soon in New York, Mr. Stroud. Mrs. Fielding, my thanks to you for your hospitality. If ever any of the rest of you come to New York, find my office. I would enjoy showing you where I live."

He turned back to Stringham. "Sir, shall we go?"

Stringham set the butt of his rifle on his thigh, reined his horse around, and raised it to a trot while Weatherby clucked and slapped the reins on the mare, and she lunged to jerk the sled south through the clearing.

The family stood rooted to watch them disappear beyond the tree line, then turned to walk back to the house. They cleaned their feet on the doorstep before they entered, and inside, Eli walked to the table to pick up the accounting document.

He looked at Lydia, then Ben. "Twenty-eight thousand pounds, British sterling. A lot of money. Enough to ruin a man. Is it too much, Ben? Lydia? Think on it."

Notes

The name of the highest god in the Iroquois religion is Taronhiawagon, which means "the holder of the heavens" or "he who carries the heavens on his shoulders" (Hale, *The Iroquois Book of Rites*, p. 74).

For the circumstances surrounding Colonel Otis Purcell, his will granting his fortune to Mary Flint, General Jeremy Hollins, and Alfonso Eddington, see volume 3 of this series, *To Decide Our Destiny*, chapter 14, page 372.

For the incident involving Lawrence Weatherby, the New York barrister, and Rufus Broadhead, father of Mary Flint, see volume 4 of this series, *The Hand of Providence*, chapter 8, page 156.

For the marriage of Mary Flint and Eli Stroud, see volume 5 of this series, *A Cold, Bleak Hill*, chapter 33, page 550.

For the passing of Mary Flint, the birth of her daughter Laura, and the role played by the midwife Parthena Poors and her husband, Abijah, see volume 6 of this series, *The World Turned Upside Down*, chapter 21, page 314.

Jamestown, Virginia
Mid-March 1784

CHAPTER XXV

★ ★ ★

*C*aptain Theodore Pettigrew came to a stop, pulled his tricorn low against the raw, westerly March wind ruffling the dark waters of the north shores of the James River, thrust his hands in his coat pockets, and faced his crew on the waterfront of the small village of Jamestown, Virginia, some thirty miles west of where the river empties into the great Chesapeake Bay. They stood in the chill, late morning sun with their shoulders hunched and their backs to the wind, heads turned to hear him above the sounds of the wind singing in the ropes and masts and spars of the deep water ships anchored in the small harbor and tied to the wharves. Fifteen feet to their right, the *Rebecca* rode low in the waters of high tide, loaded with three hundred tons of prime Virginia tobacco. She was tied tight against the dock by four, two-inch hawsers, and she was rising and falling slightly with the swells to grind against the heavy timbers of the pier. The bow of the ship pointed east, downriver, and there was one ship tied to the dock ahead of her. A squad of four armed, uniformed Virginia militia stood beside the gangplank, facing the wind with their muskets clutched in cold hands as they watched the crew.

Pettigrew's voice came strong, choked with outrage and a growing sense of fear. He hooked a thumb over his shoulder, pointing back fifty yards to the sparse, square, frame office near the center of the cluster of buildings on the waterfront, from whence he had just come.

"They've sent for the harbormaster and the taxing authority for this port. They're trying to make us think they're doing all they can to let us sail with the tide, but I doubt they intend letting us go until that additional tariff is paid."

A burly, bearded crewman asked, "When did that tariff become law?"

Pettigrew snorted. "They've had a five percent export tariff on Virginia tobacco for four years. That's not the problem. They're telling me the State of Virginia added an extra three percent that became law four days ago when we were nearly loaded."

"Was the five percent paid?"

"That was paid, half by the Scott company that sold the tobacco, and half by the Doernen company up north that bought it. But neither one of them knew about the three percent added tariff when they made their arrangements. They still don't know."

"How long to go tell Doernen, or Scott?"

"It's not how long," Pettigrew exclaimed, "it's how do we do it? Walk? We can't sail with the *Rebecca*, and I can't find a ship leaving from here for New York within the next ten days. Scott's sixty-seven miles up the James River."

Caleb asked, "How long before they can seize the cargo or the ship and sell them?"

"Thirteen more days."

"How much is the added three percent?"

"One hundred twelve pounds sterling."

"We don't have it?"

"We have less than half that much. It was never intended that we pay the tariff. That was between the buyer and the seller."

"Any chance Matthew and Billy know about this?"

Pettigrew shook his head. "No chance at all."

Caleb's face was white. "This will ruin their business."

"Ruin it before it gets started."

McKinrow's thick Scottish brogue sounded from the back of the crew. "The tides and winds are with us tonight, and they won't be again for days. What do we do? How do we get back up north?"

Loud exclamations broke out from the crew, and Pettigrew raised his hand to silence them. "I don't know yet. All we can do is—"

Suddenly Caleb gestured. "Some men up at that office want you."

Pettigrew turned to look behind him and saw the small group of men gathered in front of the office, one of them motioning with his hand. He turned back to his crew and exclaimed, "Let's go. I'll do the talking."

They strode in a body, leaning into the wind, and Pettigrew stopped six feet from a thin-faced, balding man, shivering in a thin dress coat, squinting through spectacles. The man smiled, and his voice was high as he motioned and spoke.

"Come inside. Too cold out here."

Pettigrew answered, "All of us?"

"Up to you. You'll have to stand."

The man stepped inside and held the door while the three men with him followed, then Pettigrew and his crew. The man closed the door and worked his way to the high counter that divided the room, swung the gate open, entered to his side, waited while his three joined him, then turned to face Pettigrew across the counter. The crew gathered behind Pettigrew, silent, eyes boring into the four men facing them.

The thin-faced man pushed his spectacles back up his nose. "This office never was big enough. Sorry you have to stand." He studied Pettigrew for a moment. "I take it you're the captain of the *Rebecca*."

"Yes. Theodore Pettigrew. At your service."

The man nodded. "I'm Albert Jensen. Harbormaster. I understand there's a problem with your ship."

Pettigrew's voice was flat, cool. "Not the ship. We're loaded with three hundred tons of Virginia tobacco, ready to sail with the tides. The five percent export tariff was paid, but I'm told there is an additional three percent that's been assessed."

Jensen nodded and pursed his mouth and shook his head. "Yes. A real nuisance. Caught three or four merchant ships by surprise. We didn't intend to have that happen, but that's how the legislature handled it. Not much we can do. It's the law."

Pettigrew's voice was rising. "Isn't there a requirement that notice be given before those kinds of tariffs become effective? Sixty days?"

Jensen shook his head. "Not that I know of. We've always given notice before, but that was during normal times, and these times are anything *but* normal." Jensen sighed. "But you're talking to the wrong man. I'm harbor authority." He gestured to the man next to him. "This is Peter Curtis. He handles tax and tariffs in this port. He'll answer your questions."

Pettigrew turned to Curtis, average size, receding chin, bulbous nose. "Sir, we have urgent need to deliver three hundred tons of tobacco to a New York buyer. Our ship's loaded. The only thing holding us here is lack of payment of the added three percent export tariff. We didn't even know about it until three days ago. If we don't sail with the tides, we could lose the buyers. It could cost the ship owners their company. What arrangements can we make to let us sail out tonight and pay later?"

Curtis tossed his hands in the air helplessly and spoke with a noticeable lisp. "I wish there was a way, but the law doesn't allow for it."

"Can I sign a note? A promissory note?"

Curtis shook his head sadly. "What would we do if you didn't pay? How would we collect it?"

"I'll stay here until it's paid! My crew can sail the *Rebecca* to deliver the cargo."

Curtis's smile was a mix of condescension and irritation. "And if no one returns to pay, what do we do? Throw you in debtors prison? That way everyone suffers."

Caleb saw the desperation growing in Pettigrew's face and heard it in his voice as he spoke. "Let me call this the way I see it. These are hard times, and we're here in this port, loaded with Virginia tobacco that has a buyer in New York. If we deliver it, my employer gains, Virginia gains, New York gains, and this crew gains. Your added three percent tariff became law four days ago, without notice to us or anyone else. I'll return to pay it."

Curtis raised a hand to stop him, and Pettigrew paused.

"I know all that, sir, and you must believe, I have sympathy. But what

I don't have is the power to do anything other than hold the ship until the tariff is paid."

Caleb saw Pettigrew's chin begin to tremble with anger. "A sale that will put thousands of pounds British sterling into the stream of commerce, both here and up north, save my employer, feed these men and their families for weeks. All lost for lack of one hundred twelve pounds British sterling for a tax we didn't know about. Is that what I'm hearing from you, sir?"

Curtis drew a deep breath before he answered, and all sign of friendliness was gone. "No. I am bound by the law. My authority is limited to collecting the tax, and should it be necessary, to seize cargoes and ships that fail to pay. Nothing more, nothing less."

Pettigrew's voice rose. "Then who, sir, has authority above yours?"

For a moment every man in the room stood in shocked silence, and Curtis's face was drawn, angry when he answered. "The Virginia legislature. Go see them. Your case would be considered by them within the next six months, and resolved within a year. Until they speak, your ship remains here."

Pettigrew's palm slapped down on the counter. Curtis jumped, and Pettigrew's voice rang off the bare walls. "You intend selling her within the next thirteen days?"

Curtis took one step back. "If that becomes necessary to collect the tax." He turned to the two men behind him, gestured, and they trotted to the back door and out into the wind. Curtis turned back to Pettigrew.

"Those men will return in about five minutes with militia. Armed. I have authority to arrest if it becomes necessary."

Pettigrew's head thrust forward in disbelief. "Arrest! Who? Me?"

"You're very close to defying Virginia law."

Pettigrew gaped, and Caleb grasped his arm. "Come on, Captain. You'll get nothing from these men. Let's go."

Pettigrew seized Caleb's hand and started to wrench it free, and then he caught himself and settled, and brought his rage under control. His anger was like a living thing as he stared into Curtis's eyes, but he said nothing. He was still shaking as he turned about and made his way through his crew to open the door, and they followed him out onto the docks, into the chill wind, just as six uniformed Virginia militia came trotting from the west to line up against the wall on both sides of the door, muskets at the ready.

Pettigrew turned to his men. "Come on."

He turned his back on the militia and walked away with his crew following. He could feel their weariness, and their rising fear that they were alone and unwanted in an unfriendly place, with no way to get out. They were becoming surly, and he was beginning to gauge how long they would take the abuse before they would fight back, even mutiny.

He walked on toward the *Rebecca* and stopped before four Virginia militiamen who blocked the gangplank. The crew crowded around him, hands still in their pockets, the wind moving their long hair, tied behind their heads with leather strings in the manner of seamen.

Pettigrew's voice was controlled, steady. "We need to go aboard to get clothes and some food."

The lean, thin-faced corporal in charge looked at Pettigrew, then the thirteen men with him, and he wiped a nervous hand across his dry mouth. His voice cracked as he spoke. "Sorry, sir. Our orders are that no one boards this ship without written permission of Mr. Curtis."

Caleb watched the anger leap in Pettigrew's eyes and moved one step closer, nearly touching his elbow, ready. Pettigrew's voice was so quiet it was difficult to hear him in the wind.

"You're telling me I have to get permission from Curtis to board my own ship for clothing and food for these men?"

"Yes, sir. You do."

Movement and murmuring broke out in the crew, and Pettigrew turned to them. "Back away from here and wait for me. Whatever happens, stay away from the ship. Am I clear?"

Reluctant mumbles of "Aye, sir," came from among them, but one thing was clear. They were very near open rebellion as Pettigrew strode back to the office of Peter Curtis. Caleb gave a head gesture, and the crew followed him to gather ten yards away from the ship, where they stood in the wind and chill sun, looking first at the four militiamen clustered at the gangplank, then at the office, talking quietly among themselves while they waited for Pettigrew to return. Five minutes became ten, then fifteen, before the office door opened, and they watched their captain walk out and turn directly toward them. He came striding, mouth clenched shut, and they knew before he reached them that Curtis had denied his request. Behind Pettigrew, Curtis stood in the doorway for a moment, then gave orders and pointed, and the six militiamen standing at the office door fell into a loose file and followed Pettigrew, muskets grasped before them in both hands. Pettigrew reached the crew, and the six militiamen marched on past to join the other four at the gangplank of the rocking ship.

Every man in the crew had seen battle in the war, and each was making instant calculations of whether they could cover the thirty feet between them and the ten muskets before the men holding them could cock them, bring them to bear, and fire. It would be close. Pettigrew read it perfectly and stepped out to assert himself.

"It isn't worth blood. Come on with me."

They walked west, past the office, with Curtis and the three men inside staring at them through the windows, and they stopped on the wharf with the gulls squawking and disputing over dead fish and refuse in the river and on the banks, and the wind murmuring in the masts and ropes of the ships tied nearby. The crew gathered around Pettigrew.

"Curtis will not give permission. He says the law is clear—the crew cannot go aboard a seized ship until the tax is paid. We can't pay the tax. I have fifty-two British pounds in gold in a money belt around my middle. That was for necessaries for our haul north. We could use it to buy passage home, but I can't find a ship moving north for about ten days. So the question is, what do we do about it?"

Loud talk erupted. For more than a minute Pettigrew watched and listened, gauging the temper of his men. Caleb stood nearby, saying nothing, thoughts running, and then he turned to Pettigrew.

"Let's go down to the Blue Dolphin. Get something hot to eat. Talk."

Pettigrew nodded, and he and Caleb led the way farther west to the weatherworn, unpainted tavern near the end of the waterfront. The clutch of men entered the dingy room, waited a moment for their eyes to adjust, glanced at the six men with mugs in their hands seated alone at six separate tables, then walked to the plain, blocky, harried, lipless woman standing behind a wide plank lying atop two barrels. She looked at the fourteen men, then spoke to Pettigrew.

"We don't have beds for this many."

"We're not here for lodging. Do you have hot food? Ham? A leg of mutton?"

"Stew. We have stew for this many. It'll take a few minutes."

"Do you have a room we can use?"

She pointed. "There."

"Something hot to drink while we're waiting."

"Rum? Cider?" she said.

Pettigrew nodded. "Hot pitchers of each."

"Pay in advance."

He laid money on the plank, she made change, and he led his crew to the plain, bare-walled room with air tainted by the sour smell of stale rum and salt sea air. A long, scarred, wooden table was in the center of the room, with benches down two sides, chairs at each end; a smoky fire burned in the fireplace along one wall. They closed the door, and the men took their places on the side benches, with Pettigrew on the chair at one end, Caleb on the chair at the other.

It took the perspiring woman three trips to set four large pewter pitchers of steaming cider and buttered rum on the table, with fourteen battered pewter mugs. The men poured, steam rose, the men gingerly sipped, then turned toward their captain, waiting.

Pettigrew set his mug down. "I can't find a way to get us out of here in less than ten days. I have about forty-eight pounds British sterling after paying for this meal, and at the end of thirteen days I doubt I'll have much money left if we have to pay for lodging and food. If any of you have something to say, now's the time."

The men stared at each other for a time before talk began. For ten minutes it ran on with Pettigrew listening, waiting for any plan that gave a glimmer of hope, and there was none. The blocky woman brought in two black kettles of steaming mutton and vegetable stew with fourteen pewter bowls and spoons, four large loaves of brown uncut bread that was burned on the bottom, set it all on the table, and walked back out without a word. The men filled their bowls, broke the bread, and scooped the first load of stew into their mouths, sucking air against the heat. For a time the only sound at the table was the click of pewter spoons on pewter bowls, and weary, angry, cold, hungry men working on hot stew and bread.

They were starting to fill their bowls for the second time when Caleb put his spoon down and raised his head to speak. There was a quality in his voice that stopped every man and brought all eyes to bear on him.

"Captain, has Congress passed any laws controlling all American harbors?"

Pettigrew shook his head. "None that I know of. Why?"

"Are the laws of Virginia harbors like the ones in Massachusetts?"

"Some, not all."

"What happens if two states have laws that are different, and the difference starts trouble?"

The entire crew was silent, tracking, while Pettigrew thought. "You mean if a ship from one state breaks the law of the harbor of another state?"

"Yes."

Pettigrew set his fork down. "I think the law where the offense happened would control."

"But what if the ship that offended was gone? Back to its home port?"

Pettigrew leaned back in his chair, staring at Caleb, mind working. "I don't know. I doubt one state has the right to go into the harbor of another and seize a ship. Or make any arrest. At least without the consent of the home harbor."

"And if the home harbor says no?"

"I think that would be the end of it."

Caleb nodded. "That's what I thought. If it's true, then I think we have a decision to make."

Pettigrew's eyes widened, and he suddenly straightened, then leaned forward, tapping his forefinger on the table. Murmuring broke out among the crew as their thoughts caught up with Pettigrew's.

"Wait a minute," he said. "What are you suggesting?"

All heads turned to Caleb, and the only sound was the wind drawing at the chimney.

Caleb's voice was steady and even. "We sail the *Rebecca* out of here tonight."

Pettigrew started, and his voice came hot and high. "While she's under seizure of a Virginia tariff law?"

"Yes."

"What of those ten militiamen? Kill them?"

"No. Take them with us."

Pettigrew's mouth fell open, and he clacked it shut. "Kidnapping?"

"Not exactly. When we've delivered the tobacco in New York, we pay them for their services and send them back."

Pettigrew half rose from his chair. "Take ten Virginia militiamen prisoner? You think the State of Virginia is going to stand for that? They'll have gunboats after us by morning."

"Do you think they'll fire on us when they see five of their own militia standing at each rail?"

"What? Human shields?"

Caleb's voice had not risen. "No. Observers. There's one other thing. Once on the high seas, do they have the right to fire on us?"

For a moment Pettigrew stared at the tabletop while he probed his memory of maritime law, written and unwritten. "Not without a warrant."

"How long to get a warrant?"

"Tomorrow morning, earliest. Maybe noon."

"The tides are with us until about midnight, but by tomorrow morning they'll be running against anyone who tries to sail east. That will cost them another six or eight hours. True?"

"Yes."

"By tomorrow afternoon we'll be at least twenty-four hours ahead of them. They might catch us, but we'll be a long way out of southern waters when they do, and I doubt they'll start shooting at a Massachusetts ship in northern waters and risk a war between the two states. If they follow us into New York harbor, we'll unload, get our money, pay those ten men for their services, and pay their passage on whatever ship is going back to Virginia. And we'll send that three percent tariff payment back with them."

Pettigrew was incredulous. "Where did you get this . . . wild . . . scheme?"

Caleb shrugged. "When I was a little boy back in December of '73. We had a tea party in Boston, remember? The question then was just like the one we have here. Do we pay the tax, or don't we? Only difference is, those were British taxes, and these are Virginia taxes. We didn't pay then and it helped start a war, and if we don't pay now it looks like we might start another one." He picked up his spoon. "And that's where we are. Any better idea?"

For five long seconds Pettigrew sat in startled silence. "No."

Caleb looked up and down both sides of the table. "You men have any better notion? If this goes wrong, we're the ones that go to jail, and there are so many ways for this to go wrong I'd speak against it if there was a better plan. But I can't find one. Can any of you?" He scooped stew into his mouth and chewed while he listened.

A voice called, "If we get back to Boston, can they come after us?"

Caleb looked at Pettigrew, who answered. "They have to file their grievance in Boston's maritime court and have a hearing. If Boston decides in our favor, that's where it stops."

Caleb interrupted. "Any idea how the Boston court might see this?"

Pettigrew responded. "None. I don't recall it ever came up before just like this."

"How many Virginia ships use Boston harbor?"

Pettigrew paused to collect his thoughts. "Many. Enough to make Virginia think hard before they start a quarrel."

Open talk broke out, then subsided as the next question was called out.

"Wait a minute, here. Sounds to me like this might wake up a few people so this kind of thing doesn't happen again."

Caleb looked directly at Pettigrew, and Pettigrew locked eyes with him. In that moment, both realized that the fog that had been clouding the thinking of the seaboard states had suddenly lifted to leave the frightening truth exposed where none could avoid it. Either the states become unified and stand as one, or they widen their differences and destroy each other.

Pettigrew leaned forward on his elbows and all talk quieted. His eyes narrowed and none had heard such earnestness in his voice as he answered. "It might. If it did—if it could help the states see the need to come together—it might be worth it."

McKinrow's voice cut through. "Seein' that we might all wind up in prison, I say we got a right to vote on this."

Pettigrew fell silent for several seconds before he answered. "That's fair. All in favor of a voice vote say 'aye'."

The vote was unanimous.

"All in favor of a secret vote?"

Silence held.

"All right, then. All who favor the plan of sailing the *Rebecca* out of this port tonight to complete our duty say 'aye'."

The voices came strong and unanimous.

"Any opposed?"

There were none.

Pettigrew nodded toward Caleb. "The idea was yours. Take charge."

For a moment Caleb glanced at each man in turn on both sides of the table. They were bearded, wearing worn and tattered clothing, weary, edgy, needing a bath. They were also battle-hardened veterans who had learned to live with cold and hunger and death. Most had faced superior numbers of British so many times that the art of deception and silently infiltrating enemy lines at night and the deadly use of knives in the dark was second nature to them.

Caleb nodded to Pettigrew, then spoke to the crew. "All right. Let me lay it out the way I see it. Stop me when I'm wrong. This has to be our plan, not mine."

It was half past three o'clock when they rose from the empty pitchers and pewter plates and mugs and cold stew kettles and walked out of the Blue Dolphin into the afternoon wind. They separated in singles and twos, walking slowly in different directions, unnoticed by the sparse waterfront traffic. The sun had set and evening dusk was gathering when McKinrow and Caleb met in an abandoned weed patch one hundred yards past the west end of the tiny seaport village, and two hundred yards north of the James River. McKinrow held a five-pound wooden keg of gunpowder beneath his coat; Caleb had a one gallon jug of whale oil beneath his. They dropped to their haunches in the weeds and peered about in the gathering gloom to be certain they were alone before they set the tiny powder keg and jug in the weeds and walked back into town unnoticed.

At six o'clock the curtained windows in the hamlet began glowing with lamplight. At half past six the crew came to the spot in ones and twos, dragging driftwood and broken and abandoned shipping crates to heap them high. At seven o'clock the waterfront was quiet and all but abandoned; only night watchmen remained, huddled inside shipping company offices, walking out into the cold night wind every half hour to quickly make their rounds with a lantern, then return to the warmth of the fire inside.

At ten minutes past seven o'clock the crew gathered back at the Blue Dolphin in twos and threes, walked past the four men drinking hot buttered rum at one table, and gathered in the small room at the rear of the building. Pettigrew ordered hot cider and a baked leg of lamb and boiled potatoes for their suppers, and at eight o'clock they pushed back from the table, full and warm, and turned toward their captain.

Pettigrew looked at Caleb and McKinrow. He spoke quietly. "The gunpowder and oil. Is it there?"

Caleb nodded.

Pettigrew turned to the big man with the bushy beard. "The militiamen?"

"Changed their guard at six o'clock. Still ten of them down there. Armed."

He spoke to the crew. "Did we get enough wood down by the gunpowder?"

They nodded.

"From here on, move in twos. Never alone. Watch each other's back. If one gets hurt, the other brings him to the ship. Stay out of the light. If anyone doesn't know their part in this, speak now."

For three full seconds the men looked up and down the table in silence. Pettigrew turned back to Caleb.

"Got the tinderbox?"

Caleb nodded and laid a small iron box on the table. Fifteen seconds later he laid the flint and steel down and raised the box to blow gently on the spark that was glowing in the shredded linen. It caught, the tiny flame held, Caleb waited a few seconds while it spread, then snapped the lid back on the box. "Ready."

Pettigrew drew a great breath, rounded his lips, and slowly let it out. "Let's go."

They left the room in pairs, timed half a minute apart. Once outside they glanced at the nearly abandoned waterfront, then drifted in different directions away from the docks to disappear in the dark dirt streets and work their way north beyond the last street of the hamlet, then turn east, silent and unseen. Caleb and McKinrow walked out into the wind and turned west to stand still, peering down the waterfront, watching for anyone who might be wondering about fourteen men coming from the Blue Dolphin to scatter on a night when the waterfront was all but abandoned. There was no movement, and the only ones visible were about their own business. None seemed to notice or care who was on the wharves.

Without a word the two turned west and walked into the wind with their heads down, hands deep in their coat pockets, shoulders hunched. As they walked, Caleb spoke.

"Don't I remember you had a brother? Lon?"

For a moment McKinrow looked down, then raised his head. "Yes."

"He's home?"

"No. He died. Head started to swell and he died."

"I'm sorry. I didn't mean to—"

"Pay it no mind. He's not suffering any more."

They walked on in silence, each with his own thoughts. Five minutes later they stopped at the great pile of driftwood and abandoned, broken wooden shipping crates, and reached for the whale oil and gunpowder. They cleared a small place near the center of the heap, shielded from the wind, and set a slab of flat wood on the ground. McKinrow knocked the bung out of the keg of gunpowder and jammed one end of a two-foot section of rope into it, and set it in the center of the wooden slab while Caleb jerked the cork out of the gallon jug. McKinrow stepped back while Caleb poured whale oil on the rope, then the board. He heaped more driftwood on the keg and sprinkled the pile with the remainder of the oil.

In the light of a quarter moon just clearing the eastern horizon, Caleb turned to McKinrow and silently asked the question. McKinrow nodded, Caleb drew the hot tinderbox from his pocket, removed the lid, and blew on the smoldering linen inside. Three seconds later tiny blue and yellow flames caught, and Caleb turned the box upside down on the near edge of the puddled whale oil. For a moment the flames disappeared, and then the whale oil caught, and the blue flames slowly worked their way outward.

Caleb and McKinrow stood, waited for three seconds to be certain of the fire, then turned due east and sprinted along the back edge of the town. They had covered less than one hundred yards before the great bell in the church steeple set up an incessant clanging that echoed for miles. Within seconds doors in most of the homes were thrown open. Men in shirtsleeves ran out into the yards and streets, turning their heads all directions before they saw the glow of the fire past the west end of town, away from the river. They stood for a few seconds, unable to remember anything there that could burn, then realized that whatever it was mattered less than the fact that the wind was carrying the sparks east, over the town and the waterfront. They charged back into their homes only long enough to grab coats and tricorns, and then they were back outside, running hard toward the fire.

In the darkness just beyond the back street of the town, near the east end, Caleb and McKinrow dropped to their haunches and waited, heads down, listening, hoping, and then it came. In the still of the night, the single blast seemed horrendous. For several seconds the entire west end of the town was lighted by the burning wood that was blown seventy feet into the air, and an umbrella of sparks was blasted in all directions. For a moment, awestruck men slowed to stare, then ran on.

At the *Rebecca*, the ten militiamen stopped all movement and stood like statues, the glow reflecting off the flat planes of their faces as they stared west, stunned. Without realizing it, they moved a few paces, then stopped, wind in their faces, gripping their muskets with both hands while the town came alive with lanterns and men running west, away from them, and the incessant clanging of the church bell sounding in their ears.

The militiamen flinched at the voice that boomed from behind them.

"Move and you're dead men!"

For a moment they stood transfixed, unable to understand what was happening, and then twelve men were among them, seizing their muskets, pushing them together, surrounding them under the muzzles of their own muskets and bayonets.

Pettigrew motioned. "Up the gangplank," he barked. "Move! Now!"

The corporal in command opened his mouth to protest, and instantly two bayonets were at his chest. He swallowed hard, turned, and led his column of ten thumping up the gangplank, followed by twelve shadowy men. On board, the militiamen were quickly divided, and half were taken to the railings on each side of the ship, where rough hands tied their wrists and ankles together, sat them down on the deck, lashed them to the railing, and backed up two steps to stand with the muskets and bayonets centered on the chests of the speechless militiamen.

Back at the gangplank, Pettigrew waited, listening, and then Caleb's voice came from the shadows below, on the dock.

"Ready?"

"Ready," Pettigrew answered.

Caleb trotted to one end of the *Rebecca*, while McKinrow trotted to the other. Without a word, both men swung axes hard. It took three strokes to cut the two-inch hawsers, and the two men trotted to the ropes on either side of the gangplank and swung three more times. When the lines parted, the loaded ship seemed to take on a life of her own. She was free, unfettered, and she began to move away from the dock as though responding to a need to be running with the wind toward the open seas.

Pettigrew called, "Move!" and Caleb and McKinrow sprinted thumping up the gangplank onto the deck one second before the lower end broke free from the dock and slammed dangling into the side of the ship.

"Get the gangplank up," Pettigrew ordered, and while Caleb and McKinrow threw their backs into dragging it aboard, Pettigrew pivoted, cupped his hands around his mouth and shouted to the crew, "Unfurl all canvas on the mainmast!"

Six of the twelve ran to the rope netting and in the darkness scrambled upward to the top spar, then out onto the ropes, jerking free the knots holding the furled sails. The canvas dropped, flapping in the wind, and experienced hands anchored the lower end. The sailors descended to the great spar beneath them and once again risked their lives on the ropes as they released the sail and tied down the lower end. The great sheets popped loud as they caught the wind and billowed, and the ship picked up speed.

Pettigrew sprinted to the wheel, threw aside the ropes locking it, grasped the handles, and spun it to starboard with all his strength. The bow of the ship swung to the right, and every man on board held his breath as she bore down on a collision course with the stern of the ship tied to the docks east of her. With the wind sighing in the rigging and sails, and the mainmast creaking, the bow of the *Rebecca* cleared the stern of the ship ahead by less than six feet, and as she broke into the open harbor Pettigrew shouted, "Unfurl all canvas. Bow and stern masts."

Once more the sailors scrambled upward in the nets to free and tie the sails, and the ship surged forward. Instantly Caleb was at the bow of the ship, searching out the dim, black silhouettes of the deepwater ships anchored in the river.

"Hard port," he shouted, and Pettigrew swung the wheel to watch a sloop slide past the starboard railing, and Caleb's voice came ringing again, "Hard starboard." The *Rebecca* swung violently to the right and brushed a second ship. "Easy to the port," Caleb shouted, and the ship swung back to the left, and then came his shout, "Correct to due east and steady as she goes." The ship swung slightly to the right, then straightened and cleared the last anchored sloop by ten yards.

Then came Caleb's shout, "She's clear!" and the *Rebecca* was running free with the wind, cutting a twenty-foot curl, leaving a white wake one hundred yards long in the night as she plowed east down the ever-widening James River channel. The head of every man in the crew swiveled to peer west, wide-eyed, scarcely breathing as they searched the river and the Jamestown waterfront for any sign of a ship in pursuit, but there was none. Those up in the rigging held their positions as they sped east, and half of those on deck ran to the bow of the ship to stand beside Caleb, gripping the rail, straining to see both banks of the river and anything in the water that could damage the *Rebecca*. Running with the Atlantic tides and the strong westerly wind, the loaded ship was fairly flying.

At the wheel, their captain was watching both banks like a hawk, and depending on the men in the bow to warn of anything in the water that could crack the ship's hull. To his left he saw a scattering of lights in the small hamlet of Williamsburg, three hundred yards from the river. He waited one full minute before he moved the wheel, and the ship made a swing to starboard, rounding the curve of the river to the southeast. Again he straightened the wheel, dividing the distance between the dim river banks, and held his course for the thirty-mile run to the next bend in the river. It came sooner than he calculated, and he spun the wheel hard to port and felt the tilt of the ship as she leaned east while she turned back to the north, and he shouted to the men at the railing in the bow.

"There's a light at Old Point Comfort coming up on the port side. It marks the narrows into Lynnhaven Bay. We've got to hit that Point Comfort channel dead center. Sing out when she comes into view."

Three minutes later half a dozen arms raised to point, and voices shouted, "There it is! On the port side!"

Pettigrew took his bearings, spun the wheel, and the ship creaked and leaned as she swung to port. With the judgment that comes only with years of experience, the captain made his calculations of distance and set a course that would bring the *Rebecca* past the distant light at a range of three hundred yards. He held his position to watch the light come past on the port side, and the ship was out in the deep water of Lynnhaven Bay, at the south end of the Chesapeake. Pettigrew turned the wheel once more to bring her on a course due east, and again called to the men at the bow.

"In about forty minutes you'll see a lighthouse at Cape Charles to the north and another one to the south. That's Cape Henry. Both will be about five miles away. Look sharp! When we pass between those two lighthouses, we're out of the Chesapeake and into the Atlantic."

Thirty minutes later Caleb pointed, and two of the crew turned to shout back at Pettigrew, "Lighthouse on the port side," and three minutes later, "Lighthouse to the starboard."

Pettigrew held to the broad, deep channel between the two distant flecks of light, and the crew stood still to watch them pass and fade into the distance to the west. Pettigrew judged the passing of four miles before he turned the ship due north, and she was running before the wind in the black waters of the Atlantic. A spontaneous shout from the crew rolled out over the sea, and Caleb and Pettigrew rounded their mouths to blow air in relief.

Half the crew stood watch over the ten Virginia militiamen tied to the rails, while one man climbed to the crow's nest with a telescope and the others trotted to the stern to peer into the blackness due south, all of them searching for running lights of any pursuing ships, or their silhouettes in the night. There were none. The night wore on with Pettigrew at the wheel and the crew straining to see pursuing ships that were not there, while their spirits rose with each passing mile. The first hint of dawn defined the flat line of the ocean to the east, and as the morning star faded, the call came down from the crow's nest, "All's clear!"

At mid-afternoon, two light frigates mounting twenty-four cannon each appeared on the southern skyline. By four o'clock they were alongside, flying the flag of the State of Virginia while their captains used telescopes to study the ten men wearing the uniform of Virginia militiamen, tied to the rails. The crew of the *Rebecca* stood at the rails, watching every move aboard the two frigates, grimly waiting for the gun crews to open the gun ports and commence firing, but the gun ports remained closed, and the frigates were still alongside as dusk settled into full darkness; the following morning they were not to be seen.

The *Rebecca* sped on north with the crew settling into the daily duties of running a ship, watching the American coastline slip past far to the west. Pettigrew charted their course on a map in the captain's quarters and took his four-hour shifts, with Caleb and McKinrow at the wheel while he slept. On the third day the ten Virginia militiamen were divided into two groups of five and allowed to move about the ship freely so long as the two groups did not talk with each other, and they were always under the eye of two of Pettigrew's crew. They watched the state of Maryland pass in the distance, then Delaware, Delaware Bay, and then New Jersey. At two o'clock on the afternoon of the fifth day the call came from the crow's nest, "Sandy Hook ahead, port side."

The crew watched as Pettigrew lined up the ship for the tricky passage through the bar, past the battery on Sandy Hook, then the hard turn to starboard, north up the channel for deep water ships, through the narrows between Staten Island and Long Island, to emerge into the broad, protected waters of New York harbor, with Manhattan Island and the New York docks and waterfront on the southern tip of the island, dead ahead.

By half past five o'clock the *Rebecca* was tied to a pier. At ten minutes before six o'clock, Pettigrew and Caleb walked through the door of a waterfront office with the sign DOERNEN above it and stood at the counter. A thick-featured man studied them as he walked to the counter.

"Something you wanted?"

"I'm Captain Theodore Pettigrew. I am employed by the Dunson and Weems carrying firm. I have just docked with three hundred tons of Virginia tobacco. I believe your company is the buyer."

The man's eyebrows raised. "You have papers? The manifest?"

"I do." He drew them from inside his coat and laid them on the counter.

A broad grin creased the melon face. "Can you start to unload tonight?"

"I can."

"Good. Are you the ship that came in less than an hour ago?"

"The *Rebecca*. Yes."

"I'll meet you there in fifteen minutes. Show you our warehouse."

Pettigrew nodded. "You have the pay for my crew?"

"In British pounds. Right here in the office."

"Could I see it?"

The man shrugged. "Don't remember ever being asked that before, but you certainly can."

Three minutes later, with the heavy iron safe at the rear of the office standing open, the man walked back to the counter and dropped a leather bag before Pettigrew. "There it is. Want to count it?"

Pettigrew shook his head. "No. You'll have to overlook my lack of manners. Getting that cargo here has been an experience we can talk about later. I'll go back to the ship and wait for you there."

"Good." The man picked up the bag. "I'll put this back in the safe. We can sign the releases later."

In gathering dusk, Pettigrew and Caleb walked back to the ship, hands in their coat pockets, watching the lights come on in the windows and on the ships. They reached the *Rebecca*, thumped up the gangplank, and faced the crew. They were dirty, unshaven, hungry, bone-weary, and they stood silent with dead eyes and faces, waiting.

"Doernen will have a man here in ten minutes to show us the warehouse. We can start unloading tonight if you're up to it."

McKinrow asked, "Do they have our pay?"

A smile showed in Pettigrew's beard. "In British sterling. I've seen it."

For a moment the air went out of the entire crew, and then McKinrow said, "Let's get at it."

Pettigrew turned to the ten Virginia militiamen, gathered together, listening intently.

"We're going to pay you dockhand wages for the time you've been on this ship, and then pay your passage back to Jamestown on the next ship leaving here for your home port. Any questions?

There were none.

"One more thing. We're sending the added three percent export tariff on the tobacco with you. Every one of you is going to have to sign the receipt. If the money doesn't reach Mr. Curtis, we'll visit you there. Are there any questions now?"

The corporal looked at Pettigrew, then the crew, and for a moment reflected on what he had seen them do at night at the Jamestown waterfront, and in the past six days. He cleared his throat. "No, sir. None. Your money will reach Mr. Curtis."

Notes

In 1784, Virginia did have an export tariff on tobacco being shipped from her ports (Nevins, *The American States, 1775–1789*, p. 559).

For an excellent map of the James River, Jamestown, Lynnhaven Bay, Chesapeake Bay, and the Cape Charles and Cape Henry lights, all as described herein, see Mackesy, *The War for America, 1775–1783*, p. 340.

CHAPTER XXVI

*T*hey all quietly repeated her "amen," rose from their knees beside her bed, and in the yellow light of the single lamp walked from the bedroom of Margaret Dunson. For a few moments she stood on the oval braided rag rug beside her bed and closed her eyes to listen to the faint footsteps of her children fade as they passed down the dark hallway to their bedrooms. She heard their doors quietly close and sat to remove her woolen slippers with the feeling of rightness warm in her heart as it always was at day's end, when they were all fed, prayed, and safe in their beds.

For a moment she sat still, clenching and unclenching her toes on the rug, before she stood and pulled the heavy comforter down. And once again she felt the emptiness in the room, and in the bed, and she wondered if the ache for her husband would ever leave. Nine years. At that moment she could not remember beyond the time Tom Sievers had brought him home from the shooting at Concord, with the British musketball in his lung, nor the following day when he promised they would be together again, and had died. Nine years ago. She remembered every moment of his passing as if it were today, and she felt the ache and the loneliness and the longing that had become part of her. The daily busyness of surviving in a harsh, unforgiving world muted it, but in the quiet dark of the night, she would reach to touch the empty half of the bed and the pillow that was still in its place, and the silent tears would come.

She tucked her feet beneath the great comforter and was reaching for the wheel on the lamp when she heard the whisper of slippers on hardwood, and then her door quietly opened. Her eyes widened as Prissy entered, and stood beside her bed.

"Mother, may I talk to you?"

For a moment Margaret studied her, searching for a reason that quiet, thoughtful Prissy would need to talk alone, at night. Prissy's face gleamed in the yellow light, and Margaret saw the confusion, and she moved her legs and patted the bed, and Prissy sat down. Margaret waited in silence while Prissy worked her hands in her lap, then spoke without looking up.

"Something's happening with Brigitte. I don't know what it is."

"What has she said?"

"Nothing, to me."

"Has she done something?"

"No. Well, yes."

"What?"

"Two days ago I saw her take those things she's kept on her dresser for years—the ones about Richard Buchanan—and put them in a box. You know . . . the letters, and his commission—his things. She put the box on the top shelf of her closet, back in the corner, and she hasn't looked at them since."

"That's all?"

"No. She doesn't talk. It's like she has something . . . bad . . . that won't let go of her." For the first time Prissy raised her eyes to Margaret's, and Margaret saw the pain as she forced the words.

"Mother, has she done something wrong?"

In that instant Margaret realized that her youngest was no longer a child. She had become a woman, just entering the world of intuition and emotions that were at once wonderful and exciting and confusing and bewildering and frightening, with their promise of love that could lift her to the heights of joy and ecstasy, and sorrows that could plunge her to the depths of grief and torment.

Margaret took a breath and reached deep. "Has she said anything to you about it?"

"No."

Margaret's tone was level, even, as though talking to an equal. "She's done nothing wrong."

She saw the relief in Prissy, and she went on.

"Can you keep this between us?"

"Yes."

"She is trying to deal with something none of us expected. Not her, not me, not Matthew. None of us."

Prissy's eyes widened in wonderment.

"It's Billy Weems."

For five seconds Prissy's face drew down as she struggled to comprehend, and then understanding struck, and she recoiled and clapped her hand over her mouth.

"Billy? Billy Weems?," she exclaimed.

Margaret raised a finger to her lips to quiet Prissy, and continued.

"You remember the Sunday not long ago when Billy asked to walk with her from church?"

"Yes."

"He told her he had feelings for her. Strong feelings. That he had had them for a long time. While he was away, he wrote letters to her. For over five years. Twenty-two of them. He didn't want to hurt her, so he didn't send them. When he and Matthew went into business together, he thought he owed it to Matthew to let him know, and Matthew urged Billy to give her the letters. He gave them to her that day."

Prissy's voice was barely above a whisper. "Letters? To Brigitte? Billy?"

"Yes."

"Where are they? Have you seen them?"

"She has them. I don't know where she keeps them—that's her business. But she invited me to read them, and I did."

"What. . . . what did Billy say?"

For a moment Margaret dropped her eyes and then raised them to Prissy's.

"He said everything a decent man should say."

"Does he love her?"

"Yes. He does."

"Does he want to marry her?"

"He didn't say that, but he does."

For a time Prissy could not find words. She was seeing Billy as she had seen him her entire life. Plain, homely, barrel-chested, arms and legs like tree stumps, always there, just like Matthew, letting her ride on his back or his shoulders, tugging her braids—Billy. She had never questioned that he would always be there, like the sun and the rain and the seasons, and with her awakening intuition she suddenly knew that Brigitte had always seen him the same.

"Oh, mother," she whispered. "Brigitte must be. . . ."

Margaret nodded. "She is. In a way, for her, it's like discovering someone in your family is in love with you."

"Mother, I love Billy. We all do. I can hardly think of life without him. But to marry?"

Margaret nodded. "Now you know why Brigitte put Richard's things away, and why she's been so quiet."

Prissy slowly shook her head. "I can hardly imagine . . . What is she going to do?"

"I don't know. She'll decide that, and tell us when she's ready."

"She'll break his heart if she turns him away, and she'll break her own heart if she accepts him without loving him. Has she said she loves him? Or doesn't love him?"

"Not a word."

Prissy's shoulders sagged and her head dropped forward. "I never *dreamed* anything like this could happen. How has she held herself together?"

Margaret saw the opening.

"The same way she did when she got the letter about Richard. The same way she did when your father was killed. The same way she will when her own children come, and she feels their pain in life. Maybe that's the worst of all—watching your children suffer, and you can't stop it."

Margaret stopped and waited until she saw Prissy was ready, then continued. "She'll work her way through it the same way you will when your turn comes."

Prissy locked eyes with Margaret, and for a time she stared at her mother while the first real understanding broke clear in her heart of the price nature demands of a woman for the singular privilege of bearing children. For the first time, Prissy caught the beginnings of what Margaret had endured when she lost her first child, then her husband, and then watched her sons leave to go into harm's way, never knowing if she would see them again, or if they would come home whole or crippled or disfigured. And all the while, Margaret had stood steady, unflinching, carrying her terrible burden in determined silence while she stepped up to fill the void of household leadership while the men were gone. Prissy saw her hands, hard, cracked, red from endless work, and she saw the lines that had grown about her eyes and her mouth, and in that moment she realized that her mother's silent, hidden sacrifice had been in part for her. Never had she felt such a surge of love and emotion, and her chin trembled as the tears came welling. She tried to speak, but there were no words that would say what was in her heart, and she sat silent, wiping at her cheeks.

With wisdom learned from pain and toil, Margaret remained quiet, giving her daughter time to begin the unending struggle to accept what life brings, and put it—the good and the bad, the pain and the joy—into its place and make sense of it. Time passed before Prissy wiped away her tears and again spoke to her mother.

"How do we ever repay? For what you've done?"

"For being a mother?"

Prissy looked her in the eyes. "I never thought what that meant. Being a mother."

"Repay? You repay by being a mother. A good one. And when your time comes, you will."

"Brigitte? What do you think she'll do about Billy?"

Margaret spoke slowly, with thought. "I don't know. It depends on what she finally decides marriage means."

Prissy's eyes widened. "What marriage means?"

"Yes. What makes it work. What will make it work for her. Brigitte's headstrong. She's mellowing, but she's always going to be a little headstrong. She's bright. Impatient with people who can't keep up. Sometimes she gets into things outside the home. About got herself and Caleb killed eight years ago when she insisted on leading those wagons loaded with ammunition down across Connecticut to our soldiers. You remember. They had to walk home. Nearly starved."

Prissy nodded at the remembrance.

"Well, if Brigitte has the sense—and I think she does—she ought to be coming to a clear picture of herself, and then a clear picture of Billy. Then she should be asking herself if a woman like her and a man like him can make a marriage work."

Margaret paused until she saw Prissy had caught up with her, and then continued. She chose her words carefully, and she spaced them for emphasis, and her voice was low, penetrating.

"Finally, that's what marriage is all about. When the fascination and romance have taken their proper place in the man and the woman, and they face the raising of children and keeping food on the table, the real business of life is what they must face together, every day, every hour. The love they share in their moments alone will be there, and that is important. But getting along in the business of family and living fills most of their lives. And that is what Brigitte must decide now. Is she a woman, and is Billy a man, who can carry the load together?"

Prissy was scarcely breathing as Margaret continued.

"It's nice to have a husband who is handsome and charming. But as life moves on, and troubles come as they always do, handsome and charming doesn't get up in the night to help with a sick one, or take charge of a rebellious child, or work dawn to dark to pay the taxes and fill the root cellar. Solid and steady is the one who does that. And after a time, solid and steady becomes handsome and charming, no matter what he looks like. Then one day you get up in the morning and you realize how deep love can reach, and that every good thing in life finally depends on it, and that all the troubles and the worry and the pain are worth it. Many times over."

Margaret stopped, and Prissy sat mesmerized as Margaret concluded.

"You asked about Brigitte. I've given you the best I can. She has to decide these things for herself. And then she has to be ready for what her decision brings to her."

Prissy murmured, "If she decides wrong?"

"She learns to live with it."

"That sounds so hard."

"It is."

"Did you ever regret marrying Father?"

Margaret smiled, a little sadly. "No. There were things I wish he had done differently, but he was a man and I was a woman, and on some things we had trouble. Men and women always do, because the Almighty made them that way. A woman's heart, and a man's head. Sometimes they disagree."

"Like what?"

"John had to go to war. He was a man. I understood that, but I hated it. It terrified me and I told him so. He listened, but he went anyway, and we lost him. He and Tom Sievers. Matthew also had to go. I nearly died when he left. And Caleb . . ." Margaret shook her head and lowered her eyes. "I hope I never have to endure such a thing again. I expect I'll have tears in my heart to the day I die, over losing your father. He did what he had to do but oh, oh, what it did to me."

Prissy whispered, "I never thought about it that way."

"You were young. You weren't ready for it then."

"What should we be doing for Brigitte?"

"Nothing special. Just be yourself. That's the best thing right now."

"How do you think she'll decide? I mean about Billy?"

For a time Margaret didn't answer. "I don't know. She needs a man like Billy. And he needs a woman like Brigitte. The trouble is, will they see it? I think Billy does, but I don't know about Brigitte. My own daughter. She gave her heart to Richard Buchanan when she was too young. I don't know when she'll get over it. Maybe never. But . . . if she's put Richard's things away, it means she's far enough along to realize no matter how she felt about him, he's gone, and she has to move on."

"To Billy?"

"Billy is not handsome. Not charming. Richard was. I think Richard had it in him to be a good husband, but his first love was the British army. I doubt Brigitte would have favored being the wife of a military officer. I don't know. I don't know if her independent streak will bring trouble to her marriage or not. If anybody could handle that in her, it would be Billy. But . . . handsome and charming? Not Billy. Does Brigitte need that in a husband? She'll have to answer that."

For a time Prissy sat working her hands in her lap, staring at them. "I never knew it was all so complicated."

"You're ready for it. You'll do fine. Now you better go to bed."

Prissy stood and looked at her mother. "You've changed everything."

Margaret shook her head. "I've just told you the best I can. You're the one who made the changes in yourself. You're a beautiful, thoughtful girl. You should start trying to see yourself as you are. One day a young man will come along, and he'll be handsome and charming, or plain and steady, or who knows what, and you'll start your journey through what Brigitte's facing now."

"It makes me tired to think of it."

Margaret chuckled. "If it makes you tired now, wait until it happens." She stood to face her daughter.

"You'll do well. Keep your wits about you. And for now, just be Prissy as she's always been. Thoughtful, steady, quiet, a decent woman and a born mother."

Prissy's mouth dropped open and she closed it. "A born mother?"

"There's a very fortunate young man out there right now, looking for you."

Prissy's eyes widened. "Me? Someone wants me?"

"More than anything in this world. Now you go on to bed. Come talk to me whenever you wish."

Prissy stepped forward and put her arms about her mother's neck and held her for a moment, and Margaret encircled her and held her close. Then Prissy turned and walked from the room, and Margaret listened until she heard her door close before she lay back down in her bed and turned the lantern off.

For a time she lay in the darkness while a thousand memories came flooding, of a quiet little girl with great, thoughtful blue eyes who lacked her two front teeth, and then a gangling eleven-year-old who did not know if she were a woman or a child, and then the miraculous blossoming of the child into a beautiful young lady who had come into the complexities of mature womanhood earlier than most, and who loved her older sister enough to sense her confusion, and had the common sense to come to her mother to inquire.

Margaret reached to touch the pillow next to her and let her hand rest in the place John should have been, and her last clear thought before sleep was of him—*I needed you tonight to help with Prissy—needed you as always—some day—some day . . .*

Note

The characters in this chapter are fictional, as are the events described.

Boston

March 1784

CHAPTER XXVII

*T*he Boston waterfront office door with the sign above announcing DUNSON & WEEMS SHIPPING swung open, and the March gale-force winds howling in from the Atlantic under clear, cold mid-morning skies swept into the room. Instantly the fire in the fireplace leaped and danced, and Billy Weems and Thomas Covington slapped hands down on stacks of papers piled on their desks and raised their heads, irritated, to see who had brought the gust. The door slammed shut and Caleb Dunson and Captain Theodore Pettigrew turned to take the single pace to the counter that separated the customer side from the desks and files inside the office. Caleb and Pettigrew raised cold hands to bearded faces to blow into them, then reached to unbutton the top buttons of their heavy, worn seaman's coats.

Both Billy and Covington came to their feet and strode quickly to face the two, and Billy wasted no time asking the critical question.

"You made the delivery in New York?"

Pettigrew bobbed his head. "Yes. On schedule."

"You got the money?"

"We did." Pettigrew drew a large leather purse from his pocket and laid it thumping on the countertop.

Billy was scarcely breathing as he spoke the next question. "Any trouble?"

"Yes."

Billy felt elderly Thomas Covington tense beside him.

"What happened?"

"Virginia. Changed their export tariff law on tobacco. They were going to hold the *Rebecca*. We sailed her out."

For a fleeting moment the gray brow of Thomas Covington creased, and then he grinned. "It's about time."

Caleb glanced at Covington, then at Billy. "Matthew around?"

"Any time now. He's at the bank."

"Trouble at the bank?"

"Maybe. Neither Virginia nor Maryland would release their tax seizure of the *Jessica*. The bank wanted a full report from Matthew on his try at getting her released. He's at the bank now. Due back any minute."

Caleb's face darkened. "You mean Virginia's still holding the *Jessica*? And they'd be holding the *Rebecca* if you hadn't sailed her out?"

All four men sensed the deadly spirit that came stealing. "That's what I mean."

Caleb glanced at Pettigrew. "Two ships in trouble. How far from a war between the states are we?"

Pettigrew's voice was low. "Not far."

The door to the office opened, then quickly closed, and Matthew unbuttoned his heavy coat as he walked to the gate at the end of the counter, speaking as he went.

"I saw the *Rebecca* anchored in the harbor. When did you get in?"

"About twenty minutes ago. Came directly here."

"Any trouble?"

Pettigrew answered. "Yes."

Matthew's hands slowed on his coat buttons as he looked at Pettigrew, probing, and then he swung the gate open. "Come on in and take a seat over there by my desk."

The two followed him while Billy picked up the leather purse, hefted it for weight, then followed Covington. They gathered in chairs around Matthew's desk, and Matthew came directly to it.

"What trouble?"

Pettigrew leaned forward. "We were nearly loaded in Jamestown when they told us Virginia had raised the tobacco export tariff from five percent to eight percent. They weren't going to let the ship leave without payment. We didn't have it."

For a moment Matthew remained silent while his mind caught up, and then he leaned forward, forearms on the desktop. "So what happened?"

"We sailed the *Rebecca* out."

"Without paying the tax?"

"Without paying."

Matthew stiffened. "Didn't they try to stop you?"

"We did it at night. They had ten of their militia assigned to guard her. We took them with us."

Matthew jerked back. "Kidnapped them?"

"You could call it that. They sent two gunboats after us. Caught up with us after we were out of southern waters. We had those ten militiamen on the rails, five each side. The gunboats didn't fire on us. They turned back before we reached New York."

"Did you deliver the cargo?"

"Yes. Got the money." Pettigrew pointed. "Billy has it."

"What about the ten militiamen?"

"We paid them dockhand wages for the time we had them, and paid their passage back to Jamestown, and sent the added three percent export tariff payment with them. All ten of them signed the receipt."

"Anybody show up here with any complaints? Warrants for your arrest?"

"Not that we know of."

"Where's your crew?"

"I paid them and they went home. The accounting on all this is in the purse with the money. What's left of it."

Matthew's shoulders slumped and for a moment it seemed all the life went out of him. He turned to Pettigrew.

"Only recourse I know for Virginia is under Article Nine of the Confederation. You know of anything else?"

"No. Virginia will have to file a complaint with Congress, and they'll have to appoint a committee. There'll be a hearing. That could take a year."

"Think Virginia will do it?"

Pettigrew shook his head. "No. They got their men back, with pay, and with their export tax. And if they did bring a complaint, and if the committee did decide in their favor, there isn't a word I know of in the Articles of Confederation that gives anyone the power to enforce the decision of the committee. It's a toothless wolf."

Caleb turned to stare at Pettigrew. "Wait a minute. You mean there is no committee, no authority anywhere that can enforce a decision between states?"

"That's what I mean." He turned to Matthew. "You know anything different?"

Matthew shook his head and remained silent.

Caleb gaped. "Then who dreamed up this notion of calling them the United States? United in what?"

Pettigrew's eyes dropped. "Not much. Maybe just an idea."

"Who enforces the idea, whatever it is?"

Like Matthew, Pettigrew shook his head and said nothing.

Caleb turned to Matthew. "Just so no one misunderstands about the *Rebecca*, Captain Pettigrew was not responsible for what we did. I was. If anything bad comes of it, he's not at fault. I am."

Pettigrew looked at Matthew. "That's only partly true. I was in command. I'm responsible."

Matthew licked dry lips. "Anybody get hurt?"

"No."

"How did you manage it?"

"Waited until dark. Hid some whale oil and a small keg of gunpowder at the west end of town, away from the river, and stacked a lot of scrap wood on top. Set it all on fire, and when the gunpowder blew, sparks and wood went everywhere. The whole town went down to put out the fire, and while they were busy at the west end of Jamestown, we sailed out the east end."

For a time Matthew stared in near disbelief. "You started a fire? Blew it with gunpowder?"

"Yes."

"The militiamen?"

"Came in behind them. Disarmed them and took them on board."

"Weren't other ships tied to the docks? Anchored in the harbor?"

"Yes. But we worked our way through."

"At night?"

Pettigrew grinned. "Yes. Good crew."

Matthew leaned back in his chair. "You were insane. You know that."

Pettigrew stifled his smile. "It felt a little insane when we did it." He paused for a moment. "If what we did was bad enough, I'll expect you to discharge me and file a complaint against my commercial captain's license."

Covington spoke for the first time, his high, piercing voice rising. "Nonsense. If what you did brings about a battle between Massachusetts and Virginia, so much the better." He shook a bony forefinger at the ceiling. "Right now none of us, not one shipping firm, has any committee or court that can resolve these disputes and enforce their decision. We don't know what we can do, and what we can't do. We don't know who has the rights to navigation in the major rivers, or the tax laws of each state, or what rights they have to seize our ships, and common sense has long since been forgotten. What we need is for two states to start shooting. Something—anything—serious enough to force an answer to the sick mess this country is in."

Billy spoke up.

"Our job is to keep this company in business. It seems to me the question is, how do we get the *Jessica* released, and then how do we get more shipping contracts?" He turned to Matthew. "What did the bank say?"

"They wanted to know why neither Virginia nor Maryland would release their tax seizures. I told them. After six days arguing with the harbor authorities of both states, the only answer I got was that each claimed navigation rights to the Potomac River, which gives them taxation rights, and neither one is going to do anything to change that. Until the taxes are paid, the *Jessica* remains under seizure."

"Will the bank pay the taxes to get the ship?"

"Not one dollar."

"And if we don't pay it?"

Matthew took a great breath and his words were measured. "We've got eight weeks. Then they declare our deal with them in breach and they seize the shipping firm to force a sale of enough ships to take care of it, and that's the end of Dunson and Weems Shipping."

For a time the only sound was the moaning of the March wind at the windows and doors, and the heavy draw at the chimney. Frustration became anger as the five men let their minds run with it, probing for a ray of light, no matter how small, that could lead them to an answer to the tangled confusion that brooded over the office like a great, black pall.

Billy broke the silence. "If we went to the Massachusetts legislature, could they send a delegation, or a committee, or someone, to Virginia?"

Covington answered. "The answer is no. Half the states in the Union have already tried that. The states are independent. One can't force another to do anything. Border wars, river wars, new territory wars—no end to it."

Billy went on. "Isn't there something in this Article Nine that will help?"

Covington shook his head. "No. That article provides for a committee that can hear, and decide, but it can't enforce anything."

Caleb interrupted. "If that's true, then it must cut both ways. If they can't enforce their own orders, then they can't punish anyone, no matter what they do." He glanced at Matthew. "Say the word and I'll take the crew back down there and bring the *Jessica* home."

Matthew heaved a tired, weary sigh. "I've talked to the Virginia and Maryland authorities. Only thing I can think of is to go to the Massachusetts legislature with it."

Covington's voice rang out. "You're not thinking high enough. Go see Thomas Jefferson. James Madison. George Mason. Go see General Washington himself! They're all Virginians! What do you have to lose?

The worst they can do is turn you away! The most they can do is send some letters to the right people. Something! Anything!"

For a time the men sat in silence, looking from one to the other while their minds raced with the startling thought. Jefferson? Madison? Mason? Washington? General George Washington? Could they do that? Could they?

Matthew broke the silence. "Billy?"

"Can't hurt. Might help. We'll not know until we try."

He glanced at Pettigrew, and Pettigrew shrugged. "I'd never have thought of it, but I agree with Billy."

Matthew turned to Caleb. "You?"

Caleb's eyes narrowed. "Didn't you complete two or three missions for General Washington?"

Matthew nodded.

Caleb turned to Billy. "You, too? You and Stroud?"

"Yes."

"Shouldn't Washington remember those missions? Shouldn't he remember both of you?" He gestured to both Billy and Matthew.

Billy answered. "He should. Yes. He will."

Caleb got to his feet. "I think Covington's got a point. Start with Jefferson, and go from there. If it leads to Washington, go see him."

Notes

The speaking characters in this chapter are fictional, as are the events described.

However, the Articles of Confederation agreed to by Congress on November 15, 1777, and ratified by the United States on March 1, 1781, consisted of thirteen articles covering many pages. Article IX, critical to this chapter and following chapters, consisted of seven lengthy paragraphs covering several pages, far too long to set forth verbatim herein. In essence, said article established the governmental machinery for hearing disputes between states, which included provisions for the filing of complaints, appointment of authorized representatives, hearings, and decisions and final judgments. But remarkably, there was no provision for enforcement of such decisions or judgments.

For a concise explanation of the Articles of Confederation, with some of them quoted verbatim, see Bernstein, *Are We to Be a Nation?*, pp. 27–28.

CHAPTER XXVIII

*E*li heard the rustle in the greening foliage to his left at the same instant he saw the man forty yards ahead, moving through a small clearing in the thick growth of oak and pine. And then came the great, roaring bawl of an enraged sow black bear ahead of him and to his right, ripping headlong through the early spring growth. Eli only had time to shout "Run!" before the frenzied, seven-hundred-pound mother tore into the clearing, slowing only long enough for her weak eyes to locate movement, and then she came at the man with her claws throwing dirt and decay from the forest floor at every stride while her bellowing silenced every other sound in the forest and echoed for miles.

The man dropped his long rifle and in three steps reached the nearest oak, grasped the lower branches, and swung up into the tree. He was eight feet up when the bear made her lunge. Her reaching paw caught his right leg below the knee, and he felt the five long claws punch through the buckskin leggings and drive into his flesh, and he groaned as he scrambled upward. He was twelve feet up, in the new, budding leaves before he stopped and looked down into the small, hate-filled eyes and at the yellow fangs, and he smelled her rancid breath as he watched those terrible claws rake great curls of bark from the tree as the bear tried to follow him. Slowly she settled, bellowed her defiance, and turned away, seeking her strayed cub.

Eli dropped behind a great granite shaft thrusting from the ground, cocked his rifle, and became perfectly still and silent. The midmorning breeze was in his face, carrying the wild stench of a female bear that had been in hibernation for more than four months, and who had borne a cub before the eternal warming of spring lured her from her lair. Gone was the heavy covering of fat she had gained by gorging on berries and nuts and grubs of the previous fall, until nature told her she must seek a den on the slopes of the Green Mountains for her long sleep through the snows of winter, and for the birth of the cub she carried in her womb.

Without movement, Eli watched the small black ball of fur break from the foliage to his left and come at that peculiar, toed-in running gait to his mother, to hide in absolute safety between her front legs, peering out at a world that was new and wondrous and baffling. The black mother cuffed her cub out in front of her, smelled him all over, then licked him. Satisfied he was unharmed, she grunted at him, cuffed him once more, then moved on into the foliage, searching for tender new buds, and opening rotten, fallen tree trunks with one stroke of her huge paw to lap up the grubs and ants that scrambled. The cub cocked his head to watch her, then harmlessly struck the log with a paw and watched for grubs and ants to appear. When they did not, he moved in beside his mother and licked at those she failed to catch.

Eli remained as he was, watching the mother and her cub slowly work their way into the thick bushes and disappear in the forest. He waited until the exuberant sounds of birds and squirrels resumed to tell him the bears were gone before he stood and trotted toward the man who had remained in the oak tree. He was fifteen yards away when he heard the familiar voice.

"That you that hollered?"

"Yes."

"Eli?"

"Yes. That you, Sykes?"

"That's me.

"That was close. You all right?"

"No, I'm not all right. That old girl got her claws into my leg. Can I come down yet?"

"She's gone."

Ormond Sykes dropped to the ground and limped over to pick up his rifle before he sat down. He clenched his teeth as he reached to gingerly pull his legging away from the torn flesh of his calf. He grimaced as he examined the three long, deep, bloody gashes. Eli dropped to his haunches, watching as Sykes studied the ugly purple wounds.

"She got me good," Sykes muttered. He flexed his foot, then moved his toes. "I can still move everything so I don't think she got any strings, but she got deep there for a ways. Sort of scared me. I don't fancy walkin' these woods with only one foot."

Eli leaned forward to take a hard look. "That needs stitching."

"I figger so. I'll let her bleed clean first. Then I'll close 'er up."

Eli looked at him. "You got gut? And a needle?"

"Gut. No needle."

"I got one. I better do the stitching."

"I can do 'er."

Eli shook his head. "That's on the outside of your leg. You can't reach it very well with your left hand. I better do it."

Sykes shrugged. "If you say so." He took off his moccasin, then squeezed the torn leg to encourage the bleeding, and turned to Eli. "You see her cub?"

"Heard him off to my left when I saw you. Only had time to call out before that mother scented you and came looking."

Sykes shook his head. "It sure won't do to come between a mama bear and her newborn cub just out of hibernation. Must be gettin' old. I never knew either one was hereabouts until you hollered and she let out that roar. I was one step too slow gettin' up that tree."

"You did well. I think she'd have caught most men."

"She almost caught this one. By the way, how did you come to be here, just when I needed you?"

"On my way to Boston. Business."

"Boston? You? What business you got in Boston?"

"Visit an old friend. Get some papers."

Sykes studied Eli's face for a moment. "Well, I reckon you'll tell me more when you want me to know." He paused to look at his leg. The flow of fresh blood had slowed.

Eli stood. "I'll get a fire. We'll need hot water and a fire for the knife and the needle."

Sykes groaned. "I just hate that hot knife."

Eli gathered dry twigs and branches, and worked with flint and steel to kindle a flame. He added shavings and then larger wood pieces until he had a fire burning steadily. He tossed Sykes's bedroll to him, and while the man rummaged through it for dried gut, Eli studied him thoughtfully.

Ormond Sykes was a free spirit who had roamed the northern woods since Eli could remember. British by birth, American by choice, he had no family anyone knew of, no one place he called home, and came and went for reasons known only to him. From 1776 until 1781 he appeared from time to time out of nowhere to report British troop movements to American officers, and then vanish. Twice he had been asked by American officers to risk his life getting a count on British regiments, and had stolen past their pickets, into their camps to get an accurate report both times. No one, including Sykes himself, knew his age. His hair and beard were pepper-gray, his eyes blue and watery, but he could still cover eighty miles through the forest in one day if he had to, and with a little salt could live off the land indefinitely. Eli had crossed his path a dozen times since his childhood, and the two had come to respect each other as friends.

Eli got his pewter bowl from his pack and poured water into it from his wooden canteen, set it on the fire, then went back for his needle. Minutes later the water was boiling, and Eli dropped the gut into it, then stirred it with his knife until it was soft. He opened Sykes's torn leather breeches to wash the injured leg, took a breath, and looked Sykes in the eye.

"You ready?"

Sykes grimaced. "Got a belt? Or do I use a rifleball?"

"How about a piece of wood?"

"Get it."

Eli handed him a piece of ancient, dried pine, Sykes jammed it cross-wise through his teeth, turned to lay on his left side, nodded, and muttered "Go ahead" past the wooden stick. Eli passed the blade of his knife through the flame until it was hot, and said, "Here it comes." Sykes clenched his eyes shut and bit down on the stick.

The sounds and the smoke and the cloying, sweet smell of hot steel burning human flesh, and the groan from Sykes, came together as Eli cauterized the three openings. The bleeding stopped and Eli thrust the blade hissing into the steaming water to maintain the temper in the steel before he laid the knife aside.

"I think we got it."

Sweat was dripping from Sykes. "Took long enough. What was you doin'? Practicin'?"

A grin touched Eli for a moment and was gone. "No. Maybe next time you'll get to a tree one step faster."

Sykes raised on one elbow, wiping at the sweat. "Next time you yell quicker."

Eli passed the needle through the flame twice, threaded the steaming gut through the eye, and said quietly, "Ready for the stitching?"

"No. But go ahead." He settled back and took a new grip on the wooden stick with his teeth.

For forty minutes Eli used a piece of oak wood to force the needle through the tough flesh of Sykes's leg, slowly closing the three long, deep gashes. Then he washed the sewed-up wound carefully with clean, hot water and said, "Finished."

Sykes was white-faced and trembling, and his leather shirt was soaked with sweat. He reached to take the stick from his mouth. It was nearly splintered. He raised on one elbow to look at his leg and slowly counted the stitches, in three long rows, knots in a line, the gut strings clipped.

"Thirty-eight. Ever seen thirty-eight before?"

Eli shook his head. "Not that I can recall."

Sykes began to shake. "Cold."

Eli worked Sykes's blanket beneath him, then covered him with his own. "Stay warm. I'll boil tea."

Ten minutes later Eli dug Sykes's wooden bowl from his pack, filled it with steaming tea made from leaves Lydia had insisted he take, and handed it to Sykes. He sipped at it, then looked up at Eli with grateful eyes.

"I'm beholden."

"Not at all." He laid Sykes's rifle beside him on the blankets. "I'll be back directly. You'll need fresh broth and something to pull the poison out of your leg."

Fifteen minutes later Sykes heard a single, sharp rifle crack, and soon Eli was back, skinning a young buck deer. He cut the hide into strips, then brought them and the liver to Sykes's blankets. He slit the liver open, laid it over the stitches, and used the strips of hide to tie it into place.

"That'll draw out the poison, if there is any."

Eli added wood to the fire, fresh water to the pewter bowl, then dropped chunks of fat brisket and lean deer ham and salt into the boiling mass until it thickened. He poured it into Sykes's wooden bowl and waited until it stopped steaming before he brought it to him.

"There's blood and fat there. It'll help."

Sykes sipped at it until it was gone, then handed the bowl back to Eli. "Makes me sleepy."

"You rest. I'll be here."

Eli finished cutting up the deer and hung the front quarters and single hindquarter ten feet above ground level in a tree thirty yards down the gentle north slope, then made his way back through the patchy snow that still remained on the north side of trees and rocks where the spring sun did not reach the earth. He dropped to his haunches beside Sykes, who lay on his left side breathing deep and slow as he slept, and he studied the man's color. It was returning from white to the brown of years in sun and wind and snow. Eli glanced at the sun in the western sky and reckoned the time to be about half past three. Quietly he fed the fire and set more water to boil to wash the knife and the bowl, and his hands that still showed blood from his work with the torn leg. He walked quietly to the edge of the small clearing, looking for a sapling pine that was tall enough and thick enough, selected one, and used his tomahawk to cut it free at ground level. Twenty minutes later he had trimmed it, shortened it, and lashed a cross-member at the top, then wrapped the crossbar with deerhide. He tucked it beneath his own arm, tested it, then laid it beside Sykes, satisfied the crutch would work.

The sun was deep in the western trees before Sykes muttered in his sleep, then stirred, and opened his eyes. He moved his leg before he remembered, and groaned at the throbbing pain. He raised himself on one elbow, swallowed at the sour taste in his mouth, then saw the crutch, and Eli adding wood to the fire.

"Forgot about the leg."

Eli walked to him and dropped to one knee to place his hand against Sykes's forehead.

"Fevered. It'll probably hold 'til morning. Can you eat some venison strips?"

"I kin try."

Dusk was settling and the chill of evening was oncoming when Eli came from the fire with ten long strips of deer ham sizzling on a stick, and a bowl of steaming tea. He paused to pinch a little salt onto them, then rammed one end of the stick into the ground beside the blankets. Sykes sat up and reached for the first strip of black, smoking meat.

Eli stood, and Sykes asked, "Where you going? You got to eat some of this meat."

"I'll be right back."

Fifteen minutes later Eli had a huge mound of pine boughs stacked next to Sykes and sat down cross-legged at the edge of the blanket, next to the stick of meat. He reached for the next strip, and spoke to Sykes as he chewed.

"Surprised to find you this far south this time of year. Thought you would be up by the big lakes, or somewhere east of here."

"I woulda been. But there's things happenin' up there that someone's got to go tell to Congress, or Gen'l Washington, or someone."

Eli slowed in his chewing. "Bad things?"

The firelight made caverns of Sykes's eyes and craggy face. "More like mixed-up. Confused, I guess."

"What's happened?"

"Well, there was talk goin' 'round up there about the British bringin' in muskets and cannon and shot, and supplyin' the Loyalists up above the Canadian border, gettin' 'em ready to attack from up there. Raisin' an army."

"You mean after the surrender? The British surrendered a year ago."

"I know that. But this was like they was secret in tryin' to raise an army of American Loyalists to do what they couldn't do theirselves."

Eli was not moving. "Go on."

"So I decided to take a look up there. I been up there on snowshoes since January, lookin' for this Loyalist army. All up and down the St. Lawrence, clear to the big lakes. Erie. Huron. Michigan. Ontario. Superior. All of 'em. There isn't no such army up there. Just talk."

Eli shrugged. "Talk can't do much harm."

"That wasn't all. While I was up there I took a look at all them British forts. The ones they was supposed to abandon when they surrendered. Well, they ain't doin' it. They still got their army up there, holdin' them forts, and they're closin' off all Americans from gettin' to the lakes. All the fishing and fur trade, everything. The peace treaty says they can't do that, but they're doin' it. I seen it."

Eli's brow wrinkled down in question. "Are they trying to start another war?"

Sykes chewed for a moment before answering. "You'll have to ask the British. But there's more. Rumor reached us up there that the British are also workin' with the Barbary pirates to capture American sailors and make 'em swear loyalty to the British crown."

"The Barbary pirates?" Eli exclaimed. "I can hardly believe it."

"Neither could I. Then I heard the British and the Spanish are both tryin' to shut down our ships from usin' the Mississippi River."

Eli had forgotten about the venison strip in his hand. "The British gave us use of the Mississippi in the surrender treaty. What have the Spanish got to do with it?"

"The British might of give us use of it, but that's not what's happenin'. As for the Spanish, they told us the river was closed to Americans anywhere the Spanish had control of both sides of it. And they're closin' it."

"Anything else?"

"Yes. The French got wind of the Spanish closin' the Mississippi, and they joined with 'em. Then they told us we was to quit tradin' with the French islands down in the West Indies."

Silence held for a moment before Eli spoke. "Wait a minute. The French helped us at Yorktown. Matter of fact, I don't think we'd have won without them. Now you're telling me they're doing things to hurt us? The French and the Spanish?"

"That's what's bein' said up north. So I figgered someone better come on down and tell Congress. Or someone." Sykes paused, then remembered, and went on.

"One more thing. There's rumor up in the north woods that no one knows whether Vermont is even a state. Seems like New York claims Vermont, and Vermont claims to be an independent republic, and the British was tryin' to make a deal to take Vermont as a British colony. I can't hardly follow all that. I thought Vermont was one of the United States."

"I know about all that. I live in Vermont. That'll all work out."

Sykes worked on the hot tea for a time. "Well, anyway, you asked what I'm doin' down here. That's the answer." He turned his head to look at Eli. "You live in Vermont now?"

"Yes. Near my sister and her husband. I married five years ago. I have a four-year-old daughter."

"Your wife?"

"Passed on."

Sykes's face fell. "Sorry to hear it. Sorry." He went on. "Headed for Boston? For what?"

"Business. Some money there."

Sykes's brows raised in surprise. "Money? Never figgered you to be interested in money."

"I'm not."

"Never figgered you to marry and settle down, neither."

"It happened." Eli raised the cool venison strip and took a bite.

For a time both men sat in the deep dusk with the firelight working on their faces, each with his own thoughts. Suddenly Sykes raised a hand.

"I'm goin' to be laid up here for a while, maybe a week, ten days, an' then I'm goin' to be walkin' slow for a while. If you're goin' to Boston, why don't you talk with someone there and tell 'em what I seen up there. I mean about the British forts, and there isn't no Loyalist armies. Maybe about the Mississippi, and the Spanish and French."

"You want me to do that?"

"Don't you think someone ought to know? Washington, maybe?"

"Yes, I do."

"Then you tell 'em. You'll do it better'n me. Besides, I can't hardly abide bein' in a town. Hate it."

"I'll see what I can do. For now, I'm going to spread those pine boughs to sleep on, and feed the fire. Tomorrow I'll build a lean-to. We might be here a while. If that leg goes rotten, we'll have to take care of it."

Sykes's mouth fell open. "You mean cut 'er off?"

"If we have to."

"Well, now," Sykes stammered, "that's not goin' to happen."

"I hope you're right. A day or two will tell. For now, we leave that deer liver where it is overnight and take a look in the morning."

Eli tended the supper utensils, then spread the pine boughs on either side of the fire, added fresh wood, and the two men rolled in their blankets as the cold of night set in. In the dwindling firelight Sykes's voice came low.

"Eli, you ever been west? The Ohio? Mississippi?"

"Never that far."

"I went." There was a pause. "Never saw such space. Big. Rich. Clean, like the Almighty just finished makin' it. Strong country. Waitin' out there for whoever comes. No towns. No roads. No trails. Just the Almighty's natural country. It gets a holt of you."

Sykes fell silent, and Eli waited until he went on.

"You got to go. Things is gettin' crowded here in the Appalachians. Towns like they was growin' out of the ground. People everywhere. Trouble. Why is there always trouble where there's people? So peaceful out there. Seems like man needs space to stretch. His legs, and his mind. On a clear day out there, in the spring, you can see to where the earth ends. Nothin' like it. You got to go see. You got to go."

Eli spoke quietly. "Maybe some day I will. Maybe I will."

"Better go soon, before she fills up with people, like here."

The men fell into silence, and Eli waited until he heard the slow, deep, heavy breathing before he closed his eyes. Sykes moaned once in the dead of night and Eli awakened to listen. He waited until the man settled before he went to his side and carefully touched his forehead. The fever was holding.

They awoke in the gray of approaching morning, to the sounds of the forest, and by sunup Eli had hot tea and broth ready. With the sun an hour high, Eli unwrapped the torn leg and threw the deer liver into the underbrush. He washed the leg with steaming water and let it dry before he knelt to inspect it.

"There's no red streaks moving up to your knee."

There was relief in Sykes's voice. "Git some jimsonweed. A lot of it. Make a poultice."

By midafternoon the lean-to was finished, with pine boughs a foot thick on top and on the ground below. At sundown Eli had a broth made from the venison, flavored with buds and leaves from the greening trees and bushes. In late dusk the men went to their blankets beneath the lean-to, and slept. Sometime in the night, Sykes's fever broke, and for a time he lay awake, sweating, then dropped into the deep sleep of a wounded man recovering. Morning broke clear and warm, and he sat up in his blanket to a fire with tea boiling, and he ate the last of the steaming broth like a man famished.

Again Eli unwrapped the leg and carefully cleared away the crushed jimsonweed poultice, then washed the leg clean. He reached to touch behind the knee.

"Any pain?"

Sykes shook his head. "None."

"Good. There are no red streaks. Looks like you'll be all right."

"'Course I will. Now git a new poultice onto that thing, and give me that crutch. I'm goin' to stand up."

"You're not going to try to walk."

"I know that, but I can stand."

At midafternoon of the sixth day, Sykes stood, then leaned the crutch against a tree, with Eli right beside him.

"Pain?" Eli asked.

"None. Feels good. Itches."

"It's healing."

The morning of the tenth day, Sykes sat with his leg thrust straight, and Eli used his belt knife to carefully cut the gut stitches and jerk each one out while Sykes flinched thirty-eight times. Eli used boiled water to wash the tiny beads of blood away, then stood back while Sykes came to his feet. He limped slightly as he walked several steps and returned.

"Good as new. I'll be walkin' normal by tomorrow."

"Sit down and let's see if anything's torn open."

Five minutes later Eli stood. "I think it's all healed. It'll hold."

At midday the two ate possum baked in the ground with buds and leaves, and Sykes spoke.

"You can still make thirty miles before dark. You go on. I'll be fine here. I'll stay a day or two and then go back up north."

Eli nodded but remained silent.

Sykes lowered his plate. "I won't be soon forgettin' what you done here. I owe you. If ever there's somethin' I can do to repay . . ."

Eli stopped eating for a moment. "If the bear had got me instead of you, you'd have done the same for me."

Sykes mumbled, bobbed his head once, and the two men finished their midday meal in thoughtful silence. By early afternoon Eli had his bedroll on his back and his rifle in his hand as the two men said good-bye.

Sykes jabbed a finger at Eli. "You get holt of Washington. Tell him what I said."

"I will."

"And watch out for mama bears."

"You, too."

At sunset, Eli was twenty-eight miles east of the lean-to.

Notes

Though both Eli Stroud and Ormond Sykes are fictional characters, the information given by Sykes to Stroud, concerning the upheaval and conflicts mounting in Vermont and the Great Lakes region, is factual. Contrary to the terms of the peace treaty with the Americans, the British refused to abandon their forts and were doing all possible to harass American economics, by closing down the Mississippi, spreading rumors of gathering Loyalists to begin another war, and stirring up the French and Spanish against the Americans. Such actions materially added to the already mounting troubles, and temper, of the United States.

See Bernstein, *Are We to Be a Nation?*, pp. 82–87; Morris, *The American States, 1775–1789*, pp. 470–605.

CHAPTER XXIX

★ ★ ★

*T*he threat of spring rain hung in the low, gray, late-morning clouds covering the town of Annapolis as Matthew Dunson swung the heavy door open and entered the Maryland State House. He paused for a moment to study the long, wide, straight hallway with its plain, polished oak floor, and he listened to the echo as others walked from one door to another, preoccupied, indifferent to his presence. His leather heels tapped a cadence as he walked down the hall toward a pair of great, dark double doors, aware there was very little to break the plainness of the building.

He did not know if protocol would allow him to enter the chambers of the United States Congress, and he was reaching for the large brass knob when from inside came the muffled sound of a gavel thumping the block. A moment later the doorknob turned and the great doors swung outward. Matthew stepped back as a few men hurried out, papers clutched to their breasts, talking heatedly among themselves, gesturing, ignoring everyone else in the long hallway. The exodus slowed, and Matthew approached the man standing at the entrance to the chamber.

"Sir, I have come to see Thomas Jefferson."

The elderly, round-shouldered man looked at him for a moment. "You came at the right time. They just recessed until two o'clock. Are you from Virginia? Does Mr. Jefferson know you?"

"No. I'm from Massachusetts. I'm here on the recommendation of Mr. Elbridge Gerry."

"Oh." The man turned to study those remaining in the room, and then pointed. "Mr. Jefferson is there. The tall one with the sandy hair."

"Am I permitted to enter?"

"During recess, yes. During session you'll have to use the balcony to observe."

"Thank you."

The man smiled and nodded, then resumed his position inside the chamber.

Matthew made his way through the dark desks arranged in a semi-circular pattern around the raised desk of the president, past men he did not recognize, watching Jefferson, who stood with his head lowered, exchanging words and chuckles with others in the Congress. He stopped six feet short of the small cluster of men, waiting for Jefferson to disengage. Half a dozen men slowed to eye him suspiciously, then walk on.

Jefferson bobbed his head, raised a hand, turned, and started down the aisle. Matthew took one step, and Jefferson slowed.

"Sir, may I have a word with you?"

For a moment Jefferson studied him intently. "Yes."

"I am Matthew Dunson, from Boston. I come with a letter of introduction from Elbridge Gerry. I presume you know him."

"Indeed I do. He is much respected for his work in Congress."

Matthew offered the sealed document, and Jefferson took it. He broke the wax, scanned the message instantly, and refolded it.

"Mr. Gerry speaks well of you. Very well. Is there something I can do for you?"

"I don't know, sir. I'm here to find out."

Jefferson pointed. "Let's go out into the hall, away from all this fuss." They started for the exit side by side. "Mr. Gerry tells me you served as a naval captain in the war."

"Yes, sir."

"Lake Champlain? With General Arnold?"

"I was there, sir."

They approached the door, Jefferson nodded and smiled to the doorman who raised a hand in greeting, and they passed out into the long, plain hall. Jefferson continued.

"Flamborough? Off the English coast?"

"You mean with Admiral Jones? The fight with the *Serapis?*"

"Was that the name of the British ship?"

"Yes, sir."

"Admiral Jones lost the *Bon Homme Richard* and saved himself by boarding the *Serapis?* Do I recall it correctly?"

"Yes, sir. You do." An involuntary, fleeting look of sadness crossed Matthew's face, and Jefferson caught it.

"Something wrong?"

"No, sir. I lost a friend in that battle. A very good friend."

The look of pain on Jefferson's face was genuine. "I'm sorry."

"It's all right, sir. War does such things."

"Yorktown?"

"I was there. With the French. Admiral de Grasse defeated the British Admiral Graves. It brought about the victory at Yorktown."

"Remarkable experiences for a young man."

Jefferson sought a quiet side hall and stopped, facing Matthew. "Now, Mr. Dunson, what can I help with?"

Matthew came directly to it. "I have an ownership interest in a ship that has been seized on the Potomac. Two states—Virginia and Maryland—both claim rights of navigation and taxation. My partner and I feel paying taxes to two states is wrong. We hoped you could advise us."

A look of impatient disgust crossed Jefferson's face. "You're caught in that Potomac River confusion. There is no ready answer. Do you have time to talk?"

"I am at your discretion."

"Would you mind coming to my quarters? Just a short distance from here, in a boardinghouse."

They walked out of the white statehouse into the cobblestone streets, where Jefferson turned north in the cool gray overcast. Jefferson chose to chat about little things as they went, and Matthew understood at once that this was Jefferson's way of taking his measure. He listened and responded, knowing nothing of Jefferson's origins. He was only aware there was something unique and rare in the man next to him.

Born April 13, 1743, to Peter Jefferson, a planter and surveyor possessed of five thousand acres of land at a place called Shadwell in Albermarle County, Virginia, and Jane Randolph Jefferson of the rich and socially prominent Randolph family of Virginia, young Thomas lacked nothing that wealth and prominence could provide. His passionate, lifelong quest for freedom of thought and mind and soul early led him to the works of the great philosophers of all times and generations, and then to continue his education at the College of William and Mary. It was there that Professor William Small and Governor Fauquier introduced their bright young Thomas Jefferson to one of the great legal minds of his time, George Wythe. Upon completion of his work at William and Mary, Jefferson eagerly entered studies of the law under Wythe's tutoring. Tall, angular, freckled, sandy-red hair, slightly awkward in movement and not gifted athletically, Jefferson was highly recommended to the Virginia Bar by Wythe and was granted license to practice law.

In 1769, at age twenty-six, he was elected to the Virginia House of Burgesses and soon sensed his gift was not in his limited speaking ability, but rather in his brilliant talent with the written word. On January 1, 1772, he married the widow Martha Wayles Skelton, who brought the huge inherited estate and the high social status of her family to the marriage, doubling the fortune Jefferson had inherited from his own. He brought his beloved Martha to the Virginia hilltop where he dreamed of making his home and introduced her to little more than one lone brick building and his vision of the great estate to come. He called it Monticello. With her beside him, he continued to plumb the depths of thought on humanity and the proper place of politics in life. Recognition of his rare ability to reduce deeply powerful concepts to simple, profoundly inspiring written words, steadily spread throughout the fledgling political circles of the infant, aspiring nation.

The range of his mind and his ability to write remarkably expanded as he continued in his contribution to the House of Burgesses. In 1774, with the black clouds of war gathering between the thirteen American colonies and Mother England, he was elected to the Continental Congress. Two years later, in 1776, thirty-three-year-old Congressman Thomas Jefferson, who spoke little because of his tendency toward nervousness and fright before large audiences, was placed on a Congressional committee charged with the responsibility of writing a document declaring the case for American independence. The committee included Roger Sherman, Robert Livingston, the sagacious Benjamin Franklin, and the obdurate John Adams, with young Jefferson. The committee saw the profound opportunity and potential of the document, but little realized it was to become one of the great documents of the world. Four of them were impressed that their youngest member should draft it, since his writing skills were recognized to be superior to theirs. Basing his thoughts on the Virginia Bill of Rights, created by George Mason, Jefferson drafted a masterpiece.

He was elected to the Virginia legislature in 1776, and again broadened his skills. His views on human nature and how best to govern people began to take final shape and to settle. In 1779 he was elected governor of the State of Virginia and served until his term in office expired in early 1781. On June fourth, he fled the Virginia government offices just minutes ahead of British Lieutenant Colonel Banastre Tarleton, who was bent on Jefferson's capture and the subjugation of Virginia to British authority. Although his term as governor had expired, he remained to supervise the evacuation of the government from Charlottesville to Staunton and then traveled to join his family at Poplar Forest before his return to Monticello July 26, after the British had abandoned Virginia.

September 6, 1782, he suffered the heartbreak of his life when his beloved Martha died. Jefferson was inconsolable. Despite his vow to never again enter the political arena, he accepted a Congressional appointment as a peace commissioner and took up his duties in Philadelphia to escape the painful and tender memories of his deceased wife that surrounded him at Monticello. During May and June of 1783, he drafted a model constitution for his native Virginia, for his own library and purposes. November 22, 1783, now an established leader in the American cause in the United States and in Europe, he went to Annapolis to serve in the United States Congress. December 13, 1783, Congress reconvened. What he lacked in persuasive oratory was forgotten in the reach and the power of his mind and his quill.

Matthew's thoughts were interrupted as Jefferson pointed.

"There's the boardinghouse."

They crossed the worn cobblestone street, and Jefferson led Matthew to the large, white frame house, up the front stairs, through the door, and climbed a circular staircase to the second floor. He worked with a key for a moment, swung the door open, and stepped aside.

"Please come in."

Matthew entered three paces and stopped. He was in a large corner room, with windows in two walls and a small fireplace in the center of one of the inside walls, with a bed against the wall next to it. He had been inside offices and libraries of congressmen and generals, but never had he seen what now surrounded him. It seemed he had entered the repository of all books. They were shelved and stacked on all sides of and on Jefferson's desk. Drawings, diagrams, and stacks of written documents lay among them.

For two or three seconds the men stood silent, each concluding their first impression of the other. Jefferson had never carried a sword or a musket, never fired a shot in anger, never commanded men in battle. Matthew had led men into harm's way for six years, witnessed sea battles won and lost, stood beside his men amid shot and shell, and had forgotten the number of times his own life was at deadly risk; but he had never before entered the world of politics or political philosophy. In the twenty minutes since their meeting, these two men sensed they came from worlds far distant from each other, yet there was an indefinable something that connected them. By instinct alone, each sensed he could learn something from the other.

Jefferson's hazel eyes met Matthew's deep brown eyes, and Jefferson gestured. "Take a seat."

Matthew sat in a plain, worn, leather upholstered chair facing Jefferson's desk, covered with books, documents, and a stack of maps.

Jefferson sat in a larger upholstered chair facing him, and his face became serious. "You mentioned you were with the French at Yorktown and in the sea battle of the Chesapeake."

"I was there. With Admiral de Grasse."

"Remarkable officer. Were you there at the surrender of the British?"

"I was."

"They marched down to that field west of the town?"

"Between lines of French and British soldiers. Most of them were in tears. I don't think they have yet understood how they lost the war."

Jefferson straightened. Matthew watched his expression deepen, and caught the sense that from the moment he met Jefferson in the Annapolis State House, Jefferson had been guiding the conversation to this point. Matthew had no idea what Jefferson was reaching for.

Jefferson's words were measured. "Do you?"

For a moment Matthew's breath came short. It had come too suddenly, unexpected. "I have my thoughts about it."

Jefferson did not move nor speak, waiting, and Matthew went on.

"I think the Almighty had an interest in it." He stopped, considered for a moment, and remained silent, waiting for Jefferson. There was scarcely a pause or a change in Jefferson's expression as he shifted directions.

"I take it you are married?"

"Yes. One child." Matthew paused for a moment.

"I think you previously said you went into the carrying trade—ships—following the surrender. Is that correct?"

"Yes."

"Boston?"

"Yes."

"You mentioned a problem with a ship on the Potomac?"

"Yes, sir. Our ship—the *Jessica*—seized for taxes on the Potomac River by both the state of Virginia and the state of Maryland."

For the first time Jefferson sat back in his chair and for a moment his eyes wandered over the stacks of paperwork and books and pads of drawings on his desk. "You shouldn't have to pay taxes to both states."

Matthew came erect and his expression sharpened. "Your experience—governor, legislator, in Congress—I hoped that you could advise us what to do about it."

"Us? You have a partner?"

"Yes. Billy Weems. He also served in the war. Billy was badly wounded at the Concord affair and fought in most major battles through Yorktown, where he led a company when they stormed Redoubt Number Ten. He was a lieutenant at the time of his discharge and is skilled in accounts and business."

Jefferson reflected for a moment. "I suspect you operate the ships while he handles the business?"

"That's our agreement."

"Then you both must be aware of the chaotic state of affairs this country is in right now. I mean, both Congress and the various states issuing their own paper money—most of it worthless—the lack of hard specie, the French and British and Spanish limiting and cutting into our foreign trade, bankruptcies, bank closures, border disagreements between the states, taxes, tariffs, battles over river rights, good men out of work." He gestured with his hands as he spoke.

"I know about some of it, sir. It's my deepest concern. We fought a war to be free, and now we're learning that perhaps freedom is more difficult than the shooting."

Matthew was aware his words had reached deep into Jefferson, but was unaware why. Matthew went on.

"I should also say that last month—March—another of our ships, the *Rebecca*, loaded Virginia tobacco in the port of Jamestown. Four days before they were to sail with the tides, the port taxing authority told our captain there had been a three percent increase in the export tariff on tobacco. They seized the ship."

Matthew stopped to weigh his words before he went on. "We had prepared to pay the acknowledged five percent tariff we knew about, but not the added three percent. The port authorities were ready to put the ship up for sale to collect the tax and ordered ten Virginia militiamen to guard her. Our crew took the ten captive and sailed the Rebecca out, to New York. After we collected the money for the cargo, we paid the ten militiamen dockhand wages for the days we had them, paid their ship passage back to Jamestown, and sent the three percent added export tariff with them. I thought you should know that."

A look of concern crossed Jefferson's face, then turned to a smile of admiration. "Were you there?"

"No, sir, I was on the Potomac, trying to get possession of the *Jessica*."

"The Captain of the *Rebecca* was so intrepid?"

Matthew looked down at his hands in his lap. "Not exactly. The plan came from my brother. Caleb Dunson."

Jefferson beamed. "You have a rebel brother?"

Matthew smiled back at him. "It appears so, sir."

"Well, a little rebellion now and then is not necessarily a bad thing." Jefferson sobered. "Obviously, your need is to regain possession of your ship, *Jessica*."

"I hoped you could advise us."

Thoughtfully Jefferson picked up his quill for a moment, handled it, and laid it back down. "I have the feeling you are not here to be solicited. Patronized. My sense of it is you've come here to get the best I can give you, whether it be good or bad."

The frankness caught Matthew by total surprise. "Correct."

"To do that I think I must begin with the problem that lies at the root of most of the trouble that is leading the country toward self-destruction. Do you have the time?"

"Yes."

Jefferson stood and began to pace behind his desk, gesticulating, gesturing with his hands, his face charged with passion as he spoke.

"The thirteen states are bound together by the Articles of

Confederation. Congress convenes under authority of that document. The affairs of government at the congressional level are absolutely limited to the grant of power set forth in the Articles, and therein lies the fatal flaw."

He stopped pacing to fix Matthew with glowing eyes. "The Articles grant Congress no power to regulate affairs between the states. No powers to tax. No power to regulate commerce. No rules, no policies, no power to set out uniform laws to govern contracts. No authorized establishment to enforce a single Congressional law! Nothing!"

Jefferson thrust a long finger upward. "The single grant of power the Articles vest in Congress to control disputes between the states is in Article Number Nine, and it is limited to disputes over borders and territory. It does not address disputes over rivers, and I doubt Congress would be willing to interpret it to stretch that far. Do you know what it says?"

"Not entirely, sir."

"It says Congress can appoint a committee! A committee! The committee will consist of representatives from the two contesting states, and other who have no interest in the outcome. They will hear both sides of the argument, and then they will make a decision. That sounds all well and good, until the question arises, what powers do the Articles vest in Congress to enforce the decision of the committee?"

For a moment Jefferson's jaw clenched. "None! Absolutely none! Should either state refuse to abide by the decision, there is nothing Congress, or the committee, or the other state can do about it."

He stopped and sat back down, leaning forward on his forearms. "Therein is the problem. We have created a government but denied it the power to govern!"

Silence held for a few moments while Matthew allowed Jefferson's impassioned words to settle in, and then he asked, "Why haven't the Articles been amended?"

Jefferson threw a hand in the air. "We tried! In 1783. The proposal was to grant Congress the power to tax and to regulate commerce between the states and to arbitrate disputes over the rivers and the borders. Twelve states were in total agreement! But the Articles require the thirteen states be unanimous. Rhode Island defeated the entire proposal by their single vote against it!"

Matthew was incredulous. "One state defeated the vote of twelve?"

"It did!"

"Who was responsible for the provision requiring all thirteen?"

Again Jefferson became animated. "One must understand, the Articles of Confederation were the best that could be drafted at the time. That was 1776 and 1777. You have to know, as weak as they are, they were the result of generations of learning the principles of self-government. No foreign state in the world had either the experience or the vision of the Americans when they drafted the Articles. We've learned much from those experiences, and probably the greatest lesson is how weak they are—the basic concept is sound, but the detail almost defeats it."

Matthew leaned forward, caught up in Jefferson's thoughts. "What do you mean, America was the country with the most experience in self-government?"

Jefferson turned and made a sweeping gesture to the shelves of books and documents. "It's all there. Beginning in the seventeenth century. States banding together for their common good—protection against the Indians and French, commerce, survival, food—many reasons. Finally the representatives of the colonies convened in Albany. They appointed a committee that included Benjamin Franklin to draft a proposal for a permanent union. Dr. Franklin was on the committee because he had been working on such a plan since 1751. They appointed him to draft the final document. He did, it was approved, and then the Albany Congress dissolved."

Matthew sat astonished, his mind reeling with the flood of information coming from Jefferson.

"That plan proposed a government with authority to operate directly on the citizens, without interference from the colonies. The colonies rejected it for that very reason—they feared any form of government that ran contrary to their traditional concept of the local assemblies being responsible to the people. The principle, as they saw it, was simple. Government closest to the people is the best. What they have not yet accepted is the lesson those early experiences tried to teach us. If we are to have a union—a nation—of all thirteen states, that union must be clothed with sufficient power to sustain itself. That means the power to tax, and the power to create and enforce all matters of common concern to the several states. Commerce, contracts, borders, navigation—all of it."

Matthew's mind was racing. Jefferson relaxed for a time, then said, "So you see, the simple question of how you are to take possession of your ship in the Potomac is really a part—small, but a part nonetheless—of a great flaw in the very weak document we call our Articles of Confederation. Worse, and quite paradoxically, the answer has not yet been created. As we sit here today, there is not a man alive who can give you a reliable solution."

For a time Matthew sat staring at Jefferson while his brain reached beyond any limits he had ever known in his thoughts on what was happening all around him. His voice croaked when he tried to speak, and he started again.

"You know of no way I can get the *Jessica?*"

Slowly Jefferson shook his head. "None. Absolutely none, unless you pay the taxes to both Virginia and Maryland. And that, sir, is unconscionable."

"You mentioned a committee that could be formed under Article Nine?"

"Yes. But by its own language, it does not address disputes concerning rivers. You can file your complaint with Congress. They will appoint such a committee, and the committee will first decide if they have jurisdiction of rivers. If by some chance they think they do, they will hear the case, and issue a written decision. All told, that will take between twelve and eighteen months. Then if either state, or yourself, refuses to abide by the committee's decision, nothing will be done because no one is vested with power to enforce it. That is the only remedy of which I am aware and, sir, if I were in your position, I doubt I would proceed with it because I doubt Article Nine includes rivers."

"So there's nothing to be done, except pay the double tax?"

"I know of no other practical way. I'm sorry. There is one thing I can share with you. Less than three weeks ago I was approached by James Madison—Congressman Madison—who very sensibly suggested that both states—Virginia and Maryland—appoint a committee to meet and create a workable compromise of their competing claims. Both states have agreed and are now working on appointing the committees. It's far too early to predict the outcome, but I thought you should know that everything possible is being done to settle the dilemma."

For a moment hope rose in Matthew. "How soon will they meet?"

Jefferson shook his head. "With good luck, within a year."

Matthew shook his head. "Too late."

There was a look of frustrated sadness as Jefferson nodded. "I'm afraid so."

Matthew placed his hands on his knees to rise. "I've taken too much of your time. I want to thank you for your forthrightness, sir."

"It was my pleasure to meet you."

Before he rose, Matthew pointed to the stack of several large diagrams on the edge of Jefferson's desk. "If I may ask, those appear to be maps of the east coast. Canada to Florida. But I don't recognize the lines extending to the west."

Jefferson lifted the top one and spread it before Matthew. "You recognize the thirteen states?"

"Yes."

"Those lines extending west are proposals for new states. The British granted us all claims to the lands as far as the Mississippi River. Some of our leading citizens are preparing proposals for developing those lands."

Matthew's mouth dropped open for a second. "New states? Already?"

"See here." Jefferson pointed. "This map proposes several new states, including one to be called 'Franklin.' Benjamin Franklin did not create this. That was done by some settlers in the western sections of North Carolina." Jefferson stopped to smile. "Dr. Franklin was embarrassed when he heard about it."

He spread another map. "Here we have proposals for states to be called Kentucky, Ohio, and Indiana." He reached for another from the stack. "Proposals for the states of Michigania, Assenisipia, Illinoia, Polypotamia, Metropotamia, Saratoga, and Washington."

He reached for yet another map. "Here are proposals for fourteen states yet unnamed, my best efforts at being evenhanded in colonizing our newly acquired empire from the British. This map settles the ongoing battle between Pennsylvania and at least two other states about the Wyoming Valley." He pointed. "The rich land here, bordering Pennsylvania. Too many people have laid claim to that vast valley."

For a time Matthew stood, leaned forward, studying the detail of the various proposals, realizing for the first time that Jefferson was seeing a vision for America that reached generations into the future. His mind was reeling with the vastness of the concept. The grasp of history. The lessons to be learned from hard-won experience. Correct principles of government. Westward expansion. New states. Economics. Philosophy. Were there any limits on this man's reach?

He straightened. "I didn't know such plans were being made."

"They are." Jefferson sat down. "It occurs to me there are one or two other things we might profitably discuss. Could I take a little more of your time?"

Matthew was dumbfounded. "Yes."

For several moments Jefferson remained silent as he set his thoughts in order.

"I raise the following points with a purpose in mind, and we shall come to that purpose quite soon.

"I have long sensed that this country has been steadily moving away from the traditional concepts of society. Are you aware that every country in Europe is absolutely entombed in a system of social strata from which no one escapes? Basically, the aristocracy, the middle class, and the desperate poor? In some countries the layers of society are so well-defined that to be born into any one of them is to die in the same one. Denmark, for example. Nine layers of society, and no escape from any of them."

Matthew was concentrating intensely.

"To preserve their position of luxury and power, the highest of these social strata have developed the laws of entail and primogeniture. Basically the law of entail provides that estates and fortunes must pass from one generation of the aristocracy to the next. It can never pass outside the family bloodlines."

Jefferson paused before going on. "The law of primogeniture provides that if an aristocrat should die without a will, all of his estate—the entirety of it—must pass to his eldest male descendant, and to no one else. Should he have more than one child, those born after his first son receive nothing."

Again he paused. "Think on it. The wealth and power must remain within family bloodlines, and should an aristocrat die without a will, the entire estate goes to his eldest son. By any and all means necessary, preserve the money and the power to the aristocracy! Merit, virtue, talent, ability—all irrelevant."

Matthew saw the deep rebellion arise in Jefferson. "I detest it! There *is* a natural aristocracy, and it is based on virtue and talent. It is to be found in all levels, all classes of people. *That* is the truest form of aristocracy. It has nothing to do with lineage or bloodlines. Great and good persons are found among the humble and lowly as quickly as among the privileged."

Again Jefferson paused to set his thoughts in order. "There is one other conclusion I have reached. I am committed forever against anything that attempts to limit the natural right of men to worship their God as to their conscience seems fit. I do not believe government in any of its forms has the right to interfere or dictate how a man shall worship."

He stopped and looked into Matthew's eyes, waiting for a response, but Matthew remained silent. Jefferson went on.

"Should I be granted the time and power, I will do everything possible to raise this country far above the evils of the European societies, which by their structure limit and destroy the gifted who are born to humble beginnings. I will support laws which reward virtue, not wealth and power. The laws of entail and primogeniture must be abolished. And no man should be required to sacrifice his conscience regarding his Creator at the whim of his government, nor should he be required by his government to accept membership in a faith that is contrary to his inner self. I will fight those evils until my death."

Matthew was not moving. Jefferson stopped for a moment, then pointed to a small corner desk on which were two heavy stacks of papers.

"With George Wythe and Edmund Pendleton, I was authorized to rewrite and simplify the laws of the state of Virginia. Most of it is there in those papers."

Matthew was stunned. "All the laws? You three have rewritten all the laws of Virginia?"

"Nearly all. The original laws were based on principles that offended justice and the natural rights of mankind. That is all to be changed."

Matthew could find no words with which to respond, and Jefferson went on.

"Now I state my purpose for laying these thoughts before you. You see, there are citizens in most states—Massachusetts in your case—who are considering promoting a committee that has nothing to do with any government institution. It will draw upon groups and individuals on a volunteer basis. It is to be called the Committee of Correspondence. The purpose of the committee is to keep the public informed of current political developments. Write letters. Publish articles in the newspapers. Enlighten the public of all that is being done in the world of government and politics."

Jefferson raised a finger to Matthew.

"You are in Boston. May I recommend that you inquire until you know if such a committee has been yet formed? If it has not, you create it. Tell the public what has happened to your ship. About the quarrels between the states over borders. Rivers. Tariffs. Tell them about the weakness in the Articles of Confederation. About the new states that are being mapped. About freeing a man's conscience to worship the Creator as he sees fit. Strike out against the laws that maintain the aristocratic rich at the expense of the desperate poor. Enlighten your people. Inform them. Stir them. Raise them. Promote healthy debate. Locate the Committees of Correspondence in other states and exchange ideas with them."

Jefferson stopped and leaned forward in his chair. For a long time both men maintained silence, and then Matthew spoke.

"I will, sir."

Jefferson stood, and Matthew knew the interview was over. He also rose and stood facing Jefferson, who said, "I am profoundly sorry I cannot help you with your ship."

"I understand, sir. I believe you would if you could."

"Be assured."

"I want to thank you for your time. And your effort."

"It was my pleasure." Then he looked at Matthew, and Matthew felt him reaching deep inside as he spoke.

"Will you investigate the Committee of Correspondence in Boston?"

"I will, sir. I will."

Jefferson nodded once, and Matthew saw the shine in his eyes. "Then our time has been profitable. I want to recall your statement at the outset. You said you believed the Almighty had an interest in the outcome of the war. With the passing of time and experience, I become more convinced that our cause of liberty has received divine intervention and sanction."

"I understand."

It was clear Jefferson considered their time together finished. "Please give my regards to your partner. And your wife."

"I shall."

The men shook hands and walked together from the room, down the staircase, and out into the streets of Annapolis, where they separated. The gray overcast still held, but Matthew's mind was absolutely awash in thoughts never before considered and horizons never before seen. Humbled, moved to the bottom of all understanding, sensing things as never before, he walked the cobblestone street to the Sunrise Inn, and up the stairs to his small room. He sat on the bed, staring at the floor, shocked by the realization of how limited his vision and grasp of the chaotic condition of the country had been. He was awed by the depth and sweep of the awakening that Jefferson had wrought in him. Never had he seen the nature of human beings, and of the principles of government which must bind them if they were to exist in peace, as he saw them now. That one human being should possess such a profound depth and range held Matthew in awed silence as he sat in his room, uncaring of time, aware only that each passing minute brought new thoughts that lifted him to heights and depths he had never known.

Without conscious effort, the words of Jefferson came echoing in his brain.

Associate yourself with the Massachusetts Committee of Correspondence.

Matthew's voice was scarcely audible as he murmured, "We shall see. We shall see."

Notes

In support of the biographical history of Thomas Jefferson as herein set forth, including his tutoring with George Wythe to study law, see Bernstein, *Thomas Jefferson,* chapter one. In support of his political history, beginning with his election to the Virginia House of Burgesses, see chapters two and three. For a succinct explanation of Jefferson's views on the legal principles of entail and primogeniture as described in this chapter, his views on the separation of church and state, as well as his monumental efforts in redrafting the code of laws in the state of Virginia, see chapter three; see also Bernstein, *Are We to Be a Nation?,* pp. 67–73. For the history of the attempts of the Americans to create a self-government, beginning with the New England Confederation formed in 1643 as herein described, see Bernstein, *Are We to Be a Nation?,* pp. 12–16; for a perceptive explanation of the Committee of Correspondence as described by Thomas Jefferson in this chapter, see Bernstein, p. 17, and pp. 88–90.

The states of Virginia and Maryland were in open dispute, with each claiming navigation and shipping rights to the Potomac and Pocomoke Rivers. See Bernstein, *Are We to Be a Nation?,* p. 97; for a description of the efforts of England, Spain, and France to damage the Americans economically, see Bernstein, pp. 83–85; for the facts regarding the attempts of the Congress to correct the fatal flaw of having no authority to establish interstate laws, or to enforce judgments entered against states as a result of disputes, or to levy taxes to raise revenue, and the fact that Rhode Island defeated the effort despite the fact the other twelve states voted in favor, see Bernstein, pp. 90–91; in March of 1784, Congressman James Madison approached Thomas Jefferson with a proposal that Virginia and Maryland each send representatives to form a committee with authority to meet and resolve the conflicting claims of the two states to the Potomac and Pocomoke Rivers, see Bernstein, p. 97. For a perceptive statement of the stratification of societies in Europe, including the nine definable social layers in the country of Denmark, see Bernstein, p. 3.

Virginia imposed an export tariff on tobacco (Nevins, *The American States 1775–1789*, p. 559). For an extensive and in-depth recital of the chaotic economic affairs of the states, and of their rivalries and disputes, including the ongoing battle regarding the state of Vermont and the Great Wyoming Valley bordering Pennsylvania, see Nevins, pp. 470–605; see also Bernstein, *Are We to Be a Nation?*, p. 87.

For the maps delineating proposed new states in the vast territory west of the original thirteen states, with extended discussion, including the ongoing and conflicting claims of various states for the prized Wyoming Valley land adjoining Pennsylvania, see Boyd, Volume 6, *The Papers of Thomas Jefferson*, pp. 581–668; see also Bernstein, *Are We to Be a Nation?*, p. 87.

For the participation of Matthew Dunson in the battles of Concord, Lake Champlain, the Bahamas, and the epic sea battle with John Paul Jones twelve miles off the English coast at Flamborough, as well as a definition of Letters of Marque, see volume 1 of this series, *Our Sacred Honor*, chapters 14, 15, 18, 24, 26, 28. For the pivotal battle at Saratoga in which Benedict Arnold was the most spectacular hero, see volume 4, *The Hand of Providence*, chapter 31. For the sea battle between the French and British fleets on the Chesapeake, see volume 6, *The World Turned Upside Down*, chapter 32.

The United States Congress convened in Annapolis, Maryland, December 13, 1783, with Congressman Thomas Jefferson present. He remained there until his appointment as Minister Plenipotentiary to negotiate treaties of amity and commerce, and left Annapolis on his new duties on May 11, 1784. See Boyd, *The Papers of Thomas Jefferson*, volumes 6 and 7, the Jefferson Chronology page, facing page 3.

CHAPTER XXX

★ ★ ★

*T*he door into the Boston waterfront office of DUNSON & WEEMS SHIPPING swung open. Billy raised his head to look into the brilliant midmorning April sunlight flooding in, saw the tall, black silhouette and the Pennsylvania rifle, and gaped. His heart leaped as he jerked from his chair and came trotting to the counter.

"Eli!" he exclaimed. "Eli! How . . . what . . . ?"

Eli laid the rifle clattering on the counter and the two men reached to clasp hands while Billy ran on. "How did you get here? Find us? It's so good to see you. What brings you?"

Eli was smiling as he spoke. "I asked in town. Seems you and Matthew are in the shipping business. Didn't take long to find you."

Billy was beaming. "Are you all right? How did you get here?"

"I'm fine. Walked. Canoe. How are you?"

"I'm fine."

Eli grinned. "I've never seen you on that side of a counter in an office before. Looks good."

Billy laughed. "I've never seen you in an office on that side of a counter, either. And it looks good. Come in." He swung the gate open and Eli followed him inside. Billy turned and gestured.

"Eli Stroud, I would like you to meet Thomas Covington. He sold this carrying company to Matthew and me and agreed to stay on to help for a while."

The white-haired Covington stood, slightly stooped, and offered his aging hand, and Eli noticed the swelled knuckles as he shook it gently. "It is good to meet you, sir."

"It is mine to meet you. Billy's talked about you."

Eli nodded as Billy took his arm. "Come sit over here. This is my desk."

Eli glanced about the plain walls of the austere, unpretentious office, and sat down facing Billy. "Matthew?" he asked.

"Away at Annapolis on business."

"Shipping?"

"No. Thomas Jefferson."

Eli straightened. "Jefferson! In Annapolis? You have business with him?"

"No, but we have business with the state of Virginia. Jefferson was governor there. And he's now in Congress in Annapolis. We thought he could help with a bad problem."

"You're a Boston company. What trouble do you have in Virginia?"

"We have a ship down there. But that will wait. How are things at home, with Ben and Lydia? The children?"

"Good. All healthy and strong. Most of the spring work is done. No trouble that I know of."

"The Iroquois? Mohawk?"

"Both quiet. We have no quarrel with them."

"Laura?"

Billy saw the flash of pain in Eli's eyes as he answered. "She's four now. Looks more like Mary every day. Growing. Good girl. Good child." Eli settled back in his chair. "What's this trouble in Virginia?"

Billy leaned forward, forearms on his desk, fingers interlaced. "It's the Potomac River. It divides Virginia and Maryland. Both states claim the right to regulate navigation and levy taxes. They've both seized one of our ships and neither one will release it until we pay the tariff. We can't afford to pay both states. We thought Jefferson might tell us what to do."

"Matthew's not back yet?"

"Due any time."

"Did Caleb come home?"

"Yes. He's working with us. That's another story."

"Tell me."

Billy paused to gather his thoughts. "We picked up three hundred tons of tobacco in Jamestown, Virginia. Virginia has an export tax on their tobacco. It was five percent until lately, when they raised it to eight percent. We were prepared to pay the five percent we knew about, but not the other three we didn't know about. They seized the ship. Caleb wouldn't stand for it. He and Captain Pettigrew sailed the ship out one night. Just cut the mooring ropes and sailed her out. Took ten Virginia militia who were guarding the ship with them. After they unloaded the tobacco in New York, they paid the militiamen wages and their passage home and sent the additional three percent tax with them."

Eli smiled through his beard. "Caleb's still the rebel."

"Scared us. We didn't know if we'd started a war between Massachusetts and Virginia or not. As it turns out, there is no process, no law, we could find that covers this situation. So with one ship still under seizure, and the Jamestown taxing authority mad at us over another one, Matthew went to get advice from Thomas Jefferson."

Eli's eyebrows raised. "It will be interesting to hear what Jefferson says." He paused for a moment. "How is business? We hear hard things up in Vermont."

"You'll hear worse down here. No hard money. Paper money worthless. Banks in trouble. Businesses closing all over. Farmers being foreclosed. Good men out of work. Courts flooded with bankruptcies. Dismal."

Concern came into Eli's face. "How is your business doing?"

Billy shook his head slowly. "In trouble. The bank has told us they'll have to call in their note if we don't get the ship on the Potomac released. The *Jessica.* I'm waiting now to hear what Matthew learned, because if Jefferson doesn't have an answer, I don't know what we'll do."

"Can't you get business? Cargo to carry for a profit?"

Billy shook his head. "Not easy. It's the money. The French and the

British and the Spanish have closed down a lot of ports around the world where American ships used to deal. Nobody in this country has hard money. Gold. Silver. And the foreign ports still open to us won't take American paper money. We have to guarantee payment in hard money, and that's nearly impossible to do."

He gestured to Covington, who was listening intently. "Mr. Covington had been in the business for forty years. He never saw times like these."

Covington called, "The whole business of ships carrying cargo is in trouble. All over. Everywhere. When my sons left, I couldn't do it alone."

Billy picked it up. "We've got two other contracts waiting, but we can't take them up until our bank is satisfied. If we can't satisfy the bank, we'll probably have to close our doors."

"How much to pay the bank?"

"About sixteen thousand pounds, British."

Eli started. "For two ships?"

"Six ships."

"You've still got five. Can't you use them?"

"Not without hard money. We can't get hard money without the bank, and the bank won't move until we get the *Jessica*."

Eli blew air and shook his head but remained silent.

Billy asked, "What brings you here?"

"Business. I had a visit about four weeks ago from a New York lawyer. Good man, so far as I can tell. Name's Randall Weatherby. His father was Lawrence Weatherby. You remember the British doctor—Purcell—who befriended Mary back in New York?"

Billy nodded.

"That doctor wrote a will before he died. He gave everything he owned to Mary. She took the will to the barrister Lawrence Weatherby. He took her case. Worked on it for four or five years. The American courts finally decided in Mary's favor a year or so after Yorktown. Lawrence Weatherby died, but his son Randall kept on with it. He discovered Mary and I were married and came north to find us. He didn't know Mary had died, and when we told him, he said the things

Purcell left to Mary were now legally mine. But to claim it I had to find someone who could sign a sworn paper saying they saw the marriage, and that Mary had died. I brought a paper from the midwife who birthed Laura and was there when Mary died, but I need you to sign a paper saying you saw the marriage. Can you do that?"

"I can. I gave her in marriage."

"I told him that. I'm to take these papers to New York and find this man Weatherby, and he'll get a court order giving me what's there."

"What did he say was there?"

Eli opened the leather pouch and drew out the wrapped papers. "There's a copy of the whole thing. It says there are just short of twenty-nine thousand British pounds sterling waiting in the New York bank."

Billy jerked erect, and Covington half rose from his chair, stunned. For five seconds the only sounds were the seagulls squawking as they wheeled overhead on the waterfront, and the hollow thumping of dock hands moving freight on the docks.

When he could, Billy exclaimed, "Twenty-nine thousand pounds sterling?"

"That's what he said. It's all there in the papers."

"Hard coin?"

"Sterling. Silver."

Billy's voice was subdued, nearly a whisper. "A fortune!"

Covington sank back in his chair.

Eli raised a hand in caution, palm toward Billy. "We better take this one step at a time. I think Weatherby told the truth, but that is yet to be seen. We need a court order that we don't have yet. The money's supposed to be in that New York bank, but who knows? And the bank is supposed to release it to me on the court's order, but we don't know what they'll do yet. So we better be careful."

Billy nodded. "I agree. If I'm supposed to sign a paper, what is it to say?"

"That you were there when Major Waldo legally performed the marriage between Mary and myself. That was July 8, 1778. You should state who else was there, and that both Mary and I were in sound mind and health. That's about all."

"How soon do you need it?"

"Soon. When you can."

"How are you traveling to New York?"

"Ship. There's one leaving about four o'clock in the morning."

"Maybe we can get an attorney to write the paper this afternoon. It has to be right. There's one with an office right here on the waterfront. Handles contracts for the shipping firms."

Eli gestured to his satchel. "I have a little money. I'll pay for it."

"Want to go see if he can do it?"

Eli rose, and Billy turned to Covington. "We'll be gone a while, down to the attorney. You take care of the office?"

Covington nodded and Eli asked, "Should I leave the rifle here?"

Billy pointed to a narrow closet in the corner, Eli stood the rifle inside, closed the door, and the two men walked out into the sun and the ships and seagulls and the dockhands working the ships and cargo. A few slowed to watch Eli pass in his beaded buckskin shirt and leggings and moccasins, with his weapons belt about his middle and the tomahawk thrust through. The leather satchel hung at his side on its leather loop over his shoulder.

The attorney's name was Robert Strand, and he was younger than Eli expected. Thin, small, with eyes that never stopped moving, it was obvious that his mind worked like a machine. He understood what was needed within three minutes. Five minutes later he had the essential facts for the statement—Mary Flint—Eli Stroud—adults of sound health and mind—July 8 1778—Major Waldo—Billy Weems— marriage solemnized according to law.

Strand wasted no time. "The statement will be ready by one o'clock this afternoon. Is that agreeable?"

"Yes."

"Who will pay the fee, and how will it be paid?"

Eli answered, "I will pay, in gold."

Surprise showed in Strand's face. "The fee will be one dollar."

"Done."

At fifteen minutes past one o'clock, Eli finished reading the carefully written paper while Strand sat facing him across his desk in his small office.

Eli turned to Billy. "I think it will do."

Billy concentrated as he read it. "It's all there." He turned to Strand. "Do you have a quill?"

At half past one o'clock Billy and Eli walked back out of Strand's office, onto the black, weathered timbers of the waterfront, and turned west toward the shipping office. Eli raised his voice to be heard over the clamor of the gulls and the sounds of ships and sailors and dockhands.

"I have one more thing to ask of you. Would you write a letter? A big one?"

Billy slowed, puzzled. "To who?"

"George Washington."

Billy stopped. "General Washington?"

"Yes. There are some things he needs to know."

"What?"

They pushed through the office door and through the gate to Billy's desk. Covington watched them, then went on with his paperwork. Eli laid the leather satchel with all the paperwork on the desk.

"Things are happening up in Vermont. Canada. The general should know."

"What things?"

"Coming down here, I ran onto an old friend named Ormond Sykes. Been in the mountains as long as I can remember. He hears things. He heard the British were gathering the Loyalists up in Canada for an attack on the United States, so he went up into the big lakes country and spent two months on snowshoes to find out. There is no such gathering up there. But he did see that the British have not abandoned all the forts up there like they agreed in the surrender treaty. They're still up there, and they're stopping the Americans from entering the rivers and mountains for trading. They're stirring up the French against us, and doing about all they can to give us trouble. There's also talk that the State of Vermont is negotiating with the British about becoming one of their Canadian provinces. The Americans up there are getting irritated. Short-tempered. There could be trouble."

"Vermont? British?"

"Vermont has been in trouble with New York for years over the question of whether New York owns Vermont, or whether Vermont is an independent state. Making a deal with the British would take care of the New York question, but it would make serious problems for the United States. Sykes thought Washington should know, and I promised I'd see that he heard about it. Would you help write a letter?"

"Yes. I'll need to know more detail."

"I'll give it to you."

"Good." Billy raised a hand. "You're coming to supper at my home."

"I don't want to interfere."

"You won't. Do you need a bed for the night?"

Eli shook his head. "That ship leaves at four in the morning. I'll take a room at a waterfront tavern. Maybe just sleep on the docks. I'll be fine."

"But you'll have supper with us?"

"I'd like that."

Eli eased back in his chair. "One last thing. Did you give those letters to the Dunson girl?"

Billy nodded. "Yes. I did. She's going through them now."

"She said anything?"

"Not yet. That was the only thing I asked of her. Read them, and talk to me."

"Does Matthew know?"

"I told him before I told her."

"What did he say?"

"Give them to her."

They remained in silence until Billy looked at his watch. "A little before three o'clock. Might be enough time to write that letter you want."

Eli shrugged. "Got something to write on? And a quill?"

Notes

For support of the disastrous condition of the various states in regard to hard money, border disputes, tariffs, etc., as well as the problems with conflicting claims of states bordering on a common river, see the endnotes for chapter 29.

CHAPTER XXXI

A warm, heavy spring rain came drumming in the quiet hour before dawn to wash Boston town sparkling and set tiny rivulets working their way through the cobblestone streets to the bay. In the black of her room, Margaret Dunson slowly came from the fog of sleep enough to understand the sound, and for a time she lay with her eyes closed, listening in the darkness, letting her thoughts run as they would.

Matthew and Billy in trouble—can't save their business—Caleb turning his back on the Almighty—how did it happen—what did I do wrong—John John John I need you—Brigitte hurting inside over what to do about Billy—what can I do about it?—nothing—nothing.

She moved and opened her eyes, staring in the darkness.

What do we do if the shipping business is lost—no work for the men—how do we pay for food, taxes—what do we do, what do we do?

Fear rose in her heart and she sat up in bed, wide awake. *There are demons in the dark—don't decide things in the dark—get up and get a light—and do something with your hands.*

She struck light to her lamp, put on her robe and slippers, and walked to the parlor with her single, long braid swaying down her back. She raked the banked coals in the fireplace, set shavings and kindling, and pumped the old leather bellows until flames came licking. She glanced at the clock on the mantel—twenty minutes past four o'clock—

and was walking toward the kitchen when a quiet sound from behind turned her.

"Caleb. What are you doing up?"

"Rain woke me. Better get some wood in before its soaked."

"We have more than a cord under the shelter."

"Not enough if it rains again soon. If it gets too wet it'll be days getting dry enough to burn. Better do it now while we can."

Margaret shrugged. "Get a coat on. It's chilly out there, and you'll get wet."

Caleb buttoned on his coat, the kitchen door closed, and Margaret listened for a moment to the sound of kindling sticks being stacked against the back wall before she lighted the kitchen lamp and kindled a fire in the stove. She dipped water from the kitchen bucket into a black iron pot and set it on the stove to heat, then measured out one pint of oatmeal and set it on the cupboard. She was setting bowls and glasses and spoons on the dining table when Caleb walked back in. He took off his muddy shoes and shook his coat before he hung it on its peg.

"You going back to bed for an hour?" Margaret asked.

"Hadn't thought about it."

She gestured to the dining table. "Sit down. I need to talk."

They sat down next to each other, chairs turned until they were facing, and Margaret spoke.

"I'm worried sick about Matthew and Billy. Will they lose the shipping company?"

"They could. Right now no one knows what to expect. Depends on what Matthew says when he gets back."

"Isn't he due today?"

"Yes. Or tomorrow."

"If the news is bad?"

"The bank forecloses. It's all over."

The single lamp cast both their faces in sharply contrasting light and shadow.

"Then how do we pay the bills?"

Caleb shook his head. "I don't know. I know there's eleven dollars left in the jar, and a little food left in the root cellar. The money and food might get us through the next three weeks if we're careful. From there, I have no idea."

Margaret struggled with the panic that rose within. "There's no work on the docks? Anywhere?"

"None. Good men lined up waiting."

"What are we going to do?"

Caleb tossed one hand in the air and let it fall, but remained silent. The only sounds were the quiet, steady pelting of the rain and the popping of pine pitch in the fireplace. Margaret began rubbing her hands together, looking at the cracks and the roughness. Her words were nearly a whisper. "I've prayed so hard. Every day. So hard."

Caleb spoke without looking at her. "What answer?"

She stopped working with her hands, and there was an edge to her voice. "He hasn't answered yet. But He will!"

Again Caleb did not look at her. "I don't think I'll spend much time waiting."

Margaret dropped her hands into her lap. "Be careful what you say!"

Caleb looked her full in the face. "I was careful when they shot father, but he's dead all the same. I was careful when Matthew left, but he left anyway. I was careful when I had to kill men, but they're dead. I stopped being careful, and it didn't seem to make much difference. The killing went on and on."

For the first time since his homecoming, he was opening up, and Margaret leaned forward, pleading in her voice.

"Caleb, you were so young! It wasn't fair! You couldn't understand."

Caleb's voice was rising. "Understand what? Everybody was praying to a God that didn't care? Didn't answer? That was eight years ago. I'm not young any more, and I'm still hearing prayers that aren't being answered. Either he's not there, or he doesn't care. And it doesn't make much difference which it is, because in the end it's all the same. People die. Starve. Can't get work. They pray and then make excuses when their god doesn't answer."

"He *does* answer! In His own good time."

"*After* all the killing? *After* father is dead? Explain to me 'his own good time'!"

Margaret bit down on her flare of anger, but could not hide it, and her words came hot, too loud. "None of us can comprehend the mind of the Almighty! His ways are not those of man." She caught herself and softened. "Caleb, don't offend the Creator. We need you. I need you in this house. Adam is talking. He doesn't know why you will not take your turn in saying grace at the table. Or evening prayers. He's starting to ask questions. Help him."

Caleb drew a deep breath. "Would it be better if I left?"

Margaret recoiled. "No! I didn't say that. I don't know what we'd do here without you. All I ask is that you do what you've always been taught. Respect the Almighty. Take your responsibility. Talk to Adam. Help him."

Caleb swallowed and took time to order his thoughts. His voice was low, penetrating. "How do I respect an almighty when I do not believe he exists?"

His disbelief struck into Margaret like a knife blade. She blanched white and clapped a hand over her mouth to stifle a cry and stared into Caleb's face, unable to speak. He looked at her steadily, unmoving, unrelenting, and then he rose, and Margaret reached to seize his arm.

"You didn't mean that! You were taught better. Don't say such a thing again!"

His eyes dropped for a moment, and he gently touched Margaret's hand on his arm. "I didn't mean to cause pain. But I can't live a lie. I won't." He turned and walked toward the archway, then slowed when Brigitte appeared in her robe, hair tied back, arms folded. She walked into the parlor as he passed, and she turned to watch him go, then looked at Margaret.

"I heard you talking. What's going on?" She saw the pain in her mother's face.

"Nothing. The rain woke me. He got up to keep the firewood dry."

Brigitte sat down facing Margaret. "There's more. Tell me."

"It's nothing. He's not himself. Worried about Matthew and Billy and what will happen if they can't get things worked out with the ships."

Brigitte sat back in her chair studying Margaret critically. "What else?"

Margaret shrugged. "Nothing. He's just not himself."

Brigitte shook her head. "There's more. You look terrible."

"No, that's all. He just needs time to think."

"About the business, or about . . . other things?"

"Both." Margaret drew a long breath. "Well, we're not going to solve anything for him by sitting here." She started to rise, then settled back onto her chair. "There is one thing I would like to know. Have you decided about Billy?"

For several seconds Brigitte sat still with the lamplight on the planes of her face. "No. Not finally."

Margaret leaned forward, and Brigitte could not miss the intense need. "Anything? Have you decided *anything?*"

Brigitte spoke slowly, ordering her thoughts, selecting her words. "I think I've gotten over the shock. I had never thought of Billy that way—a husband. And I think I've gotten past his appearance." She paused for a moment. "That sounds terrible. I don't mean Billy's ugly. I never really thought about how he looked. He was always just Billy. I know that appearance means something, but there are so many other things in a person that mean so much more. And I'm starting to see many of them in him. Maybe most of them."

Margaret's heart was pounding. "You're growing up!"

"I don't know about that. I only know that I have to get through this, and soon. No matter how it all turns out, I owe him that."

The quiet sound of boiling water came from the twilight in the kitchen, and Margaret stood. "Water for the oatmeal. I'll be right back." Quickly she strode into the kitchen, stirred the measured oatmeal and a little salt into the boiling water, put the lid on the pot, and moved it off the hot plate. She spoke as she walked back to the dining table.

"Have you said anything to him?"

"No."

"Has he asked?"

Brigitte shook her head.

"He's a remarkable man. He lost his father at the worst time. I don't know how Dorothy did it, raising him alone."

"I know. I've thought the same thing."

"I know right now both Billy and Matthew are worried sick about their business. If something good doesn't happen soon it will be gone."

"I know."

"How will we all pay our bills?"

Brigitte looked her in the eye. "I'll have a little money from my schoolteaching, but it won't be enough. I'm scared."

"Try not to frighten Adam and Prissy about it. They're still too young."

"I know."

"Why don't you go back to bed for a while? I'll get breakfast ready."

"I can't sleep. I'll help. Oatmeal and what?"

"If the rain lets up enough I'll get some dried apple slices from the root cellar."

"I'll get them. You know, the cellar's emptying fast."

"Too fast. I'll go down today and take a count of everything."

A strange feeling came stealing over the two of them as they sat in their robes in the predawn hour with the sound of the rain and of the fire in the fireplace, and the warmth spreading through the room. It was as though the steady sound on the roof, and the oddness of the hour, and the play of shadow in the room were drawing thoughts and reflections that needed to flow just as they were, open, without restraint.

Margaret said quietly, "How are Kathleen and the baby?"

"Good. Kathleen's frightened. Just like all of us. But she won't let it show."

Margaret shook her head. "That poor child. Think of what she had to go through eight years ago. Father a traitor. Banished. Never seen him since. Mother unbalanced. Died in England. Buried there. Kathleen had to grow up too quickly. Too quickly."

"She's done it. Beautifully."

Margaret's thoughts were coming at random. "Adam and Prissy will be out of school next year. I wonder what's ahead for them."

"Maybe college?"

"How do we pay for it?"

"I don't know. Caleb never got his chance."

Margaret lowered her voice. "I'm sick about Caleb."

Brigitte answered. "So am I. Adam's starting to ask."

"I know he is." Margaret paused for a moment. "That's what Caleb and I were talking about when you came in."

"I thought so. He seems to be drifting."

"Lost. Can't find his way back."

Brigitte waited for a moment. "I wish father were here to talk to him."

Margaret bowed her head. "Sometimes I miss John so much."

Brigitte reached to touch Margaret's hand. "I'm sorry."

"No need. I'm all right."

Brigitte said, "You talked to Prissy. About Billy."

"Yes. She saw you put Richard's things away—from off your dresser."

"She told me. She told me what you said. It helped. Why didn't you say it to me?"

There was a pause before Margaret answered. "I don't know. Maybe I thought you should make up your own mind about Billy. It's so hard to know what to say—what to do—sometimes. I've made so many mistakes."

"Not many. I don't know what I'd do without you." She ran her hand over the worn wood of the tabletop. Without looking up, she asked, "Mother, do you think I should marry Billy?"

"I don't know what to say. I'm a lot like you. Billy was always just Billy, until he brought those letters to you. Some mornings I wake up, and I still can't see him other than part of the family, and I have to start all over again. I wish I knew the answer. I'd tell you if I did."

"Prissy's turning out to be special."

"She's grown up before her time."

"Not like me. I was too headstrong."

"You learned. You got past it."

"I put Richard's things away, and it felt as though part of me would die. But it didn't. He's gone. Time to move on."

"He'll always be in your heart, but that doesn't mean you have to stop living. The day Tom Sievers brought your father home . . ."

A softness came into Brigitte's voice. "I don't know how you did it."

Margaret heaved a great sigh and glanced at the window. The curtain had changed from black to the deepest gray. "Well," she said with brusque finality, "the rain hasn't stopped, but the day is just around the corner. Sunrise won't wait. Get a coat on and fetch the dried apples and some butter and milk. I'll get the bread and jam. We've got mouths to feed."

Notes

The events and characters depicted in this chapter are fictional.

CHAPTER XXXII

★ ★ ★

*T*he evening incoming Atlantic tides were running high into Boston harbor, and seagulls and terns and egrets and grebes set the waterfront alive with their squawking as they wheeled and pirouetted in the easterly wind, then dropped like stones to snatch at the dead fish and refuse that littered the bay and the shore, and would remain until the tides reversed.

The schooner *Queen* worked her way through the few ships anchored in the harbor, spilled her sails, and settled thumping against the dock at Clark's Wharf. Minutes later the gangplank was lowered banging onto the pier, and Matthew Dunson was the first man to stride down, seaman's bag over his shoulder, wind at his back. In the gathering dusk, he quickly worked his way through the scatter of shipping crates on the mostly deserted docks, past the dark windows of the office of DUNSON & WEEMS. He strode rapidly through the narrow cobblestone streets with birds and squirrels chattering in the greening of trees and grass and the budding of flowers, as they sought the safety of their nests and holes. His pace quickened at the thought of Kathleen and little John, and he was nearly trotting as he approached the white picket fence, pushed through the gate of the great Thorpe home, and hurried up the walk to open the front door.

His heart leaped as he heard Kathleen's call from the kitchen.

"Matthew! Is that you?"

"I'm home," he answered.

He heard the hurried steps, and then she was coming through the archway with John on one arm, the other extended to him as she exclaimed, "Oh, it's so good to see you."

He dropped his bag to the floor and lifted John from her and held her close with his free arm, and she wrapped both arms about his neck. She drew her head back and kissed him, and John moved and pushed back from Matthew. Kathleen smiled.

"He's a little strange. You've been gone."

"I know."

"Let me help you with your bag."

"I'll carry it." Matthew picked up the heavy canvas bag with his free hand and with John in his other arm and Mary following, walked down the hall to their bedroom. He put his son on the floor and the bag on the bed and untied the knotted cord to lay it open. Kathleen emptied it on the bed and sorted the clothing for the wash while Matthew dropped to his haunches to talk to John who stood still, face a noncommittal blank.

"Finished," Kathleen said. "I was cooking supper when you came. I need to go back to the kitchen."

Matthew scooped the boy up and followed her back to the kitchen where she put her apron on, and opened the door to the black, cast-iron oven to stoop and peer inside. "Beef roast. About done."

She turned back to Matthew. "You saw Jefferson?"

"I did."

She stopped moving, waiting.

Matthew shook his head. "No answers. No solutions."

She raised a hand to her throat. "Oh. I'm so sorry. I hoped—"

"We all did. There's nothing he knows of in the law to help."

"What will you do? You and Billy."

"I don't know. We'll talk in the morning. I've got to find Caleb tonight. We'll need him."

"Caleb? For what?"

"I don't know yet. I can tell you that Jefferson said several things that opened my eyes to issues I've never known, or never thought of."

Her eyebrows arched. "Like what?"

"Generally, what's happening in this country, and which direction we are to go."

"Tell me."

"During supper."

She turned and lifted the lid from a pot of steaming potatoes to thrust a pewter fork into the uppermost. "Almost there."

He set the table while she put the smoking beef roast and steaming potatoes and cabbage onto platters and carried them to the dining room, then added sliced bread and cheese. Matthew lifted John to his chair between them, and Kathleen folded the little boy's arms and gently held them while Matthew said grace. As they ate, Kathleen asked questions, and Matthew steadily added detail of his time with Jefferson in Annapolis. Kathleen eyes grew larger as she caught the beginnings of Jefferson's vision for America.

"I've never *dreamed!*"

"Not many have."

Together they cleared the table and washed and dried the dishes, then Matthew said, "I need to go to see Caleb. I'll be back soon."

He put on his coat and Kathleen followed him to the door. "Don't be long."

He covered the two short blocks quickly, was hugged by a relieved Margaret and Brigitte, delivered his message to Caleb, and twenty minutes later walked back through his own door. John came walking sturdily across the parlor, arms outstretched to his father, who gathered him up and hugged him to his breast.

Kathleen asked, "Was Caleb there?"

A shadow crossed Matthew's face. "Yes. They all were. But something's not right in that house."

Kathleen stopped. "What do you mean?"

"I don't know. Time will tell. He'll be at the office in the morning."

They settled into the large chairs facing the screened fireplace with their son on the floor, investigating the fire tongs and scoop. For a while they spoke of things great and small while they watched the boy and smiled and laughed as he moved about, exploring the wonders of the fireplace and the parlor. At half past eight, Kathleen put John in his crib and rubbed his back gently while she hummed him to sleep. She returned to sit in her chair, and time was forgotten while the two talked of the little things, giving and receiving the nourishment that renewed their souls and would sustain them as life moved on. The clock was close to ten when Matthew turned out the lamps and they quietly walked to their bedroom.

The breeze died in the night, and the sun rose on a still, warm, rare, New England spring day. It was as though the world were being born anew, a green canvas accented by splashes of reds and yellows as the early flowers burst from their buds to greet the morning. People in the streets walked with a lift in their spirits, and for a little window of time the burdens of life were forgotten.

Well before eight o'clock, Matthew unlocked the office door, and he had a fire going in the fireplace when Billy arrived minutes later. Covington walked in, muttered his good morning as he hung up his hat and coat, and sat down at his desk. Caleb came in a few minutes past eight o'clock and stood silent, waiting for direction.

Matthew gestured. "Get a chair."

The four of them gathered around his old, scarred desk, and Matthew leaned forward on his forearms to speak.

"Jefferson knows of no law that will help us with the *Jessica*. He knows of no one in Virginia or in Congress who can help. He talked about Article Nine of the Articles of Confederation, but doubts it would apply. And if it did, it would take more than a year to get a decision from the committee that would hear the matter. Worse, there is no way to enforce any decision or judgment made by the committee."

He paused to give the three men facing him time to let it set in their minds. Then he continued.

"So we aren't here to decide how we can use the law, or a committee, for help, because they don't exist."

Caleb interrupted. "Isn't that the same problem Virginia had when we sailed the *Rebecca* out? There was no law or committee to hear their complaint against us?"

"Yes. The same problem."

Caleb went on. "That leaves us without a ship, and without a remedy. Wasn't it something like that that started the war eight years ago? The stupidity of a wrong being done, and no remedy except to fight?"

Matthew turned to him. "Don't you get any wrong ideas about getting the *Jessica* back."

A reckless smile crossed Caleb's face but he said nothing.

Matthew continued. "I've pondered the problem with the bank until I'm weary of it. I thought of one solution. I can put the Thorpe home up for security to guarantee the note at the bank."

Billy recoiled like he had been struck. "Have you talked to Kathleen?"

"No."

"Don't. I won't agree to it. I'll let the business go first."

Covington spoke up. "Don't consider it, Matthew. Your home is the last thing you give up, not the first."

Matthew's shoulders sagged, and for a few moments he buried his face in his hands. Then he dropped his arms and turned to Covington.

"There's one more possibility. Did anyone inquire about using our ships to carry cargo while I was gone?"

"Three or four. Four, I think. Seems half of Boston knows what Caleb and Pettigrew did down in Jamestown—ignored the Virginia authorities and cut the *Rebecca* loose and sailed her out. Most merchants admire it. They're coming here with their business, but they have the same problem we have. They must deal in hard coin, which none of us has without a bank."

Matthew turned to Billy. "What about the bank? Have they said anything lately?"

Billy's face was troubled. "Two days ago they said they're ready to call in their note. Looks like we start selling ships. Trouble is, who will buy? There's at least ten ships out in the harbor right now for sale for whatever price the owner can get. If we sold all six of ours today, I doubt we'd get enough to pay off the bank note."

Matthew looked at Covington. "Any of those inquiries in writing?"

"Three."

"What kind of cargo were they talking about?"

"Stoves, nails, screws, horseshoes—manufactured goods—from the north. Tobacco and cotton and indigo from the south."

Matthew drew a great, weary breath. "Those are solid commodities. In what quantities?"

"Could require all six ships, if it works at all."

"Reputable merchants?"

"Yes. Been in business for years."

"What would happen if we took those written inquiries to the bank? Would they consider working with us for a while longer?"

Covington shook his head. "I doubt it. They're thinking the worst is yet to come."

"Is it worth a try?"

Covington shrugged. "Can't do any harm to ask."

Caleb broke in. "Is this why you wanted me here?"

Matthew leaned back in his chair and took a moment to change the direction of his thoughts. "No, it isn't. I thought I saw something entirely different that needed doing, and you might become a part of it." He stopped and slowly shook his head. "Now I don't know. If we lose the business, it won't make much difference."

Billy asked, "What did you see?"

Matthew sighed. "I better take a minute and tell you about the meeting I had with Jefferson. It took most of an afternoon. I saw and heard things about this country that I had never heard of or supposed. The first big shock was finding out there is no government institution or committee, no law anywhere, that can force any one state to do anything! That includes Congress. The entire government structure is powerless. Almost a fiction!"

Covington was unmoved. Billy's face was set but inquiring. Caleb was a blank. Matthew went on.

"I saw maps of proposed new states as far west as the Mississippi."

"Whose maps?" Billy asked.

"Jefferson. Hartley. Franklin. Others. Those men have plans twenty years in the future! Think about it! In twenty years we could have twice the number of states we have now. If that happens, what's to hold them together? The Articles of Confederation? Those Articles are doomed! In our lifetime, there could be a war that would split this country into pieces. Just like Europe. The French and Spanish and English. Unending wars."

Covington sobered, and Billy's eyes sharpened. Matthew continued.

"Right now things are happening that are moving this country in that direction. The Virginia–Maryland conflict over the Potomac is a little thing, but it gives notice of the flaw that is leading the states toward their own destruction."

Again he paused for a moment. "The flaw is sitting right there in plain sight, but is so much a part of us we don't see it for what it is."

"The Articles of Confederation?" Caleb asked. "They can be changed."

Matthew shook his head. "Not the Articles. The only purpose they serve is to define the problem."

Covington raised a hand. "What are you talking about?"

For a moment Matthew held his peace, then spoke slowly. "The minds of men."

Billy stirred, then settled, waiting.

"Europe and the United States—all the same. So deeply entrenched in centuries of thought that they don't see it has not worked. If this country follows the old forms of government, the way the world sees them, we're doomed. Either we understand that, or we don't, and whether we survive as the United States depends on it, and what we do about it."

Covington shook his head. "You still haven't told us—"

Matthew cut him off. "I didn't see it until I spent time with Jefferson. The longer I thought on it, the more clear it became. It's his thinking that the time has come that we rise above the rule of monarchs.

The principles of government that support kings weaken the people—rob them of the very strength they need to survive."

His voice was rising. "Kings exist on the principle of aristocracy. Aristocracy depends on preserving itself. Bloodlines, father to son, wealth and power that will never be shared. The degenerate rich maintaining themselves on the backs of the desperate poor. Think about it."

Matthew did not realize the passion in his own voice. "Jefferson is doing all he can to change that. He's rewriting much of Virginia law. He's attacking the laws of inheritance. Estates can be given to anyone, not just the bloodlines. The wealth of the rich who pass on without a will is no longer given to only the eldest son. If Jefferson succeeds, the aristocrats will soon find their wealth leaving their families."

Covington was staring, mouth clamped shut as Matthew continued.

"Jefferson asks the question, what right does a government—any government—have to dictate which church a man shall join? We've always thought that right existed in government because we believed that was the only way we be certain to have a God-fearing state. Without God in government, it would eventually fail."

Caleb looked down at his hands.

Matthew went on. "But Jefferson contends that true religion consists of the relationship between a man's own conscience and his God—worship the way the man sees it, not the way the state dictates it. Can any government force its people to be virtuous? That's nonsense! And if government cannot force virtue, then it must leave that choice to the citizens, where it belongs."

Caleb spoke quietly. "What's this got to do with the shipping business?"

Matthew ignored him. "Right now James Madison and Jefferson are talking with each other. They're proposing new ideas, new ways to rise above the flaws that have the country in trouble. Conferences between states. Committees. Rules. Amending the Articles. I didn't realize this country started this process a long time ago. In 1643, when four states joined to defend against the French and Indians. The alliance didn't last long, but it was a start. There were other organizations, and finally, the

Articles of Confederation to defend against the British. We know more about this new concept of government than any other country on earth!"

Billy spoke up. "What new form of government?"

"Government based on the rule of the people, not the rule of the aristocracy."

Covington tapped the desk with a finger. "The states have it now."

Matthew turned his head to face him squarely. "Then why is the *Jessica* under seizure?"

Covington's answer came too fast. "Because the states can't . . ." He realized what he was saying, and stopped.

Matthew nodded. "Exactly. Because the states can't agree, and there is no law, no committee, no place to go for a resolution."

Billy interrupted. "Are we back where we started?"

"We're back, but do we see it differently now?"

Covington leaned back, his mind leaping. He remained silent.

Matthew waited until he knew all three men were waiting. "This country has got to find a new form of government that can make, and enforce, fair laws that bind the states together. That means the power to tax, to regulate commerce between the states, and to control border disputes."

Billy leaned forward, eyes narrowed in intensity. "You mean deny the states the power to govern their own citizens?"

Frustration showed in Matthew's face. "Some powers, but not all. Only the ones necessary to maintain peace."

Caleb interrupted. "You mean the states control the citizens, and the government controls the states?"

Matthew turned to him. "That's the direction. No one knows how to do it, yet. But either we learn it, or we watch the breakdown of the United States. Jefferson said a few of the leaders have started to encourage citizens to form a committee they're calling the Committee for Correspondence. It isn't a government committee—just a gathering of citizens who have an interest in trying to find a way out of the chaos."

Caleb shrugged and sat back down. "Jefferson thinks a Committee of Correspondence will do it? Whatever that is."

Matthew thumped the desk with his finger. "No. But if enough citizens in enough states start exchanging views, and finding out what works and what doesn't work, it could help. Remember Thomas Paine's writing, *Common Sense?* The citizens were ready for it, and it pulled the country together. Jefferson and Madison think the country's ready for the next step."

Covington spoke up. "The hardest thing to change is the mind of another man. How long do these leaders say it will take? How many generations?" Covington bowed his head in thought and went on. "You had something in mind about this Committee of Correspondence. What was it?"

Matthew shook his head. "We better spend our time finding a way to keep our families alive."

"No, what do you think such a committee could do?"

Matthew was reluctant. "Work with Jefferson and Madison and others to get their thoughts out where people can see them, talk about them. Stir people's minds."

"Like a newspaper?"

"Like a newspaper."

"A business? Print these things you're talking about and sell them?"

"It could happen. That's why I asked Caleb to be here."

Caleb started. "Me? To do what?"

"You worked with a newspaper. You wrote for your regiment in the army. You could handle the print shop."

"I could *what?*"

"Handle the print shop."

"The newspaper I worked for is gone. The one that replaced it is gone. I tried to get work there a few weeks ago, but he was closing his office and leaving Boston the next day. There isn't a newspaper in town because nobody can buy newspapers! The only question is which is worse right now, the newspaper business or the shipping business."

"Now wait a minute, wait a minute," Covington said. "Matthew, where will you get the things you intend to publish with this committee? Will you write it? Billy?"

"I think Jefferson will give us all the support he can. Madison with him. Maybe others. They see what this could become."

Billy cut in. "Start a new business. Is that what you're saying?"

"Start a Committee of Correspondence. If a newspaper will help, start that, too. If that's starting a new business, then that's what it is."

"I doubt it could ever support three families."

Matthew interlaced his fingers on his desktop. "I never thought it would. It just seemed like something we could do. Maybe should do."

Caleb stood and stretched. "With all this business about government, did Jefferson say anything that will save Dunson & Weems Shipping?"

Matthew shook his head. "We better take those three written inquiries down to the bank. It's all we have left."

Covington stood and walked to his desk. "I'll get the papers."

Billy looked at his watch. "Bank's open. When do you want to go?"

There was resolve in Matthew's voice. "The sooner the better. Thomas, do you want to come?"

"If it will help."

Matthew turned to Caleb. "You want to come?"

"Someone needs to stay here."

The three men put their coats on, Covington tucked the papers into his inside pocket, and Billy held the door while they walked out into the sounds and smells of the Boston waterfront on a calm, warm, resplendent spring morning. Caleb stood in the doorway, hands in his trouser pockets, watching them until they were out of sight before he left the door open and walked back into the office. He sat down at Matthew's desk and leaned back in the chair, working with his thoughts.

I wonder what Jefferson said that changed Matthew so much—came back thinking twenty years ahead but nothing to save the business now—isn't that what started the war?—talk that sounded so right and did nothing to stop the killing?—talk is all that's left for people who can't make things happen—we would still be up the James River with the Rebecca if we'd let the talk go on—the talk stopped when we sailed her out.

He rose to add a few more sticks of kindling to the fire, and walked to the front door to stand for a time, watching the waterfront.

Those men out there working for almost nothing—not enough to take care of their families—praying for better times—expecting an answer—can't they see that better times depend on them?—not prayer—seems like they'd finally understand that the almighty business is nothing but a way to avoid blame for our own failures—they say things are bad because the almighty has willed it for the good of his children, but none of us knows what his will is, and we won't admit that things are bad because we've made them bad, and they're not going to change until we change them, not the almighty.

He went back to Matthew's chair and sat in thoughtful silence for a time before he once again rose, impatient, irritated by inaction, wanting to come to grips with the torment they had all endured for too long. He was walking toward the front door when Billy entered, Matthew and Covington behind. They were silent, refusing to look at Caleb, defeat plain in their faces.

Caleb spoke first. "The bank said no."

No one answered as they came past the gate to Matthew's desk, where they all sat down.

Matthew nodded. "They said no."

"How much time?"

"Three weeks."

"Well," Caleb said, "that's the end of that."

Covington looked at him. "The only thing I can think of is to get one of the companies that contacted us and try to work out a transaction like the last one. The buyers and sellers arrange the money, and who's going to pay us."

Billy shook his head. "Those merchants made it clear they don't have the hard money, and can't get it. They were asking us to find it."

Matthew had his elbows on the desk, and his face buried in his hands. He straightened and dropped his palms flat on the table. "I can't find a way. I don't know what we're to do."

Billy took a deep breath and turned to Covington. "Isn't this where you found yourself when you sold to us?"

"Yes."

"Maybe we can find a buyer for the company with enough—"

The rattle of the front door turned them all to look. The door swung wide and the brilliant sunlight made a silhouette of the tall man entering. Eli Stroud held his Pennsylvania rifle in his left hand and carried an ironbound oak chest on his right shoulder. He set the rifle on the counter and used both hands to set the heavy chest beside it.

"Eli!" exclaimed Billy. He strode to the counter, followed by the other three, and thrust his hand out. "What . . . it's good to see you, but what are you doing here?" He turned. "You know Matthew, and Caleb."

"I do." They shook hands and exchanged greetings as Billy continued. "You remember Thomas Covington? The man who sold us the shipping business."

Eli and Covington nodded and shook hands.

Billy inquired, "What brings you back up here? Did things work out in New York?"

"They did. The barrister was as good as his word. Took a few days but he got the money delivered from the bank."

Relief showed in Billy. "Good. I thought you'd be well on your way back to Vermont by now."

"I would be, but I've been thinking." He pointed to the chest. "Nearly twenty-nine thousand British pounds sterling in there."

All eyes except Eli's locked onto the chest, and an electric feeling began in the plain, austere, slab-sided room.

"What would I do with twenty-nine-thousand pounds sterling up there in Vermont? What is there to buy?"

The room was deadly quiet.

"I've got a daughter to raise, but she won't need much, until she gets married. I thought I'd come back here and make an offer."

Billy saw it coming and his breath came short.

"I'll take a few pounds—maybe five hundred—on with me, and leave the rest of it here with you to run your shipping business. There will always be need for shipping on this coast, and the hard times can't last forever. If this money will see you through until things change, it seems to me you should become profitable. If you do, we'll agree on some fair way to repay the money and share in the profits."

For five full seconds no one spoke, and then Billy exclaimed, "You don't want to do that. The country's headed for more trouble, and things could happen. We could lose it all. No, you don't want to do that."

"Let me finish. I won't put it in a bank because banks are closing in every state. I don't know enough about farming to buy a farm, and I know almost nothing about manufacturing." He paused for a moment. "I don't know much about shipping either, but I think you men do. But that's not the main reason I came back here."

He stopped long enough to order his thoughts. "Things can happen. I could be gone in the next fifteen years. My sister Lydia and her husband Ben are good people. They'd see to it Laura was raised right, but neither one of them understands schools. Colleges. Matthew's been to college at Cambridge. Billy, you're trained in business. The reason I came here is that when Laura reaches school age, you two will see to it she has enough money to maybe go to college. Travel. Here. Europe. See things. Learn. Become more like her mother. Whether I'm still alive or not, you two will handle that better than I can."

The four men stood stone-still, stunned. Matthew broke the silence.

"No, Eli. We could lose it all. I couldn't live with that. I'll do anything I can to help you with Laura, but I can't be responsible for the money."

Eli's voice was steady. "Then what shall I do with it? Take a chance on burying it in the forest? The worst place I could put it now is in a bank. Any bank. Or invest it in any business. That leaves me hiding it in the cellar beneath the kitchen in Lydia's house, or burying it somewhere on the farm or in the woods."

Matthew shook his head and looked at Billy. "I've made my answer. You'll have to make your own."

Billy shook his head. "Eli, it's a fortune! Save it. Hide it if that's how you see it. I couldn't bear it if we lost it for you."

Eli raised a hand. "Then don't lose it! There's enough there to pay your bank note, if I remember right, and some left to pay for cargo. There are merchants looking for shipping. I doubt there are men more able to handle the business than you. Go ahead with your business. Just be careful."

It was too much, and it had come too fast. Not one of the four men facing Eli could find words.

Eli looked at them in turn. "Do you want time to think it over?"

Covington looked at both Billy and Matthew, but remained silent.

It was Caleb who raised a hand, pursed his mouth for a moment, and spoke casually to Matthew.

"What will you know tomorrow that you don't know right now?"

Matthew was wide-eyed. "Nothing. It just came on so sudden."

Caleb turned to Billy. "Will you be any wiser tomorrow?"

"I'll be a little more used to the idea."

A look of disgust crossed Caleb's face. "You two sound like a committee! It's time to quit talking and do something."

Eli waited a few moments before he concluded. "I've thought about this for a week. It's a good thing for both of us, but mostly me. I don't know of another way I can rest, knowing Laura will be taken care of. I'll wait a day if you want the time, but there's no reason for it."

Covington cleared his throat. "You asked me to stay on so I could advise against mistakes. I think Eli's offer is sound. Good for everyone. The trouble is it came too suddenly, and it seems too good to be true. That will pass. I advise you to take it."

Billy turned to Matthew. "What do you think?"

"At first I thought no. Now I'm not so sure. You?"

"I think Thomas is right. It came too fast and sounds too good. But it's sound. It could be good for everyone."

Matthew took charge of his reeling thoughts. "All right. I agree to it."

Billy turned back to Eli. "One thing I insist on. We go to the lawyer and have him put all this in writing so no one misunderstands. A copy has to go to Ben and Lydia so they know the money's here if they ever need it."

Eli nodded. "Agreed."

Eli picked up his rifle, Billy and Caleb took the handles on either end of the chest, and the five of them walked out of the office and turned east, toward the law office. Covington paused long enough to lock the door, then hurried to catch up. Dockhands slowed and stared at five men striding on the waterfront, one with a rifle, two carrying a strong box between them.

A stout woman with a round face and her hair pulled back in a ball behind her head gaped when the door to the law office of Robert Strand swung open and five men walked in. It was the one dressed in beaded buckskin and carrying the long rifle, with a black tomahawk shoved through his belt, that stopped her breathing for a moment and turned her face pasty white.

She addressed them all, but her eyes never left Eli. "You had an appointment?"

Billy answered. "No. But we need to see Mr. Strand as soon as possible."

"You'll w-w-wait here, please. I'll inquire."

She flew across the small room, through a door, and it slammed shut. Inside, the woman threw a hand to her heaving breast as she blurted, "Mr. Strand, there are five men out there. One has a musket. A big one. And a tomahawk. Like an Indian. And they've got a big box. Chest. They demand to see you. Shall I run for the constable?"

Strand, small, intense, with busy eyes that never stopped moving, asked, "Who are they?"

"I recognize two of them. The one with the musket and the one with reddish hair. They were here a few weeks ago. You wrote a statement for them to sign."

Strand's eyes narrowed as he forced his memory. "Billy Weems? Built strong? Sandy hair? And a tall man in leather?"

"Yes. Billy Weems."

Strand stood and followed her into the outer office. In the two seconds it took him to cross the small room he took an impression of each man.

"Mr. Weems. Nice seeing you again. Is there something I can do for you?"

"Yes. We need a paper."

Strand gestured. "Stand the uh . . musket over there in the corner, and come on in."

One minute later the five stood in front of Strand's desk, him facing them from his side.

Strand fussed with his watch in his vest pocket. "What's this about a paper?"

Billy and Caleb set the chest thudding on Strand's desk, and gestured. "This is Eli Stroud. We were here not long ago. You wrote a paper for him to take to New York."

Strand nodded grandly. "I remember. Of course."

"Mr. Stroud's back, and wants to deliver this money to myself and Mr. Dunson to be used as we see fit, provided we take care of his daughter when she reaches an age for college and travel."

Strand stared at the oak chest, with the heavy black iron straps and the huge lock. "I see. That's called a trust agreement. How much money?"

"About twenty-nine thousand British pounds sterling."

Strand froze, then dropped into his chair, staring. "How much?"

"About twenty-nine thousand British pounds sterling."

Strand cleared his throat and by force of will tried to assume an attitude of nonchalance. "Of course. Well, be seated, gentlemen. I'll have to get all the details. There are more chairs outside. Hmmmmm. Twenty-nine thousand pounds. British sterling. I can see why you carry that . . . uh . . . musket out there, Mr. Stroud."

Notes

The events and characters depicted in this chapter are fictional.

CHAPTER XXXIII

Captain Theodore Pettigrew stopped in the archway to the tiny kitchen in his small Boston home while he thrust his arms into his coat and worked with the brass buttons. His wife turned to him while she shaved curls from a bar of brown soap into a wooden tub of steaming water on the cupboard, stirred with the knife, then lowered the breakfast dishes into the froth.

"I don't know when I'll be home," he said. "Matthew couldn't say."

Clad in a common gray work dress, dark hair held back from her pretty, heart-shaped face by a white bandanna, Dora Pettigrew stopped to scoop up the baby who had crawled to grasp her skirt, whimpering. There was a sense of near desperation mixed with guarded hope in her eyes. "Do you think it might be work?"

Pettigrew's face clouded. "Don't know. Maybe." His upper lip and chin were both too long, and his eyes seemed cavernous beneath large brows. His arms and legs were sinewy and his wrist bones seemed far too large; altogether he seemed slightly awkward, uncoordinated. Yet the impression faded when things had to happen. Some could remember the day mutiny erupted among sailors aboard a ship under his command. Pettigrew strode into the four mutineers, and in less than one minute, two of them were unconscious on the deck, while the others were backing away, staring at their captain in white-faced shock. No one ever thought of him as handsome, yet, when one looked into those gray eyes, appearance faded. They were the eyes of a man honest to the bone and without fear of standing on right principle. It was the honest, principled man Dora had fallen in love with and married, not the one with the long face who danced woodenly.

"I hope it's work," she said fervently.

"I think it might be," he said. "Don't fix for me until I'm home."

She followed him across the parlor to the front door and watched him walk out into the incomparable beauty of Boston in the spring. Birds, squirrels, trees in full leaf, flower beds inside white picket fences, carts and buggies and people moving in the streets with hearts light and full in the sure knowledge that the gray, dead cold of winter was past and life had been renewed once again. He turned to exchange waves with her and was gone. He walked rapidly, with purpose, the few blocks south to the waterfront, saying nothing, acknowledging those who nodded a Boston greeting to him. He slowed as he came to the weather-beaten, unpainted office with the sign above the door, walked in, and stopped.

The sharp smell of printer's ink filled the room, and in the far left corner of the worn business room stood a printing press with its tray in place, filled with lead letters, and the press-plate raised on the great screw with the cross-arms on top. A large wooden box was shoved against the press, half filled with ink-smeared papers loosely thrown in. Two rags black with ink smears were crumpled on the print-tray. On the floor next to the wastepaper box was a second smaller box with sheets of precut paper, ready for the press. There were three desks in the sparse room, all worn and marred, and each was now piled with paperwork. The grime had been washed from the windows, and the spring sunlight streamed in to make odd-shaped shafts of light on the counter and floor. Pettigrew proceeded toward the counter, questions plain on his long face.

Matthew rose from his chair behind his desk. "Captain. Glad you could come. Bring a chair and sit with us."

Billy, Covington, and Caleb all stood to shake his hand, then Billy held the gate up for Pettigrew to enter, and all four men sat down facing Matthew. Each sensed a quiet, expectant excitement.

"How's Dora and the children?"

Pettigrew smiled. "Good. She sends her greeting."

Matthew pursed his mouth for a moment. "Things have changed since last we all met here. Let me put all the pieces out and see where we are."

Caleb settled back in his chair, listening, waiting, eyes half closed, and Matthew began.

"A friend—Eli Stroud—delivered a large sum of money for our use for about the next ten or twelve years."

Pettigrew straightened, eyes narrowed, scarcely breathing.

Matthew went on. "We paid off the bank note. This company is debt-free."

Pettigrew started. "Altogether? No debts of any kind?"

"None. We also have possession of the *Jessica*."

"How?" He turned to look at Caleb.

Caleb looked back at him and raised a hand, palm flat toward Pettigrew. "Not me! I didn't go get her. They paid the taxes. Both states. Virginia and Maryland."

Pettigrew's head swiveled back to Matthew. "If I might ask, just how much money did Eli Stroud deliver?"

"Just over twenty-eight thousand pounds British sterling."

Pettigrew's face drew down. "How did he get it?"

Matthew smiled. "Honestly. His wife's estate."

Pettigrew exhaled in relief and made instant calculations. "If I remember, the bank note was sixteen thousand pounds. That leaves you with something over ten thousand pounds."

Matthew answered, "That's why you're here." He turned to Billy. "What offers do we now have to carry cargo?"

Billy spoke slowly. "Four. Good ones. Reputable merchants. Manufacture going to southern buyers, cotton and tobacco and indigo coming to northern buyers. Banks will finance it if we guarantee payment in the event a buyer defaults. If that happens, we pay, but we also own the cargo. We have secondary buyers who have guaranteed to take the merchandise at a fifteen percent discount if the primary buyer fails and we have to buy it. To cover that possibility we've added the usual four percent fee for carrying all cargo."

Pettigrew leaned forward, his deep-set eyes narrowed. "Right now, I doubt there's a shipping company in Boston that can match it!"

Billy nodded. "Today, right now, we have enough contracts to keep two of our ships working for at least six months. Within sixty days, it looks like we'll have enough additional carriage business to keep all six ships working for at least the next nine months. Until early spring of next year."

Pettigrew was astonished. "Six? You'll be the biggest carrying trade in Boston."

"Likely. Probably in Massachusetts." Billy stopped for a moment. "Tom's had more experience than most in these matters. He's the one that put this all together over the past month." He turned to Thomas Covington, round-shouldered, gray-haired, wizened with the hard-earned experience of a thousand shipping transactions.

"What's your opinion?"

None doubted Covington. "It's sound. It conforms to all accepted rules of the trade. If you're careful, you'll be profitable from the day you start. Within one year you'll be established."

Pettigrew sat stock-still as his mind stretched to accept the truth of the unbelievable picture that had been thrust upon him in less than five minutes. "What did Eli Stroud want in exchange for the money? Does he own the company now?"

"No," Matthew answered. "We repay him in about twelve years. Right now the problem is finding crews to operate six ships."

Pettigrew came to an intense focus, waiting.

"Can you get the captains and the crews to operate our ships? Two now, and four within the next two months?"

For a moment Pettigrew reflected before he spoke directly to Matthew. "I thought you would be the one to do that."

Matthew shook his head. "We'll come to that in a minute. Right now the question is, can you do it?"

Pettigrew lowered his head and for several seconds studied the worn floorboards before he raised his eyes to Matthew. "Yes. I can."

"You will be the one to handle the crews and the ships. I'll be here to back you up. You will be paid a salary, plus the usual percentage of profits if there are any. Is that agreeable?"

"What salary?"

"Whatever is fair. You can work that out with Tom. He knows such things."

"That's agreeable."

"Do you need any money now?"

Pettigrew shook his head. "No. But could I ask why you're not the one handling the ships and crews?"

Matthew shifted in his chair. "I spent some time with Thomas Jefferson. He showed me maps of new states that are being considered, reaching west to the Mississippi River. He talked about changes in our laws and in the government—changes that will take the country in a whole new direction. He advised me—nearly ordered me—to become part of what he called a Committee of Correspondence."

Pettigrew interrupted. "A government committee?"

"No. Volunteer citizens."

"To do what?"

"Learn what's happening in each state. What's going right, and what's going wrong. Exchange ideas. Experiences. Wake people up to the hard fact that changes must come, or the United States is doomed."

Pettigrew leaned back in surprise. "That's a pretty strong statement."

"Yes, it is. The question is, is it true? Jefferson and Madison and other leaders think so."

"You intend mixing into all that somewhere?"

"Yes. If Jefferson and the others are right, there's little sense to building a shipping company that could be lost in ten or fifteen years when the United States dissolves and the disputes between them come to shooting."

Pettigrew's forehead wrinkled. "The leaders think that could happen?"

Matthew nodded. "It's already begun. And I don't intend spending my life building something that will be lost when it happens. I intend doing what I can to avoid that, and Jefferson suggests that survival of a united country will likely come down to waking up the citizenry to the fact they must change or lose it all."

Matthew stopped and gave Pettigrew a little time, then went on. "To do that we're trying to find out if Boston has a Committee of Correspondence, and we're contacting other states and cities with the same question." He gestured to Caleb. "He's had experience in a newspaper office, and writing. Does well with both. He's agreed to handle the printing and the mail."

Pettigrew glanced at the printing press, then back at Matthew and asked, "Who are you contacting?"

"Leaders who should know what's going on in their states. They should have names and addresses." Matthew turned to Caleb. "Got a copy of the letter?"

Caleb quickly went to the printing press and returned with a paper, laid it before Matthew, and took his seat. Matthew scanned it and slid it across the desk to Pettigrew. "We distributed this last week."

Pettigrew sat back in his chair and read the curt document carefully, thoughtfully, and realized he had never seen one like it. For the first time in his memory, he was looking at an attempt to reach beyond the strata of society that had always held the power of government and affairs, to the mainstream of lesser-known citizens, who did the work and paid the bills that held society and the country together.

"Which leaders? Which members of Congress?"

"Most of them. And the governors. George Washington also."

Pettigrew stared in amazement. "Any answers?"

"Too soon for answers."

Matthew changed directions. "Our ships will carry messages sometimes, depending on need and whether we have a ship going the right direction. You will be involved in that."

Pettigrew fell silent for a moment. "If all this comes together, will this office be big enough?"

Billy answered. "No. We've been looking for more space. There are two possibilities right now. Others may be coming. We'll handle it."

Pettigrew took a moment to put it all together, then suddenly chuckled. "I would never have believed all this. Within days of losing it all, and now you can't see the end of it. Getting into the committee business. Letters to congressmen and governors, and General Washington." He shook his head in wonderment. "Hard to believe."

"Sometimes I can't believe it myself." Matthew sobered. "We've got to remember, this isn't going to be easy. Many of the men who are looking so far ahead have a vision different than the others. There'll be conflicts. Troubles. We've got to keep our heads clear if we hope to find a way through it all."

Pettigrew leaned forward. "What conflicts?"

"Two I know of already. One's slavery. The other is fear of powerful government."

Caleb stirred and said quietly, "I'll have a bit to say about slavery."

Matthew turned to him with the clear image in his memory of the sick, soul-wrenching stench and sight of the dead and dying in the three feet of filth in the hold of the Dutch ship *Helga,* and of sixty-six black bodies floating face down in the Atlantic, off the Virginia coast. He said a single word to Caleb.

"Primus?"

"Yes. And that Dutch ship two years ago, *Helga.* And Stenman."

Pettigrew wondered, but did not ask. He stood. "Do you want me to start gathering two crews now?"

"Yes. Billy or Tom can show you the dates and ports and cargo that we have to start with."

"Good."

Matthew stood. "This conference is over. You men go ahead. Caleb and I have a few things to finish for the next letter."

Pettigrew hesitated for one second. "Dora isn't going to believe all this."

Matthew smiled. "Kathleen doesn't believe it yet."

Caleb rocked onto his feet and said, "Might want to wait to count the profits. Things have a way of going their own direction. Most shipwrecks are not part of anyone's plan."

Notes

The identification in this chapter by Matthew of the two heaviest problems facing the United States in 1784 were correctly stated as the issue of slavery and of the need for a powerful central government (Bernstein, *Are We to Be a Nation?*, pp. 5, 161–71).

Boston

September 1784

CHAPTER XXXIV

*T*hey came in an ancient, empty, battered farmwagon drawn by two old brown mares, clattering onto the Boston waterfront in the morning sun of a warm, late-summer day. Four bearded men in threadbare clothing and worn-out shoes, with hands too big and hard from lifelong toil with plow and pitchfork and scythe, faces burned by summer suns and winter snows and set like death, paying no attention to the dock laborers who slowed and stopped to stare.

The driver hauled back on the lines and growled his "hoooo" to the horses, then wound the leathers around the brake pole and the four of them climbed down. They hung half-empty nose bags on the horses before they entered the office with the sign DUNSON & WEEMS SHIPPING above the door, gave their eyes a moment to adjust, and stood waiting at the counter.

At the sound of the door opening, Matthew rose from his desk and walked to the counter, a question in his eyes at what were plainly four inland farmers in the office of a Boston harbor shipping company at a time they should have been at home in the beginning days of harvesting their all-important crops. Billy raised his head at his desk to listen, but did not rise. In the far left corner, Caleb stopped working with the printing press and reached for a dirty rag to wipe his hands while he watched.

"Is there something I can do for you?" Matthew inquired.

A lean, wiry man just shorter than Matthew, with deep-set eyes that glowed with intensity, answered.

"We're looking for Dunson. Matthew Dunson."

"I'm Matthew Dunson."

The man offered his hand. "I'm Nathan Tredwell. From Springfield. Glad to make your acquaintance."

Matthew shook the sinewy grip, and felt the strength. "I am happy to know you, sir." He waited while the man gestured to those beside him.

"This is Hosea Abrams, and this is Thomas Marsing, and this is Ezekiel Ottoman."

Matthew shook their hands in turn, nodded his greeting, and turned back to Tredwell, waiting.

"Are you the Matthew Dunson who sent a letter to Springfield about a committee?"

"The Committee of Correspondence? Yes. I did."

"That's why we're here. Things is happening over that way. Bad things. We don't know what to do about it, and a lot of us who's been hurt held a meeting and decided four of us ought to come tell you. Maybe you can do something."

Billy leaned back in his chair, not missing a word. Caleb stood silent, unmoving.

Matthew asked, "You own land over there? Farms?"

"Yes. Well, all except Thomas. Looks like he's about to lose his."

Matthew glanced at Thomas Marsing. The man's eyes were flat, emotionless, and the expression on his face did not change.

Matthew turned back to Tredwell. "Is that what brought you here?"

"That and more." He took a breath and began a recital in the brief, spare way of men whose lives have demanded toil, not words.

"Three weeks ago the sheriff come to Ezekiel and took the last hundredweight of flax he had, to collect a debt. Fifteen days ago the sheriff come to Hosea and took his sow and pigs. Meat for the winter. Gone."

Matthew interrupted. "To collect a debt?"

"Yes. Last week he come to take my oxen. Both of 'em. Without oxen

I can't work my land. Plow and plant and harvest. Can't do it without the oxen."

"Did the sheriff take them?"

"No, sir, he didn't. I stood him off."

"How?"

"Musket."

"Shooting?"

"No. Just had it in my hand. Same musket I carried in the war. Hosea and Thomas and Ezekiel and me, we was all in the war. We was at Saratoga, and down at Yorktown. We still got our muskets, but that's all we ever got out of four years with the Continentals."

"Has the sheriff come back to arrest you?"

"No. But he said he was. He's not a bad man. He knows he ought not be doing all this, but he says the law's the law, and he's got no choice, and he's right. He knows he takes my oxen, I lose the farm. So far he's stayed away to give me a chance. That's why we come here."

"What can I do to help?"

"Come with us. Come on to Springfield. See what we're facing."

"What are you facing?"

It was clear that it pained Tredwell to recite it all. "When we was mustered out of the army, we was given paper that said we would get paid. We went back to our families and started working our farms, and we waited like they said, but we didn't get paid nothing. We didn't have money to buy seed to get started, so we got an agreement with the merchants that we could pay for the seed with crops. That was fair."

He stopped to lick dry lips and order his thoughts. "Then the big merchants said we couldn't do that any more. We had to pay in gold or silver because they had to pay their debts to banks in Boston and New York and England and Holland in gold and silver. We didn't have it. We had a written promise, and we had paper money from both Congress and the state of Massachusetts that turned out to be worthless, but no gold or silver. We told them we could only pay with crops, and that was our agreement, but they went to the politicians and got the laws changed."

Caleb walked quietly to the end of the counter and stood still, not interrupting.

Tredwell continued. "Most of us over near Springfield is farmers, and it wasn't long before we found out that we was all having the same trouble. Couldn't pay the debts we had to take on while we was away doing the fighting. We couldn't pay, and we wouldn't leave, so the merchants started hiring lawyers. We was forced to go to court. None of us could hire lawyers because we had no way to pay. We went to court alone, but the judges wouldn't listen to us. They kept foreclosing on the farms and ordering the sheriff to come take our livestock and property, and there was nothing we could do."

The three men around Tredwell moved their feet on the floor, and their hands on the counter, and then settled as Tredwell went on.

"We sent two men over to the legislature here in Boston for help. The politicians in the legislature talked good and was quick to say we was right, and promised us everything we was askin', but we real quick found out the legislature is owned by rich merchants and lawyers. Matter of fact, half them politicians is the very rich merchants and lawyers that's taken away our farms and property. Our two men come real close to throwin' a few of 'em out into the street."

Tredwell stopped once more to gather his thoughts. "We all got five, six kids. We cleared the land where we live. We own those farms. We earned 'em. We left them for the women and kids to take care of the best they could while we went to fight for the United States while most of them lawyers and politicians stayed home. We're the ones that faced the British army to save this country, and now we're home findin' out our own politicians are taking away what little we have left. They're getting fat on what they're stealing from us! It isn't right!" His fist hit the counter top and everyone jumped. "By the Almighty, *it isn't right.*"

Matthew waited for a moment to let Tredwell settle. "You think I can help?"

"I don't know. That's why I'm here. You sent that letter to Springfield, and it was passed around. I read it. It sounded like you was not a politician or a lawyer, and that you might have an interest in what's right and what's wrong."

Matthew nodded. "Has anyone organized a committee over there? Appointed someone to speak for you?"

"Yes. Us." His eyes narrowed. "Meanin' no offense, our first question is whether or not you favor the politicians and lawyers. If you do, we're wasting your time and ours. So, sir, we'd be beholden if you'd tell us truly."

Matthew spoke quietly as he pointed. "This is my brother, Caleb. This is my business partner, Billy Weems. We were all three in battles, including Yorktown. All we want is to see this country become what we fought for."

Tredwell slowly straightened. "We liked your letter. Things over at Springfield is worse than what I can tell you. We come to find out if you are serious enough about all this to come see for yourself. All I can say is, someone better come soon or there's going to be shootin'. Killin'."

Billy stood and came to the counter to stand beside Matthew, but said nothing as Matthew answered.

"I can't come. We've got six ships carrying cargo, and Billy and I have to be here, at least through the winter."

A look of contempt crossed Tredwell's face. "Thanks for your time." He started to turn when Matthew spoke, and he stopped.

"Caleb is in charge of the Boston Committee of Correspondence. He's had newspaper experience, and he wrote regimental journals for the army. He's qualified." Matthew turned to Caleb, still standing at the end of the counter, sleeves rolled up, a badly spotted printer's apron tied around his waist, hands speckled with printer's ink, and the rag on the counter in front of him.

"Can you go with these men?"

Caleb considered. "For how long?"

"As long as it takes."

"Starting when?"

"Now."

Caleb looked at Tredwell. "I'll come."

Tredwell turned startled eyes to Matthew. "We can't pay."

"I know that," Caleb answered.

"You'll come anyway?"

"When do you want to leave?"

Tredwell looked at Hosea, then Thomas. "We can still make fifteen, twenty miles today."

Caleb reached back to untie his apron. "I'll need to go home to get some clothes and things."

One hour later Caleb strode up to wagon where the four men sat waiting. He dropped his bedroll inside, then carefully laid his Deckhard rifle beside it, wrapped and tied in canvas. "I'll be a few minutes inside," he said, and entered the office. Both Matthew and Billy rose from their desks to meet him.

"Ready?" Matthew asked.

"I'll need a little money to pay my way. I can't take food from their families. And some paper and a pencil."

"How much money?"

Caleb shrugged. "Fifty, sixty pounds."

Billy turned quizzical eyes. "That much? For what?"

"Maybe buy two oxen. Maybe save a farm. You can hold it out of my wages."

Matthew nodded, Billy counted out the silver, and Caleb put it into his leather purse and dropped it into his coat pocket as he spoke to Matthew.

"I told Mother I'll be gone three weeks or more. Might want to look in on her once in a while."

Matthew handed him several sheets of folded paper and a lead pencil.

"Come back as soon as you can. Did I see you put your rifle in the wagon?"

Caleb nodded as he slipped the paper and pencil into his inside coat pocket. "You did."

"That worries me. Don't start trouble."

"I won't."

Matthew pointed a finger. "You be careful."

"Always." Caleb's reckless grin flitted and was gone. He turned and walked out the door into the brilliant fall sunlight and effortlessly vaulted into the wagon bed. Tredwell slapped the reins on the rumps of the horses, clucked, and they moved with their huge, caulked iron shoes thumping on the black timbers of the docks, then throwing sparks as they clanged on the worn cobblestones. Tredwell hauled back with his right hand, and the wagon turned west, down the waterfront, to the street leading to the Neck that connects Boston Peninsula to the mainland. The horses and the heavy farmwagon rumbling through the streets slowed traffic until the homes and buildings thinned and they passed through the narrow land passage and were on a dirt road that wound through the spectacular beauty of a Massachusetts forest bedecked in full fall colors.

They nooned with the sun just past its zenith, in a stand of oak and maples, near a small, clear stream, and unhooked the traces to let the horses graze in their harnesses before they hooked them back up and jolted on in the springless wagon. They spoke little, in the way of men who life had trained to value results, not talk. As the sun continued its westward journey, each of the four men glanced at the canvas-wrapped rifle, then at Caleb, but said nothing.

Purple dusk had fallen before Tredwell reined the wagon off the road into a small clearing and pulled the horses to a stop twenty feet from a brook. Frogs in the cattails and bogs had begun their evening chorus as the horses were unhitched, unharnessed, hobbled, and set to grazing. The campfire was burning, and overhead, nighthawks were performing their magic, gathering insects, when the men finished their meal of fried pork belly and potatoes. The moon was rising when they went to their blankets.

Sunrise found them eight miles further west, chewing jerked beef and dried apple slices as they moved steadily on, saying little, thinking much. Midmorning they slowed at the sight of an approaching man and a woman in dusty, threadbare clothing, pulling a cart loaded with family belongings and blankets and a little food. Beside the wagon walked a barefooted, husky boy, carrying a toddler strapped on his back, and behind the wagon trudged a young, slender girl with tear streaks down her dusty cheeks. They were moving east, and as they passed the wagon, none of them raised their faces nor called a greeting. Their eyes were downcast, and discouragement was plain in their faces. No one in the wagon spoke as they passed them in the road, but Caleb saw the set of Tredwell's jaw and the anger in his face as the wagon moved on.

Half an hour passed before Caleb asked, "Recognize them?"

Tredwell shook his head. "No. But I know them. Them, and a hundred more just like them. Worked all their lives on some small farm somewhere west of us, or maybe north. The man served in the army. Borrowed money to farm when he got home. Can't pay it. Lost everything. Everything. No place to go. He's headed for Boston, or maybe New Bedford. Thinks he might find work. He won't."

Caleb glanced at Hosea, then the others, and there was outrage in them, and they refused to meet his eyes. He settled back into his place in the wagon and remained silent as it rumbled west on the rutted road.

It was midafternoon of the second day that Tredwell slowed the wagon and pointed. Fifty yards south of the road, in grass and spring flowers, was a makeshift lean-to of canvas slung over freshly cut pine poles. Inside, away from the sun, a bearded man was crouched beside someone lying on a blanket spread over pine boughs. Nearby a barefooted girl just reaching maturity, wearing an ancient, patched dress that was far too large for her, struggled with a dirty-faced, wailing child scarcely able to walk, and three other young children who were dirty, barefooted, distraught, defiant. Their tattered clothing was soiled, their hair unkempt.

Tredwell came back on the reins and the wagon stopped. Without a word the five men climbed down and walked toward the lean-to. They were ten yards away when they heard the cry of a newborn. The bearded man beneath the lean-to turned to look, then stood and came to face them. His eyes were blazing, face red, neck veins extended.

"You got it all," he exclaimed. "What have you come for now?" His arm raised and swung to point. "My wife? Children? The newborn?"

Tredwell raised a hand. "We aren't the sheriff or the law. We're from Springfield and headed home. Looked like you had trouble."

The man's face fell. "I'm beggin' your pardon for my bad manners."

Tredwell ignored it. "Sheriff sold your farm for debts?"

"Yesterday. Took all we had except what you see."

"You serve in the army?"

"Three years."

"The debt—was it to start farming again?"

"Seed."

Tredwell clenched and relaxed his jaw. "You have a newborn? When?"

"Last night. Nettie—my daughter over there—helped. Hard birth. Took somethin' out of all of us. Things is gone wrong with Sophronia, my wife. Bad. The pain won't go away. She's tried to nurse the new one but it's hard when the pain comes. We don't know what to do." There was pleading in his eyes.

"What's your name?" Tredwell asked.

"Asel Harriman."

"Can we take a look?"

Harriman stepped aside, and Tredwell approached the lean-to, Caleb beside him. They dropped to their haunches beside the moaning woman who lay holding her baby to her breast. The wrinkled, red-faced infant was wrapped in a scrap of blanket, wailing, tears running. The woman's hair was stuck to her forehead with sweat, and her eyes were clenched and her mouth clamped shut with pain. Caleb reached to gently lay his hand on the forehead of the writhing baby, and it was hot, fevered. He looked at Tredwell, and the two rose to their feet.

Tredwell asked Harriman, "You got any family nearby?"

Harriman shook his head. "Nearest is Northampton. A cousin. He's got trouble too."

Caleb gave Tredwell a head-signal and walked five yards toward the wagon where the two stopped, and Caleb spoke in a low voice.

"They're both going to die if we don't get help. How far is Northampton?"

Tredwell answered, "Four, five days. Too far."

"How far to the nearest town?"

Tredwell gestured north. "Framingham. Maybe eight, ten miles."

"A doctor?"

"I don't know. I doubt it."

"Any other towns?"

"Not near."

"I'll need one of your horses."

"You going for help?"

"Yes. Get this family busy. Get a cook fire started and heat a kettle of water. Put whatever you can find into it for a meal. Get a rag and some cold water in a pan and have Harriman keep that baby cool. I don't know what to do for the mother. I'll get back as soon as I can with whatever help I can find."

Caleb trotted back to the wagon, vaulted into the box, seized the reins, and gigged the horses into a trot to within twenty yards of the lean-to, and pulled them to a stop. He dropped to the ground and unwrapped his rifle, then unharnessed the nearest horse, except for the halter. He mounted her bareback and with the coiled reins in one hand and his rifle in the other, he kicked her into a shambling lope, with her huge hooves kicking dirt and dust at every stride.

Tredwell watched him out of sight, then turned back to the lean-to and gave orders. With the sun steadily moving west, the campsite began to take shape. A cook fire was built while Harriman led Tredwell to his old, spavined horse, hidden behind a thicket of scrub oak, next to his wagon, which had a cracked rear axle. Inside were clothing and four blankets and a few cooking utensils they had grabbed before the sheriff could get them. They dug out a smoke-blackened, dented kettle, filled it with water from a stream, and hung it above the fire. Nettie got a piece of torn rag and a canteen of water and bathed the fevered baby. Four withered potatoes with sprouts were rummaged and cut and stirred into the steaming water along with jerked beef strips and dried apple slices from Tredwell's wagon.

With the sun touching the western hills, Tredwell turned anxious eyes north, watching for movement that would be Caleb. The last golden rays of the daylight were fading before a buggy drawn by a sweated bay gelding came cantering east on the road with Caleb at the reins, a man beside him and two women riding in the seat behind, with Tredwell's tired mare tied behind, sides heaving as she labored to keep up. Caleb reined the bay off the road and pulled it to a halt near Tredwell's wagon. He dropped to the ground and helped the women down, then led them to the lean-to with the man following. Without a word one woman knelt beside Sophronia to touch her forehead while the other took the baby in her arms. The baby was still weakly crying, but there were no tears.

"Why," exclaimed the woman, "this child has no moisture left in its body! It will die!"

She stood and walked back to the buggy where she sat on a seat, turned her back to those at the lean-to, worked with the buttons on her dress, and within seconds the famished baby was nursing desperately.

Back at the lean-to, in deepening dusk, the second woman was on her knees beside Sophronia, who lay on her side, knees drawn up in pain, moaning, eyes closed. The woman straightened the legs and turned her on her back, then spread her hand on Sophronia's stomach and pushed. The groan could be heard for fifty yards. The woman reached for the pan of cool water and the rag, and began bathing Sophronia's face, talking to her gently.

"Can you hear me? Can you talk to me?"

Sophronia turned on her side and drew her knees up to her chest, moaning, and did not answer. The woman continued with the rag and cool water.

Caleb spoke to Tredwell, loud enough for all to hear.

"There's no doctor in Framingham. This is the Reverend Christopher Byland and his wife Druscilla. She's been a midwife for twenty-five years. The woman with the baby is an afternurse. Her name is Phyllis Earl. It's the best I could do."

Druscilla Byland turned to Harriman, and there was strain on her face and in her voice. "Did she deliver the afterbirth?"

Asel looked at his daughter. "Did she, Nettie?"

Nettie's chin quivered, near tears. "What's afterbirth?"

Druscilla cut her off. "You'd know if she did. It means it's still inside. We have to get it out." She drew a deep breath and gave curt orders. "Get some sheeting, or a shirt, or something. Hot water. Two or three blankets. Butter or lard if you have any. A box or a piece of tarp I can throw away. And get some light over here. Now!"

Within two minutes everything she asked for was beside her, except lard or butter; there was none.

She spoke sharply. "Nettie, I'll need you, and child, you'll have to be brave. You can't cry. Just watch me and listen and do what I tell you. We might save your mother if you'll do that. Will you do it?"

Nettie swallowed her fear and nodded her head.

Druscilla looked at Tredwell. "Take the men and children away from here and don't come back until I say, no matter what."

The men turned, gathered the frightened children, and without a word followed Tredwell south, into the darkness, away from the lean-to.

Druscilla went on. "Nettie, you get down on your knees on the other side of your mother and help me turn her on her back and get her legs up. You've got to hold her down if she fights. Then we've got to get her clothes off clear to her waist." She moved the single lantern to her side, and the light cast large, misshapen shadows on the inside of the lean-to.

"All right, Nettie. We're going to turn her."

They took hold of the arms and legs and when Druscilla nodded, they rolled Sophronia on her back. The groan brought the horses' heads around, eyes blood-red in the yellow lantern light. Quickly they drew the clothing from Sophronia, and Druscilla plunged her right hand into the hot water as she spoke to Nettie. "Now we're going to hold her legs and I'm going to have to push my hand right up inside your mother. I have to get the afterbirth out. The afterbirth is the placenta and the sac the baby was in before it was born. It should have come out right after the baby, but it didn't. Do you understand?"

Nettie swallowed hard. "Your hand? Inside?"

"Yes. Inside. It's going to frighten you. You have to be brave. Are you ready?"

"I don't know if I—"

"You can because you must, child. Now get hold of yourself."

She folded her fingers together and drew her hand from the hot water dripping, and steadily inserted it, eyes closed as she concentrated on everything she was feeling.

"I've got it!"

She withdrew her hand, and the afterbirth came with a rush. Nettie gasped but held her mother's leg. Almost instantly Sophronia relaxed and slumped, and the heartrending sounds of her pain stopped.

Druscilla wrapped it in the ragged piece of canvas tarp and set it in the dirt behind her. She washed Sophronia clean, then washed and dried her own hands.

"Now we've got to close the loin," Druscilla said, and Nettie looked at her in question.

"That means bandage her and wrap her tight."

With Nettie helping, Druscilla lifted Sophronia enough to pull the bloody blanket from beneath, and work a fresh one in its place, then settled the moaning woman onto it. With Druscilla guiding, they wrapped the midsection tight, then straightened her clothing and covered her with the second blanket. Sophronia turned quietly on her side, eyes closed, and her breathing deepened as she drifted into exhausted, peaceful sleep. Druscilla touched her face, then her forehead, then leaned close to speak to her.

"Can you hear me?"

The only response was the sound of slow, deep breathing.

Druscilla looked at Nettie, who was still on her knees, face white, eyes glassy with shock at what she had witnessed.

"Wash your hands, child," Druscilla said. "We've done all we can for now. If she doesn't get infection, she should be all right. That is in the hands of the Almighty. You did well. I'll be sure your mother knows."

Without a word Nettie washed and dried her hands, then stood and walked away to stand and stare into the darkness while her young mind struggled with things far beyond her maturity.

Druscilla called to the men, "You can come back now," and they came with the children to stand at the fire, waiting.

"We've done all we can. Her pain is gone and she's sleeping." She pointed. "One of you take that piece of tarp and what's in it, and bury it deep, far from here. It will draw foxes and panthers if you don't. This woman has lost far too much blood. She's going to need a thick broth of meat and fat when she wakes. She doesn't belong out here in a lean-to. She needs a bed, and someone to watch." She turned to her husband, waiting, and the Reverend Christopher Byland spoke.

"We don't have much, but we do have an extra bed in our cabin. She can come there. We can make beds in fresh straw in the barn for the rest of you."

The moon was rising over the eastern mountains when the reverend gigged his horses to a walk and led the way back to the road, a dull line winding through the black woods. The sleeping woman lay in Tredwell's springless wagon, propped on everything they had to soften the jolting. Harriman's wagon followed, with all the children sitting wide-eyed and silent as they slowly moved south through dark forests, listening to the sounds of the night. Midnight found them pulling rein on the horses in a small clearing just over half a mile from the tiny, darkened village of Framingham in eastern Massachusetts, where a small log cabin waited with dark windows. By one o'clock Sophronia lay slumbering on a small cot with a woven rope bottom and a great bag of dried corn husks for a mattress, jammed in one corner of the kitchen, while Harriman and his family and the four men with Tredwell spread blankets on fresh straw in the barn. Caleb stood his rifle in one corner, then walked back out the barn door, to the cabin. The reverend answered his soft rap.

"Is there a salt lick anywhere nearby in the woods?"

Byland's eyebrows raised in question. "West. Over half a mile. Why?"

Caleb shook his head. "Nothing. See you in the morning."

He returned to the barn and pulled off his boots while Tredwell turned down the wick on the lantern. For several seconds the world was blackness, and then dull moonlight filtered through cracks in the roof and walls to create a ghostly crosshatch of lines inside the barn while the men and the children settled onto their blankets, weary, unsure what tomorrow would bring.

The first gray of approaching dawn had separated sky from earth when the single sharp crack of a distant rifle brought Tredwell awake, wondering for a moment where he was. He sat upright while the others stirred and settled, and he peered into the gray darkness trying to understand that the faint sound of a rifle shot had awakened him. Seconds passed before he realized Caleb was gone, and his rifle with him. He settled back into his blanket while scenes and memories of yesterday and the night came back. He lay still for a while, working with his thoughts, waiting for the others to awaken. With sunrise approaching he heard the door to the house close, and minutes later the barn door squeaked and groaned as it opened, and the reverend entered. For a moment he stood still, before those inside stirred and rubbed sleep-filled eyes.

"I've got to tend the animals," he said.

The men tugged on their boots and within minutes had the indifferent Jersey cow in her stanchion, patiently grinding hay while the reverend balanced on his one-legged milking stool, buried his forehead in her flank, and began building a froth in a wooden milk bucket. The men were outside, feeding the sow in her pen when the reverend came trotting from the barn, voice raised in panic.

"The horse is gone! Someone stole the horse!"

It took Tredwell ten seconds to make the connections. "I don't think it was stolen. I think Caleb Dunson took it, and he'll be back soon."

"You sure?"

"We'll see."

They were shaking the straw from their blankets when the reverend's excited voice came high and shrill from the yard. "Look here! He's coming."

Caleb walked from the forest into the small clearing, leading the horse with one hand, his rifle in the other. Tied across the horse's back was a four-point buck deer, dressed and washed. With the others following he led the horse to the barn, untied the deer, and had Tredwell help him hang it from the low rafters.

Caleb turned to the reverend. "The liver and the heart and tongue are tied in the cavity. There ought to be enough fat and blood for the broth your wife spoke of last night, and fresh meat for the house for a time. Might want to get a pot set in your fireplace."

The reverend exclaimed, "Where did you . . ."

"I found the salt lick, and the spring nearby."

The reverend turned on his heel and trotted to the house, calling to his wife.

The sun was one hour high when Tredwell and those with him finished buckling their harnessed horses to the doubletree and climbed up into the wagon. Caleb raised a hand, and Tredwell waited while he walked back to enter the house. Inside Sophronia Harriman was sitting up, sipping steaming broth, while Phyllis Earl rocked slowly in one corner nursing the baby. The Harriman children all stopped to look at Caleb, while Druscilla stood beside her husband facing him.

Caleb spoke. "We need to be leaving. Is there anything else we can do before we go?"

There was nothing.

He drew his coin purse from his pocket and walked to the plain pinewood table to set five coins in a stack, then turned to the reverend. "There's ten pounds British sterling. Use it for a doctor if she needs one, and food until the Harrimans can travel." He thrust the purse back in his pocket. "That's about all."

Every eye in the kitchen was on the stacked coins. It was the first hard money any of them had seen in over two years. There were tears in Asel Harriman's eyes. "How do I repay?"

"Get her well, and raise that baby." He turned to Nettie. "You're a brave girl. Help your mother. Good luck to all of you."

The reverend said, "God bless you."

Caleb walked out the door and climbed into the wagon bed, wondering how God was going to bless him when there was an open question that God even existed. Tredwell raised the horses to a trot back to the road and turned west, with the warm spring sun on their backs and shoulders. For a very long time they rode in silence, working with their own anger and thoughts and recollections of the Harriman family, put off their farm with only a wagon with a cracked axle and a spavined horse and what few things they could hurriedly throw into the wagon box before the sheriff forced them off the only land and home they had known for twenty years. A woman beginning labor to deliver a child. Wide-eyed, terrified, barefooted children dressed in faded, worn hand-me-downs, who did not understand a sheriff and two armed deputies forcing them out onto the road, with no place to go and no way to get food without begging. The men rode in silence while outrage smoldered.

For three days they made camp late in the evening, broke camp with the morning star still high in the northeastern sky, and pushed the horses as hard as they dared down the dusty, rutted road that soon became little more than a trace in the high grass of fall. And they looked in silence at the two families that passed them, traveling east, with everything the sheriff had allowed them wrapped in blankets on their backs or loaded in an old worn wagon drawn by oxen. The men and women and children said little as they passed, and their eyes and faces were alive with fear.

On the fourth day, with the late afternoon sun in their faces, the four men from Springfield sat a little straighter and peered ahead. Caleb turned in question to Tredwell, who pointed and said, "You can see Springfield from that rise just ahead. Beyond, there's a line you can see in the forest. That's the Connecticut River. We're nearly home."

They crested the low hill, and the village, less than eight miles from the southern border of Massachusetts, stood small in the broad, shallow valley spread before them. Random clearings broke the gently rolling red and gold carpet of forest, where men and women had worked to cut timber, root out stumps, and clear the ground of hard Massachusetts rock to build homes and barns and plow and plant and raise their children. As the wagon descended the incline to the level valley floor and rolled on toward the hamlet, Caleb watched the faces of the men with him. They sat tall, peering intently at each farm and each person they passed. This was their valley, and the harvest was upon them; habit required them to know who had succeeded with their crops and who was failing in the battle for survival.

They were still three-quarters of a mile from Springfield when Tredwell came back on the reins and the horses stopped the wagon at a place where a trail wound through the trees toward a clearing and a cabin, visible one-quarter mile north. Ezekiel Ottoman dropped to the ground, and Hosea Abrams handed him his bedroll. Ottoman looked up at them and spoke to Thomas Marsing.

"Let me know what the sheriff does about your farm."

Marsing nodded but said nothing. Ottoman turned to Tredwell.

"I want to know about those two oxen."

"I'll see you at church tomorrow."

Ottoman bobbed his head, raised a hand in farewell, and strode rapidly north, anxious and fearful about his crop of wheat and oats. They watched him for a moment before Tredwell put the wagon in motion and rolled on toward the small scatter of buildings they called a town. A steepled church built of heavy planking painted white stood near the road and dominated all else. East of it was an ancient building of weather-blackened logs and mud chinking with traps and pelts hanging from nails on the outside walls and a badly carved sign above the door: WALLER TRADING. West of the church was a long, low log building with grass growing from sod on the roof and a sign above the plank door reading SHERIFF. Inside was the sheriff's office, a long room that served for holding court, and at the rear, a smaller room with barred windows that was used for a jail. Scattered about the village were a dozen log homes connected by dirt roads. At the north edge of town, away from the homes, were several large buildings, among them two with signs declaring them to be a federal foundry for casting brass cannon and an armory where thirteen hundred barrels of gunpowder, seven thousand muskets, and two hundred tons of shot and shell were stored for use by the Massachusetts militia and the Continental Army.

As they reached the east end of town, Tredwell stiffened, and Caleb heard the quiet "Oh-oh!" Instantly the others came to their knees to peer ahead, and Caleb saw their faces drop and their eyes narrow. It was an afternoon in harvest time, a time when people should have been harvesting their fields, not gathering in town. Yet, beyond the church, in front of the sod-covered building, were three wagons with horses standing hipshot while half a dozen men clustered near the door, voices raised in anger, fists clenched. Among the six, three carried ax handles, two carried pitchforks. Before them, backed against the door, were three men, two with muskets, the other white-faced as he shouted back at those confronting him.

Caleb looked at Tredwell in question, and Tredwell said, "The one against the door talking—the fat one with the beaver hat—is the sheriff. Name's Brewster. Gerhard Brewster." Tredwell raised the horses to a lope for the last hundred yards and pulled them to a halt in a cloud of dust behind the other three wagons while the gathering at the door turned to look. All four men dropped from the wagon and walked toward those clustered in front of the building.

"What's going on?" Tredwell demanded.

A man wearing the sweated, loose shirt and woolen trousers of a farmer shook his fist at the sheriff and pointed. "They got Banes! He's in there in jail! Debtors prison for sixty days. He's got forty acres of wheat and barley to get in, and they got him in jail!"

Tredwell started and turned to the sheriff. "You held court?"

"Now, Nathan," the sheriff started, "you know—"

Tredwell's voice was rising as he cut him off. "Answer! You held court?"

"Of course we held court. David Banes had his chance. He couldn't pay. The judge ordered him held in debtors prison for sixty days. Nothing I could do about it."

"What did Banes owe?"

"Uh . . . seventeen dollars, as I recall. Tried to pay with worthless paper, but Mullins wouldn't take it because he has to pay his bank in coin. Judge Devereaux read the law. Mullins is within his rights to demand coin, and if you can't pay, you go to debtors prison. Now, that's the law!"

"For seventeen dollars? During harvest?"

"Take that up with the judge."

"Where's Mullins?"

"Away."

"Away where?"

"That's not my business."

"What about Banes's wife? Abby? And his four kids? Where are they?"

"Out harvesting, last I heard."

One of the men behind Tredwell stepped forward, shaking an ax handle, voice choked with rage. "Let him out! Let him get his harvest in so's he can pay!"

The sheriff stood his ground, and his deputies with the muskets took one step forward. "You know I can't do that. The judge gave me an order."

A man with a pitchfork stepped forward, followed by two others with ax handles. His voice was loud, but steady.

"I'll sign for Banes's payment."

Brewster shook his head. "That's for the judge to decide. Not me. You know that."

The second man with a pitchfork stepped forward, the three wooden tines leveled forward, and his voice was even, devoid of emotion.

"Let him out or we'll take him out."

In an instant what had been a hot argument had become a deadly confrontation. Sheriff Brewster did not move, and the two deputies eared back the big hammers on their muskets and lowered the muzzles. For three seconds the men, armed with pitchforks and ax handles, opposed by cocked .75-caliber muskets, stood still, facing each other, waiting for someone to make the move that would set off the killing.

Caleb's voice came from behind. "How much to get him released?"

Brewster's head swiveled. "Who's talking?"

Caleb stepped forward. "How much?"

"You'll have to ask the judge. You people don't seem to understand. I'm only the sheriff. I don't decide things. The judge does."

"You better decide this one, or someone's going to get killed. Did you say seventeen dollars?"

Brewster glanced at the ax handles and the tines of the pitchforks, less than five feet from his own belly and those of the deputies. "Well, it seems to me the judge can't take it too poorly if the seventeen dollars was paid. No sense in holding a man if he's paid. And there's costs."

"How much for costs?"

"I'd have to go figure it."

Caleb drew two silver coins from his purse. "Here's twenty dollars in British sterling. That's the seventeen, and three dollars costs. Looks to me like you better think hard before you say no. It will be interesting to tell a judge that three or four men died while you had an offer of twenty dollars to avoid it. Remember. There's witnesses."

Brewster wiped at a dry mouth. "No sense in pushing this further." He took the twenty dollars and turned. "I'll go let him out."

"I'll need a receipt."

The sheriff's eyebrows raised. "Made out to who?"

"Make it out to Banes and give it to him."

The sheriff shrugged and disappeared into the office. Five minutes later the door opened, and David Banes walked out, blinking in the bright sunlight, holding a receipt in his hand. He was round-shouldered, bearded, and balding. He walked to Tredwell and stopped.

"Who paid?"

Tredwell pointed. "Him. Caleb Dunson."

Banes stared for a moment. "I know you?"

"No, sir."

Suspicion was plain on Bane's face. "Why did you pay?"

"We'll talk about it later." Caleb turned to Tredwell. "Any other reason to stay here? The sooner we leave, the better."

Tredwell raised a hand and everyone fell silent. "Let's get back to our farms. We learned some things in Boston. This man came back with us to see what's happening. We'll hold a meeting on Monday. After dark. At the church. Tell everyone you see."

Sheriff Brewster raised a hand and stepped forward, jowls quivering as he spoke. "Look here, Tredwell, you stir up trouble, and I'll have to come get you."

Tredwell turned, feet spread, and his voice purred. "You go tell that to Bernard Mullins. Him coming with court judgments right at harvest time so we can't harvest and get the money to pay him. Judge Devereaux lettin' him do it. You out here with those court papers in your hand saying you have to do what the judge says. Where was you and Devereaux and Mullins when the rest of us was away in the war? You was here getting things arranged to take our farms and our property."

Tredwell paused and for a moment Brewster blustered, then quieted, and Tredwell concluded.

"Seems like the courts and the law are whatever Mullins and Devereaux say they are. And that isn't right. The law is for everybody, and we're part of everybody, so we're goin' to see to it the law does what's right. Tell Mullins that. And Devereaux." He paused for one moment. "No, never mind. *We'll* tell 'em."

Tredwell turned on his heel and walked back to the wagon where his three companions were standing. The other men stood for several seconds, talking among themselves, then walked back to their wagons to leave the sheriff fuming at the door to his office. Behind, David Banes called to Caleb, "I'm obliged, mister." Caleb nodded in acknowledgment then climbed up to take his place in the wagon beside Marsing.

For the first quarter mile Caleb sat with his back to the side of the wagon, knees drawn up, caught up in deep thought about what had come very close to a killing. A merchant named Mullins had somehow come into control of a judge and a sheriff? He was out to ruin some poverty-stricken farmers by foreclosing on debts right at harvest time—to stop them from gathering the crops that might give them enough money to pay?

He felt the stirrings of a sense of injustice and of anger rise within him. This is why Tredwell had driven an old wagon from Springfield to Boston—five days each way—to try to find someone—anyone—who might help find a way out of the sick quagmire without bloodshed. And bloodshed was surely coming if Tredwell and his people failed.

Americans killing Americans.

With the setting sun full in their faces, Caleb spoke to Tredwell. "Who is Mullins?"

"A merchant. Speculator. From Philadelphia, I think."

"How many people owe him?"

"From around here, maybe fifteen, twenty. From other places, who knows? I know he has claims in courts clear up to Northampton and as far east as Worcester. From what I've seen, he's loaned his money mostly to farmers. I think he's after land."

"You owe him?"

"Yes." Tredwell paused. "When he came here he said he wanted to help. He'd work with us. We could pay with crops. Then when we took his loans, him and maybe a dozen others like him—rich men—got the legislature in Boston to change the law so that we had to pay in money. We could of done it, but then they said we couldn't pay in Massachusetts paper money or even Continental money. We had to pay in hard coin. There's not enough hard coin in the state of Massachusetts to pay what's owed. So now all us farmers is losing everything we own, and it's all legal."

He stopped for a few seconds, then added, "But it isn't right. And we're going to fix that, one way or another."

Caleb said, "You better be careful. The law is the law. You go above it, and you could start a war."

Tredwell didn't flinch. "That's what the British said. They lost."

The wagon rumbled on for fifteen minutes before Tredwell drew rein at a place where two ruts branched and angled south. Hosea Abrams and Thomas Marsing both dropped to the ground with their bedrolls.

Tredwell spoke to Abrams. "I'll bring your horses to church in the morning."

Abrams bobbed his head, turned, and was gone.

Tredwell nodded and gigged the horses, and the wagon rattled on. Caleb took the place beside Tredwell on the driver's seat, and fifteen minutes later Tredwell reined the horses north onto a trail that soon rounded a gentle curve that led into an arrangement of open farmyard, barn, and outbuildings to the left, low log cabin to the right. Moments later the barn door swung open and two boys who were the image of Tredwell burst out into the sunlight, stopped, then came trotting. The door to the house opened, and a woman of medium height, square shoulders, plain face, solid, walked out into the sunlight, wiping her hands in her apron. Behind her came two girls, younger than the boys, and they followed the woman as she strode toward the wagon. The woman and the children were all dressed in the rough garb of working farmers.

The boys reached the wagon first, and Caleb was startled when he could not tell them apart. They were identical twins.

Tredwell pointed to one, then the other, as he spoke. "Isaac and Jacob. This is Caleb Dunson. He's come to help."

The boys each thrust out rawboned hands that were too big and too hard for their seventeen years, shook Caleb's hand perfunctorily, and murmured, "I'm glad to make your acquaintance."

The woman approached, and the boys stepped aside as she came to her husband. She ignored Caleb for the moment it took to survey Tredwell. "You're all right?"

"Yes. Good. You?"

She smiled. "All right. Tired." She turned to Caleb, waiting, and Tredwell spoke. "This is Caleb Dunson, from Boston. He came with us to help where he can. This is my wife, Rachel." For the first time, Caleb saw the light of gentleness and warmth in Tredwell's bearded face as he spoke of his wife.

Rachel thrust out her hand and Caleb shook it. "I'm honored to meet you, ma'am."

Shy, unaccustomed to strangers, Rachel responded, "It is my pleasure, sir. I hope you can stay with us for a while."

"A day or two, thank you," Caleb responded.

The two younger girls, whom Caleb judged to be about twelve and ten, stood behind their mother, bashful in the presence of a stranger. Rachel turned. "This is Rebecca, the older one, and Ruth." There was pride in the mother's eyes.

The two girls nodded a greeting, and the older one said, "I'm happy to meet you," but neither offered their hands.

Rachel asked Isaac and Jacob, "Through in the barn?"

"Got to milk Troublesome. Then we're through."

Tredwell said, "Started the barley yet?"

"Tried this morning. Needs two more days of this sun before its ready."

"The pigs?"

"Got three down today, dressed. We'll salt 'em and get 'em in the vats in three days."

Rachel interrupted. "Finish with Troublesome and get washed. Supper will be waiting."

The sun had set when the boys walked into the kitchen to pour half the bucket of warm milk into two pitchers, and Isaac took what was left out into the root cellar to clabber for buttermilk. Caleb joined the men as they went outside to a washstand to pour tepid water and work with hard brown soap, then dry themselves on clean flour sacks. They ran a home-made, wooden comb through their wet hair and entered the kitchen.

This was Rachel's kingdom. In the fields and the barn, the men were king. In her kitchen, she was queen. They stood respectfully in the plain, log-walled kitchen amid the rich aromas of roast mutton and boiled vegetables and homemade bread, and butter churned by Rebecca and Ruth. Everything in readiness, Rachel pointed. Tredwell took his place at the head of the table, and then the others took their places, Caleb at the far end of the table, facing Tredwell. Without a word Tredwell clasped his hands and bowed his head, and the others followed, and Tredwell said, "For the bounties of this table we thank Thee, O Lord, and being safe together again. Bless us to use the strength from this food in doing Thy will. Amen."

They all repeated their "Amen" and reached for steaming bowls and platters. For a time they ate in silence before the talk began, and then it came in a flood. Tell us about the trip. Were there any Indians? How far is Boston? Did you see ships? Were there any British soldiers?

In the midst of the talk, Tredwell turned to Rachel. "You heard about David Banes?"

She set her fork down. "I heard he went to court. What happened?"

"Deveraux gave him sixty days in debtors prison."

Rachel gasped and everyone quieted as she asked, "Mullins? Was he behind it?"

"Yes."

"Right at harvest time? Judge Devereaux did that?"

"He did."

"Is Banes in jail?"

"He was until we got there this afternoon." He gestured toward Caleb. "This man paid his debt, and the sheriff had to let him go."

Rachel studied Caleb for a few moments. "That was a Christian thing you did."

Caleb bobbed his head and said nothing, while the twins stared at him in surprise.

Tredwell went on. "That's not all. When we got there, Brewster and two of his deputies were in an argument with half a dozen other farmers. They had ax handles and pitchforks, and things came close to a fight. That's when Dunson stepped in. If he hadn't, someone could have been hurt."

Rachel paused for a moment, then looked about the table. "Eat. Food's getting cold." The children scooped up food on their forks, but they said nothing as they hung on every word from their father.

"Things are getting bad." His expression mellowed for a moment, and as he continued speaking, Caleb sensed he was a torn man. "I know it isn't the sheriff's fault. Most likely it isn't Mullins's fault, either, or even Judge Devereaux's. It's just the way things has gone. Mullins's business is lending money that he got from banks. You follow that money, and it leads back to England, and Holland, and maybe Spain. I think the trouble all started when those foreign banks saw this country had only paper money, so they demanded to be repaid in hard coin. Figured they could hurt us and at the same time get land here. When they made their demand, Mullins had to get the hard money, and the only way he could do it was to do the same thing—make us pay in silver—hard coin we haven't got and can't get."

For a moment he stopped, and the room remained silent until he spoke again.

"But even if all that's true, we don't have a choice. I have to protect what we've got, no matter what. If we stand up to the sheriff and Mullins, maybe they'll stand up to those banks, and if that happens, maybe the legislature or even the Congress will do something. I don't know any other way."

He stopped again for a moment, then finished. "I called for a meeting Monday night, after dark, at the church. I expect a lot of people will be there. The sheriff knows about it. I hope he has better sense than to start something."

Rebecca murmured to her mother, "Can we go?"

Rachel said, "Your father will decide. Finish your supper."

Deep dusk had set in by the time the women finished the supper dishes, and Rachel called the twins. "Church tomorrow, baths tonight. Get the tubs out. Rebecca, get the towels and soap. Nathan, string the curtains."

Outside, the heavens were a black velvet dome filled with diamonds when Caleb got out of the huge wooden tub of lukewarm bathwater that had been used three times, dried himself off with clean flour sacks, and dressed behind the curtains. He helped the twins dip the bath water from the tub and throw it outside into the yard. In bright moonlight they rinsed the tubs at the well and leaned them against the wall of the shed where the family stored their scythes and pitchforks. When Caleb returned to the house he approached Tredwell, seated in his rocking chair before the fireplace, lost in thought as he stared into the dying remains of the fire.

"If it's all right, I'd like to sleep in the barn."

Tredwell showed surprise. "We can make a bed in here."

"I have writing to do. I'll need a lantern."

Tredwell's forehead wrinkled in surprise. "Writing?"

"Make some notes of what I saw today. While it's all there in my mind."

Tredwell shrugged. "As you wish."

It was close to midnight when Caleb put down his pencil and read the four pages he had written. Satisfied, he folded the papers, put them beside his shoes, turned the wick of the lamp down, and leaned back on his blanket. There was a slight rustle from the stalls where the two oxen lay, and then quiet, and Caleb drifted into a dreamless sleep.

Notes

For descriptions of the terrible circumstances that were ruining the farmers in Massachusetts as described in this chapter, see Bernstein, *Are We to Be a Nation?*, pp. 9, 70–71, 92–97 and Main, *The Sovereign States, 1775–1783*, pp. 452–54. For commentary on imprisonment for nonpayment of debts—debtors prison—see Nevins, *The American States, 1775–1789*, p. 456. For an excellent discussion of the practice of midwives and afternurses and "closing the loin," as herein described, see Ulrich, *A Midwife's Tale*, pp. 165–91. A federal foundry and armory had been built at Springfield to cast brass cannon and store munitions, including thirteen hundred barrels of gun powder and seven thousand muskets and two hundred tons of shot and shell, as described herein (Higginbotham, *The War for American Independence*, p. 447).

CHAPTER XXXV

★ ★ ★

*T*he henhouse rooster furiously flapped stubby wings to reach the roof of the caged chicken coop, strutted to the ridge beam, extended his neck, threw back his head, and crowed his greeting to the gray dawn of a new day. Caleb joined Tredwell and the twins in the sunup feeding of the animals and milking of Troublesome, helped hook the oxen to the wagon, then took his place at the table for a breakfast of griddle cakes and maple syrup and buttermilk. Rachel handed him clean trousers and a shirt that were tight-fitting and brushed his coat while he dressed for church with the boys. They all stood in the kitchen for her inspection, then walked out to the wagon where Tredwell helped her onto the driver's seat while the twins helped the girls into the wagon box with them and Caleb. On the ground, with the twelve-foot whip in hand, Tredwell called, "All ready," and the whip cracked over the heads of the oxen. The big splay-footed animals bowed their shoulders into the yoke and the wagon jerked into motion with Tredwell walking beside, where he would remain until they reached the church. Behind were the two horses Hosea Abrams had given Tredwell to use for the trip to Boston, haltered and tied, plodding along with resigned disinterest.

With the white church steeple showing above the trees a quarter mile ahead, the twins sat tall in the wagon, and the girls came to their knees, counting the buggies and wagons and saddled horses collecting in the village, identifying each. The twins searched for the young ladies of the valley, while the girls watched for their confidantes and friends. Caleb smiled at the realization that gathering at the church in this valley on Sunday was for a great deal more than worship. Gossip, courtship, births, deaths, illness, accidents, whose cow had calved, whose mare had foaled, who was wearing improper clothing, whose bonnet was too fancy, who had left, who had come—it was all whispered or exclaimed and added to or detracted from according to needs or whims until everyone was satisfied they knew the absolute gospel truth about everything and everyone else within twenty miles, notwithstanding that no version of anything matched any other version.

The Reverend Roger Bennett preached a starchy sermon on the Golden Rule, humbled them by his declaration that each of them was in some particular failing in this great commandment, delivered a resounding closing prayer, and services were concluded. The congregation filed out into the glorious sunshine, with the surrounding forest showing every color known to mankind. The women formed into little groups, and the buzzing began, with ladies passing from group to group, with no one being spared. Isaac and Jacob and two neighbor boys their same age accidentally found themselves near the well where blonde, blue-eyed, sixteen-year-old Mary Jane Westerman, with a large gap between her two front teeth, and three other girls her age were gathered. Mary Jane and the girls grinned their pleasure and blushed and ducked their heads when the boys approached and pulled off their old black felt hats and said, "Mornin'."

Rebecca and Ruth disappeared behind the church with half a dozen other girls their age, to giggle and exclaim and point and conjure up the most shocking ways their innocent minds could conceive to describe who had done and said what to whom, and why. Then they would shriek and throw their hands over their mouths and stare in feigned wide-eyed shock while their minds raced to invent new ways to make their startling contribution to the world of children, trying to be grown-ups.

The men gathered in the shade of the church, Caleb with them, to stand shifting their feet while they listened with stony faces to a recital of the arrest and jailing of David Banes, and they murmured aloud when Tredwell told of the anxious moments when five of the men with ax handles and pitchforks confronted the sheriff and two deputies with muskets in what could have exploded into mayhem. Heads turned to look at Caleb when Banes told of his twenty-dollar payment that prevented what could have been a disaster, and then Tredwell led them into a loud, warm, give-and-take exchange of how they should handle the meeting to be held the next night.

It was past noon when the women began to break away from their groups to find their offspring and husbands, and the wagons and buggies began to roll away in all directions. Caleb was aware that too many people were glancing at him, some quietly talking to those around them as they gestured toward him. He climbed into the Tredwell wagon and sat down, his back to the church, and waited for Tredwell to crack the whip and start the oxen for home. Hosea Abrams untied his two horses from the wagon, Tredwell nodded his thanks, and the whip whistled and popped.

The midday meal was ham and potatoes with bread and fresh cider, and when Rachel refused to let Caleb help clean up, he excused himself and went to his blanket on the straw in the barn to read his notes and add to them. He helped with the evening feeding of the livestock and milking of the old Guernsey cow, and once again went to his own blanket. In deep dusk, from somewhere to the west came the distant howl of a wolf, then another, and for a moment all else was forgotten as Caleb was irresistibly drawn to the ancient spell of the hunt. He saw in his mind the tireless pack, yellow eyes glowing, each taking their turn in the relay that would end in a trembling, exhausted deer or elk backed up to a rock or a tree stump, ready to fight a death battle it knew it could not win.

The law of this world: The strong kill the weak.

He stretched out on his blanket, jabbed at it until the lumpy straw beneath was smooth, then closed his eyes.

The morning eastern sky was gray when the barn door rattled and Tredwell entered. "Ready?"

Caleb followed him and the twins sixty yards north of the house, into the near edge of a twenty-eight-acre field of barley, heads full and golden-white in the oncoming sunrise. Tredwell and Caleb carried scythes, with whetstones thrust into their pockets. With the wisdom of a life spent learning the ways of nature, Tredwell reached to gather a handful of the heads, then clasped his palms together and rubbed them hard for ten seconds. He separated his hands, blew gently into the crushed mass, and watched the chaff lift and flutter to the ground. He opened his mouth to receive the clean, full heads and chewed them to a paste. Then he turned to the twins, eyes glowing.

"You were right. It's ready."

Without a word they walked to the west edge of the field, and Tredwell led out. Swinging his long, curve-handled scythe in the peculiar circular motion of one who knew, he started north, with the twins and Caleb behind, listening to the 'ping' sound as the blade sliced through the stalks. Caleb gave him a twenty-foot start, then followed, swinging his scythe next to the cut made by Tredwell. The twins gave Caleb a twenty-foot start, and then they began the monotonous, back-breaking labor of shocking the fallen stalks of grain—gathering an armload carefully to avoid knocking the heads loose, forming it into a bundle, using half a dozen stalks to wrap it, tying it, laying it down gently, then gathering the next armload, tying it, gathering the next, tying it.

Sweat was dripping by the time the sun rose, and chaff was sticking to their wet faces, necks, and arms. Tredwell and Caleb paused to run the whetstones five times down each side of the cutting edges of their scythes, then continue the rhythm of cutting. The sun was an hour high when Rebecca and Ruth came running, shouting, "Mama says come to breakfast." They washed, ate in silence, laid down on the pine flooring for ten minutes, then strode back to the field. At one o'clock the girls came running again. They washed and ate a light midday meal, collapsed on the floor once again, and were back into the field twenty minutes later, working with the whetstones before they began the cutting.

Four hours later Tredwell squinted at the sun, surveyed with satisfaction the sixteen acres they had cut and shocked, looked at the eastern sky for any sign of storm, and said, "We better go in. We got evening chores, and a meeting to attend after. We'll finish tomorrow and get it into the barn for thrashing."

With the silent, deep satisfaction of those who work hard for the food on their table, the men washed and took their places at the table. Isaac offered grace, and they ate leftover ham, boiled turnips and squash, and drank cool buttermilk from the root cellar like the tired, ravenous men they were. Rachel watched with the pride of a wife and mother who understood her vital place in the family and who filled it well.

Tredwell wiped his plate clean with a half-slice of Rachel's bread, glanced at her with admiration in his eyes, then put his knife, fork, and spoon rattling on his pewter plate.

"I think the meeting tonight is only for the men."

Rebecca and Ruth ducked their heads in disappointment, but said nothing.

Rachel nodded. "We'll be all right here. You four go on."

Isaac glanced at Jacob in surprise, but neither said a word at how casually their mother had, for the first time in their lives, included them in the men. They changed clothing and left the women washing and wiping the dishes as they walked out into oncoming twilight. Caleb trotted to the barn and came out with his rifle under his arm, still wrapped in canvas, and his note paper and pencil in his pocket.

Tredwell showed concern at the sight of the rifle. "You intend taking that?"

Caleb shrugged. "Just don't want to leave it here."

Tredwell said nothing, but Caleb sensed his uneasiness as they strode away from the house in a steady gait, following the trail to the road leading to Springfield; they could cover the distance to town faster afoot than in a wagon pulled by the slow, plodding oxen. It was full dark when they passed the curtained windows of the homes in town, glowing dull yellow from lanterns within. Wagons and buggies and saddle horses were tied in the churchyard, and more were arriving. The church door stood open, casting a long trapezoid of yellow lamplight on the ground and onto those who stood in twos and threes talking in the churchyard, while others moved to take a place inside. Caleb held the rifle inconspicuously at his side while Tredwell and the twins greeted and shook hands with bearded men, then worked their way inside the church with others following.

They passed through an unlighted vestibule with a shelf and pegs around all four walls for coats and hats and bonnets, and on into the church. Caleb hung back, leaning casually against the rear wall in the plain, high-ceilinged church, with its worn pews and the old podium at the front. He studied the men as they came in. Their faces were ruddy from sun and wind, serious, defiant. Most wore hard woolen work clothes and worn leather shoes; some had come directly from the fields. A man closed the door and nodded, and the reverend stepped to the podium.

"I think most of those coming are here. This meeting was called by a committee headed by Nathan Tredwell. He wants to report on his trip to Boston. It has nothing to do with the church. You're welcome here as long as things don't get out of hand." He pointed. "Nathan, the pulpit is yours."

An expectant hush fell over the room, and Nathan's shoes sounded too loud on the worn floor as he walked to the pulpit.

"I appreciate you coming. There's things need to be decided. First, I want to tell you, the committee did go to Boston, and we met with Matthew Dunson about that letter we got. The one about the Committee of Correspondence. Dunson is writing to the legislatures and governors in other states and trying to learn if the problems we have are like the ones they have. If the trouble is the same all over, he intends going to the Congress and demanding help. Matthew Dunson couldn't come, but he did send one of his men, his brother Caleb Dunson. He's standing back by the door. "

Every head turned to stare, and Caleb neither moved nor spoke. Tredwell droned on. "You know the sheriff put David Banes in jail for a debt. Dunson back there put up the money to get him out."

Banes nodded vigorously, and buzzing broke out as the men turned to peer back once more, then quieted.

"Dunson's here tonight to take notes. He's the one who runs the printing press back at his office in Boston. He'll write all this up and that's what will go out in one of those letters to the other states. I think if enough people from all over get in and support what they're doing with those letters, the Congress will have to do something. So I think the trip to Boston was a good thing. That's pretty much the report on the trip." He looked over the audience and pointed, "Hosea, Ezekiel, Thomas, do you have anything that ought to be added?"

They did not.

Tredwell ordered his thoughts and went on. "We got that behind us, so let's move on. The worst of it is what's happening around here right now. Banes got jailed over seventeen dollars. The sheriff intends taking my oxen soon. Thomas Marsing stands to lose his farm. Coming back from Boston, we passed three, four families already put off their land. One of 'em included a woman who gave birth the day after they were run off. Near killed her and the baby, both." He shook his head. "Hard to see."

He paused for a moment, then raised his head. "That's what's going to be happenin' around here if we don't do something. Now let me lay this out the way I see it. I doubt the sheriff or the money lenders like Mullins want it the way it is. I think it's them foreign banks in London and Holland that see a way to hurt us for their own gain. They're the ones that demanded pay in hard coin, which we don't have. So the banks here in Boston and New York have to demand that they get paid on their loans in hard coin, and they turn to the financiers and force them to make the same demand on us."

He stopped to be sure he had said it right, then spoke once more. "Anybody here have a different notion?"

The place erupted, and Tredwell let it run on for a time while frightened men who had faced overwhelming debt too long vented their fears and anger.

That Judge Devereaux don't have to issue them court orders throwin' us off our land—or takin' our livestock or crops—or puttin' Banes in jail—he can make orders that's right and if the law isn't right he ought not follow it—the sheriff don't have to follow them court orders that's robbin' us to make the banks and financiers fat—he can use common sense and let us pay after our crops is in and he can take meat and wheat for pay like they agreed in the beginning—the legislatures and the congress is owned by the lawyers and the rich, and they're the ones who's doin' us wrong—there's where we ought to start, and we ought to do whatever we have to to clean 'em out and start over—we beat the British for the same thing, and we can do it again with the lawyers and fat rich people if we have to.

Tredwell raised a hand and bellowed them all to silence. "All right. All right. Now let's talk sense. I don't know if what I said about the sheriff and the judge is right, and maybe Mullins too, but as I see it, if we stand up to them, they're bound to go back to the banks and tell 'em they're not going to get the debts paid in hard coin because nobody has it. Throwin' people in debtors prison and takin' their land and crops don't put hard coin in the banks in Boston and New York, and it sure won't do much for the banks over in London and Holland. If the financiers and banks here finally get hold of the fact they're goin' to wind up with wheat and barley and cattle, and no money, they'll soon enough go to the legislatures and the Congress and tell 'em to fix it."

Husky voices shouted, "Sounds right. Sounds right."

"Then we got to get organized. We all got to agree."

Caleb was still leaning against the back wall, watching everything, sensing the temper of the men in the pews nearest the podium at the front of the church, listening intently to the plan Tredwell was unfolding, gauging how the gathering was accepting it, composing notes in his mind to write on paper after the meeting.

Without warning he felt a slight vibration against the back wall, and it took him one second to pull his mind from what was in front of him to what was outside the wall behind him. He remained still, concentrating for a moment, and felt it again—something heavy moving nearby. In the heat of the words and the arguments at the front of the church, no one noticed him quietly step to the door, open it, slip into the unlighted vestibule and close the door, walk through, open the outside door and step into the darkness, rifle still held at his side.

Outside he quickly unwrapped the rifle, slung the powder horn and bullet pouch straps over his shoulder, flexed the hammer on the Deckhard, and stood still in the deep shadows by the church door, listening, eyes straining in the dim moonlight. Again he felt the ground vibration, and then he heard the creaking of a wagon coming from the east. Seconds passed before he could make it out—a dim shape approaching—and it was less than twenty yards from the front of the church, nearly to the scatter of wagons and buggies and tied saddle mounts before he saw the shapes of men crouched in the wagon with muskets. He made no sound or movement as he waited.

The driver silently pulled the two nervous horses to a stop. Other horses nearby moved and snorted at being in a strange place in the dark, with too many other horses and wagons gathered about, and a wagon rolling in among them in the dark. The driver of the wagon quietly climbed down the big front wheel to the ground and reached back to pick up his musket, while the six other men climbed over the sides and lowered themselves silently to crouch with their muskets clutched and ready, waiting for the signal from their leader.

The driver raised his hand for all to see and signaled them forward, and quickly they moved in among the parked wagons and horses, cutting the tie ropes, starting to turn the horses and oxen away from the church.

Caleb's voice coming from the darkness froze every man in his tracks.

"Might want to stop all that before I call those men inside."

Instantly the sound of seven muskets coming to full cock came too loud in the darkness, and the leader growled, "Show yourself!"

Caleb neither moved nor answered, and the leader raised his voice.

"There's seven muskets out here. Show yourself or I give the order to shoot."

For an instant a hush held, and in that moment no one could mistake the sound of Caleb's Deckhard coming onto full cock, and he spoke quietly.

"Give the order, but know that you will be the first man down."

A strangled sound welled up in the leader's throat, and Caleb cut him off before he could speak.

"Tell your men to put down those muskets in the next five seconds, and then you lead them through those church doors. I'll count three before I take off half your head with this rifleball. One . . . two . . ."

Seldom had Caleb heard the sound of restrained rage that was in the leader's voice as he turned to his men. "Do it! Put 'em down."

Seven muskets were laid in the dust, and Caleb spoke once more.

"Now open the door and lead your men inside."

Silence held for one second, and Caleb said, "Three" and the leader blurted, "Move!"

He led to the door, opened it, marched through the dark vestibule to open the doors into the church, with all six men following, Caleb behind with his rifle held loose, waist high, muzzle bearing between the shoulder blades of the man ahead of him.

At the sound of the rear doors opening, Tredwell stopped, and every man in the church turned to look. Their eyes opened wide and their jaws dropped for a moment before they clacked them shut. The seven men ahead of Caleb stopped short in the center aisle, blinking while their eyes adjusted to the light, and then the room was filled with exclamations. Tredwell's voice rose and the room quieted, and he called to Caleb, still standing at the rear of the room, just inside the doors.

"What's the meaning of this?"

"These men were outside cutting your horses loose. You'll have to ask them why."

Tredwell's head jerked forward and he nearly shouted, "What? Bring them up here."

Caleb jabbed the man ahead of him with his rifle muzzle and said, "Move," and followed them up to stand beside the pulpit, facing Tredwell, backs to the angry men behind. Caleb took a position to one side, rifle muzzle on the chest of the leader. He was a swarthy, husky man, dressed in farm clothes, with a thick, black beard and dark eyes.

Tredwell fronted the man and demanded, "What's your name? Where you from?"

The man sneered and said nothing, while the six men with him were shifting their feet, nervous, fearful. Tredwell nearly yelled, "Who sent you?"

The man stood in silent contempt and instantly the room echoed with shouts, "Hang 'em! Hang 'em!"

It took Tredwell half a minute to call them into silence. "Anybody here recognize any of these men?"

"No! No! Hang 'em."

Again Tredwell raised his voice for silence. "Get the sheriff. We got to do this right. We got to have the law on our side. Get the sheriff. Hosea, Thomas, go get Brewster."

Hosea Abrams and Thomas Marsing turned on their heels and trotted out into the darkness while inside, Caleb gestured as he spoke.

"Outside you'll find seven muskets in the dirt. Might want to gather them up for the sheriff to see."

Five minutes later the muskets were on the front pew in the church. Minutes later Hosea and Thomas returned with the sheriff, still wearing slippers, face red in anger.

"What's the meaning of this?" he fumed.

Tredwell pointed. "These seven men was found outside stealing our horses! They had these muskets. Now, those are crimes, and we're demanding you arrest them."

The sheriff padded up the center aisle to look at the dusty muskets, and his eyes popped. He turned to the seven men. "Are these yours?"

The leader growled, "Never seen them before. We was just passin' through town when that man"–he jammed a thumb at Caleb—"come at us with that rifle and made us come in here."

The sheriff turned to Caleb. "Is that true?"

Caleb smiled. "Anybody here know how to read tracks?"

Nearly every man in the room said, "Yes."

"Sheriff, I suggest you take about four of these men out there with lanterns and read the tracks in the dust, and count the cut tether ropes."

Ten minutes later the sheriff walked back up the aisle followed by four men with lanterns. He stood as tall as he could and spoke with authority.

"The tracks show these men came in a wagon, walked among the horses and wagons already here, and cut half a dozen tether ropes. No question." He turned to the leader. "You can tell us now, or tell us at your trial for attempted horse stealing and half a dozen other crimes. Who are you, where are you from, and why are you here?"

The leader sneered, "We was put upon by that man with the rifle and made to come in here. That's all we got to say."

Brewster turned to Tredwell. "Take these men to the jail." He spoke to Caleb. "You're the one who saw it, so you should sign the complaint. I'll have it ready in half an hour, after we got these men behind bars."

Rough hands seized the seven men and forced them struggling out into the night, down to the sheriff's office with lanterns casting the entire procession in a ghostly light and shadow parade, through the courtroom, into the small jail. When the sheriff turned the big brass key clicking in the lock, Tredwell turned and led his men back to the church, and took his place at the podium. Once again he raised his hand for silence and spoke.

"Now don't go makin' conclusions without all the facts. We'll know more at the trial. We got to stay inside the law. Don't get ideas about breakin' those men out and doin' 'em harm. Remember. We got to have the law on our side, all the way, if we expect the legislature and the Congress to listen to us."

He pointed at Caleb, still at the rear of the building, rifle at his side.

"You done us a good turn. Maybe this will be the thing we been waiting for to make someone listen."

Caleb nodded. "Maybe. Depends on who they are. If they were sent by Mullins, or someone like him, to steal your horses and wagons so you can't get your crops in to sell for money, that's one thing. If they were just a band of thieves on their own, that's something else. It all depends."

Tredwell reflected for a moment. "We'll see at the trial. For now, we're obliged for what you did."

Voices raised in agreement, and bearded men nodded their approval and thanks to Caleb, who stood silent.

Tredwell went on. "I think we've done what we come to do. Remember. Stay inside the law. Get word to your neighbor if the sheriff comes to take somethin'. Keep the word movin' until we all know, and we all go to the sheriff and demand he stop. Our strength is in our numbers. The sheriff and the judge can't beat us all if we stay together."

"Hear hear!"

Tredwell concluded. "Unless someone's got somethin' else to say, that's all."

No one spoke.

"Let's git back to our families then."

The men left the church, talking to each other as they tied the cut reins and ropes to their horses and climbed into their wagons to disappear in the night, still talking. Tredwell and the twins walked to the sheriff's office and waited while Caleb read and signed the complaint, then walked back to the church to wait until the reverend put out the lights and locked the church doors before they set out walking west in the moonlight. For ten minutes there was little said, and then Tredwell asked Caleb, "Would you have fired that rifle?"

Caleb chuckled. "Only once."

Isaac cut in. "What would you have done after you shot?"

"Ran."

They all laughed and continued their walk beneath the stars, through the woods, listening to the frogs and the sounds of the night. There was hot soup waiting, and Rachel sat in her robe, and Rebecca and Ruth came digging sleepy eyes to sit with their mother, listening wide-eyed as the twins told the story of the meeting. The three women turned startled eyes to Caleb as they listened to Jacob's excitement in the telling of capturing seven thieves in the dark, and of their arrest and taking them to jail. Rachel turned to her husband.

"Mullins's men?"

"They wouldn't say. We'll find out at trial."

Caleb finished his soup and bread, paid his thanks to Rachel, and excused himself. In the barn he struck light to the lantern, and for a long time he sat in the yellow light, writing, before he put the paper and pencil away, turned the lamp off, and stretched out on his blanket, exhausted from a day swinging a scythe in a barley crop, and a long walk, the drain of facing seven men in the dark, all of them armed and willing to kill him. In seconds he was deep asleep.

He remembered nothing until suddenly his eyes opened, and through the fog of a brain still half locked in slumber, he realized the rooster had once again ripped loose with his raucous statement to start the day. Thoughtfully he dressed and shook the straw from his blanket, then rolled and tied it, and slung it over his back. He picked up his wrapped rifle, checked his coat pocket for his papers and pencil, looked about to see if anything was forgotten, and walked out into the purple eastern sky toward the house. Tredwell met him at the kitchen door.

"Leaving?"

Caleb nodded. "I better get back. I think I have what Matthew wanted for his letter. It needs to go out as soon as we can write it and set the print. Will it matter to you if I use your name? And some of the others?"

"No. Go ahead if it'll help."

"Could I say good-bye to your wife? And the family? Are they up?"

"Come on in. The twins and I were just leaving for the barley. Breakfast is in about two hours. Will you stay?"

"No, I better be going."

Caleb followed Tredwell through the door into the kitchen where Rachel was boiling water for oatmeal porridge and the twins were putting on their old, battered, black felt hats against the sun. Rachel stopped, saw his bedroll and rifle, and said, "You're leaving, Mr. Dunson?"

"Yes, ma'am. I just wanted to say thank you for everything."

"You'll stay for breakfast?"

"Thank you, ma'am, but I need to get back. Matthew's waiting."

"You wait a minute." Quickly she put a loaf of bread, some cooked ham, a large chunk of cheese, and two boiled potatoes in an old flour sack and tied the top. "Take this."

Caleb reached for it as he said, "I thank you." He drew coins from his pocket and stacked them on the table. "There's about thirty pounds British sterling there. It ought to be enough to keep your oxen."

Rachel gasped and the twins exclaimed as Tredwell stepped forward. "I can't take that!"

Caleb said, "You've got to. Your plan was to stay inside the law, and I think you're right. You can't risk being in debtors prison, and your farm depends on those oxen. You're needed to help lead your neighbors. Use the money. There's one other thing. After the trial of those seven thieves, will you write and let me know who they are? I've got a hunch, but I want to know."

"I'll pay the money back as soon as I can."

Caleb nodded. "That's fair. But don't pay until you can afford it."

He shook the boys' hands, and the two girls came sleepy in their nightshirts, and he shook their hands and bade them all farewell. Tredwell followed him out the door into the yard where he stopped and handed him a wooden canteen with a corncob stopper, wet and dripping with fresh well water.

"Here, take this. Thank you for coming. Will you send me a copy of whatever you write?"

"Yes."

"Watch and be careful on the road. I hate to see you walk all the way back. I wish I had a horse for you."

Caleb said, "I'll catch some rides. I'll be alright."

With the first rays of the unrisen sun turning the high skiff of clouds red and yellow in the eastern sky, he walked along the trail toward the road. He turned once to wave, then moved on.

By nine o'clock he had his coat off, sweating, and stopped in the shade of an oak to drink from the canteen. At noon he drank and used his belt knife to cut cheese and bread and ham. At sundown he stopped again, ate, drank, and moved on. In full darkness he spread his blanket on the ground in a stand of maple trees thirty yards from the road, and slept. On the third day a rain squall moved from east to west, and he trudged through mud, hoping that the Tredwells and others in the Springfield valley had their crops safely in their barns. The morning of the fourth day he paid a farmer one dollar for a ride in a wagon filled with barrels of fresh apple cider, bound for Framingham. In the late afternoon of the sixth day, he strode onto the timbers of the Boston waterfront to the office of DUNSON & WEEMS, opened the door, and set his wrapped rifle on the counter.

Billy looked up from the growing stack of ledgers on his desk and dropped his quill as he stood. "You're back! Are you all right?"

"Fine."

Covington came from his desk to face Caleb. "Any trouble?"

"None to speak of. Where's Matthew?"

"At the lawyer's office. He'll be right back."

Caleb's forehead drew down. "Lawyer? Trouble?"

"No. We just got another contract to carry cargo. The lawyer needed dates and rates and destinations. Was your trip a success? Did you get what you went after?"

Caleb drew the sheaf of papers from his pocket and laid them on the counter. "I think so. There's the notes."

"Did you get home with any money?"

"Yes." He tossed his purse clanking on the counter. "I'll make an accounting for what's gone and what it went for."

"Later."

Matthew shoved the door open and instantly exclaimed, "Caleb! I was about to come looking for you. You all right?"

"Tired, but good."

"Did you get the story?"

"I think I did."

"Give it to us in one sentence?"

For several seconds Caleb stared at the counter before he answered. "It's only a matter of time out there until things change, or there will be trouble. Killing."

For a moment the only sound was the traffic on the docks and the seabirds arguing.

"That bad?"

"Maybe worse."

Matthew picked up the stack of notes. "It's all here?"

"Most of it. I'll write it all out tomorrow. Is mother all right? And Adam and Prissy?"

"Mother's fretting over you being gone so long. Otherwise fine. I was there yesterday."

"I better go on home. You need me for anything here?"

"No, not right now. Can I look at your notes overnight?"

Caleb shrugged. "I'll need 'em in the morning."

"I'll have them here waiting."

There was a lift in Caleb's soul at the familiar sounds and smells of Boston town as he walked away from the docks, into the narrow, crooked streets, and hurried home. He opened the front door, called "I'm home," and Margaret came at a run to seize him and hold him close.

"You had us all frightened. Thought you were hurt or dead somewhere. Oh, it's so good to see you."

"I'm fine. It's good to be home. Brigitte and the others?"

"They'll be home soon from work. Go put your things in your room and come to the kitchen. We'll talk while I finish getting supper ready."

Margaret moved about the kitchen as he talked, pausing when he told of the newborn Harriman baby and the mother, frightened when he spoke of the Monday night meeting and the seven men who came in the dark with muskets. In the midst of it Brigitte walked in the front door, followed by Adam and Prissy, and they heard Caleb's voice in the kitchen. They hurried across the parlor to throw their arms about him.

Supper was a marathon of questions and answers. Caleb said he needed to clean his rifle and was in his room when the others knelt for evening prayers. He went to his own bed early, to sleep as one dead.

At eight o'clock the following morning he opened the office door. Matthew and Billy raised their heads, and Matthew leaned back in his chair. Caleb's notes were spread on the desk before him. Matthew gestured to them.

"That's hard to believe."

"It was hard to see, most of it."

"How soon can you get it set in print?"

"Maybe tomorrow, late. Who are you sending this letter to?"

Matthew handed a sheet of paper to Caleb with handwriting on both sides, and Caleb began to read to himself.

James Madison. Alexander Hamilton. George Washington. John Adams. Samuel Adams. Thomas Jefferson. Elbridge Gerry. Patrick Henry. Thomas Paine. John Jay. Benjamin Franklin. Henry Laurens. Gouverneur Morris. George Mason. Robert Morris. John Dickinson. George Wythe. John Rutledge. Charles Pinckney. Edmund Randolph. Henry Knox. James Monroe.

Caleb raised unbelieving eyes to Matthew. "Do these men know the letter is coming?"

Matthew nodded. "Most of them. I've received correspondence from nearly all of them. They're concerned about what's happening. Do you know about the meeting to be held next March?"

"No. What meeting?"

"James Madison and Thomas Jefferson got the state legislatures in Maryland and Virginia to agree to a meeting next March, in Alexandria. The states are each appointing a committee of delegates to negotiate a settlement of the battle over the rights to the Potomac River. First time this sort of thing's happened. I think it's going to open a whole new way of thinking about how the states should work together."

For a time Caleb read the names again, pausing, thinking. "Madison and Jefferson? I thought Jefferson had been sent to Europe. France."

"He was. He left July fifth, from right here in Boston. But before he sailed, he and Madison got the states to agree to the conference. It's going to happen."

"Alexandria is in Virginia?"

"Yes."

Caleb set the list down on Matthew's desk. "Next March. Well, we'll see. We'll see."

Notes

Thomas Jefferson sailed from Boston aboard the ship *Ceres* on July 5, 1784, to take up his duties in France, as set forth herein (Bernstein, *Thomas Jefferson*, chapter 3).

CHAPTER XXXVI

*T*he midnight Boston fog swirled so thick Matthew could not see the gate to his home until he touched it, and he held his hand before him as he walked to the front door. He quietly inserted the big brass key into the lock and turned it, then entered the dark home softly. The only light was the faint glow from the coals in the large parlor fireplace, carefully banked by Kathleen before she went to bed two hours earlier. Matthew set his seaman's bag on the floor, unbuttoned his coat that was soaked with invisible droplets of water, and opened the door long enough to shake it and his tricorn hat outside, then closed the door and hung each of them on a peg in the entryway. Fog had collected thick, dripping from his brows and face in his hurried walk from the waterfront, and he was mopping at it with a handkerchief when Kathleen, wearing her robe and slippers, walked through the archway. Without a word she hurried to him and threw her arms about his neck while relief flooded through her system. For a time she stood holding him, and he her, and he was aware of a tenseness before she drew back and spoke.

"Oh, it's good to have you home."

"It's good to be here. Is something wrong?"

"No. It's just that you're long overdue. Things happen on ships."

"John's all right?"

"Fine. Asleep. He's learned new words since you left. Talks all day. Are you hungry?"

"I'll last 'til morning. Is there something to drink?"

Matthew lighted a lamp while she set cider on the stove to heat, then came back to sit at the dining table facing him.

"You had trouble getting home?"

He shook his head. "No trouble. Things went very wrong with the conference in the beginning. Set the whole schedule back."

"Tell me."

"You know that James Madison arranged for the delegations from both Virginia and Maryland to meet at Alexandria to work out a plan for navigation of the Potomac River."

"Yes. I know about the trouble with the river."

"The conference was set for March twenty-first, and the Maryland delegation arrived on time. I was there waiting to get everything I could for the Committee of Merchants letter we're sending out. I got to Annapolis the same day the Maryland people got there—Daniel of St. Thomas Jenifer, Thomas Stone, and Samuel Chase. The four of us went to the hall where we were to meet the Virginia delegation—George Mason, Edmund Randolph, Archibald Henderson, and James Madison."

Matthew leaned back in his chair. "They weren't there! It took us an hour to find out Governor Patrick Henry had appointed them, but he never sent word to them that he had done it! Nor had he ever told them when and where the conference was to be held!"

Kathleen straightened in her chair. "That's hard to believe."

"Hard to believe? It's impossible! But that's what happened. We found out Archibald Henderson lived in Alexandria and were able to locate him. He was mortified. We asked him to inform Randolph and Mason and Madison of their appointments to the committee and to get them to come as soon as he could, and he did it."

Kathleen rose and brought the pitcher of hot cider to the table with two glasses, poured, and each took one as Matthew continued.

"Henderson got word to Mason, and Mason came as quickly as he could, but both Madison and Randolph didn't hear about it until too late. The resolution by the Virginia legislature that authorized their committee required three of the four to be present to conclude business with the Maryland delegation, but Mason and Henderson were so embarrassed they suggested we ignore it and go ahead."

Kathleen sipped at her cider. "Did it work?"

Matthew drank then set his glass down. "We didn't have time to find out. Somehow George Washington heard what happened and sent a message. We were invited to Mt. Vernon to conduct the conference!"

Kathleen exclaimed, "What? Mt. Vernon? Did you go?"

"Yes. Arrived there March twenty-fifth."

"You were inside his home?"

"Every day."

Kathleen's eyes were shining. "Tell me about Mt. Vernon. The home."

"It was beautiful. The mansion is white. On a hill surrounded by lawn and gardens and flower beds. Barns, stables, outbuildings—all painted, clean. The home is immaculate inside. Carpets. Paintings on the walls from here and Europe. Words can hardly describe it. But that's not what one remembers most about it."

"What?"

Matthew reflected for a moment. "The people. The general is still learning to leave eight years of military command behind and become a gentleman plantation owner once again. He's still a little . . . distant . . . once in a while, but he observed every social grace I ever knew. A light came into Matthew's eyes, and his voice mellowed. "Lady Washington. She's a surprise—the heart and soul of Mt. Vernon. In the time I was there, everyone—guests, generals, congressmen, family, visitors—it made no difference—they all came to love her. Warm. Unpretentious. Kathleen, you'd love her. And she'd love you."

A wistful look crossed Kathleen's face. "Someday maybe I can go there." She sighed. "Go on. What happened? Did they hold the conference?"

"Yes. Started March twenty-fifth in George Washington's library. I talked with George Mason between sessions."

"General Washington conducted?"

Matthew shook his head. "No. I could hardly believe it. He provided the meals, separate sleeping rooms for each of us, refreshments on the library table, looked in on the delegates once a day to be sure they had everything they needed. He knows the Potomac River like no one else, and he has an interest in the Shenandoah and Ohio rivers, and once in a while Mason or one of the others would ask him some detail about them and the country around them. He answered all their questions, but not once did he sit at the conference table with them or even ask about what they were doing."

Kathleen raised her hand to her mouth in awe, but said nothing. Matthew went on.

"The committee made their own agenda and went to work."

"How many days?"

"Three full days."

"Did they find a way to fix the problem that had your ship held up for so long? The *Jessica?*"

"Yes. They agreed the Potomac would be a common highway for navigation and commerce for all states. Equal fishing rights, a system of lighthouses, buoys, beacons, locks, regulations for ports for both states, common defense against pirates, and most of all, they forever stopped the practice of imposing tariffs and duties and regulations that were at the heart of the conflict between the two states. A problem such as we had with the *Jessica* will never happen again."

Kathleen stared for a moment. "All that in three days?"

"All that and more. Much more."

"What more could there be?"

Matthew tossed a hand up in a wide, encompassing gesture. "They decided their commission by both states could be construed to cover other issues that had become troublesome, and they went right on. Before they adjourned they had arrived at a series of recommendations each delegation agreed to take back to their home states about such things as agreeing on the comparative value of the currency of the two states, and even of foreign currency."

"The problem of the states not accepting money from another state? They solved that?"

"Not completely, but they made a good start. They're taking back a proposal for the two legislatures to consider. But that was not the end of it. They worked out a schedule of duties and tariffs to be charged by each state."

Matthew paused to bring his ardor under control. "To put it all together, those two delegations resolved problems that will allow commerce to flow evenly, both ways. Fair, uniform, even-handed. In those three days, those men resolved what Virginia and Maryland had been battling over for years! They're taking the results back to the legislatures of each state for approval, and there's no question the approval will be forthcoming."

Matthew raised his glass to drink warm cider. He set the glass down and went on.

"Before they adjourned they did one more thing that may be the start of the biggest advance in the history of the thirteen states. They wrote a request to the President of the Supreme Executive Council of Pennsylvania—"

Kathleen cut him off. "Pennsylvania? Did Pennsylvania have someone at the conference?"

"No. That's the point. Maryland and Virginia wrote to the Pennsylvania government outlining what they had done and inviting that state to join in the plan for expanding navigation on the Potomac! Think about it! Two states inviting a third. And there's talk about inviting Delaware to come into it. Madison even mentioned delivering their work to the Confederation Congress for its approval under Article Six of the Articles of Confederation."

He stopped, ordered his thoughts, and concluded. "Will it spread? Will other states come into the open discussion? If they do, has something been started that will bring all the states together as time goes on?"

Kathleen sat back in her chair, eyes growing wider with each passing second. "It's too much for me to think about."

Matthew finished his cider, leaned back in his chair, and sighed. "That's where I've been these past several days and why I'm late getting home. Now my work begins. I have to put all this into a letter to be sent to people in almost every state."

Kathleen sighed. "You'd better get to bed. You'll need some rest."

"Have you heard from Billy or Caleb? About the business?"

"Yes. They're doing well. They have contracts that will have all six ships working in the next three or four weeks."

"Any problems?"

"They didn't mention any."

Matthew stood, and Kathleen rose with him. He gestured toward the door where his seaman's bag lay. "Let me get my bag. We'd better go to bed." He reached for his empty cider glass, and for the first time noticed Kathleen had hardly touched hers.

Puzzled, he asked, "Something wrong with your cider?"

She shrugged, and a strange look crossed her face. "I couldn't drink it." She raised her eyes to his. "There's one thing you should know."

Matthew stopped dead still, waiting.

"In about seven months, John's going to have a baby brother or a baby sister."

John Tyler of the Virginia legislature sat at the desk in his library, head tilted forward in deep thought, then for the third time picked up the document before him and read it again. Then he leaned forward once more, thoughts running.

The legislature was quick to approve everything our delegates accomplished at Mount Vernon, but they refused to send it on to the Confederation Congress for its approval. They defeated that proposal. Voted it down! Somehow we must put this before Congress! Somehow!

He laid the paper down and his thoughts went on.

If it can't be done directly, maybe it can be done indirectly.

For half an hour he neither moved nor spoke. Then he reached for paper, quill, and ink. Slowly, carefully selecting the words, he wrote:

"*RESOLVED.* That Edmund Randolph, James Madison, Jun., Walter Jones, Saint George Tucker, and Meriwether Smith, Esquires, be appointed commissioners . . . shall meet such commissioners as may be appointed by the other States in the Union to take into consideration the trade of the United States; to examine the relative situations and trade of the said States; to consider how far a uniform system in their commercial regulations may be necessary to their common interest and their permanent harmony; and to report to the several States . . . as, when unanimously ratified by them, will enable the United States in Congress, effectually to provide for the same."

He sat back and read his work, read it carefully again, and set it on the small desk.

If the Virginia legislature wouldn't send the Mount Vernon Compact to the Confederation Congress, maybe they'll send this resolution. Maybe. We shall see.

A few days later Tyler sat erect in his chair in the state legislature counting the votes, and his heart raced. He left the hall with a copy of his resolution in his papers and a sense of deep satisfaction in his soul. His resolution had passed. The legislature had set the date for convening the conference that for the first time invited all thirteen states to amicably resolve the ever-escalating troubles that had been inexorably tearing them apart.

They would meet in Annapolis, Maryland, on September eleventh, 1786.

Tyler entered his home, went directly to his library, and set his papers on his desk. He removed his tricorn, then sat down, and the thought came strong.

Will all thirteen states appoint delegates? If they do, will the delegates attend? Will they?

Notes

James Madison and Thomas Jefferson did arrange a conference for delegates from Virginia and Maryland to meet in Alexandria on March 21, 1785. The circumstances surrounding the gathering, including the failure of the Virginia delegates to appear are accurately detailed in this chapter. The meeting at Mount Vernon did occur as described.

Each delegation returned to their own legislatures, and the Mount Vernon Compact, as it came to be called, was quickly approved by each.

James Madison hoped the Virginia legislature would submit the compact to the Confederation Congress, but that effort failed.

John Tyler, of the Virginia legislature, and father of the tenth President of the United States, thereupon framed a resolution for the Virginia legislature stating that similar delegations from all thirteen states should meet to continue the resounding success of the Mount Vernon Compact conference. That effort succeeded, and the conference was scheduled for September 11, 1786, at Annapolis, Maryland. The Resolution drafted by Tyler is in pertinent part quoted verbatim in this chapter (see Bernstein, *Are We to Be a Nation?*, pp. 97–99; Freeman, *Washington*, p. 532).

CHAPTER XXXVII

*T*he Annapolis Conference—*half the states didn't bother to send delegates last March—those that did appear framed a resolution to hold another conference next May. The Articles of Confederation—a government in name only—powerless. Citizens closing down courts in half a dozen states—talk of some states seceding from the union.*

Citizen George Washington stood at the library window in his Mount Vernon mansion, staring out at the bare trees thrashing in the heavy November wind that carried sleet and freezing rain slanting beneath dull clouds that shrouded the late afternoon world in gray. He stood with his hands clasped behind his back, feet spread slightly, listening to the whistling at the windows and the sucking at the huge stone fireplace, oblivious to the costly paintings that hung on three of the walls and the thick carpet that covered the polished oak floor.

Farmers closing down courthouses to prevent further court actions of foreclosure or sending men to debtors prison—citizens forming groups to petition legislatures for reform of the entire system of money and courts—state legislators passing laws to punish them— the entire system of government in question—public and private affairs approaching chaos.

He flinched at a rap at the door, then turned. "Enter."

A short, sparse servant walked into the sumptuous library and announced, "Your mail has arrived, sir," then laid several documents in a neat stack on the large desk.

Washington nodded and the servant left the room and closed the door. Washington stared at the documents for a time before he walked to his desk and sat down with a dark foreboding growing in his breast. Methodically he went through the documents, carefully studying the names of the senders. The largest and heaviest was from Matthew Dunson. Curious, Washington set the others aside and broke the wax seal. Inside the letter was a second document, the seal broken. Washington laid the second paper aside and flattened the letter before him.

> October 24, 1786
> Boston, Mass.
> Dear Sir:
>> I write with regret, partly from respect for your much deserved privacy, partly from what I am convinced you would want to know, as follows.

Slowly Washington read on, the sad litany by now so familiar to him.

Debt, worthless money, courts—critical in Massachusetts, Connecticut, New Hampshire—citizens losing farms—debtors prison—beleaguered citizens now organizing to protect themselves—August 29ᵗʰ blockaded Courthouse in Northampton—stopped court foreclosures—unrest spreading to Worcester, Concord, Taunton, Great Barrington—on to New Hampshire—Connecticut—September 25ᵗʰ a 44-year-old Pelham farmer named Daniel Shays led farmers to shut down the courthouse at Springfield for three days—Shays a former Continental Army captain—served bravely and honorably at Bunker Hill, Saratoga, Stony Point.

Washington stopped reading and for a moment stared at his hands, confounded. *A former captain who had honorably survived such battles, now leading other veterans against his own government? Could that be possible?* He read on.

Massachusetts Governor James Boudoin issued orders—General Benjamin Lincoln to take 4,400 Massachusetts militia—put down the rebellion—defend the courts—restore order to the Commonwealth.

Again Washington stopped while he let his thoughts run, then finished reading the letter.

> I take the liberty of enclosing a letter lately received from Nathan Tredwell of Springfield, the said letter self-explanatory.

Should you find it beneficial I would be happy to receive such response as you care to make.

> Your humble and obd't svn't,
> Matthew Dunson
> Boston Committee of Merchants

Slowly Washington unfolded and laid out the second letter. The words were formed with great care, almost as though drawn, not written.

October 2nd 1787
Springfield, Mass.
Dear Mr. Dunson:

My wife Rachel writes this because I do not write good. Your brother Caleb was here. He saw what I am writing about. I think your committee needs to know things is worse since he left. Daniel Shays from Pelham led men that stopped the courts here for three days in September. Armed militia came. Farmers is organizing all over, at Worcester and Concord and Great Barrington and in New Hampshire. There's talk about muskets. Daniel Shays says the war was fought for all Americans, not just the rich. He says we got a right to fight for our farms and what's ours. If the legislature and the congress don't do something, there will be bloodshed. I believe us farmers does have right on our side, but it is hard to fight against my own flag. I hope you can do something, soon. My family sends our greetings to Caleb. He is a good boy.

> Yr Obed't Serv't,
> Nathan Tredwell

Washington raised his head and a great sadness settled on his face.

"... *hard to fight against my own flag.*"

He pushed the letters away toward the two large stacks of correspondence on the right side of his desk, then turned to peer out the window at the wind and sleet.

Men who risked all for this country—forced now to choose between home and flag—our worst fears happening—spreading—what have we done?—what have we done?

Slowly he selected a letter from the stacked correspondence on his desk, unfolded it, and read the signature. Harry Lee. Former Commander of Lee's Light Horse Cavalry that had performed so well both in the North and South. Carefully Washington read the stiff handwriting.

" . . . and there is talk of the abolition of debts, the division of property, and reunion with Great Britain. Should affairs become more critical than at this moment, Congress might call on Washington to go to the eastern States, since it is presumed that your influence would cause the disorders to subside."

Washington shook his head. *Reunion with Great Britain? Heresy!*

He selected another document from the correspondence, looked to be certain of his own signature, and read his answer to his old subordinate officer, Harry Lee.

" . . . I am mortified beyond expression when I view the clouds that have spread over the brightest morn that ever dawned upon any country. As for remedy, you talk of employing influence to appease the present tumults in Massachusetts. I know not where that influence is to be found and, if attainable, that it would be a proper remedy for our disorders. Influence is no government."

They think my presence will provide sufficient influence to end the civil unrest? And what becomes of them when my influence ceases to be? When I am gone? Who then provides such influence?

Again he reached for a document of correspondence and read the signature. Henry Knox, Secretary at War, United States. The same Henry Knox who had braved the New England winter of 1775–1776 to lead a column of men from Boston to Fort Ticonderoga and return with the cannon of Fort Ti to provide Washington the firepower to place the British in Boston under siege. The same General Knox who had commanded the Continental Army artillery throughout the war and finally at Yorktown. Bright in Washington's mind was the memory of the short, rotund man throwing his arms about his beloved general and sobbing like a child when Washington resigned his commission, and invited the corps of officers who had stood with him through it all to a farewell at Fraunces Tavern. In 1785, Congress had turned to Knox to serve as Secretary of War. True to his commission, Knox had gone personally to observe conditions at Springfield, then written to Washington.

Washington spread the letter and read.

" . . . Were there a respectable body of troops in the service of the United States, so situated as to be ordered immediately to Springfield, the propriety of the measure could not be doubted. Or were the finances of the United States in such order, as to enable Congress to raise an additional body of four or five hundred men, and station them at respective arsenals, the spirit of the times would highly justify the measure.

"I have visited Springfield and completed my investigation. I am satisfied that the creed of the insurgents is that the property of the United States has been protected from confiscation of Britain by the joint exertions of all, and therefore ought to be the common property of all. And he that attempts opposition to this creed is an enemy to equity and justice and ought to be swept from off the face of the earth."

Washington stopped reading, laid the letter down, and for a time was lost in reflection.

Secretary Knox—caught in the trap that is slowly strangling the country—not enough money to maintain an army and nothing in the Articles of Confederation authorizing him to send Continental troops to interfere in a State matter if he did have the money—and worse, contending with men who believe all Americans should share in the land we won from the British.

He stood and slowly paced back to the windows to stand close, watching the gray, late afternoon slowly darken as evening came on beneath black clouds and wind and sleet. He stood thus while twilight filled the room, and the dancing flames in the fireplace cast changing reflections on the walls of the great library.

How does one change minds that for generations have known but one form of government? One wins at war by defeating another by force of arms. But having won at war, how do we win the peace when the fatal flaw preventing it is in ourselves?

He shifted his weight, and as he stood in the somber room, he suddenly felt old, spent, defeated, useless. For a moment his shoulders sagged, and the weight of having carried his country on his shoulders for eight years seemed crushing. He raised his head, straightened his shoulders, and by force of the iron will that had sustained him, pushed his thoughts on.

Who will rise in this hour? Jefferson? Adams?

It came to him gently, naturally.

Madison. James Madison. Once a representative in Congress. Now a member of the House of Delegates. He has the intelligence, the will to work, the vision.

For a long time he stood still, working with words and sentences in his head. Then he walked to his desk, lighted a lamp, pushed aside the letters, and reached for fresh paper. He took up his quill and carefully began writing.

" . . . I applaud the refusal of the House to refuse approval for emission of paper money. I join in the hope that the House will, at this critical moment, calmly and deliberately consider that great and most important of all objects, the federal government."

Washington stopped, read his own words, then with a fervent prayer in his heart, concluded.

"Let prejudices, unreasonable jealousies and local interest yield to reason and liberality. Let us look to our national character, and to things beyond the present period. Wisdom and good examples are necessary at this time to rescue the political machine from the impending storm."

He read his words and laid the quill down beside the paper. For a time he stared at the page, searching for any words that would add to what he had written, and there were none. He signed his name, sprinkled salts on the finished letter, dusted it off, folded the paper, and reached for the wax and the seal.

Notes

Conditions for the farmers and working class people in the United States reached desperate proportions when the courts were flooded with property foreclosures and complaints to put men in debtors prison. Daniel Shays, a 44-year-old Pelham farmer, formerly a captain in the Continental Army, who served with distinction as described in this chapter, became the leader of organized farmers who began barricading courthouses all over Massachusetts, thereby preventing further court actions against them. Neighboring states joined the Massachusetts insurgents. September 25, 1786, Shays and his followers closed down the Springfield courthouse for three days. Shays preached that the land won from England was won for all Americans, not just the rich. Letters were exchanged. Harry Lee wrote to General Washington as herein described, and Washington answered as set forth in this chapter. Henry Knox, former general of Continental Army artillery and now Secretary at War, personally went to Springfield for his own investigation, then wrote to Washington. Washington answered their letters, and many, many others too numerous to include herein, all expressing alarm, then fear for what was happening.

The letters appearing in this chapter from Knox, Lee, and Washington, are all quoted nearly verbatim from their original texts. It was at the conclusion of the episodes herein described that Washington wrote his now famous letter of November 5, 1786, to James Madison, in which he implored the brilliant young Congressman to lead the House in considering the first and greatest issue before them, to rescue the federal government from "the impending storm" (Freeman, *Washington*, pp. 533–35; Higginbotham, *The War of American Independence*, pp. 446–49; Bernstein, *Are We to Be a Nation?*, pp. 92–95).

CHAPTER XXXVIII

*I*n frigid, late afternoon sunlight, Captain Theodore Pettigrew closed the office door against the freeze that had set four inches of ice reaching from the shores of Boston harbor out two hundred yards into the bay. He felt the foreboding the moment he saw the four of them clustered about Matthew's desk. Matthew was facing him and Billy, Thomas Covington, and Caleb were seated with their backs to the door. They turned to look, faces blank. Matthew gestured to an open chair, and Pettigrew loosened his scarf as he raised the gate and took his place with them.

Matthew lifted a piece of paper from his desk.

"From George Washington. Written four days ago."

Pettigrew straightened, caught by total surprise.

"Let me read from it," Matthew said. For a moment he searched, then began.

" *. . . much encouraged with the letters lately arrived from the Boston Committee of Merchants . . . informative . . . nor am I forgetful of the welcome letter received some time ago from Mr. Billy Weems concerning conditions in Vermont and locations north- ward as related to him by Mr. Eli Stroud . . . it is with much concern that I take this occasion to inform, . . . have lately rec'd letters from Henry Knox, Esq., Secretary at War, Congressman Henry Lee, Esq. . . . Congressman James Madison, Esq., and others . . . each much concerned of destructive events now spreading in many states . . ."*

Matthew paused for a moment to scan down, then continued.

" . . . *am reliably informed this date that on January 25 last, citizens of Massachusetts in the vicinity of Springfield assaulted the federal arsenal with the object of acquiring gunpowder, cannon, and muskets . . . under leadership of one Daniel Shays . . . formerly a captain in the Continental Army . . . Governor Bowdoin ordered General Benjamin Lincoln to protect federal property with 4,400 militia . . . a battle ensued . . . four of Mr. Shays' followers were killed . . . many wounded . . . the remainder fled . . . the militia followed and engaged them again in a snowstorm on February 4 at Petersham—it is feared these incidents excited them to organize and strike back . . .*"

Again Matthew stopped, raised his eyes for a moment, then finished.

" . . . *your Committee of Merchants appears to be well connected in Massachusetts . . . should it be consistent with your beliefs and goals I very strongly encourage you to spare nothing in your exertions to quell the uprising led by Mr. Shays in any manner necessary to avoid further armed conflict—induce both sides of this lamentable affair to seek their remedy through peaceful petition . . . am deeply saddened at old comrades in arms now engaged in mortal combat one against the other . . .*"

Matthew dropped the paper on his desk and looked the other four in the face. "There it is. What do we do about it?"

For a moment all four stirred in their chairs while they brought their startled thoughts under control. Matthew cleared his throat and continued.

"If General Washington has taken the time to write us, this whole affair must be bad. I think we'd better pay attention. Someone better go over there and see what can be done."

Caleb cut in, anxious, eager. "I've been there. The Tredwells live at Springfield. I'll go."

Matthew nodded. "What about the rest of us?"

Billy spoke. "We've got a business to run. A big one."

Covington raised a hand. "I'll stay. I can handle the business end of it."

Matthew looked at Pettigrew, asking the silent question.

"I'll stay. We've got four ships carrying cargo now, and contracts for the last two. Someone has to be here to handle it. I think Tom and I can do it alone for a while."

Matthew glanced at Billy, and Billy said, "The general didn't say it in his letter, but I think he's remembering assignments he gave us. Hard ones. You and me and Eli. I think he's expecting something from us."

Matthew pointed at the letter. "I think it's there, between the lines."

Billy said softly, "We'd better go."

Matthew turned to Covington and Pettigrew. "You sure you can handle this for a while?"

They were sure.

"There're a few things I have to do here, and I'll have to go home to help Kathleen. Cut some firewood, be sure she's got enough food in the root cellar. I can be ready by morning."

Billy nodded. "I'll have to do the same."

Covington broke in. "You'll need a way to get over to Springfield. Take one of the light freight wagons and two of the horses. We can make do while you're gone."

Caleb stood. "Mother isn't going to take this very well, and there are some things I should do at home. Any reason I can't leave now?"

Matthew shook his head. "You go on. Meet at the warehouse in the morning, eight o'clock. I'll have the wagon ready. All right?"

It was.

"Bring your own food. Billy, you bring some coin, and this letter from George Washington."

At four-thirty that afternoon, Caleb walked out of the office into the setting sun, and at five o'clock Matthew and Pettigrew wrapped their scarves and followed him into the gathering twilight. Covington turned to Billy, still hunched at his desk, working to bring all books of account current.

"Want me to stay?"

"No. I'll be a while. You go on when you're ready. I'll leave these books on my desk if you need them. Lock the door on your way out."

At twenty-five minutes past six o'clock, Billy closed the last ledger, stood, stretched, yawned, and walked to the safe where he counted sixty pounds in coin into his purse and stuffed it into his coat pocket. He banked the coals in the fireplace and was buttoning his heavy coat when the front door rattled. He stopped, puzzled at who would be calling at this late hour, then walked to the door, turned the key, opened it a foot to peer out, and froze in shock. Facing him in the yellow shaft of light, clad in a heavy coat with a scarf wrapped tight and a heavy knit hat pulled low, was Brigitte Dunson.

"Do you have a little time?" she asked.

"Brigitte! What? . . . Come in here." He stepped aside, and she came through the door and he closed it.

He was nearly scolding. "You shouldn't be on the waterfront alone after dark. Don't you know—"

"I know. Caleb said you're leaving in the morning. That there could be trouble. I had to talk to you before you go."

The grab in his stomach took his breath for a moment. *Here it comes. Ten years. Here it comes.*

He led her to the fireplace and arranged two chairs facing each other. The fading coals and the single lamp on Billy's desk cast the room in a shadowy twilight.

"Is this all right?"

She sat down. "Fine." He sat down facing her, straightened, brought his eyes to hers, and waited. Never had he felt so inadequate, so plain, as he listened.

Holding her hands in her lap, she said, "I hardly know where to begin. You know you are a part of my life. When I look back, you're there in everything, like Matthew. Caleb. If I try to take you out of my memories, there's a hole that leaves it all a little disconnected. Can you understand?"

He nodded but remained silent.

"It never occurred to me that I loved you, just as I did my brothers. When they brought you home from Concord twelve years ago, shot, I died inside until Matthew said you would live. I would have felt the same about Matthew if it had been the other way around—if you had brought him home half-dead."

Never had Billy seen such need in Brigitte's eyes, heard such earnestness in her voice. She went on.

"I look back now and wonder why it never occurred to me that those feelings could be anything other than what they were. Then you gave me those letters, and nothing in my life had prepared me for the shock. It took me days to understand what it all meant."

She leaned forward, searching Billy's face before she continued.

"You know the feeling I had for Richard Buchanan. Ten years ago— I was young, he was young. We knew the difficulties, but we were certain our love would allow us to rise above the fact he was a British officer and I was an American girl. We couldn't see it was doomed. Then he was called away, and the next message I received was that he had been killed in battle."

She stopped, and Billy saw the pain in her eyes, and he could do nothing but remain still and silent.

"I loved him. When he died, something in me died with him, and there was nothing I could do about it. In a real way, I still love him, and I think always will. But now, I know that I have to put it behind me and move on. Life flows. It won't wait. I've mourned Richard too long."

Billy held his poise. Brigitte took a deep breath, and in the dim light of the glowing lantern and the dying fireplace embers, looked him in the face and quietly went on.

"I've nearly memorized your letters, and your feelings are clear. Before you leave for what could turn into a shooting war, I think I must tell you of my feelings. I love you, Billy, for the good man that you are, but not in the way I loved Richard. I wish I could, but I can't. And there will always be a part of me that belongs to him. Do you understand?"

He nodded faintly but said nothing. Brigitte went on.

"I believe that what I feel for you, and what I think you feel for me, is enough to make a marriage. A family. The question is, can you accept me, knowing what I have told you?"

Billy straightened, struggling with what Brigitte had offered. A heart divided between a living man and a dead one. Compromised. Less than complete. In all the months and years Billy had yearned, waiting, he had never expected it. For a time he sat in the gloom of the office, head tilted forward, eyes downcast, while he put her words in the scales and weighed them, again and again, while she sat still, waiting.

The realization came to him slowly at first, then quickly, that he had never truly considered the depth of her suffering over the loss of her first young, imprudent, impossible love. Only now did it come to him that she had lived with life's worst pain in her heart every day for ten years. With that understanding came a realization of the wrenching turmoil he had caused in her when he forced his letters upon her. Then it broke clear in his mind that she had reckoned with her own broken heart and seen what it was doing to her life, and she had risen above it. He could only guess at the price she had paid to come to the waterfront at night, to open her heart to him as honestly as she could, not knowing if he could accept that there would always be a part of her that belonged to Richard Buchanan. A lump rose in his throat, and he waited until he could speak before he raised his eyes to hers.

"I never dared hope you could see me as you do. My heart is yours, Brigitte. I'll spend the rest of my life in your debt. When I get back, can we talk of marriage?"

Brigitte's chin trembled. "I'll be waiting."

Billy stood. "I'll see you home."

She rose to face him, and she stepped close and reached for him, and he wrapped his arms about her, and he held her close, heart pounding, and she drew her head back, peered into the plainness and the strength and the goodness in his face, and she kissed him, and he kissed her.

There was little said as they walked steadily through the cold streets, linked arm in arm. He left her at her front door and walked back to his own small, austere home, where his mother and sister were waiting with hot soup and homemade bread. Dorothy saw the change in him, but waited for him to speak of it. He finished the last of his bread, then gestured, and Dorothy and Trudy sat down at the table, waiting.

"Today we received a letter from George Washington."

Dorothy's mouth fell open, and she exclaimed, "General Washington?"

"Yes. There's been fighting over at Springfield and Petersham between the farmers and the militia. The farmers are led by a man named Daniel Shays from Pelham. Four of Shays's followers were killed, and many more were wounded. We talked about it at the office. It's clear Washington wants us to go do what we can to stop it, although he did not say that directly. Matthew and Caleb and I have decided to go. We leave in the morning, early."

For several seconds neither of the women moved, then Dorothy said, "Shooting?"

"Yes. But you're not to worry. They've sent more than four thousand armed militia. There should be no more shooting."

Once more Dorothy bit down on the fear in her mother's heart, as she had done so many times before. "You'll need food. I'll put some things together." She started to rise, and Billy raised a hand to stop her.

"One more thing. Brigitte came to the office tonight just as I was leaving. We were alone. We talked. When I get back, she and I will discuss marriage."

Trudy gasped and Dorothy blurted, "Marriage?"

"Yes. We will be married."

Trudy threw her hand over her mouth and began to sob. She didn't know why. Tears welled up in Dorothy's eyes, and for several seconds she could not speak. Then she stood, and Billy stood, and she embraced her only son and buried her face in his chest, shoulders shaking in silent tears. Billy held her until she quieted, then stepped back and raised her face to his, and there was a light in her eyes Billy had never seen before.

"Billy. Oh, Billy. You can't know how happy I feel."

He drew her to him again, and for a time they stood in an embrace, while Trudy sat staring through tear-filled eyes, not knowing if she should stand and join them or give them their moment, as she struggled with emotions she had never felt before.

They waited until they had accepted the newness of it, then cleared the table. While Dorothy and Trudy washed and dried the dishes, Billy went to the frozen wood yard and stacked the kindling, then split half a cord more and stacked it before he came back in, face white from the cold, hands and fingers numb.

"There's enough firewood out there for about three weeks. Is the root cellar all right? Do you have enough money?"

"Yes. We'll be fine."

"I'd better get packed."

The morning sun was an icy ball on the eastern rim of the world when Billy opened the front door and paused long enough to wrap Dorothy, then Trudy, inside his arms. "I'll be back in two or three weeks. Don't worry about me."

"Be careful."

"You know I will."

He draped his ammunition pouch over his neck, shouldered his bedroll, picked up his musket, and walked out into thick frost that crunched underfoot and turned sunlight into tiny, numberless jewels of red and green and blue, and they watched him stride out the front gate with a great cloud of vapor following from his breath.

The wagon was waiting at the waterfront warehouse of DUNSON & WEEMS SHIPPING, with two Percheron draft horses hitched and waiting, long, shaggy winter hair hanging from their jaws and bellies. Steam rose in clouds from their nostrils as they moved their feet, thumping on the timbers, anxious to move, to be in action, in the piercing cold. Billy dropped his bedroll and musket into the wagon box next to Matthew's, and at that moment Caleb came in his swinging gait to lay his bedroll and rifle beside the others, all the while looking at Billy.

Billy waved Matthew over and faced the two brothers.

He swallowed and ducked his head, not quite able to suppress a smile. "Last night Brigitte and I talked. When we get back from Springfield, she and I will be discussing our marriage."

Matthew stood stunned while Caleb grinned. It was Caleb who broke the shocked silence. He thrust out his hand and seized Billy's and exclaimed, "Brigitte told us last night. I can't tell you how happy we feel. Mother and Prissy laughed and cried half the night. Adam thinks it's nonsense. But, Billy, I couldn't feel better about it. I give you my best congratulations."

"Thank you."

Matthew moved as soon as he could, and he wrapped his arms about his friend who was dearest in his heart, and Billy clutched Matthew to him for a time, before Matthew drew back, grinning.

"You don't know how I've prayed. You don't know."

No other words passed between the two of them, because none were needed. They stood in silence for a moment before Matthew broke it off.

"Ready?" he asked, then climbed to the driver's seat while the others got into the wagon box. Matthew slapped the reins down on the rumps of the Percherons, and they lunged into their collars, snorting in the cold, stepping high, anxious to be on the move.

The days passed beneath freezing sunshine, the nights in bitter cold. The three men took turns driving the team as they moved steadily west, jolting in the freight wagon on snowy country roads frozen as hard as Massachusetts granite. They stopped at midday only long enough to feed the horses, build a small fire to heat water for tea, eat bread, dried beef strips, and cheese, and move on. At night they built a large fire and boiled potatoes and turnips and frozen mutton, then went to their blankets fully dressed. In the afternoon of the third day the wagon rattled through the town of Springfield, where the men sat in silent awe as they passed the armory and the foundry, with broken windows and smoke-stains on the walls. Minutes later Caleb turned into the lane leading to the farm of Nathan Tredwell. He hauled the wagon to a halt in the frozen, deserted yard and was climbing down when the window opened and the muzzle of a musket was thrust through. Caleb stopped in his tracks and raised his hands.

"Hello, the house," he called. "It's Caleb Dunson. I'm looking for Nathan Tredwell."

The musket muzzle disappeared, and the voice of Rachel Tredwell came across the yard.

"Caleb Dunson? Is that you?"

"It's me, Mrs. Tredwell. I have my brother and a friend with me. We need to talk to you about what's happened."

The door swung open and Rachel Tredwell, with a shawl thrown about her shoulders, took two steps into the yard. "Come on in."

They walked to the door and followed her inside, where Rebecca and Ruth stood quietly, near the hearth. A fire burned in the fireplace with a large kettle hung on an arm, heating.

Rachel hung her shawl, then turned to Caleb.

He gestured as he spoke. "This is my brother, Matthew, and our friend Billy Weems."

Rachel shook their hands in turn. "You're welcome here." She turned to Caleb. "Do these men work on that committee? The one that writes about the trouble?"

"Yes. They're the ones who started the paper."

"Is that what brings you here?"

"Yes. That and a letter from George Washington."

Rachel's eyes opened wide. "He wrote to you?"

"He did."

"You wanted to talk to me about what's happened?"

"Yes."

"Nathan and the boys have been gone since January."

"Are they in town? Springfield?"

"We don't know for sure. They was there in January when the battle was fought at the armory, and then we heard they was at Petersham early this month when the militia come during a snowstorm and there was another fight. We haven't heard where they went after Petersham."

"They've been gone since January?"

"January twenty-fifth, at the fight at the armory in town. Four farmers was killed, twenty hurt. Nathan came home only long enough to get food and some gunpowder, and he and the twins left, and then we heard about Petersham. Haven't seen 'em since."

Caleb could not miss the fear in her eyes, nor the concern in the two girls.

"Has anyone said where they might be now?"

"Some of 'em went to hide in Vermont and New York, but last Sunday the reverend said he'd heard they was coming back. Things was happening over in Sheffield. West of here. Might be they're gathering there."

Caleb turned to Matthew. "Shall we try Sheffield?"

Three minutes later Caleb waved his good-bye to Rachel, standing in the dooryard with her arms folded against the cold, then straightened in the wagon box as it rumbled down the lane, and Billy swung the horses west onto the frozen ruts they called a road. On the second day all three men sat silently as the wagon moved on, watching the frigid skyline for large smudges of gray or black smoke, the sure sign of the presence of an army of four thousand camped in the dead of a Massachusetts winter. On the third day Caleb's arm shot up, and he exclaimed, "There! North and west! Smoke!"

The sun had passed its zenith when they rolled through the tiny village of Sheffield. Half an hour later they were passing through the southeastern fringes of a sprawling camp of Massachusetts militia, with soldiers reaching for their muskets to line the road and stand hard-eyed as Matthew held the horses on a steady course toward a huge fire that burned near the command tent. They were slowing near the fire when Billy murmured, "Keep an eye out for Eli. He's likely here somewhere."

Two pickets brought their bayoneted muskets to bear while the three men climbed from the wagon and stood facing them. Their leader, a surly man with sergeant stripes and a huge beard, challenged them.

"Who are you, comin' in a wagon like farmers?"

"Matthew Dunson, of Boston. This is my brother, Caleb, and our friend Billy Weems. We represent the Committee of Correspondence in Boston. It has lately become known as the Committee of Merchants. We need to talk with your commander."

The picket scowled. "Committee? No committee's got nothin' to do with us. You better keep movin' before you're mistook for the farmers we been shootin' at, and git yourselves kilt!"

"Is General Lincoln here? Benjamin Lincoln?"

"In the tent. But you aren't goin' to see him."

"Tell him we're here because George Washington wrote to us. Tell him."

The picket's face fell. "Washington? Wrote a letter to you?"

"Tell General Lincoln."

Within minutes the three men were standing inside the command tent, across a small, badly scarred desk from a bull-necked, surly, gravel-voiced, suspicious General Lincoln. A small, iron stove glowed a dull orange in one corner.

"George Washington sent you?" Lincoln raised doubtful eyes.

Matthew reached inside his coat and drew out the letter. "This is his letter."

Lincoln laid it out on the desk, and his lips moved as he read it silently, then looked up. "What is it you want?"

"The General wants an end to the bloodshed. We intend doing what we can," Matthew said.

Lincoln grunted, "Huh! I've got my orders. We stop when they surrender."

"There's no way to sit down under a white flag? Avoid all this?"

"Not after they attacked the armory and foundry at Springfield."

"Those are federal properties. Not Massachusetts. Why not let the federal government handle their own affairs?"

"Because they can't. No money, no way to raise it. Massachusetts isn't going to stand by and let that rabble close down the courts. You should know that."

"I do know that. Washington and Madison and others are holding a conference in May to take care of it. If the farmers will agree to stop what they're doing until that conference is finished, will you?"

"That's not for me to say. I have my orders, and I'll carry them out until I get new ones."

"You're a field commander. It's in your power to order your men to stand down if in your opinion that will best achieve your orders."

"You a military man?"

"Six years on the sea. I was with de Grasse at Chesapeake Bay. Billy Weems here, fought from Concord to the storming of Redoubt Number Ten at Yorktown as a lieutenant. Caleb, my brother here, helped Morgan take down Tarleton at Cowpens. Yes, we're military men. And I'm telling you, sir, you will better discharge your responsibilities if you will get this stopped until Congress tries to take care of it at their conference in May."

Lincoln leaned back in his chair. "Tell that to the rabble out west of us. In the meantime, I know my orders. Is there anything else?"

Matthew picked the letter from the table. "Not at the moment. Thank you for your time."

Matthew turned on his heel and walked out of the tent with Caleb and Billy following. He was folding the letter as they walked back toward the wagon, all three of them with eyes moving constantly, probing, memorizing the camp: the mess halls, the regimental flags hanging limp in the dead, freezing air; the commissaries; the half-buried powder magazines; the cannon standing muzzle to muzzle in two long lines; the shaggy horses with steam rising from their nostrils and hides; the men huddled about fires or cutting wood or dicing beef and potatoes into steaming pots hung on tripods. The familiar feel and smell and sounds of a winter military camp came back as though it had not been six years since Yorktown.

Matthew mounted the driver's seat while Billy and Caleb settled on their knees in the wagon box, eyes moving, watching everything.

Again Billy said, "Watch for Eli."

Matthew gigged the horses and held them to a slow walk, working them carefully to the west edge of the camp, then north until they passed the last of the tents and pickets. He swung the horses back to the east, then south, down the eastern edge of the camp to the place where six hundred horses were being held inside a rope corral that marked the south end of the camp. They were one hundred yards beyond the last pickets when Matthew drew rein and the steaming Percherons stopped. He turned to Caleb and Billy.

"We've got to make a plan."

Caleb spoke. "For which side?"

Matthew answered, "Neither side. A plan to stop this thing if we can."

Billy hooked a thumb over his shoulder, toward the camp. "We know where the army is, but we don't know where the farmers are or how many they have, or how they're armed, or how willing they'll be to lay down their arms. Until we do, any plan will just be a guess."

Matthew straightened in the driver's seat. "Then we go find Shays's people. Lincoln said they're somewhere west of here."

The sun was sitting on the western treetops before they saw the smoke staining the blue above. Minutes later they saw the first pickets. Watching, making estimates of numbers and munitions, they passed tents with sullen, suspicious men watching, on to the center of the camp and stopped. A man of medium height, large nose, and thin beard, dressed in shabby clothing and an old coat came from a tent to meet them. At his side was a second bearded man, shorter, thicker in the shoulders.

The taller man spoke. "Who are you?"

The three climbed down from the wagon, and Matthew faced him. "Matthew Dunson from Boston. I'm here for the Committee of Merchants, which used to be called the Committee of Correspondence. These men are with me. May I ask, sir, who are you?"

"Daniel Shays." He glanced at the shorter man. "This is Andrew Bouchard. Did Lincoln send you here?"

"No. We were there. We left his camp over an hour ago."

"What do you want?"

"The same thing we asked of General Lincoln. To find any way we can to stop all this. Congress has arranged a conference in May to try to work out a peaceful plan. Is there any way to get you and your men to wait? Give Congress a chance?"

Shays shook his head. "They've had six years. They've talked it to death. We've got over four thousand men here that are through talking."

"You've already had dead and wounded, and there will be more. May is just ninety days away. Are more dead worth ninety days?"

Caleb and Billy were watching Shay's eyes, his expressions, as he spoke.

"Can you promise Congress will do what's right?"

"No, I can't. But I can promise there are powerful men who will do everything they can."

"Who?"

"Washington. Madison. Franklin. Hamilton. Morris. Mason. Others."

"Where they been this past six years?"

"Working at it."

The man shook his head and smiled. "They didn't do very well. We already had two battles, and we're getting ready for one more."

"When?"

"Soon."

"Wait. Give Congress one last chance."

"They've had one last chance."

"Is there anything to stop this?"

"Tell Lincoln to take his men home. Tell the courts to stop taking away our land. Tell the legislatures to make fair laws. That'll stop it."

"That takes time."

"Or muskets. Go on back to Boston. No need you getting hurt." Shays and Bouchard turned and walked to the tent and disappeared, without looking back.

With the sun gone and dusk settling over the frozen camp, Matthew took the driver's seat while Billy and Caleb climbed back into the wagon bed. Matthew gigged the horses and walked them past campfires and tents, angling north and east to pass through the rest of the camp. He was fifty yards past the north edge when a shadowy figure in a wolf-skin coat with a parka, and wearing beaver-skin moccasins that reached to his knees broke trotting from the woods with a Pennsylvania rifle in one hand, grasped the side of the moving wagon with the other, and swung up.

"Nice to see you all again."

Billy gaped. "Eli! How—"

"Saw you pass through camp."

Matthew turned in the wagon seat while Caleb recovered enough to exclaim, "Nice to see you, too."

Billy asked, "You were in this camp?"

"Both camps. What brings you here?"

Matthew hauled back on the reins and stopped the wagon, then handed Eli the letter from Washington. Eli held it close to make out the words in the fading light before he handed it back and spoke.

"You been to the militia camp?"

"This afternoon. General Lincoln is stubborn."

"So are these men."

Billy leaned forward. "You've scouted both camps?"

"Yes."

"How do you see it?"

Eli wasted no words. "Lincoln is spoiling for another fight and so are Shays's men. From the camp talk I've heard, it's likely to be tomorrow morning. The Massachusetts militia have about four thousand men and about eighty cannon and horses to move them. Their cannon are just south of the middle of their camp. Their powder magazines are off to the west. Most of their horses—maybe six hundred head—are in a pen at the south end of camp. If their attack is for tomorrow morning, they'll start hooking the horses to the guns in the night and likely start loading the cannon with grapeshot. They'll have their men fed and ready to march before dawn and be moving before the sun rises."

He pointed. "The people with Shays have just over four thousand men here, and others not far north. But they have no cannon and only a few horses. Most of these farmers were in the Continental Army until six years ago, and they know about battles. But if the militia gets those cannon in place and use grapeshot, any battle could become a massacre."

Billy gave him no pause. "Is there a way to stop this?"

Eli shook his head, and his eyes dropped. "Four of us, stop eight thousand stubborn men? No chance. The best we can hope for is to save some of them."

Matthew said, "Do you have a plan?"

"I've thought about it."

"Go on."

"I think the militia intends surprising the camp here about dawn. So the battle will be right here. If we can get into the militia camp around three o'clock in the morning, near the cannon, we'll know when they start to hook up the horses to the guns. If they do, we'll know they're getting ready. That's when we blow two of their powder magazines and run the horses through camp and scatter them in the forest."

He paused to order his thoughts. "When those powder magazines go, every farmer in this camp will know it. That's when we move in to their leaders and tell them that we've probably slowed down the militia, but not for long. If they've got any sense, they'll scatter—get out of camp so the militia will find no one here when they roll their cannon into place. Save their men to fight another day, and maybe, just maybe, that future day will be after May when the Congress meets in Philadelphia."

He stopped and drew a breath. "That's the best I can do."

Matthew asked, "How do you plan to be in both camps within minutes?"

"We split. Two go to the militia camp, two to this one."

"Which two to which camp?"

"Billy and I have done this two or three times before. We'll work on blowing up the magazine. You and Caleb work on getting this camp to scatter."

Matthew said, "Anyone have a better idea?"

Silence held for a time before Caleb said, "You sure I can't help blow those powder magazines?"

Eli smiled. "I thought you'd like that."

Matthew cut in. "I doubt we can do better. We better eat what we can and get wrapped in our blankets before we freeze."

At midnight, beneath a quarter moon in the east and a blanket of stars overhead, Eli and Billy dropped from the wagon bed to the ground, their weapons in hand, and started east with patchy snow and frost crunching at each step. At half past two o'clock they stopped to study the fires and the pickets at the militia camp and picked their way through silently, to drop flat on the ground at the north end of the lined cannon, muzzles gleaming dully in the moonlight. At three o'clock they watched the dark forms moving in the moonlight and heard the sounds of horses being harnessed and hooked to the big guns. At twenty minutes past three o'clock, they stopped again, on the west side of the nearest powder magazine.

Eli reached inside his wolf-skin coat to draw out his hatchet, and Billy waited for the muffled sound of the flat side of the hatchet head striking a skull, then moved quickly to Eli's side. Without a word they used the fallen picket's musket to pry loose the lock on the powder magazine and within seconds were inside with the bungs knocked out of three huge powder barrels and a heavy trail of powder leading from the stacked barrels to the door. Eli kept watch while Billy struck flint to steel, blew on the spark in the charred linen, then dumped the glowing lump onto the powder trail. As it began to burn, they darted out the door, shouting, "Fire in the magazine! Fire in the magazine! Run! Run! Scatter!"

There was no shout that would terrify soldiers more than "Fire in the magazine!" and the militiamen instantly dropped everything and ran for their lives, scattering in every direction away from the doomed gunpowder. Billy and Eli waited until the nearest men were safely more than fifty yards away before they turned from the door and sprinted south. They had covered one hundred yards before the first explosion blew the sod covered roof off the front half of the magazine, and they were scrambling on hands and knees when a second, horrendous blast blew yellow flame and dirt and shattered timbers four hundred feet into the clear, freezing night air.

Within ten seconds the camp was bedlam. Stunned militiamen were running in every direction, shouting, pointing, with no reason or plan. In the midst of the tumult, Eli and Billy sprinted south, dodging through the falling pieces of shattered wood, knocking soldiers left and right. They reached the rope horse pen and Eli was swinging his tomahawk while Billy worked with his belt knife, cutting the two rope lines as they ran, circling the pen, shouting, waving their arms at the frantic, terrified horses, driving them north to stampede through the camp. Running blind, the crazed animals bolted over men and through tents, turning away from the great fire where the magazine had been.

Billy and Eli fell in behind the horses, running. Following the swath they cut straight through the middle of the camp, to dodge off to the right to the second powder magazine. The pickets had long since disappeared in the panic, and Eli used a huge rock to smash down the door. Within two minutes Billy dropped a ball of glowing tinder into the gunpowder they had scattered at the door, and once again the two ran from the doomed magazine. Ninety seconds later the blast leveled tents fifty yards away and knocked wagons and soldiers sideways. The tower of flame and burning debris lighted the world for two miles. Three minutes later Eli and Billy stopped and dropped to one knee twenty feet inside the tree line of the forest. For a long time they watched the frenzied militia running in every direction as their officers tried to shout them to a standstill and restore some sense of discipline and sanity.

It was approaching five o'clock before the militia had what horses they could find hitched to twenty-eight cannon and had their infantry around campfires, eating burned sow belly and hardtack.

Eli said quietly, "We better go see what's happening with Matthew and Caleb."

To the west, Matthew and Caleb strode past a thousand men, standing bareheaded in their coats, staring wide-eyed at the great glow to the east. The concussion from the first blast had rolled through their camp just seconds ahead of the roar, and they had come from their blankets thinking they were under siege. Then, as they watched in wonderment, another blast turned the eastern sky to day for several seconds, and the concussion and sound of a second explosion thundered through the camp. Struggling to understand what had happened, none paid attention to two men striding toward the command tent.

Caleb at his side, Matthew stopped before Shays.

"Two of the powder magazines at the militia camp just blew. Their horses are scattered. It means they're getting ready to ambush this camp before morning with cannon and grapeshot."

"How do you know this?"

"Two of my men did it."

The man gaped. "Your men did it? Why?"

"To stop as much killing as we could. You can't fight cannon and grapeshot because you have none of your own. If you have any thought for your men, tell them to scatter. Vermont. New York. Reassemble later in the spring. Save themselves."

For a time Shays stood in silent thought. "I doubt they'll do that. They've waited too long to end this thing."

Matthew controlled the flash of anger. "Tell them! The militia will be here before the sun's an hour high, and they'll be coming with grapeshot."

Caleb could remain still no longer. "I was in Springfield with some of these farmers before the fight at the armory. They're good people. You let them get slaughtered by militia cannon, and you and I might have to discuss it personally."

Shays came to an instant focus. "Are you threatening me?"

Matthew stood silent, watching.

"No, sir, just stating a fact. You want me to go tell them what's coming?"

"You stay away from my command."

"I'll wait until I hear those militia guns rolling in. Then I'll do what I can to get these men out of here, back to their families."

Shays's voice was ugly. "I'll have you shot if you do."

"That depends on whether you can give the order before I fire this Deckhard."

Shays's eyes widened as it broke clear in his mind that Caleb meant exactly what he said. He wiped a frosty sleeve across his mouth and for a moment lowered his eyes. "I'll take care of my command. You two get out of camp." He walked back into his dark tent and dropped the flap.

Matthew gave a head signal to Caleb, and they walked away, toward the commissary. They took up positions outside the rear of the dark building and watched as the glow in the eastern sky dwindled and the men around them came back to life and started to move. With the predawn gray defining bare branches on trees one hundred yards distant, Matthew nodded to Caleb, and they walked out to the center of the clearing, where Matthew raised his voice.

"Those explosions were two of the powder magazines in the militia camp. Their horses were scattered. By now they've recovered, and they're on their way here with cannon and grapeshot."

Men slowed and stopped, then began to gather, while Matthew continued to shout.

"I'll repeat it. Early this morning two of the men with me blew some powder magazines in the militia camp east of here. They also scattered their horses. By now the militia have recovered from it and are coming this way with cannon. They have grapeshot. Their plan is to ambush this camp. We've only slowed them down to gain time so you can save yourselves."

Caleb was watching the faces of those gathered round, estimating their number. There were close to one thousand. Matthew continued.

"Right now it doesn't matter who's right and who's wrong. What matters is that you save yourselves. You can't fight cannon and grapeshot with only muskets. Take your weapons and your blankets now and scatter. Disappear in the woods. Go home. Get back to your wives and families. Live to fight another day."

Murmuring began and quickly turned to a rumble, when Caleb saw the crowd opening to his right, and he saw Bouchard barging through the mass toward Matthew. Without a word Caleb turned and walked directly toward the oncoming officer. He met him twenty feet from Matthew, Deckhard still in his left hand. He was five feet from the man before he saw the pistol in Bouchard's coat belt, and then Bouchard reached for the handle, and he had the weapon nearly drawn when Caleb's right fist caught him flush on the chin and the man went over backwards, arms flung wide, and he hit the ground on his back and did not move. Without a word Caleb picked up the pistol and trotted back to Matthew's side. No man spoke nor made a move to interfere as Caleb passed. Matthew glanced at his younger brother as if seeing him for the first time, then turned back to those gathered around.

"Gather your bedrolls. If you've got a wagon, hitch up the team and load up with others and get out of sight. Do it. Now!"

A commotion from the east side of the gathering turned all heads, and Matthew stood tall to see Billy and Eli coming in at a trot, weapons held high above their heads. Men moved aside to let them pass and they came on in to stop before Matthew, panting for breath, vapors rising in a cloud. Billy gasped, "They're coming. Twenty-eight cannon. Maybe three thousand infantry."

"You got two of the powder magazines?"

"Yes, and scattered the horses. But they've recovered. They're coming. You've got about twenty minutes. Thirty at the most."

Matthew straightened and raised a hand high, shouting. "There's still time! Disperse! Disperse! Get your belongings and scatter! Go home!"

A few men turned and walked, then trotted away, but it was as though most of them were caught up in a cloud of indecision, unable to make a choice—torn between their anger and the common sense of scattering into the woods. Caleb, Billy, and Eli gathered around Matthew, backs to him, facing the crowd, weapons cocked and ready as Matthew tried one more time.

"Make up your minds!" he shouted. "You have no more time. You'll be facing cannon and grapeshot! Half of you will be killed or crippled. Get your belongings and go home! Gather another day when you can win! Disperse! Get away from here!"

Matthew stopped and watched, desperate, not knowing what more he could say or do in the minutes that remained. More men began to murmur, then shake their heads and walk away. But the great bulk of them stood where they were, unable to decide, a few beginning to call out, "Get into battle formations and be ready!"

The pounding of two incoming horses brought all heads around to peer east, and all muskets were raised to the ready. Two blowing plow horses came in at a lumbering gait, and those on their backs hauled them to a stop as they slid to the ground running, shouting as they came, "They're coming! Five minutes behind us! Cannon! Get ready! Get ready!"

Instantly Matthew screamed, "Disperse! Get away from here! Get away!"

For three seconds that seemed an eternity the mob of men stood stock-still before they finally broke, running in all directions. They threw their scanty belongings onto their spread blankets, rolled them hastily, caught them under an arm, abandoned their tents, and with their muskets in the other hand, ran for the woods.

In the clearing, Eli raised a hand to point due east. "There! Five hundred yards!"

Billy and Matthew and Caleb followed his point and saw the movement through the stand of bare trees. Horses coming at a run, pulling big-wheeled cannon carriages, with crews running alongside to keep up. The four men watched the militia catch up to the running farmers and then they were in among them, stopping the horses, turning the cannon, lowering the muzzles. The popping of a few muskets echoed in the forest, and then more, and then came the first blast of a cannon and then two more and then a rolling volley of cannon fire.

Horrified, sickened, the four men stood still as they watched farmers buckle and go down while the cannon crews reloaded and the big guns bucked and roared again and more men stumbled and fell.

Billy grabbed Matthew. "Get back to the wagon! Those militia don't know who we are! They'll turn the cannon on us."

The four of them turned and with Eli leading, sprinted into the woods and dropped to their haunches long enough to be certain they weren't followed before they rose and ran on, to their freight wagon, where they dropped to the frozen ground. The firing of the cannon and the rattle of sporadic muskets moved on west until it faded.

After a time, Matthew stood and led the way back to the nearly deserted field of battle, and the four of them walked through the scatter of broken bodies and shattered trees. They looked into the dead faces and the staring eyes of bearded men in ragged clothing, and they said nothing. Billy stopped at the edge of the clearing, and in the frozen silence said, "There's nothing we can do here."

They walked back to the wagon and stopped, and Eli spoke to the others.

"I need to go home. Vermont. You go on back to Boston. Tell them what we saw here. What we did. We saved some, on both sides, but the dead died without need. Tell them."

The others gathered to him and shook his hand and said their farewells, and they watched him walk northwest into the trees, and he was gone.

Billy climbed to the driver's seat while the others mounted the wagon box. He turned the big horses into the morning sun just clearing the eastern skyline, and the wagon moved across the clearing. For a time they said nothing, and then Caleb spoke.

"Eli was right. It could have been worse. We saved some. Many."

Billy asked, "Did you get a count?"

Caleb answered. "Twenty-nine farmers. Three militia. Maybe a few more in the running fight away from the clearing."

Caleb spoke to Matthew. "If the militia had caught them by surprise, it would have been hundreds. Six, eight hundred. You saved some."

Matthew looked at his brother and nodded once and said nothing.

They pushed steadily east until early afternoon, then stopped to eat cold food while they let the horses graze on what grass they could find in the frozen, patchy snow. After a few more hours they made evening camp, somber, with images of cannon flashes and falling men in their minds.

Morning brought a gray overcast and a rise of twenty degrees in the temperature, and Billy said, "Weather coming," while they ate fried bacon and potatoes and drank steaming coffee.

Midmorning, traveling in the jolting wagon, they faced an easterly breeze that brought the first flakes of snow. They nooned in falling snow, and before they remounted the wagon, Matthew spoke.

"We saved some of them, but maybe we did more than we think. Maybe this is what is needed to force Congress to do something. They're going to hold that conference in May, in Philadelphia. If we write all this in a letter—everything—the battle—the insanity of Americans killing Americans—make them feel it and see it the way we did, maybe we can shake them hard enough to quit talking and actually do something."

Billy took his place in the driver's seat, and the other two climbed into the wagon box. Before Billy started the horses, Matthew spoke once more.

"There's one other thing. We're bringing Billy back home safe and unharmed. I want to be there when we deliver him to Brigitte."

For a moment Billy did not move. *Brigitte!* His heart leaped at the remembrance of their precious time before the dying fire in the office and the touch of her as they held each other and she kissed him and he kissed her. He said nothing, but his mind raced as he talked the horses into motion, traveling east, into the lightly falling snow, toward Boston, and home, and Brigitte.

Behind him, jolting in the wagon box, Matthew sat with his knees drawn up, head bowed, eyes closed, vapor rising in the freezing air as his thoughts ran heavy.

Thirty-two men dead—frozen in the snow back in that clearing—thirty-two good men who fought side by side for six bitter years to be free from the British—and now they're dead because we're killing each other! For a moment he raised his head and peered over the tailgate as though by the looking he could somehow see beyond the miles back to the clearing to where the frozen bodies lay, dark and still and twisted in the white snow.

Is that what we fought for?—to kill each other? What happened to the dream? The dream of freedom?

He grasped the top of the wagon box and set his jaw, and a light came into his eyes.

It is right! The dream is right! It carried us through the worst that a king could do to us, and it can carry us until we learn! Free men can govern themselves—change the world! They can! The last great challenge is the learning. We must hold to the dream until we learn!

Notes

The three battles between Shays's followers and the Massachusetts Militia commanded by General Benjamin Lincoln occurred on January 25, 1787, at the Springfield armory, then on February 4 at Petersham, and finally at Sheffield on February 27, 1787. Four of Shays's men were killed at Springfield, none at Petersham, and more than thirty at Sheffield, where cannon and grapeshot were used by the militia. Three militiamen lost their lives. There were several wounded on both sides. History records these events and others related to it as Shays' Rebellion. Though the rebels lost each battle, their actions served to shock the general population to take action, and prompted the Congress that gathered in Philadelphia in May of 1787 to seek laws that would avert further such tragedies. Shays's record of military service as a captain in the Continental Army, with honorable service in several major battles, is accurate. The parts played in these episodes by Matthew and Caleb Dunson and Billy Weems and Eli Stroud are fictional (Bernstein, *Are We to Be a Nation?*, pp. 93–95; Freeman, *Washington*, p. 534; Higginbotham, *The War of American Independence*, pp. 447–48).

BIBLIOGRAPHY

Bernstein, Richard B., and Kym S. Rice. *Are We to Be a Nation?*, Cambridge, Mass.: Harvard University Press, 1987.

———. *Thomas Jefferson.* New York: Oxford University Press, 2003.

Bowers, Claude G. *The Young Jefferson.* Boston: Houghton Mifflin, 1945.

Boyd, Julian P., ed. *The Papers of Thomas Jefferson.* Volumes 6 and 7. Princeton: Princeton University Press, 1952.

Bunting, W. H. *Portrait of a Port: Boston, 1852–1914.* Cambridge, Mass.: Harvard University Press, 1971.

Busch, Noel F. *Winter Quarters.* New York: Liveright, 1974.

Claghorn, Charles E. *Women Patriots of the American Revolution.* Metuchen, N.J.: Scarecrow Press, 1991.

Cutler, Carl C. *Queens of the Western Ocean.* Annapolis, Md.: United States Naval Institute, 1961.

Davis, Joseph L. *Sectionalism in American Politics, 1774–1787.* Madison: University of Wisconsin Press, 1977.

Earle, Alice Morse. *Home Life in Colonial Days.* New York: Grosset and Dunlap, 1898. Reprint, Stockbridge, Mass.: Berkshire House Publishers, 1993.

Edgar, Walter, *South Carolina, A History.* Columbia: University of South Carolina Press, 1998.

Eyewitness Accounts of the American Revolution: Valley Forge Orderly Book of General George Weedon. New York: New York Times and Arno, 1971.

Fisk, Anita Marie. "The Organization and Operation of the Medical Services of the Continental Army, 1775–1783." Master's thesis, University of Utah, 1979.

Fitzpatrick, John C., ed. *The Writings of George Washington.* Volume 27. Washington, D.C.: United States Printing Office, 1938.

Fleming, Thomas. *Liberty! The American Revolution.* New York: Viking, 1997.

Flexner, James Thomas. *The Traitor and the Spy.* Syracuse, N. Y.: Syracuse University Press, 1991.

———. *Washington: The Indispensable Man.* New York: Little, Brown, and Company, 1998.

Flint, Edward F., Jr., and Gwendolyn S. Flint. *Flint Family History of the Adventuresome Seven.* Baltimore: Gateway Press, 1984.

Freeman, Douglas Southall. *Washington.* New York: Simon and Schuster, 1995.

Graymont, Barbara. *The Iroquois.* New York: Chelsea House, 1988.

———. *The Iroquois in the American Revolution.* Syracuse: Syracuse University Press, 1972.

Hale, Horatio. *The Iroquois Book of Rites.* 1883. Reprint, New York: AMS Press, 1969.

Harwell, Richard Barksdale. *Washington.* New York: Simon & Schuster, 1995. A one-volume abridgment of Douglas Southall Freeman, *George Washington, a Biography,* 7 vols. (New York: Scribner, 1948–57).

Higginbotham, Don. *The War of American Independence.* Boston: Northeastern University Press, 1983.

Jackson, John W. *Valley Forge: Pinnacle of Courage.* Gettysburg, Penn.: Thomas Publications, 1992.

Jobe, Joseph, ed. *The Great Age of Sail.* Trans. Michael Kelly. New York: Crescent Books, 1967.

Johnston, Henry Phelps. *The Campaign of 1776 around New York and Brooklyn.* New York: DaCapo Press, 1971.

Joslin, J., B. Frisbie, and F. Rugles. *A History of the Town of Poultney, Vermont, from Its Settlement to the Year 1875.* New Hampshire: Poultney Journal Printing Office, 1979.

Ketchum, Richard M. *Saratoga.* New York: Henry Holt and Company, 1997.

Klein, Herbert S. *The Atlantic Slave Trade.* Cambridge, Mass.: Cambridge University Press, 1999.

Laguerre, Michael S. *Voodoo and Politics in Haiti.* New York: St. Martin's Press, 1989.

———. *Voodoo Heritage.* Beverly Hills, Calif.: Sage Publications, Inc., 1980.

Leckie, Robert. *George Washington's War.* New York: HarperCollins, Harper Perennial, 1992.

Lumpkin, Henry. *From Savannah to Yorktown.* Columbia: University of South Carolina Press, 1981.

Mackesy, Piers. *The War for America, 1775–1783.* Lincoln, Nebr.: University of Nebraska Press, 1993.

Main, Jackson Turner. *The Sovereign States, 1775–1783.* New York: New Viewpoints, 1973.

Martin, James Kirby. *Benedict Arnold, Revolutionary Hero.* New York: New York University Press, 1992.

Martin, Joseph Plumb. *Private Yankee Doodle.* Edited by George F. Scheer. New Stratford, N. H.: Ayer Company Publishers, 1998.

McCrady, Edward. *The History of South Carolina in the Revolution, 1780–1783.* New York: Russell & Russell, 1969.

McCullough, David. *John Adams.* New York: Simon & Schuster, 2001.

Milgrim, Shirley. *Haym Salomon, Liberty's Son.* Philadelphia: Jewish Publication Society of America, 1979.

Morgan, Lewis H. *League of the Ho-de-no-sau-nee or Iroquois.* Vol. 1. New York: Dodd, Mead & Co., 1901. Reprint, New Haven, Conn.: Human Relations Area Files, 1954.

Morris, Richard B. *The American Revolution Reconsidered.* New York: Harper & Row, 1967.

———. *The Forging of the Union, 1781–1789.* New York: Harper & Row, 1987.

Nevins, Allan. *The American States during and after the Revolution, 1775–1789.* New York: A. M. Kelley, 1969.

Parry, Jay A., and Andrew M. Allison. *The Real George Washington.* Washington, D.C.: National Center for Constitutional Studies, 1990.

Pool, Daniel. *What Jane Austen Ate and Charles Dickens Knew.* New York: Simon & Schuster, 1993.

Quarles, Benjamin. *The Negro in the American Revolution.* Chapel Hill, N. C.: University of North Carolina Press, 1996.

Randall, Willard Sterne. *George Washington, A Life.* New York: Henry Holt & Company, 1997.

Rankin, Hugh F. *Francis Marion: The Swamp Fox.* New York: Thomas Y. Crowell Co., 1973.

Reed, John F. *Valley Forge, Crucible of Victory.* Monmouth Beach, N.J.: Philip Freneau Press, 1969.

Stokesbury, James L. *A Short History of the American Revolution.* New York: William Morrow, 1991.

Tower, Charlemagne. *The Marquis de Lafayette in the American Revolution.* Vol. II. New York: DeCapo Press, 1970.

Trigger, Bruce G. *Children of the Aataentsic.* Montreal: McGill-Queens University Press, 1987.

Ulrich, Laurel Thatcher. *A Midwife's Tale.* New York: Vintage Books, a division of Random House, Inc., 1991.

———. *Good Wives: Image and Reality in the Lives of Women in Northern New England, 1650–1750.* New York: Vintage Books, 1991.

Von Riedesel, Frederika. *Baroness von Riedesel and the American Revolution.* Translated by Marvin L. Brown Jr. Chapel Hill: University of North Carolina Press, 1965.

Wallace, David Duncan. *South Carolina: A Short History.* Chapel Hill: University of North Carolina Press, 1951.

Wilbur, C. Keith. *The Revolutionary Soldier, 1775–1783.* Old Saybrook, Conn.: Globe Pequot Press, 1993.

Wildes, Henry Emerson. *Valley Forge.* New York: Macmillan, 1938.

ACKNOWLEDGMENTS

Dr. Richard B. Bernstein, internationally recognized authority on the Revolutionary War, continues to make his tremendous contribution to the series, for which the author is most grateful. Jana Erickson has again spent much time and effort on the cover and the artwork. Richard Peterson has exercised his usual great patience and careful work of editing. Harriette Abels, consultant and editor, has guided the author with her wisdom and insight.

However, again, the men and women of the Revolution, whose spirit reaches across more than two centuries, are truly responsible for all that is good in this series.

The work proceeds only because of the contributions of many.